DON'T THE MOON

LOOK LONESOME

DON'T THE MOON
LOOK LONESOME

A Novel in Blues and Swing

STANLEY CROUCH

Pantheon Books / New York

Grateful acknowledgment is made to the following
for permission to reprint previously published material:

Edward B. Marks Music Company: Excerpt from "Fine and Mellow" by Billie Holiday. Copyright © 1940 by Edward B. Marks Music Company. Copyright renewed. All rights reserved. Reprinted by permission of Edward B. Marks Music Company.

Warner Bros. Publications U.S. Inc.: Excerpt from "When It's Sleepy Time Down South" by Leon Rene, Otis Rene, and Clarence Muse. Copyright © 1930, 1931 (copyrights renewed) by EMI Mills Music, Inc. All rights reserved. Reprinted by permission of Warner Bros. Publications U.S. Inc., Miami, FL 33014.

Library of Congress Cataloging-in-Publication Data

Crouch Stanley.
Don't the moon look lonesome: a novel in blues and swing/Stanley Crouch.
    p.   cm.
ISBN 0-375-40932-7 (hc)
1. Interracial dating—United States—Fiction. 2. Women jazz singers—Fiction.
3. Jazz musicians—Fiction. 4. Norwegian American women—Fiction.
5. Afro-American musicians—Fiction. I. Title.

PS3553.R575 D66 2000
813'.54—dc21   99-048835

Random House Web Address: www.randomhouse.com

Book design by JoAnne Metsch

Printed in the United States of America
First Edition
2   4   6   8   9   7   5   3   1

For

ALBERT MURRAY,
RALPH ELLISON,
AND SAUL BELLOW,
MENTORS ALL

With Gratitude

TO GLORIA NIXON, my wife, whose astonishing fine brown beauty is equaled by the bright and enduring spirit, mother wit, insight, and pure soul of her personality. What a poetic combination of honey and hot sauce.

TO GEORGE GUTEKUNST, who made sure that Beryl Markham's *West With The Night* was brought back from obscurity, and who showed such loyalty to this book that his close, critical reading was essential to how it turned out. From the sustained passion of his efforts, I learned another set of things about the meaning of true friendship.

TO NATHAN SCOTT, a great scholar, whose explanation of what was wrong with the second half was so clear it helped me get it together.

TO RUSSELL LARKIN, who gave me some very good pointers early in the process of bringing this whopper on home.

TO JUDY JOICE, whose knowledge of food service and sailing helped me caulk the hull of one chapter.

TO JEANINE PEPLER, my resistant secretary and true assistant, who is also a mighty savvy reader.

TO ERROLL McDONALD, my editor and the one who was there fully ready to let it ride as the bets got bigger and bigger.

And, IN MEMORIAL REGRET: LEON FORREST and DARCY O'BRIEN, two marvelous writers and close friends, who were also invaluable competitors with whom I had hoped to joust until we were all far too old to do anything other than joke about who put a whipping on whom—and when.

Do not look around you to discover other people's ruling principles, but look straight to this, to what nature leads you, both the universal nature through which things happen to you, and your own nature through the acts which must be done by you.
—*The Meditations of Marcus Aurelius*

I was feeling right up to it. Could it be done? Yes, I could do it.
—Aretha Franklin, "First Snow in Kokomo"

Don't let it get fair now. No telling what you might see then.
—anonymous Negro

Contents

Prelude

Some he and some she wanted to hear a story from the streets that dipped down into the basins of society. They wanted to be taken with words to where some of the people who were light and some of those who weren't could meet. Tease us with a tale, they said, of walking outside the skin you were given and the skin you were told meant something particular.

They waited. They waited. Oh, well.

A story showed up, looking like a Midwestern lady. A woman and her world right now. Oh, she had some adventures. Her soul was informed by epiphanies. She learned how to listen. She learned how to think. She learned to raise up out of herself and become an adult. She learned that memory is an instrument of return and that the human heart is always going back to the times when it was most deeply touched, when it was pierced, when it grew wings and took to flying.

So you, like that some he and some she, will get to know the motion of a soul, and the Chinese-box rhythm of that motion is what we will call her story.

Part One

THE YOU AND ME

THAT OUGHT TO BE

I

GEE, BABY

When CARLA flew to Houston with Maxwell to meet his family, there were a lot of brief stares. The flitting attention spurred her to remember, as she now preferred to forget, that she was so Norwegian looking. Her sandy hair was flat as a piece of paper, her skin just short of chalky but robust, her blue eyes the perfect tint to match the veins in her arms and legs; but he was very dark and bulky, with close-cut woolly hair, his eyes drowsy and nearly decadent in their cast.

This contrast, which they used to joke about, meant too much right now. That put a gash in her spirit. They were no longer so damn superior to the dank rhetoric of racial talk. The two had been together for five years. The first four were so good they presently seemed like no more than an elaborate fantasy, a tale she told to herself about an idiotically wonderful life she had never lived. Over the last ten or twelve months, the supreme closeness of their love was suffering. Their home, as if from nowhere, was invaded by emotional disorder. It might linger, it might not. She hated most the mystery of wondering just how long that divisive prickliness would dominate his mood, then infect hers. If she *had* to experience the sudden spread of this interior cactus, Carla preferred the times when it disappeared almost immediately and Maxwell became himself again, not a perfect guy by any means, but her man. Then, sure, there was reaffirmation in his tone of voice, in his touch, in the way his eyes put themselves on her, as if she were now clear to him again, not a blue-eyed fog he could almost see through, knowing no warmth, no substance. At first, it always felt like a gleaming gift to know that her soul and flesh had risen from beneath a dehumanizing abstraction and had returned to their rightful place. Way inside, however, her heart eventually felt like a rubber band that had been pulled and pulled until it could not go back to its original size. Some hard, hard bitterness went with that.

It had gotten pretty ragged and pretty nasty by the time the couple arrived in Houston. Everything each one knew about the other had nearly become secondary to his being black and her being white, neither one individual, neither one human. That was where they were. But, for all of her feeling that things were just about over, she didn't accept what she sensed was his idea that it was *natural* for them to become alienated, an unmatchable boot and slipper. This girl from South Dakota and this guy from Texas, as far as Carla was concerned, were not instinctively doomed to lose each other just because she couldn't become what he was. She would die before she would accept some garbage like that.

While the two silently moved through the airport to get their luggage, her mood began pushing her mind around. That was how she did it; it was her impulsive way to get herself together. She always handled the moment she was in by constantly shuffling back and forth between the past and the present whenever the pressure was on. Carla knew that her life, *just like everbody else's,* was a detective story. So she was a person who always wanted to figure out if a problem gaining ground was a matter of personal blame, or if some shortcoming in combination with the slippery nature of life had landed her on the abundant curve of buttocks that made this white woman, like her mother but not her sister, such an anatomical anomaly. There was always a reaction to those soft twin glories below her waist, usually one that was funny or endearing or, well, kind of insulting.

At this luckless moment, Maxwell was walking toward the baggage claim as though he was by himself, all by himself. That was *so* mortifying. He might have been at home in Houston but he wasn't making any attempt to let her feel as if she was, or could be. What a chickenshit. It sure wasn't like that when they were first really getting it together and he took it upon himself to make her laugh and feel good.

Maxwell used to nickname her "Tailback" or "Back in Action" or "Black Bottom" or phone her from on the road and ask, "How are those Viking grandes dames doing?" That enchanting fanny also got its measure of attention when they traveled through the night clubs that were part of his Manhattan kingdom—Sweet Basil, the Blue Note, the Village Vanguard, the Jazz Standard, Birdland, Iridium, Smoke. There was that time she often recalled with a secret fondness that was just as secretly embarrassing. An older drummer friend of his, so deep in his cups, said to Maxwell one night as Carla sat down next to him at the bar of the Vanguard after returning from the lavatory, "Boy, now ain't *you* a bitch? You got a blonde with a black ass. What is this world coming to? Now you got niggers so white a brother afraid to go out with a *real* white woman can get a black one black as a stovepipe hat and the black woman talks and acts just like the pinkest lady the Lord ever made. You seen 'em: all proper and shit, all baby-food smooth in the mouth—cultivated, bubble-butt blackstrap molasses-looking women all the way up from the gutter, with *no* kind of jungle left. *No* soul to go home to. Just so nice. Ain't got a speck of fire sitting in their panties. Only thing wild left over is that barbwire pickaninny hair. But you, Maxwell Davis, nigger, you stumble your bodyguard-looking self out here and find a white woman couldn't *nobody* tell was white if all they got to see was the shadow of her profile. You know I ain't lying. She ain't got no regrets about it either. I seen her walking with that big ass banging and prancing along like she's proud of it. I'm telling you, I seen me some changes made in this man's world. Now you got black girls proud their hair is nappy and white girls happy they asses ain't flat as pancakes. I need another drink. The end is near—near *you*."

As she now looked at Maxwell exhibiting his commendable manners by stepping so gracefully between the other passengers as he pulled his and her luggage off the ramp and made sure that he neither bumped into nor struck anyone with their suitcases, she, for absolutely no reason, saw him as he was before they became lovers. Before she finally gave up her apartment and began living with him, before they got so close that, it seemed, when one inhaled the other exhaled.

It was the indelible blue spring morning a year before their romance moved into hot couplings. Maxwell was very carefully lifting Bobo, who could no longer walk, and taking him to the cab that would carry his friend to the Veterans' Hospital. My God, my God.

There was still one more piece of luggage to get and Carla, as a clear pearl of sweat appeared on Maxwell's neck, heard the way he played the saxophone and thought of how attentive he could be and how much, while not feeling even a smidgen of inferiority, she admired him for the force of his sensitivity and the confidence he brought to his art and to the life they had together when nothing unreasonable was mashing down on them. What a mess they were in, the two of them heading for the rental car counter, no closeness distinguishing the air between them. They breathed separately. She was angry and she was insecure but there was also, down in the war room of her soul, a sureness that if this thing could be made right, and if the making it right depended on her, she could do it.

This woman was prepared to take all the necessary hard knocks for what she wanted because of the way she had already lived. That's right. Houston was just another stop. Her life had largely been a study in sturdiness, or the destruction of it: a body and soul graph of stability and instability, of difficult rises and hard falls. That was it. There was nothing to whine about, however. This wasn't particularly special. No way her life was so different from everybody else's. No way.

Carla, something of an adventurer when she thought about it, had been among so, so many different kinds of people that she had no doubts about certain things. None. The world was a tough place and anybody who stayed around found that out, in spades, clubs, hearts, and diamonds. Call your trumps. The rules of illumination, satisfaction, disillusionment, thrills, surprise, joy, shock, and heartbreak were the same for everybody. But it was also just as true that the individual was still that human being out there feeling it alone.

That special aloneness was like getting out of a car back home in South Dakota. Back home on one of those windless days and one of those roads that had cost so many young lives when kids, drunk and looking for any kind of excitement, mistook the empty space for a boundless plane of safety and managed to kill themselves.

Out there all by yourself, there seemed to be no worlds of existence other than your own breathing, the feeling of your body, above and below the skin, and that horizon, stretching on and on in flatness.

That exquisite solitude was warming because one could pretend that God had made all of this for no greater purpose than to provide just one person with a big target for musing. You could be that vain if you were comfortable with it.

The high-toned flummery one could get into back home when nobody was around for miles and miles had little to do with the over-crowding that she had known for a while now. Carla was breathing down the neck of forty and had been residing—with a break of a couple of years—in New York since her early twenties, arriving there with an unshaped desire to sing but not the nerve to sing what she actually felt. Her out-west ethnic background had something to do with it; she wasn't sure she could measure up. Even though the world of Negro music had attracted her since she had been a surprised girl in church, and even though her love of the music had taken her deep into the human side of the Negro world, where there were those she liked and those she couldn't deal with, Carla the new arrival trembled inside about being mistaken for a person unlike what she actually was.

That lack of sureness during her early and mid-twenties prompted the woman to make some mistakes along the way by trying to avoid seeking what she really wanted; by not stepping into the aesthetic line that pulled her most strongly; by not facing the reason but looking for something in which she could be authentic and white and accepted and accepting of herself; by, finally, not taking the chance on failing.

The girl from South Dakota had overcome that while listening to a little portable radio on a long bus ride. The music told her what to do. From then on, color be damned, she called upon the same will that had provided her with the discipline to become a local skating whiz with championship potential when she was a high school girl. Second by second, note by note, and beat by beat, Carla had made herself into a jazz singer, one who had been getting some light attention for the last few years. There was a blessing there.

That attention, those nightclub jobs, and the recordings that were now looming made her relationship to Maxwell quite different from what it was at the very start, when he was being called with job offers all the time and she was rarely the person the caller wanted to employ.

The telephone was the enemy then. It consistently defined the career limitations of the woman in the house, which was why she hated to hear it ring and turned down the speaker on the answering machine, choosing to find out what was going on later in the day, perhaps before dinner, or even later.

Such petty tactics made her feel she was a combination of a bitch and a coward. So let it ring. Let it ring. Ring. Pick up the receiver and act like a fully grown person. There. Her envy, that brittle cousin of awe, subsided to a great degree.

Envy hadn't taken up much space at all when Carla was a kid out on the plains, but New York had made her resentful of the success of others—almost anybody, regardless of career—which was something she hated and fought every time that covetous mood made its way to the front of the emotional line. Consequently, it was easy to be thankful for the fact that she was much more confident about herself as an artist, and now usually carried her accomplishments with the modulated authority she had been introduced to during her grade school years as Miss Popular.

That unintended preparation worked well for her when she was interviewed by the nincompoops who wrote about jazz, almost all of them guys who made the art into a revelatory mistress they bloated with the chocolates of their sentimentality or tortured because it so clarified their own inadequacies. Oh, she knew just how to play them. Easy as unsalted butter melting on a skillet. Clarified. Absolutely. Add to that the truth that the greasy spoons and the top flight restaurants where she had waitressed were finishing schools for her and any other woman who needed to learn how to express an amalgamation of dignity, good cheer, ease, humor, and appreciation—with just enough of the perfume of sex to make a man tip better and feel closer but not close enough to say something so unsavory it would draw a snippy admonishment that might be compressed to a contemptuous razor of light in the insulted one's eyes.

Carla's demeanor convinced every jazz journalist who wanted to do a profile of her that he was discovering fresh material. Because Maxwell, no matter how good he was at handling them, never wanted one of those guys to ever set foot inside their home, her interviews were given in a coffee bar or she visited one of their overstuffed apartments full of the information that these men absorbed and too frequently displayed in place of souls. They were so unlike what she had dreamed about back home, when the South Dakota girl had her imagination tweaked by the exotic force of Eastern European men who were gutsy and physical. These nerdy jazz writers might have been pure New Yorkers, most of them Ellis Island stock to a man, but they never reminded her of the young Tony Curtis in *The Sweet Smell of Success* (whom her mother thought was one of the handsomest men ever born and never failed to look at with a special enjoyment when *that* movie was shown on TV). If being muscular or athletic or sexy was the subject, well, they sure as hell weren't Mark Spitz, whose very name made the girls shriek in the locker room showers at the health club when she went back home for a visit during *his* Olympic year of great conquest. Still, any one of these journalists, zhlulbby or not, badly dressed and unconvincingly poised, could be useful. The bean pole or the shorty or the average build or the zhlub of the moment would be taken by her humility and her shining appreciation of the fact that *he* had chosen to sprinkle some ink about the way she sang and the way she was. In the middle of those interviews, as with who knows whatever else, something human might take off.

The variously formed love both she and the interviewer had for jazz could redefine the context in the direction of camaraderie. Then a real mood punctured the game and flattened it. This resulted in the singer believing that much more in what the music was about and what it could do—and how you, no matter what kind of a tricky plan you had, must bow down in your feelings before this thing whenever the right question was asked or implied with enough oomph to stimulate what it felt like to hear someone really take off, or what a miracle it seemed when you were on a bandstand and the swing lifted up.

Any time she was reminded of that swing during an interview, the girl from South Dakota knew she was lucky. Yes: quite. In some personal place, she also felt ashamed for looking down on someone so far outside the way it actually was, especially since there was no way on the entire earth that this woman could ever set her mind to forget how terrible it felt when she was trying to get into the jazz world and had exactly no idea which way to go. She might have had a big rubber butt but she sure wasn't hip. Besides, as Maxwell said, "Never get *too* hip, baby. Two hips *always* make an ass."

9

As it emerged from her like a tantalizing musk, this unspoken realization went to the head of the interviewer, shifting the gears of his enthusiasm into overjoy. The written results, putrefied by clichés, lacking in musical insight but delivered with all the quirks of unearned superiority, were embarrassing but also the substance that underlay a brief but very definite period of gloating. Yep: she was a gloater. Always had been. So while Carla wasn't sure that she would catch Maxwell, there was no doubt that she was going to get much, much closer to his level of success in only a few years. Well, *maybe*. If you're equal to your desire, *maybe* is just enough to bet everything on, just about enough.

Maxwell in all his power was no joke. Not that big boy. Stepping up to where he was would take some doing. She had learned the details of his substance by the day. His winning of jazz polls, the recording dates as leader and guest artist, the copious attention that had fallen on him over the last few years, and all that made his success were not come by simply or naturally. Those who believed the hazy things he said in interviews and thought his music was something achieved through no more than the will of his breath had been totally duped. Playing the part of the idiot savant was a mask Maxwell never removed among those he knew wanted to bite big plugs out of his style or take high positions in the critical circle for breaking down the essences of his methods. He had contempt and slight regard for such people. Her man was an old-timer in the sense that, like a master magician, he only displayed the puzzling charisma of the illusion, never revealed what it took. Not this guy. Those who would truly know where he had hidden the secret crowns and mirrors of his accomplishments had to have the heart to dig for it. He had no intention of using Santa Claus as a model because there had been no reindeer on the roof waiting while his prowess was delivered for no more than the price of wishing on a star or mailing a list to the winter wonderland of the North Pole. The language of the music that was literally at his fingertips resulted from unrelenting homework. Being gifted wasn't enough for him; he flogged his substantial talent; he set fire under it; he spurred it. Maxwell had mastered his horn through a discipline that pushed Carla from admiration to replication. His playing had fluidity in every key. Simple to complex chords were no barriers to his self-expression because of the time spent deepening an already highly perceptive ear. He knew entire recordings and could pick up his tenor, play the saxophone solo, the trumpet solo, the piano solo, the bass solo, and whiz very close to the drum solo.

Sometimes, to show off, he would attach the horn to the hook of the everpresent neck strap and put on a Duke Ellington recording, playing through every note in the arrangement, having learned the work so well that he knew the individual parts played by each of the trumpets, the trombones, and the saxophones. To further intimidate Carla, he would play the recording through yet again, this time blowing in unison with the bass player and laughing when the bassist either missed a chord or made a pedestrian choice.

The obsessive posture of his studying meant that he would examine new rhythms, melodic ideas, and harmonic intervals over and over, making himself into an aesthetic juicer that left nothing behind, not even pulp. When he was all the way into something that had no chance of eluding him, Maxwell would finger the air as he slept or sometimes sing out bits of phrases. Those were periods of increasing grouchiness because he was at war with his own limitations and saw new information not only as an area of intrigue but as an opponent. Maxwell believed that the things you didn't know were *trying* to stay beyond your grasp. He had said as much. Weird. So there was a fusion of curiosity, determination, anger, and superstition as he worked and worked at the details until he had them down. Her man ceased being irritable and made fun of himself once his fluency in a new area of expression had been brought home to his horn. The tail he pinned on himself was that of a mad scientist scrambling around in his laboratory. With a melodramatic tone, hunched over and limping, he'd play one of the ersatz Gypsy themes from *The Son of Frankenstein,* then scream, "Ah! He's lost his mind!" He was funny. She loved her a man with a sense of humor. Geez.

Watching Maxwell on the bandstand cleared up why he had become one of the main men on his instrument. The mystery ended very quickly. After staring at the photographs of Coleman Hawkins, Sonny Rollins, Ornette Coleman, and Thelonious Monk, he left the dead kitchen that was the dressing room in the Vanguard and walked to the bandstand through the tables on the red carpet, or came past the cooking staff of Asians and West Indians through the kitchen from the dressing room that used to be in the basement of Sweet Basil but was now right next to the back of the club in a small place that was once a watch repair shop on Bleecker Street, sauntered from the spacious and mirrored dressing room down the stairs of the Blue Note, emerged from the office-like dressing room to the right of the bandstand at the Jazz Standard, walked up the short hallway from the narrow dressing room at Birdland and through the doors near the waitresses' station across from the stage, came from his dressing room at Iridium where they served the musicians fine food and moved toward the left side of the bandstand, rose from the bar at Smoke and stepped up on that stage as if everything each person in the room possessed actually belonged to him. Hand it over. His dark fingers touched the horn like it was part of his jaw, not hanging from a neck strap. A reed he was wetting in his mouth had a functional role that even a non-musician could be sure of as he pushed the shaved piece of bamboo cane into the mouthpiece of his saxophone and turned the little screws that held it in place. Then he zigzagged across the instrument to see what was up.

The sound Maxwell got from that big brass tenor always stopped the talking when he began the first tune without introduction, never using a microphone because the size of his tone moved up under the paint on the back wall of a room. Yes, that tone was big, *full,* not loud and offensive. It was a statement in and of itself, which was what he had aimed for, explaining to Carla that the musicians who could play the very fastest weren't those who shot out scads of notes, lickety-split. Not them. The champs when it came to speed were actually people like Louis Armstrong and Ben Webster because the very sound each of those special people made was an *immediate* musical experience; no phrase was needed. They didn't have to build up. You were taken away instantly. One note against the ear. Boom: There. Instantly. You can't play faster than somebody who *always* has the sound of music in his horn.

Carla already knew that her own way but his saying it with such insight made her think more deeply about how true that was of all great singers as well. You had to get the sound of music in your voice. Then each note and each phrase was gravy.

He said important things to her about being in charge. As with the true masters of the bandstand, Maxwell led his musicians through his instrument, guiding the piano, the bass, and the drums in the directions that he wanted to hear. "Otherwise," he told her, "you're an employer, not a bandleader." Yessiree: this guy was a leader. He was also a mobile listener who told his musicians that you always had to play as if every other instrument on the bandstand was part of your instrument in order to create the feeling of a group giving spiritual order and fire to the moment. Then, on every level, all of you seemed to be playing something preordained but the art of it was actually the outcome of improvising beyond your individual ego into the collective soul of the music. "It's not magic," he said, "but it should seem like it is. It's about listening and responding and creating on the run. That's why the great freedom of the groove sounds impersonal, like a dream better than any fucking thing we know once we stop playing."

For all that, the particulars that Carla heard in Maxwell's improvising tended to dominate. His rhythm was perfect—or so close to perfect that you could never be sure whether or not he had gotten lost or tangled up. Sometimes he would play under the tempo, rumbling like a train beneath the ground shaking the glasses in a bar. Then he would pick up speed, reducing the tension, and move in line with the rest of the musicians.

The kinds of ideas he had were endless. He might work through the harmony as though it were a staircase and each chord was a step to be danced on, or apply pauses, letting some chords go by, to give the impression that he was taking the stairs two or three at a time.

His melodies might be long balletic bounds of sustained notes that sailed up over the meter. He could use staccato phrases that transmogrified the saxophone into a tuned gathering of drums from which came brutal honks or kidding pats and mock punches or tap-dancing stanzas in swinging rhythms.

When feeling the limitations of the material, he might slither through the music with ideas that took him far outside the key, creating an ambiguity as ominous as it could be playful.

A monster when it came to form, he could dismantle a tune and throw away everything except a phrase or two, or he might repeatedly play the bridge over and over until his band recognized that he was only dealing with those eight bars. In the middle of one song, Maxwell could suddenly move into another, then back, then add one more song, twisting them up against one another in a maddeningly fierce weaving of motifs, strip them all down to a couple of blues licks and dive down into that funky-butt lushness, eventually returning to the first song he had begun working on.

It didn't always come off perfectly, and sometimes he sat brooding in the dressing room because he had failed, but the audience lost control of itself whenever he brought such an adventure off, which he did seven or eight out of ten attempts.

At certain times, he created dialogues with himself, singing out notes from the upper register, then responding in the grumbly bottom, only to use the middle range to wrap up the tale he was telling. Or he optioned to play the upper part of the horn in a shrill manner and retort from the lower part of the instrument with breathy lines that were part air and part pitch. He could reverse the process and play uncommonly high notes that were wisps of lyricism contrasted by roars and honks from the lowest register.

The control he had over the notes themselves allowed for a musical version of the well-cut diamond, which catches and holds such a large degree of light it becomes a kaleidoscope. Beneath, or run through the intellectual detailing, the passion, and the boudoir lore was never less than a mystical quality that gave his work the impact of overhearing very intimate prayer. There was a blue star in his tone.

Seeming to be stalking inspiration, restlessly walking about the stage or standing in different places in order to change the angle from which his sound was projected, Maxwell used his tenor with so much power and intensity, from penetrating stage whispers to nearly bellowing, that a light gray suit, inching down from the shoulders to the knees, would turn charcoal gray with his sweat by the last number of a set, when he could feel his socks squishing in his shoes.

Two or three changes were necessary when he worked clubs, always beautifully dressed, each part of his outfit matched, shoes, pants, jacket, shirt, and the tie visually aligned with his socks.

Watching that dandy become a laborer right before your eyes was reminiscent of seeing the fight films he had of Sugar Ray Robinson so smoothly entering the ring with his hair coiffed into delicate waves and crests but leaving with his hairdo reduced to a riot of limp quills and his body shining, his trunks sticking to his legs, and his opponent completely done in for the night.

By the final note of the evening, Maxwell's band members knew they had been on a job in which revealing the heart through musical form was neither a simple nor a flippant thing. This man gave another meaning to playing for keeps. If you don't want to give it all up, don't go up there.

"Some guys," Maxwell said to Carla after they had eaten a dinner of chitlins, potato salad, and three kinds of greens he cooked with slab bacon in their Greenwich Village apartment, "they hide behind what they know. They study up on putting a wall between you and them. The information is a barrier. These kinds of guys don't want you to see who they are. That would fuck up their program. I like music because you can be everything in public. You can be scared, you can be mean, you can wish for things, you can remember something dirty or something perfect. I mean you can be free. Dreamy. Serious. Confess if you want to. Fuck it. All the atoms in your heart can come alive on a bandstand. The bandstand is not somewhere you should bullshit. You also shouldn't come up there if you don't have something to contribute. You had better be right when you get up there or it could be a little painful. You might get your pride shattered by a foot deep in your ass."

If one of the older masters came up there to sit in with him, Maxwell was all respect and heavy affection. His admiration for they who had made the language or had become notable individuals couldn't have been more apparent. He would almost make them blush when telling the audience of their exploits. The look that he had on his face, tightening and sucking his upper lip as they played, was one of pride in those men and in the music itself. His nods and smiles had an incandescence both boyish and full of the absolute recognition wrought by his endless studies, his hours upon hours of analyzing what made the best the best.

At a moment when one of those older men hit an especially individuated note or passage, Maxwell slightly jerked as though stung by an invisible bit of magic. His own playing as they listened to his story was then the epitome of that communal authority at the root of jazz. Carla never got away with dry eyes when she found herself in the middle of listening to that. That was the feeling she wanted and the feeling she knew she had.

But there was another side to his playing, too.

Audiences went wild for Maxwell, and the other tenor players lined up at the bar or over in the corner or sitting right down front would shake or slowly turn their heads, if not look at him with the mixture of awe and hatred that is reserved for those artists who make their fellow practitioners feel as though the only thing they will ever get out of the race against them is a chance to eat plenty of dust or pant just close enough to feel an acidic fart contemptuously cut in their faces.

The ones willing to bring their horns on his bandstand and raise the flag of battle would be toyed with at first. He laid back, smiling, cool as a new block of ice while they put out their hottest stuff. Then, the beast awake inside him, he would begin to play in their styles, improving upon them, little by little, before tearing their heads off the way a cat does after he has had his fun systematically bloodying a captured mouse.

If they liked to play fast, he played faster, more intricately, and with greater precision; if the blues was what they did best, he got so rowdy, insinuating, and greasy the house flipped out; if they liked to lope along, he found a boody-bumping groove that lifted the bandstand up to the moon; if the ballad was their forte, the romantic tones coming from his horn became such a celestial strain of interior perfume and perspiration that everyone within hearing distance was made to experience how love felt at its most tender state of naive ache and its most satisfied recollections of the rhythm key and the velvet lock.

The bandstand was Maxwell's kingdom and those interlopers who chose to enter it knew that their fate was execution.

Carla understood that equaling him in her own realm was no easy task, but she grew to believe she just might, if her luck was as strong as her will.

She sure had a few things going for her.

To the good, beyond the voice and the hard work she did on it, Carla's looks weren't starting to fade just yet, though her skin didn't have as much moisture and textural flare as it had only two years ago. The three angel rings on her long neck were deepening at a slow and inexorable tempo but, for now, still added character and weren't so grooved she might feel forced to wear turtlenecks and scarves to mask what seemed unattractive wrinkles to her, if to no one else. The singer maintained—except for a little bulge of belly Maxwell found stirring in its round softness—the same size she had been when completely filling out to womanly contours by high school graduation.

For someone experiencing the evaporation of her late thirties, this was fine fortune in the visual department. You heard right. No matter how much she hated all of the sex-object stuff, and it was a *serious* pain, Carla knew that a woman's looks were indisputable assets in show business. There it was. *Face the world, young lady, or it will roll over you every last time you're looking the other way,* her mother always said.

Since junior high, guys liked to give her the gander and she had always appreciated being the focal point of their fantasies—as long as she didn't have to find out what those imaginings actually were.

Sometimes, as though mercy were no more than a myth in the world, you were forced to know their poisonous dreams.

One late evening, back in the early days of her adventures in Manhattan, not so very far from the southern tip of the island, she had almost lost her life because of one of those fantasies; she had nearly made it to the starring role in an autopsy photo; that had wrecked her for a while and, even now, she repressed memory of that night when the moon was an uninvolved witness to terrible things below, when all the great distance from the security she often associated with her mother's arms was as meaningless to the city at large as one of those unseen night boats splashing through the water that encircled the town, where neither pity nor hospitality was competing to distinguish New York.

So much for that.

She had still gotten through.

Yes, she had.

Well, well. How do you like that?

All of the studying in the conservatory in Chicago, all of the dues she had paid, the jam sessions she had gone to, the numberless hours upon hours she had spent listening to players in the flesh and on record until the parameters of the art took on specific technical angles at the same time that its magic deepened for her, well, every millisecond of every bit of it gave her power right now. As it was not in the beginning, she had crossed the suspension bridge between the Lutheran church and the nightclub bandstand, between those choir rehearsals at which she was told that she sang like an agent of the Lord and those rooms where the audience was right in your face, hoping to be elevated but, particularly in the world of New York, endlessly quite ready to feel disappointed to the verge of outrage.

Carla was now on the other side.

She was at one with the people she wanted to join in the task of making jazz music. This was nobody's boondocks girl hopelessly trying to find the sweet groove. This one had cut her way out of that cocoon of unfamiliarity with the essentials of her art, which nobody was born with anyway. Some were better prepared to swing by their upbringing. With the right help, Carla had made up for that.

Her harmony was immaculate. Carla knew chords backwards and forwards.

The Italian voice teacher in Chicago, the voluptuous and slightly humpbacked Roberta Clemenza, had commanded her pupil to wear both earplugs and shooting-range gear over them in order to bring her silently in tune with exactly where the notes came from in her body, which also meant that her sound was far larger and more precise than that of the average jazz singer.

The lovely and supreme accomplishment was that she had gotten all the way into the pulse, the interior of the rhythm. She could twist around in the time, pushing it forward or falling behind or laying right on the center of the beat. The moment she strode onto a bandstand now, the audience and the other musicians knew that someone was up there who was ready to get the job done with enough swinging feeling to make the occasion an exchange of passions and stories.

When it worked, the emotion given musical logic pulled the audience members into the hotter and more reflective aspects of their own lives, while the responses of those listeners—verbally, visually, and through the mood they created when sufficiently moved—liberated Carla to look inside herself for more life to which she could give order and narrative on the jet wing of the moment.

When it didn't work, the result was a whole lot of trouble inside, a feeling of frustration or defeat. Some of that was basic to the insecurity singers had because, suddenly and with no explanation, your voice could disappear and you were left with a mangled version of it, one that had trouble staying in tune, one that was short some notes in its upper and lower registers, one that just wouldn't get into the rhythm.

Usually this voice did what it was supposed to, but when it didn't, no amount of ego could keep you from feeling small enough to dance on the point of a needle. Yes, thank God, her sound wasn't inconsistent. Her voice rarely failed her. It worked.

But everything didn't work. That would be too much like perfect, wouldn't it? The blues had been waiting for Carla and Maxwell. It was right there vamping until they had to give it full attention. Their problems—she still couldn't fucking believe it—were the results not of who they were but of *what* they were. That was how harsh it was. Color stuff was intruding and Maxwell was *letting* it intrude. That infuriated and humiliated her.

Whenever she brought it up—his surrendering to some clichéd bull-shit—he took an express to the land of denial, but she knew all the way down to the very last space in her soul that he was starting to lose faith in the two of them being together. This man wasn't really comfortable with her in public anymore. That was sharply obvious to Carla. Now, when he looked at her, it seemed that the kind who thought them fools for even trying to make something lasting had an ally. Him.

It appeared that he wished she could be something else. If she was lying, she was flying. Well, she didn't intend to become anything else, even if she could. She wasn't like that. She goddam wasn't.

Carla felt neither shame nor regret about growing up where she did or evolving into the person that she had become. The merry message that Maxwell could only mock these days was American. That was it. This nation was everybody's. There was nothing at all wrong with being from Indian country, where she had a pre-adolescent fantasy of herself as a buckskin Lakota princess wearing her sable hair in braids. On the ridge, sitting atop a wonderful pinto, only a blanket separating its muscular body from hers, the more reddish than brown princess thought of the crush and grief she felt for her brave and fallen Indian warrior. He had died of measles, a sign of their world ending, which meant nothing to the millions of mindless buffalo, way down east of the ridge, shaking the ground like an earthquake. Though these beasts would not live long either, it didn't seem that way then. They covered the land like hump-backed snow; there wasn't a blade of grass or an inch of earth visible in any direction down there, only them, their fur, horns, and hooves. What that land and those skies had seen. Yes, thank the Lord, her roots were all right with her. She could no longer be made to feel insecure or regretful about that. What she was had become obvious over the years. As an American girl, when she was still young and woozy, her mind impregnated by as many movies and books as any other citizen, she had also imagined herself a pioneer woman in a wagon train heading west and ending up in the Great Plains, ready to face the heartbreak of that pitiless landscape. Putting the guys in their place by being sure-shot Annie Oakley wasn't too bad either, her trigger finger and eye confounding the men who were so much stronger than she but had to learn that it didn't take all the hurly burly muscle and bubble-gut to lift a rifle: Sorry, you half-blind gathering of polecats, this shooting iron doesn't know and doesn't give a hoot if I'm a girl. Or traveling by the stars that determined the path of the underground railroad—and leading runaways through the swamp as Harriet Tubman, General *Moses*—was a super thrill to think about. What could you say? Maybe nothing is the best answer. This country is just too big to worry about where you get your start. You didn't vote on that in the womb anyway. That put no change on the fact that she didn't want to lose him either. Please, God, help us stay together. This was a frequent prayer, full of begging and selfishness.

Now, her pride scorched, she ruefully understood how desperation, like a whiff of bad air, surprised you. That added a deep vein of anxiety to the snarl of anger and frustration.

If she could just get on that straight line from the bandstand to her private life, from the acceptance she had gotten among the musicians to the same kind of assurance from Maxwell, everything would be, not perfect at all, but worth all the emotion.

Maybe all life ever came down to was finding out if what you wanted and what you had done and were doing was worth all the feeling.

That sense of herself, even as she felt a brooding fear quite unfamiliar, was what now sailed her from the rental car lot in the imposing Houston heat back to that unenchanted time during her senior year when Carla was a cheerleader and the girls had to take the big yellow bus home with the high school football team. It was an oblique memory but came to mind because that was a signal time when she understood something and made it into a philosophy. She didn't know it then but there were a lot of things the teenager didn't know, sitting there in her blue-and-white cheering outfit, with pompoms to match, and briefly smiling at the stylish little bells she had attached to the laces of her white tennis shoes so that her movements in front of the parents and students in the bleachers had a ring to them that only Carla and the other girls could hear.

Surrounded on that yellow bus by the sweat and the bruises, she had never felt more female. It was different from how her handsome guy and the others looked when they were fresh and their hair was smoothed back, their uniforms clean, and the expectant zeal of forthcoming competition was all over them. Now that they had won away from home by just a little, little bit, all the boys were filthy and quite proud of their pain, maybe drunk on it, muttering and shouting, their eyes childish and monstrous.

Something primeval slid itself into the air as she listened to them and smelled their funk. In the darkening light, the team's voices in her ears, Carla stared with counterfeit offhandedness at the brown blood. It marked the football uniforms almost forever but, she smiled to herself, actually only short of washing machines. Above all, an aspect of masculinity revealed itself through the brutal joy filling the bus as if it could blow hot breath on the windows.

She felt an awe just short of gooseflesh because it must have been that way when so many battles had been won and history had changed through the skilled use of violence and the willingness to stand in front of terror. The plastic helmets with the face guards, the broad, protective shoulder pads under their jerseys, the skintight toreador pants, the exposed calves, and the short boots with loud cleats were all something more, expanding outside the clunky bus to a place where her emotion soared on the magic carpet of historical association.

But Carla had not felt inferior nor had she ever wished to exchange places with those battered teammates. Looking and assuming an understanding of the seen and heard was plenty. Removed from all of her ideals, her disillusionment, her anger at the impersonal surprises of fate, and all of her tightly wrapped loneliness, the soft and dreamy world in which Carla the cheerleader cuddled her heart was good enough for her. It remained stationary in the middle of the smell of those young men and all that their thrill of victory made her contemplate.

She didn't arrive at any of those historical revelations upon first coming into Houston. There was too much other stuff. It was odd enough already. Burdensome. As things were, Carla wouldn't have expected Maxwell to even want her to go there with him. He was so busy shutting her out of his life, why would he take her back to his down-home beginnings? There was something strange going on.

Anyway, traveling in summer to the Southwest had its own reality. There were Delta plane tickets to buy and reservations to make.

Maxwell considered himself the world's best navigator. From childhood he had been fascinated by maps. As a professional musician, he had worked his way up from the cheesiest airlines to intimate awareness of all the very best ones. Numerous tours had made him an expert on the railway system and hotels of Europe, and he even knew the quickest ways to get around Japan as well as the finest of the very small restaurants where the Nipponese brought a live fish to your table, whacked off its head, and made your freshly dead delicacy right there.

That traveling pedigree was insignificant.

Carla always took over and handled the logistics when they went out of town together. That was her domain. There was a lot of enjoyment in making an itinerary, looking up hotels, haggling through arrangements on the phone, putting everything in her notebook, the whole bit ordered so well that a trip became a specific set of expectations. She loved it because nailing dates and destinations in place always gave a direction to time. You seemed to be going somewhere, not just moving through each day.

Further, at least at the beginning of a trip, she was never less than happy to go just about anywhere with Maxwell because they traveled in high style and it always felt good to get everything packed the afternoon before, at her insistence, order a driver to come pick them up, watch her man's bulky form take the bags to the door, and survey their street in Greenwich Village before stepping into the car.

She hadn't been so happy this time for more than one reason.

Bad luck had fallen like a storm of excrement. It was as though she were swimming upstream in raw sewage. A recent lunch with her sister at Grand Central Terminal while Maxwell was working out of town had been such an unexpected horror that, once it had been slowly and angrily examined for every bitter motivation, every symbol, Carla refused to remember the reunion. No, she would not.

Tired from the plane ride, distracted during the drive from the airport, and falsely cheerful from the moment she got out of the car, Carla was soon busy trying to learn about Maxwell and his family as people down on the ground, not symbols.

Their ice blue stucco home with black metal awnings was quite nice and in a part of the Houston suburbs where Negroes, in a fairly recent past, had not been allowed to live. The home had a two-car garage, a manicured lawn, a large backyard with a toolshed that his father had dismantled from the old house and rebuilt for another function, since it was once a little clubhouse Maxwell and his brother had sawed and nailed in place, board by board.

The inside of the home had walls that were painted in gradations, starting darker at the bottom and moving toward lighter tints on the ceilings. Fancy. Carla longed to take a seat as soon as she saw the big, comfortable leather chairs and an enormous leather couch that would have dominated the living room if it were not balanced by a glass and shining steel coffee table.

There were televisions on wheeled stands behind each of the three bedroom doors and small portable radios hanging from pegs in the two bathrooms. The dining room table was stained pale oak with chairs to match.

On the backyard grass not far from the toolshed and the lawn chairs was an oil drum converted into a barbecue pit. It had the emphatic silent presence, sitting on its welded legs, of a musical instrument. There was a quiet but powerful relationship between that barbecue pit and the big table with benches on either side that sat on the screened-in veranda under the extended awning at the rear of the house.

As Carla thought of all the coals that had been burned, all the meat that had been cooked, all the carefully mixed sauce that had been splashed on, all the smoke that had risen into the sky, and the mounds of ashes left behind, she felt the same delicious hints of mystery about inactive powers that Maxwell had opened up in her consciousness when he said that every musical instrument had secret tones hiding inside, all waiting to be discovered or rediscovered.

No one, he pointed out, had ever put a new tone inside a horn because no instrument could produce something that wasn't already there. Forgetting anything distinctive just turned it back into a secret that was then hiding out once again until it was tracked down and nabbed by the one who lost the memory or by somebody else who either got on the case or stumbled up on it.

Secrets, by the way, didn't care if you remembered them or not; they did all right on their own. But the secrets were full of mischief, which was why people knew what they were talking about when they said their memories played tricks on them. At that point, memory and secrets were hooked up in a conspiracy and running a fast one on you.

After that foray into Maxwellism, Carla then promised herself that she wouldn't float here and there in her mind so much that she might miss important aspects of what was going on around her during this first visit to Houston. Her tendency to contemplative dreaminess had sometimes been mistaken for aloofness or disregard and she had no intention of giving these important members of her man's family those impressions. That would hurt him, it might disappoint them, and it would surely, in the long run, hurt her.

Still, she knew she couldn't actually stop the marching legions of memory as they came to attack or rescue or soothe or mystify. All she could do was promise herself that she would try to avoid the habits of mind and sensibility that had been with her since she was a child. Carla wanted to move closer to Maxwell, if she could, by getting to know his parents and what they had given to him or what he had rejected and how that might help her make something more durable of their disintegrating love. Yet who was she to look for allies among these two people? There was no way Carla could know if she would be accepted by Maxwell's mom and dad.

They had always been cordial but brief on the telephone, which he just handed to her on a holiday to say something that didn't add up to much other than the ritualized polite exchanges about Christmas and the New Year. That little telephone fluff didn't happen every year anyway, since Maxwell wasn't always home for the holidays. Beyond that, he didn't talk with them much, or at least he didn't when the two of them were home at the same time. Carla always said she was looking forward to meeting them and they responded in kind. That was it.

Now she wondered if they—like the dummy their son was becoming—cared what she was on the surface of her skin, in the tint of her eyes, the texture and color of her hair. The way things were in the world today, one never knew. Prejudice could come from any direction. It probably always had, long before there was ever an America.

True as that had to be, she was nowhere other than where she was, all of her difficulties prickling and pricking her spirit in ways that arrived with such dismal accuracy they seemed specially ordained. So this trip was a big deal right now. If the parents of her man didn't like this particular woman from South Dakota, she and Maxwell were finished for sure. His parents would then corroborate his own misgivings. Whew.

The very thought of that made her throat burn and her eyes hurt. It would pain her so badly if it happened, so badly, but Carla also knew it wouldn't kill her. There!

Well, she had faced up to a lot before and she would face up to this, trying to win those two people by being herself. Herself was all she had, and when she was disoriented at her very worst times, that was all she had ever wanted to have. It might do; it might not. That, without a drop of varnish on it, was the meaning of her blues.

2

ME AND THE DEVIL

Maxwell's father was a deacon in the church and had been an automobile repair man but some years earlier a tire had exploded on a machine designed to fix flats and the flying slivers of metal from the rim inside the tire had nearly reached his jugular vein, which led to a nice sum of money and living in leisure, the squeak from damaged vocal chords always a reminder of how, as usual, it hadn't come easy.

Ezekiel Davis was different from his son in that his dignity had no elements of the combative. He was lean and the scars on his face, some dark, some pink and freckled, appeared to be symbols of his travels, which included fighting in the Korean War and working for a few years in the aircraft plants in Los Angeles ("It takes years to build some of them dadgum planes. They don't pop up out of no toaster").

Carla felt an invisible glow coming off Ezekiel but assumed it was no more than her own sentimentality, her overwrought affection for anything she considered pure. When Ezekiel and Maxwell were in the same room, it was obvious which of the two was a boy. Something happened to her man in the presence of his father that she found both delicate and muscular in an internal way. All of Maxwell's troubles seemed to dissolve and the various faces he wore disappeared. The power of his father baptized him so that the sweetness and the strength of his personality were liberated. He was so much more naturally poised because his father didn't care a whit what kind of a name he had in the jazz music world, which became obvious when Maxwell was reeling off a list of his tours and awards at the dinner table on that first night.

"That's all well and good, son, but you know me: my big concern is how your soul is doing."

"I guess it's doing all right, Pop. I haven't heard any complaints lately."

"Hope it's doing better than your baby brother's. Aaron called here just a few days ago and told us he had that AIDS, you know."

"Yeah, I know," Maxwell said with neither feeling nor trepidation.

Aaron was Carla's friend, the only homosexual she had become close to, had felt some kind of good feeling about. Whenever he came to New York she had a ball running around with him. He was so witty and so masculine and so oddly feminine. They were perfect buddies during those visits, and Manhattan was their town, nobody else's.

It hadn't started that way. She met Aaron on the telephone.

"My brother there?"

"Normally people say hello."

"Well, I guess they do."

"Who is this?"

"Baby Aaron."

"Oh, you're Maxwell's brother."

"I bet you that Carla girl."

"Yes, I am."

"White, ain't you?"

"Yes."

"You sound pretty. You sound just so sweet and pretty. I bet you pretty to look at, little white girl. I bet you pretty. You pretty, ain't you?"

"How can I answer that?"

"I know anyway."

"How?"

"Uh-oh."

"Something the matter?"

"Sure is: I can see that fishing pole."

"What?"

"I can see it. Lord, I can see it."

"What are you talking about?" she asked, smiling at the humor in his voice and blushing.

"I can feel that hook in Baby Aaron's ear. Oh, my dear. Reel 'em in, reel 'em out. You want another compliment, don't you, girl?"

There was silence. She felt him chuckling all the way out there in San Francisco, where the men loved the men and so many women were irrelevant. Carla felt she had to say something.

"Well . . ."

"Well is a hole in the ground."

This one was odd.

"Anyway, you just tell Maxwell Baby Aaron called him. Baby Aaron. Tell my big brother I appreciate that money he sent out here to me. Tell my big brother that I'm still out here living the way I want to live. Tell my big brother, God bless him, that I won't stop until I drop. He'll know what I mean."

"I'm glad somebody will. You can be sure of that."

"Oh, wait a minute. I want to tell you a secret."

"Why?"

"I won't tell you then."

She didn't know what to say.

"All right. I can tell you the confused type."

"I am not."

"You am not then," he said with a minstrel inflection that allowed both to laugh.

"I'm just kind of shy sometimes, and sometimes I don't know what somebody is going to say and I don't know if—"

"That's too much."

"Too much what?"

"Honeypie, I didn't call to get **your** story. I called to have me some jokes with my big-head **brother**. And I called because my first mind told me something. It say to tell you that old rascal loves the hell out of his white woman."

"He told you that?"

"Maybe he did, maybe he didn't."

"Oh."

"If he didn't, I'm the kind would try to make you think he did say all that."

"*You like to trick people?*"

"*Sometimes people need to be tricked into feeling good.*"

"*That's not very fair, is it?*"

"*Fair is a bunch of cows, pigs, and horses in tents.*"

"*You really have your own way of talking. Kind of weird, though.*"

"*I'm just copying. Heard it all when I was little boy, before I became a pretty boy, long before I got my calluses on my knees. Sometimes a lie, pretty girl, is the sweetest thing in the world.*"

"*You really believe that?*"

"*Listen to you, girl. You don't have to get serious the first time you talk with people.*"

"*I try to be serious all the time.*"

"*Look, pretty girl—*"

"*My name is Carla.*"

"*Well, excuse the stink off my shit. It's about damn time.*"

"*Aaron?*"

"*At your service: Baby Aaron on the other end of the line.*"

"*Are you trying to make me feel bad?*"

"*Oh, no.*"

"*Well, if you were, you were doing a good job. Sensational.*"

"*What you mean?*"

"*You just make me feel insecure.*"

"*I didn't mean to do that.*"

"*I don't know why but people will always say that they didn't mean to make you feel bad but they seem to be so good at it.*"

"*Has your time out here been that hard?*"

"*I've had some moments.*"

"*I like you.*"

"*Oh, you! You just made me blush.*"

"*Good.*"

"*Do you like being embarrassed? I'd like to know that.*"

"*Sometimes I feel like I wish I could get embarrassed.*"

"*Oh, you're beyond the rest of us out here, aren't you?*"

"*No.*"

She knew better than to follow up on that one.

"Guess you know your sister, Malena . . . guess you know that, too."

  "Know what?"

"She lost herself out there—"

"Lost herself?"

"Sure did: on that crack up there in Chicago."

"Oh, no, Daddy," Maxwell said with an emotion much like that of a child who has just learned about the horror of death.

"Malena was slow-dancing with the devil in the dark, you know. When you with the devil, son, black dark can get much, much blacker."

With those words, Carla felt a chill. Maxwell seemed petrified. Ezekiel, almost in an abstract mood, continued.

"Oh, my baby girl. Whew. My baby. Seemed it was all all right. Nothing new to that. Always seem like that. Ha. Let me tell you something. Everybody is some terrible future's clear and perfect fool. I know that. Everybody."

"Now you can see why I married this man," Eunice said, each syllable enunciated with the same quality of emotion heard in her husband's words but incontestably shaded with a completely different personality.

Ezekiel looked directly into the eyes of his son's lover.

"Now, Carla, I don't want you to feel left out. So I'm talking to you at the same time I'm talking to Maxwell. You here with us now. If you good enough for my son you good enough for me and Eunice."

"Let her know, Ezekiel, let her know. That's right."

They had said that so perfectly, as far as she was concerned. It was her trouble as well as their trouble. That made the evening more easy for Carla, though the story she heard told by Ezekiel was another of those in which someone is admiring a mural of a loved one and the wall falls forward, crushing the person under its destruction.

"Malena is the middle child."

"So am I."

"Three children?"

"Yes. Three."

"Mm-hm." Ezekiel paused for a moment.

"Three's not a crowd when it comes to having babies," Eunice said. "Birth is always a full house. When you pregnant, then *one's* a crowd. A crowd inside you, swelling up and turning over and all that mess, until you lay down and give birth to that darling child."

Carla then assumed that Maxwell's mother was another of those thinkers whose intellect rises out of common experiences. She knew people like that in South Dakota: they could squeeze new drops out of subjects you thought were drained of interesting ideas. Her head turned from looking at Eunice because she felt that Ezekiel was about to say something.

"Now, Carla, you know Maxwell done probably told you Malena and her husband, old Pretty Boy Floyd, was doing real good."

"Yes, he told me," she answered, eyeing Maxwell, who seemed to have left the room while remaining seated.

"Yes sir, doing *real* good. Had a house, two cars, just like me and Eunice. They both was working and making that nice money. Making babies was right around the corner. Grandchildren."

Maxwell had been at the wedding in Chicago. It took place just before he and Carla seriously started seeing each other. So she missed that one. But there were pictures prominently displayed in their Manhattan loft, none with Malena looking straight into the camera. She was either in the background or turned in the other direction. Malena was in profile, the veil still over her face, when Maxwell, Ezekiel, and Eunice were posing for the camera. In another, Maxwell stood smiling between Baby Aaron and Malena, each of them staring off with hot eyes at something beyond the border of the photograph, his brother to the left, his sister to the right. There was one in which Maxwell had his arm around Floyd, who could pass himself off as the very definition of happiness; stocky, medium brown, his eyes large, and every aspect of him subservient to the big grin of a man who had finally found his angel child, his angel girl, his angel woman, all three fused into one long-necked dark beauty who, like Crazy Horse, seemed somehow beyond the abilities of the camera.

Maxwell saw the two of them when he went out to play in Chicago, which was once a year—maybe. The music business was like that, a musician was only as employed as the last job. There were no guarantees, nothing regular, just surges of employment and periods of waiting for the phone to ring with an offer that had to be debated unless it was too good to risk losing by trying to haggle. When a job came up in Chicago he and Malena would stay in touch every few weeks or so after Maxwell returned to New York. Yet Carla found that she had always been gone from home whenever Maxwell talked with Malena over the phone. What bad luck. She could never avoid feeling that a telling fragrance of personality had entered her home and passed on through the window, leaving her no clue as to its impression. Carla wanted to put a voice to all the stories she had heard and all the affection her man had for his sister. She still felt gratitude for a kind of luck because it lifted her inside to hear the feeling Maxwell had for Malena and to see how pleasant an effect talking to her had on him.

But that had been a long time ago. Maxwell was traveling so much now that he compensated by sending his sister and his parents expensive gifts, avoiding telephone calls so that he didn't have to explain why he hadn't been in touch for so long. His ways were his ways. When problems piled up with anyone close to him he settled each of them with a grand gesture as a prelude to taking a vow of silence on the trouble. That usually succeeded, but there were occasions when the grand gesture could lead to trouble.

Almost any time Maxwell took Carla out of town it always resulted in him spending too much money, pretending that he was doing better than he was and making her feel like a queen while the trip was going on but a guilty burden after they got back home with far fewer dollars than their immediate living expenses demanded. So they went from extravagance to penny-pinching. Yet she couldn't stop herself from answering in the affirmative whenever he looked into her eyes with whimsy and asked if she wanted to go with him wherever it was that he was working. There would be steak, lobster, champagne, and a beautiful dress or some radiant piece of jewelry. They would find themselves in a very fine hotel and she would be in his arms at sunrise, inhaling the entire world and feeling as complete as she ever did. Then, usually during the packing and the checking out of the hotel, they would both start to descend from the euphoria of their mad study in living beyond their means, each of them somewhat uneasy about the other, him seeming to be peeved at her for coming along, her irritated at him for tempting her and rankled by her own willingness to jeopardize the quality of their next few weeks at home. At such times, she wished all of his jobs were like the ones in Chicago, where he didn't have to try and impress Pretty Boy Floyd and Malena. Carla also wondered if Malena carried any of her brother's ways into her marriage and—were she to handle difficulties *with Maxwell's methods—if her Pretty Boy found it compatible to go along with such spendthrift approaches to domestic life.*

"Yeah, they was doing good, very good," Ezekiel said. "But they got knocked over the head by that party appetite. Floyd called here crying on the phone, couldn't hardly talk. They started using that cocaine: just a little dab. Having what they thought was some fun. Every now and then out in the suburbs. They out there with the good-doing white folks and these Negroes taking *dope,* can you study that?"

No one said anything, but Eunice, who had a nervous habit of barely patting her hair now and then, ruefully nodded her head, a stern dribble of unintelligible whispers leaving her lips.

"Can't put a head, can't put a tail on it myself. Terrible times is all and not paying enough attention to God."

"I know that's true," Eunice said with force.

"So that party appetite creeps up. It *will* creep up now. Started with a little bit. Then some more. Should have stopped back before they started with any of that muckty-muck. No. That seem too much like sense. Then they went into that crack because it was cheaper. Cheaper to keep using. Cheaper. Sure was cheaper. Lost everything. The house. The cars. Their good-paying work. All of a sudden, they was flapping in the wind. Didn't nothing mean nothing but getting that crack."

"How come I didn't know this?"

"Well, Maxwell, calling every six or eight months, ten, eleven, you miss a lot."

"Be fair, sweetheart. Now we do have, Ezekiel, we have us three full scrapbooks of postcards from Maxwell right there in the living room. We got all those presents from all over the world. You know that."

"He know that, too. That ain't the subject on the table. I'm talking about calling. The telephone. Good invention."

The twist of Ezekiel's wit prompted Carla to lightly cough into her fist, hiding a laugh of bitter empathy.

"What's it been now, fifteen months, a year and a half? More, which it could?"

"I been busy playing my horn."

"Imagine you have."

"How come you didn't let me know about my sister?"

"Boy, fast as you always moving, where was I going to catch you—

and if I had of caught you, what was you going to do? Malena ain't no saxophone. You couldn't control her. We didn't hear about it until it was over."

"What do you mean, *over?*" Maxwell tried to be indignant but his father's eyes crushed that out of him.

"I don't mean she dead, son. Sorry if you thought that. My fault. No, I mean she gone. Disappeared. Just like a little drop of sweet water in a dusty wind."

Gloom started hissing up like steam.

"Sweet water. Ha. You don't remember, son. Doubtful. But sometimes Malena would get up sad in the night."

"Got up *all* the time, Ezekiel, not sometime."

"Darling, you right on that. Was just a little girl. The only thing could put her back to sleep and make her feel right was—"

"A glass of warm water with a nice teaspoon of sugar stirred up in it. That was her favorite. Girl held that teaspoon in her mouth just like a thermometer so she could get all the sweet off that spoon before she enjoyed herself that glass of sugar water. Yes, she did. Then she could go back to sleep."

"Hmmph. My darling said it. Yep. That's it. But can't nobody calm her down now. Nobody knows what kind of trouble she in. Oh, Lord God, it happened *so* quick."

Ezekiel appeared to inhale the story in bits of broken glass as he paused, his eyes successively moving quickly from blank to hurt to angry to compassionate to ambivalent. Maxwell obviously did not want to hear any more tales about Malena but also found himself caught, exactly like a person trying to revive a beloved someone who has drowned, the unchanging fact of the demise fought against with ever-weakening and anguished attempts to bring back this disappeared soul, this animate fact of spirit that has moved just beyond reach, leaving only a brand-new cadaver, one already terrifying in the sunken visual texture that arrives as life departs and the temperature of the flesh begins the descent toward becoming as cold as any stone. Carla saw that Eunice obviously had lived the story her own way and her mood had, for all of her previous low-keyed fervor, the quality of very-cold liquid brass filling her insides, pushing out all of the sorrow, leaving only a small cloud of tragedy in eyes too impassive to even work for a poorly done statue.

"They was down there dirty as two sewer rats," Ezekiel said, "but Floyd started pulling himself up. Mmm-hmm. God took pity on him."

"Praise His name," Eunice said.

"But, as both of you all got to know, there always explanations *somewhere*. I was reading this thing."

"Floyd just loves him his newspapers and books. I bet I tied up a ton of those papers and magazines. We still keep those *Jet*s though. Crazy."

Carla read *Jet* as if her soul depended on it. *Jet* was the only way she could get a sense of how black Americans lived, week to week. With Maxwell, she had met Negroes in Harlem, Philadelphia, Pittsburgh, Boston, Baltimore, and Washington, D.C., who had entire closets filled with issues stretching back thirty or forty years. One time she had a dream in which entire families of Negroes flew through the sky on magic carpets made of the magazine, the pages flapping like the wings of angels just above the head of the world. As soon as they arrived at the Davis home from the Houston airport, Carla assumed that those boxes stacked up on shelves in the garage were filled with endless issues of *Jet*. *Jet* held a grip on Negro culture because it was a set of notes on the history of the group and a set of notes on the moment. Kind of an outline. Smaller than regular magazines or comic books, it was easy to carry and one could read it very quickly. The copyediting often showed off the illiteracy of the employees, but that didn't matter. *Jet* told the story. Everything, from high governmental appointments to estimable scientific accomplishments to scandals to prestigious or commercial awards, the deaths of the great and the petty, the amount of money *anyone* was paid for *anything—if* it was substantial, a week's "best photo" if it had a black person in it, a history page with two or three important historical dates connected to the particular week of the issue, a "beauty of the week," which was a pinup of a Negro woman in a bikini, who was a hair stylist but spent her leisure time doing things she enjoyed, such as "reading, horseback riding, and photography." There was an all-American shamelessness to *Jet* that gave it such an epic quality Carla could almost always perk herself up by reading the magazine from cover to cover because something of absolute grandeur or absolute materialism or absolute absurdity would reveal itself in a line, a story, or a photograph so unprofessionally achieved that a ghostly personal texture would sting up off the page as if a rising soul was unintentionally pinned to the paper. Every now and then she would consider getting together with the white girlfriends of a few other black guys and see what the group of them would make of some her favorite issues of *Jet*. But Carla felt so ashamed of herself for considering any such thing that she actually hoped Maxwell would never realize just how much she liked the magazine, fearing he would see her as some sort of a voyeur, something like those white women who made bagging the testicles of Negro men into sort of a safari, replete with tales of urban outback oddities.

"Well, we might keep all of those *Jets,* Eunice, but you know I reads all *kinds* of stuff."

"I already told the girl that."

"Never been any different."

"Sure hasn't."

"So, as I was saying about this thing I was reading: seem to me like it can give us some light on the way these kind of people like Malena feel about doping themselves up all the dadgum time. Read every word. Read it twice. Read it again after that. Thought about it. It was an article about pleasure in the brain centers. Right up there inside your skull. It wrote women have more dopamine. Much more. The thing what makes you feel real fine is dopamine. Sensual. Clear up there in their brain. So when they get going on some of that drugs, they suffer from the female curse. Goes all the way back to Eve getting sweet-talked by the devil in the garden of paradise. Women always got to watch having fun; they never know how close they might be to destruction."

Carla felt as if a rage the size of a coconut were trapped in her throat. She was new to this Southwestern Negro world and didn't want to embarrass Maxwell, but she was extremely tired of the casual disrespect women had to put up with, especially from older people who were oblivious to all that had changed in the world. At the very same time, she wanted to smile—but didn't, obviously—as she recalled something Maxwell had said, which endeared him to her, that off-angle sense of humor he had.

The two of them were watching a television show about Renaissance art. At a central point, the screen was filled with Masaccio's painting of Adam and Eve getting booted out of paradise, given what was once called "the bum's rush" before its meaning was later inverted. Carla had mentioned, jokingly, that when she was doing some studies about the women's movement she had seen a cover of an old **Life** magazine with the words "Was Eve Framed?"

"Well," Maxwell said, "that's incorrect."

"What do you mean it's incorrect?"

"I mean just what I said."

"Aw, man, you obviously, you missed, you just missed the whole point of a basic concept of feminism: Men blame women for everything."

"I heard all that."

"So what's incorrect? Tell me that."

"The cover should have said, 'Adam Was Set Up.' "

The way he looked at her and the tone of his voice caused her to laugh, even though she wasn't at all sure what he meant. Carla raised her eyebrows in a way that let Maxwell know she was asking a question.

"Look at it this way: If God didn't want Adam to sink all the way down into the hot, hard dick rhythm of temptation, why did He jump up and give Eve a nice, tight, juicy vagina?"

"Well, you weren't there. You didn't see Him 'jump up.' How do you know it was tight and juicy?"

"Because they were in paradise."

He stared at her, smiling.

"Do you think you are in paradise?"

His face took on a stonewall assurance mooshed up with humor and erotic underplay.

"No, I don't think I'm in paradise; I **know** I'm in paradise."

"You do?"

"I feel good. I got you. All of this is good. You my bird of paradise. You not sweet sixteen, but, as B. B. King said, 'I love the way you spread your wings.' Oh, yeah. That's a fact."

Carla felt so satisfied by what he had just said that she forgot what they were talking about.

"Anyway, following my point—not the point I'm soon going to have to follow into you—"

She casually smirked but knew she was blushing. Blushing was as unpredictable as anything else. It also had as many meanings. This *blush was not one of embarrassment. It was one of anticipation. She knew how to meet a man skin to skin.*

"—Eve could have been down there between the legs just like those store-window dummies; sealed off, nothing open. Now the mouth is another story, but you get the point."

"Oh, I get it all right. So you're saying God was behind it all."

"That's exactly what I'm saying. First of all, God designed the world and He designed snakes, and if it wasn't for that slick snake design, the devil wouldn't even have had a clue about how to dress in the first place. Now you must remember this: it was a whole new situation. Dew was all over everything. The whole world lived in the morning. Fresh as you can get it. Fresh. Nobody knew what was happening, except God. And, if you look at it a little closer, the snake got a worser deal than women."

"My, my. Is that so?"

"I'm serious."

"Sure you are. Sure. Big insights arriving here."

"Look at it this way: When they want to call somebody a scumbag, they call him a snake; they don't call him a woman. Furthermore, you got women governors and all that kind of thing. One thing you can bet your bottom dollar on, you can be sure there will never be a snake governor."

"But there is that all-purpose word bitch, isn't there?"

"Uh, by the way, there actually is."

"Well, I guess that finishes that off right now."

"Yeah."

There was, to her ear, a delicious nuance of defeat in his voice. She would fix that.

"Let's go to paradise."

"Your move, baby. You got the power."

She took off her blouse and bra in nothing flat and pulled his mouth to her breast, one of the places where it belonged.

3

KNOWN ALONE

At the stained oak dinner table picked by his mother, in his father's house, with the plastic cartoon black cat clock on the dining room wall ticking as its tail went back and forth, Maxwell took on the dour melancholy Carla recognized whenever he was very disappointed or very hurt. She was sure he was thinking about his sister. The gusto he brought to good food gradually removed itself as Ezekiel talked. He began to eat his smothered chicken much more slowly, dawdling with his sweet potato and his green beans. He ate none of the hot buttered cornbread pancakes that Eunice had made especially for her oldest son. Carla recalled how her man said that Malena loved sugarcane when they were growing up; she would go through tube after tube, long after the sweet had made Maxwell almost sick. Never bothered Malena, the girl could go on and on. Once, however, he caught her throwing up from it, trying to hide, but she just drank some water from the garden hose, gargled, spit out all the bitter, laughed, and went right back to her tubes of sugar. That was an omen.

"She could pitch her ass off, too," he once said, talking about her superior athletic energy, which included being the fastest runner in the neighborhood and a girl who could knock the hell out of mannish

boys until she got more interested in dancing with them "and spend-
ing plenty of makeup time in the mirror. Plenty is what I'm saying.
You know plenty? Well, she made it real. You couldn't believe it.
After she started closing in on getting finer than a motherfucker,
Malena put the v in vanity. Let me tell you this. If you could wear a
mirror out, if anybody could do that, she would have needed a new
one every week—every damn day. By sundown, the mirror would be
ready for the mirror coffin."

It had become quiet as the four of them sat there, each now undoubtedly going over Malena's tale while eating. Maxwell's mood encircled
him in an atmosphere much like one Carla had experienced with him
before, where his irritations and his moments of helplessness were
somehow resolved by his memory of his sister, who could pop up in
conversation at the oddest angles. The conversation could start with
sports, move to the subject of racism, shift to sex, and conclude with
some artistic revelation connected to Malena. Along the way, she had
her own complexities of response to Maxwell, since life had produced in her a set of ways that had been outgrown by the desire to be
more her actual self every second and less the manifestation of the
defenses that helped one keep in the game.

For instance, while enjoying Eunice's cornbread during the long din-
ner table silence, Carla recalled one New York afternoon, perhaps a
year or so after she had moved in with Maxwell. The South Dakota
girl and her beau were walking farther west in Greenwich Village to
the White Horse, a willfully grungy bar on Eleventh Street and Hud-
son. They had left the Waverly Theatre on Fourth Street and Sixth
Avenue, pausing for some minutes to watch the furious rhythm with
which Negroes played basketball in the public court across from the
movie house. At one point she thought she noticed that a few of the
white guys who were athletes, there and ready to play, had the same
look of awe and indignation she had seen in some of the white jazz
musicians when they were listening to a band of Negroes turn into a
scalding band of angels.

    "I remember when some brothers got beat up over there around
those courts."

    "Over basketball?"

"Over Sylvester Stallone."

"Who would want to fight over him? He's so boring."

"Nobody wanted to fight over him. But Stallone knew what he was doing."

"Whatever he knew didn't have anything to do with talent. Oh, he's just the worst actor."

"There was no one close to a white champ, so he gave them one. The white man was the underdog. The brother—Apollo Creed—was on top and he was lazy and he was making fun of the country."

"You really paid attention to that garbage, didn't you?"

Maxwell looked at her with such pity that she gazed away, sensing that the conversation was going to evolve into a confrontation of some sort.

"Those were summer movies, you know?"

"If you say so."

"The Italian guys with the white T-shirts—you know the kind I'm talking about—they would get wild after those goddam Rocky movies came out."

"Oh, come on. These are just bad movies, you know that."

*"I'm serious. You had to be careful. A black guy had to be careful. They might try to become Rocky on **your** ass. I hate Stallone for that. He made the wop natives restless. Then they wanted to whop the shit out of you."*

With a professorial tone she found quite bizarre for him, Maxwell explained to Carla that in the first of the films, Rocky lost after putting up a good fight. But the movie got the Academy Award. White people wanted to see somebody stand up to these uppity niggers. That's why it was considered so inspirational. Then Rocky got a rematch and became champion in the next one. The Italian boys in New York really went nuts after that. It was a mess. Maxwell wouldn't go into the details but Carla knew—by the splash of bleakness that swiftly moved across his eyes and the timbre of his voice—that something had happened to him during that period. He might have been fighting for his life near those very basketball courts. It was the kind of unexpected, terrifying image that always made her feel as though she was about to urinate on herself. Carla wished to say something comforting but didn't know what that would be and found no way to slip in her compassion because everything Maxwell *said at that point was so large and expressive, even in its pauses as he looked her directly in the eyes, that she remained in an unusual silence, aghast at what her man had said and equally puzzled by how much detail there was to the thought he had given those ridiculous Rocky movies.*

The saga went on. Well, she assumed, it must.

After Rocky lost to Mr. T, who was the bad guy, the Italian Stallion had to get some training from the black guy who had lost the title to him.

"Who?"

"The guy who was based on Muhammad Ali. Apollo Creed?"

"Why did he have to do that?" (This one had better be good.)

Why? Because Stallone found out how big the black movie audience market was and he gave the world the bad nigger and the good nigger: the bad nigger is the one who will draw the black kids to see him whip your white ass mercilessly; the good nigger is the one who learned the error of his goddam ways because you whipped his ass and now he will help you satisfy the white audience by teaching you how to whip the ass of another buck-wild bad nigger. Ebony and ivory putting a double-clutch foot in a bad nigger's ass. A pure work of commercial genius. It pissed Maxwell the fuck off.

Even though his tone of voice never rose much above normal, Maxwell's morose analysis finally became a bit much for Carla, who, suddenly full of the trickster, decided to mock him in a covert manner by pretending that she found it unimaginable that anybody could live so intimately in terms of how sex or race was depicted in a commercial arena defined by its very crassness. That would turn things around. She had the scoop. It was now rather obvious what he was rolling out. Maxwell was just doing an ethnic version of a guy thing. They always loved to teach you something, or think they were. Might as well have some fun with him. Her mood now modulated to another emotional tonality, Carla decided to use some good old Midwestern wisdom that had been delivered to her back in the time when she was a kid athlete licking the batter spoon in the kitchen after practicing all Saturday morning with her big sister. Mom, whose baked goods were the talk of their church, lit a Camel, sucked her teeth, and said to Carla, "It's good to be underestimated. Keep that going as long as you can. Stay on it. Let them be as snooty as they want. Sure. Just you be humble, work so hard you almost get sick from it, then give them unfiltered hell when the time comes for it."

This mocking trick of laying in wait for your moment intersected with what was an interior battle strategy she maintained for the first few years of their living together. Her state in the very beginning of their romance was way down indigo. Grief was putting internal injuries on her emotions and any time this woman was terribly gummed up and blued up it always took her some time to fight her insides into order, to get free of what kept Carla from making it all the distance into what she considered the best of herself. One of the stratagems through which she conducted war on any kind of anguish or loss of confidence or repugnant discovery of something terrible within her spirit was to script a way of being and remain inside that character. There she could resist the terror and rage that had the complaining strength to fill her heart with a coagulating purple goo. Self-pity was always the melodramatic enemy. It had the power to corrupt any feeling, even that of true grief. She wasn't having that.

She wasn't going to let her guy blather on and on the way he wanted to about Sylvester Stallone either. Consequently, Carla played possum and enjoyed wearing the mask of the clunky white girl who didn't quite get it. Clueless blues. That invariably made Maxwell go into a Mr. Cool kind of pomposity and set himself up for a surprise that brought them closer together whenever she would later show off some of what she had found out about a world he thought she was largely unfamiliar with.

As Maxwell walked to Seventh Avenue and West Fourth Street with more of a swagger, stopped for the light, and went deeper into his chosen position as her instructor in the racial ways of the world rendered in pulp drama, Carla applauded herself again for the Negro cuisine she cooked with such imperial kitchen authority he couldn't believe what he was tasting in that first year of them living under the same roof. That let him know something. This girl from South Dakota could hang tough in the kitchen. She chained his heart more securely with those pots and pans.

But there was no mention made of sweet home Chicago when he had asked where a white girl like her learned to cook like that. Here and there was the answer. Nothing more. That was an iron doctrine. Unless they both knew him well, Carla never talked with a new man about an old one. Do unto others. It was always horrible enough to imagine yourself becoming part of some former sweetheart's repertory of tales he entertained his newest lady with, using you to make a point about something bad or to create a standard for behavior that would result in the next woman hating you the way people hate rules. Maxwell wasn't told all of that and only smiled that here and there was a helluva good goddam cooking school. "You already carrying that snow white Hottentot boody and now you're going to cook like you was born in a skillet of fish grease. Baby, you're the top." He rose from the dinner table of their loft in his ribbed, sleeveless undershirt, a toothpick in his mouth, and hugged her then with such dewy heat that a courtesan might have blushed at what she began to think. Then, the braggart rising in his mood, Maxwell spent the next few months inviting friends over to experience his woman's culinary skills, him sitting there with those sensuous eyes and looking at her as though she were as rare as a snow leopard. Exactly: just as she had a battle strategy to handle her heartbreak she had her wiles, too. So, she realized he was still saying, did Stallone. Yikes!

The great wop Rocky went to Russia and became the great white hope peacemaker.

Shuttle diplomacy, I presume.

Yeah. Exactly.

With boxing gloves?

You said it.

Absurd.

Not quite.

Absolutely stupid.

Uh-uh.

Have it the way you want it, Maxwell.

No, no. There were dramatic reasons for this: Rocky's very own good old white man's nigger had been hammered to death in the ring by the fists of a cruel Russian so big that just the wind from the sickle of a hook that missed would knock you out. That did it. Rocky wasn't having it. He had to avenge his faithful nigger. The nigger meant that much to him. Rocky came back from a monstrous beating to put his foot deep in the ass of the Russian. (Carla, her teasing gear fully in place, thought about asking if the Italians had then begun to attack Russian immigrants.)

That was bad enough, right?

If you say so.

But it didn't stop there.

How could it?

Rocky got the full stadium of Communists to applaud his idea that the USA and the USSR could get along if they tried. White ego, Maxwell said, had completely run amok.

Then the subject of Malena entered the conversation, which was a relief to Carla, who wanted to back out of her mask as a novice in need of knowing how things really worked. That had become tired. She was then made somewhat uneasy by the combination of her lover man's eccentric theories and the increasing severity of his anger over some dumb movies. He wouldn't be moved. But since she didn't go to see that kind of crap, she couldn't really say he was wrong. His doing a guy thing that she resented didn't matter. All that his theories added up to was something brutally ridiculous if he was right. It wouldn't be the first time. The brutal and the ridiculous—thank you very much—were good friends. They went back together, had warred against a whole lot of things as allies, had pouches of babies' hands in common, belts of shrunken skulls, lampshades of human skin. You name it. Carla, as the daughter of a history teacher who also taught the classics, and as a student of culture herself, was thoroughly aware of how much influence the film industry had on mass behavior and found it almost withering to again discern that no more than pulp examples of opportunism might result in even one person being attacked by some louts with skull-crushing clubs and bats. It could happen. All that crud went together, Carla sighed within her mind, the films that made men think they had so much entitlement, the films that put a celluloid ring in the collective nose of the German people during the Third Reich's moment, the crabbed images of American ethnic groups, the calls to war or to bitterness or to sentimentality. The experience of the air changed. She and Maxwell, now holding hands as they walked west, seemed so small at that moment, a couple of fiery molecules trapped inside an imposed misunderstanding, with nowhere to run, nowhere to hide, at risk in their invisibility, at risk in their visibility. Tales of Malena were welcome. Anger of her own was creeping into Carla, not as strong as Maxwell's but it could get like that if it kept going. You had to strike back if it got too dangerous, even if it meant nightmares upon nightmares. You couldn't lay back and enjoy it. You had to slash back or else. Stories of Malena would get her mind off of that. If not, the girl from South Dakota could calm herself and forget. She had been doing a good job of it for years. She could stick to her script.

Just as they were about to enter the White Horse, Maxwell slowed the pace of his walk as he told Carla that Malena's getting interested in boys made him kind of sad because she had been his brother and his sister in one package before the hormones started moving on her.

"Aaron was a sissy-assed faggot from the first day he was born."

Carla, unpleasantly used to his contemptuous way of talking about Aaron, noticed that some of the other customers in the White Horse had heard what Maxwell said as the two of them were sitting down. At first, the others took on the demeanor of people caught in an express subway car as someone begins to heave up the undigested stink of a particularly greasy meal. Then they began to recognize Maxwell, and Carla could see that both the desire to express their love of his music and the impulse to voice their disappointment in the man were wound up in an absurd brawl. Ambivalent silence mediated a longing and hostile draw.

"It was just in him," Maxwell said, sipping his cognac, then sipping his tap-beer chaser after they had ordered. "Aaron always liked boys and men in a homosexual way. I guess he did. It got past me for a long time. But my mother knew it, my daddy ignored it, and all the women in the church knew it."

"This makes me kind of curious about one thing, you know?"

"Yeah?"

"How did the church women think about it?"

"Funny that way that you asked."

She stared at him. He kissed her on the forehead.

"Your curiosity makes you very pretty, you know? When you want to know about different things, you look so different. It keeps your face from being boring."

"Thanks. Boy. Who ever heard anybody say that?"

"You."

They laughed.

"But what about the women in the church?"

"You want to know about that, huh?"

"Sure."

"Not like how bored you were about Sylvester Stallone."

"Well . . ."

"Don't deny it. I know how you are."

"That's why I love you. You know that, too."

"Oh, yeah."

Maxwell then kissed her on the lips, sat back, and put a worldly look on her that made Carla feel so safe and wanted her breathing went shallow. That look carried over into the sound of his voice, which had a cosmopolitan quality that belied the crude way he began talking about his younger brother.

"They had feelings for Aaron. The church women accepted him. They always accepted homosexuals. They didn't talk about it but they did it anyway."

"That's very strange to me. So odd. What another world. I always thought church people of whatever Christianity you want to name—you name it—I thought they back away from gay guys and lesbians."

Maxwell appeared to ignore what she had said. She hated that.

"Besides, dig this, Aaron could sing so pure. I'm telling you. So pure you couldn't believe it. Perfect notes, nothing too much, nothing too little. No vibrato. Something else all right. Aaron had it. His spirit was like a skyscraper. Soul on every floor. He put a very touching atmosphere in the air when he opened his mouth to sing. The holy voice of God came out of his throat."

Maxwell became silent, looking out the window onto Hudson Street, and Carla assumed that Baby Aaron had his first affair with the choir director. Those guys could be notorious for that. They had to be watched closely. The predatory ones were almost as bad as the priest she had read about. That priest was kicked out, got married, had kids, very cute ones, and tried to live happily ever after. As a man of the cloth, back in his barbaric days, he had his way with many boys. During a trial which Carla couldn't remember in exact detail, one of those who testified against the former priest was now grown up with wife and children. When he was young and terrified, things had happened that weren't evident in his clean-cut mature look. The former priest who sat there in court so calmly with his wife used to force this man to the floor of his office when he was a kid, rip his *pants down, and create an indelible nightmare. The bastard. Carla missed something Maxwell said.*

"The women in church will tell you some things. They will pull you aside when you don't understand what's happening. Then they might whisper. Those whispers are full of information. You got to listen then. 'You got to watch God. Watch Him. He will part the Red Sea in your soul and let something good walk through in perfect safety.' They will tell you stuff like that. They know what's happening."

He went on to say that Malena had always been so strong and so sweet. Maxwell recalled how she danced up and down when his mother was bathing her. Before she could talk she could sing. He heard notes coming out of her. If he could remember them he would play them right now. His sister's songs were based on odd scales and they didn't have any feeling in them other than the feeling of living. They weren't happy and they weren't sad and they didn't have any kind of meditative thing going nor did they seem to know the conditions of fear and pain that decide the directions of so much music. They meant nothing. If Maxwell could imagine an angel humming as it went about heavenly work the other side of anything we fixate on in the world of the flesh, that is what one of them just might sound like. He was pretty sure of that. The feathers of angels' wings were probably a bunch of different hums stuck together. They fly along on those hums because those hums are untouchable and they are invisible, like everything that means anything, like the soul, like the mind, like emotion. There he went, unintentionally charming Carla again.

Malena, he said, started off with mud pies and got as dirty as anybody could get short of being held by the back of her foot and deepdipped in quicksand. You couldn't tell that looking at her in church or listening to her flat little voice singing along, just under the adults', always trying to hide out of shyness but also penetrating with a feeling that had a glow in it. She loved books and lived in a wonderland. She wanted all the dolls in the world. One of her fantasies was to have a doll barn up on a very tall hill. In that barn, all of the dolls in the world would live once their owners fell asleep. In the doll barn they could all relax and it could be quiet. When they got tired of it being quiet, they would tell Malena all the stories of their different lands and they would tell her all the secrets of all the houses they lived in.

Her coordination allowed his little sister to learn to juggle immediately. She was a good public speaker. She leaned into an audience. One time he saw a picture of himself playing and realized that he leaned his saxophone into the people in the seats and wondered if he got that from Malena. Her cooking wasn't bad either. Maxwell didn't mind putting his feet under a table that had, hot off the stove, her food on top of it. Carla, teasing, told him it sounded like he had a crush on her. Maxwell didn't find that amusing. He made it clear that there had never been any kind of incestuous feeling toward Malena. The idea of that made him feel like he had stuck his finger down his throat and beat himself over the head with a hammer at the same time. But any time he would look at the muscles in her legs or watch as she got her sports rhythm going and her forehead became glossy with sweat, " I thought I was looking at something sacred. I'm serious now. I still have that feeling. I never loved anything in the world, even music, more than I loved my sister."

Carla was envious. She wondered if Randy Jr. ever felt that way about her. She would have sensed it if he did. But he **could** have. She didn't know for sure. It wasn't a positive thing. Now the corkscrew of worrying about it started turning inside her. Did Randy Jr. ever love her like that? Did he? That was another something she would never know.

Maxwell, after ordering himself another round, then confided that he had a secret aesthetic rescue technique. It gave him total power when he was working in a nightclub or on a concert stage or in the recording studio. If he wasn't being fed inspiration by his fellow musicians and he couldn't inspire himself, all Maxwell had to do was just concentrate with all his will until he got the clear, broiling image of Malena running so fast on the relay with her head back, or if he could see her out there in the hot sun leaning forward with the ball behind her waist and getting ready to go into the windup, her special little laughing squint in her eye: "Suddenly, Carla, I'm telling you, I start playing like a motherfucker. Notes start coming from everywhere. The tenor opens all the way up. So **much** emotion. When I'm pressing down the keys on the horn, they feel like velvet and notes seem to come out from under my fingernails. Malena does that for me. She always got the power. That makes the memory of her, well, I know it's strong as an angel looking out for me."

Carla felt lightly stung by those words. Her jealousy rose up much higher. She ordered another white wine and wished she could be Malena for somebody, anybody who would be creatively invigorated by the simple act of recalling her the way she had been once upon a liquid time in the sieve of the past. It was obvious to her, like it was to everybody else, that some kinds of memories were demons but she had never thought of a memory as a guardian angel. At his best, Maxwell was always easing her into unexpected areas of illumination. That was more important than any games either of them played, moving inside of and around each other's defenses. There were kinds of knowing he revealed to her that hurt as deeply as she had ever been hurt; there were also kinds that made her heart balloon and move out of its most recent measuring, even the loose and shapeless gowns of sensibility Carla assumed would allow her to—

Ezekiel stood up after everyone had finished the peach cobbler and ice cream desserts and invited Maxwell for a walk. The silence that had prevailed was done. His son rose up from the table, leaned over, and kissed Carla on the forehead. He rubbed her gently on the neck and said that he and Daddy would be back soon. Ezekiel smiled with the approval of a father who felt that his son had become man enough to know how to treat a woman. He joked with Eunice that she and Carla had better *be* there when the two of them got back or he was going to send the law out looking for them. Eunice replied that if he was going to do that, he should send the police to the airport because "if we leave here, we *really* going to leave."

As she was helping Maxwell's mother with the dishes, which she resented but did because she was in a foreign country called Houston, Texas, Carla noticed that Eunice, this still quite beautiful but stout lady of the house, moved around at such a deliberately slow pace that she was soon doing nothing other than toying with her diamond rings and her gold necklace while watching her son's ladylove cleaning up.

Carla's miniature anger at the obvious turning of the racial tables was transformed into a sort of humility as Eunice said to her in a timbre of voice she had never quite heard, "You doing good, girl, you doing good." The sound was pleasantly heated and it made Carla feel as though she were standing naked before this woman and being embraced for something older and much more mysterious than picking up plates, scraping what was left on them into the trash, washing and drying the cooking utensils, the silver, the plates, and glasses before placing them in the dish rack, where they remained until Eunice, now seated and picking her teeth, gestured toward the higher cabinets, the silver drawer, and the lower cabinets where the pots and pans were kept.

"Come on over here, girl. Come on now," Eunice said, standing up.

The lady of the house put those meaty arms around her son's lover in a way that made this newcomer feel as she had when Carla was small and her hair was being toyed with by her mother as they looked out the window at the South Dakota snow and sang Christmas carols very softly because, it was explained, Santa Claus didn't like drunken bellowing disguised as the holiday spirit. Yes, Mom was an easygoing aristocrat who loved to give everything just a little bit more refinement. She didn't come from money but everything had to be as good as one could make it; otherwise, human beings might as well be bestial ships moving along according to the rudders of instinct. Choosing things very carefully and getting everyone to the dinner table while the light was still alive and special, or reading a paragraph from a novel over and over, or memorizing Emily Dickinson, or taking the girls for walks and telling them what the name of each flower and each tree was, such were the kinds of things that Mom put her attention to, which created a particular kind of relaxation that had welcome written all over it and smelled of clean sheets and cleaning fluid. Carla, for no reason at all that she could see, wanted to cry but felt so stupid in that Houston kitchen because all of the feeling that appeared to come from Eunice could have just, in its reality, been so much less than she wanted it to be. Skepticism, even so, didn't stop the desire from remaining stationary in its familiarity.

Back in the time when women who looked like Eunice had visited her family's Lutheran church to sing, Carla had desired their approval. The perfectly dressed little girl smelling of soap and one wet fingertip of her mother's perfume behind each ear didn't know why she wanted them to love her but, even so young, she was already aware of the politeness that children get in place of affection, especially from strangers. Carla's trouble was already in place: nothing outside of herself was ever completely believed and nothing was ever enough. Some might say she suffered from excessive expectations. So, as with many people and situations, those black or brown or mustard or cream-colored big ladies were always just beyond her. She tried to vaguely nuzzle up to them and would receive a compulsory pat, but Carla felt that those women never took the people from her background seriously. It was their duty to God to sing His praises wherever they were invited but, as one of the Negro preachers had said when he gave a guest sermon, "Some folk spend so much time putting Vaseline on and swimming in motor oil it's hard for true goodness to get a grip on them. It's hard. They got to wash themselves clean first. But that kind of *sin* oil—the kind *I'm* talking about—that kind *hurts* to come off. Oh, yes it does. You got to be *willing* to stand *naked* with the blood from your scraped-off sins gushing right on out. You got to go there by yourself, not with your brothers, not with your sisters, not with your mother, not with your father. You got to be alone and you got to be grateful to be *known* alone. Known alone."

Those two words: known alone; known alone; known alone: rang like a clapper in Carla's sensibility—first as a child, then as a girl, last as a woman. That Sunday they rang during her girl time as the hulky Negro women and their men began to respond to the preacher, a separate ritual taking place right in front of those gathered in Carla's church. They began to shout back. They punctuated his statements. They became part of what he was preaching. They became known together. Together they became known. He said, then they said. Carla became excited but the look on the faces of her mother and her older sister were at a remove. Mom and Ramona were not disdainful; they just seemed unimpressed. Dad rocked a little in the rhythm, his smile giving Carla more confidence in what she felt. Randy Jr. seemed a bit frightened. He clung to Carla's arm. She was ashamed of him but knew far better than to try and push him away.

The visiting minister had moved from behind the pulpit now and was stalking the gathered. Sometimes one knee went up as if it were a cocking mechanism setting the next sentence in place. He turned to the choir. He walked to the left. He spoke out to the center. He boomed out against the right wall. He stage-whispered. His work of life was nowhere else but up there on that Sunday. He was following the call. Its existence was his essence. There was no other thought, no other thing, no other world.

"The Lord comes quiet, the Lord comes loud, the Lord comes

invisible, the Lord comes clear as day, bright as the sun at the noonday hour. I say, 'Amen.' The mysterious wonders of His ways should not never be forgotten. His eyes *never* close; *He* can see the littlest, teenanchy speck of dirt on your soul. *He* can see you reaching to scrape it off, too. Oh, He *knows* how hard it is for the heart out here in this lonely world, this world that can be so cold, this world where every door is closed and every path is blocked. But the Lord knows something else, too. I say He does. *He!* Oh, yes. The Lord knows every last one of you *can* stand up to the pain. Great God, I feel *good* this morning."

"Praise His name."

"Oh, you *can* stand up. Great God, I feel *good* this morning. Seem just like yesterday. Uh-huh. Looking everywhere for proof of the Word. Yes, yes. I feel *good,* I said. Oh, yes. Little me, just like little you. Wandering the wilderness. Desert far as you can see. No wind. Hell down here on the ground. Caught in a crisscross but unaware of the *true* cross. Seem like yesterday. Then I found the Word and the Word found *me*. It could happen to you. Uh. Yes. Don't get lost. Don't you get lost. Oh, I say you *can* stand up. Good God a'mighty, you *know* you can. You can put a *handle* on that pain. You can hold that pain in the skillet of your soul and you can pour it *out*. Just like it's hot grease. You can pour that pain in that Crisco can. The sun of the Lord will be the flame to heat the skillet of your soul if you let the grease of that pain settle and cool off and turn gray on you. When the face of your soul has turned gray, you better know you are in big trouble. Don't get lost in what I'm saying. Keep your eye on the sparrow of the Word. Listen to what I'm saying. A gray soul is a dangerous thing. Got to put some heat on it; got to melt that pain; got to pour it out. But if *you* don't know it, you *lost,* you *blind,* you mumbling in the wilderness. You will *never* know the in-time, on-time, timeless light that stands, forever heated up, behind the eternal Word."

It was finished; he moved backward and sat down. The presence of his sermon and the sound of his people still lay heavy in the room. It was something Carla knew nothing about other than the fact that she had never felt quite that way when she came to church. It was not more beautiful than what she was used to; it was just differently beautiful. She had discovered that she could be touched in a new way.

Over time, for there were many visits, Carla sensed that those

Negroes thought all these people descended from northern Europeans who had suffered like hell to get where they settled—fighting the weather, the Indians, starvation, bad luck, and each other—were not on the spiritual A-list. Nothing was ever said. There were no supercilious looks, but Carla believed that none of them assumed that the Swedish, Norwegian, German, and Dutch people in that congregation would ever get tickets to ride on the glory-bound train. It was inconsequential how surprised people like the Norwegians on both sides of her family had been upon discovering the horror and the excruciating labor this strange new land imposed on all willing to enter it. The bones out there in the American wilderness—the cannibalism of the Donner party, the massacres, the high infant mortality—meant nothing to the Negro Christians visiting Carla's church. Suffering in and of itself was not enough. The black people, so often sweating and patting themselves with handkerchiefs, were distant even though they seemed jovial and warm. Their distance didn't have the feeling of a trick, a mask; it was just a queer kind of sadness that never left their faces and gestures unless they were talking with themselves. Then their burdens seemed to lift, just as their burdens lightly arrived whenever they were approached by a member of this white church or stood among them talking. Not being among those sanctified Negroes always made her sad in a very special way. It was a hurt that had no name on it. Far inside her, Carla hoped that Eunice's embrace meant that she had been accepted, that the fleshy warmth, the perfume, the mascara, and the baby powder that she smelled were all central to a spiritual recognition that she had needed for so, so long.

4

SHOPPING FOR NOTHING

Eunice loved to go shopping, even if she didn't buy anything. Malls, which Carla hated, were special microcosms to Maxwell's mother and she walked through them as though they were her very own castles. Carla found something moving in the way Eunice would stand on an escalator or how she would peruse jewelry, blouses, underwear, and sigh with self-deprecating humor at the dresses now too small for her. Rare had been the time since college when she saw a woman so confident, or at least one in whose self-assured company she hadn't experienced the equally self-defensive impression that being allowed to tag along was some sort of favor.

The wife of Ezekiel spoke of the shops with a possessive pride, of what they had to offer, and of how high the quality of the merchandise was. One would have thought that she was bragging about something she owned, especially since it seemed that every proprietor and every employee in every shop—Negro, white, Mexican, West Indian, Vietnamese, Pakistani—knew Eunice and spoke to her with an affection that had none of the taint of business. They talked about nothing, absolutely nothing—the weather, what had been on television the night before, what movies they intended to see, how their cars were running, and whatever else—but somewhere beneath the surface of the words, even when the mutilated immigrant English was far the other side of easy comprehension, somewhere in the rhythm of the speech and the way the voices swooped up and down the registers, there was a connection that had a luminosity, one that made the trivia of the conversation sort of a code behind which there was substantial fraternity, compassion, affection. Carla felt chagrined for trying, so often, to find a way to look down on what were quite high-level doings. She knew that opening her heart was always the challenge and—a long drop from a welt-covered high-mindedness—always the mushy approach of the naive who wanted the world to be a lot sweeter than it ever fucking was. Maybe the various things going on around Eunice weren't such impressive emotional codes in a perpetual sense. They couldn't *always* be. There had to be those who talked about trivia who actually *were* trivial. It would be frightening to think that all of those people whom she had found so boring over the years weren't truly boring at all, just types whose ways of communicating had gotten by her and who resided in a land of far greater meaning than her own gleeful smugness could comprehend. Yeah, right.

Seated and eating huge hot fudge sundaes with Eunice at the top level of the mall, Carla was suddenly amazed at how she was able to see the many floors and the many shops through the eyes of the woman she hoped would someday become her mother-in-law. Some sold gunk, some sold better gunk, but others sold good things and the air-conditioning made all of the discoveries of who had what and where it ranked much more relaxed than such explorations would have been out in the hot Texas sun. And beyond the way the people who staffed this place related to Eunice, something was going on. There was sort of a community to the mall because the template of Southwestern ease and humor got up over the racial fences and made these long-term and newly arrived ethnics sort of a modern American tribe broken into different styles. The connectives were commercial, which meant that what some would only see as the crass arena of the merchandise, the price tags, and the cash registers actually brought together what would have been nearly a Tower of Babel, since the nation was, again, remaking itself as people from other places brought their backward customs and their optimism into the culture, irritating the mainstream that had to adjust as much as it could to what these new people understood and did not understand, what they did well and what they did badly, how they tried to get with the way things were done and how they stubbornly resisted dissolving into Americana once they found out that this was a country in which you could abrasively move along if you remained within the law of the land and the locale. That was the adult stuff. The conflict between the symmetrical and asymmetrical was always central to the mutating national biography, which was why youth culture based itself on asserting an angularity tied to offensive trends, attempting, at least since the middle fifties, to give its insecurities a symbolic relationship to the feeling of the immigrant alien, however little the young, being ahistorical and narcissistic, knew about any of that. So the children in the mall all shared the same torpid language of boredom, attraction to bad taste, the desire for a secret distance from the world of grown-ups that was symbolized by their headphones and their rocking to something nobody else could hear; but that weird adolescent sort of sullen fervor could turn into something fresh and pure if the kid got just a little bit of attention with some feeling on it. Unlike in New York, which always extended some sort of a dare, the overall energy of the people was caressing or more like a solid handshake or even a good-willed slap on the back.

Not only. Eunice told her, as if countering what Carla was thinking but not saying, that there was also a violent thing in Texas. It came from all the wild white folks who immigrated into this territory and fought the Indians from over here, who were pretty rough redskins themselves, known to butcher each other and the Scotch-Irish intruders in possession of reputations throughout the South for biting each other's ears and noses off and thumbing out each other's eyes over plenty of nothing. And everybody knew that Mexicans had a taste for blood since they loved them some cockfights and bullfights, which was also exactly how the people Eunice came from were—the worst of them bloodthirsty, by the way, since her roots were in Louisiana and Mississippi, where some certain kinds of Negroes would cut you or shoot you just as soon as look at you. So any kind of peaceful behavior was doing good, which was usually how it actually was, though there could be times like back some years ago, during the eighties, when there was the summer drought so bad people ended up sitting by their air conditioners with guns to make sure they didn't wake up to a fast car or pickup truck taking off with their air-cooling box and leaving them to face up to the threat of a heart attack if they were too old to stand the kind of heat they knew too well from long ago when they were children and nobody, even the rich people, had anything other than some fans to handle the season.

That fit perfectly with everything else, once Carla took in things with a little closer attention. Her sense of surprise and wonder stayed in place but it changed emotional color as some hurts were added. Now it was seeming complete. She could surely see the unhappiness here, the adulterous meeting there, the naiveté that was jubilantly cruising for what would someday be a terrible bruising, the child who had a combination of sadism and self-absorption in his or her eyes, the man who had grown tired of his wife because she had disappeared into bovine slovenliness, or the woman who was suffocatingly bitter because sex, frequent or infrequent, had been drained of all romance and passion, resulting now in the hollow climaxes that sent the troubled woman—once she knew that she had failed again at finding any love pushing her to orgasm—into the bathroom, where she might weep for half an hour with the shower running and the door closed before she could return to that cold, cold bed. Life weighed the same even if the scale it stood on was inside of an air-conditioned mall. My, my, wasn't she just the gauche girl on vacation down in Texas?—which she *had* been to, once upon a time in another life, when she was singing country-and-western music terribly and was known as Tammy Lee because one of her guys thought, like they *all* did, that she was as hot as a hot tamale. Maxwell didn't know about that. Why should he? Her past was her own.

"Carla," Eunice said as she finished her sundae, "I could almost live in here. It's the whole world except they don't sell cars and tires. I could wear new dresses every day, sleep my big butt on one of those sure enough wonderful mattresses, eat here, eat there, go to the movies—they're two floors down—and just have myself a time. But even if I mentioned this idea to Ezekiel, just sort of playing, you know, he would give me the pity-that-poor-woman look. Sometimes, he's too serious about anything you bring up, anything that happens on this earth. But I might as well get to it. Do you think you love Maxwell?"

"I know I do."

"Love don't stay the way it looks at the start, you know."

"I know."

"Oh do you now? I don't think that's quite possible. You too young. You don't know what I'm saying."

"I hope I can learn to understand what you mean." She wasn't that young and Lord knew that life had left its thumbprint on her.

"I hope you can learn, too; it'll keep the both of us from wasting time. Dumb, you know, is so slow it hurts. But you ain't dumb anyway. Back to the point: What I mean is love has some funny ways. Very funny."

The odd strains and difficulties that came with deeper affection were forces Carla knew well. She could speak on those herself.

"You got to leave it so many times. You got to have feelings don't seem to have nothing to do with it. Isn't these sundaes good, girl?"

"You said it."

"Boy, oh, boy. Yum-yum. Love don't stay sweet like this, you know. Not at all. Sometimes you get so far away from where you started, you never think you will get back. I'm serious, serious as the last breath of a baby. You can get far away. I have truly felt that way with Ezekiel. Numerous of times. He's a hard man to love because he's so strong. You can't find the little weaknesses women love to squat on. With him, you got to stand up. You got to rise up above yourself."

Before Carla could ask Eunice what she meant, Eunice began telling her the story of Malena. Everything about these people was like Maxwell. On your mark, get set, go! Now, mind you, remember to notice that you aren't now going where you were going. What a crew of oddballs.

Always beautiful, Malena had expected to get everything she wanted but had never been the kind of woman who liked the men who got anywhere. Oh, no. That would be too much like sense. She had a preference for the low type, thick men with gold teeth and Jheri-kurls, men who had bad thoughts on the boil and plenty of bad memories swelled up inside them. Somehow—you better watch out—the men always had grace, kind of an animal ease in the thoroughness of their power, and Malena appeared to always become little more than a perfumed cigarette that they French-inhaled with relish and snubbed the light out of. Bringing her back from that had always been rough. Hard as pulling walrus teeth. Terrible. She would stop talking much about anything. Silent as a coma. Her room would become her prison cell, where some recording about love got played over and over and over until Eunice had to demand that she put on her headphones. But Eunice was the mother and she was the child and Eunice knew how to pat and rub her daughter and sometimes just hold her hand as they looked out the window. Or she would order her to go riding and take her way up to East Texas, where some of her favorite relatives were, the old folks, and Malena would warm as she sat slumped in the seat. When she got out of that car and felt all that love she had known since she was as small as it was possible to remember, the girl would start to come back to herself. Some of that peach cobbler and ice cream would lift her right up. Chicken and dumplings in the expert style. Collard greens from right behind the house. They would get her to talking that *tut,* the language Negroes invented to keep the white folks outside of knowing anything, with words like dud-a-mum, which meant damn, and fuff-o-square, which meant fool. Put those together. Mmm-hmm. That Texas Negro: nothing like it.

Then, on the way back home, the world out the car window just passing by, it would bust out: all the humiliation and the loneliness that came of not being with a man who had convinced her child that she was *his* heart and who, with all his devilish ways, had become *her* heart. Eunice would listen as the blubbering got louder and louder, sometimes almost to the point of Malena shrieking that she couldn't stand it, that she would go somewhere and stay if she knew where to find that somewhere. Eunice had learned to have a purse full of handkerchiefs. She would pop it right open and put them on the seat. If Malena didn't notice, she would take her right hand off the wheel and put one in her daughter's left hand. Handkerchiefs were more personal and the Chanel perfume on them seemed to work on the feelings like Ben-Gay did on the sore muscles. Slowly and slowly, Malena pulled off that snakeskin of heartbreak but Eunice always knew that snakeskin was hung up somewhere in her daughter's mind as a memory no one could help her get rid of, fangs still attached. Eunice thought Malena was kind of like steak. Instead of it getting harder the more you beat, what you end up doing is tenderizing it.

That idea put a tightness in Carla's chest. It clarified something that made her quite uncomfortable. The next thing Eunice said was so shocking Carla didn't respond. Eunice looked at her, let it seep its way in, and repeated herself, using exactly the same words.

"One married the girl and tried to kill her for the insurance."

"Tried to kill her?"

"You heard me. Son of a something. Knew everything about cars there is to know. Ezekiel first started thinking he had a future. Nothing impresses him more. My husband loves him a man can lay up under a car. Out there fixing and fixing until the car gives in. Until it throws up both hands. Until it decides to do right. But Ezekiel also gets him those angelic telegrams. You best believe me. These are when he's sleeping. The bed gets wet. Big mess. First I always think he's peeing all over me. He's not, praise the Lord. Oh, no. Not that. The Creator is baptizing him in the future. That's my husband. Yes, it is. Sat up fast as a switchblade one cold and lonesome night and said, 'Malena better get away from that man. Get away! He got total harm on his mind.'"

Carla had the feeling of being caught between the real and the unreal, the true and the hallucinated. There was nothing she could say. It sounded absurd but she had learned that just nodding to mean that you had heard what was said was a way of not lying while not insulting the person telling you something.

Eunice, her mind suddenly a pinwheel of memory, spun the tale in a different direction as Carla heard her tell that she caught Malena, her only daughter, with her panties off too early and they battled like two hurricanes, the daughter telling the mother that she loved this worthless dicky who was so much older than her: "His years would have had to bend over backward and hold their ankles before they got down to where she was." As Carla expected, Eunice won out: "She wasn't going to mess around and end up bringing no tiny snot machine in *this* house. Oh, no. Not in this house. Not here. Not in this lifetime. Finally, mad as hell that I had to do it, I told her how to protect herself because there was just no use to looking out for Malena: That child was born to run the other way."

Eunice paused and vaguely scrutinized the empty dish of her sundae, toying with the plastic spoon and waiting for the strength to tell the rest, or maybe just rummaging her mind for the right words. Carla felt very uneasy in this public place because there was no clear reason why this family intimacy, however disjunctive, was being offered. Then Eunice patted her on the hand and looked into Carla's eyes, tears running down her brown cheeks. Her eyes were closed as she breathed deeply and held Carla's hand. Passersby looked on with a certain sympathy or ominously snatched their children as the tots started to giggle, point, or ask a question about why that lady was . . . Then, after a bit, Maxwell's mother began to speak.

"Ezekiel told Malena to get her fast tail away from that Rodney. She couldn't live here and stand up to her father like she did to me. I'm the only one can stand up to Ezekiel. The only one. So Malena left the house right then and got her own apartment in a nasty pink stucco building in the Fifth Ward. Worst part, not the best part, like we used to live in before Ezekiel's accident money came through, which was due to a white lawyer down here who sniffed the cash piling up and chased the ambulance right to our house. Pecos Andy Bill Jackson. Known for riding them law books like bronco stallions. Hard to throw him. Rough in the court. Makes the other guys cry a trail of tears as they leave court after they been told how big a check they're going to have to sign. Got us done *plenty* right. Cold as a straight razor on a January morning. But nobody can do *everything*. Even *he* couldn't help Malena when it came time for her to get help. She didn't *want* him to do nothing. That's understandable, however, if you think about the place she went to just so she could be with Rodney. That tells you just how much she loved that Negro. The place is just terrible, with all the screens torn, the babies crying, and the men drunk, high on some kind of dope and waiting to fight. Now Rodney now, he wasn't *none* of that. Got to give him that. *Got* to. Oh, yes, got to give him *that*. All of that boody-butt fool acting them other boys made their specialty, well, girl, that was—you better believe it—a few notches *below* him. Rodney had him a *job*. BMW: black man working. That was Rodney. Greasy Negro sweated all day and partied all night, which is why, for instant, he had beginning bags under his eyes much, much too early for a young man."

Carla began to see Rodney, slightly, but nothing said about him had the substance of willful homicide. Of course, she remembered that there had been tests given to the man in the street—pictures of jurors and of murderers. No one could ever tell the difference. How different would Rodney look from Maxwell—who had his own "beginning bags" under his eyes—or from any other bulky guy whose charisma arrived through the power of conviction? The part about her daughter was more palatable. On the way to the mall,

Eunice had already taken Carla through the Fifth Ward and slowly drove past what the South Dakota girl now realized was the pink stucco place where Malena had lived until she got a home with Rodney. Eunice had shaken her head as she looked around. It was noisy, some of the young mothers cursed at their children, and some boys with expensive Jeeps sat up on the tops of the front seats, stockinged feet on the dashboards, radios blasting and waiting for the young mothers to come to them. Some were shirtless in the heat and had the ugly dark scars left from gunshot wounds and the surgery used to patch them up. If quicksand had a mood, that was it.

"Rodney finished off Ezekiel with the white 1948 convertible Cadillac. Finished him. Gone. My husband could not have been any more impressed if that boy had started dancing on the sun and came back to earth cool as a cucumber. Rodney had worked on that old Cadillac until it was looking brand new. Showroom level. Pretty thing shined and floated down the road. Still silly to me, though: all that time under a car. Actually, I'm *sorry:* I have to laugh—hee-hee-hee—because I always wanted to ride in it myself. Ain't I a mess? What can you say? You should have seen it, Carla. I bet it would have got to you."

Carla couldn't imagine it. She had never been attracted to primitive men, which was what Rodney sounded like, but there had been times in her life when a man showing his sophisticated relationship to some kind of machinery gave him that added kind of force, where the primal and the refined got so mixed up together that what this female from South Dakota considered truly masculine made her come to attention.

"Ezekiel and his friends called it *the iron horse.* But beautiful is all you could call it if you called it right. And Rodney with my poor lost Malena stuck to him like a postage stamp. Well now. His big hat and his Jheri-kurls. No never mind to nobody. Through the night streets on the weekend, there he was riding and smoking and spitting and rattling those gold rope chains around. Oh, he was a mess."

"This was when she was in high school?"

"Oh, no, college, girl. Malena was still living here, though."

"When had things happened with the older man?"

"That was in high school. The girl didn't learn nothing from that, nothing at all. Maybe her trouble is she never did get older than she was then. I mean older inside of herself. I don't think to this day my daughter ever got a good enough kind of recognizing going on to see what was wrong. The man took advantage of her. She was abused. He was a white teacher. White as they make them. His name was Childress. John. Blue eyes. The man was just as handsome as he was no good. I *never* told Ezekiel, not even a little bit of something. Everybody would have ended up crying if I had done that. I just told Mr. John Childress the truth. I told him Ezekiel would *kill* him. Old Mr. John's eyes got to hopping around then. Oh, he was shook. He had seen Ezekiel. He knew what he was looking at. Pulling down that zipper was opening up a grave. Oh, he backed off that girl. My baby knew damn well better than to tell her father. Malena's wild but she's not crazy. Ezekiel would have murdered the man and the white people would have executed him and it would have been the biggest mess since they gave a whole herd of elephants two buckets of Ex-Lax one by one. No, no: we had to hold that truth back. Her and me had to handle that heartbreak. But Malena knew about men then. She knew the feeling of the flesh. I had to teach her what to do. If I didn't . . ."

Eunice's eyes now had the harsh calm of a serial killer as she folded her arms. There were no more tears. Her soul appeared to have evaporated. Carla had known that experience, that internal blank slate, and had learned how to keep things to herself because nobody other than you would ever have any idea what lethal fury the fear of death could bring out. She, Eunice, and Malena had something private in common. Eunice nodded in acknowledgment of the unspoken and continued.

"Pitiful. Try as we may and try as we could, Malena wouldn't hear nothing against him and married Rodney way too soon. Way, *way* too soon. Then they got it in their minds to go on an insurance spree. Well, I know he must have put it in her mind. That's right. He got her mind right where he wanted it. Devilish man. They got all kinds of insurance. Insurance for this, insurance for that. Policies on top of policies. Insurance up the rooty-tooty. I doubt they missed insuring the fishbowl."

A midget laugh leaped free of Carla's mouth before she could stop it.

"Well, I may laugh and joke, but I don't play."

Carla became quiet and looked Eunice right in the eyes to let her know, once more, that she didn't play either. Their intimacy clenched like a fist of mutual recognition. Eunice half smiled and went on.

"Before you knew it, that gold-toothed pot of evil had got under the wheels and fixed the brakes on Malena's car. Fixed them for death. Planned it for rush hour. She was right in the middle of traffic fast as the law allows. He wanted my baby girl dead in a car crash. Now that's what he wanted, ain't no doubt about that. That's what he wanted. This Negro was so cold, he was so cold and in lack of the compassion of the beating heart that he could stand up in our faces smiling while he wanted me and Ezekiel to have to bear witness to Malena's destruction as she lay dead cold and crushed up on the terrible cooling board."

Then, Eunice had a light of mirth enter her eyes. It startled Carla, who was thinking about how hard a trip that would be after the phone call. My God: wishing all the way to the frigidly impersonal morgue that the body with a tag on its toe was the corpse of somebody else. Praying the entire distance to feel relief instead of horror when the sheet was lifted up, wanting to see a mangled stranger, naked and stiff, nearing the time of the autopsy knife.

"Maxwell never heard one word about that. We knew that hothead he got. Just like Ezekiel. He still don't know, and he never *will* know. Right now, long as it is later, if he found out, he would go looking for Rodney. Right now. Right now. Oh, yeah. Talking sense wouldn't do nothing about it. Maxwell would find him, too. He still around. That fool just hasn't found anybody to murder for some stack of damn money, so he's going straight as he can, still driving that iron horse."

The first night that they had arrived, after Maxwell had pounced on her like old times and she had met him with her own fire, each of them quivering against the other at the end, every kiss remaining on her body like a fading brand that had sweetly sizzled under her skin, Carla was still awake and looking out the bedroom window at the moon when that white 1948 Cadillac had slowly rolled past the house on its white-walled tires, shining under the full light of the sky, the top down but the smoked windows up. Now she knew why it had frightened her.

Carla was wondering exactly what Rodney had done to the car to make the brakes fail but she didn't ask. This was no time for pushing. Obviously, Malena had survived. There was a haze to it, which made the guy seem like an evil demon in a fairy tale who had secret but deadly magic.

"Rodney. Negro must have looked at some old movie. I know it like I know my name. With John Garfield and Lana Turner, something about a postman and some ringing."

"*The Postman Always Rings Twice?*"

"That's it, girl, that's it! You ever seen it?"

"Yes, I have."

"I used to be just that Lana Turner size, you know, but I wouldn't give up one teaspoon of gravy to get back to that kind of old skinny and pretty. I may be big enough to shake a house but I can shake a man's heart, too. Believe me, girl. I can do that."

That kind of self-assuredness in a world where slim, slimmer, and slimmer than that were the ideals repeated over and over in the media always beguiled Carla. She had put in more than twenty years adoring the Bessie Smith song about being a big fat mama with the meat just a-shaking off her bones, and every time she shook, some skinny girl lost her home. But Carla also remembered how clearly she had once seen herself as a blonde icy Venus of the sort Lana Turner was—the sexy nova who confronted John Garfield with the genre of contempt every woman should show toward the obvious intentions of crude men. As a teenager, Carla had cultivated a low-pressure version of that knowing haughtiness, not enough to appear repulsive but an amount adequate to make it clear that there were no free rides coming and one had better be ready to be charming or sincere enough to melt the adolescent heart of a teenage girl who, behind the demeanor of a difficult test question, didn't actually know very much at all. As a woman in the fullness of her heat and power, Carla had no nostalgia for that phase of innocence. She just wanted Maxwell to never forget who she really was.

"Something wrong?"

"No, not really. Just a dark cloud went through my mind. It's gone now. Go ahead, please tell me more. I'm so intrigued I'm almost ashamed to say it. You really make me feel like I'm part of your family, Eunice."

"Like Ezekiel said, you right here with us. We can tell. But you know all that."

"I still appreciate it."

"Now you making me feel self-conscious, girl."

"I'm sorry."

"Don't be sorry, just be steady," Eunice laughed.

Carla couldn't help smiling and was quite happy that she couldn't.

"Anyway, back to that Rodney. I'll go to Jesus believing it. I will. I know it *had* to be a movie on his mind because Rodney didn't read *anything*. Basically, the man was ignorant, which Malena— except when it came to men—was not. He wasn't stupid. Just ignorant. Didn't get educated. Didn't think he had to. Thought he knew all he needed to know. When you come down to it, the man wasted his brain. It was a shame. This was a real shame, girl, that hairy chest and that velvet black skin going to waste. Yeah, he had the look of charm to him, low-down dog with snake eyes, hypnotize you if you look too long. That man was made to make you think the wrong things. Get you to feeling so safe he could kill you when you wasn't looking. Malena didn't believe it. She did not come back home to us until after it was clear that the man had intended to destroy her. But he couldn't take his little ninety days in jail and go. He couldn't near about do that. So Rodney almost lost his own no-good life, prowling around here. Around *here,* do you hear me? Then he was standing at the door, holding a can of Old English, drunk as Noah, no shirt, his belly hanging over his belt. He stands there with eyes red as blood just cursing me and Ezekiel and Malena. Crazy, huh?"

"Well, it could be something else."

"What else is that?"

"Maybe he wanted to get hurt."

"He came to the right place."

"From what I've read, maybe he felt guilty for the hurt he had caused all of you."

"He should have felt guilty."

"He probably did. So it could be that, too, Eunice. Don't leave that out, you know. It could easily be something like that: He could have been asking to be punished by pushing and pushing until someone did something to him."

"Smart. Smart. That could be just right. It could be. I guess it could. But it didn't matter at *that* time. There was no thinking in this house. I had a gun in my hand but I just didn't choose to send him home to Satan right then. If we hadn't of had that thick gate door, though, if he could have kicked his way in, well, it would have been hell to tell the captain."

As Maxwell drove Carla through the Negro community in the rental car, he pointed out that those who were doing well, just like his mama and daddy, all had "prison doors" on their houses to keep the criminals out. He said to her that prison doors were the cost of being black during these days. It was a bitch. Black people used to be prisoners on the plantation, lifelong property of the white man, unless he decided to sell them off to some other white people. Now black people were prisoners in their own homes because the criminal niggers that had all their guns tried to run the neighborhood nigger plantation by scaring the hell out of everybody. These niggers wanted your property, your ass, and maybe your life. Just like the white plantation, these niggers—who used nine-millimeter pistols and Uzis instead of whips—wanted what your labor produced; they wanted your body if it appealed to them, and they could kill you if you got too uppity when they were ripping you off. They could destroy families with their dope; they could turn the girls into crackhead whores up on the auction block. Plantation redux, like a motherfucker.

Carla was shaken by the dark description of life under the constant threat of crime, but she felt that she had to remind him of the walled-in white communities in Miami, all of them reminiscent of similar things in Third World countries, where the rich protected their property and their leisure with armed guards, barbed wire crowning the concrete walls that surrounded their estates, and the most savage dogs that money could buy. They were trying to hold back the hellfire. If the criminals were ruthless or rugged enough to take their chances, something far from light and easy was waiting for them on the other side of those walls. With a little dagger of sarcasm in his tone, Maxwell said that the people those white people were trying to protect themselves from were niggers, too, which meant that maybe things had finally gotten more equal in the United States: Black people and white people were both terrified of wild niggers.

"So with this velvet black Negro howling at my door, all right now: I had to hold back that hate, Carla, I had to hold it back. With all my will, I had to hold it back. If Ezekiel had been there, all the nights he scared me near to vomiting, us laying up in bed and him muttering so coldly about this boy trying to murder his baby girl. I know the cold in that feeling. I know it. I was there and I heard it. So I don't have no doubt that my husband would have taken that gun from my hand, pushed me aside, and made sure that Rodney would be dead as Abraham Lincoln. Blown back from the door with a big hole or two in that hairy chest. Just like he deserve to be. Oh, he deserve it. Believe me, he *deserve* to be dead."

The silence then was a pocket deep enough to hide the world in. Carla was sure that the worst would have led to the blood on their porch and the police cars everywhere, the cops, full of superiority and disdain, knocking on the door and asking questions you didn't want to answer, while all you wanted was to back away from the red night experiencing only the fusion of regret and a sense of accomplishment, of not having been transmogrified into a flesh-and-blood whimper. Then that thing nobody wanted to go through, which was all of the publicity, with the people you didn't know now knowing you and turning your every appearance away from the inside of your home into a spectacle. Good this woman hadn't had to go through that.

Eunice looked in her hand mirror, patted her hair, put on some lipstick, squeezed some drops into her eyes to take the red out, and suggested that they go walking around some. She told Carla that another hot fudge sundae would be too good to pass up if she sat there any longer, so the best thing to do was get away from that rich temptation. They went to look at some linoleum, some curtains, and listened to a guy explain why satellite dishes were the future of television. Many more channels. Far better reception. Eunice knew about the satellite dishes already but she allowed herself to become intrigued because, it was obvious, *more* was one of her favorite words.

As she and Eunice were moving around, Carla recalled the morning when she was lying in bed about ten years ago, snug and convinced she was in love with Bobo Williams, the first one she had known with dreadlocks. She had been in New York for a few years and was shyly trying to find her way into the music scene, wanting to sing but afraid to let anybody hear her, working as a waitress, and wishing there were still taxi dance hall jobs so that she could be held all night and hear those good old Broadway tunes. In her fantasy, Carla didn't care about the risk of clumsy guys stepping on your toes or the numbing fatigue at the end of the night. That was a small price in order to be held. There were fantasy compensations. Taking a long, long bath, then sitting down on something perfectly comfortable, then soaking your feet before sleep would most assuredly have been three of the great pleasures in the world.

When she had daydreams of that sort back then, Carla laughed at herself, since she lived in a tiny space five floors up in an East Village apartment building, the best she could get and the most she could afford. While one could just as easily dream in the East Village as anyplace else, it was silly to try and Miniver Cheevy your way through a time when collapse, degradation, and all manner of pretense were the constants. Carla, repulsed by the casual filth of the streets and the buildings, found herself wandering among the poor Puerto Ricans, the old Jews left over from blue-collar poverty, the lower-class Negro families here and there, as well as the many so-called avant-garde types in music, theater, dance, and writing. Somewhere there had to be a strengthening emotion for her, an event or a person or a movement that could turn all the burners on in her soul and her mind. That was as hard to find as a good man. Too frequently, other than knowing how to ask what a customer wanted as she waitressed in one of the cheap restaurants, Carla felt as though she had become mute, crippled by her inability to stand up to the city with the strength she found that it demanded. She could hear, she could absorb, but she couldn't really say to anyone who she was or what she wanted or where she had already been.

All the confidence of her past was on hold somewhere in her sensibility. Carla felt as though New York had tied her self-assurance up in a chair and punched holes in it with an ice pick the way robbers had done an old cook from Harlem she used to listen to tell stories about the glory days of the Village, when Charlie Parker walked the earth. At other times, she didn't feel made into a Swiss cheese of intimidated inertia. She felt as though she were something else altogether. Looking at the moon one spring night when the city seemed to be singing itself to sleep—both gutturally and with a shrill display of undaunted *ineptitude*—Carla, her heart plummeting, believed herself to be the central character in the story of a homemade fish swimming in a part of the ocean made so dark by extravagant self-love that eyes were irrelevant. The thought smacked her groggy. The woman at the window of her tiny East Village apartment shook off the internal blow and became a spectator looking at the image of herself: Carla the fish started to swim upward and, along the way, discovered how to cut through the closed eyelids and begin to see. At first, she saw nothing but her own blood, then, moving past the melodrama of the entire metaphor, the South Dakota girl was humbled by how much life beyond herself there actually was. Manhattan, in that sense, was perfect for her.

New York was the only place she knew of where the sheer weight of the human intensity wore one down to fatigue, made you feel as though you had done a job. This was true even if all you had done was take a long subway ride and gotten out somewhere uptown, looking for another one of the town's many moods, its special tone of feeling that was determined by wealth or ethnicity. Ethnicity, trips around town taught her, was the endless riddle because every group had so, so many versions of itself, from the bottom to the top, from the top to the bottom. When someone said, "I'm a . . ." it didn't mean anything of particular substance until you got to know the person. It was usually no more than a perverse party favor, an effect, an attempt to simplify a moment in the conversation. Of course, Carla was not doing too much talking, but she saved enough money to purchase a middle-range wardrobe that allowed her to go in many different kinds of places and seem a regular. That way she was able to study the neighborhoods and the people, east and west, from the downtown seaport south of the city through all the ascending blocks and hills up to the northern borderline of Harlem, which she didn't have the nerve to enter because no one she knew downtown had any idea what was going on up there other than hostility, protests, and a complete lack of interest in the rest of the city and any of the good things it had to offer. Well, that was what people **said**, black and white. Harlem was a cultural cadaver. What did she know? What did they know? Harlem could just as easily have been an urban garden of kaleidoscopic souls like just about everywhere else in Manhattan, but Carla needed someone to take her by the hand and knew not one person who could.

She had some very rough times for a period, hid out in her apartment, ran around with an out-of-town crowd, sublet her place while she went on a wild-goose chase, then came back, like some sort of backwards lemming who couldn't stay gone, who had been turned into a denizen, no matter how unpleasant some of her life had been in the East Village. At the time that she returned, the Asian women in New York, much further along in numbers, were accepting the era they were in and wore the same kinds of provocative attire so many of their sex at large had taken as a natural way of dressing since the era of the miniskirt, the period when everything was allowed to hang out. Carla found it touching to see these women whom she had always thought of as so visually dull take their very own ethnic stall in the beauty and boody sweepstakes of a city where the female, with so much pushing against her, could exude a peculiarly radiant quality because she seemed such a respite from the immutable noise, the concrete, the traffic jams, and all the rest of it. Now the Chinese, Japanese, and Korean women were rising from novice bad taste into what would inevitably become, for the very best of them, high style with slanted eyes and that incredibly beautiful dark, dark hair. There were some white women grousing about how these inscrutable bitches were sneaking in and getting some of the best guys by pretending to be so pliant. That was until they had them hanging from their small-busted bra straps and lowered the black-widow boom, not killing them off softly but paralyzing the will and turning those men into grateful wimps, gone for good. Seated near the waitress station where anyone on that shift could hear them, a group of college girls who attended school in the Bay Area of California were talking about this with their bejeweled mothers at a fancy restaurant where Carla worked on the East Side in the thirties. They were sure, like all the other girls who were not stupid enough to be taken in, that these Asians had started their tricks by pretending to have no interest in feminism whatsoever. They gave the impression that their only desire was to become updated and educated geisha girls there to satisfy their men. This drew the guys already tired of the sexual rhetoric into their silken webs, where the boys were spoiled and wrapped up at the same time. Well, Carla thought as she took their orders and caught lots of their complaints and their anecdotes as she served them or stood at the waitress station observing her tables, here we go: somebody always has too much to say the goddam second you decide to do something they don't think you have the right to do. She wanted to hawk and spit in their food but knew that was too trashy to even consider for more than a delicious second. It was a secret but satisfying reply plenty of waitresses and waiters made to nasty customers, but since these people had perfect manners, the girl from South Dakota knew she didn't have the right to change the seasoning of their orders just because she found their attitudes hateful.

When Carla patronized the loft concerts of journeymen and those who were supposedly exploring frontiers, she was usually disappointed, unfortunately expecting something that would make her feel that the trip to New York had not been in vain. Then she heard Bobo, who swept her off her feet with his drumming, which was the percussive equivalent of fugues masterfully executed with cymbals and drums: themes of rhythm and timbre set against one another, chasing and playing with and around the four parts that his independent coordination of hands and feet made possible. Always holding his head up, sweating until he began to gleam, Bobo was playing a duet with Maxwell Davis, who was on fire, flames coming from the bell of his horn and creating huge shadows on the walls, but all Carla could hear were the drums, the drums: so many patterns powerful or soft or building combinations of both with the cymbals creating a drone beneath the beats played upon them; the metal rims of the drums, the cymbal stands, the sides of the drums were also used here and used there for different colorings of rhythm in this overall pattern of time stated and time hidden, time building and time dissolving, all of the force coming from the hands and legs of this man who imposed ambidextrous passion from the limbs above and the limbs below, breaking up and defining everything as intricately as the shapes and lights of the midnight Manhattan skyline, then bringing it all home to something very simple, just the four/four beat on the ride cymbal, the stick tipping with a velvet touch and no other sound coming out of his kit until the sock cymbal fell in on two and four and the bass drum humped its way in with feathery lowness, then the snare drum, capable of so many timbres from that left hand, turned around inside the beat like the whistles Carla had heard used by exquisitely marching, stamping, and turning drill teams. Wow upon wow silently left her mouth. Then it began, as it always did, with the two of them find-

ing a way to begin talking. He saw her looking at him and he looked back at her. That part was settled.

She was immediately taken by the sound of his voice and the way he walked, which made him look as if he was partially marching and partially sprinkling himself forward. Bobo had a majesty to him and he made love with a refined fury that pulled the same thing out of her, a delicate feel for human skin and a gasping for life that almost made her feel ashamed at the same time that excitement and passion took on actual meanings of an order that were innovations of identity for Carla. With Bobo, she learned to be a woman; finally, everything coy and comfortable slipped away. Even her displays of enthusiasm ceased to intrude themselves: there were no moments when abandon became a mask for a lack of concern about the specifics of the other person. Her own personal brand of soul stood up on its hind legs and took over.

In the air-conditioned mall, Carla felt sad, emotionally hyperventilating as she rose on the dunking stool of memory while looking at Eunice, who was trying out a big motorized leather chair. The big chair could be put in different positions with one set of buttons but it also delivered focused back rubs when another set of raised plastic circles were pressed. The way Eunice looked as the big black chair hummed and rolled against her back, from the lower spine to the shoulders, made it clear to anyone with half a thimble of sense that the leather seat with the interior masseuse would be in the living room of the Davis house someday.

Though she resisted, Carla was dunked again into the vast liquid of a past that seemed to drown her optimism at the same time that it forced her to soak every aspect of her sensibility in what living to this point and becoming a grown woman had added up to. This was not what she wanted to do. All Carla wanted was to pay attention to where she was and what it meant. She could not have explained to anyone why, at that moment, watching Eunice stroll around the motorized chair as though it was a breathtaking piece of sculpture, nothing could stop her from remembering more of what it was like before falling in love with Maxwell—what happened as Bobo stood up on that ominous morning, sort of muddy golden in color, when somebody loudly knocked on the door of his storefront loft in the East Village.

They knocked with such force that the wires on the belly of Bobo's snare drum sizzled. Something was surely wrong. There was no doubt about that. Oh: them. She could hear the voices of Satan's Children telling Bobo that he had two weeks to move out. Carla didn't need to see the jerks because she had become familiar with the low and rasping sound they used, something kind of like the exaggerated nastiness of television wrestlers.

"We see you bringing these white girls in here, man."

"So?"

"We don't like it."

"So?"

How dare such people say anything about anyone? All they did was drink, get high, disturb the peace with their motorcycles, and ride off, hugged from behind by those scrawny, dirty-haired sluts or the battered tubs of tattooed excrement that always seemed in advanced pregnancy, whether they were or not. Trash, the worst kind. Satan's Children weren't to be confused, as some nitwits did, with other kinds of people. For instance, Carla had always loved folk music, the moonshine part of America, the bluegrass banjo plucking and the cowboys farther west, the twangy-talking, common but vital people who had given the nation so much of its heart. Stubborn, compassionate, full of flair, reckless, clear about heaven, confused about hell, half racist and half not, overrun with pedophiles, violent, but also as sensitive as one of those poor boys living his life out in a plastic tent because he had no protection against germs. For all the memories of loving Patsy Cline like she was a goddess, singing the lines of Flatt and Scruggs, living on Jimmy Martin like he was water in the desert, or shooting pool and drinking beer in West Texas as her brand-new cowboy boots seemed bent on destroying her feet, Carla had never been able to abide unadulterated trash, those people who were so close to animals, so spiritually spavined, so ignorant, so hating of anything that suggested life could have something sweet inside it, something refined. When she was with Bobo, his unapologetic tenderness had the power to reduce every last bit of her to a translucent sigh and a startling, reluctant squeal, something like an anger at the fact of loneliness itself, a rage that spanked the flank of her orgasm as it ran free. Lying there during the first few weeks of being with him, remembering herself in such embarrassing detail, she was aghast at her own capacity for feeling, at least until it became a normal condition of passion, something she had neither looked for nor expected, not to be the way it actually was.

That atmosphere of clear emotion lying next to Bobo often led her to relive the smarting remark that Ramona, her older sister by four years, had made to Carla when they were both again in the house where they had grown up. It was the tip of South Dakota fall and the college town was filling up with kids come to learn what they would learn and go on to do what they would do, if lucky enough. The house was still big but its size now, for the two sisters, was sated with the bygone spirits of two untested girls arguing, laughing, talking about boys, joking about ugly girls, fretting together when they had high school or college classes hard enough to hack away their grade point averages. If that list wasn't the past regaining itself before them, it was the past of the two complaining about their younger brother, and going through the rituals of endless practice when Carla was getting groomed to become the Olympic skater Ramona had all the tireless will for but not the talent. That surpassing talent on Carla's part threw up an electric fence between the two of them and the fence remained from that point forward, its current never any less strong.

Admiring the texture of her skin, the color of her eyes, the naturally knowing shape of her eyebrows, and her not-one-more-pound-since-high-school-figure, Carla, who had been out in the big wide world for a while now, was obliquely implying how good she was with the guys as she and Ramona prepared to go to dinner with their dad. That was the time when they were both visiting home determined to get their dad to set aside the martinis that made his once so handsome nose into a ruptured red and blue confession of self-abuse. Dad had always had a taste for the sauce, which Mom kept in check, but her death had sunk him in it and neither of them was going to let him drown. Their task, however important, didn't stop Carla from genuflecting before the mirror. That did it. That broke it. Listening to her small-shouldered sister compliment herself as though she were a spiritual kept woman who had never gotten beyond living in high school, Ramona looked at her with the same resentment she had tried to hide during the period when Carla's body almost sang across the ice on her skates. That sibling hostility disheartened Carla now but, when youthful victory was all over her, she enjoyed recognizing that jealousy as much as she did the best of anything. It was a slice of heaven on a plate. She loved to gobble it down but pretend she had never—ever—seen or touched it.

Ramona's face evolved quickly from that of a competitive sister to one that contained the contempt of a military drill instructor. She looked at Carla as if all that she had wanted to say for every second since the days of skating was finally given its head: "Well. Well. So you say. So you say. I don't doubt it, little sister. I don't doubt it at all. I don't doubt that you are just as good-looking as you always were. But that's not where it stops. It doesn't stop there. Not quite. You know there are other things out in the world here right now. A barn full of other things right now."

Carla suddenly felt like slapping Ramona, and the emotion frightened her. She kept her face blank, however, and stepped closer to her sister in order to make her physical presence a challenge to the insult she could hear coming. If she was going to get it, Carla intended to take the whole goddam enchilada at close range.

"Here's one for you to fry in that egotistical brainpan. Listen closely. We know how hard that is for you. It's not easy, listening to other people. Try, though. Just try. Other people do exist. They have things called feelings, too. But the point is not really that. I'm saying something right here you need to know. Yah. When you wear pants, you can't hide behind them. When you wear a dress, you can hide behind it by lifting it up. I'll take the pants."

Recalling that always put her into a capacious snit. But what in the holy fucking world did Ramona know about men? Sometimes the only way you could escape being yourself was by having sex. When she was by herself and the big feeling came over her, Carla could briefly mist up at the fact that she wasn't trying to get away when she was with Bobo. Once she became accustomed to being with him, Carla wondered, with sort of a stoic glee, if the entire conception of refinement might well have bloomed, so many centuries ago, out of no more than a caring touch. Some people didn't like that kind of living at all. They tried to pull you down. Trashy bikers. Just who the hell were *they—standing at the door and talking to her Bobo in growls—to say anything about anyone? Who were they? She would like to know that.*

"Tell me that one more time."

There was silence that seemed to pucker with imminent violence.

"Do me a favor: just one more time."

"You hard of hearing, man?"

"I might be."

"You got two weeks to move out, man. We don't like this mixing of the races."

With only his head exposed, Bobo reached for a long leather bag that leaned against the corner of the front door and unzipped it with one hand. He noiselessly took out a pump shotgun with a short handle instead of a stock. Carla became so spooked she wanted to run into the bathroom and throw up.

"Two weeks?"

"That's what we said, dude."

"Right. Hmmmm. I'll tell you white boys something."

"We're doing the telling, buddy. You got two weeks. Fourteen days. Now what you got to say, Mr. Nigger Motherfucker?"

"Two weeks?"

"Two weeks!"

"How about two days?"

"What did you say?"

"How about two minutes?"

"Oh, this nigger's a tough guy."

*"How about right motherfucking now?" Bobo said, standing nude before them as he pumped the shotgun. "Don't not one of you sad motherfuckers move: white boy brains **will** fill the goddam street* **this** *morning. Mmm hmm. So you supposed to be some bad white boys; you supposed to be some **bad** motherfuckers. Let me tell you crusty motherfuckers something: there are **no** bad white boys; there are **no** bad **white** motherfuckers. But, to be fair up in here, let's get frisky. Oh, yeah. Let's get all the way down to the shit, the grit, and the mother wit. Mmm-hmmm. Let's see what you loud-knocking crackers* **got.** *That's what I want to know. I want to see how bad you funky-assed white boys are right motherfucking* **now,** *with your too-goddam-loud-motorcycle-riding asses. Say something! Just one peep."*

There was another silence. This one was strained tight with trepi-dation. The palsy of apprehension gave Carla the flutters. All she could do was shake and listen.

"Well now. Well now. All right. There you go. Do anybody except me notice how quiet it done got? Quiet as a white man when it's time to give a nigger some credit. Do anybody except me notice that? Say it loud. I thought so. Get the fuck on. Next time I'll kill every one of you as soon as I see you."

Carla felt terror, something she had never known. It was very different from being extremely frightened, even petrified and in fear of losing one's life. Nothing like that had ever happened so close to her. Actually . . . but Carla never thought about that. This was now and she couldn't conceal one degree of her discomfort. Then Bobo, with infinite delicacy, calmed her down, his tools very small kisses and melting hugs. It was one of those bizarre East Village moments, in retrospect, because Bobo was standing in his doorway naked with a shotgun and nobody seemed to have seen it or called the police or anything.

"Bobo," she later asked him, her voice almost shaking, "would you really have shot one of those creepy guys?"

"I'm from East St. Louis, baby low. I came here not to give in. They was as close to getting taken out of here as one wrong word can get you. They came over here thinking I was a nigger fucking a white girl—a white girl much finer than any of them will ever get. But now they know—if they lucky—I wasn't none of that. This motherfucker here was none of that. All I was was one thing: death standing right there with my dick hanging in the wind. No fucking going on."

When he was finishing his time on earth in the dreary Veterans' Hospital, Carla felt so angry at Bobo because the shared needles used to shoot up the dope had taken him all the way down, sapped away the beautiful body that she loved to look at as he slept and bring her lips so close to she almost kissed him but didn't, fearing that he would wake and the special privacy of her just loving him through her eyes would be destroyed. The scar from a Viet Cong bullet in his left thigh and the one where lead had passed through his right shoulder, clean and breaking no bones, had inspired recollections of the jungle and the battles as she rubbed them ever so softly, hoping they would go away, back in the days when they were alone and the world seemed so dominated by their feeling for each other.

*"It was a death game. It didn't seem like a war. But I guess a war is a death game all the time. But there's always a game going on behind the game you think you in, and that game behind might be working for you—because somebody is trying to use **you** to separate some heavy stuff. You look like you don't know what I'm talking about. Why should you know? Here's how it could be over there. Sometimes, when they was getting ready to put something rough on us, word would get secretly snuck over to the niggers."*

"Do you have to use that word, Bobo? I hate to hear it. Do you have to say it all the time?"

"Yes."

"Could you, just as a favor to me, not say that around me? It makes the air feel dirty. I really don't like it."

*"I grew up with the word nigger in my mouth. It seem natural to me. But it never seem natural when a white somebody drops it on your plate and the smell of shit starts coming out of it. Then you got to clean up that mess with something that **might get just a little rough**. Anyway, the Cong would send out word some kind of way, until it got to be nigger to nigger: **Night Wind. Night Wind. Night Wind.** Believe me, niggers rose up out of there easy as Jesus floating back to heaven. We figured out how to get as far away from where we was as we could."*

Carla had never imagined Bobo running from anything. Instantly, he became less mythic and more of a man and that much more of a person she could love with a bit more of the precision that comes with understanding.

*"The white boys would be left to take that sudden whipping. They took it, too. But they wasn't like Satan's Children; those white boys were **men**. They would shit in their pants and cry to the Lord, trembling and trembling, then the ones who had heart would come **up**. They would snatch that overcoat of fear off of them—throw it away!— and do something to **save** a motherfucker."*

She smiled to herself as he used those terms because Bobo had written them in "Throw It Away," one of his attempts at free verse, describing fear as a very heavy overcoat buttoned all the way up, the wearer lacking hands, sweating, sweating. Most of the writings were amateurish or incoherent but that one was very good and Carla sometimes sat reading it over and over, drinking her Irish breakfast tea. At the deli once, with Bobo's words in her head, when she asked for the tea, the guy behind the counter went and got her a Budweiser. He didn't hear the word "tea" and thought she wanted a liquid Irish breakfast. They both laughed. Quite a difference. Quite a difference.

"Didn't make no difference what color the motherfucker was either," Bobo said. "The white boys with heart would show you something. They got up to try and bring that man back. Sometimes they got took out on the way. A hole just as big as your head blown in their chest, but they was coming for you, they was coming, little punk-seeming white boys. That's right: shit you couldn't believe. Sometimes they would be dead and running and get to the man they was trying to save and, suddenly, they would fall flat dead as they was when they first got hit. Just like that: Their will clicked off. Up on that tip, you learned that the dead **can** walk. A man is in deep trouble and then you see death walking to save him **from** death. I seen two of them go down just like that coming for me. Just like that."

Bobo went on to say that he believed that one could only become a man, or learn what a man was in battle, if everything inside of him and everything outside hurt because he's so scared but he **had** to move; he **had** to show what it means to be brave. It meant to have **real** love for your buddy, even if the buddy was a stranger or he was some simple, pain-in-the-ass motherfucker. War had its own jagged game going. It was about killing strangers and about saving strangers: "**Somewhere** along the way. Shit. All them bullets flying? All the men crying out as they go down? Death was picking mother-fuckers out for **fun**, baby low. Well, your buddy might die and **you** might die, but the two of you can be sure you done something God wants **everybody** to know."

When Bobo spoke to her like that Carla was returned in emotion to the way her childhood nights had been as she was under the covers with a flashlight, reading some beautiful fairy tale full of monsters and princes and endangered girls with golden hair waiting for some-one to love them enough to risk their lives, no matter how many times they had to if those sad and sweet girls were ever to be pro-tected. But how did one reckon that on some evening one of those girls grown up to be a woman might find out that she had to be ready to take care of herself, and forget she had saved herself, and keep on forgetting in order to keep on living?

Bobo said that when there was no **Night Wind,** which was most of the time, the Vietnamese sat up all night singing some kind of yong-yong music that sounded like they couldn't tune up: "We who are about to die salute you. That goddam noise would definitely make you want to go home. Then, for a split second, you would hear that heart in it. Then, when dawn got up, it would get all the way quiet. Too quiet for you to miss any sound in the world. Sometimes I thought I could hear all the way back to East St. Louis. You could feel it was almost there. Death lollygagging out there some place you couldn't see.

"That's how it usually was. You couldn't see them. It's like we were out there trying to kill the wind. Yellow ghosts. It happened like that before. I didn't know anything about that until a long time later. See, Maxwell got a book about fighting Indians. I read it. Yeah, I read it. **The Crimson Prairie.** Up in there, the man says the Indians out there on the plains fought just like the Cong. Motherfuckers appeared and then pulled you out behind them. Slick. Then they broke up into smaller and smaller units until they disappeared. Gone, baby low. Not quite. It wasn't going down no way like that. They reappeared with a surprise for your ass. They was on your flanks and in the rear carrying death on horseback. But they had some new shit for you over there in the jungle. Out there in all that green, which was a different green every couple of yards maybe. So many different greens. Endless different green. That was a lesson in variety you wouldn't forget. A man out there learned how something beautiful could hide the crying sign of death. Just like the South. Same situation. You go down to a place like Mississippi and you can't believe all that evil was happening in all that beautiful land. Can't believe it. Not this beautiful. But the strange fruit of a nigger hanging from a tree was a real thing. White women pregnant and coming to lynchings to get fingers and toes for their children so they could have a souvenir if lynching went out of style before the little white kids could see one. Nothing like a mother's love. When I first got to 'Nam, we took a funky-asssed village and this woman came out of a hut with a baby wrapped up crying and handed it to the commanding officer. He did a hands-across-the-nations number. White boy. She just stood there smiling *like the beginning of the world. I'll go to Jesus with that smile in my mind. The baby was covered with grenades. They blew him, her, and the baby to pieces. It wasn't nowhere near right, but that's why I believe some of the guys over there went crazy and killed everybody. That's why. I'm not making no excuses for those guys who became real cool killers and had too much murder in their hearts to give a damn who they wiped out. Like I said, they was all the way into being wrong, but you still never knew who the fuck you were looking at. That's a feeling I know. Myself, baby low, I felt like killing **everybody** white when they took our weapons and kept us under guard, all the niggers, rank and no rank. Kept us segregated for about a week after Martin Luther King got iced. We didn't know what was up because they kept it a secret and they knew niggers were tearing up America so they didn't know what to expect from some fighting niggers they had trained to kill. Now I can see why they would be scared to hell and back by us. I ain't near about bragging but we definitely knew how to do a monkey to death. The white man did a good job. He made us professional hit men in combat boots. We could stop a beating heart for good. All kinds of ways. The white man was right. You better know how to get together with some murder when the battle is on and the Cong started moving on you—looking mad, looking scared, looking hypnotized—and you start putting that heavy lead on them. I'm talking about killing now. I'm not talking about playing. Goddam! You not ready for that, but you **get** ready. Now it's just like football noise after the hike, except that the grunts and cries are deeper. They're sitting on top of wounds or they're sitting on top of death. One way or another, them backing up or you backing up, it gets to the end."*

Carla got very excited as Bobo built to those crescendos but she hoped her face didn't show it. She wanted to look impassive because she hated war, everything about it. She wanted to seem above what he was talking about, even nearly disinterested. It was all twisted up in how she felt about so many things. Guys had always gotten on her nerves when they talked about "the doings of men," as her father teasingly called it. They wanted to stick their cards to a private club right in your face. Bobo wasn't doing that, not at all, not with those tears appearing in the corners of his eyes, but Carla recalled how her father and her brother would be so proud of themselves in their camouflage suits when they came back from hunting deer or boar with bows and arrows. So, so manly: two Norwegian Indians with light green eyes and a camper, patiently waiting for James Fenimore Cooper to immortalize them. Coop would know just what to do.

If they returned late in the morning and the meat was being prepared some time that afternoon for dinner, she never felt less than mortified by the obviousness with which her brother always figured out a way to stand before her with his palms dripping blood as he pretended his nose itched so he could rub it with the back of each hand. That was on the same line as how he would put cockroaches in all of her vanity boxes once he knew they terrified her. Catching the insects must have taken some time, but he always got the payoff as she irrationally screamed at the sight of one, living or dead.

When her dad and her brother went mountain climbing, she feigned vague interest but was never less than fascinated by their gear—the boots, the hammers, the rope, the nails, the special belts for equipment, the thermoses, and all of the expectation that must have been very close to the excitement the Wright brothers felt bubbling up when they were on the verge of conquering the air. The feeling that came with them after they returned from a mountaintop was different from the mood they brought with their dead animals. That other mood fit inside the room. This one seemed bigger than the room. It was enormous. It had had the passion of accomplishment extended beyond the walls by a rather strange and unforced humility. Carla wished she had been with them as they described how it got colder and colder as you got closer and closer to heaven, panting on the top and looking farther than you ever believed you could see standing on two feet.

"Randy and little Randy, you hungry guys sound like you've been talking with angels. All you two, big man and little man, have actually done is climb a mountain and return home with nothing to show for it," her mother would facetiously bray, serving some spoon bread, some ham sandwiches, and the chicory coffee she had picked up a taste for during a vacation in New Orleans. It was from her mother, Sue of the blue eyes and the exotically fine figure, that Carla had gotten the atypical backside that was so Negroid in shape, so much so that one of Maxwell's friends always created a passing anxiety by referring to her as "the Empress of the Caucasian Boody Rebellion."

His hair gone, the brownish-black dreadlocks she had often joked
of as making his head look like a West Indian mop, the scabs all over
his body, and a light sweat rising, Bobo, who had once been the defi-
nition of strength for her, could no longer even whisper through his
dry, dry lips, but she knew that he wanted her to hold him. As Carla
rose from the metal chair in the Veterans' Hospital where she had
been weeping, then sniffling to try and control herself, her eyes feel-
ing as though rubbing alcohol had been thrown in them, she found
herself captivated by what had become an increasingly sorrowful
magic: his eyes never changed. The power remained in place, reduced
in form to a pair of dark brown lights that begged for nothing. While
Bobo might have begged for her forgiveness whenever he swirled out
of control into the dark universe of drugs, he was never one to ask to
be spared his serving of pain. He always stood and took it like it
came. She had no choice other than to love him.

"Now you have to understand something about Ezekiel," Eunice
said, backgrounded by Thelonious Monk's astonishing interpretation
of "Sophisticated Lady" piping through the mall. It was an unexpected kind of mall music but the guy who played from noon to one
every day on a huge Steinway in front of the store that sold musical
instruments, sheet music, and books about musicians, well, he got
friendly with the fellow who handled the sound and found out that
this guy loved jazz and opera. The fellow in charge of the sound at the
mall sent the piano player on the mission to buy some good-sounding
compact discs. So one might hear Maria Callas followed by Billie
Holiday, Debussy followed by Ellington playing his *Melancholia,*
Billy Eckstine's entire *No Cover, No Minimum* preceding Kiri Te
Kanawa's *Songs of the Auvergne,* the purity of *Bailero* sometimes
stopping shoppers dead in their tracks, its spiritual eroticism oddly
reinvigorating them to pull out their plastic cards of acquisition with
a second-wind gusto that shot up sales as though the Christmas holidays were there and it may have been the last time to get those gifts. It
may be the last time.

The mall's piano player was a trim, muscular, dimpled, slick-
haired, handsome Irish guy in a tuxedo and patent leather shoes. He
was from Hell's Kitchen in New York. Confidently twisting to the
beat as he worked the keyboard and his feet danced on the pedals, the

piano man—no matter what he was presently playing—always broke into "Rocking in Rhythm" when he saw Eunice, who would snap her fingers and do some kind of jitterbug or fox-trot or something with such grace it appeared that the god of merriment had taken her into his arms. In return, once a month or twice or even four times a month, Eunice brought that Irish guy a butter-filled blueberry cobbler and joked that she was waiting for his belly to get fat so she could identify with him.

"Ezekiel," a seated Eunice said, only briefly sucking on the plastic spoon she had used for the hot fudge sundae purchased with humorous glumness after they had returned to the ice cream parlor, "he could have told you both at the dinner table what all that he knew happened to Malena but my husband's too proud and he's too shy. Shy as he can be sometimes. Yet in still, he also stopped it to keep me from sobbing like a helpless fool. When he and Maxwell went for that walk after that meal, or on *one* of these walks, he's going to tell him. The truth of life is this, Carla: *Somebody* got to tell. It might be you, it might be your mother, it might be your father, it might be your brother: *Somebody* got to tell. Now, I'm going to tell. You see, when Floyd started pulling himself up, God bless him, the poor man had to get as far away from Malena as was possible at all. Pretty Boy left Chicago and went back to the protecting and forgiving arms of his people in Mississippi: because my baby girl was slipping down deeper into darkness. I never told Ezekiel, but, so help me, I had a dream with Floyd rising on muddy wings and our loving girl singing dirty songs as she went down slow in black quicksand. The quicksand was just like black sugar and powdered glass. It scraped and it cut."

Carla's breathing took on the shallow quality she always experienced when she feared something for someone other than herself. She had some idea that what was coming was already so powerfully implied that it would not actually shock her, but the way Eunice said what she said made Carla feel as though she was helplessly looking on as something too terrible for words was actually rising from a secret world into the objective space of language.

"The whole thing is she got to loving that nasty little pipe. I don't understand it but I guess it's a snake bite people keep wanting to repeat. Poison over and over. Now Pretty Boy said before he went back home that she just got *filthy*, which I could not believe because nobody on this God's earth loved a bath more than Malena. Lord, she drove the whole house crazy as a basket of betsy bugs staying in the bathroom, soaking and washing, soaking and washing, all the way back from when she started bathing alone and had the nerve to lock the door."

Carla recalled how it had been for her when she was a little girl and stood before the floor-length mirror on the back of the bathroom door looking at herself with the door locked as she brushed her teeth or dried herself off after bathing and placing her towel on the rack Dad had installed just for her as he had for her older sister. These were only for Ramona and Carla then, none yet for Randy Jr. Her cotton nightgown with the pink angels on it and the terry cloth robe could have been red cashmere and white ermine as far as she was concerned. She was clean and she was ready for her bedtime story. All was smooth and well in the little crystal ball of a world where she lived just before falling off to sleep.

"Floyd said she forgot all about that cleanliness. Her teeth got dirty, those pretty teeth she almost brushed the enamel all the way off. She smelled for three city blocks. Her skin started to break out with blackheads. My baby's hair looked like a dust mop, so filthy dirt flew if she turned her head fast. This is what Pretty Boy said. And I could tell it hurt him to tell it because I was listening on the other line when he was telling it to Ezekiel. So Floyd goes one way and Malena goes another. Once he got himself standing straight, he said he was looking in the mirror one day, and he saw tears coming and he knew he had to go back to Chicago. He had to go back in that black hell looking for his woman."

There was no Malena to be found when Pretty Boy Floyd began searching for her. That petrified his heart with fear and broke it in two. He was feeling guilty for leaving her alone but he was also relieved that he had become strong enough to go so near all of that dope and not fall back by the wayside. He prayed for strength every step of the way. The smell of the burning temptation didn't make him waver as he went from crack house to crack house, well remembered by all of the kids who had dropped out of school and were sitting on cars with cell phones ready to alert the dealers if the cops were on the way. The kids always had new baggy clothes or jogging suits and new tennis shoes, untied as was the fashion, bounties of oversized jewelry, this one and that one actually grinning with sympathetic pride and mouths full of gold teeth at the obvious fact that Pretty Boy Floyd had gotten himself together. He had returned from the world of the dead who do not know they are dead. The crack house lookouts could not articulate to the comeback Floyd what they felt in words other than "okay, yo"; "yeah, yo"; "getting' up, yo"; "go on, yo"; "got it right, yo"; "hey now, yo"; "be strong, yo"; "hey*hey, yo.*" Yes, as immature but hardened witnesses to monumental self-destruction, they had seen how far down chasing that high had taken him: all the way into the fuming grave of the crack pit when he and Malena were busy losing their cars, their home, and their jobs, incinerating themselves with glass pipes.

"Finally, one of them boys wearing enough chains to make him a humpback pointed to a house across an empty old lot. The house was facing the other way. When old Floyd went in there, the little bottles they sell that crack in—you seen them on television—they was breaking under his feet every which way he turned. He could smell that stuff burning like sulfur. Wasn't much light and he didn't know exactly what was there. He felt some fear. Yes he did. With those dope-using kind of people, you better off being scared than sorry. Way better off. So Floyd went from the back to the front door and didn't see nothing. Empty everywhere his eyes turned. Not a peeping, mumbling thing. Nothing. He was stumped, he said, and his heart was hurting more than a little bit. Where in the world was his baby love? He would do everything he could to pull her out of hell. He would die for her if he had to; if it took his life, he would give it. That's what he said. It made the earpiece of the phone turn hot against my head."

Carla's heart sped up and she had no doubt that her face was going flush. The heat coming from Eunice was close to palpable and she remembered herself how often the touch of something soaked in a hot potion of memory could seem wet and on fire at the very same time.

"Listening to Floyd talk to Ezekiel, I felt so bad for that boy because I knew then just how much he loved my Malena. He had the real feeling for her heart none of them other ones had. None. Not a mumbling one. He felt love for my girl. Oh, he loved her right up there with me and Ezekiel. Then Floyd stopped at that crack house door and he said he felt some strange kind of salt getting rubbed in the wound of his loneliness. He felt the kind of hurt that bites inside you. He hurt and he couldn't do nothing but hurt. Floyd reached for him the doorknob of that old empty house. He paused. Something told him not to turn around, told him not to turn around, told him *not* to turn around."

Eunice paused, a look of incensed exasperation commandeering her face. Carla wanted to ask her what was wrong, then nearly cringed inside at the idea that one could ask what was wrong in the middle of a story that was about nothing other than what was wrong.

"But, just like a lot of men that do not know—any *kind* of way— how to follow their first mind, Pretty Boy Floyd turned himself around," Eunice said, her arms folded as if, responding to a chill, she were holding a shawl over her shoulders. "Oh, he turned around, yes he did. He noticed he had missed a door over to the side of the staircase. It wasn't open; it wasn't closed, just cracked a little bit. He could hear feet crushing crack bottles. Some people was in there, walking. Moving against his first mind, Floyd opened that door."

Eunice gulped for air as though she were drowning. She had to have her some water. Carla went to get it for her. She drained three glasses and went back to exactly the place where she had stopped.

"Thank you, Carla. There was men lined up and holding two dollars in their hands, and there was our only girl, our baby. Our baby. There was our Malena, skinny as an ice cream stick, dirty as a pipe cleaner. Raggedy, down on her bloody, bloody knees from those broken crack bottles. She was breathing deep and breathing deep and sucking, globs and globs of that stuff dripping right down from her chin. Floyd cried out. He said the hurt in his soul filled the whole room. Malena, her eyes just as bitter as salt, looked up at that poor man in stone-cold, cold rage. Next thing he knew, one of them guys or two or whatever, had knocked him blind. He woke up with his jaw broke, his pockets empty, and those broken bottles cutting through his clothes every which way. Malena was gone, disappeared, nowhere to be found. If she's living, she's surely out there in hell somewhere."

An empathy, a horror, and a terror so strong came over Carla that she momentarily felt that she would swoon. But this was not the time for her to sit in awe of this terrible story and emotionally leave Eunice alone at the top of the mall. Frightened, she was well aware that no words would do, none. With all the heart Carla had, she reached and took Eunice's hands, her touch containing the kind of painful softness she hoped would be an offering of her entire presence, everything she had outside, everything she had inside. Then Eunice, whose eyes had closed and whose head had fallen forward, lifted that still beautiful face and looked at her, not as someone entranced by the terrible fate of her own daughter, not someone who had just given this South Dakota girl a tricky test built upon the heartbreak of real people, but as a woman who could, very, very clearly, see Carla as the sweet, fragile thing she could never stop wanting to be.

THE GIZZARDS ARE MINE

EUNICE FELT like driving when they left the mall and she took Carla through every part of the city, her mood changing as she commented on the bad driving of the other people and gave her son's lover little tales of how this became what it was and why these people lived in one place and those lived in another. Carla felt appreciation for the very smooth way that Eunice handled her four-door red Oldsmobile, rolling along, turning and braking so that all of the accelerations and decelerations were executed as though driving was always supposed to be no more than perfectly timed motion, an experience of flotation at various speeds. This woman gave an Olympian quality to the four-wheeled technology that carried them from place to place so that what was actually a whirlwind tour had the feeling of moving with the unobstructed freedom of a cloud. Again, Eunice spoke as though she owned everything that she talked about, or had been there where there was trouble, had been the center of the joy when something jubilant had taken off, and was the force to which this Southwestern mix of life had to answer, second upon second, minute upon minute, hour upon hour, day upon day.

When they got back to the Davis house Carla wondered if Maxwell had been told what had happened to his sister while he and his father were out picking the two free-range chickens that had been killed, plucked, and made ready for their dinner position on the grill before the two women returned.

"Before anybody says one word—" Maxwell began.

"The gizzards, the liver, and the necks are for me and my son."

"I guess that means the case is closed," Eunice said with a surpassing haughtiness.

"It means what it means."

"Well, Ezekiel Leander Davis, Jr., I know that if I want me a gizzard or a liver or some old chicken neck I have me my rights as a consumer to lift one of them onto my plate."

"Time out. C'mere, son. Conference time."

The two men went out into the backyard and seemed to be having a rather spirited exchange, but when Carla looked closer, she noticed that they weren't talking at all; they were just making huge gestures and smiling. Suddenly, they both broke into "All Right, O.K., You Win," singing it in harmony as they sort of shuffled back into the house, Ezekiel serenading Eunice, Maxwell Carla. The father sang in a high, sweet tenor, right on pitch; the son in a Billy Eckstine baritone that was mockingly just a little off every few notes or so. Then Ezekiel called his son to attention.

"So now what do we have to say, young man?"

"We got a lot to say, Pop."

"We better say it then."

The two started a chant they must have made up hours ago.

"Oh, oh, we got the best women." Then they clapped once. "We got the best, best women." This time the claps accented the repeated word "best." They then had it going. The syncopations started moving. The accents were delivered with stamping feet and the clapping became more complex as they looked at each other and mutually felt the coming of a new shift in rhythmic emphasis. With nothing to determine where or when, they stopped at the same time and went back into "All Right, O.K., You Win," this version a country-and-western interpretation that flooded the room with syrup. Then they stopped.

"We are men working and these kinds of mountain-dew shenanigans must be brought to a stop, young man."

"You said it, Pops."

"Let us now continue to cook dinner."

"Let us continue."

"There is chicken to be barbecued."

"The chicken must meet the pit."

"There is potato salad to be made."

"And I shall make it."

"In order to have a balanced meal, we will have a salad."

"A salad must be had."

"Are the eggs boiled?"

"The eggs will be boiled, Father."

"Will your potato salad be worth eating?"

"It will definitely respect the taste buds, Dad."

"Son, yonder awaits the sweet potato pie I will bake."

"Seems impatient for the oven to me."

"Boy, your observations seem just about right."

"I want to thank you for that, Father."

"And the bowl sits there to be filled with my special salad."

"Dad, there will be—"

"Lettuce, tomatoes—"

"—steamed brussels sprouts, grated carrots—"

"—radishes, cucumbers—"

"Cool cucumbers, sir."

"Cool cucumbers, raisins, and cabbage—"

"Sliced."

"Son, I did say what I said: I said sliced-into-very-little-pieces cabbage."

"You did not, Pops, but you *would* have if I had not so rudely interrupted you, sir."

"Correct. To our duties we must go."

They turned and went to work.

Though she and Eunice had practically laughed themselves daffy, Carla was now sure Maxwell had been told what had happened to his sister because he had a way of turning his head as though he had a crick in his neck when he was really bothered about something. He did that every so often, in the kitchen and throughout the delicious meal, which was followed by very pleasant conversation in the leather chairs of the living room. Eunice said it would all have been better if the two Mr. Men had fixed some homemade ice cream to go with the sweet potato pie. Ezekiel took a theatrical deep breath through his nose and said that there was nothing like the appetizing scent of true appreciation.

Eunice stood up, walked over to him, bent down, and loudly smooched her husband on the lips. "I couldn't agree more with nothing you ever said," she softly laughed, many layers of satisfaction ringing out of her voice, each layer a statement on marriage that was public and private but mostly some business she and Ezekiel knew far better than anyone else, as the only people who are ever aware of what is truly going on between a man and a woman are the he and the she.

6

ALL NIGHT FOR A PIG

THAT NIGHT Carla awoke to see him sitting on the edge of the bed. The moonlight and the shadows formed a garment of the visible and the invisible. From the sound of his breathing and that private timbre of intense unhappiness, she was positive that Maxwell was thinking about his sister and that he was probably crying. But there was no normal reaction from her. Carla felt so unnatural without the buffers of his parents that her being was as leery as it had been years back when she was taking her baby steps into the jazz world. His refusal to talk with her about how he felt took away her own courage to live through this hurt with him. It hadn't been like that for the first four years. No. Usually, when either of them sensed hurt or turmoil or the unexpected internal bleeding of some sudden loneliness, there would be a way to say, I'll live through this with you. I'll comfort you, if you need it. I won't run, and no matter what it is, you will not be diminished in my sight. I'm with you, whether life is comfortable or choking.

Here, welcomed by Ezekiel and Eunice at every instance and even with him acting as though he loved her in the old way, Carla didn't know at that moment, as she felt Malena swelling inside his silent heart, exactly what to do. She couldn't decide if she should despise herself for taking the cowardly choice and leave her man alone with the palpable loss that rose from him and lay in the air as a dual nightmare that neither of them was mentioning. There was that side of their relationship. It had depreciated that goddam far. She just didn't fucking feel free to love him. Rejection could shoot out of Maxwell right then and that would crack something inside her after what she had shared with Eunice. Carla wished to be forgiven because the back she would have run her hand down as a signal of empathy when everything was in better shape might as well be a row of razor blades she was so afraid to touch him.

There were also those moments when he would tell her things she had never heard before. Sometimes he was just so weird and comical and lovable. Once, a few years after she had moved in with him, she was trying to do something with her uncooperative flat hair other than put it up in berets and was quite frustrated. A permanent would not do because she hated them. She was also nearing her period and her skin looked, to her, embarrassingly pale. When Carla was that pale she didn't always feel comfortable being seen in public with her dark-skinned man. It was one of those irrational chains she whipped herself with like those guys walking down the street in Iran during the hostage days. At least, she pondered, they had religion behind what they did, behind the blood that started to appear on their shirts. All she had was discomfort and a shame that she could explain to no one and that no one could explain to her. As she was on the perimeter of tears, Maxwell appeared in the mirror with an impish look on his face.

"Now, Carla, let me tell you something."

"What is that?"

"This is something you really need to know."

"Well?"

*"You are a **real** white woman. I mean even with that super unwhite boody."*

By irritating her, he had saved her from her shame. She could get away from the feeling that was doing her in.

"What is that supposed to mean? All right, all right: I've been too pale the last few days."

"Oh, no, none of that. I mean this. I mean you."

"Yes?"

*"You are a **real** white woman."*

"As opposed to an unreal white woman?"

"That's my baby. Now you're getting hot."

"What is an unreal white woman?"

"Oh, you know, these Jewish bitches and these Italian bitches."

"Maxwell, I told you I **hate** it, I **hate** it, I **hate** it when you use those words."

"All right then. That's cool. I'm a cooperative kind of guy."

"Well, you sound like a full-fledged jerk right now."

"Anyway, I like to keep it smooth."

"Sure."

Carla's back was still to him as he kissed a certain spot on her neck, an inch or two below the hairline, and she saw her face turn hot pink in the mirror. That sort of thing—in person, over the phone, in gifts, in words on paper—was all she ever wanted. Carla, more ashamed than ever, felt a sob of affection wanting to burst out.

"What I am trying to explain to you is the truth about Jewish and Italian fe-males."

"Which is what?" she said, hoping to sound sarcastic but hearing instead a little tremor in her voice. Maxwell, fortunately, didn't notice, and went on in the same mood and tone of speech. Unlike Bobo, he didn't have emotional perfect pitch.

"I'm telling you, they are not real white women. That's why they're so frustrated. That's why the aggressive ones are so goddam aggressive. That's why the bitter ones are so goddam bitter. That's why the snooty ones set world records in being snooty balooties."

Carla laughed, feeling so much better.

"But that's all right. It does not matter if they are aggressive, if they feel bitter, if they try to be snooty balooties: they will never get there."

"What?"

"That's it. They'll never get there. They won't."

"Get **where**?"

"To the top. Wait. Hold up. Please, baby, don't ask me the top of what. Don't do that. I'll **tell** you the top of what. These Jewish and Italian broads—I mean **women**, I mean **women**—they know that the top level of the white people don't believe in them, not as being white women they don't. The only people who believe in them as authentic white are these ignorant niggers in the jazz world. That's why they come around here: so they can pass for white."

She had turned and was looking at him as though he had smashed a favorite dish.

"Maxwell, you sound like you've lost your mind."

"Maybe so, but I haven't. Not at all. Maybe we should approach this subject here from a humorous perspective. I think that will do the job. Yes, indeed. By the way, have you heard the one about what's the difference between a pig and a jazz musician?"

"No, I haven't. Thank God."

"Now you see how you're getting and you don't even know what I'm getting at? That's okay. You are a very brilliant woman. You will come around. Here's how it goes. It's very simple and simple things sometimes tell the whole story. You don't have to be intellectual; you just have to know when to listen. Information is always passing through. That's the job of information: to pass through."

A tinge of insecurity colored her emotion because she wondered if Maxwell thought that she, too, was a snooty balootie who missed things because she didn't have the ability to listen. She hoped he didn't think that. Not that. Gee whiz: what a little menstrual cycle can do to you.

"Stop looking so serious. This is funny. It goes like this, a pure work of genius: What is the difference between a pig and a jazz musician? Come on. Come on. No idea, huh?"

"None at all. Not my kind of humor."

*"**Anyway:** A pig won't stay up all night trying to fuck a jazz musician."*

Maxwell began laughing so hard, coughing and turning around, that Carla was afraid he would break some of her toiletries. She didn't find that joke, if he called it that, funny, not even vaguely. Still, she understood what he meant because, almost as soon as she began going into the New York jazz world, starting her preparation to learn how to become a serious jazz singer, Carla had often been stunned on a long and slow burn by how much attention frumpy white women would be given by Negro musicians and Negro hangers-on, hour by hour. Having usually been one of the more attractive women wherever she went, this felt like some sort of bizarre defilement. A kid in her middle twenties, Carla was perplexed and pissed off. One given to talking a good game about the insignificance of looks, she was vain. It wasn't her fault, as far as she was concerned. God had been good. Go argue with Him.

That weird thing with these guys and their hothouse wallflowers happened in all Greenwich Village clubs, but it became most clear in Good Henry's. This was the insider's insider's room over near New York University, where the musicians played to provide the last thrust of swing for the lower Manhattan night creatures in search of a groove that felt as strong as the city itself. Everybody who wanted to get that last taste of jazz, like some hot ambrosia before bed, made it in there, gathering from all of the other places that had closed at 2:00 a.m. The musicians played four hour-long sets, 10:00, 11:30, 1:00, and 2:45. During the space between the start of the third set and the beginning of the fourth, the last audience was able to get there, buy drinks, settle in and relax, perhaps order food before the kitchen closed at 3:15.

The nickname of Good Henry's was "the pharmacy" because so much dope passed through there, at least two or three dealers in the house by the last set every night. The dealers were jovial, brittle, or sometimes so taken over the hill into derangement by their product that they either couldn't finish sentences or had impassioned faces that were at remarkable removes from the mishmash of their words. About half of the musicians bought the cocaine and about half didn't; the same with the listeners, though the dope buyers might have been no more than ten or fifteen percent, actually. It could all depend on the night. The cocaine was good for business because it hopped people up, dried their mouths, and they then tried to slow their rushing hearts by purchasing a number of drinks. In the bathrooms behind the closed stalls one could hear dope snorted off of thumbnails or up diagonally cut straws throughout the night. The sniffling and the gnashing of the teeth were signs that the white powder was inside the body and having its way.

Carla was attentive enough and well read enough to know that by the early eighties, about the time she arrived in town, there were a good number of cocaine whores in the culture, jazz or not. These women were willing to pull down their panties or enlist their sucking mouths in erotic service just for the sensation of the white powder that sent them flying so astronaut-high. That alone, she laughed to herself, could keep the trade coming and going. The drug dealers talked to the good-looking coke whores as though they were prized pets and to the others as though they were irritating hags, perhaps once quite attractive, but now only on the hustle for some free narcotics. These white-powder whores were always excessively friendly to the guys with the bottles of "girl" or the caches of aluminum foil folded to hold the dope in twenty-, fifty- and hundred-dollar portions.

At one point, perhaps ten years later, musing as she looked out her window at the moon and wondered if she should start seeing Maxwell so soon after Bobo died, Carla speculated that the whole cocaine thing must have a remarkable effect on sexual relations. What a boon the happy dust must be to all of those unattractive and fumbling guys who could get pretty girls to do intimate things with them that they would not otherwise. That did not stop Carla from, while holding her cool, struggling not to become uncontrollably enraged at the way some of those jerks and some of the drug dealers had talked to her when she first came into the scene, assuming that she was available to them, even though one or two of the drug dealers were good-looking guys with something that surely approached class, especially one big, dark, immaculately dressed engine of fascination from Harlem, he who wore mufflers or subtle and beautiful silk scarves to conceal the black, ropelike leavings of a razor cut across his throat. But Carla couldn't put class together with selling drugs nor freedom together with using them. She was tight like that. I'm not that creative, the girl from South Dakota smugly said to herself. Every now and then, however, when she was at the limit of her beers or tired of seltzer water, the god of dreams sitting heavy on her head, she wondered what it would be like to suddenly pep up the way those other women did when they returned from the bathroom to the bar or to their tables. Curiosity was as far as it got. She ordered a cup of coffee.

All in all, Carla loved coming to Good Henry's more than any other place in New York because the ethnic mix was so pronounced. In the other clubs, somewhere below five percent of the audience was Negro, but it was different in that well-kept shotgun room with portraits of jazz musicians hung on the left. On any night, America and its admirers might turn out. Many Negroes, Italians, Jews, Irish, sometimes Puerto Ricans, Austrians, Japanese businessmen, sumo wrestlers, the odd genius painter, and whoever else arrived, from the *movie star trying to pretend he or she was another person to the almost immediately bounced loon who would suddenly stand up and begin singing a religious or patriotic number in the middle of some serious swing.*

In there, with so many of so many kinds ready and rooting for the music, a feeling unlike any other took Carla over. Whenever there was an affluence of top-flight Negro musicians in the house, coming there after their own jobs had ended or turning up to see how well the trade was being handled, those who were swinging for their supper would pull out their best abilities, often raising up their swing against the pressure of the city with something akin to combative prayer, or they inspired viscous howls from the Puerto Rican women who held their heads so high and were so distant but geysered warmth when a certain kind of Latin beat was dropped in place—not to mention the times when the musicians provoked the magic of that good old greasy belly-rubbing, which sometimes took place when it got down to the late, late show and the women would allow the men to dance with them, the masterful, improvised notes putting that vital sheen of particular sensitivity on the feeling of romance. Carla was then in hog heaven (especially that time when Maxwell, who had been looking at her all night, rose and they danced as a slow blues wove itself through the room and she realized, even in her grief for Bobo, how deeply she wanted to be held and gently led in that way that dancing allows a woman to follow but be equal and to measure a man by his ease and his sensitivity to her body and its rhythms).

As she lay there next to Maxwell in Houston, leaving Good Henry's behind, Carla wondered how Ezekiel and Eunice had made it through so much. They were so strong but maybe they came from a time in the world when people were more convinced of how things were about to go. There was God and Satan and the world being tugged at by the two. Actually, the world wasn't being tugged at by the two; Satan was trying to tug the world from the grasp of God. Carla thought at that moment that she might have figured out the reason why the devil was so concerned about the world. What else could he struggle against God for? Could he command the stars or create something beyond infinity? There were two options: to rule where he was, satisfying himself with inventive and eternal sadism, or to try and take at least some of the pleasure from being all-knowing. The torture of the damned would have to be boring because human beings and their capacity to suffer in a rigged situation where death was not a possibility would get stale pretty soon. If Satan could keep God from relaxing and continuing to create infinitely and with ease, that would be some sort of victory. But there was the distinct possibility that the battle was on a much more cosmic scale and involved far more territory than could be imagined by those who wrote all of the religious texts that arrived before astronomy.

The territory was first revealed on the Sunday evening that the visiting Negro minister was having a ham and mashed potato supper with the Reverend Knute John Orison, the pastor of their Lutheran church in South Dakota but a man who looked as though he could have played Paul Bunyan, tall, broad, huge neck, enormous hands, but given to a gentle quality that had the communicating ballast of all that muscle held in check by his spiritual concerns. When Mom mentioned that this supper for the colored preacher was taking place in a few weeks and that she was going to make one of her peerless apple pies for the occasion, something kept telling Carla that it was important to be at that table, even though only a few adults were supposed to show up. About the age of ten and already stubborn, she begged and begged until Mom and Dad submitted. Well, not exactly. Things didn't go that way in that household.

*Pulling Carla into her and Dad's bedroom and closing the door after she caught her child gloating, Mom made it clear, with eyes as hard to look into as marbles were to chew, that she and Dad **decided** to try and fit her in at the special supper table. They weren't doing it because any whining girl was going to tell her parents what to do. That was something she had better recognize this very second unless she wanted to stay home for sure. If anything, she would be allowed, they would **let** her go. Humbled by the tone of her mom's voice, Carla softly told her mother that all she wanted in the world on that day was to go there with her and Dad. Fine, just don't ever be arrogant about anybody else's generosity. Do you understand? Yes, she did. She understood. Good. Gloating is not my notion of grace. It is not. That'll be enough.*

This meant, when it got down to cases, that Mom and Dad had to ask Pastor Orison if their youngest daughter could come along. Sure, bring the little lady. See if she can sit for an evening with no other kids to play with and keep out of everybody's hair. Oh, she can do that. She'll be quiet. Bring her on. Please do. Ramona was left to baby-sit Randy, which her big sister did not like but definitely preferred to looking down or straight ahead in familiar, blank-faced irritation, this time while listening to some pastor whose style did not appear to appeal to her.

*Following the slices of ham, the mashed potatoes, the gravy, and the green beans, the ministers got into a discussion about people out there in the world who thought God didn't exist. Reverend Orison observed, with dry hostility, that the idea of God being dead came out of Germany and was all through the schools now. The Negro said it didn't matter **where** the idea came from, what those kind of people thought was only one more example of how rarely understanding went along with the passage of time in this age. Besides, he said, looking right at Carla, understanding is a condition of wisdom, not a flight of years. She bowed her head, nervous. They were all eating Mom's golden-crusted pie with vanilla ice cream. The Negro complimented Mom on how good it was. Carla felt proud of that, proud of her mom. The visiting pastor continued after eating a bit more of it. There was another thing that had come to him one night when he was out walking and looking up at the stars, his mind on the source of all we know and do not know. God, actually, did **not** exist because God **created** existence, just as one who drew a circle on a piece of paper was not **on** the paper. God was like that, outside of existence, in some state of reality beyond the things that were on our minds, things such as the world and the universe. To God, regardless of how complicated they were in our corner of life and death, these things such as existence were no more complex than crude doodles on a piece of paper. Language, the way we put our logic together, caught us up and made it hard for us to address that concept of **how** God is real. **We** thought everything was **inside** existence. Right, everything is—except the Creator. God was like that. Above all we know. Beyond existence. Praise His name. Mom had no visible reaction, but Carla had never seen Dad smile like that or his head move up and down that way. Some-*

thing mysterious had been said and she heard the words the moment they came into the air. In her middle twenties, she began to understand what the visiting minister meant, and when she did, things were never the way she saw them before. A spiritual freedom to which she was a complete virgin cascaded inside, as if her soul had a bloodstream and she could then experience the motion of every drop.

Her head began to hum and she touched Maxwell, who put his hand on her, seeming to know she wanted his touch, even though he was not awake. That was comfortable. It was an interlude between memories of him and her learning periods inside Good Henry's.

For all that vibrant late-night ritual, Carla still saw many examples of the fact that a jazz musician would stay up all night to bed a pig. There was a surreal quality to all of these guys chasing after these unattractive women and there was an arrogance in these unattractive women that Carla had never, ever, seen before. They sat as though they were aristocrats in some gilded court, or they decadently rolled their eyes at some of the musicians or some of the hangers-on, or they rather stuffily looked upon Carla when she would come in and try to be sociable. They had no interest in her at all and did their best to make her feel as though she was an eternal outsider.

There was one Italian woman, short and not bad-looking, who was described as "a white lady who has moved far beyond the desire to screw the race; she is going about actually doing it." She and her sister had been run out of Jamaica, Bermuda, and Haiti by the local female populations at the threat of death—machetes at the last stop—because in each place, they "had set up a pussy factory so constant, I must tell you, that the damn thing, you got to know, was running there twenty-four hours a day; so much laying down and legs gapping open, all this going on so furious that one nigger getting himself up to leave the pussy was immediately hit in the back with the doorknob at the base of the spine by the next nigger coming in. There was much near crippling going on, you know."

That Maria of the legendary pussy factory, she who, clearly on certain nights, had slept with every one of the twenty or more black men presently in Good Henry's, always said to Carla, just before laughing,

"Hello, Miss S.D. How are you going to keep them down on the farm?" Carla tried to get in on the joke but couldn't.

Maria, however much a devoted debaucher, was at the high end, ever tastefully dressed and literary, far from stupid. Many of the other white women of Negro choice were mediocre at best, incapable of grasping anything subtle, coarse in their self-expression, bleary-eyed and desperately trashy far too often. Here and there, of course, there were white women—skinny, slim, shapely, voluptuous, fat, or otherwise—who were not only nice but who obviously didn't feel that all those Negro guys were one penis of adjustable lengths and thicknesses that had various bodies behind it. Some of them were married to their musicians and had the gaze, so clearly purified by serious affection, of women who had soldiered through all the cold hostility that could now come from anywhere, white or black. These women had soldiered through, using their love to keep them warm. As with the black women who befriended her, Carla had good feelings for those women.

The others could put something on her, though. She had even been snubbed and verbally abused by two walking Jewish houses of oral joy (known behind their backs as Rotund and Rotunda), one contemptuously blowing cigarette smoke in her face at every chance, the other asking Carla whatever made somebody like her think she could fit in the New York scene. Both expressions of disdain had hurt her more than she was willing to show, especially since those women had been around the jazz world for a few decades, servicing musicians with drugs and blubber. But Carla had been strong enough to ignore their nastiness. She used an old technique she had practiced since junior high school: play dumb and you will be left alone.

Carla's pride was involved as well. During the days when she had modeled herself on Lana Turner, Carla had been homecoming queen and there had been these girls at her high school who wrote down her clothing combinations every day, every single day for three years, and if one of them was sick and missed school, she made sure that she got details from one of the others. That was back in the period when she had started the Fashion Club. Carla felt it was time for young women to take a stand. They met in her homeroom after school once a week for about an hour, discussing issues. She and all twenty of the other girls concluded that things went bad after the forties, which was the period that had the highest quality of female attire. They then dedicated themselves to maintaining the lofty standards so faultlessly set when Coco Chanel had been at the apex of her powers and influence. Though they were too young to have been there as more than toddlers during the Kennedy years, Jackie Kennedy, pushed by Carla, was their patron saint. In a speech she was extremely proud of, Carla made it quite clear, passing her Jackie scrapbook around, that this was a woman who had never—not once— given in to bad fashion. There was no record whatsoever of her ever having been seen in anything at all that was not in the very best taste. She was a model for the ages and would someday be recognized for all she had done when it came to seriously picking her outfits, from the quite classy and formal to just what you would throw on to take a walk through the park.

During her three years as president of the Fashion Club, the four girls who had not been allowed membership due to their bad taste made Carla their obsession. What a hoot. They recorded the colors of her blouses, of her sweaters, her skirts, straight or full, her socks, and her shoes. Synthetic fabrics were out: wool, cotton, and the infrequent silk she saved money to buy from her summer jobs. Blobby Marsha, ruler-shaped Sharon, buck-toothed Laurel, and big-nosed Kate, whose dentist father once had tuberculosis—all fruitlessly working up to the status of wallflowers—wouldn't have done badly in the jazz world if they had followed Carla these many years and miles in order to still see what she was wearing.

But they would not have known what she was thinking, even back then. From junior high school forward, at the point that her beauty had started to fiercely pronounce itself, Carla alternated between a low-keyed autocratic demeanor and working hard at pretending she thought she was just like everybody else, and she usually succeeded. On both planes. People looked up to her while feeling that she was somehow right there as one of them. Most of all, after the joy Carla took from doing so well in all of her subjects—especially music, language, history, and math—she knew she was good-looking and that, from boys to men, getting her attention had been on the minds of a good many guys. Now, among dope dealers and proud trollops, she found herself in a world where her looks and her home state might *reduce her to some kind of stereotype, the kind of white person Dan Aykroyd had made his career lampooning: meticulous, stiff, empty, doofus, hilariously lacking in informed feeling.*

The fusion of serenity and giddiness Carla felt as Maxwell, still asleep, embraced her more tightly, was reminiscent of the camaraderie she felt for her very special buddy, who was now so far away, as far away as Carla was in the unrecoverable past when they had come to know each other.

Her favorite girlfriend, Leeann, was black and looked like some lean, breathing, and mischievous piece of ebony sculpture. She had taken Carla in after they struck up a friendly conversation at Good Henry's one night. Leeann broke down all of the codes for her in long telephone conversations or walks all over Greenwich Village, pointing out this and pointing out that. Carla was still presenting herself as a timid waitress then and making do with that inside-out mouse's hole of an apartment in the East Village where the bathtub was in the middle of the room with a board that could transform it into a disastrous dinner table. She had been through some very rough times over there, one so terrifying that she had cut herself off from everyone and everything for a couple of months, just sitting at home and rocking, listening to her favorite records, singing along with them, calling out for food, studying harmony, eating alone and rebuilding herself into socializing shape, measuring her way back into the world, where she kept that sharp edge of midnight trouble to herself and became so strong she could refuse to remember it. Leeann, to be sure, was beyond such things. She was a model who went to the Middle East, to Paris, and to Italy, earning big money and living a very swanky life, some of it made possible by shrewd investments at the advice of an old boyfriend who remained loyal to her well-being though they were now snugly inside the platonic lane. In her wild and profane way, Leeann had become the sister to Carla that Ramona had chosen not to be once they got their dad off the bottle and helped him face the fact that martinis were not going to make him into something other than a widower.

"You girls have no idea what you have done for me," Dad said to them as the three sat down to the table where they all had gathered

for so many evenings in the past. The light was just going and there was no more than a bit of the initial turning of color to be seen in the leaves. They had a dinner of steak, potatoes, and broccoli, his meat well done, Ramona's medium, and Carla's so rare it still had a few moos left in it. "When your mother died I had no place to go. You have no idea how good those martinis tasted and how wonderful I felt when I was drunk. I didn't feel bad, not at all. I felt just grand, top of the heap, perfect. I wasn't, of course, but I felt like that. It was the same when Randy Jr. died out there in those mountains and I found him frozen where he fell. As I have said many times, Randy, well, he looked just as if someone had slapped him on the back by surprise. No pain, just surprise. I drank then. Your mother stopped me. Sue knew how to do things. Your mother was that sort of person. The knowing kind. She was so above but she understood so much below. She filled my heart many times, girls, many times. Your heart is the kind of thing that can feel like a big empty cask if somebody as close to you as another human being can ever be suddenly has the worst bad luck and dies. As is pretty obvious at this point I tried to do that thing you can never do, act like my insides were nothing but a goddam gas tank that ran on martinis. So stupid. It was also insensitive to you girls. I should have been a better man about it. I should have and I would have but I just couldn't. Couldn't do it. Then, as the way things will go, I had the kind of luck you can have if you just have it. You two came back home to stop your dad from being a bad boy. Who deserves that kind of love? I mean it. Who does? Oh, stop looking so serious, you two. Come on, stop. I love you two girls. You're all I have and I love you beyond measure."

When they were sitting in Leeann's West Village town house one afternoon, Carla told her of the way she had been treated by Rotund and Rotunda. Leeann's eyebrows reached for her hairline, she stuck her lips out, set down on the polished redwood living room table the mint green glass plate covered with a delicious layout of mango slices, and commenced to run the voodoo down. As she spoke, Leeann accompanied and punctuated every word and phrase with a twirling and stabbing fork so beautifully designed it momentarily became a stainless steel distillation of all the creature comforts that Carla, on every visit, envied so deeply but—thank God—never resented: "Those two fat motherfuckers? Fuck them bitches. Ugly don't like *pretty. They just mad because you represent everything they didn't start with and everything they, for goddam sure, ain't never going to have. But they got on one good shoe, though. Two fat-assed fashion jockeys: the bitches know how to ride the style. They got to know something about them blubber-rubbing niggers who chase after their balloon asses. Either those brothers got something crazy going on in their tops, or they just black men who believe that fat meat is sweet and greasy. Now I know, **okay,** that you got to understand that about the mysterious entity known to one and all as the Negro. The Negro draws **no** lines. **All** pussy is good. **All** shapes are fine. The Negro has the most democratic johnson in America."*

"In a way, I think that's kind of nice."

*" 'Nice,' you say, you say, '**Nice**'?" Leeann said, strutting a Jewish brogue that made them both laugh.*

"What I mean," Carla went on, "is that it gives a woman a chance to be appreciated for herself. That's how it seems to me. It really does. If the guys are like that, thank God, a woman isn't automatically locked out in the cold by her looks. There's some more freedom there. There's something to that, don't you think?"

*"Good point. Always the kind that pretty women make. Always. Pretty girls like you always have **so much** sympathy for the bulldogs of the sex. **Right.** We will return to that point, simpatico Susie with the blue eyes."*

"You know my mother's name was Susan."

"See, we're coordinated, Carla. But where was I?"

"Bulldogs. That kind of thing."

"Right. But, like every other red-blooded American narcissist, I have to sing my own song on this theme, which is just a little bit different. More than that, actually," Leeann said, a little penknife of unhappiness opening up a thin but lengthy cut in the texture of her voice.

Carla wondered what that song could be, since Leeann was so sophisticated and had so much going for her, such superb taste and such access to the very best of New York. Carla didn't know what a perfect life actually meant, but Leeann came as close to it as anybody she had ever known. Everything for her began at the top of the line. She never took subways or cabs because she didn't want to worry about some fools trying to mug her. Not hardly. That would force Leeann into using some very, very nasty things that she knew how to do extremely well, all of them achieved with disguised weapons that were almost on the Rube Goldberg level but grounded in serious to deadly wounding. Cabs were out because there might not be any available on certain nights or stormy days or, Kiss my **black** ass, she just might have to put up with being indignantly asked where she was going—or, worst of all, **passed up**—by some fucking foreigner who couldn't even afford to handle her weekly cleaning bill and had no idea that this black woman right here **always** tipped five bucks until she soon got good and tired of living in an Alfred Hitchcock movie whenever she raised her arm in the street and saw those yellow cars for hire coming in her direction. Hitchcock had said that when some people sit down to a table and it blows up, that's a mystery. When there's a bomb under a table and nobody knows it, that's suspense. She didn't know what kind of taxicab blues she had, but one of them was enough. Too bad, too bad, tut, tut, tut: "Can't be on the auction block and a good-paying customer at the same time. Two tears in a bucket: fuck it." So Leeann, always on the guest lists of the very best parties and openings and private lectures and dinners with exceptional people, traveled by private car, moving along behind smoked windows.

Her driver of choice was Boris, a dark blonde Russian from the Ukraine with remarkable lead-colored eyes. Nearly handsome, he was made like those muscular and powerful men who had always done the brute work of building civilizations but carried themselves like lyric tenors or had the easy stroll and the suave intensity of gesture exhibited by the most subtle of pantomimists. The way Boris stepped out of the car and came around to open the door had a pervasive gallantry. If a bum was moving on one of his passengers, he had only to look, his gray eyes filling with acid, and the derelict knew that Boris would abide no begging and that he did not intend for those passengers entering or already inside his car to hear any panhandling. There was silence from the bum and a backing away, sometimes with a salute snapped off that made Boris laugh softly. As he then gestured to the military derelict to return and gave him a few coins, there would be another laugh, this one a bit louder, the Russian familiarity with madness, grandeur, consuming landscapes, hunger, and inconsistency fluttering inside his chuckle like the blind ghosts of *history that never cease to suck the blood of a people or brutally stumble into them.*

*Leeann preferred Boris because his stories were unusual and they had the stain of life that she found lacking in so many of her business encounters, where all someone was talking about was which model was sucking whose what, and who was on what drug, and what designer had made himself into a heterosexual by, supposedly, switching over all of his blood with a dialysis machine so that he could duck AIDS (then, born again with his dick pointed in a different direction, the chump married one of the spiritual maggots that sprouted wings and buzzed around the shitheads with too much money). Once you had heard the themes, the variations became monotonous. Gossip, gossip: the secret talk shows about people with upper-class bucks who woke up with the blues three different ways, two minds saying to leave, one mind saying to stay. Usually, theirs was the hollow-log blues and reminded Leeann of the end of **Le Père Goriot,** where the youngster who has come to the city and is solely attending the old man's funeral sees the empty carriages sent to represent the daughters of the deceased, both identified by their crests. Carla also knew Balzac was saying that the country boy who had been so impressed by the big city and those high-class women saw then the literal emptiness that symbolized the spiritual vacuity of those who shimmered in such luxury at the grand balls. Leeann nodded; she always remembered that book: it reminded her of New York. Same funk, different time cycle.*

From all that garbage, Boris was a relief. Leeann nicknamed him "Soul Brother Pushkin No. I," which always produced a laugh from Boris that, if solid, would be like a terrific ceramic piece that emerged from the heat of the kiln shaped exactly like freedom. Normally, his eyes in the rearview mirror possessed the cynical melancholy of one who had killed more than a few times and who had been disillusioned all the way down to the soles of his feet. Carla knew she had seen that look in Bobo's eyes. Boris—"myself one more of the number of us too big to know"—had grown up finding the bones of soldiers killed during the German invasion. Those bones were everywhere, just below the earth: "not far so deep in any of the directions where we played." There "were included weapons brown of rust" that the kids used for games they invented, sometimes also rotted old boots and pieces of uniforms. Soul Brother Pushkin No. I remembered one day a kid found some kind of land mine and killed himself playing with it. Yes, there was fun; yes, there was danger to playing. Others had pieces of themselves blown off. This early in children's life, they had right now the looks on their faces of war veterans but no war known to them; bad luck only.

"A joke I see now was the school."

Leeann and Carla, heading for a huge whoop-de-do in a town house on the East Side near the water, perked up their attention. Boris smiled that way in which only the right side of his mouth rose. The joke of school: It was important, in Communist time, he said, to learn the things about truth. Tests had to be shown. So children were told in school to ask God for candy, pray and hold back no desire, no passion, to use their wills in entirety. None came. Not candy, even single piece. Ask again. Still none. Once more. Pray more now. No candies for them. No candies. Children then became sad. No attention from God. They were then told to ask President Stalin for their little sugars, bad chocolates and such. Candies arrived with much pomp and cheer. In such objective contest, God lost; Stalin had victory of winning.

Boris had been in the military, not too high up, not too low; close enough to power to learn in detail how it all worked. He kept Leeann current on the twisted-up gangster ways his country had gone since the Soviet Union was busted: totalitarianism had taught the men in the military, the police, and the secret service how to adapt themselves into highly skilled gangsters. What were once ruthless yet official underground ways that weren't focused on the profitable remained underground but expanded themselves and became, at once, even more criminal and, for the first time, extraordinarily profitable. This was because the professional criminals who had successfully evaded capture in a country that had no individual rights came together with those who enforced policies with methods that, in theory, should have completely destroyed crime. Now the murdered died only because they were in the way, not because they threatened the vision of the state. Now the ideology was the freedom from ideology. There was, it should be recognized, the determination to do whatever *was necessary in order to maintain intimidation but also have the public and private fun that goes with hedonistic luxury. Included was the possible end of the world aided in perfection by very bitter persons from the old Soviet Union: exactly these people sold doomsday nuclear weapons only because of being the guards at the secret top of the military with nothing else to use for economic social uplift. These had auctioned off six or seven big boom devices into the hands of unknown men, could be Arabs, could too be maniacs from the West or suicide cult leaders from the East for whom nerve gas in the subway was not enough, could also be ones who had done all they were able to think of with their very high walls of money and now took huge joy from knowing that, as their aging inclined them closer and closer to death, they might find the right place near stockpiled weapons to bring in this time the Gotterdammerung that would have already happened if Hitler—as the Reich began to decompose under the invading boots of the Allies—had the tools to bring on the total fire and the final, universal darkness.*

What a world, Carla thought, feeling uncomfortable behind the dark windows of this sumptuously comfortable limousine. The words Boris spoke transformed her and the girl from South Dakota became much like herself when she was a teenager in the early winter air and began walking home from the pool among her buddies, all of whom had climbed the fence at night on a dare, jumping like fools into the chill water and paying the cost of not having towels, which would not have changed the weather anyway. In Carla's mind her teeth were chattering and the ruthless bodily sensation made it seem that warmth would never return and that perhaps one version of hell was just that—the earth turned to ice, the wet skin and the wind working together against you, the trees become burnt down stumps, and the sky painted over with lead-colored clouds of dust, a shield behind which the sun hid itself from the artificial wilderness made true by these weapons so massive in their ability to close off all fun and games in an iron-hearted world sentenced by mad men who themselves would not live long. Wow: all the dreams and nightmares of medicine and technological miracles are coming true. In this case, the kinds of loony tune scientists and arch villains little Randy Jr. pretended to be when he ran around in a spattered painter's smock that was his lab coat, imitating his Fright Night television favorites, Bela Lugosi or

Vincent Price, and waving Dr. Pepper bottles of a Kool-Aid secret weapon mixture that would make him master of the world or its complete assassin—these characters invented to satiate the public's appetite for the entertainment of ritualized fear had jumped off the screens and were now out in the streets or the back woods somewhere.

All this kind of thing, Boris went on, because those from Russia trusted with the life of the mother earth now had nothing to defend and nothing to trust other than how much money you own. A new dishonesty was normal. "Our country is now run by Cossacks of people in all of underworld," he said, which Leeann observed was "better than a crocus sack."

It was feeling very good lying there with Maxwell embracing her. For a bit it seemed as though the world was doing just fine and they had their place in it, visiting those who might be her future in-laws and lying alone in the Houston night, nothing moving in the street and the sky preparing to lighten up as dawn geared up to bust out with a sunrise. Carla couldn't tell if she had been asleep or not but knew that all of this thinking would probably make her somewhat groggy tomorrow, so much so that all she would be waiting for was the chance to take a nap, which one couldn't do for a number of hours since she had never seen anyone say that he or she hadn't slept well and was, now, going right back to bed. Maybe things would work out so she could go someplace with Maxwell and get in a swim, which was always the most pleasant experience with nature she ever had. Nothing came close to the feeling of being in the water, doing all of the different strokes, moving forward in the regular way, then using the breaststroke, then the butterfly, then swimming backwards or going under the surface and feeling the water against her as she slowly parted the invisible liquid curtain, loving how the coordination of her arms and legs gave such sublime locomotion. For some reason which she could never get straight, Maxwell had never liked Leeann. He never said anything about her directly, but there was always something snittish in the air between them, even as each of them smiled so brightly an onlooker could feel the need for dark glasses. If Carla could have a dream right now, she would ask him why he didn't like her friend and he would probably tell her that he was jealous of the affection she felt. Men can be that way about a woman's friends. But just as Maxwell had his way, Carla had her buddy and she wasn't about to give her up. Sometimes all Carla could think about was Leeann, wondering what it would be like to live so privileged a life, not just be a guest or a girlfriend.

Leeann had flown first-class so many times, always arriving just five minutes or so before the plane doors were locked. Airports were boring; the little dinky clubs for first-class passengers were nothing to write any damn body letters about. Some coffee, some fruit, some newspapers, couches and stuffed chairs, televisions on news channels you couldn't change. So what? In lovely flat shoes and one of the velvet or suede or terry cloth or satin jumpsuits she wore for airplane travel, Leeann preferred to joke with the skycaps or the black women on the staff, listening to their stories and making up some outlandish ones of her own, since she didn't feel that it was necessary to tell the truth to strangers in order to be interesting. Dawdling like that, wherever she could and with whomever she could, allowed her to go right on board at the select moment, pretending that she didn't know she was about to miss the plane and making her entrance once everyone else was seated and buckled in.

*So many were such occasions in first class that Leeann claimed to have forgotten that there was anything beyond the curtain behind the first-class seats other than the tail of the plane and maybe some resting places where those flight attendants who were turning into sagging and pruned-up hags could talk about the good old days when they looked like something worth laying a gander on ("I have to say it, Carla. I have to. Forgive me, sweetie, but the truth is the goddam **truth**. Time whips white women like the plantation overseers whipped them some **very** uppity niggers. You know what I'm saying? With absolutely **no** mercy"). Deferred to by those who had seen her in magazines, satisfied to be last, ready for an immediate mimosa, she relaxed and looked out the window, always the window. Consequently, Leeann claimed, with what might have been an angular twinkle in her eye, that she always wondered where all those pushy goddam low-class people with their carry-on luggage suddenly came* *from after the plane landed. Maybe they buckled them into seats on the wings. Peasants.*

None of that made certain social elements of her life any different, she said, from those of every other black woman. Carla didn't really buy that but she was accustomed to how New Yorkers, no matter how well they did in the world, were able to make themselves into victims of some sort. It was another strategy for maintaining a way of talking in which the first person took over every angle of experience, whether I'm only doing as well as you or I'm doing as bad as you or I'm as ambivalent as you. All bases covered. Leeann got to her any-black-woman's blues by extending, sometime later, her observations about jazz musicians and pigs. She had invited Carla to her town house after a particularly pleasant evening in Good Henry's, filled with champagne, dancing, and handsome men who left with other women.

*"Now in my case, **how-some-ever,** I would be walking around with mucho unused pussy if I was waiting for these jazz club niggers to get around to **me.** All I got going on, it don't mean a damn thing. Too tall, too black, hair too short, eyes too big, and too much mouth going twenty-four/seven. Of course, I could slink the rink over to Brooklyn and play the bogus bongo African queen role for my peoples. I would have to dress the flowing-robe part with the Hula-Hoop earrings and the gold bone in the nose, and get a dick here and there, but that would be a little too crazy—even for me. No, not my cup of nigger business. That ethnic stuff wears me all the way out, being the one-legged black girl in an official ass-kicking contest. Then I **really** feel that I've worked like a nigger. So, if we don't mind getting real, I'm stuck with white boys and I'm stuck with white boys sticking it to me."*

*Carla had always seen Leeann with white American guys or Europeans, never making much of it, just assuming that they were the men she met in her upper-class life, where there might not have been as many available Negro guys. Leeann's guys exuded the power of a casual familiarity with privilege, even in the way they inhaled and exhaled cigarette smoke, the certitude shown as they picked up and parted menus, how they addressed people in positions of service, the manner in which their faces became combinations of masks and revelation as they spoke of where they had been and what they did in business. These men all gave the impression that in their world of achievement, Carla, **not** Leeann, was the exotic. Miss South Dakota* *had yet to achieve anything of note, and they could sense it because she tried too hard to be relaxed, which made her a bit clumsy and ungainly, her grace under siege by her own insecurity. At those moments, when the jig was up, Carla felt most like the little girl who wants to hide behind her mother's skirts. She didn't want to take cover behind Leeann or constantly talk about her great black friend in order to give herself a social anchor or some moorings. It will not always be like this, she promised herself. But promises don't change the facts of where you are. The rich looked at Carla with amusement since they were surrounded by or involved with those who were obviously on the way up or were already quite accustomed to the money that had come down to them through the bloodline of the family sluice and the thunder of conquest.*

Intimidation aside, they weren't Carla's kind of men. She had already been there. Among them she could have been no more than another of the blonde arm-charms lifted from social hibernation every time one of those guys wanted something pretty to accompany him someplace. For a little while she had a real romance with a courtly Irish guy, but these men usually didn't care if the girls were screwing them or their reputations or their credit cards or their credit lines as long as the bimbos knew when to lie down in the dark and do what they were told. No, not her type. She guessed they weren't really Leeann's either, but didn't have the temerity to ask. Some things, she had learned in the very hardest ways, one waited to hear. It was always dangerous to ask for information you weren't ready to get.

Still, she wondered. In fact, Carla remembered reading a perspective from a New York black woman who had a rich white husband. The woman loved self-assurance; that attracted her more than anything else in the world. Her preference was men with clout, not no-clout men. As this woman would have it, there were no black men, once you scratched the surface, who had the confidence to move in her and her husband's world of long-term wealth, oil sheiks, studio heads, diplomats, Wall Street tycoons, and those beltway insiders who shook and moved the world.

Carla laughed out loud as she read what that woman said, turning heads on the subway to Brooklyn, then thinking first of her college years back in what became sweet home Chicago, where Rondo Jackson moved among the rich and famous or rich and unknown when *they came into his blues club on the South Side, giving them the impression they had better be happy they even got in. "Traveled all over the world has you? Made all **kind** of money," Jackson joked to one financier who used to stand every great once in a while at the bar drinking boilermakers, with his entourage of the Chicago elite, all game to sweat and look on and shake their heads from side to side on the wrong beat. "Yeah, I know: traveled all over the world, talking with kings and queens, making all them goddam deals, but you got to come on back up here to get that **real** feeling. I know how it is: if I was in your shoes, I'd be doing the same damn thing myself," Jackson said, moving along, moving right on through his packed house, dressed in lime green from head to toe.*

After watching and contemplating some rowdy kids and thugs for a bit, Carla couldn't stop reading the black woman's article, even as she walked toward the Brooklyn Botanic Garden to meet Maxwell that very first time, trying to ignore an excitement that was fanning up and down her body. The very rich Negro woman with the white husband, falling back on the gauche fairy-tale metaphor, described herself as living far up on the mountain that became oiled emerald glass in that last stretch before her castle. No-clout men couldn't make it. They either shriveled up and passed out very quickly from the thinner air, or they slipped and went plummeting down, their rageful and intimidated screams filling the valley. In New York, however, one sometimes gets the chance to see if the pudding proves to be as good as the baker says it is. When Carla encountered that brown-skinned woman with her hair frizzed up at a private showing of deca-dent fashion photographs that Leeann took her to, the South Dakota woman concluded that the lady in question was extremely deluded, since she was clearly no more than a thickly made-up and snooty extension of the gold and platinum watch her Jewish husband wore and made sure that everyone saw. Her eyes had the self-obsession and the swelling, then receding, sadness that Goya had caught in his court paintings, where the truth of human frailty cleaved raw even the hearts of the outrageously privileged.

"Let us not get lost in the polka-dot boody shuffle."

"The what?"

"What I'm saying is simple, country girl: going out with white men does not take your black ass even one mile closer to paradise,"

Leeann said, opening up another bottle of champagne as the morning star went through its glimmering paces. "That's the fact of it. No matter how much shit they know about this and know about that—been here, been there, done this, done that—I have had to get used to their ignorant, red-pimpled asses, too. Whitey riding darkie. When it rains, it pours; when it's not yours, it's Dinah Shore's. But that's—let us stop right here—another story. That story is sometimes sadder than a funeral for twins, which, as you must know, is twice as sad as the normal kind. Still, let us not forget, this chickenshit farce is a knockoff-funeral bargain: it is two little coffins for the price of one heart. Another story."

Whatever the tale was, Leeann had already taught her running buddy something so important about the sadness doubled up like that grief for twins, which was the power of Monet's **Water Lilies.** She took Carla to the Museum of Modern Art one day when Miss South Dakota had been complaining of how slowly things were going and how difficult it was to make a career in music. The music was like a whirlwind, you could feel it but you couldn't hold it or control it. The frustration made you wonder if you should have gone after something else. Carla could tell, taking a breath as she complained and complained, her only power the measure of her disappointments, that Leeann was beginning to show a particular kind of fatigue—the version that comes of listening to and recognizing how being excluded has created an overwhelming self-obsession in the speaker. All the individual hes and shes can think about is themselves. What is wrong with **them**? Why aren't **they** understood? Do **they** have what it takes? What do **they** have to do to slip by, to get in, to become one of those who cruise along in the golden lane of the accepted? Is there anything like fairness in the world? And so on all the way down the long, long tunnel in which the listener is dragged behind the talker, who holds a spotlight over his or her head with the determination Hitler showed when he stuck that arm into the air and would not waver as the troops marched and marched and marched right past their führer. Triumph of the arm. Leeann did not say that she had heard enough; she said that she knew just what her buddy from the Midwest needed. She would say that, Carla thought, miffed by Leeann's confidence and admiring her at the very same time.

When they turned the appropriate corner in the Museum of Mod-

ern Art and the **Water Lilies** swept up against their eyes, an extraordinary, elevating repose took over. They were immediately as at ease as
everyone else who was already there, some of whom sat on the
padded benches for hours, transported by the power of those brushstrokes, the ones most deeply touched crying the meditative tears of
exultation. Leeann told Carla that Good Henry's was the best place
to rise up out of the nighttime blues but that there was nothing better
to get the daytime blues off of you than those **Water Lilies**. They had
what this model from South Carolina considered the ultimate power
of art. The flowers on canvas could lift you into the region of spiritual
confidence that radiates from beauty so pure one would think those
brushstrokes could turn a jar of piss into apple juice. That experience
could transform anybody's soul into that of a rugged angel who
knows the untended hurts and the cold narrow prison of the spiritual
night but recognizes, "without one fucking blink whatsoever," the
russet power of dawning revelation. Those **Water Lilies** had done
plenty, plenty for Leeann on many bad days, especially the kind that
made her feel that all she wanted was something that reminded her of
the warmth of her dead mother, the touch that lifted the pain off of
you. That's right. Say it. The sophisticated upper-class colored girl
with so much dirty mouth at her whim sometimes felt so grateful that
she had to resist falling down on her knees and thanking God that
someone had been blessed with the power to help so many people the
moment they turned that corner.

Later, over coffee in Trump Tower, slumming on Fifth Avenue,
Leeann said that as far as she could tell, most of the niggers who
guarded all the great paintings and sculpture in New York didn't
think any of it was shit and could be noticed pitying the people who
made so much of this old painted shit, this marble shit, this metal
shit: White folks, goddam, goddam, always paying top dollar to get
chumped off. This, Leeann joked, was good because, trifling motherfuckers, these niggers would have probably disgraced the race by
clumsily trying to sneak home with some of that goddam artistic shit
they knew they didn't know a fucking thing about anyway. Then,
reversing herself once the joke had set in, Leeann told Carla that
what she had said about the guards wasn't true. Many of them were
artists and did know what they were looking at and could give you

some pointers on what was good, what was better, what was best, and what was even better than that.

"Now, as far as what Maxwell said, he was busting out facts, not farts. Kikes and wops are not official white folks."

Carla had made herself become accustomed to Leeann using the word nigger, which she could not abide any more easily from her than from anyone else, but accepted because, as she continued to find out over and over, no black person would stop using it just because she didn't like to hear it. Part of the power they assumed was to determine when the word was destructive and when it was painful, even when it was neutral or joking or an appellation of honor. That satiric offering of honorary status was what Maxwell meant when he would sometimes playfully say to her at night, "Bring that nigger ass over here, pink girl," or congratulate her for the luck of not being one of those white women he said were members of "the well-known white organization, the N triple A—NO ASS AT ALL." Those two syllables, as any kind of term—even when she had to laugh and laugh herself—finally gave Carla an unpleasant feeling, and she thought black people rather naive about the word because, not once in her experience, had a white person used nigger with anything less than a demeaning intention. This was true of even the white boys who imitated the swaggering simian moves and gestures, bad taste, and worse behavior of rappers and so embarrassed Carla she wanted to become invisible whenever she saw them. Leeann using racial slurs for other people was even worse. Carla didn't have the nerve to call her on it and knew she would lie in bed later that night wondering if she should try to get Leeann to stop that kind of insulting talk when they were together. She was such a great and loyal friend that Carla wouldn't want to lose her camaraderie over a couple of words. Well, she sighed, that must be why so many others accept such things from their friends. They weigh it all and let the words go by. Those words were the mold in the corner of the bread. It should be cut off, but sometimes that moldy bread was served.

The whole trouble with just listening to those words, Carla finally said to Leeann, reminded her of how she had to quit working a jazz club on the Bowery, where the lights in the bathrooms were the same color as blue veins, which discouraged junkies from going in them to *shoot up. It was the night when the burly Irish owner, who spent most of his evening time at Plato's Retreat while his wife worked behind the bar, showed her, a South Dakota girl still fairly new to Manhattan, what to do with some molded cheesecake. The room, which had once been a thing of well-kept beauty, with hardwood floors that shone, had become a dive under his ownership, the floors dull, the bathrooms constantly breaking down. He didn't believe that the public should get any more from his concrete Irish ass than it could muster with drilling equipment. This was one of those who had cheap liquor put in all of the bottles in the afternoon and told the staff he would have their knees broken by his hoodlum Italian friends if they ever uttered a peep about it. If the customers complain, shrug you don't know what the fuck they're talking about.*

On the evening of her cheesecake lesson, the club was filled. The work was demanding but the tips were beginning to pile up. It was still early and Carla knew she would go home just fine, her money hidden in a pocket she had sewn inside her jeans, no purse, and a box cutter hidden in her hand as she walked home with her arms across her chest. The Irish guy looked at her. One of the brutal forearms that had repulsive horns of bone for elbows and looked misshapen but deceptively tapered into especially handsome fingers was rubbed across his forehead, just below the gateway of tenacious balding. He shook up a can of whipped cream and, with a soft-pedaling but demonic contempt, heavily sprayed it over the green patches of mold, creating lovely curlicues that went on across the entire top of the slice of cheesecake. Carla looked at him. She looked at him as he held out the plate. She looked at the pure white whipped cream. Then, abominably angry at what he had just done to her, Carla took off her apron, ran her hands back through her hair because she needed the hell out of that job at that time, and turned around. She knew that Irish bastard. He would say nothing. No complaints. No anger busting out of the top because the club was filled to overflowing. He would serve it himself and play the waiter that night, digging in like the bulldog son of a bitch that he was. No one fucked over him. Not, as he said, the circumcised bastards or the goddam uncircumcised bastards.

"I'm glad you explained all of that to me. It made the bubbles in my champagne pop with more seriousness."

"Well, take it or leave it."

"Now I know to leave some cheesecake with whipped cream on top. But I'll choose my own diction, thank you very goddam much, and I'm still more interested in talking about these white women passing for white."

"That's ridiculous. You sound like Maxwell."

"I don't think so. Not on this lady's dime. What's happening right here at this moment is that you better **recognize**. I mean do you really believe," Leeann smirked with something of a cruel satisfaction, "that white folks think Barbra Streisand is officially white with that neon schnozzareeny and that seriously nappy hair? I beg to differ if you think they do. These white folks love her funky drawers when it comes to her singing—and they should, the woman is gifted, gifted way over into the extreme when she opens that big-assed mouth. But that girl's nose, in profile, have you spent three seconds peering at **that**? Ain't no **Water Lilies**, baby. Very low on the uplift. Looks like a goddam staircase fucking a ski slope. Now let's talk about this completely insane shit, as far as them white folks in Europe is concerned. To them, hey, Europe stops at the eastern borderline of Poland. Catholic Poland, where the pope was bowling his ass off when he got the call after they sent out the smoke signal at the Vatican. Except for him, those Poles don't give a goddam about no Jews of any kind, the stacked-up Auschwitz version or the ones walking and talking. Nobody can make them feel guilty even after fifty years of appropriate whining and crying and finger-pointing. So you know, behind closed doors, ain't no Russian no kind of way included in this deal. Italians got in and got booted out a long time ago. So, hell to tell, girlfriend, when you break it and shake it out there in the world of them white Protestants and northern European Catholics, the best them Jew and Italian women can do is hope to be considered—silently, mind you—white niggers, if you please."

"I have never ever, ever thought anything like that. Never. It seems ridiculous to me. So stupid!"

"Now don't get defensive. Don't get the red face on me. Fine. You like people. You're one of the luckiest people in the world. Puts no patches on my black ass. Must we travel this road again?"

"What road?"

"Okay, we will travel it. **You** are not prejudiced. You're not an anti-Semitic bitch looking for some prejudicial gravy train to ride your untalented ass on to glory, which is where the dick behind that kind of fucking in the ass comes from, dildo or au naturel. You are a good citizen. Fine. No more applause. No more parades. Hooray for you."

Carla didn't like Leeann making her the brunt of that blowtorch humor. She was proud of not being prejudiced. It shouldn't have been something to be proud of, but as long as things were not ideal and you found yourself trying to embody something the other side of common ignorance, it wasn't such a bad thing to feel pride for adhering to principles that lifted you above the great fall of common hostility to all that was different or anything that demanded a bit more patience if you were to achieve human understanding. She felt no pain about saying that.

"But what does your not being a bigot have to do with the bumpers on a big frog's ass?"

"I'm lost in here."

"What I'm saying is that nothing about you makes any difference to the people I'm talking about. They don't do phone surveys to find out what **you** think. They do their own shit and they keep that shit going on. Why? Because all over the world it feels good to tell somebody, 'No, **you** cannot come in. Get the **fuck** away from here.' White folks don't do that better than anybody else. They just get more attention. But white people like you sure don't know much about the ways of white people."

Carla knew more than Leeann thought, but she wasn't interested in talking about it because the prejudice, or the indifference, was always too close to home and it hurt too much. She had learned heaps about white folks that she didn't want to know, just as she had learned a lot about Negroes that she could easily do without. But it was Leeann's move in the conversation and Carla, as usual, was fairly happy just listening, for the most part.

"I know me my people, you can believe that. I started at the bottom, climbing my ass up out of a greasy boot in South Carolina. I can open up on some niggers now. I can holler. I can tell on them. I can holler."

"Can you whisper?" Carla asked with her own sarcasm, feeling a bit more even as her friend seemed just about stunned by the question. A big smile spread its teeth inside Carla.

"I prefer to whisper," Leeann replied, her eyes becoming imperious. "But sometimes you got to shout. Oh, you got to shout now. Maxwell knows you got to shout on these niggers. You got to shout on these niggers because they got such bad taste in white folks."

Carla somehow felt a twinge of humiliation, the sort that made her realize that, for all of her talk about the primacy of individuals, she could be slapped with the goods. A few words could make her forget that she was Carla and transmogrify her into just another white person taking offense at a Negro talking too long and too strong about those other whites who had nothing more to do with her than the accident of skin tone. At such times, she wondered if she would ever be able to even accept herself as a person every single second, never hiding behind her group, never feeling something abstractly protective or defensive or proud. Would she forever remain behind the eight ball of dark moods or have to know the creepy feeling that, aided or not, she was always ready to lead herself to some kind of psychological Alamo? Did anybody really need history in order to make their human passions important? When it was black-dark and tenderness lay over the air like a mosquito net, keeping the stings of the petty at a distance, what did how she and Bobo or she and Maxwell touched or lay next to each other have to do with history? What did it have to do with the wonders of early womanhood in sweet home Chicago?

"I'm losing you, girl. I'm losing you."

"Oh, sorry. No. I mean I was listening. I'm right here."

"Say what you want to say. Now you got *me* lost with that funny look on your face. Where was I?"

"I believe the subject was shouting and bad taste in white folks."

They both burst into laughter.

"Anyway, Negroes out here know so little about anything connected to anything. I mean anything further behind, further back than the last time they took a do-double-dooky. They don't know the difference between history and hot sauce. That's why they treat these crude, rejected, penniless, third-string white whores like they're queens. Now is that some motherfucking shit or is that some mother-fucking **shit**? These bitches would fuck a beer bottle if it was black and it could talk some niggerese. Nigger, **please**. Can you imagine how much money has been spent? How many drinks been bought?

How much dope has been paid for and snorted in order to get these crusty, splotchy, flat-assed white bitches in bed?"

Carla again felt assaulted. It bothered her when Leeann said things of the sort she read in black novels. The white woman. The white woman. The white woman. Do they think about anything else?

"Now that's another place where you step off from them, Carla— that hooty-spooty boody."

While Carla didn't like it when anybody other than Maxwell talked about her rear end, her history, her caboose, her background, or any of the other terms for it, she felt just fine and a member of the party when Leeann complimented her on her form. Then she experienced that sisterly emotion and the thought of Ramona echoed up from a serious hole in her spirit.

"But one woman can't get all the smoking in the stroking; we sure know that. Plus—mind the rhyme, keep the time—there's a magnificent sliver of justice up in here."

"You caught me off guard, Leeann. I must say. I must say."

"Must say what?"

"I'm glad there's something of value in all of this."

Leeann's eyes turned to mock-brown discs of ice.

"Did you say you're glad that there's something of value in what I'm saying?"

"I did: something of value. Can it be? I mean do you really think we can get a sliver of something good out of all of this black-white stuff?" Carla chided.

"You heard what I said. I didn't stutter. A sliver. And, yes, it is magnificent. It really is. Along about now, that's the best female thing about integration, in and out of the jazz world: it helped ugly white women get handsome Negro men and ugly black women to get handsome white men. The exotic is damn sure erotic. Might seem crazy, but, hey, this is America."

7

YOU, TOO

CARLA KNEW from crazy, inside and out. It had to do with what she wanted to be seen as and what she didn't. That question of the image had been on her mind for a long time. Such stuff might have begun when those girls were looking at her every single day of high school, her very own drooling paparazzi using paper and pen instead of camera, film, and flashbulbs. Everybody wanted to be seen as *something*. Usually something beautiful or handsome. As an example, the pure, natural gifts that could make most singers hide under the bed were only part of the Streisand tale in the tub of butter that was her place in the culture. What the woman did when she became a movie star was a whole other thing. As one who remembered when all she surveyed seemed as close to her grasp as the consistency of her will, a snap of her fingers, some long nights studying with the fury of a lawyer preparing a brief for the Supreme Court, or an inexperienced vamping cast of the eyes, Carla lay there confident that she understood quite well the appetites of the golden-throated Brooklyn woman Leeann ridiculed so fiercely for her profile. Costarring opposite one seriously good-looking guy after another—each one scripted to lose his mind over her—Streisand had successfully pushed her way into a private club of public glamour, just like Fred Astaire. There it was, men first, as usual: the great dancer, who hadn't been all *that* much sweeter to the eye than the homely Woody Allen, was probably the initial guy nobody would consider attractive who still got a special pass into the club of romantic leads. Then, she supposed, Bogart and Sinatra. The graceful Midwestern feet and legs; the upper-class hard-boiled sweetheart; the Hoboken beanpole baritone. They made another Mount Rushmore of types for girls to get crushes on. As ever, for all its American brevity, here was a tradition. But Streisand, who confessed in middle age to having always been insecure about her looks because of her deprecating mother, was in no way like the Negro singer Maxwell had joked about one night at Leeann's when she was, again, reviling the queen of the Jewish nose. The very thought of his undercutting dig made Carla laugh almost loudly enough to awaken her man. This other lady, Maxwell claimed, was so unattractive that a guy, one who had been enchanted into spending the night by the sumptuous magnetism of her sound, awoke the next morning and, upon looking at that unadorned, sleeping face, said, "Oh, Lord, *please* wake up and sing something."

As she snuggled up to Maxwell, his sleeping embrace warming her, his barely audible snoring mixed with the sound of the air conditioner and the Houston crickets, she spiritually groaned as something told her that there was a fatal cancer inside their love, that she would never be his wife, that there would be no children, that she would, again, find herself alone and looking for somebody who had a feeling for her and who brought Carla's feeling all the way up to the top, where she wanted to live, come high water, come hell.

She snuggled closer: an odd, becalming quality of safety and confidence now rode the cool air rattling into the room that had been Malena's but was now cleared of all memory. Everything boxed up out in the garage, all the original furniture gone, now a pure space made into a guest room. It would still have seemed sadistic to have Maxwell sleep in his sister's room if there had been any other choice. Eunice had turned Maxwell and Aaron's room into a quilting, darning, and sewing factory, with a dressmaker's dummy, an ironing board built into the wall, shelves filled with patterns, fashion magazines, and the coloring books of all sorts that she loved to work her way through, having started to collect them when those about Jackie Kennedy had first come out. She had every one of them that Carla had bought when she was a teenager. Sometime soon, Carla thought again, Eunice would have that massaging leather chair from the mall either in the living room or, just as easily, in her sewing room, losing herself in her thoughts, the comfort, and the relaxing pressure as a new kind of electronic slave did her bidding.

Malena was far from gone, however. In one section of the living room there were all of her junior and high school yearbooks, her miniature skyline of trophies, her white leather Bible containing the words of Jesus Christ in red letters, her maroon high school graduation cap with tassel, and a few photographs in braided gold frames, one picture of her leaning into the finish line at the Olympic tryouts, where she was so far ahead of everyone else in the sprints, the long jump, and the high jump, but had suddenly left because of some trouble with a boyfriend, athletics forever behind her.

Her, too. My God. Whoever knows? No one. No one at all.

It was her senior year and a few weeks after the homecoming ball. The sweet and hot froth of it all was still in place. Late autumn was there, with so many subtle browns and golds, not the many colors of the Eastern Seaboard. Out in the South Dakota world were the flatland grasses and the shelter belts of trees, which were planted in surrounding squares to protect the fields from the winds that would otherwise blow away the topsoil. There was the spreading quiet in the falling temperature that was so characteristic. As if in a drill, the season was preparing to make its exit, to withdraw its forces and let old man winter lie down in white until there would be those days when you came outside and the moisture in your nose froze so quickly that your breathing had a rattle to it.

Hungry as she walked down the hall with all of the other kids who were just as ready to eat, Carla was taken by her outfit of thick white cable-knit sweater, short suede navy skirt, white cable-knit knee-socks, and navy suede shoes with off-white laces. The mirror in the girls' bathroom had pleased her immensely. It was easy to see. Her time as a full-fledged woman was surely around the corner.

Carla was leaning over the water fountain in the bright and noisy high school cafeteria, after a filling but abominable lunch, when a dumb Dutch boy who was pushing the tall metal contraption that held stacks of trays decided to cut the fool this time by speeding up his pace, running, then standing on the back of it. He almost zoomed past her as she turned the fountain's handle and the water rose, but the flat bottom edge of the tray rack, bumped and bumped loose from the screw above the wheels so that a rectangular blade was in place, slashed the Achilles tendon of Carla's right leg and it rolled right up.

A down-mustached lesbian named Alice Olson who lived with her nurse, owned many tweed suits and the cutest matching felt hats, was the school doctor. She was on the spot immediately, moving through the bewildered kids, taking over with a comforting professionalism that was very compassionate. Miss Olson didn't realize what had happened with the tendon and merely stitched the wound closed, a mistake that wasn't realized until two days later, when it was too late. The strength necessary to carry out her Olympic plan was now gone; contrite apologies and get-well cards made no difference whatsoever. Carla should have had corrective surgery immediately. Her leg was never the same and she had a limp so slight it was virtually imperceptible, the calf just a shade smaller than the left. If winter was on the way, she could feel it sooner than other people. Part of her body was now a barometer.

In her bedroom, sitting up one afternoon with pillows at her back and the sun shining as it did no matter what happened to anyone, Carla felt needles of tears were flying around inside her like the frozen water in an ice storm, but she would not cry. She would not. That was not part of the deal. Not this time. The cut, the blood, the furor, and the screaming in the cafeteria had taken her to a place beyond the satisfaction of weeping. Crying had not a blessed thing to do with it. Carla's face was still and blank and everyone's voice seemed to barely arrive in her ears. Her boyfriend, luscious Paul Munger, had left for football practice and she was now there with her family, every one of them. Her thoughts were an Eastern drone, a broken record, a typing exercise that used all of the letters, over and over. The troublesome fix was in. Carla would never recover to the point where she could satisfy herself by being so poised at the top of the stand, her gold medal around her neck and a girl lower on either side, one wearing silver, one bronze. Never. That was the slit-tendon fact of it. Her mother and father were saying that it was just one of those terrible things that we all have to live through at some time or another. Little brother Randy seemed inexorably shocked by recognition of the razor-thin moment when everything assumed invincible could stop forever. He fidgeted with a new kind of youthful paranoia.

But Ramona, who rushed home from college, stared at Carla with a gaze of smoldering empathy yet one that also said, *you may now have some indication of just how much I have hurt all of these years because I was so incapable of doing something I would have given the world to be able to do: I cried inside and won't stop; neither will you. Now I cry for you because we could have both been on that top step as I swallowed my bitter, bitter pride and hugged you to me, my sweet little sister in such splendid victory. That gold medal was something special for us. It would have given us another chance. Then all of the times we were happy for blizzards and for so much ice would have meant something nobody else would understand, even Mom and Dad. The big thermoses of coffee, the peanut butter and jelly sandwiches that gave you so much more energy. That pitiless reflection in your face once you had warmed up and were going through your exercises. So snooty and fearless. The pretty little predator. Cut the others down with the skates you loved to sharpen once you got the hang of it and did it only your way back there. I can say for sure you couldn't say what you were really thinking without blushing. It was too hard. Bet you it was something similar to the way those Negro people, the Church of God in Christ people, you know, the kind of way then that they talked when they came to sing for us. The women were as fat as our local Dutch wives and that guest minister had his loud way with those kinds of phrases they use. Victory on my mind is what I'm guessing you would have said. If you could be honest, honest just once. One time. All of those championships you won out here and pretended you were shy and humble. Nobody was as good. My God, Carla, I was* so *jealous of you every second. It was a very bitter curse. God, it was bitter. The bitterness was unbearable. I walked lightly under the weight of it because I was so terrified. I didn't want anyone at all out here to notice how much I wanted to have what you had.*

Sometimes, late, when we had finished your practicing and walked home through the snow, I would be angry with that cold supper in my stomach. I would be angry having to study so late before bed. I would be angry because I made sure nobody but me was going to back up all your coaching and be there with you when coach Lolly Johnson was home with her family and you still wanted to practice and make things just a little bit better. I would be angry from telling jokes and giggling with you at the kitchen table with everybody else there asleep already. I would choke my wet, salty anger into the pillow when I knew you were asleep. I was so jealous, you know? To be honest, I can say that. I was excited at how you showed that you were so happy, so built for speed, for leaps, for control, and snapping up into your triple axels. You had, even under that bright gloating you so unsuccessfully tried to suppress, everything any future champion would ever need.

I can hardly look at what luck has done to you now. I bet all the baby fat in your mind is gone down the drain right now. Right now I feel that one of those ice skates is spinning its razor edge right on top of my heart here. Yet I can't try to look away. I must try to be with you all the way for right now. Right now will go, too. It will go. This won't last. I can tell right here. We both lost something. We lost a chance to come closer together. We lost the chance to learn each other's hearts through the excitement of that victory. With your gold medal just behind us, we could start to try to love each other as sister and sister again. I know we could have. So much is now gone. I could kill that trashy stupid boy. I feel that I could kill him. We were robbed. That's what happened to us. He destroyed us. Dutch bastard.

So when Carla migrated to New York nearly fifteen years ago now, she had finished college as a music major, hoping to become a composer, but she didn't want to go into concert music because she didn't like the impact of the twelve-tone approach. Schoenberg had wasted his time as far as she was concerned. The music always sounded too depressed, either autopsies in action or someone fidgeting with plentiful scabs. It was also ironic that the Schoenberg sound had ended up as background music in horror movies by the middle fifties, just as whole-tone progressions, alternating with imitation Gypsy stuff, were the rage of monster movies a decade or so earlier, and Stockhausen along with his crew got their horror moment going into the late sixties and seventies. Yep, the public never accepted European avant-garde music as more than accompaniment to tales of fantastical worlds. If you went that way, all you could look forward to was writing scores for outer-space displays of cinematic technology—awed flotation, dread, suspense, and terror the dominant conditions.

Even so, twelve-tone music had become an academic ideology and she didn't like the response to it, which was minimalism, a few things repeated until you felt aesthetically raped by an army of clones. To Carla's ear, Bartók was the soul man of twentieth-century concert music, and so much more skilled than either those writing second-rate Schoenberg or those ridiculous, yucky-bearded guys carrying themselves like endlessly joyous or grave hippies who knew everything but had so bravely shorn themselves of all sophistication in favor of a rankling humility, or who were now on the level of Eastern gurus—and sported the appropriate prayer beads as well as the lame wardrobes—but wrote, for the purposes of tedious repetition, very little material, not a single note of it interesting or touching. Save that for the pig trough.

The big upshot of it was that Carla, as much as she loved *Music for Strings, Percussion, and Celesta* or *The Miraculous Mandarin* or *Concerto for Orchestra,* couldn't figure out for the life of her how Bartók's kind of music-making would work for a girl from South Dakota who had studied composition in Chicago and felt most internally vital when she wore her hair in a ponytail and was dancing in one of the blues clubs, slow or fairly quick. Something in that blues sound took her back to her childhood wonder when those sanctified Negroes visited her church, singing and speaking of God as though He lived right next door. It was in one of those blues clubs that she was first called "baby girl" and felt as if she immediately dissolved into her tennis shoes.

The Negro who said that to her was a saxophone player in a band that got the business of joy so hot that the club went from high fun to majestic ritual. As Big Boy Franklin cooed or shouted, sometimes spinning around between phrases, falling to one knee or looming over the audience on the elevated bandstand, the tenor saxophone man cut riffs out of the air or slipped in little ingenious melodic phrases. When featured for a chorus or two, he stood there with his clothes sticking to him, magically seeming taller, and played with such unabashed sensuality and recognition of love in lines so tuneful and so harmonically deft that hot got hotter and bright got brighter.

During the break, when she was trying to be nonchalant as she lifted her ponytail up off of her neck and fanned her face with one hand before taking a swig from her beer, the tenor player stepped up on her, not too close but close enough for her to smell the scent of heavy, inexpensive cologne and a kind of sweatiness that Carla had to admit was decidedly Negroid. She wasn't as bothered by that as she would have been some teenage years earlier when she was a billboard-carrying liberal threatened by the idea that there was any difference in people other than skin color. She got one part of the lowdown from a music student friend of hers, Kentucky Daisy McCord with the square teeth, the red hair, and the endless freckles. Dogpatch Daisy worked at an expensive hair salon on Lake Shore Drive and told her that Negro, white, and Asian hair were as different as bubble gum, bricks, and baseballs. They hold water different; they respond different; they manage different.

"We may well all be the same on the inside, in our hearts, Carla, but I can tell you this, blondie rondie, we are definitely different on the outside," said Daisy one Saturday afternoon when they had finished jogging and were sitting on the grass in a park near the conservatory, enjoying their mutual exhaustion. As she was wont to do in private because her beliefs made her seem so hickish to the sophisticated, enthusiastic, witty, magnetic, condescending, and unbelievably competitive Jewish kids in the music department, Daisy went spiritual with her South Dakota buddy: "God, let's face it, is a creator and we are all variations on His theme; the heart and the soul are kind of, sort of, constant—but who knows how the outside will go? In case you're wondering, buddy-buddy-buddy, I know a gynecologist who works at a Cook County public hospital and he says that, without a sorrowful doubt, all female vaginas smell the same. If they're clean. Don't laugh; it's true. Come to think of it, if these freckles could have been pushed closer together, and if they were followed up by enough more, I could just as easily as you please be a Negro. I could be a black, a colored, or some kind of not-white something, with this stubborn ringlet hair staying just the damn same." Smirking with a fun look on her face, Daisy reached into her memory for one that must have come from her Blue Ridge childhood: "Little Orphan Annie, we will get your fanny." Then, with her face much more serious and suddenly romantic, Carla's redheaded play sister lay back and began peddling an invisible bicycle with bewildering sensuality, saying as she stopped, sat up, and looked her confidante in the face, "Lordy, Lordy, I wouldn't mind my fair share of that, if it was right. Little Orphan Annie would like someone to come get this fanny. I'm absolutely sure you know what I mean. There is nothing more, Sister

Carla, I would love on this very night than to be gracefully manhandled by a fellow who felt some very sweet things for me."

The tenor player, Jimmy Joe Lee, excited Carla as she stood leaning against the rail where one could drink, since there were no chairs in the club. All of them had been taken out, one by one, until the club became a miniature dance hall, selling Styrofoam plates of barbecued ribs and barbecued chicken served with greens and a choice of potato salad or secretly seasoned beans at the tables outside in the back, where dancers could get a little of the heat off of them and taste some of that good old home-home cooking. "I say *home-home*," Rondo Jackson, the owner of the club, explained at the microphone every time the band took a break, sucking his teeth for the symbolic sound of pleasure that follows a delicious meal, "I said I say *home-home* because what we got, as which you all know, is twice as good as what anybody else got. Hell to tell the captain, sometimes you just got to speak the *truth*."

Carla found the portly Jackson comically elegant because he always wore one color from head to foot—red hat with red feather, red shirt, red tie, red jacket, red pants, red socks, red shoes. The colors other than red were light to dark, dark blue; light to charcoal gray; mint, lime, and shamrock green; lavender and canary yellow. In the summers he wore unbuttoned silk shirts with the silk undershirts showing, and a gold chain with a floating heart. "I wear this," he once said to Carla, pausing with the counterfeit familiarity self-absorbed club owners show frequent customers, "I wear this because, just like every goddam body else, I don't know where my heart is going. Emotion, let me tell you, is not a stable thing." She knew he was trying to "drop something heavy" on her, but she also knew that what he was saying was rather intimidating. Who actually knows the destination of the heart?

"You better watch that Jimmy Joe, little girl," Jackson said to Carla as she was obviously preparing to talk with the tenor player, "he's a real killer-diller. That's right. Whoa, now, little girl, he's known to make the women into oh so shameful squealers. Band of angels come to wash out my mouth with soap. Don't let me get so low, don't let me get so low. Excuse me, Mr. Lee, for tattling out reality. Let me hold myself *back*. Let me get to stepping on up the way. Rondo, let's *go*. Claustrophobic here. This space between you two

beginning lovebirds is much too tight. I feel like my hat crushing in."
He paused, picking his teeth before firing off his windup: "You know
I take me very good care of these *chapeaus*. Don't you know it now?"

Carla and the tenor player laughed because Rondo Jackson had
helped move them closer, more or less stripped away the prattle that
begins most conversations when a hot man and a hot woman meet,
both trying to be cool at the same time that each of them wants to let
out a little indicator of steam so the other person knows—without a
doubt—that there is taut fire down below, not cold fish, not baggy
hoonyang.

"Say, baby girl, what is *your* name?"

She just stared at him, slowly putting her beer bottle to her mouth
so that something might chill off at least some of the feeling that his
baritone voice aroused in her. Then she decided to just go for broke
and be herself, let her face look like whatever it looked like. With a
little trembling sound of expectant tenderness she said, "Carla."

"What brings you up in here?"

"I love the way you play." She couldn't believe that he had never
noticed her. That was impossible.

"Well, thank you, Miss Carla. I love playing."

"You sound as though you do."

"I hope I do. It would be a hell of a shame if I didn't."

She didn't feel comfortable talking about him so pointedly at that
moment, so she switched directions.

"What I guess I'm really saying is that all of you, this whole band,
it seems so sensitive and it has so much power."

"Well, we're playing the blues, baby girl. Blues is, truth be told,
sensitive and powerful music."

"I guess that's what brings me here so much. That care and that
strength. When it's slow, it's so painful and so sweet."

"Well now: somebody's not deaf. You hearing with your heart,
baby girl. Which, you know, is what we want."

"When you guys speed up, I know I can't help dancing. I'm just a
real fan here. The music makes me feel alive. What can I say?"

"You could tell me why you're looking at me like that."

"No, I couldn't," Carla said, lifting her eyebrows, "because it's
what you think and so much more than what you think."

He smiled, then laughed. Jimmy Joe, his force delectably prickling her skin, seemed like he was made out of life. Carla would bet there wasn't a dead cell on him anywhere. Still, she couldn't believe she had just said what came out of her mouth. She excused herself and went to the bathroom, where she hooted at the fact that this was the very first time she had ever heard something that sounded exactly like the words of a woman pass beyond her lips. What had come over her?

Well, for one thing, she wasn't drunk and never got drunk, one or two beers was the limit, seltzer water from then on, or seltzer water all night. Carla wanted to stand apart. The loose way she saw some of the women get—some of the white women—bothered her and she didn't want to become one of them. Oh, some of the Negro women were pretty loose and wild, too, in their straight tight skirts, their painted-on pants, their wigs, and their heavy makeup, bumping and grinding as though they were sent to earth to do no more, no less, letting those men know that *if you think you can handle all this heat then put your hot hands where your mind is right now, goddamit*; but they, unlike those trashy white women, never had that look of condescension, narcissism, and depravity flashing on and off in their faces. That look was spiritually ominous. It said something about a ritual that Carla wanted to have no part of, one in which some slick-looking Negro with expensively prepared hair that was being done in by the heat would keep buying the bleached blonde drinks and they would dance and dance with so much sexual obviousness that their clothes seemed to fall away and the club was made witness to them in bed, the couple oblivious as two cats or two dogs. What was odd, however, was that those very couples, like any who had the blaze of the beat slip into their bone marrow, could spark the band; they could take over the direction of the sound; everything could gradually appear to exist only for them, at which point one of the Negro guys might gently kiss the sweating bottle blonde or the woman might make an expansive and affectionate gesture so pure that she was liberated from her fundamental crassness, inspiring the rest of the room—through the rising drive of the onlooking and singing and blowing musicians—to dance that much more truly with the ones they loved or the ones they were with.

Carla never went home with any of the guys who danced with her, black or white; she was too scared. Her courtships had to take place in public some other way. Even though she was already fully aware that only the two people ever know what their coupling means, she backed away from the handsome and the not-so-handsome and the unattractive guys who could intrigue her because of the confidence with which they carried themselves and the finesse exhibited in their arms and feet as they held her close and the choking flotation of tenderness came over her, making Carla almost want to beg to be taken to some home on the South Side where she could release those sounds that she didn't know were inside of her until she had gotten as physically close to men as she could get, starting in her cheerleading days when Carla had studied everything that was available about contraception before dating the fastest guy on the track team for one year, the best basketball player the second year, and concluding with the captain of the football team, he who was so poignant and so strong, mostly fogging the car windows by himself when they finally got alone after she had been announced homecoming queen. That last high school beau, the cuttingly handsome Paul Munger, would probably have gone on to become a star professional quarterback if he and his buddies had not been out roaring drunk one night after graduation and driven forwards and backwards around the lake as fast as they could until a mistake no one remembered flipped the car over and over down a hill where it turned into a U around a tree, leaving every one of them a permanent and disgusting cripple.

Yes, Carla immensely liked each one of those early lovers but never really thought about them because they were part of a time in her life that she preferred to edit or blank out. If she recollected the athletes with whom she had learned about sex, she would eventually start recalling how it had been when Dad brought little Randy's body back wrapped in a blanket tied round with a rope that was a first cousin of the one she and Ramona used to play with and jump over when they were girls; of how it had been shortly after she returned from the land of country and western when Mom was suddenly stricken with terrible back pains and was dying from cancer of the spine within three months, her eyes like two hot pieces of metal the night she left for the arms of the Lord, repeating, in a wheezing voice, "I never thought it would be like this." She would begin reliving how depressing that last year in school had been after her accident, even though everyone genuflected before the gallantry with which she faced her life after all Olympic dreams were slit to death. They thought she was brave and couldn't believe her good humor, how much more earthy she had become; the way, like a princess, she had begun to pull the unattractive girls into her social circle; her fervor as a cheerleader; the increased power of her public speaking; the immersion in music. Beneath all of that, Carla felt, day upon day upon day of her final two semesters, as if she had been kidnapped and blindfolded and was waiting in a room to be threatened, raped, and tortured again, the horror stopping just below the point of death. *Why not make the most you can out of bad luck?* she, in Houston, thought about that period and of the deaths that followed, reducing the family to Mom, Dad, and the two girls, then Dad and his daughters. It was what the Indians called "the time of long suffering." However, her exaggerated sense of loss in the last nine high school months of that unregainable past was in direct proportion to what her dreams had been. There could be no arguing that. She was not one who intended to say, as she had heard far too many in her hometown say, "It's good enough for me."

That may also have been part of why she felt a bizarre sort of satisfaction when Paul and his buddies had such a stupid car accident—just like handsome athletes, always thinking themselves invincible, ever able to get out of it, sure somebody will pick up the slack, bend the grade, do the math, write the paper. They were that way. The world bowed because of their physical prowess, but injuries being the impersonal things that they are, sometimes one with a sense of importance will have to learn a lesson about the frailty of all concerned, how the goods can be damaged on the assembly line by poor workmanship or finished off on the way to the showroom floor. Blue-black-haired Paul, with the bull neck, the warrior's jaw, and the port-wine birthmark on the left side of his chest, could not have known her bitter turmoil. Impossible: Carla was just shy of excessively sensitive as he adjusted to the hopelessness of his future. But nothing ever sounded more comforting to her than the day, maybe a month after she and Mom returned from Europe, when Paul said that he didn't want to see her anymore. It made him feel too bad and too foolish and more crippled than he already was.

Carla, as an ongoing emotional regimen, used all of her will to avoid diving into that ice pool of memory. Even now, the death of her mother was blocked out, only an image coming in every so often.

Some dips into that sky blue water had to be avoided in the interest of holding it all together. That wasn't cowardice in her book because there was nothing more to learn from how suddenly her mom had left the world. That stuff was always after you. One did not have to sink or dive into anything, however. It might attack on the ground. You could put that in its place, too. So the bullying nostalgia that had pushed her through so many head-ringing gauntlets of memory was conquered, finally. She was a match for all of it, and her mind was what she essentially wanted it to be. Mom was thought of exclusively as she was at full force. Carla knew that was right. Even if it wasn't, that was how she was going to do it. The strength not to break down, which had come to her that day she sat in her bed after the cafeteria accident, was now an interior property.

As for her time in that toddling town, unless she came to the Chicago blues clubs with dates those long-gone years ago, when the light of the world was revealing itself to her, Carla would leave all by her lonesome, every erotic nerve ringing, the smell of some guy in her nose, the feel of his hands vibrating on her skin, the literate or illiterate words he had whispered to her rising and falling in her mind, but her so terrified of being mistaken for a natural blonde tramp from South Dakota that all she could do once she got home was quickly undress, stand under the barely warm water trying to shower the night off of her skin, look at herself in the mirror for any sign of trashiness, brush her wet hair until each arm nearly fell off, then, feeling something as comfortable as an anvil in her chest, slowly drop into bed, where she fought her desires until Carla began to touch herself under the covers, eventually went into a spasm, and fell asleep, heartbroken and horrified by the feeling of an empty orgasm.

Anyone interested enough to see how she looked Jimmy Joe in the eye on that special Friday evening would be assured that Carla had no intention of settling for any agony on this night. His tenor saxophone had told her all she needed to know. So did the sound of his voice and the gentlemanly quality that he seemed to have been taught at the right times and in the right places. At the very least, Jimmy Joe knew how to keep her from feeling nervous. But it wasn't only about him: he wanted this young music student to tell him at least *something* about herself. As if bored with it, Carla laid out a meat-and-potatoes biography of where she was from, that hers was the middle place of three kids, and how she had always had talent for music and for ice skating but that music had won and brought her to his town a couple of years ago to study. She had no interest in dutiful sympathy: Carla said that her family didn't see anything serious in ice skating so she could only go so far with it and put the whole enterprise behind her as a high school senior. It had become boring anyway, skating every day, from the end of school all the way to eleven o'clock, coming home each evening to a cold supper, everyone in the house asleep, no one to talk with, nothing to think about but misbehaving, which she couldn't imagine doing anyway. Yeah, she had some division championships, but they didn't mean much to her, even though she had beaten some kids three or four years older than her when she was only twelve. Well, maybe she was kind of proud of that. But in the end, so what? Athletic glory is a very fickle thing. It was nothing compared to music. She would rather hear somebody play the blues any day of the week.

Done with that, Carla got to the interesting part: she asked Jimmy Joe about himself. He was a local boy, his family line running south to Laurel, Mississippi, the same place Leontyne Price was from. He had studied music right where Carla was studying but he didn't want to play or write anything like *none* of what they were teaching. All he wanted were the tools so he could catch the first thing smoking to New York and let them have a taste of all the tenor he was practicing. He knew he was that good and he wanted some of that Manhattan action. But he didn't like New York and he didn't like what they were playing. "If they weren't running chords up and down like a fireman going up and down a metal ladder, they were running scales up and down, up and down, same thing. Pentatonic to death. Coltrane—great musician now—messed them up something terrible. Didn't intend to, probably . . . probably not. But they still lost the taste for melody. Didn't seem at all like music to me."

Then, he said, there were these other people who couldn't play nothing—but, boy, oh, boy: they could talk enough stuff to make the moon come down and sit in their bedrooms. Words were their specialty, not notes. Dictionary time when they got to talking. The newspapers and the magazines called them avant-garde. He *really* didn't like them. When they played instruments they sounded like they were trying to tear them up. "You know how today people think destroying is the most up-to-date thing? Why tear up your furniture so you can sit on something different? You might puncture your ass." Carla burst out laughing immediately and was glad her swig of beer had gotten down in time so that she hadn't sprayed him.

In reality, he continued, there were many musicians who *could* play. They could play all kinds of ways. Some, a handful, could even work that avant-garde stuff into music: they could swing it, they could blues it, they could pick up an instrument somebody had worked hard to engineer and somebody else had made work and they could refuse to misuse it. Those kind had worked just as hard as he was working to make himself ready for the call to action. But, for all his preparing, New York gave him a very rough time when it came to trying to get in with the really good musicians: the doors were closed as tight as the bricks in a wall. Too many of them were connected with dope and Jimmy Joe wasn't going over *there;* it didn't matter how good they could play. As far as the others went, there was a long line to get in their circle. You had to be willing to wait a while. So, in just a few years, he found himself coming back to Chicago with his tail between his legs. He didn't have the patience necessary to be great. He didn't have the patience necessary to get as close as he could to the great. He just didn't have the goddam patience to stay around and live as an outsider in that extra fast town. Jimmy Joe had taken that special New York ass-whipping, which—couldn't be avoided— stripped him of his confidence. For a long while he could do nothing but think about how wrong he had been about himself. There would be those times, from morning to night, when he would just stare at the saxophone as if it had beguiled him, then betrayed him. It looked liked it had been designed by bad luck to do bad luck's business. The bell, the pearl buttons, the neck, the mouthpiece, and the overall shape had something sneaky about them. Tricksterism. But grits and gravy make their own demands. You got to eat. Then he started working with the blues bands, the migrated Mississippi power of this man's Chicago, the howl and the purr, the scream and the sighing whisper that had come up from the backwoods and got itself electrified, ready for the big-city joy, the tall buildings, the fast troubles, the massive loneliness, the predatory winter winds, and the inevitable transubstantiation of love into the meat of a man and a woman stuck together and trying to rock all right in a big brass bed.

Suddenly, up in that sweat and up in that beat, he knew he was home, just like the prodigal. "Sometimes, when we get going, I feel like my chest is near about to bust open with feeling. Sparked up like that, I can slip all that studying in. Bring it on home with me. Not too much, not too little, just enough. That's my standout in this music. Tricky and right. Kids, they always ask what to do. Now I know: Get a good tone. Some expression. There's plenty of good tones hidden in that horn. Plenty now. Don't nobody know: maybe a brand-new one waiting just for you. But even if you can't get a good tone, don't ever mess around and miss that melody. Go horizontal at all costs."

"What was the last thing you said?" she smiled, liking the phrase and wanting to hear him say it again.

"Go horizontal at all costs."

"Hmm," Carla said, rubbing the back of her neck and the left side of her face in one motion.

"You like that idea?"

"I might."

"Well, baby girl, I hope to be nice enough to get you to try it."

I've been going horizontal all night. Every time you played something that touched my heart. I only wanted to know that you might want me just as much as I want you, is what Carla immediately dreamed of saying, but instead she said, "Is that so?"

"Oh, it's truly so."

She just looked at him, the head-to-toe warmth that was radiating from her body giving Carla the impression that everything about her was exposed. Quivering a bit inside her heart, she was ashamed of none of it. Something pleasant had netted her and she had no intention of trying to get out.

"Baby girl, you got a special glow."

Her ego taking over, she said, "Tell me about it."

"It can float up on a man and it can carry a man."

She liked that.

"I'd say it's even stronger than how pretty you are, and you look *damn* good."

She liked that even more.

"Although," he playfully smirked, "sometimes you have your nose so far up in the air that you look like you would drown if it rained."

She couldn't repress a quick giggle, blushing at what she knew was her aloofness and somehow happy that he had said it so plain. At that moment, introduced to herself anew, she realized that her low-pressure haughtiness was a form of shyness, an aspect of fear, maybe a velvet kind of imprisonment. The way he was now looking at her made for a surprising bit of discomfort, as if he knew what she was thinking.

"Other times you look like that special glow is getting ready to bust up out of that bushel."

She didn't know what to want to say: Jimmy Joe had apparently seen through her and had made her like it. He had brought this South Dakota girl home to sweet blue Chicago.

"Times like that, baby girl, right up on that bandstand, Miss Carla, you make affection tremble up inside me. In the old days, I think they called that a crush, didn't they?"

"They did call it that, Jimmy Joe."

"Well, baby girl, here we are, saying strange things to each other. But they're true."

"You're the one saying the strange things. You're the one, Jimmy Joe. You're the one."

She put her hand on his and knew that she was beginning something, a walk up the stairs to where all the rooms were reserved for the women, her luggage neither too heavy nor too light.

8

SEEING IS BELIEVING

Maxwell was surprised when he, Carla, and Eunice went to the de Menil Museum, where he saw so many of the African pieces of the sort that had so influenced the work of giants like Picasso. In a section of the museum not much larger than a studio apartment in Manhattan, what some joked of as compartments, not apartments, were pieces so brilliantly selected that the viewers were given a compression of African art history.

"Dang," he said, "right here in my hometown. Look at all of this stuff. In Houston. You could never have gotten me to believe this. I never paid attention."

"Well, you never came back home enough to find out."

"Yeah, but this is the first time you came here."

"I'm not the art type. You supposed to be. So, seems to Eunice, you should have been over here and told me about it instead of Carla saying why don't we come. Girl, if you could have gotten Ezekiel to cancel fishing for this, you would have been a miracle worker. He'd rather look at nothing coming out of the water all day than stand up here and look at something on a wall."

Carla laughed with Eunice. Maxwell smirked. He very rarely laughed when his father was the butt of a joke unless Ezekiel told it himself, then father and son whipped up so much noise Eunice had to make it clear that she didn't think it was all *that* funny.

"So, anyway," Maxwell said, a false seriousness coming into his voice, "now I'm living in New York looking at these pieces in books and they're right here. Almost all of this I've seen already. Now this is strange. Looks like most of those photographers came to this one corner and took almost all of their pictures. My African heritage, lost, stolen, and strayed way down home to Houston. Lord have mercy."

Eunice strolled around the pieces with not too much interest of one sort or another and said she was going to look at some of the other stuff, then step outside for some air. Maxwell kissed his mother on the forehead and remained with Carla, the two of them looking closer and closer at this part of the de Menil collection.

Carla found the African art interesting but had never been as taken by any of it as she had by the art of the Far East or what she felt when she was in Italy that first summer after high school and saw the rise of the belief in humanity and in God arrive together in those structures of such magnificence. Architecture, masonry, painting, and sculpture were all used to serve the powers of the unseen and to make the person down here on the ground kneel inside himself or inside herself. Yet the African pieces had a sense of strength and of terror and of having been photographed. The fantastic figures, such wild improvisations on proportion, sometimes made her think of work done by wooden cameras, the lenses and darkrooms made of knives, clay, and dyes. While the European statues usually seemed as though they were the result of models posing, the African pieces had another kind of dynamic, sort of a lurching in place, all the exaggerations were plastic exclamation points, like what Bobo had taught her about rhythms and what the juggling of accents could do to them.

When she and Maxwell found Eunice outside, she was looking over toward another gray building, her curiosity apparently aroused by those going in and coming out.

"What's that there?"

"The Rothko Chapel."

"Chapel? He a religious man?"

"I don't know. That's where they have some of his last work."

"Dead, is he?"

"Yes."

"Let's go see that. I still can't believe you two come down here and have me out looking at paintings and statues. I feel cultured now. Maybe I'll hold my head up a little bit higher when I get back to the mall," Eunice laughed.

"These paintings are black, Eunice."

"Black?"

"He colored?"

"Not quite, Mama."

"His work is sort of an extension of Rembrandt's black backgrounds, at least, some people think so."

"I know Rembrandt. He's the one painted people from way long before him but had them wearing the wrong clothes. I guess like if you painted some colored people from slavery times and had them in the cotton fields wearing dark glasses, jogging suits, and Air Jordans. That's the man you mean, right, the one called Rembrandt?"

Carla and Maxwell did everything they could to keep from exploding into laughter.

"What's wrong with you all? That is the Rembrandt man, ain't it?"

"That's him, Mama."

"Thought so. Mmm-hmm."

Carla was taken by the tranquillity of the chapel, where the fourteen large dark paintings seemed to have no connection to a man who had committed suicide before this octagonal gray structure where they were to be shown had opened in 1971. There was nothing like gloom, only a feeling of electric mystery. Perhaps some were right that this had been the end of all that could be achieved in certain kinds of painting once the figurative image had been done away with by the abstractionist of further and further flight from the external world. Actually, that wasn't true. Dad and Mom had pointed out the odd distortions of clay and the strange colors around the smelly openings of the hot springs when she was an adolescent during a family camping trip when they all went to Yellowstone National Park for Old Faithful's high-water act.

"The guys who think they're so modern," Dad said, "they're painting these kinds of things and we're supposed to believe that nothing of the sort has ever been seen before. Indians were looking at these things before there was one art gallery in America."

"But those painters and their followers live in New York, dear.

We're just the Silent Majority out there. The peasants. I imagine they think the land is peasant-like, too. Not tall and concrete enough. Those gorgeous mountains don't mean anything to them. The smell of this air out here. The feeling of a forest covered with snow. Those New York people don't know anything about America."

Mom went a little far with that one, Carla thought as she tried to comprehend what Rothko was doing in these huge, one-dimensional canvases, which might have been no more than rectangular sections of silhouettes he hoped to infuse with humanity through his painterly touch. This was just as American as anything else. Everything in America was American. Nobody really wanted to sit in the witness chair and tell you what America was—because who the hell knew? Not a blessed soul; it was too big. In fact, how could anybody who ever traveled this country have the nerve to think he could truly be president? Running this leviathan of place and race and religion and culture and conflict and cooperation and dream and nightmare wasn't what the Founding Fathers had in mind, if anybody was interested in thinking about it, by the way. Had those racist and sexist men in their long coats and stockings and buckled shoes known it was going to get this big, they might have settled on designing a benevolent monarchy rotating from the military to the legislature, a great soldier appointed until he died, a great legislator appointed until his death.

But as Carla brought herself back to the room she was in and her place among those who moved through the chapel with such slathering appreciation, there was one thing she realized was true about what had happened since the figurative image had been fractured beyond even sympathetic recognition: the mood of sheer paint on canvas became the issue. It was a one-to-one relationship made successful or a failure by the third factor, that painter just as alone as Daniel Boone shouting at the top of a valley, that painter hoping that his brushstrokes would echo outward from the canvas, telling the world that he existed and telling himself who he just might be for that splendid piece of time in his smock. Even so, that was not enough for Carla's taste. There was so much that could be done, and since the contemporary painter had a cornucopia of choices, closing himself or herself out of the world at large in favor of a small array of symbols seemed a very, very little sense of work. She turned around as her shoulder was ardently tapped and saw Eunice with her eyes misted over.

"Something wrong?"

"Something's right!"

"I don't understand."

"Come here, Carla," she ordered.

They went to the wall facing into the room.

"Look from here, girl. You'll see something."

Under the sun arriving through the skylight the paintings had something to them that was startling. There were forms beneath the dark surfaces, and those forms, far from stationary, were much like blue, pink, and violet clouds that moved at the solemn tempo of clouds. But they were also jubilant and giddy, playful in the way that they were revealed from this position in the room. There was also the elephantine majesty of the night sky with barely perceptible images gliding across it. Carla felt the pressure of those paintings on her spirit and she brought Maxwell over to where Eunice stood, dabbing her eyes with a handkerchief.

"Uh-oh. Hey. Hey. Okay! Now. Uh-huh. Oops. *Yes. Now* I get what he was doing. All right then."

"That's just beautiful. This man knew something, Carla," Eunice said. "He knew something, Maxwell. Oh, yes, he knew something. That's what they mean by the spirit in the dark. Look at that spirit moving. God is holding control in this house. I'm going to bring Ezekiel in here. He won't want to come, but when we get in here, he won't want to leave. The spirit in the dark, I tell you."

"Well, you know, Blind Lemon Jefferson said he could tell his dog by the way it barked and he could tell his woman by the feeling in the dark."

"Blind people say all kind of things."

"Some of them are right, too."

"Well. A broken clock is telling the truth twice a day."

Carla saw them smiling at each other just as she thought the mood was going to become unpleasant. The light coming from the sky made the paintings into something else yet again. This must have been what was meant by chromatic black, all of those tones and shapes as varied as what lived and moved in a rain forest when the sun went down.

9

LIGHT RAIN, LIGHT RAIN. BABY FALLING DOWN

IT WAS far from light that New York winter after Bobo died, however, and she carried him around unless she could get her mind off of the way they had been together and even how it had been as he started to fall apart, that great strength evaporating as he turned into more and more of a skeleton, finally unable to even sit up behind his drums, scabs all over his body, her in a panic when they found out what was wrong and that she, somehow, hadn't contracted the virus. She was thirty-two years old and her health was perfect. Some kind of blood had been splashed around the doorway of her body and the plague had not come in. She had been protected, and for that, the girl from South Dakota found herself trying to answer a wordless riddle asked by a spiky, arthritic guilt during those cold, irregular moments when it didn't seem as if her insides had been cut out once Bobo expired. Her Bobo. She imagined him fixed in distant cruelty right next to her as his ashes were emptied into the Atlantic Ocean, the spring day of the boat on the curling liquid force leaving nothing but a memory of the dust that was once her man now disappearing so quickly in the salt water and the cries of the seagulls in agitated conversation just above her head. All of that pushed her into a hole of depression, and whenever she got to the bottom there was no exit other than a greasy pole.

But Carla could work her way up out of that hole if she tried hard enough, if she could diminish the grease with each attempt to climb up, if she could just distract herself, if she could even become self-centered to the point where the uppermost concern was being recognized for what she had going. In her mind, pulled down into gloom so, so often by the bubbling reminiscences of Bobo, she decided to become some kind of temptress, a courtesan, a hot streak of urbane sensuality rubbing an image of itself on the air. She didn't intend to actually become promiscuous or anything like that—or even have sex—but Carla wanted all kinds of attention, everything that could make her feel less alone, more important, not a woman by herself sitting in an apartment where she kept Bobo's cymbals in the closet because looking at them was more than her soul could handle. Leeann told her once, "Sometimes, girl, when trouble comes stalking you, you have to smack it in the goddam face. You have to tame it. You have to let it know who's boss. Rock it right out of your bed. Put on your black leather, get out your whip, pull out your brass handcuffs, and spank trouble until its ass turns cherry red." Very good advice: Go to war.

So Carla, all battle stations in action against the blues, was in an especially high-styled mood one night in Good Henry's. It was as if her insides put italics on the feeling of superb. The woman battling grief had gotten herself so together and worked extra waitress shifts until she had the money in hand to buy a gray overcoat that had leered at her out of a window in SoHo, daring this South Dakota passerby to see if she had the discipline to save the cash and put on its padded 1940s shoulders, its design down the front that had a flap which could cover the buttons or be turned back so that the pinkish pearl circles with the navy blue stitches coming through the buttonholes remade it into another coat altogether, the length proceeding down to half of the calf, and the back distinguished by a pleat that held its place in the middle but opened up to a pair of pyramids, one above, one below. The inside of the coat was covered with red silk, which made her joke—only to herself, of course—that she was some kind of an honorable scarlet woman. In black boots and a cap made of black Persian wool, her body was covered with a long dress of many colors. Now that dress was slit at the sides for comfort (and to show off her finely shaped legs in heavy tights), lined with silk, and made of glove-soft leather and suede. It had been sewn to order rather cheaply by an East Village Korean tailor from remnants picked up in the garment district at knockoff prices.

Walking on the west side of town from place to place in the upper Twenties and then into the Thirties had paid off, particularly since she always enjoyed the congestion of the area. It was titillating for her to look at the way the Negro and Latin guys pushing the garment racks shuffled along like boxers or walked like dignitaries in disguise. She enjoyed feeling as though she were being accepted or rejected by the sexy to repulsive Jews who sold the remnants and looked at you as though a thousand of exactly your make appeared before them every single day, all lacking, none quite right. The thickets of anxiety and raucousness that came with the fierce traffic were too much to believe. Anything might be screamed out of a cab window. The messengers, always Negroes or Latin guys on bicycles, wove through the deadly traffic at daredevil speeds, wearing—locked across their chests like metal sashes—the heavy gray or dark chains they used to protect their bikes from thieves. They were experts at missing accidents or death, but they didn't always weave so successfully. Sometimes one of them would be in an intersection bleeding and writhing, small spears of hurt coming from his mouth, or Carla would walk upon a bike turned into a pretzel and a street corner covered with pints and pints of blood, no witnesses left, no story, only the sinister proof of fatal collision.

The cabs themselves looked as though they were literally trying to drive through the trunks of one another, and with the decline of the Jewish and black drivers as more and more immigrants from the Middle and Far East came into the game, there were new dangers. The owners of the cab fleets were climbing the walls because more cars than ever before were destroyed by these people recklessly driving over potholes. There was also the ever-potential beating any fast-mouthed New York woman might get from some guy whose country did not allow women to be so aggressive. One such bastard, Carla was told by an ancient Jewish cabdriver, had been brought up on charges, thrown out of the business, and jailed because he turned around in his cab and repeatedly smacked a woman who talked to him in a way he didn't like. "You don't sometimes like nasty talk from a few of your customers—or a lot of your customers. This is the truth, obviously, and anyone that cannot very easily see this, this is not your kind of job. There is also this: taking gallons of shit from these wild, brassy women is what you might say is no more than our chivalry over *here,* if you know what I mean." Finally, there was the inevitable quirkiness and expectation and disillusionment that moved in the air like invisible mobiles if you found yourself nearing the Port Authority, where the buses came in and where they left, bid 'em in, bid 'em out. All through those streets and between those tall buildings, passing the porno shops on Eighth Avenue and looking with flippant disgust at the men who walked in or out, Carla had gotten just what she needed, experiencing the impulse to back-flip with excitement the first time she stood before the tailor's mirror and saw just how unbelievably good she looked, even if she knew she could never go any further than silently gloating to herself.

Sometimes looking good can make you feel good, she had once been told by a Negro saxophone player with caramel-colored skin and a profile like the Indian on the long-discontinued buffalo nickel. Whenever she looked at the guy, Carla thought of how her dad had once given her one of those nickels for good luck. As a teenager, she had a small hole driven through the nickel so she could wear it on a chain around her neck, but never would these days, since so many people were looking for any excuse to say you were prejudiced against them, or insensitive to their feelings. Watch your step, watch your step, watch your step.

That saxophone player's profile glowed for a mile and he was always exquisitely dressed, wearing his hair so close that its visual texture was like tight grain in smooth wood.

So I know you must feel good all the time, fine as you are, Little Miss Blue Eyes, he had continued, so disappointingly missing how *her* moods worked, complimenting Carla in a way that made any intimate connection between them impossible because it was obvious that this man could not, as sensitive as he was to fabrics and the subtle mixing of colors and textures, see the tremulous aspect of her heart that was so goddam basic. That was too bad because what that tenor-playing marvel of sartorial style had that made him so magnetic was the ability to swagger while standing or sitting in place, using only his eyes, his thick-fingered hands, the tilt of his head, and the way he might stretch his neck while listening and barely grinning as if some top secret sort of talk was going on. Oh, well, oh, well: it is a small number of them that can get you right.

But what Mr. Spiffy himself said—in the absolute abstract—about looking good and feeling good was right in line with her strategy when he said it, and it was right on that particular night when the Manhattan chill justified Carla leaving her East Village apartment looking as elegant as she could, proud of herself, ready to vamp the moon out of the sky, athrill with the idea that on this night, if that great moment would come, she just might find herself talking to a guy so interesting and so interested in her that she could stop trying to protect her insides with wit and good cheer and start toward being ready to give out every other feeling she had as well. The wind hit her eyes as she thought about that, walking along toward Greenwich Village with a step of the sort she had only when she was on the way to where she thought she might become happy, if not through the men, then through the music and her friends.

Then she was there.

Carla felt like she was some sort of a miniature queen in her microscopic part of the jazz world when she walked into Good Henry's, took off her cap, shook out her hair, and stood, more or less, unmoving for a long, long moment, pretending to look for a place to sit so that the other women could take in her brand-new coat before she bemusedly walked the length of the bar and hung it, with the red silk showing, on one of the hooks that extended from the wall near the piano, displayed for everyone to see and too obviously there to be stolen, however safe things always proved to be in the club. Low-quality drugs might be sold now and again, but there were never any thefts. That was part of what gave Good Henry's a home feeling of safety in which the musicians provided the pleasant warmth, the dreamy but slightly acidic romantic coziness, as well as the log-stacked crackling and blasting of a fireplace, which might also be turned in feeling to the experience of taking some kind of a trip below the luxury and battle decks of the good ship Manhattan, all the blue way into her boiler room, where the metal doors opened and the coal was flying into the flames from enormous shovels handled by men of inarguable grace and syncopated rhythm. What year was she thinking about? All of that naval stuff was long gone.

Carla took a barstool next to jet black Leeann, who had on a yellow cashmere sweater dress and ice blue boots, a martini at her side with four speared olives submerged in the white liquor, her ivory cigarette holder from Kenya working it with some kind of black cigarette from Europe, and a very subtle rouge that gave her dark skin an even livelier quality.

"Look out now, Carla, you whipping it on them tonight, girl."

"Thank you, I just threw something on."

"You did what?"

"I just threw something on. Glad you like it."

"You're getting more like me every day," Leeann laughed. "What will it be, beer or seltzer water?"

"I'll start with fizz water and work my way up to the heavy stuff."

"Bartender, give my glowing homegirl from South Dakota the light end of what she likes. Not too much lime now. We don't want her falling on her face."

After a number of seltzer waters and a lot of laughs, Carla had to go to the bathroom and went in so quickly and absentmindedly that she didn't hook the door. As soon as the yeasty smell of the liquid stopped leaving her, she heard the door open and heard it locked. There was some spirited tittering. Then she heard the telltale snorting of cocaine. Carla didn't know what to do because whenever she had stumbled upon people using drugs they responded to the presence of someone who wasn't into the powder with baleful looks. Those looks were unpleasant and she always got away from them as quickly as she could. So Carla decided to remain quiet and hope neither of the two people—whose different sighs and tongue clickings clarified their number—would check themselves in the mirror, do whatever the fuck else they had to do, and leave her to herself, ready to wash her hands, check herself in the mirror, and rejoin Leeann.

"Hey, girl, what's wrong with you?"

"Huh?"

"You heard me. You look like the husky dog been dragging you around feet first."

"Huh?"

"Feet first, like your butt was the sled: so you could raise your head and look right up at his shitty Yukon ass."

"It could be that. Whoa. Whoa."

"You all right?"

"I don't feel good."

"Don't feel good? Hmm. Hmmm. This Bolivian flake cocaine? Are you serious?"

"I don't mean that. No. Uh. Let me see. Whew!"

The woman breathed deeply. There was no sound other than the two of them sniffling.

"I mean my emotions are all messed up."

"Congratulations."

"Don't say that."

"Don't say what? Everybody's feelings are messed up. All. You know. They are. Right. Know what I'm saying?"

"Maybe. I guess maybe. Yeah. I guess. But I lately . . ."

"Lately. When is lately? Lately what?"

"I just feel like I don't get enough feeling."

"Now I *know* you gone. You putting me on."

"No, I'm not. I wish I was. Oh, I wish I was."

"Are you crying?"

"You know I am."

"What's wrong?"

"You're my best friend. I don't have to hide it."

"You know you my heart. You my tightest tight friend."

"I know. I know. But I'm scared to say it."

"Come on with it. I don't back off."

"You don't." Her voice had become so shy.

"Not me. When it comes to you."

"Well, like I was saying, I just don't feel like I get enough feeling."

There was silence and Carla could tell that the friend was just waiting for the words to continue, aware that there was nothing to be said until the other woman got to where she was going inside herself. The woman on the edge of confession cursed, loudly and impotently.

"At least it's coming out."

"Not at all. I don't mean it that hard. Excuse my faking. Oh, Lord. Whew. It's all inside." Her voice quavered now.

The other woman softly made a sexual joke, trying to gently pull her friend up with a bit of bedroom humor, taking off from "It's all inside."

Only one laughed.

"Oh, yeah," she said, her voice jaded, full of exhaustion, and slightly hoarse. "I get myself plenty of dips, girl, some of them kind of sweet." Then with a conspiratorial giggle soaked in brine and run through with a wistful gallantry she said, "I can get all kinds of attention paid to my lower lips, very good attention. Almost *too* good, if it can be like that. If it can be. Maybe so. Maybe. But I want a little more, just a little more. Something fair, you know? You know what I'm saying? Something fair. You know, just a little. It's not that much. I know it's not that much. I just want some attention paid to my *heart*."

"Oh, girl," the other woman said with an empathy that revealed as much about her as what her friend was saying.

"I feel kind of oppressed, you know?"

"I know just what you saying."

"I go out, I get charmed. We dance. You know how beautiful New York is at night with the brother you hope is right. It's all nice. Everything's good. It's good. Yeah, it's good. But still nobody wants me with my *heart*."

The other one let out a deep breath and Carla imagined that the friend was hugging the woman in constant sorrow, being as kind to her as she could.

"Lately, it has got to be too goddam much," she said, sobbing softly.

"You know you going to be all right. Get a little grip there, play sister. Come on, now you know you took over the whole division of visitors' services. Not one of us ever did that. Not a black woman. Close, but you, you put the brass ring around your finger, baby. That's right. How about that? That ain't no light thing. Those white bitches don't let loose one iota of power without a fight to the death. So you know how strong you are."

"Right. I know that. I'm proud about that every day. I never lose pride about that."

"Now you see: there we go. Back on that track."

"I don't think so."

"Aw, come on."

"I wish I could. I do. But I can't. I guess what I'm saying is I hate feeling abandoned the moment . . . Whew. Anyway, I wish pride could save you. Self-esteem, all that bullshit. What I feel has nothing going on about that. Nothing at all. No way I can see." Angry tears were audible in the woman's voice.

There was another silence. It had a sad and bitter feel to it. Carla's knees lightly trembled she was so embarrassed sitting there. She wished she could seep through the wall and back out into the club. She had heard enough.

"I don't think it's that much, you know? I don't think so. It's not fair. I feel like I been gutted, all my insides cut out. I feel like I'm about to cave in because nobody wants me. I just want somebody to want my heart. I hate the way I feel. I really do. I feel trapped somewhere. Oh, I don't know. I don't. But I guess it's not hard just to say it to you. It just hurts so bad to say it: I just want the freedom to be sweet."

Carla heard the door pulled on the stall.

"Somebody in there? I'll be damned. Is this some shit?"

Carla raised her panties to the right place and stood. A period was taken to compose herself. She flipped the latch and pushed the door open. The room felt like a furnace. The two black women, each of them extremely good-looking—one tall and willowy, though full-breasted, the other just below average height—stared at her like they wanted to kill her. The drugs had been put away but they had involuntary sniffles and appeared to be rubbing their tongues against the roofs of their mouths. Carla went to the washbasin and turned on the water, put some soap on her hands, and held them under the faucet. She couldn't look in the mirror because she would have had to face their eyes.

Then the stage whispers began.

"Let me tell you something," said the tall, light brown one in the tan leather pants suit with a permanent that was auburn and as smooth as Steuben glass, and whose large butterscotch eyes were still red from tears, "you could have coughed to let us know you were in here, bitch. But you wanted to eavesdrop your white ass off, didn't you? Yeah, you did."

Carla said nothing. She pushed back the faucet handles, stopping the water, and reached for a paper towel. Her hands dry, she turned around.

"You ought to slap the shit out of her. We should fuck her up and say she called us some niggers," the other one said, stepping in front of the door and making sure it was locked. Then she took a knife out of her purse and opened it. There was white powder along the blade. Below the magnificently styled braids, above the long chocolate brown neck that rose from a red and green sweater tucked into black leather pants, were now not the eyes of outrage but those of someone contemplating just, precisely, precisely, how much physical hurt would do the job in such a way that nothing would be misunderstood about the insult of silent intrusion.

Carla wanted to scream, she wanted to run, she wanted to cringe in a corner and beg them not to hurt her. But all she could do was stand there, shaking harder and harder and harder.

"I don't think so, girlfriend. Naw. Uh-uh. She would love us to whip her ass."

"Not hardly. I came up hard. I can *always* go back. I don't think she would like my hands on her snooping white ass."

"Yes she would."

"Not the kind of ass-whipping I want to deliver. Make her *recognize!*"

The two women looked at each other and Carla fought off the turning of her stomach.

"No! You're missing how it is."

"How what is? All my life I've wanted to knock the shit out of a white bitch like her. They might wear soft coats but they're hard, dog-assed bitches underneath. They'll fuck over you every time they get a chance." She closed the knife, put it back in her purse, set the purse on the floor, and took a step toward Carla. The other one moved in front of her.

"That would make her day. Heard that shit, took that shit. Masochistic motherfucking bitch. Then she could collar us as another pair of crude nigger bitches. Now I *know* how you flimsy bitches think. Look at me, you white piece of shit, or I *will* knock the fuck out of you."

The cursing spiraled something in Carla. Her pride came up. She was in the wrong but she wasn't trying to hurt the woman. As if she were Bobo, Carla concluded that they could bring on the pain. Carla raised her head as Bobo would. He was there with her and she was by herself. She had to be there by herself. Carla knew then how all of those felt who would not grovel before their executioners. That pushed in more spunk. She ceased shaking and felt the she-bear of her pride stand up to full height on its hind legs. There would be no fainting, no feigning, no looking for an opening. Carla put all the dignity she could muster into her eyes and met those of the woman who was railing at her. What she saw actually made her feel horribly justified in begging forgiveness, but it had gone too far for that. She hadn't coughed. She hadn't rattled around in the stall. It was like that.

"Bitch, *you* are the crude one; *you* are the fucking eavesdropper. You didn't give me a choice. No choice. None. You didn't give me one. I was just a crying nigger girl on display. Do you know," the woman asked—tears starting to rush down her face, the sound of her voice zooming back to adolescence—"how much that *hurts?* You raped my privacy. You did. You did. It's not fair. It's not fair."

Humiliated, Carla saw that this was not the anger of a clearly sophisticated lady somewhere in her middle thirties or just above them. Perhaps twenty years ago she had begun taking that internal beating that comes of not getting enough feeling. She knew where she was in the blue world, and now, right in Good Henry's, one person too many knew. This gave the black woman the surprising expression of someone who so subtly seemed to look as though she wanted to know if a stranger and a friend rolled into one had appeared out of nowhere, a person willing to take the crucifying edge off of her anger, rescue her from an unexpected aspect of hurt by some sign—a nod, some cast of the eyes. Carla couldn't step up to that. She would *not* step up, and the woman, intangibly sagging, quietly said to her friend, stage whispers finished, "Let her go, let her go. God bless her."

"The stars were on your side tonight, you funky-assed bitch."

When Carla returned to the bar, she had to use all of her capacious will not to shake, not to cry, not to go back, free of all dignity, and ask those women . . . She didn't know what to do and could only look down when the two left the bathroom and stared at her as though their eyes were flame throwers. Leeann knew something was up but let it pass, sensing that Carla did not want to talk about that one.

"Don't worry," Leeann said, "I know it was just one of those things. Some kind of wild shit. Women and women can be like that. Rough."

Those words heard in the bathroom stall were on her mind for a long time following that harrowing night. Carla's thoughts were like all of the balls on a pool table as the break sent them going in every direction. Some of the ideas were dropping into the pockets, most weren't. What the woman said, those words, went around and around, hitting the rails, cracking against each other, sometimes waking her as she lay in her apartment alone but not wanting to be alone. The freedom to be sweet. Maybe that was what any woman in the world who wasn't just an evil bitch wanted. It could be. Up under all of the talk that they traded back and forth and all the complaining they could do about men—who, by the way, were deserving of *all* the complaining—there was probably that desire for a kind of freedom that didn't appear in any books that Carla knew of, not even in the myths and in the various religions. They all talked about love and about compassion and those sorts of virtues. But being sweet, that condition of being as an *expression* of freedom, as what lifted you up out of all this bullshit that style and pride and success didn't protect you from, that was a kind of victory nobody ever trained you for or even made you want to go looking for. Oh, there were all kinds of admonitions about humility and doing unto others and such. Sweetness, even so, was another kind of thing. Every mother's child, actually, had heard the words "Be sweet" when he or she was acting terribly. That was where you first heard the direction. It was there, almost always with your mom. Nothing maudlin about sweetness when it took on its force as a real nuance, one that wasn't hiding behind sentimentality, or mistaken for it. There was surely a power to that unrestrained sweetness, and who wasn't afraid of it when the force of that aspect of being pushed itself into how you acted and what you wanted and what you wanted to do and how you wanted to do it? Yet sweetness was always, after all, not very mature, kind of childish or adolescent, wasn't it? Sort of like the problem in German culture, that it was too much like German chocolate cake, heavy and gooey. Well, not really. It was the luminescent cream on top of goodness, which didn't have much of a functional place in the world of right now when "tough" and "fuck everybody except me" was how people wanted to present themselves, either crudely or with layers of decadent sophistication in places at the top of society, or in those intellectual circles where there was nothing worth believing in other than one's ability to make fun of anything that might seem elevated. Elevation was a trick, an opiate of the people, a set of cotton-candy conceptions that stuck to the roof of the world's mouth, sickened its stomach, and rotted out its teeth. Real sweetness actually saved your teeth and wasn't edible by anything other than the spirit. It was what made the smile a universal expression of something at the center of both the secret and the obvious story that flesh fought its way through. What an authentic liberation, just to say "I'm sweet and I'm here for you." Carla wished she could thank that woman with the auburn permanent and the butterscotch eyes for helping her up the road as she sat there too stupid to make enough noise to ensure that her presence was known. Sometimes it was so confounding that you couldn't help crying because you had to so deeply hurt somebody you didn't know in order to learn just a little bit more about the human heart.

A very troubling night for Carla arrived during that period of thinking. All of her recent experience was in place and she was so lonely. Bobo had been with her in that bathroom but he wasn't with her in the flesh. He knew right now what she was figuring out anyway. He had already said it. Bobo told her once that what he was looking for when he was playing was "that sweet groove" because, "Baby low, you can get all tied up in the excitement of yourself and not play for the *band*. It's not even about you not knowing what's happening: the excitement of you *is* exciting. All that power in your body is firing hard with your blood and all the muscles and nerves and all the organs. The power of *you* is going on all the time. You can get hopped up just thinking about that monster. Yourself is a mighty machine and it's *also* got feeling and thinking. Shit, you know you can get tied up in *that*. But the sweet groove, now that's some other stuff. That's the third plane. The first plane is me, the second one is you, the third one is *us*. That's the one when you're with everybody else and you never play only for yourself, not one second, not a single goddam beat. The *entire* me comes out then because I can hear everybody and play with everybody at the same time. Then I get chills. My feet, my legs, all up and down my arms and in my face and my fingers. When I feel that, I know I'm in the sweet groove. That's the most expression. You back off yourself and yourself comes through even more. Hot diggity motherfucking dog. I don't now how to explain it but that's the way it is."

That made her think of all the times she had heard him play, healthy or sick, straight or on drugs, with his whole drum kit or just the parts that were left after he had hocked enough to get some dope. Bobo could be fighting against slumping into a dope nod when off the bandstand, but as soon as he sat down, he became erect and a military calm smoothed itself over his face, as if he were standing at attention during a rigorous inspection. The boxing-glove hands that were a by-product of heroin always delicately held the sticks, and when the tempo was counted off, he opened up like a flame thrower squeezing its heat through a small glass tube. It was refined but red hot, no imprecision, no excessive volume, nothing that drew attention to itself unless it was lifting the music up through his multileveled conversation with the rest of the band members, his interpretation of the form, his ongoing variations on motives from the tune and from the other improvisers, and his swing, his almost giddy dance beat that rode on the metallic steam of reverberation from his cymbals and remade itself into wood, plastic drum heads, and the beater on the bass drum foot pedal. There was a moan to his beat and there was an undefiled joy. In a jam session at Bobo's loft, during a rehearsal, and in the environment of the clubs where he got more and more jobs before the sickness overcame him and he couldn't summon the strength to be himself, Carla experienced combinations of emotion listening to his drumming. He could make her feel as though she was in a church that gave way to a carnival that transformed into a splattered emergency room that became an autopsy unit given authority by the presence on every table of fresh and rotting corpses that transmogrified into the pushes and screams of birth as new life popped out like a champagne cork.

Yes, it was that way then. Now he was gone and she was by herself. The sad feeling, like all deeply sad feeling, gave the impression of forever. Carla rose up, went to the window, and opened it slowly, the cold winter air goose-bumping her skin. She wanted to sing. It was so late nobody could hear, and it was New York, where it didn't make any difference. In her silk slip, with no man to love and no man loving her, she heard something like freedom slowly chugging its glorious and bloody way up the rails of her spine to the throat that was now and so suddenly sore. She could be no sadder, she could be no more herself. It came out, each syllable sticky with what felt like all the longing in the great big wide world:

> Don't the moon look lonesome shining through the trees
> Don't a woman look lonesome when her man gets up to leave

10

AMAZING GRACE

As EVERYONE in the Davis household was preparing for church,
Carla became a little moody. She thought about how her emotions
were going as she showered and washed her hair. The remarkably
sensual and layered gauze of Marvin Gaye's *I Want You* album
was coming through the portable radio on the peg in the bathroom,
its sound making her feel good again since Gaye was her favorite
rhythm-and-blues singer. His passion was the most complex, the
most conflicted, the most adult. Carla hadn't understood it when she
was a kid, only that she couldn't stop dancing when he sang and that
his rhythms went with everything she was doing as an adolescent
coming into the spring of her femininity. By the time she was Miss
Knockout in high school and had picked up all of the Detroit dances
from a chunky black girl named Lorriane who was one of Dad's students and dreamed of being a symphony conductor someday, Carla
was able to sense her way through Gaye's music and understand his
concepts. Much, much later rather than sooner, the adult Carla loved
the effect of such inventive overdubbing, with Gaye avoiding gim-
mickry while achieving another level of intensity because the elec-
tronics allowed him to do his own matchlessly poignant backup
vocals and sing his own counterpoint, mix in a few sweet nothings,
some guttural inflections, an unintelligible but bubbling kind of

mumbling, even some female sounds that were far too nakedly pornographic for Mom or Dad to hear back then but fit perfectly with her sexual experiments.

Always in love with having an edge, Carla taught Randy Jr. the dances she had learned from Lorriane as though they were her very own inventions, and the two of them, after dancing as only a competitive sister and brother can, imagined what it must be like to see one of the big Motown shows up in Detroit or Chicago or one of those kinds of places. What could it have been like being the two marshmallows in a wonderful chocolate pudding of a party—the only ones! Wow. Wow. Wow. What could that be like? Could it be like the weekend Dad and Mom had gone to Chicago when they were in college, him staying with relatives and her with a cousin who was a party girl ready to take them out dancing at place after place until they ended up on the South Side, four white kids partying at some nightlife guy's jam-packed house, then having chicken and waffles in the morning and riding the elevated El train back to where they had started? But since the urban race riots had taken place, it probably wouldn't have been safe. If it was safe, it would be different. If it was different but friendly, it could still be a lot of fun. *Can you believe what kind of fun that could be?* So that was how it went and as far as it went. Out where they were, Boondocks of America, you just had to dream and bear it, make do with 45 r.p.m. singles, albums, televised images, and fan magazines. Life might be sweet and easy, but it sure wasn't exciting and greasy.

Often, during her junior high school time and in that last year before Ramona left for college in Southern California, the silent contest between the two sisters took a hike as they lay on Carla's bed and looked out the window as the popular music played. They just sang along and used that singing as another way of talking because, whatever the sentimental tune might be, it provided a perfect closeness worth so much more than what they would have clumsily or hesitantly said about growing up and missing the childhood times when they could sit on Dad's lap, which was now off-limits, first to Ramona, now to Carla. They weren't little girls anymore, and would never be again.

Nor would that atmospheric condition of having exactly the same unspoken emotions repeat itself between them, for by the time she returned from her freshman year at college Ramona started changing, becoming a bit more remote, not just from Carla but from everyone. Her older sister's taste in music had switched over to the Beach Boys, country and western, and an aggressive school of rock. She started traveling in a snooty group of college kids whose parents Mom and Dad had always considered old guard and behind the times in all of their social attitudes. Ramona never apologized for them or spent any time talking about her new friends. Her preference in conversation was the desire to go into law and clerk in Washington, D.C., so that she could be at the fountain from which all national policy flowed. Something brittle was spreading inside her big sister. It was during this time that Carla really had to suppress her arrogant confidence in an upcoming Olympic gold medal, and went even further beyond how good Ramona could ever be. Carla once heard Ramona crying behind the door of her room with such caustic intensity that the outstanding athlete of the household was afraid to go in and ask her big sister what was wrong. She didn't tell anybody else about it. It was too private-sounding. But later, when Ramona appeared at dinner, she was as neat, witty, and as clear-eyed as the president of a welcoming committee once the festivities had begun. Her little sister really admired her then. That was exactly the way the baby daughter wanted to be.

The bathroom filled with steam while she danced and rinsed off, then stood turning the left faucet for hotter and hotter water, loving it until she reversed things and let the cold water from the right faucet wake her up completely and make her skin feel utterly alive. That was Dad's way. When Carla tried it around the age of twelve, both Mom and Ramona thought she was crazy, but it worked for her and became her preference. At that time, Carla was sure that she and Dad were more clean and more fully conscious than anyone else in the house. It was their little pact. Later, Little Randy could be heard yowling and shrieking in the shower, but no one paid any attention to him and he never sat down to the table as though that way of showering had become his.

"That was Marvin Gaye, ladies and gentlemen, brothers and sisters, brothers and brothers, sisters and sisters, lovers and loved ones, youngsters and oldsters. M.G. Marvin Gaye. You can't beat that with a stick. Now that brother *always* knew what's going on. That's why *his* oldies are *always* goodies. Just imagine how much good, good loving *that* brother instigated. That loving feeling was all *up* in his voice. Hey. He didn't get people to pull the covers *off;* he got them to pull the covers *back.* Let's not get too risqué, or risky as some of my friends say. You get the point. *I Want You.* What else is there to say? Clear as the summer sun. Now let's continue this Marvin Gaye special with *In Our Lifetime.* Got to be: we don't know any *other* lifetimes. If you're like me—and I *know* you are—you just *heard* about them other lifetimes. Better hold on to this one as long as we can because the future is always a fuzzy dog that *could* have rabies. I know: let's drop the cracks and get back to what used to be the wax."

As she started dressing while Maxwell showered and Ezekiel could be heard humming and warming up his voice, Carla considered the fact that church had not drawn her for quite a long time. Something about New York had done that. It made Carla more dependent on herself, at least spiritually speaking. That was just how her life went in Manhattan. There had been no plan. She hadn't declared anything. This was no comment on corrupt ministers or the result of her having been too busy to get there regularly. Carla just didn't go. She had, most assuredly, always believed in God and had, measure by measure, grown to feel especially blessed by Him, particularly with her intelligence and the will to get through the disappointments that could only be perfectly described in deep breaths and the periods of unfocused dread that sometimes ate at her as though she were covered with honey and army ants. Somehow, New York seemed to tell her that God wasn't going to be held in anybody's one house of worship. He would drop in, dressed up as a vessel of serenity or a drill instructor or a cauldron, let the believers have what they needed, then move on out to the grand metropolitan feeling that seemed some immense bell of life that never stopped clanging. That was why Carla always experienced a closeness to God in New York, much closer than she had felt anywhere else, even on those dry cold nights back home when there had been a blizzard so terrible all electrical service was out and the candles gave their place the light and the shadows of a Renaissance painting as Mom, Dad, Little Randy, and Ramona, remaining themselves but recast as her very own biblical characters, spoke and moved through the house while the pale moon shone over the snow with what seemed a permanent connection between the winter purity of the elements and heavenly illumination.

That was there in South Dakota; New York was now.

When she was freezing in her apartment, when she counted the different kinds of green that arrived with spring, when she was frying in the summer—the concrete holding so much heat and the millions of air conditioners blowing out hot air—yet found herself correctly but oppressively reluctant to wear something so skimpy the Puerto Rican boys would get even more belligerent, and when the yellow leaves of autumn moved about in swift cones of wind, Carla felt that she had heard of God through the mouths of men but now she saw Him. As much as she loved nature and would never forget one morning upstate when she was staying with Leeann in her gorgeous redwood summer house and all of the birds, one kind after another, began to declare themselves in song across the pond in the back of the place, gathering, standing apart on the ground, flapping up, taking to branches, red feathers, blue, brown, and yellow, Carla always, when the calm of reflection was on, found that the true God of her heart was urban, praised in steel and concrete, in glass and speed, in traffic jams and overcrowded streets, in deceptively bad manners and outbursts of bliss when Times Square was full of people ready for the old year to drop dead. She couldn't help it, New York had made her like that and she loved it.

Breakfast was ready. The smell took over. There was nothing else one could think about. Eunice had cooked some grits. She scrambled a pan full of eggs with some cheese. She fried enough ham steaks and sausage to leave little space on one of the big serving platters. Moving in the kitchen with that balletic confidence all great cooks have when they are in the hot corner of their domain, Eunice brought out a couple of stacks of corn bread she had fried in a skillet for time's sake and for that specific taste. Carla set the table, then put the glass pot of coffee and the pitcher of lemonade within Ezekiel's reaching distance as Eunice winked at her just before declaiming, "You all better get here before Carla and I throw all of this good food in the trash if it gets cold. You have been warned."

"My, my, Eunice, this is an incredible breakfast. They would love your cooking in London. They serve huge breakfasts over there, too."

"Well, chappy chap chap then. But my feeling is you don't need to be sitting there thinking about the Lord with your stomach growling. When you eat good and when you make food taste good, you just imitating how good the Lord makes the world work. Don't get sloppy now. You got to keep that devil out the kitchen."

Putting a special little fold on Ezekiel's napkin, which was checkered blue and white instead of red and white like the others, Eunice said, "I can cook all kinds of food, you know. I took me some classes over to the cooking school. Don't let me get loose. But Ezekiel, he's one of those you got to sneak in on. I can't make him something he ain't never had all by itself. Never will work in this world. It got to go with something he knows. When I sneak it in like that, he gets a taste for it. Then one day he'll ask me to whip up some of that—he can never remember the name but that man has never had any trouble describing something he likes. That's how he lets me know. Then my work will be affirmed."

Laughing together, Ezekiel and Maxwell came to the table. Ezekiel said grace and they began passing around the food that Eunice had made. Everyone dug in for a few minutes.

"My Lord, what a morning," Ezekiel said, "you have outdone yourself this time, darling. Everything you did for this breakfast is perfect."

"Thank you, dear, just for you, for Maxwell, and for Carla, my brand-new friend."

"I think you all better come down here more often. I didn't know the best could get better. Can you cook, Carla?"

"Yeah, Dad. She can rattle some pots and pans."

"Thank you, Maxwell. I do the best I can."

"Carla can cook as good as she wants to and better than she should."

"I guess so if you say so. How long have you two been together now?"

"Four years."

"Five years, Maxwell."

Bobo had died that spring before and they were together a year later.

"Five then. You know a year can slip past if you don't watch out."

"Might slip by you men, but a woman remembers every last second whenever and wherever she been."

"Some men remember every last second, too."

"They might."

"They do—if they got something good to pay attention to, darling."

"I appreciate that, but I sure hope you are not telling this girl that the reason your son dropped a year of life out the window is because she's not worth paying attention to. I know you not saying that."

"You know right. I didn't mean that, not at all, Carla."

"Oh, I didn't think you did."

"I didn't mean that either, baby. I guess everything just went so fast I didn't realize what I was saying. You know, time passes fast when you're using it; it passes slow when it's using you. No, my Carla doesn't bore me. Not at all."

Carla thought then of how those performers who took possession of time, of the present, exactly as if they owned it in every direction, always seemed larger or taller than they really were. She smiled at Maxwell, realizing that the audience saw the person in the proportions equal to the commanding emotional width laid across the moment. The invisible inside expanded the look of the outside. God, did she love this guy.

"You could have brought her down here a long time before now, if you ask me."

"That's right, son."

"I couldn't afford it."

"They got trains, planes, and automobiles. Good inventions."

"I fly first-class."

"Well, excuse me."

"My feeling is straight and easy. If you're going to die in a crash, you might as well be comfortable."

"Don't talk about death at this table, boy."

"Oh, Mama, what difference does it make?"

"Everything begins with words."

"A lie is words, too. It didn't happen and it's not going to happen."

"Son, you never know. I don't care what we talk about myself, but your mother means—"

"I mean I don't like death at my table. Death gets enough attention as it is. We don't have to give it more."

"But, Mama—"

"You heard what she said. That's it. Now let's have us some more of this good breakfast and stop yacking about one subject when we have so many to talk about. For instance, Eunice says you all had a heck of a time when you went over to that demolition museum."

Maxwell and Carla flipped into laughter and Ezekiel chuckled.

"De Menil is the name, Ezekiel."

"After all the talking you did, I think demolition is right."

"Why is that?"

"Because it blew up your mind."

"Oh, you're so old-fashioned. Nobody says blew your mind any-more."

"I'm talking about what they say *now,* thank you, not the foggy slopes of yesteryear. When they say somebody is *blowing up,* these kids out here in the streets mean he's betting bigger. Expanding himself. So that's what I'm saying: your mind got *blown up.* The inside of that pretty brain got bigger."

"You got me there."

"You got me a long time ago and I been watching closely ever since."

"Oh, Ezekiel, you know what to say."

"And you know what to do, and when you put that together, darling, it makes one and one equals a two. But that two is one, and that's how it's supposed to be."

There was silence at the table then. Who could say anything else? All the four of them could do was eat more of that delicious breakfast. What a morning. What a morning. Two is one. Carla had felt that before. She knew exactly what Ezekiel was saying but she couldn't imagine it being that way for forty years. How would the heat maintain itself? In her moment, with so many circling a mirror over and over, only one's own image and one's own feeling maintaining any significance, in this period of such narcissism that the self had become a God, when all of the meanings from the past were scraped off of the backpack of bricks that one was forced to carry into life, the weight of loss cutting into your flesh, hunger intensifying when you went to the places where you were supposed to be fed, thirst arriving the way it does when one is told the saltwater ocean is what one must drink, and the whole fatigue of this technological time squashing you down as you were deafened and incinerated by the false fire of vulgar hysteria, it was hard to sometimes believe that two could become one. But two could do it. Carla knew they could. She had been there many times with Maxwell, but when she had really been there was when Bobo took her into his heart and she knew the terrors he had seen and was transformed through his trust into part of him and into a fuller version of herself. It could happen to you. If you were ready for it. You had to stand up to that power. It was no kind of play thing at all.

Bobo had told her, on one of those nights when the feeling of the East Side hadn't been so abusively severe, one of those nights when his profile with the little caterpillar scar on his left cheekbone had been so magnetic, a time late on the clock when they had walked west on Houston and down the Bowery past all the butcher-block and home-appliance businesses, tiring feet moving them into Chinatown, strolling and holding hands and him sometimes suddenly turning to waltz with her as he hummed, grunted, and sang "Lover" into her ear, embracing her so closely and so gently, then the couple holding hands and swinging them like two kids until they were at the ocean under the Brooklyn Bridge, where the very night itself seemed to be the slurping water accompanying Bobo in the wind as he had said that God to him was the power to pay perfectly close attention. The world, he laughed, didn't do much of that, and most of the anger he felt had to do with that ice-cold not-a-fuck-giving fact. He wanted to explode so that people would notice him. That was how it was. See me! Bobo said that once he recognized that there were legions of people like him—most people, maybe—he whittled down his fighting side as much as he could and remembered what it had been like in Vietnam on the days and the evenings when the napalm, the trees, the animals, the gasoline, and the people had stopped burning in layers of smell on every open space in his memory and his consciousness because he was so busy being taught the treacherous wonders of Charles Wilcoxon's drum books by this nigger whose head was so big Bobo nicknamed him Charlie Brown.

Working on that music, all of those beautiful patterns and accents, such marvelous applications of the rudiments, the two soldiers seemed more than free of what had come before in battle and what would always come once anybody's blue war got declared. People want something good, up above themselves, Bobo had said, which was why he began to practice with so much passion, searching out the syncopated poetry of those beats until his hands began to strengthen through the increase in pain that was the definition of developing muscularity. That pain delivered power and the distinctions of nuance into his fingers as well as the first couple of inches above each palm, eventually moving throughout the forearms, the biceps, the shoulders, and the chest.

At that moment of the morning's wee small hours, Bobo raised his head to an odd angle and his eyes took on the demoralizing cast of Michelangelo's *David,* which made Carla want to back away from him but she had, instead, stepped closer and taken his hand, looked up at her love, raised all her fingers until they softly touched his dreadlocks, pulled his head forward, and delivered her best kiss of fire.

"Baby low," he said, hugging her, "baby low, baby low. You got hold of all the sweet details in the world, ain't you?"

"When it comes to you, Bobo, I hope so. I hope so with all the heart I have." Something ached inside her when she said that, it was the hurtless hurt of love that suffocated at the same time that it flooded the lungs with oxygen.

Nodding, he ran his hand over her flat hair so softly she only slightly felt it, took a deep breath, and put his own best lips of flame on her. Hugged up, they had then their silence, the raw quiet as the New York night became a dual birthday suit. Manhattan was the two of them and they were all of it. Then, some immeasurable time after they had seated themselves on a bench, spooning as they used to call it, her man, as inevitable as the blues, gave more words to the shape of his blood memories and took Carla on another tour of Vietnam. The girl from South Dakota didn't really want to hear more of his brutal past but she was glad to, as certain things were said. He clarified a gloomy misunderstanding on her part very quickly, as if he was aware that she was making nice but was also disconcertedly dragging that misapprehension around. Charlie Brown knew about more than the drum books of Charles Wilcoxon. He knew things as dark as a line of midday corpses in a freshly blackened field burned down on patrol. He knew things like that. Up under his back-home humor, his country-boy pride, and his stainless bravery, he also knew all there was to know about authoritative savagery. Charlie Brown. It was this deep brown master drummer, with those mahogany eyes on ice, the yellow buckteeth, the mole not quite hidden in his left eyebrow, the shaved and sweating head, who also taught Bobo the martial arts, the most deadly, which was the real reason why her man had stood at that door facing Satan's Children with that shotgun on that unforgettable morning: if he hadn't had the wood and metal line of that weapon between those four white boys and himself, Bobo could have killed them all so fast somebody would think their dead bodies had been mysteriously dropped on the sidewalk and he was just opening the door to see about all the goddam commotion. Charlie Brown had schooled Bobo in those murdering arts that meticulously well, stripped down to his undershirt and drawers, his face still filling the front of his big head but now as far out of town in its disposition as the eyes of the Negro torturer the command brought in, he who came with two razors in each of his shirt pockets whenever a captured Cong wouldn't talk. Yes, Bobo said wearily, his fingers and his hands were instruments of immediate destruction. Immediate. That was why he had to talk so much shit to Satan's Children, too much shit, a wagonload of shit: Bobo had to get the impulse of that killing feeling out of him.

That feeling went away in Vietnam when he was practicing his drum exercises just short of making his hands too sore to precisely function if trouble came walking like sudden battle. He began snorting a little heroin then. Just a taste. Not much. All he wanted was to relax, but he found out something he didn't expect. The heroin high was the only thing that was close to the emotion that fell over Bobo when everybody in the troop knew the enemy was somewhere near and, as fully aware of that danger as he was his name, the future drummer of multidirectional explosions—he whose beat had a cry inside of it and whose cymbals could sound like metallic or crystalline gusts of wind—out there in the middle of war, would set aside his helmet, put his dog tags in it, strip to his waist, remove his boots, and begin to wander away from camp, armed with nothing but a bayonet, wander out one yard and crouch in stillness, then another, then slow steps that didn't get much faster, then stick the bayonet in a tree as quietly as he could so that he could move farther out unarmed, his hands and feet his only protection, Bobo now all the way back to the beginning when the man himself was the solitary weapon. It was during those wanderings, sometimes as far out as three hundred yards, that he perceived his existence most fully, one step at a time, his mouth dry, his breathing unapparent. He could hear *everything,* maybe even a beetle walking on a leaf. He could see pure distances and distinguish what appeared to be every inch traveling outward. That step by step taking the chance on his life going down in blood by stumbling into some of the enemy, stepping a bare foot on a booby trap, or filling the crosshairs of a high-class sniper made Bobo feel as though his whole body was constructed of pinpoints sparkling with heat.

As Carla listened to Eunice humming and put just a little last-minute rouge on her cheeks, she didn't know if she could sing well enough to keep people from turning in her direction, looking at the flat-haired girl trying to get it right. Wrong. It was silly to think that way. She was a singer, after all, and what was she trying to do—*look* for something to make herself uncomfortable? What a psychological vocation. Still, there was that contrived sound of would-be soulfulness that Carla always fought against in herself, the thing that so often made white musicians seem as though they were more intent on acting and posturing than releasing their personalities through the order and shape of musical logic. But she had heard far more than a few Negroes sound just as phony baloney. So what she wanted was not racial; it was just something hard to do but if you were a Negro and grew up within *a certain kind of Negro background,* you had a head start, just as the white kids who had gone to good schools before college had a head start on the Negroes taught by less good teachers. At first, they didn't seem as smart, but if they had the will, the gap closed and, by junior year, they looked the white kids in the eye with another kind of confidence.

So what she was worrying about was really pretty silly, wasn't it? After all, things were going along rather well for her at this point in her career and her sound was standing on its own. There was work; she was up there on her own bandstands; respect was unfolding. It was also silly to try and make herself feel insecure because Maxwell had long loved to satirize the preachers, the church services, and the out-of-tune singers. He once told her that when a French interviewer had asked him if he believed black people had natural musical ability, Maxwell had answered that only a white person could ask that question. The interviewer couldn't understand what he meant and got a little huffy. There was an attitude there: "After all," Maxwell said in Margaret Dumont's voice, "he was *French,* you know." Then Maxwell went on to say that he told the guy that when you went in a black church and saw those people in robes sitting up in the front behind the preacher, they were what was known as a *choir*—the people who *could* sing. The rest of the people in church *couldn't* sing, and that had been discovered through that good old all-American technique of the *audition.*

Carla had laughed back then, but as the four of them got into Ezekiel's brilliantly shining black Lincoln—the leather seats as soft as butter, men in the front, women in the back—she was still unaccountably anxious. It was a balm to her nerves that Eunice patted her hand in that accepting way and she, who loved seafood so much, listened with her mouth watering as Maxwell's mother chatted and stage-whispered about this place that the two of them had to go in order to get away from the men. Go anytime. Anytime. Oh, there was serious catfish served. The best catfish dinners and potato salad. Skin-and-bones fellow had him a catfish ranch and raised nothing but catfish and you could sit inside under the air-conditioning and look out at some nice, nice trees as the taste of the Coca-Cola with fresh mint leaves let you belch out all of the gas into the top of your fist and prepare your insides for the plate which was the last home of the golden-fried creature that looked like he had once had himself a mustache.

Carla knew she was falling in love with Eunice the way a younger woman can feel so much emotion for a true lady whose sole ambition seems to be to make everybody comfortable. Well, of course, it wasn't that simple, given the story of Malena that Eunice had told her. That was damn obvious. Sure, Eunice knew a lot about pain; she just wasn't interested in passing it out. As he drove her around late-night Houston and took Carla to one of the tree-lined spots near some water where he used to try and get teenage girls to take their clothes off when he was in high school, Maxwell—so freely himself, as he almost always was before they were having their troubles—also told her that his mother and father used to fight like two earthquakes, screaming and hollering, throwing stuff around and breaking dishes. Maxwell stoically mentioned that he had a scar under his hair on the left side of his head from a dispute when he got too sassy and his mom smacked him as hard as she could with a serving spoon. Eunice told her son that there was only one man in that house and that *he* wasn't him.

So there had been periods when Maxwell and his mother were so angry at each other that all they could manage out of their mouths was such forced cordiality that it was insufferable, which led Ezekiel to say, "You two got to do better than that. Myself, I think it got to be a far, far better choice for you two to give up speaking at all until that poison drains out of your words. It hurts my doggone ears to hear it." Eunice had no trouble with Aaron and always seemed to be in some sort of conspiracy with Malena, which led Maxwell to believe that there were always secret things going on between them, just as there were always secret things going on between women. They loved and hated and supported and sabotaged each other behind a door that was closed to men.

"You see," Maxwell said, "all of that's just like some of the things that I know she told you and that you aren't about to tell me anything about."

"How do you know I'm not telling you?"

"That's the way women are."

"You know so much."

"I don't need to know much. I'm a man."

"Is that special?"

"No: it's manly."

Carla laughed and Maxwell kissed her, first softly, then with the sort of emotion she sometimes thought would blister her mouth. The rented car parked at Maxwell's own private lover's lane began filling up with atmosphere, the moon sliding into and out of cloud banks, the June bugs putting up a mighty counterpoint to the frogs, and the two of them now free in the singular way that romance liberates a man and a woman to become most individual at the same time that their passion seems a compression of all surrounding circumstances.

"Right now," he said, "in a movie some white man would have to come over here with a badge and a gun to mess up our little groove. Don't leave a black man and a white woman alone. No, no, no. Corny. So, you see, sometimes life can be better than the movies."

They chuckled in near unison.

"I'm glad so many things have changed. Imagine how guilty people must have felt during segregation. I'm glad that's over. We don't feel unnatural. Most people don't think it's unnatural either."

"No: only about two hundred million," he laughed, suddenly tickling her and making her giggle until she pushed his hands away.

"But my dad—"

"Yes, your dad . . ."

"You're making fun of me."

"No I'm not. I'm serious as a big check."

"You're not. I think you are making fun of me, but, anyway, my dad always says that when society goes forward or goes backward or stays the same—any of those—people are agreeing on what they consider natural at that time."

"I could have said that myself. If I had thought it. I'm doing all right anyway. Here we are. You and me. Natural to the hilt."

They kissed and kissed and held each other. Then Maxwell had his arm around her and they looked out the window into the sky.

"You know, I feel in a good mood but something is still kind of bothering me."

"What's that?"

"Babe, it's hard to say."

"But I bet you're going to say it."

"All right, I will. It just seems you have some very deep animosity toward your mother."

"Absolutely not."

"You sure?"

"What did I say?"

"Absolutely sure?"

"Who knows me better than me?"

"But I didn't ask you that, darling."

"You didn't have to ask me for me to say what I just said. Do I need to repeat myself?"

"Hardly. I don't know why you have to respond this way. Damn. Babe, I don't know. I just like the idea of all four of us being together, your mom and dad, you and me. There's something nice to that. And I always like it when you don't feel under any pressure. Then it's like it was at the start. Totally relaxed and sweet. Gee whiz. We're supposed to be vacationing here. But some of the things you say. You can say things, you know? You can. But you do have to be aware of this: I know you. I don't know everything about you and I never will. But, Maxwell, I do know something about the way your heart works. I play close attention to you. I love you."

He kissed her very softly and ran the back of his fingers up the front of her neck and under her jawline. There was something taciturn in the air. That mood moved on out.

"Okay. All right. Eunice and Maxwell. The parents' corner and the children's corner. It wasn't a cakewalk. Oh, no. She could make me feel like a golliwog. You know, those monster dolls they used to make of black people? Probably not. A minor gap in your education."

"I don't appreciate that. You don't have to spoil this by condescending to me, Maxwell. Babe, why can't we just be nice to each other while we're talking? It's such a beautiful night and I feel so good being here with you."

"I'm just playing. I'm just playing."

"You don't have to play like that."

"You're right. You're absolutely right. Correct. I agree. Please, baby, forgive me. Sometimes I make you feel something different from what I mean. That's not even close to what I'm intending. Forgive me. *Please.*"

She had been gazing out the window and turned to him, looking Maxwell up and down, his face, his bull neck, his broad shoulders, his big arms. Carla leaned herself into him, embracing her man as she kissed him on the neck, the cheek, then his lips, her breathing raised up just short of steam. Then she pulled herself back and let him know through her eyes that she was ready to listen to whatever he had to say.

"Goddam! I like that kind of forgiveness. Whew."

There was sex inside them and its heat was moving to reconstruct the molecules of the atmosphere. But those two pairs of lips could wait; those two bodies could hold back. There was talk to be done and both of them knew it. Words were coming up. Somebody had to tell.

"But let us return to the battleground. The rocket's red glare; the bombs bursting in air. That's the way it was. I'm serious. On an emotional level, hey, this was Pug City. Eunice and Maxwell. We had our fights. *Definitely.* This was when I was a kid because I'm not the kind of man who can feel comfortable under a woman and my mother is not the kind of a woman who can have it any other way. At least, not with some kids. Now my father's a different story. She never could be over *him.* I don't even think she wanted to. My mother was just a fighter. But my father had an advantage that a son can't have."

It became silent and Carla waited and waited as Maxwell looked off and played with his nose as if he were barely massaging it with his fingers. There was still no talking going on. Abstraction was beginning to take over as the feeling of being near an important point started to give way. Finally, miffed a bit, she started to say something.

"Hold it. There's more. I can see you're tired of waiting. I just had to get myself together to express it the way I believe it is. Actually, if you just think about it, it was simple what Ezekiel had over me."

"I'm thinking about it and I still don't know what you're talking about."

"My father was having sex with her. That's an advantage. A son can never equal that. She was having sex with him. Malena could never equal that. And Aaron, he was a sissy; who knows what he was thinking about? But my mother changed a lot after my daddy had that accident and almost died. That did it. When that tire exploded in his face and the metal cut his throat, something was completely over. Gone. I think she seriously prayed her way into that one. Eunice *had* to do that. She worked on it until she got *softer*. She didn't love any more and she didn't love any less. But she got *softer*. When she found out that was where her strength was—being *soft* with all kinds of power in the center—mama stayed just like that. You couldn't resist her then. She had you. And you *liked* her having you."

Putting all of it together made Eunice much, much more compelling to the South Dakota girl come to visit those she hoped would someday know her as their daughter-in-law. Eunice was surely something. What a force. So. So. There was more to Maxwell's mom than the Negro earth mother white women like herself were so frequently seeking to complement their own mothers, to provide folk insights, humor, and tales of bewildering disasters limited in their effect by an immutable stoicism rinsed in the blues and shaped up as the gospel bird of rhythm that rose up from the frying pan of hard times and flapped heavenward, headless and featherless but dripping buckets of greasy soul. Were these big Negro women no more than ceramic mammy cookie jars remade in human flesh and thought to contain everything from vials of syrup to chocolate-covered coffee beans that could make the heart race at an addictive tempo? Sugar, wisdom, and thrills. Step right on up, honey. Carla knew, as she actually always had, that the answer was in the negative column. You could pretend people were whatever you wanted to pretend they were, but they would always be people, separated from you by no more than style and outlook, which might be repulsively or gruesomely alienating or might not be all that different once you got down to it. So Eunice was not down-home sweetness personified but, actually, one whose heart rode on a saddle made of her mortal soul, which was strapped to a tiger that Maxwell assumed had been tamed. Hold that tiger. Basking in that realization and conspiratorially chuckling within herself, Carla felt perfectly at home until the car stopped and Ezekiel said, his voice so solemn, "Here we are at the house of the Lord."

From the very second of her footfall on that first step as she walked into that building of tan brick with an actual steeple, Carla was put in the condition of awe that came over her as a child when the Lutheran mass—which was never called a mass—began and people she knew, or had come to know, transformed themselves in order to get as close to God as they could. Even before things began back home she could see the shift of spirit as they walked up the twenty steps into the eggshell stucco church. There they set foot after foot on the burgundy runner leading them to the wooden benches that had no pads and faced the pulpit beneath the single window that was a big stained-glass cross. In that turn of spirit, their individual and collective posture changed and it seemed as though everything they wore had been picked out and put on or pulled into place with the extra measure of pressure that defined the "Sunday-go-to-meeting" look, which was furthered by the smells of soap and hair not quite dry. Mom made it clear to Carla that since God had given human beings a world so beautiful, it was doubtless their responsibility to enter His house made up and dressed up like a multiple creation the Lord could feel proud of having blown life into. The Lord didn't care if you were rich or poor, if your clothes were old or new, if your shoes had been bought last week or had cardboard in them to fill a hole, if you had a hundred shirts or blouses or only one that was ratty but, by the fact of necessity, good enough to seem special.

"Carla," she said, "being human is so hard all you can do is try to better yourself by purifying your heart. Everything else, mind you, might remain pretty rotten. I laugh and joke all the time, you know, horsing around. Ha. Still, I have my own burdens. Inside me is a hot temper you will never see if I can maintain control of myself. As you know, I hate imperfection. I'm not a child, however. I know that we can never reach the perfect. It's too far away. That's why we have such a deep longing in our hearts. But if we learn to live with grace, we can make all the imperfections just a smidgen easier to tolerate. Isn't smidgen a queer but wonderful word, don't you think? I think so. Any*who,* the little difference is subtle, but if it's better all the effort is worth the trouble. That's why dressing up for church is an expression of grace and respect for God. You bathe and scrub. You get all the dirt off your skin, from between your toes. You clip your nails and your toenails. You pick every article of clothing carefully. You *don't* mismatch. *Never.* Religion, worship, is not a casual thing. This isn't some people kind of sitting around drinking beer and telling stories. Religion is serious because you are seeking the spiritual state of joy. There is nothing more serious than joy when it's about the right thing. Like your father and me dancing."

In that house, on that morning, Carla sat down near the front row between Maxwell and Eunice. This was a ritual forum that she immediately recognized once her eyes went down the little program printed on a single sheet of folded blue paper that had the sign of the cross drawn at the top and a barely skilled drawing of roses with exposed thorns on the border. Throughout her own experience she had never thought of these things as rituals because Carla's impression of this Negro style of Christianity was focused solely on the sermons she sometimes heard over the radio or the gospel songs she loved. The context out of which those forces rose into being were foreign. Here, at The Ark of God In Christ, was where the spirit would appear or not appear. The form was there. All it needed now, as the congregation took its seats, was the people to begin the dialogue with the evidence of things unseen.

PRAYER

Begins with prayer that is a half an hour before the service, which prepares the church for the presence of God; it ushers in the presence of God.

Carla thought of her mother and father cutting a rug as Ezekiel and the other deacons lined up in front of the pulpit and began humming some hymn or gospel tune she did not know. There was no music other than their voices, which contained the sound of invitation, the very same sound that Carla loved in jazz music. The male power and the ancient opening of a timeless door reached back to Africa, to Asia, to Europe, to every place in the world where sound was used to state an attitude of spirit and to create a communion that was complete in its allegiance to all things good and cosmic and its admonitions about all things internal and external that one had to gird oneself against. Carla's mother and father appeared in her mind on the night that she had worn her crown as homecoming queen and carried a glittering scepter, her hands in white gloves that went all the way to her elbows, the full-length evening dress ice blue, the evening pumps soft gray. It was the high school dance in the gymnasium with banners hanging from the walls, and one would have thought that Mom was the queen and that Dad was her king. Carla felt a bit upstaged by the way they moved with such intimacy and such pride, such refinement and abandon, but she was soon emotionally beyond their presence and so involved inspecting the resentment and the admiration of the other girls as well as the untempered affection Paul Munger showed her that night, mustering gallantry and finesse from out of nowhere, becoming for that occasion a prince charming of the sort he had never been before, carrying himself as though his quality as a young man, not his looks and his achievements as a football player, was all that could make the homecoming queen feel satisfied and particular. She knew heaven on earth that night, the way it touched, the way it tasted and smelled, its texture and substance. Her heart was partially filled by all the ceremony, and the filling was completed when she and Paul were finally able to be alone together and the tones of passion that rose from their throats seemed as pungent and aromatic as the smoke from pine needles on a bonfire.

Carla looked at Maxwell, inwardly grinning and grimacing at the same time, as she chastised herself for thinking such impure thoughts while the church service was starting. Maxwell seemed bored and gave the impression that he had better things to do but was well aware that if he came to Houston, Texas, he was going to attend church, at least on Sunday, every week until he left. His assenting nods were untrue and the gaze in his eyes was proof of how bad an actor he was when deep but distant feeling had him in its clutches.

Yet, with the same look on his face he had when telling her how irresistible Eunice was when she softened, Maxwell was surely captured by the unaccompanied singing of those black men. Their voices grew in power, not volume, and left no hiding place in the church.

They were swaying from side to side, leaning back, raising their heads, slightly squatting to get some low notes, rasping, sometimes nearly shrieking, then hitting harmonies that had the bracing finality of closing the door on everything other than majesty. The sound started rising around Maxwell and Carla, Eunice's voice joining in with a quality of emotion Carla had not heard, regardless of all that she had listened to, from the terrible tales to the jokes and memories made so different by this woman's speaking voice. The sound of the congregation moved like an invisible surf from one end of the room to the other, surging upward and receding, whispers exorcising next to shouts of exultation, long notes that were near to moans but had no pain inside, thick, thick harmonies of pitch and timbre, everything from perfect to far from perfect intonation, a whole lot of mumbling going on, little chirps, very nearly, from the children, a rolling form of feeling, in toto, that was intended to usher in the presence of God, to make way for the sap of salvation to run free and easy, to slip all the masks off of every soul, to let the faces on the surface, the faces of the unseen, and the feelings of the congregation stand unencumbered. Carla heard her own sound add its character as all those present, through generations of voices young and old and in-between, fused into a force that used no words, that spoke only in the language of tone, that pried the roof off so that there was nothing between heaven and the people. A half an hour of that passed. The deacons then ceased the opening and welcoming incantation, each one now reaching for a handkerchief and sopping up the perspiration covering his face and neck. The church was much warmer. God was in the house.

LITANY

A scripture is read that will foreshadow the sermon of the day.

A fellow Eunice told Carla was the assistant pastor came to the pulpit. He was very dark and wore metal-rimmed glasses. The sweat made him into a shining man. His shoulders were shifted back and forth in a rhythm that had something of the athlete's last period of warming up just before the games begin. There was a smile on his face, then a frown as he thumbed his Bible open, scrutinized the page, cleared his throat, and looked from one side of the church to the other, staring all the way to the back of each head, seeming to see through each person for a second or two in order to make sure that no ears were dancing around to private tunes that had nothing to do with the business of the spirit that was surely at hand. He coughed. He greeted the assembled.

"I like this New Oxford Annotated Bible. Yes, I like this. From over in England, you know. Oxford. Plenty of knowledge. Good translation. Just as good as the King James, if you ask me. Anyway, these are the wonderfully anonymous words of the Letter to the Hebrews, words from an unknown source of holiness, nobody claiming it, just the truth. I'm talking about Hebrews 1:10 to 1:12."

The assistant pastor said, then they said, phrase by phrase, line by line:

> And,
> Thou, Lord, didst found the earth in the beginning,
> and the heavens are the work of thy hands;
> they will perish, but thou remainest;
> they will all grow old like a garment,
> and they will be changed.
> But thou art the same,
> and thy years will never end.

THE WELCOME

Pastor will then welcome any visitors.

To Carla's surprise, the preacher she had seen so many years ago in South Dakota, who had touched her and made her feel as she had never felt in church before, this man came to the pulpit, his robes dark, his hair driven-snow white, his girth rounder. Yet the same face was sitting on his neck, perhaps shaped a bit more like a cherub's but now creased and dense with another kind of spirituality that she knew had come from the years of working on his cosmic mission. She whispered her astonishment to Maxwell, who turned and said to her, "Could be. He's been around. This guy used to work up there trying to bring Indians to Jesus. Never got scalped. He had a church up there before he came down here. Most of the church was black, though. Yeah, he got around. You could have seen him." Then Maxwell smiled at Carla as though he didn't quite believe what she had said but thought it fine that this guest of his family now had something else to think about during what would be a monster test of patience.

"We want to welcome all visitors today," the pastor said. "We even have somebody returning to visit us this morning who used to play right up here in our church band. You remember him. Little boy with a whole lot of talent. Whole lot of talent. Nothing could hold him back. Praise the Lord. There he is right there. There he is. You know him. Maxwell Davis. Used to stand right there with that saxophone, playing for the Lord. Blessed. Now he's all grown into manhood and traveling all over the world and making recordings and becoming known here, there, and everywhere. But he's still ours and we're still his. You can only go so far from home and home is always waiting for you. That love is stationary, praise the Lord. Stand up, Maxwell, let the people see you. Don't be shy, boy, stand up. There he is. We know Ezekiel and Eunice Davis are proud of him, and we are proud of him, too. Pride everywhere. Praise God. You went a long way, young man, but you started here and *here* will always be with you. Maxwell has with him his friend. Stand up, young lady, if you please."

Carla didn't feel the least bit shy as he called out her name and the church people looked on with approval. This was her home, too. They made her feel like it was. She wondered if the minister recognized her. That was so long ago. She was so different then, still short before that burst into her full height that took place at fifteen and brought with it a bustline that had to accept the industrial look of the bras in those days. Those cardboard cones that held yarn were what somebody designing them apparently had in mind. Icky to even think about it.

"Those of you we don't know, understand that we welcome you all and that God welcomes you and that welcoming you is doing God's work and that's what we are here for. So, to one and all, let me say just one more once that this house of the Lord is *your* house of the Lord, praise God, and that we know how to hold you to our bosom with love and never let you go. Never let you go. I said, '*Never* let you go.' We're serious up in here. I say thank God right now and let's go forward."

PRAISE AND WORSHIP

Instrumental music kicks off with different people grabbing the lead in the audience. There might be transitions between five or six different songs in a single tempo, with one person after another entering and introducing a different theme as though the songs are a form of discussion, a way of looking at spiritual issues from different perspectives.

The pastor left the pulpit and, with no warning, the drums, tambourines, piano, organ, and bass went into a rocking tempo, instantaneously hot, beyond warming up. The church members began singing songs that no one called, most standing and clapping and getting straight on the various corners of the beats, some hitting the tambourines with their palms, smacking them against their elbows, others quickly licking their thumbs, which they ran across the tambourine skins for smears that were followed by thumps against their forearms. The women who remained seated used the floor as a drum they clattered against with the heels of their shoes as they clapped in a counter-rhythm. The polyrhythms grew in muscularity as a variety of clapping patterns defined the beat in timbral melodies of syncopation. In some kind of unpredictable antiphony the songs were boomeranging throughout the congregation, picking up one voice here, another there, leads and backgrounds rising into the air. Then, while one theme was being sung, someone would suddenly begin another song, which would create a round as it edged up into position and took over, the whole congregation turning a musical corner on a tonal dime and flipping into another key as the piano, organ, and bass modulated and laid on those triplet overlays of chords and percussive phrases until some giant voice from somewhere in the church burst into yet another tune, demanding another modulation, other voices to reinforce the lead, another backup of chorus work that immediately broke into two parts, one stating, another answering, both underlining the direction. Spiritual combat was the dominant theme—"Soldier in the Army of the Lord," "Call on Jesus," "Victory Is Mine." Carla was dizzy with astonishment and didn't know any of the songs but discovered that Maxwell did as he went with them, his voice becoming stronger and stronger with each shift of melody, text, harmony, and key. He was singing for the two of them as far as she was concerned, and somehow she loved him more than she ever had.

*comes to the microphone and sings in slow tempo until a new and
meditative type of song takes over.*

He who had read the text came to the microphone as the swirl of
spirit and song had risen to a level of steam so distinctive everyone in
the church was beginning to look as though he or she was nigh unto
wet enough to have just been baptized. The assistant pastor rocked at
the microphone for a bit, then stood still and began to intone, over
and over, the word "yes," drawing it out, drawing it out, using his
voice as a moist blanket. The congregational fire began to lower as
he moved to the words "Mary," "Martha," "Lazarus," each name
pushed into the air with a brawny but lyric baritone, stretching out
the syllables, no tune clear until he sang "oh" three or four times in a
specific tonal place and the congregation shifted over into "Oh,
Mary, Don't You Weep." Carla knew that one and joined in as everyone reached a condition of full but spiritual quiet, sort of a calm that
lifted itself out of the notes as the song ended and the gathered seated
themselves. There was business to talk of now.

"We'd just like to bring something special to everyone's attention,"
the assistant pastor said with a nearly conspiratorial enunciation that
preceded a chortle of beckoning community. Then he slowly moved
his head from side to side. "Oh, yes. Something is coming up. You
better know it. Oh, yes it is. My, my, my. Now let me make it plain. If
you love this church and you love the members, then you won't want
to miss this. Not if you can do anything about it. We don't play
around when it comes to this kind of stuff. In three weeks, in just
three weeks, we will have our annual summer picnic."

The congregation responded with the emotion of students who had
been told school would end a month early and everyone was already
guaranteed the very highest possible marks.

"You heard me. You're right to start oohing and aahing. You're
right. You know. In fact, I don't even have to announce where, since
we always go to the same place. If it fits right, no adjustments are necessary. We know where to repeat and we know *what* to repeat. There
will be the typically enjoyable events such as the showdown when the
pastor and his team take on the Deacon's Board. There it is. Some
softball *will* be played. Oh, yes. We'll see just who can back up with

action what's in the center of all this talking going on. Oh, we'll know by nightfall who can hit and who can pitch, who can field and who can run some bases. There will be no argument. It will all be over and it will have been witnessed. As you well know, Deacon Ezekiel Davis is dangerous on that mound. A rough customer. Mighty rough. He can make it so chilly out there a mouse would be afraid to run across the plate looking for some cheese. *Mean.* It could depend on him. But you know how it is. You know with Elder Merlin Menefield coaching the pastor's team this time around, one never knows. *Do one?*"

Carla could imagine what a sight Ezekiel made out there putting all of his attention on the batter and the strike zone. It had to be an awesome sight of pure authority—the wind, the light, the speed of the ball, and every bit of energy, from the catcher to the outfielders, centered on that mound. Ezekiel in command. There was no doubt that he had been the one who taught Malena to pitch so well. How he must have loved watching his girl when she was such a fine athlete. Carla remembered how it had always been difficult for her to conclude, once the game started, which side she should support because there was such wondrous beauty to a great pitcher and an equally compelling grandeur was radiated by the hitter determined to use that slender bat and make telling contact with the ball. Her favorite times reached up into drama when there was a battle of concentration between a pitcher and a hitter, the pitcher throwing all of his best stuff and the batter knocking one foul after another until, long beyond the full count, one of them miscalculated or leaned too much in one direction or lost footing and became the loser yet one who had done so well that any fan of baseball had to commend him for the quality of his effort. *"Now that's sport,"* Dad would say, *"that's sport. You have two men and it all comes down to measurements. There's judgment there, too. It could be food; it could be physics; it could be warfare. Proportions are the whole story. I like the televised thing of it, really, really do, but there was always something more for the actual, personal imagination when we had nothing. I don't mean nothing. We had plenty enough. Our baseball cards, the photographs in the newspaper and the stories in which a Jewish guy like Hank Greenberg, well, now he was a combination of Joshua out of the Bible and just about the dream of any American boy. Then you had DiMaggio hitting like it was the most natural thing in the world to get to first base. Geez! And, sure, we had our newsreel images of these baseball guys. Godfrey Daniels! Then the radio, my gosh, it became a thing of absolute magic. This is far out of the usual thing, you know. Far outside, way into the woods you could even say. Outer space. You heard these things. You saw these things in your mind. These baseball guys, these legendary guys, were too big for you to ever really see them. You couldn't do that. Giants in the earth. Right here. I mean, quite naturally, Hector and those guys couldn't really see Achilles. All they could see was what they had heard about him. He couldn't fit inside their eyesight. Too big. Same with our time as young people. When your mom and I were in college over in Wisconsin, we would go to the baseball game at my cousin Dave's house. He was well off you'd have to say. Well off. What times those were. Over there with the hot dogs, the Cokes, the popcorn. Dave and his wife Martha. Those big console radios were the top of the line then, the absolute best. Nothing like it in this world. Sitting there seeing nothing—not a blasted thing—and us jumping up and down. The make-believe was our heritage. Ballrooms. Ball games. Radio shows. There'll never be anything you can imagine like that again. It was a world of the ear and the mind. That's gone now. The mind is losing its place these days. You could even say the mind is losing its mind."*

"Now," the assistant pastor continued, "I know what you're thinking about and I'm about to say it right now. Here it is. Stand up, Mother Harris, let everybody see you since they will all be coming to thank you for what you will do with the menu."

Mother Harris, wearing a purple dress and a small purple hat that looked like a velvet helmet, was tall and deeply black, old with white hair, furnace heat in her eyes and immovable ditches of seriousness lined one atop the other on her brow. She stood and turned to survey the whole congregation. Her smile seemed difficult to produce and her dentures appeared to pain her. She also seemed very weary as she fanned herself and looked around with something in the emotional range of yearning. But Mother Harris also had the hearty, secretive grin of a publicly acknowledged master. Carla wondered what her special dishes were.

"Woman can cook now," Eunice whispered, "cook good as she want to and better than she should, but the world is going to keep on turning when her body is laid to rest."

Carla nodded but thought the statement rather odd. Maybe Eunice thought *she* should be the one everybody was praising.

"That's right. Get excited. You know you better ooh and aah. You *better.* Good as that Mother Harris food is. Victory is assured in the kitchen, among the pots and the pans, in the world of the recipes. I don't even want to *think* about it. I might fall down and go into a cold sweat. You know what I'm talking about. Oh, yes. We will also see how many in this church are still spry enough to involve yourselves in *any* form of activity after eating all of the fine, fine food that is guaranteed by this woman's culinary gifts, about which no one has *ever* complained. So you keep that on your calendar. Get ready. Get ready to get ready. Get ready to get right over there and have yourself a good old good time. All right now."

CHOIR

This is their moment. The select singers truly announce their presence.

As the assistant pastor seated himself, there was a blare of glorious sound from the back of the church. The force of it lifted Carla's insides and she was completely surprised by the opulence of the harmonies and how dramatically they were made to fit inside the rhythms played by the musicians. The unfathomable joy had a transporting effect. This was the music that had been rehearsed and these were the singers who had been picked by the choir director to stand up in front of everyone and let all concerned know just how good the people who were chosen to distinguish themselves as members of the choir could sound. There was a charismatic pride in the way they sang what they sang, and the phrases arrived with the collective confidence that hours of singing together brings, including the trips to gospel conferences and the harmonizing on buses, the warming up in the hotel rooms, and the putting on of robes and makeup and the combing of hair and all the preparation that goes with arriving in a strange place to sing up against all those who have arrived for the same reason you and yours have. There was history in the notes and those notes had the tonal presence of a sonic rainbow, glowing right up into the air, way up into the middle of the air, wheels of sound within wheels of sound. The choir, swinging its robes and walking in a rocking march, smiling and looking at all those seated, moved on up to the pulpit. As was usual with any representative gathering of Negroes, they spanned the color range, from bone to blue-black, and their body types ranged from thin as a pencil to grossly overweight. The hairstyles were epic as well, braids, Afros, weaves, shaved heads, permanents, and Jheri-kurls. By the time they had come up the red-carpeted aisles and taken their places behind the pulpit, a thrill was once more in place. They let it lope on down into a hum that sustained itself as the subsequent part of the ritual began, cushioning that next dimension of spiritual ceremony until it was time to gracefully shift into something different.

OFFERING

Pastor greets everyone and calls for the offering.

"Good, good morning to everyone. Good, good morning. As this is the offering, we are getting ready to honor the Lord in giving. Giving is our opportunity to imitate the ways of the Lord and to recognize the meaning of our Savior, Jesus Christ, and to make it possible for some part of our collective mission to achieve itself. We have already begun to offer all that we possess in our hearts and our souls. Now is the time to support the work of the Lord from that which you have gathered with the sweat of your brow. If you work, you sweat. From the blue-collar level to the computer world—let me say it again—if you work, you sweat. You labor. And from your labor you receive what is necessary to handle the material things of this material world into which we are always trying to inject the richness of the word of God and the ways of God. As you know, we are working on a building, we are expanding. We need more room. This old church has gotten too small. We have two services today and could have four if people were willing to keep coming and we had the stamina. But we need to expand our space so we can bring in more people and provide more services to our community, from the young to the old. Home is all we are ever thinking about. Let the young feel safe, the poor feel supported, and the old feel loved and respected. That's the kind of home God wants us to provide. So there is a blue envelope in front of you that will accept whatever help you want to give us, which we will appreciate and God will appreciate."

The ushers then directed the congregation to the table where the offering pans were held by the deacons and there was a big box for the tithing. While people were marching to the table, the choir seamlessly moved from the humming and sang "Amazing Grace." Carla had put twenty dollars in her envelope, and the blue rectangle of paper felt nearly alive in her hand as she carried it to the offering pan, making sure that she put it in the one held by Ezekiel. His eyes were now those of a deacon in the middle of his work and they had another cast of emotion as he looked at her. Carla felt as though he thought she might be capable of something good but mysterious. It was the oddest feeling, having nothing to do with anything connected to the world she knew. Ezekiel was, at least so it appeared, assessing her soul in some way that was intimate and general at the same time—how that soul worked within her and what it meant in the overall context of spiritual things. The weight and the elevation of this religious attitude brought a prickly sense of proximity to what could only be considered a gimpse of everlasting grace. It was amazing.

MINISTERING

Pastor begins to talk about things that are on his mind, such as events that are in the news, even personal recollections connected to the life of the spirit.

"I think now, I feel now, I know now that this world of ours is suffering on a rack of turmoil," the pastor said, standing again at the pulpit. He looked out into the congregation as though he was also looking through the walls of the church. "We see everywhere around us a sense of loss. The air is full of grief. Melancholy seeps from the leaves of the trees. There is sadness inside the water. Weevils of ill will walk through the food. Memory is rotting in the streets and everywhere around us. Men have forgotten how to be men—"

"They sure have!"

"Now ain't that the truth!"

"—and women have forgotten how to be women—"

"Trouble in the world, trouble in the world."

"—and *both* have forgotten how to do the many things you *have* to do if you want to raise children up to be something other than savages."

"Amen to that."

"Now, children, *our* children—*all* children—they have forgotten how to *be* children. They have been deprived of the right of innocence. I said 'deprived,' and I meant deprived. Oh, they have been victimized. Innocents left in the wilderness until the wilderness became part of them. They are old before their time and they are out of touch with the meaning of time."

"Umph. Umph. Umph."

As the pastor continued, the responses became milder, more contemplative, and created a lyrical accompaniment that reminded Carla of what one hears when a blues band shouts up to a climax then begins to back down in sighs made immeasurably deep by the softening intensity of the textures.

"We have jobs to do and we see neglect in every direction. Running, running, running. The heart is suffering in this world. The soul is wounded in this world. The past is eaten alive in this world. All we know how to do in this era is make fun of everything and make everything equal by turning it into dirt and water. If it can be covered up with mud it can be loved. Vulgarity and virtue are twisted all up until you can't tell one from the other. We need another perspective, another position on the hill, a way to see into the promised land. We need to take the time to get in line *with* time. We lose time because we forget time. Oh, things are bad. Yes, they are. But we have to remember what Paul said. He had been blessed with the power of accurate recognition. You put that with love and that's the biggest blessing in the world. Praise the name of God. Now Paul said in Second Timothy 4, verse 2 to 4—'preach the word, be urgent in season and out of season, convince, rebuke, and exhort, be unfailing in patience and in teaching. For the time is coming when people will not endure sound teaching, but having itching ears they will accumulate for themselves teachers to suit their own likings, and will turn away from listening to the truth and wander into myths.' So there you are; somebody always knew. Recognition and reckoning are Siamese twins. Somebody got to tell. Somebody. Somebody got to tell. Praise God."

The pastor seated himself and a hum of yet another disposition went through the church as his words settled into the sensibilities of the worshipers. Maxwell had a bored look on his face once more and was silently muttering to himself as he did when he was musing his being into a place at a far remove from where he was. He turned in his seat with a subtle restlessness, his sense of etiquette too well in place for him to embarrass his mother and father. Carla's reaction was quite different. The ritual was well worth the trip. Maxwell had his attitude; she had hers. Eunice patted Carla on the hand and the connection they had been developing grew just a little more.

SERMONIC SOLO

Someone is featured singing a beautiful song.

An adolescent boy who reminded Carla of Aaron stepped from the choir into a solo position. This was Baby Larry. His hair was cut close and his body gangly, somewhere between its earlier stage and its destination. There was an atmosphere of ambivalence to him. He might have been a homosexual; he might not have been—but his gestures were right on the line; they could have meant masculinity as easily as they could have been the expression of femininity. Everyone in the choir looked at him the way jazz band members look at the finest improviser among them, the one with the goods: the special note nobody else can play or find, the phrases that have the ability to completely fill the balloon of the moment and, thusly, transform it into a conveyance. This boy, rubbing his throat with his fingers, looking down, and becoming a statue as he stood in the silence that preceded singing, was just the other side of shy but appeared to have things on his mind much deeper than arrogance. Baby Larry had a sweet floating quality to his presence and one could imagine that clouds were preeminent in his thoughts. It was obvious to Carla that, from the very way that he stood, firmly but ready to climb right up in the air behind his notes, this boy could sing. She could not have been more correct. As soon as Baby Larry began to let out his voice, Maxwell whispered into her ear, "This is weird. He sounds just like Aaron. Oh. Oh. What? I can't believe this. It's weird. How could this be?"

The boy sang "I Won't Complain." His eyes found a place on the ceiling and they never moved from there.

> I've seen some good days,
> I've seen some bad days,
> I've had some hills to climb

and oh, so much pain
but the Lord has been good to me
He's opened doors that I could not see
It could have been me, outdoors
With no food and no clothes
But I just want to say thank you, Lord
Thank you, Lord, I won't complain.

As the boy went into more and more verses, the notes so pure that it sounded as though he was very nearly singing a different song from the choir, tears began to mist up in Maxwell's eyes. He was somewhere back in a time that Carla would never experience with him or with Aaron, no matter how much she cared about either of them. But she took his hand and held it tightly, feeling Maxwell's emotion seep into her and hers into him. Right in front of them and the whole congregation, something all of the church people who remembered that singing Davis boy had to realize, was a recycling, in virtually the same form and the same sweep of passion. Here was Baby Aaron returned to a point of glory in that period before he had dived so deeply into a world of promiscuity and such pervasive danger that his very existence was now some sort of a miracle.

A few months before they came to Houston, Maxwell had asked Baby Aaron something during one of his visits to New York. The brothers and Carla had drunk three bottles of champagne and there was an easy feeling of mirthful and intimate camaraderie in the loft. In their home, Carla didn't mind drinking and even getting drunk during a very exclusive gathering of a few people, but never in public. She always wanted to be able to walk straight and hold her head up high in the world.

The champagne, botttle after bottle, was a perfect taste and sensation at the end of a very long day. Aaron and Carla definitely needed something after they had spent many hours together, him first getting a close, snazzy haircut at Avalon and playfully threatening to sue if accosted by "the savage beast" that was Maxine, a tiny dog given free run of the salon because her master was the owner. Then the two of them walked half a block west and decided against waiting to get into

Tartine, where the lines outside were just too goddam long for Baby Aaron, regardless of how good Carla said the food was.

West Fourth Street had become another restaurant row in New York, beginning where, in the typical Manhattan way of confounding expectations, the eastern border was West Tenth Street crossing Fourth. Moving west to Charles Street, Perry Street, Eleventh Street, Bank Street, Twelfth Street, and ending at Jane Street and the Corner Bistro, which boasted a formidable burger, there was one excellent eatery after another. Carla's favorites were Anton's, la metairie, Chow Bar and Grill, Chez Ma Tante Cafe, Titou, EQ, The Place, Café Fés for what Maxwell called "that good old Moroccan grub," and Seville for the sangria and the joyful rowdiness of the crowded atmosphere even more than the food. When she and Maxwell were on that street together, seeking out some lunch or some dinner, she experienced an easy sense of all being well because you could always depend on the quality that lifted food to the poetic level above sustenance. In any of those places, the miracle of bread often snapped her fully awake. How had it been discovered? The discovery and control of fire made the cooking of meat inevitable. Easy as pie to deduce. But how did our ancestors ever look at a field of wheat and come to the conclusions or the discoveries that produced the staff of life, a loaf of it having no resemblance at all to its source? She could probably find out but Carla had never wanted to, preferring to feel just a little hot pinch of humility whenever she picked up a good piece of bread and realized again just how wonderful were so many of the things passed down to us all. Such culinary blessings were some of the superior reminders of God's grace that did a fine job keeping in check any tendency toward forgetting that good fortune outside the world of corruption was just another way of saying divine mercy. These were not subjects for afternoons with Baby Aaron, whom she adored for his buoyance and the sizzling wit of his company.

Turning away from Tartine, they commenced strolling and window shopping, having coffee, joking and snacking all over the West Village before walking leisurely on East Third Street to the address of one of his friends, Maurice Arthur, who had been nearly killed due to a splash of foolhardy and sadistic narcissism. This fellow had begun telling his latest tiresomely obnoxious Puerto Rican boy that, as good as he himself looked, the only reason any time at all was spent with crude and ignorant Latin kids of this current boy's sort had much more to do with curiosity and bad taste than meaning. Nigger though he was, Maurice said, he wanted there to be no doubt that he was an excellent caliber of man and that his sensibility was none other than that of a spiritual dinge queen. You are nada, he said, compared to me, **nada!** Sullen and excoriated, the Puerto Rican kid said nothing. "There may have been a tear hidden in the corner of his eye somewhere. The pretty little bitch. An **acid** tear," Maurice said to them as they drank some chilled bottled water that tasted wonderful after walking so much already, then coming up the six flights to his apartment. Their host continued the tale, setting the bottle of water down on a circular table, its top glass-covered lapis lazuli decorated with the carved image of a sword partially concealed within a toreador's muleta that was inlaid red marble. The Spanish boy, Mordreno, the pretty little bitch, got some gasoline much later that evening and threw it on him while he was asleep, waited as he awoke coughing and choking, then stood in the moonlight near the door of the bedroom with a Zippo lighter until Maurice the sinfully handsome, who was a luminous dancer and an actor, had gotten on his knees sputtering and wheezing and begging and apologizing to the diablo kid who was now sobbing and hunched over like the ape of death, choking out the words, "Nada y fuego, fuego y nada." Maurice groveled. He humiliated himself. He promised the boy everything he had. All the money, all the clothes, all the jewelry, the credit cards. Don't hurt me, baby, please don't hurt me. The surly Mordreno's voice glinted like the blade of a razor with a small line of blood across it as he repeated the same words he had been saying—"Nada y fuego, fuego y nada"—seeming to have heard nothing that Maurice said. The solemn sound created an even more intense design of terror, a violent black hole chewing the space of the room into it. As the descent into the suffocating sink of fear reduced him to convulsive trembling, Maurice screamed for mercy, soiling himself. A zero rolled through the air in silence. It encircled him and tightened. Nothing doing: The Puerto Rican's opposable thumb changed the world of Aaron's friend for good. He was now, even in his dimly lit apartment, a monstrosity, his handsome features mortally wounded by the young Mordreno.

Maurice hadn't the money to get all of the plastic surgery, which might not have done much for him since his burns were third degree anyway and it was just a cruel piece of no good goddam luck that he didn't die in the first place. When Carla went to the toilet, she noticed that there was a room just next to it in which photograph after photograph of Maurice in his beautiful days was mounted, creating a monastery, an island of images devoted to what he had once been and what he had lost because he chose to talk far, far too much shit to exactly the wrong person. So Carla and Aaron were quite happy that Maxwell wanted to take them to dinner then come home to a refrigerator that he had filled with champagne while they were traveling about, East Side, West Side, all around downtown.

Maxwell had finished a lucrative tour and was quite ready to lay out some cash for some big fun. The three had gone uptown on the West Side, to Dock's on Broadway, one of Maxwell's favorite restaurants, where each of them had a huge lobster and Carla knew that she was going to have to take a long bike ride the next morning while Maxwell and Aaron jogged near the pier before settling in at Aggie's on Houston Street for one of the best breakfasts anybody could get downtown. But that was all for tomorrow. They were at home now, the dinner behind them, the third bottle of champagne finished, comfortably listening to all of Aaron's favorite singers—Billy Eckstine, Nat Cole, Sarah Vaughan, Tony Bennett, Billie Holiday, and Aretha Franklin, whose first gospel recording he couldn't get enough of, drunk or not. Carla worshipped the Queen of Soul, too. What an intimidating inspiration that woman was.

"Say, Aaron, you remember how you used to sing?"

"Must I try and be modest?"

"Be yourself."

"Exactly. Nobody who heard Baby Aaron will forget him—not even Baby Aaron."

"You're right. Absolutely right. Right. I know what you mean. But how can you be what you are now?"

Carla recognized the mean attitude that liquor could pull out of Maxwell.

"Whatever do you mean?"

"You know what I mean."

"Oh: that."

"Yeah, Aaron, **that.**"

"Where shall I begin? Here I go. I was what I am now right back then. Deep in the heart of Texas. I just hadn't spread my wings or spread my cheeks."

"Aaron, you're a nasty guy, you know that?"

"No better than you know it."

"That wasn't very nice. My girl is here. She didn't have to hear that."

"Maxwell, I don't —"

"Carla, this is me and my brother talking. You can listen or you can leave. I would prefer for you to stay. But this is my brother. Is that understood?"

She nodded, her insides broiling with a feeling of humiliation.

"Don't mind him, Carla. Negro's just drunk. He gets that way. Indian in the family. Wahoo. You know what I'm saying?"

"We're not talking about me. We're talking about you."

"I love to be talked about. Talk on."

"Fine. What I want to know—I really want to know this—is how could you get from the great singer you used to be to the faggot that you are now?"

Aaron might have sensed where things were going, but he had been verbally slapped. Oh, he was definitely surprised. There was a flaming pause in the conversation. Maxwell seemed pleased. Carla felt imprisoned by her vow of silence until she saw that saucy light come back into Aaron's eyes.

"I must confess, Maxwell, that I had to work at it, dear brother."

"You sang such pure notes. Those notes were pure as a motherfucker."

"I **was** a bitch, wasn't I?"

"You might be more of a bitch now."

"Oh, no. You don't understand."

"I don't understand what?"

"Back in the day, under the full moon that was the true yellow rose of Texas, Baby Aaron thought he was a girl disguised in a man's body. Now I know better."

"Which means what, by the fucking way?"

"I'm a man who enjoys men. That's all. Mad about the boy. He's funny that way. Lover man. Someday he'll come along. **They'll** come along: the men I love."

"So that's supposed to be it?"

"It's not **supposed** to be it, Maxwell, it **is** it. Stop being so ignorant."

"I'm not ignorant. I'm just asking a question. I want some answers, not some bullshit. There's got to be more to it than that."

"It's supposed to be **my** life, but why don't you just tell me how it **actually** went. Hurry. Suspense is pissing all over me."

"Somebody had to do something wrong to you."

"Wrong is an answer in a quiz show. Oh, I know this is going to break records in sophistication."

Maxwell blankly looked Aaron in the face.

"You and I, man, we used to run together. We were athletes. You were my brother. We were a team. We built our own little clubhouse. You know that's what we did."

"Yes, that is what we did."

"Then you started getting like you are now. Tell the truth. Come on now. Be truthful. One of those guys in the choir or something like that. Somebody took advantage of you. It had to be something like that."

"Sorry, sorry, sorry. Not that dramatic and you know I love me some drama. Nope. It's actually simple. Nothing complex. Make of it what you will. Obviously, you still don't feel comfortable with me being around and being such a hard-core sissy, but, you know, I think you should give yourself a better life and get over it. Lift your country ass up and get over it. I am **going** to be what I am going to be, and I **was** what I was going to be when I didn't have **any** idea that there was anything in the **world** like what I am right **now** or already **was**— THEN. Okay? In the beginning, I was a sissy. Furthermore, for your information, Mr. Man, I can still sing the black off my ass. Baby Aaron can hold on to just as many pure notes now as I did during that time of the me and you that used to be. Now I saves those pure notes for myself. I sings only at home. I couldn't never adjust enough to church life now that my knees aren't dusty from praying. I don't care how good the niggers sound. They would never accept me and that's **their** loss. They can stand in line and kiss me where the sun don't shine."

"All right. Good. Fine. You've made your point. But I still want to know one thing. This is what puzzles me the most."

"If I knew it was going to be like this I would have at least demanded some goddam Cristal champagne. You see, Carla, niggers are always trying to fuck over you in the cheapest way. That's why they used to cut each other up so much. They didn't want to spend the money on guns. Always looking for bargains, ain't you?"

Carla had expected Maxwell to tell Aaron to keep her out of it, but he seemed to have not heard his brother or to have decided that he wouldn't be sidetracked. Maxwell was going his way and that was where he was going.

"Sometimes I lay awake at night thinking about this."

"Dear me."

"That's right. I'm the one up in the middle of the goddam night, not you. You got me wrong. You don't know how I really feel about all of this. Sometimes it scares me because you're my brother and I love you and I'm actually not ashamed of you. You're just weird. But I live in New York, which is full of weird people. In New York, you're not even weird. Try to get a prize in New York for being weird. You'll never win. So think about that. But this one thing keeps coming up in my mind."

"How long, how long, Maxwell, will it be before you say what it is?"

"Don't make fun of me. This is serious."

"Well, get your ass serious then! Get serious. You think I'm playing. You think I'm bullshitting. You think I'm not already tired of this conversation five minutes ago? Go on, you big-head fool. Waiting is driving me off the deep end."

"Relax. All right. Sorry. Don't start crying on me. Then I know you'll be ready to fight."

"I have better things to cry about, much better things," he said, with tears coming down his face.

"Carla and Aaron, my lady love and my brother, I guess it's time to apologize. I completely fucked this up. It's just one of those things: Alcohol, alcohol, how low you make me fall."

Aaron, his eyes full of affection, crookedly smiled at Maxwell.

"This is what I have on my mind all the time. **All** the time. As many times as you've been on your knees and as many times as you had your

boody busted, I just want to know how is it that you have had AIDS
for six or seven years and you haven't been sick **one** *goddam day?"*

"Nigger, is that all you want to know?"

"Right. Explain that one."

"I'm a medical miracle."

"But how is that?"

"Do you really want to know?"

"I can't wait."

"It's very simple."

"Break it down then."

"I don't know if you can stand it."

"Let's see, little brother."

"All right then."

"All right now."

"Simple: some coons can and some coons can't."

"Did you say what I thought you said?"

"I sure did."

"Some coons can and some coons can't?"

"Thank you, Jesus."

The two of them began guffawing and playfully sparring until Maxwell embraced his brother with a familial intimacy that Carla wouldn't have missed if she was offered a penny for every foot, feather, hoof, claw, and fin in China. From that point on, the relationship between the two of them was so, so different. They now had a closeness Carla had never thought possible, and when all three of them were somewhere together Maxwell had no response to those who stared at his brother and never showed any kind of reluctance to introduce Aaron to the men who dominated the jazz scene, which was, essentially, a man's world, but not one that welcomed men who loved men in the overt way Aaron did.

Carla wondered if Maxwell was thinking about that particular night in their home as he listened to the kid sing with the choir. But she knew that sibling relationships are so thoroughly complicated that there might be something close to an infinite number of things a brother could be thinking about a brother or a sister could be thinking about a sister or the kids of both sexes could be thinking about each other.

SERMON

The message—now that the way has been prepared—is given.

The pastor began by saying that his sermon for the day was "Maintaining Time."

"Well," was the reaction from the deacons, deep, elasticized into a long tone heavy with vibrato and followed by a "Mmmmm" from Mother Harris. Eunice whispered to Carla that the woman was *always* showing off.

"Now I already told you that I know we have all manner of turmoil facing us in these times. But we have to *recognize*. We have to stand up. We have to be ready to get ready. We have to know that time is our time. Today is our time and yesterday is our time and tomorrow is our time. The reason that is true is because God is a creator and a creator has no trouble with time. Time has trouble with him. A creator is superior to time. A human creator who's an actor can sound like a child or sound a hundred years old. He can handle the innocence or the sophistication of time. He can walk the high wire of time and not fall. A creator doesn't have to worry. Our Lord is a creator. Our Lord is *the* Creator. You know I'm right. You know it. Now I remember one minister who gave a sermon called 'The World Series.' He was getting down to something. He had a good grip on recognition. The World Series. It was the Lord's team versus the devil's team. Each team only had seven men because the pitcher and the catcher were neutral. They worked against both teams. Time was the pitcher and he was always winding up, and eternity was the catcher because eternity catches everything!"

They started responding.

"Now the Lord—you got to watch that heavenly Father. Praise His name," the preacher continued. "You got to know that G-o-d is the truest way to spell great. You got to know that. I say, 'Amen.' Does anybody out there hear that? Does any one of you hear what I'm saying up here on this clear Sunday in the house of the Lord?"

"Oh, yes, oh yes."

"I hope so up here. But *you* better hope so."

"You better *hope!*"

"I said it and I mean it: you got to get ready."

"Get ready now!"

"You got to get *ready.*"

"Better!"

"I'm talking about *ready!*"

"Yes!"

"Here it comes."

"Bring it on down."

"There was a king once upon a time, praise the Lord."

"Amen."

"This king, oh, my Lord."

"Lord, Lord, Lord."

"He was known. Yes, he was known. He was known as Ethelred. He was known as Ethelred the Unready."

"Make it plain."

"Listen to that. I said, *'Ethelred'* I said, 'Unready.' "

"Tell it!"

"That's what I said: I said, *'Unready.'* "

"Mmmmmmmmm."

"Ethelred, he was *un*ready. Born, good God, born all the way across the water. Uh-oh. Way over in England. Way back then. Uh."

Bring it on up."

"Way back *but* you got to watch it. Time is a *tricky* thing. It passes but it repeats itself. It goes off and it comes back. The *truth* is a returning thing. Time is the truth. It repeats. So, good God, you got to know. King Ethelred, he was unready. He didn't know when to move. He couldn't get up and do his job. He wasn't ready. We got plenty of people out here just like him. They pray and they think about God but they don't do what they are supposed to *do.* They are unready. Don't try to hide the truth behind history. You better understand something. Then was never *only* then and now is never *only* now. Listen to what I'm saying. The Lord works in *layers,* His wonders to behold. So you better put your mind on that wonder so you won't wander through the wilderness and lose contact with the path that is your task. History is all the people in you right now. The past is nothing but an exhaled breath and you're still breathing so it's coming right back. You got to know when *then* is right *now.* I'm telling you something. Way up *there* is right down *here* right *now.* "

"Clear it on up. Tell it all. Tell it all."

"So you can't outrun time, and you definitely can't outrun the assignment put on you in *your* time. Oh, you can run. *Jonah* tried to run. Ha. No good hiding place out here under God's heaven. Mmmm-hmmm. You can't hide in the *past*. You *can't* hide in the future. You can't *hide* right now. My Lord is real. Uh. My Lord is the God of time; my God is the *Lord* of time. So you got to be *on* time. Seems like a misty morning. If you not *on* time, time will be on *you*. Seems just like afternoon. And you cannot, oh no, handle the *weight* of time. No, no, no. Nightfall is coming. Oh, yes it is. You got to be *humble* to walk softly on the *truth* of time. I say, 'Walk now.' Those are your feet and they will not fail you; and they will not fail me. The moon is rising. The truth of time wears *iron* shoes and those shoes are *big* as the con-stellations that fill the heavens. The stars are too bright to count. You better know that dawn is on the way. Uh. The truth of time is that an irresistible force passes *through* an immovable object. Seems like a misty morning. Keep on stepping. Uh. Big, I say: feet going on forever. Stay on the case. So you can't be late. You got to be *ready* to get right. You got to *get* ready to get right. You got to get ready to know. You got to be on time."

Some were standing and turning now. The organ was underlining the preacher's words. Mother Harris and other older women up front sat and waved handkerchiefs. They rose and turned and turned and sat. Their cries of response were unearthly. That unearthliness was picked up by other older women, all of them ping-ponging sounds that were neither happy nor sad but were a music Eunice joined in making, an announcement of just how long they had been close to an inimitable potency, one that had answered the mysteries and held back the deluge.

The preacher moved from behind the pulpit now and he was hold-ing a cordless microphone. He went from one end of the altar to the other. His body illustrated every word. Ezekiel and the rest of the dea-cons were heated up. The power with which they had begun the ini-tial praying and singing was intensified. The pastor was letting them know how it went. He was the messenger of the moment. The spirit had him and it was making everything plain. The congregation was taken through example after example, Genesis to Revelation, Old Testament to New Testament, of those who had not done their jobs, who had fallen by the wayside, who had not understood that theirs was a task to be done in a certain time. There was a beat to existence and you couldn't come in too early and you had better not come in too late. Every man, woman, and child had better get on the right part of that spiritual rhythm. This was no kind of play thing. God made the minnow wiggle in the sea; He made the farthest invisible galaxy. Billions upon billions of light-years were the smallest measurements of His creation. Which He could make larger or smaller at any time He wanted. Alpha was His name; Omega was His name. He was God. We, fashioned in His image, could live in a drop of water if it was time for us to be done that way. Time was a weight, time was a weapon, time was a pair of wings flapping into the arms of the light of revelation.

"Oh, my God. Speak through me with just a pinpoint of your might. Oh, Lord, oh, my God, on that cold, cold day of the soul when the Savior was in a sweat and his tears were burning down his face, on his knees all by himself in the Garden of Gethsemane, when it touched him that all he knew of time and the feeling of living that it had given him, at the moment that it crossed his mind with the power of a boulder crushing his chest, he did not want to join God in the reality of time that is beyond the time beyond time. Our melancholy Savior. Sadness lay upon him like the many plagues brought down upon the Egyptians. It was raining unhappiness. It was bleeding unhappiness. The fountain of his soul was filled with the frogs and locusts of loneliness. Every firstborn wish was slaughtered by the approaching feet of the Roman soldiers. He was on his knees begging for something he would not get. The bitter cup of doom was something he wished would pass his lips. He did not want to taste the dark wine of death. He was the Son of God and he was guaranteed a place in heaven at his Father's side, but the sorrow of the flesh facing the ending of breath brought him to his knees. His heart bled a pool of terror. More than we know. There were whippings. There were thorns. There were nails. There was a spear, and what gushed from the wound of that spear was a key to the door. More than we know. Not more than the Savior knew. Oh, he knew. He was truly a man. That was why he felt fearful of the end of his life in the world of the flesh. He even questioned his fate when he felt forsaken as he lay crucified upon the cross. None of that mattered. His job was preordained. It was his time. Somebody got to go. Somebody got to go there for you before you can stand up and go for yourself. To save the world, to make it possible for us to struggle and meet the beds of cactus that are the troubles of our time, our Savior stood up to his time. He knew he had to die. He accepted it and he fought it. He was a human being but he would return as a lion."

The pastor started heading home. The flare of his sound had embraced everyone and now he was closing in on his conclusion.

"This is a date for which you can*not* be late. Too important. Satan the devil snatches the *tardy*. Did you hear me? I said that Satan, I said that the devil, I said he will stand *outside* time and *snatch* the tardy. They who are too tardy will remain late and lost forever. I say you *better* be hearty; I say you better *not* be tardy. I say when it gets late in the world you must remember that time is told by the movement of the earth around the sun and that time moves around the sun of the Lord who is the God of time and that the devil is the coalmine lord of darkness and that is why Satan is *outside* of time and will keep you—*if he can*—from being there for the appointment your soul *must* keep. You got to pick a number and you got to be in on that number. You better snatch these words and keep them on your mind. You better march. You better get up off your knees and do the proper do. You better know that time past and time future and time present and all motion in the eternal rhythm of existence begins and ends inside the mind of *God,* which is the infinite storehouse of light. Make sure you don't find yourself outside of time in the coal mine of the devil digging for lumps of darkness. Watch yourself. It could happen to you."

They were joyous in their seats now. They were enraptured on their feet. Handkerchiefs were raised and waved and waved and waved. There was so much crisscrossing sound, so many voices, each of them known together, each of them known alone. The congregation, now one moan made of flesh and sweat, was slowly calming down as the organ and the piano delivered concluding trills, and those who had stood up and turned around and around or jumped up and down, who had come so close to possession by the Holy Ghost, were fanning themselves and looking on in wonder. Carla herself picked up a fan and started whipping the air onto her face as the essence of the ceremony stretched her insides, made her feel as though she was enlarged by what she had witnessed and what she had experienced. Seemed just like yesterday. Carla was taken back to the morning when she was a child praying with her mother and the power of God pushed itself inside her like a hot gust of wind. Carla had floated up above the church inside that passage of illumination and was able to see everything from the crest in space where she and everyone she knew lived in motion to the very end of the universe. Nothing was said at all but her mother turned to her daughter, words glowing out: "There is no beauty like the power of God. Is there?" Mom knew. She *always* knew.

CALL TO DISCIPLESHIP

Invitation to you who do not believe in Christ to come forward and give your life to Christ.

"There may be in this house on this morning some people who have never known the meaning of our Lord and Savior," the minister said with a vocal tone and a mood much different from those upon which his sermon had been built. There was a gentle seducing sound to what he was saying and it lulled you in his direction. "Oh, yes, there are those who missed the teachings. They might have been playing in the backyard when the Word was at the front door. They might have been swimming and water was in their ears when the Word passed over the swimming pool. They could have been looking to the left when God was passing on the right. They didn't know. But if you didn't know and you know now, feel no shame and come on forward. Come on and join this gathering that lives to make the most of what was brought right on down to us by Jesus Christ. He was sacrificed for all of us and we must make the most of that sacrifice. That blood must not have been shed in vain. That torture must not have been felt for nothing. The nothing I mean does not diminish the victory of love, compassion, and sacrifice eternally represented, enacted, and perpetuated by our heavenly Father and His only begotten Son. They did their part with characteristic perfection. So when I say nothing I don't mean anything about God or about Jesus Christ. I'm talking about your making it in vain for yourself. We cannot crucify the truth in our hearts by remaining outside of the church. Our time is our time. Come with us. Make yourself whole."

This was not a morning when there were those in the house who were yet to be converted or who were willing to be converted. The preacher looked around and around, his eyes stopping for a second or more on Carla, who did not have to go forward. Her beliefs were steady, even though they didn't take her into any church very often— in fact, never. Everything about life had been affirmed for her, but she was as close as she wanted to be. If she had gone forward, she would have been submitting to the ritual, not the content, which, in itself, was all right with her, plenty. Truly wonderful. Carla sat where she was, holding Maxwell's hand and holding Eunice's.

OPENING THE DOORS OF THE CHURCH

Those who have been saved but wish to become a new member of the church come forward and are welcomed.

All of the ushers stood, as did the deacons, as did the entire leadership of the church. The pastor's wife, a voluptuous light-brown-skinned woman in a cream-colored straw hat and matching cream-colored dress with beige pumps and gold-flecked tan stockings rose and walked to stand in the rostrum just to the side of the pulpit. The pastor stood above her, saying, "If you already know the Lord and Savior Jesus Christ as your personal savior, and desire to establish a church home, we would be pleased to give you the right hand of fellowship."

The congregation applauded as a number of individuals came forward, a few families with three or four kids, all of the youngsters clearly fatigued by the ritual or shy about walking down the aisle and being looked at by row upon row of these people they didn't know. The pastor greeted each of the new members, introduced them to his wife, and announced that the circle of the Lord inside this house had been expanded, by divine grace, praise God. He then opened his Bible to a passage that those eyes had probably fallen upon so many times that the words might easily and immediately gather in his mind whenever he thought of that very verse as it appeared on the variously made and differently sized pages of untold different kinds of type and printings of the scriptures that were opened on the numerous Sundays and other days when he had read them: as a young man, as an adult, as he had been when Carla was a child and saw him delivering the guest sermons in South Dakota, as his travels had made him before he settled in Texas, and as he was now, older and more mysterious in this church than he was so long ago, primarily because his presence seemed now to have an even stronger grip on the central living factors of the moment. He was a conductor on an invisible train of glory and it didn't matter whether you could see it or not, the sound of that locomotive passing on the celestial rails set everything in this house vibrating on a very subtle plane of perception this morning of worship as things were at an end. The pastor read from Acts 2:47: "And the Lord added to their number day by day those who were being saved."

BENEDICTION

The whole church delivers it with the minister.

Everyone stood and Carla relished the experience of being surrounded by so much fortitude and softness, such interior muscle and fluffiness. She felt as if her insides were being massaged with sweet oil. The musicians began the last song of the ritual and the congregation sang:

> Praises to God
> From all creatures
> From heaven and below
> Praises to God
> Father, Son, and Holy Ghost

There was a pause in the music as the pastor, with a lifting, lifting timbre to his voice, said, "May the Lord watch between me and thee while we're absent one from another." Then the congregation sang "Amen."

It was finished. The ritual was done.

At that point, the congregation slid into normal conversation, chatter, joking, discussion of the message, hand-shaking, back-slapping, and embracing, with children tugging parents to go home for Sunday dinner. Teenagers were giving each other the romantic eye, boys to girls, girls to boys. Single men who were sweetening up on single women either sat in conversation with them or were on their feet making the kind of talk that would lead to walks, drives, dinners, and, one never knew, maybe even hitching up into holy matrimony.

Young children started chasing each other around. An usher came in and shouted, "Who's got Sister Mamie's car blocked?" People were taking turns shaking the pastor's hand and hugging him. They loved his message because he always made them feel the spirit and think new thoughts. Eunice turned to talk with some women she obviously hadn't seen for all of a week, introducing each of them to Carla, and there were people coming up to Maxwell reminding him that they knew he was going to turn out to be something a long time ago, back when he wore his same old pressed dark suit and his brown tie that some kind of way could never be kept in place but he still, little boy or not, played the saxophone with the kind of gift only those favored by heaven above ever really get a chance to feel and pass on, know it in their own hearts and use it to touch other hearts. Now that he was getting some of the attention, Maxwell came right out of his own private bog where all that bubbled up from the waters was apathy. He wittily reminded people of what *they* had been like then, too, and some of the things they had done together on a few memorable church occasions. It was as it always is when the past is regenerated: no one seems to have ever left home.

Now there was something going on over near the pulpit. Carla couldn't see what it was but there was a noise from a couple of voices that had a dissonant relationship to the euphonious atmosphere. It was hushed at first but took on ever more sound space, causing people to turn in that direction. The pastor was talking to some congregation members, smiling and patting his forehead with a handkerchief as his wife and an usher came up, their faces grave. In stops and starts the congregation began to pick up on the problem. Trouble was in the church. Eunice was craning her neck to see if she could make out anything, and Maxwell looked in that direction because the people around him turned and started to stare toward where the mysterious difficulty was taking place. Carla, suddenly as curious as a child, wanted to stand up on the bench in the row where she had been sitting.

"You know what's going on?"

"No, Maxwell, I don't."

"Something. Look at those people. Something."

Ezekiel appeared and started telling people in a voice full of command that they needed to get back and that there were professional medical people in the congregation who were going to have to come to the front of the church and they would be slowed down if the membership didn't at least get itself into the rows. People began to clear the aisles but they remained standing, which made it impossible to make out the trouble. Three men hurried up the aisles; all of them, Eunice told Carla, were doctors who had been members for a long time. "Umph. Now those going there are nurses," she continued. "Something bad is going on." Then the startled whispers and the ordinary speaking levels started to weave themselves from the front to the back of the church. Mother Harris had been felled by a heart attack. Death was trying to get inside the church. Sorrow and muttering and prayers began to recast the atmosphere. The congregation was asked to seat itself.

Maxwell began to edge along the wall and Carla followed him. Mother Harris was lying still on the floor just beyond the front row. Her face was twisted in the distortion of stroke and her feet had been placed on a stack of hymnbooks. One of the nurses gave mouth-to-mouth resuscitation while the doctors were handing out keys as they ordered people to go get the medical bags from their cars. Emergency was being called and the pastor was calming down Mother Harris's family, her son and her daughter, their spouses, and her grandchildren.

Mother Harris responded to nothing. Amyl nitrite was put under her nose. She remained still but her bladder released all of its water. She lay there in a puddle spread below her waist. There were grunts of despair and more prayer as that news was passed through the congregation. The emergency people sped up the aisles and did all that they knew how to do. These two waves of help, from inside and outside of the church, had failed. There was nothing to be done. Nothing. Mother Harris was gone. None of her vital signs acted out. People began weeping and repeating her name as they felt the grief bloat itself inside them. The Harris family was in shock. The young children kept asking their grandmother to get up, Gran-Gran, to get up, please get up, Gran-Gran, and the daughter was sobbing beyond the reach of consolation as her husband, his eyes red with tears, held her. The son, like a wild beast, was storming back and forth. Holding his mother's hat by the purple ribbons that had been tied beneath her chin, he was silently shouting, as though madness had snatched him. His wife, coughing and crying, seemed afraid to say anything to her husband. Ezekiel got to him and said, "Come here, boy, come here." The son of Mother Harris looked at him and ran to Ezekiel, who embraced the man as all the loss and terror came out in stinging whimpers. Maxwell looked down, his own eyes full of tears, and Carla felt both hot and cold with fear and trembling.

The pastor stood in front of the pulpit, an incalculable gravity upon him. He gave out a long, long sigh. Then he walked over to where Mother Harris lay as immobile as she had been when the whole process of death and its victory over medicine had begun forty minutes or more earlier. One side of her face was so terribly turned while the other appeared so calm that she took on, in death, the visage of horror and peace. The pastor stood over her body and breathed as if his own last breaths were being taken.

"I have been told that Mother Harris has gone home to God. That is what I have been told. Yes, that is what they say. But I feel something else in this room, in this house. I feel something else. I don't know what it is but I *do* know what it is. Everyone in this church knows what it is. You know. I know. I feel *life*. I feel the breathing spirit of our Lord and I feel the merciful wetness of the blood of Christ. Let us not fear this moment too much to pray."

The pastor paused as he looked at Mother Harris.

"Lord, we have been talking about the dark wine of death this morning. We have been talking about the bitter cup of the last silver minutes into which that final taste of doom is poured. In this house, we have been talking about all of that. Yes, we have. Yes, we have. So, Lord, like us all, I know that in the final analysis Your will for me is death. Yes. I know that Your will, in the final analysis, is death for Mother Harris. Yes. I know that death is Thy will for every member of this church and every visitor and every new member we have given the right hand of fellowship this morning. Yes. But I *still* want to pray. *We* want to pray. We still want to *beg* for Your mighty compassion. We want to get down on our knees."

Everyone went to their knees.

"God, we know that our salvation was made possible by the blood of Christ on that cross where Your only begotten son was sacrificed for the soul of mankind, he who was born in that manger in Bethlehem, unwelcome, arriving among pigs, cows, and horses. Taking his first breaths in front of three wise men. Dying between two thieves.

We have spoken of that, too, this morning. But we have to ask You something. There is no other way. We have to ask. You sent us medicine. You sent us doctors. You sent us nurses. You made it possible for the emergency men to get here and work like Trojans. But Mother Harris lies before us responding to nothing. This church could be an old, old tomb her body is so still and so in place. She only just an hour ago stood before us, and now she has been spirited over the wall of death. But we know. Yes. We know that her body will respond to Your will. We know that Your will, and Your will only, is the will of eternal life. We know that eternal life awaits us when we wear the robes that will fit us well because we put them on at the burning gates of hell. But, in this house, on this morning, we would like to ask You to be merciful and let us have this wonderful woman among us for as much longer as You decide she should be here. We want to ask that. We want to ask that You will reach across the eternity that is Your creation and that You will grace us all by letting this woman live on the microscopic speck of dirt that is the earth we know in our frail and deeply terrified mortal coil. For these things, for this divine compassion, we are willing to humble ourselves and beg."

The pastor, still down on his knees, now became silent.

The hush settled every active thing in the air.

It was as if the elaborate stillness of death were the only reality within that church, now and evermore.

It was too, too quiet to hear anybody pray.

Focused fully upon the corpse of Mother Harris, confronted with this mournful lull, they were all kneeling before the unbeating telltale heart, the red silence of unmoving blood, and the pursuing troops of bondage that were the concluding admission of cold, cold, bottomless defeat.

The preacher, his forehead touching his clasped hands, his collar and tie soaked through, his dark robes now symbolic of the final winding sheet, parted the silence.

He began to hum, and the hum that was his beginning of song became the word *yes,* and that single word, moving itself through a melody that Carla learned as it was sung over and over and over, the solitary syllable becoming stronger with each repetition, transformed the feeling of the room once again. Inside that isolated word was the entire story of everyone in the church and everyone they had ever heard of, living or dead. That *yes* was the compression of the tale of the human organism that seeks out sustenance and joy, that wants for food and for a release of the dopamines that give all sensual pleasure, the organism that flees pain and builds all of its civilizations on a meal and a groove, but also the organism which steps up from the small cage of its survival and tries to fly outward, where the glittering strength of its existence will be equal to that of the stars and its wings will find, *somewhere,* the source of all light and the source of all pain and the source of all acknowledgment—that very greatest of *all* great conceptions: the idea of a force capable of *absolute* recognition, supreme comprehension, He whose eye is on the sparrow *and* on the eyeless fish in the black dark ocean, on the microbes *and* the births of new stars, He whose rightful name is not just I AM but I KNOW, not just I KNOW but I *DO.* They were all asking now, in that *yes* so finely tailored up with soul and filled with innumerable variation upon variation, spirit reaching out in the chords of timbre that are inevitable when so many different human tones and different throats and personal ways of breathing support and push forth the pronunciation, the invisible essence of request become a drone of many colors moving along, slowly and with the burden of sorrow, but just as much with the strength of having known that *that* which is horrible may not be *horrible* forever, may *not* hurt for too, too long, could *possibly* just turn around and become something altogether different from what it was thought to be *if* faith would only raise itself up, impressed not one iota by the shadows of the valley of death or by the eclipse of life that arrives when the moon of demise slides in front of the sun and all we know goes so *black* as the body becomes as cold as any stone and as hard as the fear of the rigor mortis that symbolizes the end of all softness.

Then the body of Mother Harris began to twitch. Yes. She was then covered with the shine of dew. Yes. The moisture gathered up. Yes. It flowed then and flowed until she was soaking. Yes. Then she turned to the right, turned to the left, quaking. Yes. The twisted side of her face moved as though it were an ebony piece of clay being made straight. Yes. Her eyes, which had been closed and would never see again, then opened. Yes. Mother Harris suddenly sat up and screamed a "yes" that went through the roof of the church. A gasp spread and everyone was now standing and shouting, or weeping again but for yet another reason. This was a pandemonium of happiness so outsized that it turned in quality toward hysteria. The ushers, while thanking God after each sentence, began asking that the congregation remain where it was and not come running forward. The embracing and the crying overtook everyone. Carla was in Maxwell's arms and she was sobbing and so was he.

The pastor stood and began walking back and forth, one arm in the air, his white hair slicked to his head by perspiration, and announced that it was time for the professionals of the medical world to get on with their job.

"Oh, yes," the pastor said, "oh, yes. I said, 'Oh, yes. Oh, yes.' We have seen the mighty power of the Lord this morning. Oh, yes. I say, I say, 'Yes, we have seen the power of God.' Oh, yes. Hallelujah. This church has been blessed. Amen. We have all been blessed. Praise his name. We have to be *thankful*. Oh, my Lord. We have to be *thankful*. I said, '*Amen.*' We have to remember *one* thing, we have to remember that *He* said, '*Ask* and it shall be given you; *seek,* and ye shall find; *knock,* and it shall be opened unto you.' *Hallelujah. That's* what *He* said. *His* will be done. Oh, my good sweet Lord. *Praise* His name. *Praise* His name. *Praise* His name. Good God a'mighty. His will be *done. This* morning!"

The pastor turned around and around, clapped his hands, shook his head, then, in a voice of velvet supplication, asked Baby Larry to sing. The young man, who had taken off his robe as he began to pray on his knees, slipped his robe back on and sang "Oh, Mary, Don't You Weep" as the emergency workers began to lift Mother Harris onto a stretcher and she was moved on out for an appointment with a recovery room, her family following as though their feet did not touch the floor. Baby Larry looked again to the ceiling, his eyes stuck on something no one could see but that everyone knew had just been seen and had just been felt and would forever be recalled with such intensity that there would come a day when those who had stayed in bed and missed that service, out of laziness, out of fatigue, out of having done too much fun the night before, all would curse themselves for not having gotten everything together, their clothes crisp and clean, and gone on to meet the Master of All Masters at the Ark of God in Christ. Each word and each note melted or evaporated in the pure force of Baby Larry's singing. That force pulled them all. Every voice lifted and sang along with Baby Larry, the collective joy mixed all up with a collective exhaustion. Tell Martha not to moan.

Carla was in pain: she had been on her knees so long. Maxwell's shirt looked as though he had just been baptized. This wasn't quick, like in the movies. It was a miracle but it had taken time and work. So many souls had to step down from the heights of their pride and humble themselves for somebody else. They were known together and they were each known alone. Death had been told to raise up and go someplace else, to trail behind life a little while longer. There was no point telling anybody in New York about it. All Carla could do was sit there in a state of something mightily close to actual grace as Ezekiel drove them home. After they had all showered and changed into something clean and fresh, relaxed and recalled the miracle from each of four perspectives, all seeing the same thing, all seeing something a little different and feeling the atmosphere in a personal way, a few hours had passed. Then Eunice called upon Carla to help prepare a marvelous dinner of red snapper, collard greens, beets, and sweet potatoes. My Lord, what a morning.

THE BLUES THREE DIFFERENT WAYS

T HAT SUNDAY night Carla lay awake after she and Maxwell had made love with a fresh empathy, in which the layers of sensation were like old times, but something better. She was more than satisfied but sleep wasn't moving in just yet. It would have to repeat itself, that feeling from him, and repeat itself and repeat itself for some time, a good while, before Carla could even start to believe that they were truly getting back together, that he was *with* her. She would have to have all of those affirmations and reaffirmations. Then it would be clear that they could stand up against *anything* intent on separating them or defiling what they had so as to uphold an ancient but acid abstraction, the one into which all individuality dissolved and you were as fused to everyone else in your group as the molecules of liquid measured off in a vulgar, heartless gutbucket. No, Carla wasn't about to begin declaring victory now. It wasn't time to jump and shout for joy. Maxwell had made it like that. He had faded in and out too many times over the last year. This was no occasion to rush into gloating, since the two of them might only have been experiencing the sweet aftershocks of a miracle. Her time out here had let Carla know that victories, moments of closeness and recognition, have no guaranteed relationship to permanence. Life had slapped the taste of naive confidence out of her mouth often enough to stabilize that piece of understanding.

She rubbed her face, stroked her upper lip, and felt under her chin for the very little sag that would eventually grow to take the beauty of her long neck from her. Carla could hardly feel it, but the incipient pouch burned her finger and sent a hot drop of tart fear into her stomach. Would she ever get a face-lift if she couldn't stand it? Was she that vain? After all, she *was* in show business. No. No. She figured she would just live with the face that life gave her and hope that it made her a little more humble, instead of desperate and resentful of younger women. How pompous. St. Carla of the Order of the Humble Heart. Yeah, right. Ha. But, way inside the quiet places of her spirit, there was, however badly she said it to herself, the daunting prayer to inhabit humility yet have the strength and the resilience living up to her dreams required. It was so, *so* hard. She took a deep breath and let out enough air to make a cloud the size of a pillow.

Maxwell, probably none of this on his mind, was in the land of dreams, "hanging out with brother Morpheus," as he loved to say. Now she, after orgasm so transporting it might have been no more than a deceptive form of hope, was caught remembering one of those crazy arguments the two had had when Carla was—quite rationally, by the way—going on about misogyny. She knew she must be thinking about it due to her persistent doubts about the future. Her soul cried out for another subject. There was a blankness that came in, eventually. Her spirit became quiet. She just listened to the air conditioner and felt the muscles on Maxwell's arms, those arms that had held her so often and that she had looked at when the two of them met in the Brooklyn Botanic Garden, him making her begin to feel on that spring day what she had wanted to feel after Bobo had been dead for the year that seemed a decade, leaving her out there all by herself, on some ridge where her life was reduced to a silhouette: all passion become dark and indistinct, recognizable only by outline until a memory came up and took on all the color of a past that could never be tied to the rail of life again. Her argument with Maxwell was still knock, knock, knocking on the door of her mind. Leave that silent. Don't answer. She remembered how Mother Harris had such a brittle scent as she was carried out of the Ark of God in Christ. The fabulously grand sound of Ezekiel's voice at the dinner table carried her along, as did Eunice's unimpressed assertion that Mother Harris—no matter how long the woman lived after God had let her return to this world—would never cook any fish or any greens as well as the ones getting fixed right now.

The heating and frosting joy came through as Carla forced herself to recollect the time she was singing "Blue Skies"a few years before Bobo died and he was there with her, behind the drums in his loft— first sweeping with his brushes, then tipping along lightly with his sticks, leading her and rhythmically talking to her in percussion language—as the South Dakota girl started to get with all of the tricks he had taught her about triplet subdivisions inside triplets and accents that juggled the beat: each note that she picked out of the chords going by in her head was coming out of her body and falling into place with actual swing, swing for the very first time. Yes, dear Lord, it was swing.

That had taken so long and she had worked through so many songs and gone to so many jam sessions and felt so bad so often. On bandstand after bandstand, Carla was just another white girl standing up there and dropping the swing when it was her turn to take center position in the sound. She could hear the beat she wanted to sing but it wouldn't come out of her mouth. The expressions on the faces of the other musicians brought her down from a deceptive euphoria those infrequent times when she thought she had caught the rhythm.

During those low years she sang with her head down or seemed distracted on the bandstand, and never looked out at the audience unless there was a dumb society job to be done where everything was show and swing didn't matter: all you had to do was bully the rich with a brash cabaret twist and they would love the dirty insides of your oldest shoes. Carla hadn't noticed the position of her head when she was singing jazz until that morning, when she turned around and looked straight at Bobo, feeling herself internally rise into that syncopation and step up into the music as a dark, blues-speckled texture slid from her mouth that was real, not a pose. They were swinging together then, together for the first time. She had asked him later on that first day of swing how he had put up with it for the last couple of years.

"Say what?"

"Oh, me trailing you around to your gigs and sitting in with all the guys giving me that cold eye. Or, well, you know all the times it took me a whole day to understand some of the rhythms you were playing. Sweetheart, how did you put up with that?"

"Something told me you would hear it."

"Really?"

"You know it did."

"Well, I guess."

"Most definitely. If it didn't, I would have said that you need to do something else. Oh, for a long time, you sounded like a crime against singing, but I waited for you. Just like people waited for me when I couldn't play."

"I can never imagine you not being able to play, Bobo."

Bobo looked at her as though she was the biggest fool ever born. He began laughing as though he couldn't stop and Carla felt as though her eyes were going to water because she was afraid that he thought she was just too silly for words.

"Baby low, I used to drop beats, rush, drag the tempo, fuck up all *kinds* of ways. Turn the time around. Name the mistake—any one—I made it triple. I was lucky if I got it the *fourth* go-round. Hey, you think people look at a singer funny when she ain't doing it, try being a drummer. They really hate your ass because you *never* stop playing. You, the bass player, and the piano player are there from the start to the finish. The rhythm section runs the whole length of the tune. We should get that extra money. We do the most work."

He had said that to her before—how *many* times had he said that?—but he had never told her that he thought her singing wasn't good. Carla, in a heavy sweater, her wet hair wrapped in a towel, wearing some jeans and a pair of cuddly slippers with dog faces and floppy ears dragging the floor, was just beginning to react to that statement. She looked down at her feet and had to silently laugh at how stupid those slippers looked and how surprising it was that Bobo would have gotten them for her when she complained of how cold it got in the East Village loft that was now warming up as the pipes percussively kicked out the heat hissing through the radiator with the emotionless indignation of machinery. A laugh wasn't all that was inside her. It hurt to have him say that she had sounded as terrible to him as she had to herself. At the same time, her chest was filled with a brand-new goodness of experience because she was now really feeling the rhythm as a participant, not just a listener.

"About what you said, it was a long wait, you know?"

"Had to be. You got to know how to wait and you got to know when to wait and you damn sure got to know who to wait for. Isn't that, baby low, what they call the learning process?" he laughed and grabbed her up in his arms.

She couldn't stop laughing and smiling that day. Carla had climbed over the wall into the party, mostly, when it came down to it, because she had had the courage to wait for herself. As it always did when she was lucky, her life was starting over. She now comprehended what Bobo had once said about the time. They were cuddled up in her dinky place, where she had cooked a Christmas turkey with corn bread stuffing, collard greens, mashed winter turnips, salad, and plum pudding. The two had just watched Bobo's favorite version of *A Christmas Carol,* Alastair Sim starring on her miserable little black-and-white television. Those ghosts giving old Mr. Scrooge the blues took Bobo back to the point in his life when the whole question of time started taking on a clearer presence of meaning.

It came to him through his strengths, which were math and music. Those were the two classes in which he was exceptional while a school kid, never finding much to his liking in literature or history or the sciences, subjects Bobo avoided failing but for which he never did the work that would earn him above average grades. The symbols in math and in music sent his head up above the clouds. When he found out in junior high school geometry that a line had no start and no end, he lay awake throughout that typical East St. Louis evening, noise out in the street, records playing, cars speeding by, people shouting and laughing and threatening their various ways through another Friday night. God must have been a line that started nowhere and ended nowhere, more even than alpha and omega. But God was a line that you lived on and that spoke and did things. It didn't just lie there, not the spirit of God. That line had something to do with time but it was something that Bobo didn't conclude until much later, after he had truly learned how to play and was able to conceive exactly what he was in the middle of when the smoke was rising up off the bandstand and everybody was tuned into everybody else. Then he saw the crucial element of difference.

In European music, you got paid good bucks for sitting there doing nothing for a long time. What? That was what being a "percussionist" meant in that music: I don't get to play much. Don't get him wrong: they played the hell out of whatever they got to play, great technique and power, but that music didn't usually use drums for anything other than rare "coloristic" effects and moments of drama. The pace and the articulation of the meter was controlled by the conductor. The number of beats in the meter wasn't stated separately the way it was in a jazz rhythm section, which made the beats of a bar and the harmony come alive unto themselves as independent and collective agents of interpretation. She didn't get it. "Since you *are* what you play, baby low, you become the time or the harmony or both when you're on the bandstand." That was something for Carla to think about as he said it that way. The motion through space which is what we call time is divided by the bar in music. That's pretty obvious, she thought. Where is he going with this? Where does he think I've been all these years, studying cosmetology? One of the first things you learn in music is that the tune keeps going and it doesn't stop just because you don't know where the fuck you are in the form and in the time. Was he giving her a lesson too basic to be interesting? So? But, Bobo said, in jazz, the time doesn't just pass as it's defined the way it does on a ticking clock or a metronome; it *interprets* the tempo through swing, propels you, supports you, and it *talks* to you, comments on your own activity, and *you* talk with it.

A little wow filled her heart as she thought about that, assuming, with a bit of humor, that she had been a dunce for who knows how long. Little wow or not, this thrill, actually, was beyond any single kind of defining. This sudden hurling of her consciousness into an area of virgin recognition must have been close in the chill it gave her to what Columbus felt when he first saw the Western Hemisphere. Realizing how bizarre it is to stand beneath the stars with such a charitable attitude toward yourself that you think you really know anything, using your misunderstandings as far too serious little chess pieces of rationalization, Carla was glad that she hadn't let anything stupid slip from between her lips as Bobo spoke to her about another world of time. Saved by the bell of her indignant silence.

When the girl from South Dakota and her man from East St. Louis were making music together from that day forward and she felt the nuances of what he meant as his contrapuntal beats interacted with her phrases and her phrases interacted with his percussive commentary, Carla knew that her waiting it out had resulted in the discovery of a new road of artistic light and a fresh understanding of life itself, one in which the human being was able to actually converse with the motion through space that was time: the durations, which were usually so oppressive in their swift, meaningless, and impersonal tickings, became symbolic partners in your life. You stood up to the motion of time, all of it, the past and the present. So improvising for expression and form was more than summoning up the past through memory, searching for lost time; it was more than dreaming or wishing; it was achieving the full emotion of pure existence while in cooperative dialogue with time. That was what the party was all about. You swung together. And when there was a bass player jamming with them, interpreting the harmony and the rhythm as a double force, his rhythm and his harmony *spoke* to you and *you* spoke to them, since the chords were also entities unto themselves that could take on surprising distinctions of interpretation. So the bass part was in cahoots with how Bobo's rhythms inside, around, over, and under the basic beat of the time might arrive, either as one angle or two or three, his conception being that improvised polyrhythm was the percussive version of the ongoing voicing of chords, something he discovered studying Max Roach, Art Blakey, Roy Haynes, Philly Joe Jones, Ed Blackwell, and Elvin Jones. In the center of that, singing her own line while responding to the other musicians, rhythmically and harmonically, Carla began moving on up to higher musical ground. She was also discovering another wide-open room in the meaning of home.

Still, that New York conversation with Maxwell was pushing its way in. Finally, submitting to what seemed the separate will of her own memory, Carla went back to an afternoon in their West Village apartment when she was walking around in some red long johns Maxwell had bought her and hidden under the blanket on the bed so that she would find them when she got ready to turn in. That was his habit, always buying her little surprise gifts he would stash in the medicine cabinet, in the pockets of her coats and dresses, under dishes left on the sink. Bracelets, earrings, watches, pins, brooches, normal house slippers, all of them things she loved immediately, none of them given to her directly. Every now and then months might pass before she found something. Whenever he went on the road, she could be sure there were concealed presents around the house, ones that were easy to find and made her not only miss him more but cherish, up just another notch or so, the sweetness of his feeling for her—which was, of course, why that argument, another one of his dismissals of feminism, made her so angry. Her point was, as usual, just a simple one, something obvious, nothing to spark an argument. But he came right at her, the sound of riled patriarchy shooting out of his voice.

"You don't have that right."

"You would know."

"Right: I would."

"I can't believe how arrogant you men can be."

"I don't know about all of that. But I know that what you're saying is way off. You don't get this one right. None of that stuff you're saying is correct."

"So you think black people can tell when they're being made fun of or they can tell when somebody is subjecting them to some goddam hateful contempt but women can't?"

"I'm not talking about race."

"This is just an example of—"

"It's wrong. *You're* wrong. Misogyny starts on a different plane altogether, which is something you women might *talk* about, but what I'm talking about is more personal. It doesn't have *anything* to do with society structures and all of that stuff."

"That is preposterous."

"Oh, yeah?"

"Absolutely. Misogyny is built into the culture."

"Maybe so. That part you all know about—and that's *all* you all know about. But there's another side. Oh, yes. There is. What it really has to do with is what happens when a guy just starts taking a woman out, you know?"

"No, I don't know."

"Well, this guy—*any* guy—he's just getting to know about women and he expects something and she gives him the impression that he *should* expect something. You know how women lead a guy to believe they're all so far up on the fucking shelf."

"There's nothing wrong with self-esteem."

"Nothing at all. I support that. Good. But let's *continue.* So this guy and this girl—"

"Why does she have to be a girl? Why can't she be a woman?"

"Let her be a woman then."

"I'll accept that."

"I'm glad you will."

What an ass he seemed right then.

"So this young guy and this young woman talk on the phone, they take walks, they go out here and they go to this place and that kind of place. Courtship and all of that. Every bit of it. The guy is patient; he tries to be entertaining to the woman."

"Is this nameless Mr. Him doing her a *favor* by not being dull?"

"Not at all. A man is *supposed* to be entertaining to a woman."

"I'm glad we agree on that. Go on."

"Mm-hm. She gives him the impression that he's closing in on something too hot to talk about. Her arrogance and her little pushing away tells him that. Then she puts that acid kiss on him and he's *done* for. Now his mouth has that *sweet* burning. He starts dreaming about her when she's not there."

That was unexpected.

"As far as our boy is concerned, this woman has so much soul everybody ought to know it. This woman didn't need nightfall. Her soul was glowing in the *daytime.*"

Sweet, very sweet. Oh.

"She walks around all the time right inside his mind. He really desires her now. He's really loving her now. He's seeing double. The whole world is just two different things now: her *all* the time and *then* everything else. He couldn't stop thinking about her unless he got some goddam brain damage. Then what's up gets broken down. Busted: the guy and the girl go to bed and he finds out the pussy's not shit."

"You know I don't like those kinds of words. I don't like that dirty-mouth stuff. It's degrading. To you and to me. We don't have to climb down the toilet, Maxwell, just to talk. Besides, I hate the direction of this conversation."

"That's just a little too bad. I have a point to make."

"You haven't made it yet?"

"No, I haven't."

"Well, if it's not any more interesting than what you've already said, I don't want to hear it. I don't want to hear it at all."

"Oh, it's interesting. But you have to give something a chance.

Now let's get back to that moment. The moment in *bed*. *That's* where misogyny starts: when a guy goes through all of that and the pussy's not shit."

She couldn't believe she was living with this man.

"Now to God, Original Sin might be getting in the bed in Eden in the first place, or in a bed of leaves, or wherever Adam and Eve got down to business. But to just a man out here, hey, what Original Sin is *now* is that the quality of the pussy is not worth the trouble. I know Adam thought about *that* when he was out there busting his ass after he and Eve got eighty-sixed from paradise."

"I want you to know that I hate what you're saying."

"Right."

His smugness put a higher boil to her blood.

"Anyway, I know what Eve gave him couldn't have been any good. And that's *still* how it is. That's why so many guys are out here frustrated at this very minute. Right now. This very second. Poor guys. Damn. They're having all kind of wild-assed sex but nobody's giving up any *pussy.*"

Carla's face could have been an orange flame.

"Are you crazy? Do you have any idea what kind of bullshit you are talking right here in our house? In our *home,* where we sleep together? This is infuriating. This is *such* bullshit. It isn't about somebody *giving* somebody else some *pussy,* as you so repulsively want to call it. It's about two people communicating with each other and creating something from the heart."

"That's what *I'm* saying."

"It is *not.*"

"Oh, yes it is."

"Be serious."

"Listen. You can do it. Try to listen. You can do it."

"Don't insult me, you jerk. Don't talk to me like I'm a child."

There was a silence as he looked at her, his eyes moving further and further beyond the surface of her pupils, until she felt inhabited.

"Stop looking so angry. Come on now. I'm talking to you, baby, like you are the one and only Carla, which says it all."

That softness took her off guard.

"Now listen. There's a class struggle and there's an ass struggle, and what *I'm* running down is coming straight out of the jungle."

"What? Oh. How profound—or should I say primal?"

"Makes me no never mind because I mean the he and she that will *always* be. I'm talking about the voodoo of the battle over the quality of the boody. Laugh that haughty laugh if you want to. But here it is: All these women running around out here and they know all these tricks and all kind of positions and whatnot. Hoochie power. Hoing up and hoing down, hoing all around the town. Very good. They worked at something. They studied. But not *really,* because they don't know how to give up some *serious* pussy. They don't know how to take all their clothes off and push their hearts through their bodies. That's some *pussy.* That's what *I'm* talking about. I mean *serious.* Sometimes with that snooty balooty shit you talk I forget—just for a second now, only a second—I forget just how sweet it is to be loved by a woman who knows how to put her entire heart all the way through her body. Her entire heart. Every last sigh and whimper of how she really feels. Her complete heart. I mean you. Your heart, baby. Then I got to meet you with mine. I have to equal *you.* That's what I'm talking about. That's what I want to do. That's what you *make* me do. You don't leave me with *any other choice. That's* why I love *you.*"

She just stared at him. There was nothing she could say. Maxwell kissed her on the lips very softly, so softly his mouth seemed to become part of hers.

"Look, I'm going to the store," he said, slipping on a sweatshirt. "You want me to bring you anything?"

"What did you say? Oh. No, I'm fine. Nothing. I just want you to come back here, babe, and be with me right here. That's all I want. That's all."

Her mood in Houston was happy again and lonely again. Well, that was *their* side of the story, she thought, turning in the guest bed, rubbing her leg against her man's, feeling neither full nor empty, and listening for a bit to the air conditioner, which had a hobbling bossa nova rhythm that would always mean the Davis household to her if she heard it anywhere again. She couldn't see Maxwell but had the willed hallucination that his body was in perfect outline, that she was watching him sleep, which he enjoyed in reverse when she was completely crashed out and, according to him, moved her mouth as if she were alternately whistling and sucking on something. She doubted that his description of her in the land of Nod was more than a veiled come-on, but, yep, all that he had said about the disillusionment of sexual encounters wasn't *all* there was to be said on the issue. How the hell could that be? Huh? The truth under the ruckus was that so much of what had happened between men and women in Carla's time was based on how unsatisfied *her* sex was with the performances of the guys who carried themselves like they were such hot stuff but presented the fairer side of the species with unfair memories that they could have done without. Maxwell could have been teasing her. That wasn't impossible. Maxwell. What a satirical gadfly. Carla knew she had as much love for being teased as hatred.

She now felt as though she were enveloped by a melancholy lullaby, but one that held her back from sleep. It had no notes; it had no words. It was just a lullaby rocking her but moving nothing at all.

Speaking to him in a silent way, as she sometimes did while he was dozing, the girl from South Dakota sat up, her thoughts directed at Maxwell. They might not have actually been thoughts. Perhaps just a mix of associations, impressions from up against the wall of her life, the kinds of things she wanted him to sense about her and that he did when she was lucky. Some were autobiographical, some she had listened to, others had carried her into worlds she didn't ever expect to enter or to leave so suddenly, even desperately. Right now she really wanted him to hear her. Just listen. Oh, God. If she could wake him up and tell him about herself in another pattern of greater detail, they might get into something else, a fresh galaxy of understanding, a place where she was less mysterious to him and more evident even to herself. Yeah, sure. Their delicate situation, in frosty truth, might not benefit anyway. That didn't stop her from meditating, traveling neither by land nor by sea nor by air. She slid back down and let her mind have its way. Once more recollection was victorious. Why shouldn't it be? Who the hell was close enough to care? There was no one there in her head but herself. She might as well do some traveling all alone.

Instead of saying Good morning, blues, I might as well say Hello, Mr. Memory. Mr. Memory, how do you do? Mr. Memory might not be a glamour-puss, but he sure knows how to open a sarcophagus. He doesn't listen to any self-pitying wail from a frail, because he's an ice-cold, savage hellhound on my trail. He doesn't shoot you down with any kind of lead, he just snatches your brain and buries it among your dead.

She clearly was lying on a bed of evil nails this night. She might as well get on with the gloom, she might as well, like they say, dust her broom. It never took long to get back to where you had been. All the tickets were express and either first-class or no-class. That's right: traveling all alone. Let's go.

In that period of insolent and defensive promiscuity, when she was doing a stiff-upper-lip number, at the point where she pushed herself beyond the effects of a nearly fatal calamity that had kept her out of public view for a while—around the angry time that she had wanted to slap Ramona in the face after they had come home to see about backing Dad away from the burden of white liquor, the Bombay martini grave of alcoholism he was swallowing himself into—Carla had learned so much that she didn't want to know. Most of it had to do with being made a spectator to the erotic repertory of the Manhattan guys from whom she sought the intensity of attention that had been so basic to her high school years as Miss Thing, swinging along and examining a daisy chain of admirers, each of them hoping to smell good enough to be singled out as someone the female pride of the campus would notice, then pin to her social apparel.

Mr. Memory, like a truant officer with bulldog tenacity, searched through those bedrooms and those nights, those smells and those gasps so sensual but so filled with the funky blue air of dissatisfaction. Pulling the empty loving along by its ear, Mr. Memory then took the girl from South Dakota out of that montage of insufficient touches and decisively brought her to a school of feeling much, much nearer to the time in which she actually existed. Whew! Leeann, Cecelia, Toots Celestine.

Oh, what a night.

She touched her sleeping man and wondered what Maxwell would have thought if he had gone out there with her and her ace boon buddies on that evening which had been put under the microscope of sour romance, picked over by the magnification of the blues and dressed down by a blues shout in a town house. Glee spread inside her heart and she chuckled, shaking her head.

Then, her nose toying with the scent left on her skin from their lovemaking and the idea of getting up to take a shower having its own attraction, she knew that late post-Celestine gathering at Leeann's was no place for him or for any guy, off-limits. Well, separate experiences were still part of the law of the way she had lived, *only* Carla knowing everything about where she had been and what she had done. There had been no amendments.

Law or not, it felt a little tight now in this Houston night and there was still the desire to confess herself closer to Maxwell and pretend that telling him her story was a way of being intimate. Ha. She actually didn't believe that interior hustle. It wasn't about that "I'm confessing" bullshit. From her perspective, love so frequently had most to do with standing behind somebody and correctly sensing who they were and letting them have all of the privacy that they needed. It always came back to how private she was. That wasn't the happiest of the two or three truest things she knew about herself.

A fact, yes, but she was having herself a good time on that night of extra schooling at Leeann's. How about that? Her experience was *not* just one miserable gathering of irritation, distrust, and anxiety because all was far from well with her sleeping saxophone player. There was more going on than wanting to maybe get married and maybe have a baby or two before it was too late. The more was something to say thank you for. The instant she said that, Carla felt the sensuousness of life preening itself all over her as she went into the bathroom and got into the shower, loving the wetness falling on her like big warm stars that became liquid light on contact and washed some of the darkness out of her heart, let her relax as she enjoyed the disappearance of dryness that transformed her into part of the hot water and made the reliving of the hot conversation such a perfect retort to Maxwell's erotic theory of the trouble with heing and sheing. What a wacked-out vision of misogny's beginnings. Nutball. So stupidly and indisputably male, which, when it came to understanding, so often rhymed with fail.

Maxwell would have been straightened out if he had been there. Cecelia would have swallowed him like a hog does a snake. No doubt about it. A song started coming up, beginning right where her feet touched the tiles, but it wouldn't be respectful to get loud in the house of Ezekiel and Eunice the way she could showering at home when her man was dead to the world and nobody else could hear anyway. So she just hummed softly from the bottom of her throat and went back to Manhattan.

It was girl talk that night, maybe inconsequential to all the guys but apropos of what Carla considered the catty-corner mood up on a high plane of pleasure. Dames all, talking about the tribulations of looking good and what they liked to wear, they were on their game. Oh, did they all meow about the ups and downs of this and that, the who, the how, the why, dishing out stuff that was way above the dirt.

"Now we got the Viagra curse," said Leeann's cousin up from Washington, Cecelia, who was copper-colored, buxom, and especially beautiful, her burnt-orange hair worn in a very smart Afro of angular crests, and her green eyes alternating a fire equal in the height of its volatile contemplation to the sophisticated deeps of an unwavering tenderness. The three of them, full of the night, were sitting around in Leeann's town house after an evening of running through the city, drinking, eating, dancing, and flirting a few weeks before Maxwell returned from the road and the plans were made for the trip to Houston.

As always, they had greatly enjoyed each other and Carla was happy once again to see Cecelia, whom she had known now since around a year before Bobo's death, and who, even though nothing was ever said, seemed to disapprove of her going out with Bobo and Maxwell. Well, she wasn't the only black woman like that. You took that in stride. Even so, it was obvious that Cecelia liked her because that woman seemed incapable of putting on a mask or spending an evening in the company of someone whom she held in low regard. Cecelia now had a long-distance love affair going on with an expatriate writer named Kelvin Thomson but usually had troubles with men because, she once said around the time Leeann introduced her, "they think I'm too much work. That's what they tell me. I don't think about it much, though. No, I don't. If I did, I don't know if I would find time to think about anything else. I would end up laying back in a big puddle of sorry for myself. So I spend a lot of time watching myself being myself. It's not the same as being myself with somebody just a little special, but that's the best I can do right now. Yes, that's the best I can do."

The best that Leeann, Cecelia, and Carla could do on that recent night, however, had been pretty damn good. Each of them was in a mood before the groove came around. Something wasn't right in the world. They dodged specific discussion of the wobbles and foibles, though. Late in the afternoon they preferred discussing their hair and what they were going to wear that night and the various kinds of fights they had seen men having with women over the years, invariably concluding that, when it got down to the last bitter corner of the bottle, they might get plenty tired of the ignorance so endemic to the opposite sex but wouldn't trade the high-flying sides of their romances for the ostrich style of staring at worms and moles. No worm sandwiches and rodent burgers for them.

By the time they left Leeann's, all three were laughing and joking and taking on that sort of luminous quality sophisticated ladies have over all others. As Kelvin Thomson, who could get philosophical about anything, said to Carla and Maxwell, "Those who don't know that purity and virginity have nothing to do with each other miss the high-toned polish of the blues. Wisdom, my friends, is the highest form of purity because it understands the meaning of *all* the losses, every shit-filled spot of blood you can't wash off the face of your soul."

The girl talkers weren't thinking about any kinds of losses—no, no, good Lord, good Lord—after they had taken in the city through their pores and, at Leeann's insistence, had capped off their outing with a trip to the Upper West Side apartment of Toots Celestine. The New Orleans trumpeter was the king of New York jazz at the moment and Maxwell's biggest rival, the one musician whom he was transparently jealous of, no amount of cool or silence masking how demoted Carla's man felt since this Crescent City wonder, marching on it for fifteen years, had systematically turned the town into a pretzel with his playing, his compositions, and his command post at the Manhattan Arts Complex, where he was the artistic director of the most important jazz program in the world.

"Don't mean a thing to me," Leeann said in the car, "all that stuff between him and Maxwell. That's between the boys. The girls are out tonight and I be's well aware that New Orleans man knows how to give a good goddam party. If you coming up there with me bothers Maxwell, have the nigger call *me*. I'll tell him all kinds of ways to get to the next day."

Carla didn't say anything. She just looked at Boris's gray Russian eyes in the rearview mirror and wondered why it should make any difference where she went, given the way things were now. Besides, she was curious as to how Celestine's party would go. She had heard they were swinging almost off the deep end and that he lived in a swank situation of the sort that didn't preclude the trumpeter playing his horn whenever he wanted or having huge gatherings in his place, which Carla had been told was filled with awards, paintings, and portraits of Louis Armstrong.

As they walked through the front of the blue-doored West End Avenue high-rise, passing the black-coated, white-gloved doorman and sinking just a bit into the gold and maroon carpet, Carla could not believe that a jazz musician was living like this. Glass paneling. Good paintings in the lobby. Big leather couches and leather chairs. Wealthy people walking in and out. How was this possible? Some of Maxwell's jealousy rubbed off to such an extent that she could feel the snooty balooty taking over her chest and putting her head at a tilt. As she fumed on the elevator up to the thirty-fifth floor penthouse, it struck her that this was the way those musicians who looked at Maxwell's clothes and his deportment felt as they stood near him in the clubs and saw him in the streets or stared bitterly at the big posters hanging from the ceilings of Tower Records, advertising his recordings when he was there signing newly released compact discs.

What put the real turn on her, however, was the smell that came from the partially cracked door as soon as they got off the elevator. The door had what amounted to a comical coat of arms painted on an ebony square of wood. Louis Armstrong's face as the King of the Zulus at Mardi Gras was in the middle. Beneath Armstrong's face were the words:

Gully Low:
S.O.L.

In the top left corner of the ebony square was a chicken, across from it a shrimp, in the right corner below a red bean, and at the bottom on the left was a grain of rice.

As far as Carla could see, at least for this night, it was actually a menu. Celestine had his cousin in the kitchen, a huge reddish-brown Negro with a thick Crescent City accent and a long black cigar, unlit, stretching from between his teeth as he cooked big pots of gumbo, red beans, and rice. The trumpeter was in the extremely large main room of his long, T-shaped apartment. He sat at the piano, with huge windows filling two walls behind him. Wickedly snickering or bursting into laughter between phrases, Celestine was playing and singing a dirty, dirty blues as Leeann, Cecelia, and Carla—like three of the finest women God decided to tantalize the world with—came into the crowded party. Since it was spring panting up on summer, they didn't wear any wraps. Immediately the girl talkers had glasses of Veuve Clicquot La Grande Dame shoved into their hands by some high yellow drunken buddy of Celestine's who, muscular enough to be a bouncer, was playing butler, server, and announcer, shouting, "Make way for these three graces. My, my, my, it couldn't be sweeter if it was homemade apple pie."

"I like this already," Cecelia said. "Cheers."

They sipped their champagne.

"Lord have mercy, this is good!" said Cecelia.

"What did you expect—Mad Dog 20-20? You're with Leeann, baby. I know where to take my favorite cousin and my best friend."

"Here's to Leeann, queen of the night," Carla said.

"And the morning and the afternoon," Cecelia added.

"Amen," Leeann intoned with a grim look on her face before guzzling the glass empty with the parodic loud slurp of a fast-tailed hussy.

The three laughed like they were being paid for it. Their laughter hit the air at the same time as that of those who were listening to the concluding verse of Celestine's improvised dirty blues.

The party became something else altogether as the cooking was finished and the paper plates and plastic forks started filling one pair of hands after another, taking the smell of Louis Armstrong's hometown throughout the entire space, which was overrun with soulful-looking men and women, every color, every kind of hair, apparently representing all of the species. The age ranged from youngsters in their late teens and early twenties to those in their seventies. Some were musicians, others visual artists; there were dancers, actors, Celestine's hoop-shooting buddies from the neighborhood, listeners, models, lawyers, hangers-on, writers, filmmakers, students, veterans of the

New York night, tale and tail spinners, those who knew the meaning of riding the rails and could tell stories about the Great Depression, others who acted as though contact with that particular backside set of cakes would change your life even though the more expensive spread wouldn't melt in their mouths. Those plates pushed them all together in combination with the music and the greasy, enveloping, concentric circles of the groove. Crescent City, truth be told, the gumbo and the beats and the good humor removed any lines of superficial division. You couldn't tell the shrimp from the chicken or the chicken from the sausage or the sausage from the shrimp. It was all good.

This was Carla's kind of party. There was no denying it. She loved the taste of the food and it was nice to be getting plenty of attention from some guys other than Maxwell in an atmosphere that was so seductively convivial something inside her wanted to stand up and holler like a mountain goat. Before the girl from South Dakota knew it, she had downed about three glasses of champagne and was having her second plate of gumbo and rice. Hold on. This was a little loose for her. Carla got some chicory coffee from the kitchen to steady herself. She wasn't about to get tipsy. Leeann was over by the stove teasing the cook and flirting with him.

Cecelia was the first to start waving a handkerchief and strutting when Celestine and the musicians began playing "Liza Jane" in second line fashion and the party members got to marching through the apartment, ending up back in the main room and hugging up into each other as the host gave a golden rendition of "Embraceable You." Carla—now fully rebelling against Maxwell's jealousy—wanted to go over and sing with him but had to sit in the bathroom first, where she found herself humming "I'm Gonna Wash That Man Right Out of My Hair."

When Celestine saw Carla, he called her over to the piano and said, "Now I know you're going to sing one of those good hot blues numbers with us. We got all the musicians here."

She stepped out of her shoes and stood with the backdrop of the New York skyline behind her. She wasn't wearing stockings and the carpet felt just right under her feet. She stared at him and said, " 'Fine and Mellow.' B-flat."

"Uh-oh. You want to get serious, huh?"

"Let's hit it, Mr. Man."

"Yes, I see. I better get armed for this. Bubby, take over this piano. I see I'm going to have to get my horn."

"Aw, man, I don't want my red beans and rice to get cold."

"Come on, Bubby. We'll put some hot blues up in here and keep everything warm, from the food to the flesh. Oh, yes. Now if you all still feel like dancing out here, well, this is where you supposed to be. We party up in here," he said, picking up a specially designed trumpet that weighed five pounds and had the mouthpiece built in, like a bugle.

Carla counted it off but Celestine took over with an introduction of one long twelve-bar phrase of twists, slurs, high notes, and sheer blues melody that singed her ear. She didn't stutter. She answered him.

"My man don't love me/Treats me oh so mean," Carla sang, a totally unguarded timbre lightly sanding and growling into her sound.

Celestine laid some trumpet notes on her shoulder as if to say, "Yeah, baby, I know just what you saying," while Bubby stroked off a keyboard trill that pushed her further into the blue terrain her soul had been walking for nearly a year.

She almost whispered the next line as if it were a secret going public and followed that up with an acidic accusation in the rhyme as she expanded her voice.

> My man, he don't love me,
> Treats me awful mean.
> He's the lowest man
> That I've ever seen.

"Sing it, Carla, drop it down," Leeann said while dancing with one of the massive kinds of rock-hard Negroes she always joked would have gone for five thousand dollars in 1840.

Celestine took one note and, imposing color upon color, squeezed it repeatedly as if it were an entire song.

The girl from South Dakota gripped the rug with her toes as she went to each of the pitches that laid out the story under the words. That prehensile grasping at the bottom somehow helped her get the emotion into each line as Carla stepped up her register going into the repeat, painting those pants on that handsome man and coming down so far into the meat-to-meat recollections of the blues by the next rhyme that the skin on her arms almost cooled and pimpled.

> He wears high draped pants
> Stripes are really yellow;
> He wears high draped pants
> Stripes are really yellow.
> But when he starts in to love me
> He's so fine and mellow.

She heard an alto saxophone, then a tenor join in, and a drummer had put down his plate to sit behind the traps, laying out a wide, medium-slow pong-pong-pong-pong on the cymbal, the reverberation stepping into her bloodstream as a bass line, with grease-laden harmony made of shadows three feet deep, took over the lower side of the rhythm. Oh, she was feeling it now and she was surrounded by the same kind of masculinity Carla had observed as a high school cheerleader when the clunky yellow bus was taking the victorious football team home and she had never felt more feminine. This time, though, right in the middle of the blues, everybody was equal to the action—no room for squares—and she was the quarterback, calling the plays and throwing the passes out of her throat, which was, like her heart, all the way open. She told a tale now that she had seen and absorbed out there in that air-conditioned jungle. But the statistics and the photographs and the pratfalls between barstools became spiritual as Carla raised herself up beyond observation into the ambiguity of passion where music becomes a voice of the unspeakable, where words are only beginnings, touching points, entrances to the unknowable that can only be understood if there's enough soul to go the distance. Her classical training allowed for a sound of such magnitude that the guys didn't have to back away in order to allow this woman the freedom of space that keeps a singer without a microphone from being smothered. She was meeting them, and as they touched in the invisible huddle of the rhythm, Carla called some gutbucket verities into the room, hitting the next to last word of the third line with a correct and saucy illiteracy that inspired calls of approval from the dancers: "All right now, get below sea level."

> Love will make you drink and gamble,
> Make you stay out all night long,
> Love will make you drink and gamble,
> Make you stay out all night long.
> Love will make you do things
> That you know is wrong.

Then there had to come the promise and the hard threat that she was living but had never made to her man, her man to whom she was not even talking at this moment. Instead, she was experiencing the full brand of existence that only arrived when the music started and there was no fooling and jacking around. Not goddam now. The human accuracy in the art of organizing the throes of the spirit was—from note to note, beat to beat, nuance to nuance—being gracefully handed back and forth as though clumsiness would remove some big chance out of the life that was going by at this instant. In that oh so expensive apartment overlooking the city, with the smell of gumbo, red beans, and rice in the air, with the pale moon shining down on all that was happening—fair, foul, and beyond giving a fuck—there was a single but collective shot at making the spiteful present, the meaningless thrust of time, submit to a story and hold back its arbitrary disregard, all the while putting that woman's head on that man's shoulder, tightening this other guy's arm around the throbbing waist of his partner, and pushing one pair of navels after another into contact. This—if there were actual justice in the world—was the way it was supposed to be. No matter, baby. No matter, sweet cakes. No matter at all. Just rest up against this heart. The whole band seemed to be inside her as the next stanza swelled out of Carla, heating her throat and mouth.

> But if you treat me right, baby,
> I'll stay home every day;
> If you just treat me right, baby,
> I'll stay home night and day.
> But you so mean to me, baby,
> I know you're gonna drive me away.

The musicians were patting her on the back and embracing her and agreeing through their instruments, Celestine now using a rubber plunger and vocalizing the brass out of his horn, the alto and the tenor twisting up blues knots of stark, crooning melody, the drummer coming down on a backbeat that wasn't too strong while he had a sexy little triplet bouncing off of his snare that made her feel as if time were gamely patting her on the ass, and the bass fiddle, as grave as it was ebullient, created for Carla the sensation of passing its harmonies into her chest. Her voice was all the way into precise freedom now and she was able to build, first throwing off the initial line with incipient hostility, then making the second a more chilly perception as well as a prelude to an admonishment, a communal wound making plain the mortal fools we can so easily be. She hit the last word and the last note up above the head of high C and flared it out into an ominous thorn, not as a stunt but as if she were actually trying to toot her soul up through the roof.

> Love is just like a faucet,
> It turns off and on;
> Love is like a faucet,
> It turns off and on.
> Sometimes when you think it's on baby,
> It has turned off and gone.

"I say all right now," Celestine crowed with high regard, "we got somebody right here in this room who knows what's going on out here. She knows the blues is a traveling thing and a waiting thing. It goes with you and it waits for you. Oh, yes. What? Be serious. It's not over. Hell, no. Not tonight. Now we're getting ready to do some *swinging* up in here. What? I heard you. I know. Yeah, you right. You right about that, too. You better believe it. You know we're not going to let this woman go. She's not going to put her shoes back on and get out of here without a whole lot more singing. Excuse me. That is, if she feels like it."

Oh, she felt like it. Carla had to sing, sing, sing until the party had thinned out and it was almost time to go. As the musicians got some more to drink and to eat, a small woman from the Far East came up to her.

"I am singer, too," she said, "and you give me courage tonight."

"Courage?"

"Courage, yes. I am from Japan, as you can see. This music is not from Japan but it is in my heart."

Carla nodded.

"I work very hard to sing but I did not think I could get this right until this time when you were singing. It was so beautiful what you have the things that are too much for the Japanese people. They do not like the too much colors and smells when Billie Holiday and Dinah Washington are singing. That is not many of their records there in the stores. They like all the smooth singing in Japan. You have the smooth, very smooth, which I, too, have. But in the way you make the note is the colors and the smells that I did not think I could get ever at all. Now I have *courage* to *try*. Now I have. It is now I am willing to work hard for the extra that you sing so *very, very* confident. I want to thank you for this. You are very wonderful for someone who wants to learn."

Carla thanked her with as much warm grace as she could and went to the bathroom, not able to understand exactly what the woman was saying to her. Was she talking about race? Did she mean that seeing a white singer do this made her feel that she might be able to get up there and swing and sing the blues? It was probably something like that, which Carla both appreciated and resented, knowing the Japanese were too polite to say it that directly. In this case, polite was the right way to go, since her color was the last goddam thing she wanted to hear about. If she hadn't had herself such a time singing; if she hadn't so enjoyed coolly kicking back on the couch in her bare feet and explaining to the musicians how using triplet eighths and other subdivisions *within* quarter-note triplets allowed her to swing completely different kinds of rhythms while *right inside* four/four; if the girl from South Dakota hadn't suddenly remembered, as she sat schooling the musicians and the Japanese singer again smiled at her with such admiration, how she herself had listened, in the tiny apartment and at Bobo's, to her own homegirl over and over and over on *Basin Street Proudly Presents Peggy Lee,* struck every time by her ease, her swing, her understated manner, her humor, the confidently tasteful eroticism and the spiritually fluid intensity of expression Lee was able to bring off through subtle varieties of attack and vibrato, an artistry so thoroughly soulful that it convinced Carla—which no other white woman singing jazz ever had—that maybe she, *too,* could actually get there with complete freedom, just like the established Scandinavian babe up on the Basin Street bandstand, the bluesy blonde who had been christened Norma Egstrom and reared equally far from blues and swing country; if all of that passion and reflection had not come around to her, this party girl out on the town with her buddies would have been extremely pissed off. As it was, since the trouble with Maxwell meant that she no longer enjoyed being a symbol of anything of any sort other than her individual self, the idea of becoming a Statue of Liberty beckoning with a sticky handful of chitlins to those immigrant masses who wanted access to the power of the gutbucket was still somewhat bothersome.

What *masses?* she laughed to herself while sprucing up her eye shadow and putting on some lipstick in the very bathroom where, according to Leeann, one of Celestine's many women, a very, very beautiful black executive from Boston who earned a fine living selling Negro memorabilia, fell to her knees for a groaning mouthful after she, while cold sober, became so heated up about her trumpet man at one of his parties that she pushed him behind the door before she could stop herself. Was that the kind of thing that Maxwell wanted now, a gorgeous and successful black woman so oblivious to the outside world that it didn't matter who knew what she did and where she did it? Well, this one right here was not about to be that way. Neither repression nor prudishness was the problem. When it came to the sticking place, she had plenty of ragtime in her soul. He knew. But would Maxwell ever remember now that they had done things almost like that Boston woman and more, childishly extending the excitement by taking the risk of getting caught in the hallway of her funky apartment house with the door keys jiggling in her hand and her red lace panties caught around one ankle as they made love against the wall, or with her best black evening dress pulled up to the top of her thighs, the sapphire and silver bell earrings he bought her tinkling and him lying back in one of the deck chairs up on the town house roof of the East River place owned by one of his wealthy fans while a party—so expensively catered it seemed like a dream—was going on full blast in the backyard down below, or kissing and hugging sometime after dawn when they had taken a long walk all the way from the Village to midtown following the last call at Good Henry's and, caught up in the feeling, sought doorways and hiding places behind bus stops where they could feel each other up with more and more fervor until the returning destination of his place or hers needed to be fireproofed before they entered? No, blondie rondie, he might not be remembering that right now. This bum is thinking of a big, big sandwich of something else he's hungry for instead of you.

"Carla," Celestine said as they were about to leave, "tell Maxwell to call me. I want him to go out on the road with me as a guest in my band. All over the world. The whole world. Yeah. He's been on my mind for a while. Next year I want to write a big, long piece for him to put all that Texas soul on."

"Sounds good to me. I'll tell you what. Let me find it. Hold on. Where is it? There. Here's my card. We have the same phone number. It would be better if you told him what you want to do."

Carla, furiously jealous, wondered when Celestine might want to use her as a South Dakota soul-girl guest all over the world. She thought the hell with it, fought off acting stiff when he fraternally embraced her, kissed her on the cheek, and said how much everybody appreciated her lifting up the music and letting them know—yaz, yaz, yaz—that singing wasn't a forgotten thing.

Disappointed after all of that groove, Carla was in the mood for the catty corner when they got back to Leeann's. The sweet side of life just couldn't make it into the end zone, could it? Dead on the two-yard line.

Now, with the sweep of whirlwind fun behind them, the three girl talkers were relaxed big-time and the wee small hours were getting larger. It was not so far from dawn and the big moon that had fully starred throughout the cloudless night was getting ready to fall down before the rising of the sun. With increasing acrimony, they were discussing the Manhattan and the nation that were theirs to take and theirs never to have, each writing her bitch list on the air with a red-hot poker of feeling. When they got back around to men and what was happening in the hour of their discontent, Cecelia launched into a fog of passion that made the moment of her expression have less to do with clearly seeing anything than getting beyond seeing to experiencing the private station of a person's spirit: all of the observations and picked-up details from friends amalgamating with her own autobiography, the central temper one formed of a yearning that could slip by your recognition if you got stuck in the words themselves and the deprecating tone of Cecelia's voice. That was what Carla had gradually learned about the combative street-corner posture that Dad said came into being and took on more and more space in attitude and social exchange after the assassination of Martin Luther King: these black people often had a presentation abrasiveness of manner and talk that gave off much less actual emotion than you thought. This presentation personality reminded her of certain kinds of New York Jews and Italians in that it was sometimes a test to see if you could actually pay attention, if you were truly interested enough to listen for all of the notes of the dense human chord, not just the obvious ones, the triadic edifices of prickly clichés. Cecelia nearly always forced Carla to listen that way because she was, like Leeann, a very, very smart woman with a very, very profane mouth.

On that particular night, for all the high fun at Celestine's, the voluptuous fifty-year-old copper-colored beauty who hadn't been married for fifteen years, oh, she was gone and she pulled the other two women right along with her. The still steady years with Kelvin Thomson weren't even referred to; those were beside the point.

They had moved from Leeann's long dinner table, all of them barefoot, and were sitting in her soft leather chairs. As Cecelia got into the broil of her emotion, she stood and began to pace back and forth with rum and Coke in hand, pausing now and then to take a sip, giving the impression that she was talking not to her friends but to a jury that was hearing opening or closing statements. Sometimes, in midflight, Cecelia scorched the space before her with the look of someone staring at the most reprehensible defendant who had ever pissed between two shoes.

"That's what I said: the Viagra curse. These same tired motherfuckers who been doing the same tired shit for thirty years, who haven't thought about one new position, one new thing, one something that could make it a *partnership*, now, after you have had to put up with their trifling shit for who knows how many times in the bed, now they get old and what used to be torturously boring is finally over in twenty minutes so you can go back to fantasizing about having somebody who touches you and makes you feel so special you want to cry. No good. Not that kind of luck anymore. These niggers go get their little blue Viagra pills and you have to put up with four *hours* of that tired shit. *Now* the niggers get to running around and waving their dicks at everybody again. You got to go through that *all over again*. No rest for the weary. But it doesn't stop there. Why should it? It never has before. Now these little airheaded bitches who flip their fucking shoulder-length hair around because they've gone and made Asian and Filipino hair a new colonial cash crop that's imported and *fused* to their nappy heads with plastic and a special pressing iron, strand by strand—that's right: *strand by strand*—these little tiresome young fools, who are yellow or wish they were but, at least, can now compete, flip for flip in the hair battle, these black, brown, beige, and bone bitches with their glossy lipstick and their batting eyes and their fucking inferior or superior positions in the pigmentocracy of Washington, D. motherfucking C., they can end up under some powerful nigger who might be *your* nigger and who used to leave them alone out of default because he had *finally* gotten to the point that he *couldn't* fuck but one woman anymore. And *if, if* you do get somebody who's good-looking and grown and seems like he knows how to handle himself—you know, a brother with some actual charm, not just some bullshit—most of the time you have to lie there and become a member of an audience of one as you observe the brother get *down*. Instead of applause, you come. The niggers would *bow* if they didn't have one little dot of discretion moving across the seventy-foot screens of their egotistical goddam minds. Left to themselves, though, they would take off their black derby hats and wave like Melvin Van Peebles did in *Sweetback* when he tamed the big-assed white girl who was in charge of all those scroungy biker motherfuckers, nothing but pissy-drunk Klansmen rolling on two rubber wheels apiece. Oh, now Miss Pink Lady was rough and she was tough and she could lift a whole motorcycle by herself and all that shit, but when she laid her flat ass down and he dropped on top of her she got so hot and so helpless she had to call the nigger by his *name*. *Sweetback*. A minstrel with a hard dick. *Always* onstage."

Wow, Cecelia, she thought as it began to move toward another Houston dawn and Maxwell was still hanging out with brother Morpheus. Well, here she was, clean and fresh, too tired to do anything about sleep—not the type who ever took pills for anything unless nearly forced—and thinking about what Cecelia had said. Sometimes it goes like that. Cecelia was right. You could surely be made an audience member instead of a lover, Carla thought as she finally fell asleep.

SKY VIEW IN BLUE: CROSS TIME CATCH-UP

Y EAH, SHE WAS familiar with what it meant to be an audience member. That was the way Carla felt in her twenties. As she slept now, her mind avoided bringing to the visible surface that is a dream any of the romantic elements she had neither been reminded of nor thought about during this Houston visit so filled with stories and memories. Lying next to Maxwell with the morning light on her sleeping face, she had only so much space for overt mental involvement and was already exhausted, heart and soul. She needed nothing else to trouble her, no more blues, no more worries. Her mind knew that quite well, just as her mind, now a sleepless dog catcher, knew that her twenties were forever alive, so much so that a few words such as those she had recalled Cecelia saying could whistle those years up and that period of the well-kept pet would come panting in with the newspaper of that part of her life in its mouth. She didn't need all of that, not the muddy tracks clearly visible, not the headlines, the editorial columns, the restaurant reviews, the society page, the gossip, the sports section. This was not the time. Consequently, there was not even the vivid mystery play in which what takes place turns the sleeper, upon awakening, into a befuddled detective who must decode the emotions disguised in strange images. Carla saw again exactly what had happened, but only through touch, the hand of recollection run over those objects of experience as if she were blind, or as if she were a swimmer moving through a dark, dark water of varying temperatures. This allowed her to feel the whole period of high-class serving positions and high-class experience but forget it by the time she awoke.

It was a bit withering, what she peeped out. It was thirteen or fourteen years ago. It was the city's fault as far she could see then. It wasn't her normal way but it became normal a little bit too fast. New York would do that to the unsuspecting. Blame it on the spiritually maiming buildings and the population and the intolerable impatience invisibly snaking around you.

The density of Manhattan put something on her mind that the girl from South Dakota had never thought of at home and didn't have to bother about in Chicago. In a couple of years, the idea of being a stranger and pioneering her way into recognition lost its appeal. Finding out she wasn't all that special actually startled her. New York hit you with blunt objects and made you acknowledge blunt things. Just like every other woman in New York, Carla had the same love bush and wanted largely the same good treatment and was, finally, either available like almost every single woman who didn't hate men, or wasn't, like the few single women who were at war with their own loneliness and didn't want to be taken prisoner by the needs that could lead them to humiliate themselves.

Now Carla wasn't exactly humiliated when she found herself in the bedrooms of guys who had done well in the world of work or who could take her to their Long Island homes or up into Connecticut, where she rode magnificently bred chestnut horses and experienced the greenery surrounding an estate where a sailboat moored down the hill leisurely bobbed back and forth. No, there was no direct humiliation, but she learned what it felt like to be made a spectator whose orgasm was no more human to the guy than a clay pigeon exploded with a trick shot of some sort. In the phase of her life for which the holy Ramona had such contempt, Carla knew, way low in the underbelly of her loneliness, that it was a game always played by two: she was opening her legs and hiding behind her body and the rich guys were dropping their pants and hiding behind their erections.

There could also be more.

You could be touched.

Yes, you could be touched.

From what she knew of it as an outsider, coy to herself at first, the yachting and horsey and tennis sets weren't really her cup of tea. But adapting wasn't the hardest job in the world. It was actually kind of easy, especially since the help she got had such a gleam.

In that arena of life, Carla had some bona fide big fun with one you could only call a man's man, the square-shouldered, witty, well-read, athletic, and sexually powerful Barton Mulhaney, a fourth-generation Anglo-Irish broker. He was not a forgettable man and neither was the set of moons that surrounded the Jupiter of his privilege. His was a nose-bleeding world of high, high social prominence, incredibly well-appurtenanced living quarters, sportsmen with tall tales of land and sea, and women, a good many who knew about the best of everything, some who were new forces in the world of business, others who worked for their favorite charities with the unrelenting energy of Inca messengers propelled by the cocoa leaves in their mouths, and too many of whom spoke of looking like raccoons in Brazil following their face-lifts, if they were beyond a certain age.

What a world. So long ago, so far away. So different from the lakes of the Midwest and the Indian ponies. Those lakes had another taste and the water felt different on her skin. The ponies were descended from the small doses of horseflesh that lived on grass instead of grain, were light, and drove the heavy-horsed cavalry boys crazy when the wars with the Indian nations were on. Up in this other strata, where even the country greenery of the bushes and the trees seemed in the service of wealth, other things were on top and made *you* feel on top. There was nothing at all like the full scent of the ocean, the sunlight turning the water into a shining thing, the feel of a boat moving under you, or the satisfied exhaustion that came after riding, when the inside of the jodhpurs had been sweated through, leaving an embarrassing outline of your private parts in dark perspiration—except that you could pretend to an urbane and gamy sense of life far beyond what you possessed.

After first lifting your hot hair off of your neck for a minute or so, taking in the smell of athletic females, and drinking some lemonade instead of a Bloody Mary, you could smile with counterfeit knowing while listening to the older women laughing at the club after the horses had been taken to the stables. At first, the atmosphere was very butch; everything associated with being powdered, rouged, lipsticked, and perfumed into a lady was washed off by the riding and the sweating. The hair stunk, as did the underarms and the crotch. You were dusty, gritty, and in that riding club the feeling was one associated not with refined females but purely with strength and the love of it, the ability to rein in and handle one of those dangerous animals, the confidence that came of the inner thigh muscle buildup necessary to remain well seated as you went into a gallop, the knowledge of the line between sadism and sparking that came with proper use of the riding crop, and the rugged delight of being almost worn out as you dismounted but were emotionally far more ready for life than you might feel a good deal of the time.

A cloud of salty mirth swirled in once the women were comfortable in the afterglow resultant from the panting, bouncing, wind-filled return to a state that was nearly animal in its nature but remained aesthetic in that skilled balance between safety and abandon. Before they saw their horses on the way out, while they were downing the Bloody Marys and preparing to be driven home for the soaping and scrubbing and standing with shampoo in their hair for a bit, the tone of the club changed. It became much more loose, *much*. Yes, it did, particularly if one of the riders made a witty remark about the stain darkly defining the passion flower that was somebody else's warm valley. Was it, oh, just the ordinary result of exercise or, heaven forbid, could it possibly be an advertisement, or a signal of distress, or, as Frank Sinatra said, a tender trap? Say, do any of you girls remember when a sight long common to stable boys abruptly went national when Elizabeth Taylor wore those jodhpurs in *Giant?* It was during the death scene of Mercedes McCambridge, her nemesis, of course. What else could a woman who looked like that be? Beauty and the Beast. Goody Two-shoes liberal Maryland Liz, and cowboy-booted, spur-using Mercedes, pure Texas trash. Sparks between the high-minded and the low-minded wealthy. Minor-league doings, however, *so* minor-league. That part of the drama couldn't be compared to the fact that this was the very first and the very last time the lips of a major star's tangle of secret triumph was so well defined for the public eye. *True* National Velvet. What gut-busting laughter! Then, those in their late thirties and forties, even fifties, the married ones and the divorcées, began joking about just how helpful that doric outlining had been to the mating ritual strategy of bagging some guy whom you so deeply wanted to give you the sweet eye.

Carla, uncomfortable as she sipped her lemonade, thought herself in the smelly middle of a bawdy scene written by some guy for the theater, not quite real to her. Then things changed again as she heard another element in what they were saying. This lighthearted stage trampishness might also be referring to something a little heavier than the South Dakota girl understood much too quickly. It could also be, moving past the vulgar in a magical flash, an unprimped moment of primal glory. Just like the blues: When you were right there as butch as you could look and smell, the private part—made so public by the wet shadow of that androgynous horsemanship— returned you to the position of a prize that was *all* woman, *all* lady, all lover, and awfully prepared to be tenderly wooed.

That was an aspect of one side of it. There were others.

The moral center of engagement in that universe was liberal Democratic politics, not Republican. These people firmly believed that those below should get more than the drippings from the fatted calf. A number had actually been in the presence of Martin Luther King— "a *very* sexy guy by the way"—or recalled listening to the horror stories told by civil rights workers in overalls at gatherings held within mansions. The express purpose of those afternoons and evenings was raising the kinds of funds for bail and legal assistance that these upper-class people provided by writing hefty checks, coming together in their wealth with the Jews who not only supported the voter registration movement but fretted day and night when more of their children than any other whites decided to go South. As things became too radical and crazy, with young people unaccountably saying they wanted to overthrow the country, the children of highly successful whites and minorities raising their fists in the air, clubbing innocent people in the streets, sending out bombs, burning down banks, and living underground, a pall of depression fell over the liberal rich. A collective dream echoing back to the steps of the Lincoln Monument had been thrown against the wall and shot. But, being Americans, they recovered from the violent disillusionment, philosophically accepted their exceptional luxury, just like Tolstoy, and went back to doing the best they could for the downtrodden, expecting less than before but realizing that the world, after all, never stood still long enough to be fitted and dressed in a many-colored suit of social perfection.

The polished frenzy and reflective repose of all that privilege could blot out Carla's dreams of being some kind of a singer, yet never quite so much as those soothing times when, for instance, Bart would recite Sir Thomas Wyatt while bathing her in the huge tub that sat on gold eagle's claws, had an eagle's head of gold for a spout, and gold wings for hot and cold handles. Then, as she stood, scented water, mineral salts, and soap bubbles sliding down, he dried her off with a series of arousing pats and rubs delivered with big, soft terry cloth gloves.

It had begun with that Wall Street lover of Elizabethan sonnets when Carla got off work one night from the Sky View Room, which was in a Rockefeller Center building on the sixty-fifth floor, a destination arrived at by express elevator. The room was an art deco masterpiece. The spirit of the New York that had come to thunderous power in the thirties as the skyscraper went East was all over the place, its doors, its windows, its bathrooms, its lighting. At first she worked the bar known as the Sky View Promenade, which drew midtown executives, lawyers, high-class mistresses, and top-of-the-line gigolos, all very good tippers who tended to be out of there before the tourist crowd came in around eight, their deals made, their drinks had, their assignations arranged, their break-offs begun. In a few months, the cabaret room called the Premier Landing was her gig and she longed to be behind the microphone singing her own two shows during the week and three on the weekend. The sixty people who were there and dressed to the nines sat in the intimate horseshoe arrangement of tables around musicians who had the benefit of a perfect sound system and a classic Steinway A piano, either to sing in front of or to arrange their instruments near. Finally, she was in the grand space, the Sky View Room, with ceilings that went up fifty feet and enormous windows that made the architecture of Manhattan even more of a player in its atmosphere than in the other two spaces, all three of which gave the customers the feeling that they were truly on top of the planet, in the very highest of all horizontals, beyond even the mountains. Between the Sky View Room's windows were marble panels that held bas-relief images of constellations, gods and goddesses, centaurs, flying horses, and minotaurs. The dance floor held the bandstand and the tables went up on three tiers, each successive one proof of how much less money you had spent than the people just below you, since proximity to the dance floor and the musicians reversed the whole idea of above and below, something like Lower Egypt being above Upper Egypt.

The kitchen that supplied the light menu for the Promenade and the full dinners for the Premier Landing and the Sky View Room was at least five hundred feet long. It was something out of a nineteenth-century novel of filth and grease contrasted by all of the stainless steel and the masterful staff that turned out six hundred dinners a night, everything from absolutely fresh sushi to steaks so tender that they made knives more instruments of light gesture than necessity. There were at least twenty-five magnificent chefs and a bevy of what were called *ex-terns,* unpaid people from culinary institutes or equally unpaid rising talents in the class-act kitchen world who did a lot of the shit work just to have the experience of learning at the elbows of such virtuosi. More than a couple of times during the evening, no matter how she felt, when Carla went into the kitchen to pick up an order, she was struck for an instant. The sheer power of that many people focusing so much precise attention on food so as to maintain a varied product that could meet the approval of cultivated palates seemed a compression of the forces that underlay Manhattan's interplay of the vile and the sublime. The Sky View shadow world out of which those spectacular appetizers, entrees, and desserts came was a culinary version of the sweatshop, an ugly caterpillar made of salad bowls, pots, pans, skillets, griddles, ovens, refrigerators, and food that the staff used to create the preliminary cocoon from which the butterfly of cuisine would rise, its body on a plate, its wings the aromatic perfume of the superbly prepared.

Carla had to think about *something* because the waiters in the Sky View Room were some of the nastiest bastards in New York. They hated women and a woman working that room usually lasted no more than a week. She left broken, defeated, and feeling battered. Since Carla had plenty of trouble on her mind at the time that she had gotten into the Promenade just a few months ago, the intrinsic difficulty she faced on this level helped her stand up to the city again, come out of hiding in her apartment, go toe-to-toe.

It was more than a cake walk, however. The waiters who gave her so much grief were standing up for their principles, as barbaric as those principles were. The unwarranted transformation from such suave fellows out in the big room to sadistic creatures nearly put the chill of surrender on Carla as soon as she discovered where life had taken her. Old Jewish and Italian guys, each waiter had been there before the establishment had submitted to an employees' union that included those in serving positions. Every man had all of the memories that were casually burned into him by owners who had never had jobs of the sort that might give them any insight into the problems of labor or any respect for those who earned their livings in the salt water of their own sweat. These people the waiters cut their ethics under were oblivious types who grew up in mandarin houses with pedals and buttons that rang the live-in help—never the servants!—from every floor and room. Vile conditions below weren't vile conditions to these people so high in the evolutionary scale that they defecated vanilla ice cream and urinated ginger ale: such conditions were just the way it was for those who hadn't made something powerful of themselves in the world. So this cutie pie from South Dakota had her nerve to think that she could come in there, just breeze in on a smile, and work comfortably in one of the New York rooms where the biggest tips were left. Not among these bums, girlie girl. The old waiters had come to a consensus about these matters so long ago that they went on automatic when a woman arrived because they felt that their fraternity shouldn't be intruded upon by some dame who didn't have anybody to back her up. These guys would short you on your tips and hand you your money with a look that told you there was nothing you could fucking do about it. They would bump into you. They would trip you when somebody important was near. At such times, the flying plates seemed to crash even louder and made you feel as though the sound of them hitting the floor was still ringing in the air as you were brutally chewed out for not being more careful.

But they didn't count on the instinct that had made Carla such Olympic skating material. Bruised and humiliated at the end of the night, she went home and sat for hours in the tub. The next day, the black and blue marks were covered over with makeup. Eyedrops were at the ready so that she could squeeze them in that night and remove the red if something particularly terrible sent her into the bathroom, where she was free to release the suppressed tears. All right, okay. Take a deep breath. Well now. They just didn't know, did they? It seemed that they really didn't. These assholes had no idea just who in the belly of hell they were trying to screw around. Pity the fools. This was a girl who had hit the ice many, many times, skinned her knees repeatedly, pulled muscles, and twisted her ankles on the way to becoming a merciless swan who took steel dominion over the rink. These waiters were just some more competitors who wanted to make this job into a contact sport.

Well, let's play then. She developed the ability to anticipate a trip or lifted up the vendetta instinct to give tit for tat by spilling a cup of hot coffee on the jerk who was trying to mess her up. Her skill at turns on the ice was transmogrified so that this innocent-looking girl, feeling she had no other selection, might jostle a rude scum-sucking pig and send him to the floor with no sign that he had ever been touched by this gentle young woman. The tougher they got, the meaner she became, always jovial, always whistling, always asking to be excused, offering to help, and ever waiting for the act of dirt that would be returned with serious pleasure. Total war with a smile, no sign of gloating, no impression of self-satisfaction.

At one point, with the percussion of breaking and crashing turning the service into a slapstick comedy short of laughs, an orange-haired and bandy-legged Irish manager, a Jimmy Mullins known to take pleasure in dressing down the incompetent, this little guy whose fore-locks were always falling forward when he got hot under the collar, had a simple question. He wanted to know if everybody had developed jelly fingers or some such shit. Too goddam much food was being spilled on the fucking floors, which meant that roaches and rats were rooting for youse to set a new pace for the feeding of vermin. He wanted to know if anybody could explain what was going on. There was silence. The manager Mullins stared with ascending fury at the head waiter. One could see that the glum Gianni Chianella—nick-named Punch for his lithe days in the boxing ring when he was so fast "you couldn't hit him in the ass with a handful of rice"—was a man of power. No matter. A statement full of contempt and bent on making this veteran grovel before those below him was on the way. The quite proud head waiter braced himself. Just before the manager spoke, Carla asked if she could say something. Sure, young lady. Then Carla very softly apologized for her own part in the matter and told the manager that she did have to say that no job of hers prior to this one had such a crackerjack staff of waiters. There was no group of people more willing to help and teach a newcomer to the kind of room that *anyone* would be honored to work, not just because of what it paid but because of what it *was*. In some odd way, every snippet of bitterness in her life inverted itself so that she was absolutely convincing. The manager, touched, uncocked the rhetorical pistol that he was obviously about to fire into the prominent skull of the head waiter and said that this girl had the kind of spirit we needed from everybody around here. Timidly, Carla told him that she had to beg his pardon: the Sky View Room truly had that spirit already. She just knew it. Everyone was simply having a bad week. We'll see, young lady, we sure the hell will goddam see. Back to work, all of youse.

That turned them. The head waiter, who was the cruelest of them all, so changed his demeanor that the look of a prince slapped aside the predatory stare of a beast. Carla had shamed him. He patted her on the shoulder with genuine feeling. She became one of the gang. It was a victory she never spoke of to anyone but a triumph that Carla would never feel less than proud of, as proud of it as anything she had ever done.

The girl from South Dakota got off the elevator one night, having had a few beers with the waiters and the rest of the staff when the room was closed down. Behind her was a share in the mood of victory brought on by an extremely generous stream of customers. Oh, what a night. The Sky View was a job where you could earn as much as three hundred an evening, and this had been even better than that. The winning mood swept through what was still a mess at the edges and awaited the face-lift of those who cleaned up the sixty-fifth floor and made it, once again, into a gleaming citadel of visual pleasure. Outside the elevator door was a man in a driver's hat and coat. He handed her a note that read she was invited to dinner with Barton Mulhaney on any night she wanted and at whatever place she chose. She nodded to the guy and took a cab home down Fifth Avenue, which she loved at that hour when the epic loneliness of the city seeped in like a long note held by a stringed instrument about to break under the pressure of the emotion. That big feeling of isolation was much like sitting in the middle of a cornfield back home, when nothing but the stalks, the sun, and the wind seemed to exist, when even you, for all your self-obsession, didn't seem to be there, when only some perceptive part of your consciousness had made it through and you were inside a sliver of freedom, a nameless space between the worlds represented by the cars that were not passing and the stalks that—like the buildings of this city so different in tone because of the lateness of the night—had nothing to say about anything at all, were only proof that something had been planted or something had been built, facts which were big enough to fill any heart hoping to have some sense of what it would be like when the last fair deal went down. Yes, she felt as though she owned the night. There was, as well, another fresh tingle of emotion inside her. The note in her pocket had a strange warmth to it, nothing actually coming from the paper, of course, just a chance at something that might be a blessing right about now. Carla was still kind of wary. She had learned that you have to be careful in New York. Your life could depend on it. No way was she going to meet this guy anywhere other than a big, loud, brightly lit place that she could leave and get home from very easily. Safety was more imperative than ever. So the choice was Gallagher's on Fifty-second Street, where you could see the steaks stacked up and waiting when you came through the door. It was a restaurant she had intended to treat herself to one day as a result of talking to the guys at the Sky View about who put the meat on the griddle best in midtown. Carla did not give her phone number, only left word with Barton Mulhaney's secretary that she was always free on Sunday and Monday and that any messages for her could be phoned in to the job.

Carla recalled that night a number of times. Barton was all charm and knowing. This was a man of class given magnetism by the effortless and far from abrasive air of entitlement that enveloped him and was projected in whatever direction he cast his eyes. He was a masculine pearl and knew it, which was why she enjoyed the look of surprise on his face when she offhandedly made it clear that she had never noticed him in the Sky View. Well, he had sure seen her. Picking up waitresses wasn't something he did, but as she must have known, anybody could tell that there was much more to her than whatever it took to be a first-class server of food, pourer of wine, and bringer of desserts. Luck had given him a sense about such things and no one with any of that acuity could miss the intelligence that was as opulently poised within her as the style she brought to her job of work.

What a slick one. But she liked it. She could stand some nice talk right now. Some appreciation would help reconstruct her. It would complement the adversity that had most recently done its part through the waiters. So Mr. Barton Mulhaney got her whole story rather easily, or, at least, as much of it as Carla presented to those she had just come to know, all the cigarette burns of experience kept from view. She was soon his girl and found herself moving through another part of New York society. Barton had inside relationships with people in the fashion world so that Carla was loaned stupendously beautiful dresses to wear at very special events and felt about her looks as she never had when her image, extended by that evening wear, filled the full-length mirror on the closet door in her East Village apartment, where she still lived, refusing to be put up in a better place, loaned money to do so, or anything of that sort. Sure, there were plenty of mornings when she awoke in Barton's Park Avenue spot, but Carla had no intention of becoming any rich guy's kept woman. She liked him a lot and would leave it at that.

There was nothing more fun with her rich beau than leaving Horse Neck, Connecticut, on the sailboat and coming down into Manhattan. That was the capper of the capper, another sense of presence and rhythm, a novel experience of the air and of the smell of the sea, of the birds, of the sun itself, the moon, and the night stars. Again, she recognized that no more than where you were could put new coats of pigment, arriving from an unexpected palette of feeling, on the commonly known elements. A charming man who knew how to touch her and a sailboat in the moonlight, what more did she need right then?

Bon voyage!

The *Dublin Son,* so ridiculously named but so perfectly crafted, glided on the water in the Long Island Sound down through Plum Gut, leaving the sound and moving into Gardiners Bay, then to Three Mile Harbor, which was in East Hampton, port to plenty of other boats and the owners who knew Barton well and had respect for his seamanship, whether older guys or those in their middle thirties, as was he. After hanging around there and having some food and a little drink, they went to his big place on the beach, where the ever-changing form of the sea and the light on it looked magical to her. She played poker that night with Barton and some of his buddies, starting off with a few hundred dollars and winning a little more than five thousand because, refusing to accept that she was good, they kept raising the stakes and losing and losing. Her boyfriend was amazed, she was told after they left, that he was traveling around with a blue-eyed Midwestern card shark. She offered to have him give the guys back the money. Give it back? If those bums weren't so cheap underneath all the brag and show, you would have won *fifty* thousand dollars. The hell with them. They just paid a little money for a good story. They'll be talking about you for weeks to come.

After breakfast the next day, they headed back out through Plum Gut for a twelve-hour sail to Oyster Bay. This was the long one. If she was going to get seasick, now was the time. Carla did not and Barton told her, his background the sound of the wind in the sails and the squeaks from the rigging, that for all he imagined her to be as she appeared to him in the Sky View, the very thought of her being a sea goddess, too, did not cross his mind even once. When she thought about it, Carla was sure that all of those spins on her skates, day after day and night after night upon the solid water, had prepared her for the seawater that refused to remain still. She didn't tell him that, though. Let him imagine her as a goddess. Let him adore her. She could use it.

The couple stayed overnight in Oyster Bay, her heart filled with all the myths of water that she could recall as they remained on board and felt the pulsation of the sea beneath them throughout the resting time. The sources of those myths became more real as she remembered the way that your nose and your ears became increasingly sensitive to the wind, which allowed you to know where it was, the direction from which the invisible—benevolent, indifferent, dangerous—was coming. The spray had a delectable quality, those fine drops in your face or a full splash amounting to, for her, a very enjoyable soaking. There were also the big sounds of the metal in the rigging that could frighten at various points. Attuned to it all, Barton preferred a tiller to a wheel and let her understand why. She, with enough coaxing and explanation, held the tiller and actually felt the rudder in the water, knowing right off that those who had been to sea many times had another level of sensual experience in which the parts of the ship, as with one's own body, sent the messages of pressure and motion back and forth, back and forth, swelling and falling. That night in Oyster Bay, he cooked for her and *did she* enjoy being treated so sweetly and so well.

The next day's trip continued past Execution Rock, where events used to take place that gave the pile of stones their name. On they sailed, under the Whitestone Bridge, entering the East River and moving toward the Throgs Neck Bridge, Barton explaining on that first voyage that over to the starboard side was the Triborough Bridge, which they could not see but that connected Queens, Manhattan, and the Bronx. It hadn't been finished at first because one of his countrymen by mass bloodline, the dapper champagne-and-caviar crook Mayor Jimmy Walker, had fumbled around like he was some goddam African dictator. This stain upon the reputation of the Irish people stole too much of the money to finish the job, which perhaps made it rather clear that the Third World shenanigans presently exasperating those dummies at the World Bank were as common to the worst imported eaters of potatoes as to the contemporary consumers of African yams. That Walker was an example of how corruption had become decadent, too godawful greedy to achieve what was necessary to maintain power *and* the trust of the people. The *better* grade of highly placed political criminal understood that what you did if you were to sustain a civilization—or generate one—was merely charge two or three times what was called for but *get the job done, build* the goddamn bridge. Or, upon taking the IMF loan, skim off as much as you possibly could, then *do* for your ex-colonial people what you said you were going to do when you went before the European bankers with your hat in your hand and a tear-jerking tale of the burdens of underdevelopment. Those most selfish Africans will meet Walker at the place in the abyss where the bad Irishmen go.

Barton, the spray coming up on the port side of the boat and some hard flapping going on in the sails that he had to eliminate by getting the position of the craft right, told Carla that he had friends who worked the Street and were quite angry about being left out of some of the strange business a few of the black guys in securities were able to get into just because of a little more melanin that the next person.

He didn't have any truck with that kind of stuff, but there were unceasing rumors that powerhouse Africans wishing to smuggle gold and diamonds into the US of A had a penchant for dealing from under the bottom of the deck of the law with only the brokering descendants of those who had been sold into slavery by other Africans back on the balmy beaches of history and grimacing black gold held in cages. Bygones were bygones. No bitterness at all. Cheers.

There could, however, always be a scent of trouble. Barton laughed that a Negro buddy on the Street said that what actually separated him from Africans wasn't any kind of credit line; it wasn't a tribal line; it was a *funk* line, the appalling, foggy stench that he couldn't adjust to because the white people in the American booby hatch had corrupted him with soap and deodorant. He had been had by hygiene. When he was obligated to be downwind among his wealthy and cultivated brothers and sisters from the original homeland—their dresses so fine, their suits so well tailored, their shoes scuffed and rundown as though they hadn't been in the culture long enough to become important articles of elegance—this guy took a global perspective as he fought to keep from passing out. Like Londoners, the Parisians, Arabs, and the Indians of the East—these beautiful people rose all the way up into very high refinement while sustaining the stink that kept them in symbolic contact with the odors of the lowly. Carla said to him that she remembered feeling the same way when the psychedelic generation came to flower and very smart kids set aside all the niceties they had been taught by society, preparing food with dirty hands, which made them sick, and not washing, which made them unpleasantly ripe to the nose.

"Well, here's to armpit aristocracy," he toasted, taking a sip of Bushmills from a bottle with an orange label.

The *Dublin Son*, free in its motion from any conversation, continued on through Hell Gate, which the Dutch called "hell's channel." As far back as the early part of the seventeenth century, boats began going down because the rock-filled narrow strait was basically a drain of the Long Island Sound, easily affected by the Atlantic Ocean and the tidal currents in the East River and the Harlem River. In 1876, the same year that Custer met the big measure of death, the U.S. Army Corps of Engineers set off what was then the biggest bang of all time in order to make smithereens of those underwater rocks upon which hundreds of ships had run aground before gathering for bed on the ocean floor pallet laid out by Davy Jones. For all that blasting, Hell Gate was still far more than a little tricky. You had better know what you were doing when you got in there, and Barton Mulhaney did know what he was doing, which didn't remove the suspense because the concentration in his eyes, the way he stood, and the delicate care with which he steered assured Carla that he wasn't one who mistook sailing through there for anybody's toying activity. As they got into the East River, the couple traveled alongside the FDR Drive, named after the man who had supplied the money for the Triborough to be finished and had put many New Yorkers back to work during the Depression by federally financing all manner of building. The Irish guy and the Norwegian gal went past Gracie Mansion, the mayor's digs, and on under the Fifty-ninth Street Bridge, sailing on a line now parallel to the magnificent homes of Sutton Place, which had once been tenements full of Negroes who were moved out and up to Harlem, this quite a reverse of the process at the time but one that predicted the nature of urban renewal, something the comedian Dick Gregory referred to years ago as no more than an aphorism for Negro *removal*. To the port side was Roosevelt Island, once known as Welfare Island and a place that had still standing the shell of the building in which Typhoid Mary was held until she ended her days in this world. This, like much of what Barton said to her, was his own mixing of willful mistake and fact, a characteristic she realized far later was much like what she loved in Leeann at her most playful.

The sights stood on their own, finally, as anyone lucky enough not to be blind always had to thank God for. When they got to the southern tip of Manhattan Island and looked toward it as the sun was about to slip on down, there was the bizarre but beautiful image of nothing but skyline and concrete, not one blade of grass, not one handful of earth, no sign of a neighborhood, only something so huge that one experienced the fearful premonition that the millions upon millions of tons could only sink right now under its own terrible weight, vanishing like an Atlantis that had gone just a bit too far in cramming one thing next to another and another and another and another and another, up and up and up, on and on, so much construction, so many buildings, 722 miles of subways, endless phone lines, universes of electricity—all of it amplified by the squirming drive of the people themselves, who were barely equal to but far from intimidated by the finger of civilization pointing south that was the ageless rock upon which they lived. Something inside Carla kneeled in terror but felt immediately replenished the first time she saw that image as they rounded the island, went past the green Statue of Liberty, and docked in the Seventy-ninth Street Boat Basin on the Upper West Side, where Barton had a spot for the *Dublin Son* and a car waiting for them.

On the ride after that first time that she had sailed down from Horse Neck with him, Barton, his diction and sound slowly transforming, told her he had a good funny story. Another one. She wasn't really interested in hearing anything. She wanted to think of how the water had looked, what it felt like to be in the middle of the wind, and that sense of coming in contact with, as her handsome sailing instructor had said, something that didn't care whether you were there or not, lived or died, had a good time or hated being on a boat. The park and Fifth Avenue had reminded him of something. That was why he was going to tell her this story. No luck. Why couldn't he sense that she just wanted to ride snuggled up with him? Why should he? It was his world, all his, and she was just along for the ride. A little bitterness was foaming, like a partially digested smidgen of a good meal trying to make an unpleasant return to the top of the palate.

In the backseat of the Jaguar, with Barton's heavy arm around her, Carla was now very tired from the sailing and feeling herself pushed toward irritation by the sound of his voice, which was beginning to seem enamored of itself. So what? Soon she would be in his place and settling into that bathtub, her feet up on the gold wings for hot and cold, and a blue washcloth on her breasts, the feeling of being home all over her soul and, doubtless, a little bit of unhappiness needling its way in due to the fact that she was a woman who had a trained singing voice in her body that no serious direction had been given to, only a bunch of speculations that were perhaps the flags of surrender cowards designed and pretended had the same meaning as will and risk. There was no need to hurry up to unhappiness. It would be there waiting. The first five notes of "Never Let Me Go" went through her mind. *Yes.* If he would only kiss her, everything, at least for now, would be all right. What a jerk. His hand was on her face, his mouth was on her lips. It was true and the inside of her chest was melting. A whole serving of freedom was delicious within her. He could tell her anything he wanted to now. He had felt her heart without a word. After a sufficient amount of hugging and kissing, she asked him if he was going to tell her his story. Story? The one that the park and Fifth Avenue reminded you of. Sure, sure. His arm didn't feel heavy on her now.

Let the hunting story begin. Ready, go!

Barton and his buddies met a son of the Old Testament at a rifle and pistol club where everybody went to keep their skills up. The Hebrew bastard could *shoot*. He had the feel for it. For him it was only fun, something he got interested in one day and just started doing once or twice a week. He was the only Jew he knew who was interested in marksmanship, the *aesthetics* of it, not like Israelis, who learned to shoot for, well, unfortunate reasons. This was said with a twinkle of pride. Well then.

The guy was also bright and sparky. Brilliant, to be more precise. His favorite opening to a funny story was, *This will make you laugh*. They took a great liking to the cut-cock son of a bitch. Besides, his name being Barney Bergelheim made up for the little bit off the top. He was, too, one of the very few with money who loved his country and his fellow man. Like all of them, this guy was a very serious contributor to social causes that went the gamut from race to saving or protecting those things in nature that certain kinds of men in business could give a shit about. This guy was well aware that a Brink's truck never followed a hearse. You couldn't deny him his heart, his feeling for the world. He became a real buddy. He went out with them to some of the joints so Irish they didn't even serve British gin.

One word led to another, as they became more friendly, and they eventually asked him if he wanted to go duck hunting with them. They were all eating mutton at a private club over near where they did their shooting as members in the underground basement of boom, boom, boom. Clay pipes were racked in the ceiling, maps of the Emerald Isle were everywhere, and it couldn't have been more relaxed. He didn't answer. Come on, what about going out hunting some ducks with us? Well, he didn't know. Aw, come on. Get up early for some fun this once. The hell with early rising for the office only.

Get out in the wild. Shoot something *real*. Watch it drop from the sky and have it on your plate for dinner. Nothing like it. After acting like the most sought-after guest in Manhattan, he agrees to come along and there is no doubt that a fine time will be had by all.

So this guy, like all Jewish guys who might be athletic but are not sportsmen, shows up in brand-new gear, looking like he had come to life from the window of Abercrombie & Fitch. Not one thing had ever been used before. At first, he had the look of a man with full pride in his good taste. All of the right stuff was in the right place. About that, he was more than correct. Then it hit him. There he was with some seasoned guys in their favorite this and their favorite that. Not one new shotgun among them. Nobody ratty but every mother's son in something pulled on and pulled off many times. Dammit. He was the outsider. Again. Oh, holy hell. What a terrible, terrible feeling. True, quite true, but the nature of things is that it didn't stop at him. It did not stop there. *No es possible.* There was also the matter of the dog. The dog? Yes. The retriever. This Jewish guy had a retriever that had grown up as nice as you please on Fifth Avenue and had never been any closer to the wild than Central Park, no closer to water than the lake inside it, not a beast familiar with the woods but one well acquainted with the paths where he was walked to take his dump once a day and maybe chase a Frisbee every now and then. The real hunting dogs, the ones all these Irish guys had, they sniffed the beast. Sniffed him as if he was up for sale. Then they looked at this panting and pampered *true* son of a bitch as if he should get the hell all the way back to where he came from and leave bringing in the birds to them.

The Jewish guy, sensitive, so sensitive, empathized with his animal, whom the Hebrew must have imagined also felt as suddenly out of place as he did, this whole Daniel Boone business as big a mistake as the South seceding from the Union. Incalculable disappointment was guaranteed.

So there they are, once all the driving is over, waiting for the big birds to come flying south from Canada, all of them forming the glorious chevron that is the pure math of the genetically instinctive realized in feathered flesh and blood. This is something as gorgeous to see as it is to hear the sound of their wings lifting swans up in East Hampton. But our subject is ducks so big they seem like 747s when they come into sight and are moving toward you. Ducks, by the way, give you the impression of being below an avian Chinese restaurant because they always seem to be arguing with all the goddam quacking, one asking when they're getting there, another responding that they'll get there when they get there, another saying he's been flying as long as anybody else and has no interest in overhearing snide remarks, the one at the point of the chevron telling them all to shut up and let him do the leading, one after another wanting to know why the hell he's at the point of the chevron in the first place.

The entire mood of the morning, at least from the Hebrew fellow's perspective, was an object lesson in the wacky nature of social alienation, even among enlightened Americans. The Jewish guy's family had arrived in New York from Germany and Russia over a hundred and twenty years ago and every one of the Irish guys on the hunt had families that didn't go back more than eighty. Just by virtue of being experienced sportsmen, they caused this guy to think he was an interloper and not a special guest, something that Yankee blue-blood sorts had enjoyed doing to the Irish as long as they could, always referring back to when the dawn of 1700 or earlier had cracked its way into the Eastern Seaboard calendar. This was surely not what Mulhaney and his friends were trying to do on that morning, though, pranksters all, they deeply enjoyed it, even pretending to be talking about this Jewish guy among themselves when he couldn't hear exactly what they were saying. He didn't get it just yet. All of that was over, dead as Robert E. Lee. Farewell to all that high-hat-in-your-face bullshit. People who had come up now didn't need to feel required to meet the standards of some other people. No matter how far your family went back, *you* weren't there and *you* didn't do whatever it was that you reminded other people your *ancestors* had done so damn well.

Then the Jewish guy takes down the lead duck, which does that odd twist before falling. The Irish guns start going off and other birds are hit, twisting and falling, twisting and falling. The moment of more than truth is here now. Something about existence itself will be made clear. Up or down. Fido, don't fail me now. The Fifth Avenue retriever looks at the Jewish guy. The Jewish guy looks at the retriever. The retriever looks at the falling duck. The Hebrew fellow has the face of a guy ready to be embarrassed beyond belief. His eyes are insistent, imploring the animal. He seems about to cry. The retriever looks toward the falling duck. Well. *Well?* A wailing wall would fit the moment. Oh, no: *zoom,* he's gone, right into the water, right to the duck, right back, rising from that water with the duck in his mouth and dripping everywhere. If Barney Bergelheim could have paid a dog a million dollars for bringing back a dead duck, the dog would now be sitting even prettier. One can be sure that there is a sum set aside for him big enough to choke a grand stallion, or for the erection of a statue somewhere in Central Park that will commemorate this beast's recognition of his canine roots through a highly detailed bronze so realistic that one will nearly be able to smell the woods, feel the air, and see the water falling from this magnanimous creature that proved, with no more than a dead duck in his mouth, that a dog is a man's best friend, even if the man's Jewish and kingly as Jesus Christ.

What a sense of humor this courtly guy had and how much Carla loved to laugh with him. She needed the invincible lilt of some wit. Mmm: how much he helped her get back to herself and something close to the way she wanted to be. It could be more than that, too. There were always signs. Barton Mulhaney was there for her having, if she wanted him. This purported hunting story, which probably didn't happen anyway, must have been his style of telling her that she was welcome to all of this. His manners were too good for him to say that directly. It would have been as though he knew how out of place she felt. Could be. He had the right kinds of senses. It could also be that he was uncomfortable in the silence, like those guys who have to make your ears or the air itself cater to them and their presence. There was probably some of that, too, some of it. Still, the door to a castle seemed to be opening. Think about it. Maybe this was where she would end up, his wife, with a legion of children and fantasies about being some latter-day Rose Kennedy, Norwegian version. It could take that shape and end like that, with her one day before death looking from the window in Connecticut and thinking of what it must have been like back in the mornings, afternoons, and evenings of those now long gone, they who traded with the wild and stately Indians, had none of the modern conveniences, hadn't been housebroken with our sense of cleanliness, and arrived in a time before they could be blessed with our naive confidence that our offspring would live beyond childhood. Or, at the finish line of mortality, she might be musing upon how she herself had been when Barton was alive and they were young, perhaps what it had been like to become parents of such a brood and to learn the ways of each, growing to accept disappointment about some and the blessings of superior ability in others, moving all along the life from a young mother to a decrepit grandmother, even great-grandmother, then reading Sir Thomas Wyatt as the light came in and feeling the final coldness begin to make its sharp way up from the feet, closing off existence with every inch until the heart was reached and the unconscious beat, fighting, ceased to go on.

That was *her* version. There was also another. It wasn't really funny but she responded as though it was.

Carla found herself laughing almost hysterically inside when Bart's mother told her the very best way to conclude the story. They were having tea and cake out on the back lawn; downhill the sea was toying with the sailboat. The widowed Mrs. Patricia Mulhaney had prominent wattles where her jawline used to be, a long neck of sagging smiles all the way down to its base, and a freckled brown hide instead of skin. This proud lady, who refused to have anything surgically lifted or altered, explained that there was no better death at all than to expire on the court with your racquet in your hand and your outfit perfectly white, your deep tan superbly even from the game and from boating and riding. So much good sun and good sea air. Obviously, a stroke on horseback could be too messy because your boot might get caught in the stirrup and the poor dumbish animal, spooked to full gallop by the presence of death on its back, could easily drag your lifeless body into something so horrible the coffin might have to remain closed at the funeral.

That put the curve in.

When Carla actually contemplated this world of expensive preparation and faced the emotional evidence that she absolutely and breathlessly adored all of the luxury, the South Dakota girl then felt a sting at the bottom of her heart and got out of that circle as fast as she could, trying to make herself into a country-and-western singer on the run, traveling through the South and all the way into West Texas. There was no pretense to epiphany. She recognized that the whole shift was driven by panic. Her intention was to move as far in passion and manner from the world of the Mulhaneys as she could. What a close call. She was too hot and greedy for that privilege not to cool down once her soul came back to her. Bart was ever so deeply hurt and didn't understand but that was of no significance. None. *She* understood, sublet her apartment, and was gone on the first thing smoking. Three hundred bucks a night in tips at the Sky View had supplied her with plenty of cash. There was also the money won from Bart's poker buddies. This time the dream could be on *her* tab. Nashville, here I come.

Nothing, however much she loved the gumption and tart sorrow of country music, touched her anywhere near as deeply as the feeling she had gotten dancing to the blues bands in Chicago. It just didn't. The sanctified texture of the blues was always in her ears. It became her shadow. Wherever she woke up and with whatever Camel-smoking, whiskey-drinking guy—his tattoos having just about rubbed off on her if they made love hard enough—the blues, always the blues, was right there waiting. She might as well have been followed by the Blue Ridge Mountains themselves, something so solid and always there. They would never let her go. All day long. All night long. They bent the glitter of the rhinestones, hid in the fringe, in the dressing rooms, under the stitches in the seams of the jeans, just below the surface of her lipstick, washed through her hair, lifted up in the smell of a man, tracked her from behind the thick eyebrows of a passerby. But she couldn't sing the blues, not that Chicago way. She knew she couldn't. My Lord, my Lord. God, please send me a *break*. Let me go. *Please* let me go. There were luscious facts in the middle of all this trouble. Her voice was plenty good enough to make something of, and her range was fine. She didn't have perfect pitch but her relative pitch was strong enough to keep her well in tune. That was pretty damn clear. Still, this failure of soul in the spiritual environs of Patsy Cline and Johnny Cash made her feel wilted and stupid for even trying. New York was where she had to do it and where she had to find the sound that she could pull out of her body and stand behind as it slowly got strong enough for Carla to call herself an actual professional worthy of uncrimped respect.

THE EMPEROR OF
THE EVENING TIME

EZEKIEL AND CARLA took a walk while Eunice and Maxwell prepared dinner. It was Monday and Mother Harris was in the hospital. Church folk had been calling the Davis home and talking about it all day. Carla had spent most of the time lounging around and recalling that miraculous Sunday. Maxwell was drained and lay in bed a good deal of the time until he and his mother went shopping for the food they were going to cook. Before he and Carla left, Ezekiel had joked that if the kitchen, much less the house, was still there with the two of them working on something together, then good luck was just as real as the Lord. They had walked a few blocks when Ezekiel, who had been chuckling to himself mysteriously, said something.

"You know, Carla, I think my son might make a man of himself and get right on down to the business of making you his wife."

"I don't know about that."

"I think that boy sees something in you special. He puts his eye on you a particular way. That's the way he looks at something important to him. I know that look. He's my son."

"I don't understand."

"I know one thing, women always come up with a fishing pole and they'll stand at the water until they reel in a big batch of compliments."

"Ezekiel, I don't know what to say."

"You know what to say. There's not a woman living don't know what to say. It's how she says what she says. Some will talk. Some will move a certain way. Then you got those who push on you with their eyes. But they talk plenty. You know what to say. You got a lot of feeling for my son, hasn't you?"

"Yes."

"But you two wasn't doing too good when you came out here, were you?"

"I wouldn't say that."

"You didn't need to say it. Me and Eunice can see. We been together rolling back and forth through hell four or five, six or seven times. Almost lost each other. We know the story from the first word to the last. The story of a man and a woman is what I mean we know."

"But that story isn't the same for everyone."

"If they ain't crazy, it's close enough to be the same. I mean in life all you ever look for is what you like in a different version. Then you done had an experience. If it's really exactly the same you, hmm, well, then you have moved on up the nowhere road to nowhere. It's just like what makes a new day beautiful. You know what that is?"

"No, I don't know what makes a new day beautiful, Mr. Ezekiel Davis. Do you?" Carla asked, hearing the echo of Eunice in her tone.

"Yes, I know *I* know. You *sure* you don't know?"

"Not exactly. You tell me."

"Well, what makes it beautiful is it hasn't been used yet."

They walked along exchanging no words for a while. Carla was confused by that one, not by what he said but by what it meant within the context of the conversation.

The summer heat had leveled off and there were people passing in cars who looked at the two of them, a few waving at Ezekiel or lightly honking their horns. He waved back as though he owned each block or lifted his fishing hat with the grandeur of a man who lived up on the hill but had come down into the valley to see just how the other people were doing. She could feel the fatigue from having stayed up so late rambling around with Mr. Memory.

"I used to be a fighting man, you know."

"A what?"

"Oh, I used to know how to rumble. Knock a man down *hard*.

Hurt him. When I was in the streets in the Fifth Ward, I was a knuckle-head. Skull hard as teakwood. Ways just as hard, too. Mmm-hmm. But I never cut or shot nobody. That's because it just never came up. I had me a knife with a matchstick broken off stuck down in the opening so it didn't close *all* the way. The tip was still out. I practiced with that. I could pull that out and open it up with my thumb so fast you would have thought it was a switchblade. I was rough. Did me some gambling. Had me all *kinds* of little wild girls. I can hear how they sounded in the dark right now. "

In the black night of their home, Maxwell always endeared himself to her when she lay naked on her stomach and he slowly rubbed and gently squeezed her backside while whispering, "I know my dog by the way he barks, I know my baby from the feeling in the dark."

Carla smiled to herself before speaking.

"This is very surprising. I mean I'm shocked. I really am. This is so strange."

"Mmm-hmm. All of that was before I got saved. When the Creator came and got me I was in the hospital after getting cut right across my arm gambling in the bathroom of the movie theater. Right across the muscle. Caught off guard, winning and full of that gin. Between the white man and that white liquor, a Negro was in a world of trouble. My arm wasn't supposed to work again. That's what they said. Said it with a whole heap of confidence, too. Sorrowful. Of course, you know *they* know everything, them doctors. Everything. I was supposed to be a cripple for living ignorant. Then He who separated the light from the dark came right in that hospital window on the wings of the wind and told me to straighten up and I would be taken care of. My chest nearly busted open with the truth. Soon as I got baptized I was a better man. I started flying right. But me and Eunice still used to fight like World War II. Not all the time, but when we did fight, oh, my Lord, did we go at it."

"Maxwell told me."

"I expect he did. You're his woman. You *supposed* to know what he knows. That's what makes you his and what makes him yours. He supposed to know what you know, too."

"We talk a lot. We tell each other a lot of things. But he never really told me about the two of you. He never even said that we should come down here to visit."

"Well, if he finally got around to it, it must mean something. All these years he's done been gone from home Maxwell didn't show up much—and when he did, he didn't bring nobody *else* down here."

"Really?"

"I see you fishing again."

Carla blushed.

"You know you just turned pink?"

"Yes, I know. I can feel that."

"You know, I think I read somewhere that Thomas Jefferson thought that there was something wrong with my people because we don't blush if we ain't mixed enough—you know: yellow in the face."

"He did believe that. Or he pretended that he believed it. That didn't bother him when he was having children by the slave women. I guess all of the human feeling that he found so lacking in the faces of black people didn't matter when he was having sex with them. I guess it was fine right there to do whatever he wanted to with them and never acknowledge their humanity. Mr. Jefferson didn't care about how those women felt. He had other more important things going on. He lived his life so far above those black women. He was always in the company of white people who looked at them as animals. That doesn't seem to have been on his mind."

"Could have been. But he might not have been able to stand up to his own feelings. Lots of people are weak like that. They feel good about you but they can't *treat* you good. They know you're no good but they're afraid to let you *know* it. That's just the weakness of a human being."

"That might be so, Ezekiel, but it doesn't make being treated badly feel any different."

"Now you're right about that. You couldn't be any more right if you turned into an angel and said that from way up in the middle of the air. Still in all, the weakness of the human being is the struggling part of the story. Old as I am, if I knew exactly where some people was shooting some dice right at this minute I would want to get down on my knees with them and see if those dots could add up to some big money. I could go right back to being a fool on all fours. I would *love* doing it, too. You couldn't tell me I wasn't in heaven, no dadgum matter how loud you talked or how long. I would be all the way down in that. Then, once I got going, I would like to have that gin burning down my throat. I would like some secret little girls, many as I could get. What these Mexicans mean when they say your home is *la casa*, but the ones with the extra little girls, the little hot side dishes, they're *las casitas*, the *little* homes."

Carla stopped walking she was so stunned. Ezekiel seemed possessed, the turbulence of demonic appetites in his eyes. Then another power ejected that from his gaze.

"You can start back to walking. I ain't so much above anybody else. That don't make me a hypocrite neither. I just ain't so much above. I'm just a man out here with all my weakness trying to make sure I don't leave my final mark as a weak man. I want to die fighting the devil in me. Whenever I don't do what the weakness in me *wants* to do, I know that the devil is howling like that boy James Brown used to howl about how he had *lost* someone. Devil had me and I'm *gone*. Got away. Thank the Lord. But Satan *still* stops by to see if he can take me by the hand so we can walk side by side until I'll do everything wrong I want to do until I'm satisfied. When me and Eunice used to fight so much, that was him doing the best he could. But you see we still together. He lost that one."

"That gives me some hope. It does."

"Good."

"I really need that. Thank you, Ezekiel. It is true. Maxwell and I are doing better now. I think we are. I really hope so. Gosh, I don't know. I'm confused. Coming down here for this visit has really been something I didn't expect. But, to be honest about it right now, there have been some times when I thought he was going to leave me. I was so terrified of losing him. I still am."

"That boy ain't going nowhere."

Carla didn't want to seem as though she were fishing again, but the desire to ask him why he was so sure furiously itched inside her. She had to ask another way.

"You might think he's not going anywhere but Maxwell told a friend of mine that being with a white woman didn't make him comfortable."

"I expect it wouldn't."

"I felt *so* humiliated."

"I wouldn't expect any feeling different from that. It's always a surprise when your favorite hat turns into a crown of thorns.

Always one. But that's the world, the flesh, and the devil. That's those three."

"But I don't know why Maxwell and I have to be judged by some people and then he has to go along with the idea that he's supposed to be with one kind of woman. I don't know why we all have to go through that at this time in the world. We're supposed to be so advanced. That's so stupid."

"Stupid works around the clock. You never see it in the unemployment office. The consequences is pretty clear. You know you got all kinds of people out here running around telling other people what to do and who to do it with and all of that kind of mess. Always been here, you know. Always. *Somebody* knows better than *you* know. They can sit back and tell you what to do. They can read your skin like a Gypsy woman supposed to be capable of reading the palm of your hand. The reason you have to be strong is they *might* be right. But they might be *wrong,* too. You have to hold on until you find out. Hold on. But I got faith in my boy. He ain't going nowhere."

After an exquisite dinner of moist meat loaf, turnip greens, cauliflower, and macaroni and cheese, with Eunice and her son nodding to each other across the table in recognition of how well they had worked that kitchen action, Maxwell wanted to go over to the Gathering Place, a juke joint where there was a little band that played some old down-home blues. He wanted to get in on that number. His body was hungry for some blowing and this was a side of Houston he hadn't shown Carla. These were pork-chop-and-collard-greens Negroes all the way. These were the blues people. They were where the blues got its thrust and its substance. Sometime around the turn of the twentieth century, their feeling needed an aesthetic form and that big feeling in a three-chord structure was large enough to tell the story of the nation, in one permutation or another. Blues was like the moving air: it went everywhere. Still, Maxwell explained to her, there was no room like the Gathering Place in New York; that part of the black past was dead and gone or it arrived back East in downtown clubs where white audiences did the very best they could to pretend they were tuned in when they stomped and hooted in imitation of what someone they knew somewhere had seen Negroes do in a time before this one and a time when all of the grand old blues men were still alive and out there playing, each of them capable of lining the country fences in the air and making an audience witness to the religious power of the spirituals given secular form.

BLUES TREATISE IN DIALOGUE TEMPO

When Cecelia brought her drunken writer boyfriend who lived in Paris to a dinner party Leeann gave for him, just about everybody got into a discussion of the meaning of the blues. Bobo was in his last illusory days of indomitable strength then, high but well in control, and Maxwell was traveling in the company of one of the Brazilian girls he attended to as though she were as rare as a snow leopard. Kelvin Thomson wasn't smashed that night, but he was on his thinking pedestal and Cecelia was so proud to be in his company and he was surely proud to be with a woman so beautiful and so unflinchingly smart. Kelvin Thomson had promised Cecelia that he wouldn't embarrass her, but the writer wasn't exactly on the wagon with his legs dangling off and his arm in the air as he waved goodbye to all that excessive guzzling: he had, however, one foot firmly on the golden cart of discipline, since he only drank heavily watered whiskey. The point of discussion, after tale following tale and each big laugh giving way to a bigger laugh, was how to look at the blues.

"The blues is just as happy as it can get sad," Bobo said.

"That's right," Maxwell said. "Which means you can get the blues and be in a deep, deep groove. Ain't that right, baby?" he asked of his Brazilian girl, who was part Japanese, one of the million Japanese Brazilians descended from the workers brought in around World War I as an antidote to the lackadaisical attitude of the locals, who were Indians, Portuguese, and African, or either a two-part or three-part mixture. Earlier, Maxwell had joked that since her ancestors in Brazil were rhythmically indoctrinated by the land of the samba, they probably went back to Japan, every detail of ritual perfectly retained from the original homeland, then screwed up all of the ceremonies by going along with everything until they started beating out samba beats instead of the solitary strokes on Buddhist bells ringing in clear skies.

"Samba is a groove, too. It on many occasions has very unhappy lyrics to dancing rhythm. Samba is a lot a sad dance that is happy also."

"But it doesn't have the **philosophy** you get from the blues," Kelvin Thomson said.

"What philosophy, baby?" Cecelia asked, snuggling up to him.

"The secular and the sacred perfectly resolved instead of slugging it out."

"That's interesting. I never thought of blues as being in combat with anything," Carla said. "All I knew was that when I came in contact with it in Chicago, real contact, it made me feel like one part of my belief in life that hadn't been spoken for was getting its chance to be heard."

"Carla is a South Dakota **blues** girl, you know what I'm saying?" Leeann laughed, bringing everyone with her, including Carla.

"You know what Bessie Smith said, **Any** Woman's Blues."

"Tell 'em, Carla," Bobo cheered, at one with the good feeling of the evening.

"But what **I'm** saying is something else," Kelvin Thomson continued. "I'm talking about what we get from Mr. W. C. Handy in 'Aunt Hagar's Blues.' Right there it's all compressed and ready to roll."

"I play that all the time, the one Louis Armstrong did on his W. C. Handy album," Bobo said. Bobo was exaggerating. He didn't play it all the time, but Carla had heard him play it enough times to learn it herself.

"That Mr. Armstrong version is as good as anybody ought to want it," Kelvin Thomson responded. "It doesn't matter who's singing it. The philosophy is clear. Listen to those lyrics." He began reciting them but, without much of a pause, Bobo began singing them, joined by Maxwell, then Carla, which caused Kelvin Thomson to bust out the words with melody notes from his baritone register. Leeann and Cecelia began leaning from side to side as they silently hummed and snapped their fingers, which Maxwell's Brazilian girl joined, clapping with charisma.

Old Deacon Spliven
His flock was given
The way of living right
Said he no winging,
No ragtime singing,
Tonight.

Up jumped Aunt Hagar and shouted out with all her might,
all her might.
"Oh, tain't no used to preaching.
Oh, tain't no used to teaching.
Each modulation
of syncopation
Just tells my feet to dance and I can't refuse
When I hear the melody called the blues,
Those ever-loving blues."
Just hear Aunt Hagar's children harmonizing to that old mournful tune
It's like a choir from on high broke loose.
If the devil brought it,
The good Lord sent it,
Right on down to me.
Let the congregation join while I sing those loving
Aunt Hagar's blues.

"Now that's the entire engagement, the whole whoop-de-do," Kelvin Thomson said after they had finished. "What we have is something very odd for Western thinking. You got to watch that Negro."

"Baby, do you have to use that old-fashioned word?" Cecelia asked.

"Somebody has to call the Negro by his rightful name. But let me get back to my point, you copper-colored moon dream. You got to watch that Negro. The sacred and the profane might get mixed up for the betterment of mankind. You got to watch what he'll do when he knows who he is. That's why any movement away from the true grandeur of the Negro is welcomed by all concerned. "

"Amen to that," Leeann said.

Carla felt a bit uneasy but repressed it, assuming that if she weren't one of the crowd she wouldn't be there.

"Keep that nigger boy running. Ralph Ellison knew what he was talking about. Give a Negro a letter to deliver that says he is to be treated as though he is not shit. But don't let him open that envelope. Then he might come to himself and return to the level of what W. C. Handy had his hands on. Check yourself before you wreck yourself. That's why those lyrics are the Negroid manifestation of an odd idea in Western thinking. This is the Negro winging in after Western civilization moved up out of paganism to the point where good and evil were sent to their separate corners and came out slugging when the bell rang. Very odd. The first thing is the melody called the blues."

Carla had always loved that phrase: *the melody called the blues.*

"Here's the curve ball. What those backwoods church people looked upon as the devil's music turns out to be something sent from the good Lord himself."

"You know," Bobo said, "I thought about that plenty of times. Goddamnit. It seems like the devil got tricked. The trickster got tricked. The bullshitter got bullshitted."

Bobo floated over to Kelvin Thomson and resoundingly slapped his palm.

"All right now: while he was trying to trick you," Maxwell said, slapping Kelvin Thomson's palm much more lightly, "he brought something down here that was way too good to be from **him.**"

The hand-slapping made Carla feel as though these guys had to create a closed circle separating them from the women in the room. It was their nature. Funny. They were clannish that way.

"That's exactly where the profundity is. Here we have a total reversal of what Milton's Satan says in **Paradise Lost:** Rather to—"

"—rule in hell than serve in heaven," Carla, Leeann, and Cecelia said, joining Kelvin Thomson like a chorus.

"So that bad boy Satan creeps around with a gutbucket of blues and thinks he's pulling the people down when they start to dance."

"He must have creeped up on me many times," Leeann said.

"But the blues is played to get **rid** of the blues, not to hold **on** to the blues."

"I remember," Leeann said with a tremor, "my mama used to say she was going to rinse that nigger out of her hair with some blues."

Everyone paused and looked at Leeann.

"So let's not lose our point. Since the devil can only bring something bad, like Maxwell said, at the **exact** moment that Satan thinks he's doing you in, the devil is being turned into what he hates the most of all: a messenger boy for God. It's just what happens in Luke 11:15, when somebody notices that Jesus casts out demons by using **Beelzebub,** the **prince** of demons."

"So you mean when I'm shaking my black ass to some blues I'm casting out demons?" Leeann asked after exhaling a cloud of Balkan Sobranie drawn in through her ivory cigarette holder.

"That's right. That's what the brother's saying," Cecelia answered, snickering and looking Carla in the eye. "You got to watch that wagging black ass."

"You know I know **that**," Leeann said with such mock snobbishness and a theatrical shaking of her tail feathers accompanied by vaudevillian eye-popping that everyone laughed.

"So," Kelvin Thomson continued after almost choking on his own laughter, "we have something else right down here in the gutbucket. I mean **down** there, brothers and sisters. Something that reverses the common meaning and the common understanding. Even more than we've already said. I meant get down, turnaround. This blues power is everything we've already said it is—plus: it's also a first cousin of communion, nearly a goddam twin."

"What?" Cecelia asked, her eyes as serious as a mortician's. She had converted to Catholicism ten years earlier, stayed in it for nearly five years, and still wasn't going to sit there and hear anything goofy about the Eucharist. Better watch yourself. Those eyes nailed her attitude to Kelvin Thomson's forehead and he could feel it as he put a twinkling gaze on his St. Louis woman.

"In communion, sweetest, you are following what sounds like, on the surface anyway, the cannibal instructions of a nonviolent messiah."

"Well, he wasn't always nonviolent," Bobo said. "He whippped the shit out of them money lenders. Knocked all of their tables over and took a serious lickin' stick to them motherfuckers. They got kicked to the curb. He wasn't there to go for no bullshit."

Bobo had closed the conversation down for a moment as everyone turned to him and, seeing a dark pugnaciousness flare up in his face, understood that this was the Jesus with whom he most identified.

"But what do you mean about communion?" Carla asked, seating herself in her Bobo's lap and leaning back into his arms, perhaps challenging Cecelia to look askance. Her question was quiet and soft but the feeling was urgent. When she was still young and on her knees waiting for the wafer and the sip during the Lutheran mass, the moment of Holy Communion always had the feeling of heavenly magic. Never failed.

"I mean people frown on communion because they take what Jesus said literally. You can't do that. People who hate or don't understand Christianity do that. They miss the blues poetry. It was already blues poetry when he laid it down in symbols. The man was still alive. And he sure the fuck wasn't telling his disciples to put him on the menu right then and have some fun later on when the Romans put his body in a cave. That's why it's blues poetry. That's why it's another version of playing the blues to lose the blues."

"All right now," Bobo said, squeezing Carla to him and kissing her on the back of the neck. A speck of ice came into Cecelia's eyes.

"I understand the people who are repelled by the words Jesus used because the truth of the Last Supper is based on two of the worst things you can imagine, chewing on human flesh and guzzling human blood. But instead of turning your stomach they turn everything around. They become the symbols of connecting to the holy spirit of God and salvation through that ritual grub of bread and wine."

"Mmmm," Leeann moaned as if she were in church.

"I say another amen to your moaning amen," Kelvin Thomson said, mimicking a Negro pastor's sound and getting a fat laugh before he went on. "The Last Supper was something, girls and boys. Something. Rough stuff. Futuristic. Jesus was nobody's philosophical bum. This man was a long way past the primitive custom of slicing off a piece of the king's carcass and gobbling it down before putting on the crown and letting that power mash creases in your head. That so-called issue of flesh, that kind of snack stuck around in castles and behind closed European doors long after Mary wept over the body of her crucified son. No: Christ was flying out from another nest. He was serving symbols of everlasting life at his last table."

Carla felt as if a shaft of light had thrown open the shutters of her heart.

"We're talking major reversals of perception here," Kelvin Thomson smiled as Cecelia proudly grinned at him. "Get down turnaround. That's the ultimate power of God anyway: reversal and redefinition. That's why I'm saying the blues is nearly a twin of communion, **too**. That's **exactly** what Mr. Handy understood perfectly, brothers and sisters. Exactly the same thing. **Major** reversals. He was right on the goddam money: "If the **Devil** brought it, the good **Lord** sent it.' From where we are now, I don't think we're going to do much better than that. Hell no. At least not in terms of pulling down a better sense of how quirky the relationship is between good and evil, the shadow and the act, the crack of doom and some fat back. You got to watch that Negro. He'll upset you."

There was a pause in the talk as everyone appeared to be thinking about what they had been saying. Leeann moved around refreshing drinks and emptying ashtrays, wiping corners and quickly moving on to something else, maintaining order but with a fluidity that defined her as a great party giver. The image of Leeann wagging her bottom and parodying herself at the same time came back to Carla as she rose from Bobo's lap to get a glass of water. The girl from South Dakota wondered if she would ever become so at ease about her own backside that she could make fun of it and be proud of that flesh at the same time. Well, she was proud of it, that was for sure.

"You know, it's like in those Road Runner cartoons," Maxwell said, "where the coyote takes all of his Acme stuff and makes this crazy invention to get the Road Runner and ends up getting his ass kicked by his own designs."

The others realized that he was still thinking about the blues.

"That'll do, too. That's right across the plate. You're still thinking about that stuff."

"I like to keep going."

"So do I, brother. Check this out. Another interesting part of that section in Mark **and** Luke is that Lincoln got his 'house divided against itself cannot stand' line from there. Except that in the Bible the subject was the house of Satan being divided against itself by the finger of God," Kelvin Thomson said, hugging Cecelia with one arm as he drained his glass of sacrilegiously watered single malt and the sheer intensity and softness of her affection for that man created a torrid mist of tenderness that Carla wanted to turn her eyes from, it was so naked and so vulnerable. But it made her think she knew, for the first time, what she herself must have looked like when she was with Bobo and all her love for him had unashamedly come to full life, pushing every particle of shyness aside in the sweep of its completeness.

The night ended with **Ellington Indigos**, so many alluring ballads in succession and everybody dancing close, Carla so pleased for Cecelia but also—quite against her will—somewhat interested in

Maxwell Davis, who turned out to be far more intriguing than she would have thought when they first crossed paths, back on that epiphanic night when he performed in duet with Bobo but she could only hear the splashes, rolls, pings, thumps, chattering, snaps, and brushes of the drums. As everyone was relaxing in a collective groan of pleasure which was surely a prelude to coupling, a rather dashing German aristocrat and filmmaker named Ekkehard turned up to have one last drink with Leeann, who used his arrival as a cue to shoo everybody else to the door so that she might find out just what would turn the face of her baron cherry red.

The Gathering Place was just outside Houston on a back road with a large parking lot surrounded by a metal mesh fence. Before driving there, Maxwell and Carla relaxed in their bedroom after dinner, while Ezekiel did the dishes and talked with Eunice, who didn't really approve of blues joints but didn't really dislike them either. She just never stuck her head in one. Ezekiel, of course, knew them inside out, sideways, and upside down, but he couldn't step back into that realm of temptation; the pull was too strong for him. So when it came time for their son and his woman to leave, Ezekiel and Eunice gave off the feeling that two people they loved were going into dangerous territory, where anything might happen. Maxwell laughed off any possibility of that, asking when was the last time that something bad had happened out there. Can't remember had been the answer. The youngsters had taken over all of the shooting and cutting, shooting mostly. Well, unless some rappers rushed in looking to kill each other, Maxwell said that he felt pretty safe. If he didn't, there was *no* way that he would take Carla over there.

Over there was stucco painted the color of red brick. Inside they served cheap wine and cheap hard liquor, put potato chips and pretzels on the bar and at the tables. There was also a popcorn machine and one could get a very, very greasy sausage sandwich with some potato salad when it got late. Was not served before late. Late didn't have no time; late was when it got served on a paper plate with a little colored napkin and a white plastic fork. You better be glad you're getting anything.

All of the tables were old, the chairs in disrepair, and the hustlers who hung out there were old as well, still walking those ancient street struts and dressing in loud outfits that were not quite up to date but could make for a hilarious image, such as the pock-faced, pot-gutted guy who was wearing a purple linen motoring cap, scads of gold chains, some white long johns, a red belted and zippered pouch right under his belly, gold house slippers, a deep purple cape, and an enormous diamond ring on each hand. He was accompanied by some ladies of the night who had surely seen better times but were still ready to lie down or immediately go to their knees if the price was right. But there were also mostly older workaday people who wanted to hear them some good blues before they met the white man the next morning and continued to spend the rest of the week daydreaming about Friday night. They wore the mishmash of jogging suits, straw caps, overalls, pants suits, T-shirts that made them walking advertisements, and all of the combinations that older black people, confused by the oddball fashions of the day, found themselves sporting in public. That was just as true of the bad wigs, weaves, and braids on the heads of the women.

The conviviality in the air was solid with familiarity and the timbre of bad news heard and shared, then dismissed in favor of another drink or a sudden story that had nothing to do with the subject under discussion. Everyone, from hustler to straight-life customer, looked Carla up and down, the hustlers trying to figure out if she was a prostitute, which would lift Maxwell to the sky in their eyes; the others just wondering what this boy was doing bringing a two-apple-assed white woman in this place like she belonged in there, which she couldn't, but, actually, she could, since nobody gave a good goddam about a white woman coming around anyway, particularly since those white blues-listening-to kids from the schools and the ones thought they might play them some of this shit themselves could flood up in the Gathering Place on Friday and Saturday every once and a while, making so much motherfucking noise and whooping and spinning around you would think they got the Holy Ghost and the up-tempo palsy at the same time. Whole lot of shaking long hair going on.

The band was led by J. D. Pettibone, who was at least seventy-five and sat down onstage with his guitar in his lap and a rhythm section of younger musicians behind him. Some of the rhythm section guys had plans to quit everything they did to make money during the week and break out for Chicago, where they said a man could still make a living playing the blues. Pettibone called Maxwell up to the band-stand as soon as he noticed that the saxophonist had his instrument and told the people he knew this boy from back when the boy couldn't do nothing but slobber through his horn. Done got famous now. Somewhere out there. New York, probably. Some kind of place. Can't keep up with everything. But you don't have to keep up with the blues. All you got to do is feel them the right way, and before you know it, they'll come prancing out of you like you didn't even have to sing them or play them. Happy, therefore, to have somebody used to sneak around and listen to the old heads play that rocking good music. Happy as a sissy in Boys Town. All right, Maxwell Davis. Let's get it on.

Afterward, someone came in who was very dark-skinned, burly, and had on an open shirt with his hairy chest showing. He was wear-ing gold chains, Jheri-Kurls, and a big white Stetson. The man was no stranger to the room and had the demeanor of one who was admired by all who frequented the place. Carla didn't have the slightest doubt that this was Rodney and was made perfectly sure when she heard somebody over there at the bar call his name as he laughed and laid down his money, taking charge of his space and all who were in it.

Maxwell, fortunately, was the kind of musician who didn't wander around in a club after he had played. He sat down in a place where he could see everything and allowed the listeners to come to him. They might be invited to sit down, if they were effusive enough about his playing or had the scent of intrigue. So everything seemed pretty safe for the time being. Neither Rodney nor Maxwell paid any atten-tion to each other. They were both too egotistical. Someone pointed Maxwell out to Rodney, who didn't even look in his direction, only said that he was on the way somewhere and didn't want to get hung up listening. He had just come by for a nasty drink before putting some rubber on the road in town until he found a place and a woman who caught his attention. Then he would pounce. The intermission was interminable and Carla, having drunk many glasses of Eunice's splendid ice tea before they left, had to use the bathroom so badly she thought she would urinate on herself if she didn't go soon. When sure that neither of these two guys would get within even ten yards of each other, she made her move.

Carla went to the shabby ladies' room, which had some dusty plastic flowers stapled to the wall around the mirror, an old rusty machine that once disseminated Kotex, a very weak lightbulb, and some sandpaper bathroom tissue you also had to use after washing your hands in the sink, which had water coming ice cold from one faucet and boiling hot from the other. She took some perfume from her purse and sprayed a bit in her hair and quickly across her neck and the front of her dress. When she came out, Maxwell was gone and so was Rodney.

"Where did Maxwell go?"

"Oh, he and Rodney went outside. That's the door," the bartender said, pointing as if she could have forgotten the entrance through which they had come into the place. Asshole.

The infamous Cadillac was parked in a spot all by itself and the two of them were near it. Carla ran over to them.

"Maxwell. What are you doing?"

"I wanted to see this guy's car and I wanted to tell him something. You can go back in. This is between us."

"I'll stay right here."

"Carla, go back in the bar."

"I'm not going anywhere unless you're with me."

"Yes you are."

She didn't move.

"Well stand right there then."

"Quite a little girl you got."

"That's between me and her. Let's you and me get to the real deal."

"What's that, brother?"

"I know who you are."

"Everybody in the nightlife knows Rodney. I'm the emperor of the evening time."

"I know what you did, Rodney."

"I did a lot of things."

"Yeah, right. I'm only talking to you about one thing, though. The others I'm not giving a fuck about. Just one thing."

"So what is that?"

"You tried to kill my sister."

"Who told you that?"

"I'm talking about Malena. You tried to kill her."

"Maxwell, let's go."

"Carla, I told you to go back in the club."

"No."

"Look, you're making me very angry."

"I'm angry, too. Why are we out here in the first place?"

"That's my business."

"It is not. It's our business."

"I love you, baby, but if you say one more word, I swear I'll have to slap the shit out of you."

"Then I guess you will. We have to go. Maxwell, let's go."

"Go on with your girl, boy. You don't know nothing about down here. She's right. Get your ass out of here. You're edging up on thunder."

"On what?"

Rodney tilted his head back.

"What the fuck did you say?"

"Thunder! And when Rodney cracks, lightning comes out."

"Maxwell . . ."

"I have just have one thing to say to you."

"Say what you want to say, say *all* you want, but you better not try to put your hands on me, saxophone boy."

"I'm just telling you this. You better be glad I didn't know about you when you tried to kill my sister, when you tried to get her killed, you jive-assed motherfucker—"

"I'm not going to hear but *one* motherfucker."

"You better be glad. . . . Anyway, I just want you to know this: the me who was walking around when you tried that shit, he would kill you right here."

"I can die anywhere. Ain't no special place set for me. Ain't no special time. But wherever I die, I'll be dying a *man* and no stringy-haired white girl with a nigger ass is going to be nipping at *my* heels."

"Maxwell, let's go. Leave this piece of garbage to himself." She tried to pull Maxwell but couldn't do it. He was there, like a telephone pole, a tomb, a heavy safe. She tried to pull him away again, then looked at Rodney, hating him for being there and for everything he was and would ever be. If she and Maxwell could just get beyond this moment. If they could just start moving on away.

"Will you leave us alone? You bastard. Leave us alone. Please let us go away from here."

Rodney didn't look at her. His eyes were on Maxwell, whose anger was still mounting and whose cheeks were starting to wiggle with the heat of his rage. That didn't mean anything to Rodney. He now looked at Carla, whose eyes were almost watering.

"I do think I'm in the wrong. I believe I am. Yes, I am. You can call me names. I don't mind. I deserve that. Mmmm. Mmmm. I shouldn't have insulted this woman. Not at all. She's just trying to help you, man. She's trying to stop the blood from puddling. I deeply apologize, Miss Lady. All my heart is in everything I'm saying. *Please* accept my apology."

Through her fury and her alarm Carla felt pierced by the implacable charm that had brought Malena to the edge of the burying ground. Maxwell vibrated as he stared at Rodney, who now backed up to his car and leaned against the fender of the iron horse that had been so prized by the mechanics and automobile collectors for so long. In its hard white shininess, even under the nearly starless sky, the Cadillac was a solid piece of 1948. It was an impartial part of history that might, one more time, bear witness to bloodshed, just as surely as it had rolled past places and over roads where murder, hot or cold, had already been done.

"Listen to me, Mr. Davis. Just give me a little bit of space, just a corner. Keep a-hold of yourself. I know you heard what you heard from these niggers around here."

"I heard what happened."

"They say all *kind* of shit. They just fighting the silence with some *lies*. Now you and me about to pay the cost."

"Well, I *believe* what they said."

Carla stepped between Maxwell and Rodney, looking her man in the face, so much violence coming out of him it could singe her dress and her hair.

"Ain't *this* a wagonful of bitches? Something to tell the *world*. I swear the nighttime is the *right* time. Now you see what kind of a woman *you* got. You see that. You better look a little closer. I think you better. We *all* want that. I mean I don't know *nobody* who don't. I hope you know what you holding on to, boy."

Maxwell moved to push Carla out of his way but she dug in and threw her arms around him.

"I'm not going to let you do this."

"Well, in that case, I ain't neither," Rodney said, moving around to the driver's side of his car and opening the door, the rolled-up black windows just below his chest as the sound of untold pride forced itself upward. "You know, we can start marching toward the hospital. Or the morgue. You and me, Mr. Davis. Makes me no never mind. I'm not trying to be late for my funeral. But I'm running from *myself* tonight, and there ain't no way, saxophone boy, that you can catch *Rodney*. I'm the emperor of the night, god*dam*. That's who *I* am!" He was then behind the dashboard and the motor turned over with a walloping snarl as the wheels began to sputter gravel and the man who wanted to murder Malena for her insurance money was gone like the father of the wind.

"Carla . . ."

"Yes, sweetheart."

"You know you couldn't hold me if I didn't want you to hold me."

"I know."

"But I would have had to hurt you, baby."

"Yes, you would. Right here."

"I love you too much for that."

"I know that. Maxwell . . ."

"Yes, baby."

"God, I don't know. I just love you. I just love you *so* much. That's all."

Maxwell sighed out the sulfur of limitless anger, closed his eyes, and started massaging his forehead.

"I think I need to go back in there and play me some more *blues.*"

She hugged him, knowing that there would have been nothing she could do if two men that big had decided that the point was to make sure that the other guy never breathed another fucking day in this world. That would have been the death dance. She would have fought. She would have screamed. She would have been hurt or broken up as they went their violent way. Death had whistled, twanged, and whizzed past her ear. She had never heard that terrible music before. Not like *that*. Then Rodney turned the corner with his wheels howling, rolled up on the sidewalk, nearly scraping the mesh fence right next to the parking lot, and shouted "All *right!*" with all his enormous might, gunned his motor, lifted his white Stetson above the smoked windows, and sped on into the blackness of the road, the two red lights on the back of his Cadillac diminishing in size until they were invisible. The blue light of the sky was Carla's blues and the red lights were her mind. Maxwell laughed. It was over. Her man was shaking his head and chuckling.

"What a *wild* motherfucker," he said to Carla, lifting her up and turning around and around. Maxwell didn't feel to the touch like he had when she was trying to pull him away or when she embraced him as her last resort. The pace of his heartbeat was slowing and he was no longer trembling.

"Do I have to say it again?

"Say what, sweetheart?"

"That I think I need to go play me some *blues.*"

There were some people near the door. Their eyes looked like tongues that were ready to lick up some blood if any had been spilled. They parted so Maxwell and Carla could go into the Gathering Spot. The band was just back on and hit one of those pure blues grooves: a-wookata-too-too-too, a-wookata-too-too-too, a-wookata-too-too-too, a-wookata-too-too-too. Uh-oh: there it was. The rhythm train was calling for all those who could to step right up those stairs of blues time and get on board. Carla sat right in front of the little band-stand, pooped out. A nice cold beer was brought to her that she hadn't ordered. It was ambrosia. Some people were immediately dancing. Maxwell attached his neck strap to his tenor saxophone, which now looked like a magnificently curved and pearl-buttoned medallion instead of an instrument, a symbol of accomplishment and a way of saying just who he was. The first long note that he squeezed out was more masculine and more tender and more androgynous and more than male or female or happy or sad or frightened or brave or knowing or befuddled than anything she had ever heard her man play. Carla burst into tears with all the feeling of what had been clogged up during the struggle out in the parking lot, but she laughed as she simultaneously experienced a rising much like the one that had happened when she was praying as a little girl in South Dakota, right next to Mom, and traveled up through the Lutheran roof to where eternity was as smooth and as easy to cross as the glittering floor of a transporting ballroom. This was their Houston night, all of it; Maxwell was her man, and they had made it through to the blues glee that was presently booting its way out of his tenor. The music was a shelter and a traveling place and a temple with all of the stories well told on the walls of its sound. Nobody, a little while before, might have known the trouble that was between them, but now they all knew, everyone sober or moving up on tipsy or drunk as a skunk, and it was clear in note after note that just the two of them were now wed in some way that was special beyond even the most elegant ceremony.

Part Two

BACK IN

THE APPLE

13

A SPONGE, NOT A SIEVE

As ALWAYS in Crescent City, things were right and so was she on this homecoming Sunday. The piano had been tuned, the musicians were swinging with her, and Carla was in very good voice. The songs she chose were "Please Don't Talk About Me When I'm Gone," "I'll Be Seeing You," "Mean to Me," "I Remember You," "You Can Have Him," "Remember," "Body and Soul," "You and the Night and the Music," "Ill Wind," "Ghost of a Chance," "There'll Never Be Another You," "This Time the Dream's on Me," and "I Cried for You." From the first beat, Carla knew that it was all the way *on* this afternoon. It was *on*. Things were so high-flying the lady could pat her foot on the light and the dark sides of the moon. Something new happened to her body: the rhythm of the swing was inside her right leg, which rose and came down on the toe as she reached for certain phrases. Then it was in her left leg. The sigh and the howl of life were bursting inside the purr of her soul and freedom was everywhere. She could have been the wind stalking through the music. She hit every note she heard and brought off almost every phrase she tried, sometimes starting in the second eight and moving it all the way up into the modulation and across the bridge until she was in the last eight before taking a breath. Deal with that.

The musicians were obviously happy with the way she was getting the job done up there and her mood was exultant. Her story was so clear it felt as though it were coming out of her pores. There was nothing like singing the blues away. The people were in there, too. This audience was her favorite kind, mixed to almost a United Nations condition, and they were with her, clapping at the right places, keeping their conversations below the distracting level, and rocking with—not against—the beat. Just looking at them was another aspect of inspiration. What a groove. This was what she came into music for.

Doing all right could definitely be her theme song right now. What she sang and what you heard was what she was. That had gone through her mind when she was getting ready to go to work, picking out her dress, her shoes, putting on her makeup, dropping in her purse the stuff she would use to freshen up her looks during the break. It was lonely in the loft with Maxwell gone back out on the road already. *Anyway:* over that last two and a half years, up there on that bandstand and in the back rooms of clubs, the girl from South Dakota became one of the guys. All by her lonesome. They were dealing with her, not her as Maxwell's girlfriend. She was right in there joking, complaining about out-of-tune pianos, doing parodic imitations of the club owners. She was discussing chords, rhythms, who could play and who couldn't. She was making smug fun of the jazz writers who didn't really spend that much time in clubs listening to the art they sat in judgment of, content to argue with each other about recordings and, though musical illiterates, write reviews as if they knew enough music to truly evaluate somebody's harmonic conception, melodic gifts, technique, or rhythmic approach. Since things between the two of them were back in the trash, waiting for the garbage trucks to haul them away, Carla tried to keep her mind on herself as she strode downstairs from their loft and started walking east toward Crescent City. No, she didn't want to think about him and the ambivalence that started stinking up their home as he turned his back on all that had brought them together, all that had moved them up to higher ground in Houston. Her hope was, essentially, gone.

Thinking about him was not something to do. But she did as her thoughts about the nature of show business turned in his direction. He was so stealthy, so brilliantly stealthy. Maxwell was such a devious master at dealing with the jazz critics, always cordial, joking, and giving them the secretly cruel but tactical impression that they were insiders while keeping a scrapbook of the stupidest things they wrote, which he used for his amusement and read aloud to other musicians when he gave parties, all of them finding it was better to make fun of what oppressed them than spend a lot of time pissing and moaning about the kind of problem Duke Ellington called "a complaint that has no future." Ellington sure knew how to name it.

Now, during the Crescent City break, sitting in her dressing room and relaxing among the liquor cases, still trying to keep her mind off of Maxwell, she was desperate for an emotional breather, a little space, some fresh breeze in the unventilated room of anxiety that was her consciousness half the time. But there was the bandstand. Yes, there was. All the romantic trouble overshadowed what was going on for her until times like this chance to stand most like herself in the music. As of this very afternoon, her confidence was in place and the overall arc of her life was coming into first light, as if she didn't even *need* to know how widely her universe existed apart from her present difficulties. It might be best to see just how long other sides of her life could claim squatter's rights on her memory as opposed to worrying herself about this man of hers who just might not be there too much longer. She decided to do that. Wash him out of her hair.

It was sort of a game Carla would play with herself, hide-and-seek with thoughts about her lover, who had been so good to her for so long she assumed too much of the world was there for this particular woman. Remember who you are and how much you have. Carla might as well have been back in the bed in Houston, up late and thinking about the night of girl talk and the party at Toot Celestine's. That was a very good night up in the northern New Orleans head-quarters of Manhattan, but she was sounding even better this after-noon. Perhaps she was in one of those periods of swift growth that pushed its way in and dragged her talent up the road so fast it almost bloodied her knees. Your God-given ability could take care of you, if you took care of it.

She was soon joking for a bit with Jed Corsakoff, one of her favorite bass players. Maxwell didn't hire Jed anymore; he only used black musicians now. Well, those were his jobs. This one was hers. No time for mood indigo. Jed was chiding her for singing such perfect harmony, which made Carla, of course, an imperfect singer, since so many of them, he said, wouldn't know the right chord if it walked in their dark bedroom after midnight with a Day-Glo condom on. Clearly a Freudian banana peel wrapped around the meat of the metaphor, he laughed. The bassist rubbed his hands together, took a theatrically loud deep breath, and told her he was about to psychologically lasso the big Texas blonde at the bar, then escort her home for some Manhattan rodeo-romping, kosher style. Open sesame, little doggy. Determined, Jed left in a hurry.

Mickey came in and was effusive about how wonderful her sound was this afternoon. She was always more than good, he told her, but today she was singing as if she were a sweet angel in heaven. She was divine. He wished his father were alive to hear her.

Mickey owned Crescent City, a restaurant upstairs on Broadway near Union Square. The place was designed to look as though it were in New Orleans and the food was especially delicious. Mickey's given name was Michael Latagano and he had spent an entire evening a couple of years ago telling her and Maxwell how much he hated the Mafia and what shame they had brought to the Italian people. As a kid he had hated them. Who were these guys walking around frightening the neighborhood and demanding money for being willing to hurt people who had done them nothing?

Like he always did, one day Mickey the schoolboy came back from school into the store of his two aunts on Mulberry Street down in Little Italy. It was the middle of the afternoon and there was no one there. No one. This was not what he expected. He wanted his daily piece of pastry and his cappuccino. He had been thinking about the taste so much he almost stepped into a big pile of crap in the street. So here he was. A hungry schoolboy with his books feeling like iron. He set them down on a table and looked the place over. Nobody. It felt like ghosts in there. Dull blades started twisting in his stomach. Evil was quivering in the air. What was going on? It was quiet as the inside of a coffin. What should he do? Go home and tell his mother to come there? She would know. Wait. He looked behind the counter. Jesus Christ! There they were, his aunts, these two large Italian women, lying on the floor. Still as death. Still like they was laying embalmed in the funeral home. Oh, my God. Then he got surprised again. His two aunts sat up when he whimpered and they asked if the body of the dead man was still out there. What did this crazy kid mean there was no body? Did he have horse manure for brains? They were in a rage. This was not the time for joking. Not on this day. They were serious. No idiot monkey business. Look for yourself. Use your eyes. Out there on the floor. On the floor, dumb head. Out there is a man in the corner. The man has his brains blown out. Neither stood but both lifted their right arms and pointed. Stupid head. In the corner! Not so. They were crazy. Total nuts. They were wrong. There was no man. There was no mess. Mickey could see Carla was confused. He paused. This thing is something. It is their way, these people. You must understand, these piles of horseshit they were talking about could murder very neat. It was their business. Where the man had been sitting was as clean as the mind of a newborn baby. But the tablecloth, there was their mark: it was gone. That was the cost of a dead man to them. A tablecloth. The next day a big man with pocks all over his face and broken teeth, this man with a big scar on his throat, he gave me a bag for my two aunts. A new tablecloth was in it.

Mickey, who drank seventeen cups of espresso a day and was sure he would ultimately destroy his kidneys, had heard from a certain musical guy that Carla was a very good singer and asked her when she was in there one night with Leeann and an Italian textile million-aire if she wanted to work at this place, which was going to have music on the weekends, Saturday and Sunday afternoons.

Sure, she said, if things are right. It's hard for a singer if they're not right.

In this place, he said, they will be right.

Did he want to hear a tape or anything?

No, he had his ways of knowing what was going on.

Really?

Sure.

Let's talk about money.

Let's.

"If my father, if my father was alive, Carla, my father, he would go crazy for you this afternoon. Just crazy. Finished. Gone. Insane. It would be too much for him. You in my place. That angel voice in your throat. Who could ask for anything more?" Mickey said, leaving her alone in the dressing room.

Grateful for what Jed and Mickey had said to her, that support, Carla thanked her lucky stars, knocked wood, and crossed her fingers before taking another sip of her beer as she relived the scintillating spiritual experience of just how much *she* had done with the expressive quality of her voice once Maxwell explained that he didn't really start playing the tenor saxophone until it hit him. The hell with hiding. Forget trying to stop thinking about him. He's part of you. His story is part of your story. All the stories you've heard are part of your story. You been a good old contemplative, gloating sponge too long to try and be a sieve right now, girl. That's right. You know you remember what he said. You will never forget that. Ever. It happened to him in New York. He had just learned how to fill up that horn, not send a hollow string of sound from his mouth all the way out of the saxophone's bell. On that day of new information, he laid up on a nice round B-flat, playing it again and again, putting all kinds of thick tenor grease on it. Then he knew something. It was a revelation.

"Every instrument ever invented," he said, "is a dead serious commentary on the limitations of every other instrument any goddam where on the face of this bitter earth. You're bright; I know you'll understand this. My baby with the big brain and the big heart."

He kissed her and continued talking. What a lovely moment. He was so supportive then. She needed that. Carla couldn't deny it.

"What I'm saying, Carla, is if something besides the tenor could do exactly what the tenor did, line up with it all the way, there wouldn't be no tenor; you wouldn't need it; it would be redundant. Yeah: every instrument has its own very special abilities. Once you find your personality inside of *that,* you can start truly playing something."

She didn't have to hear that twice.

From that point on, Carla was always listening for the sound that was really hers and began using her voice to do the things that instruments couldn't do. Diction then became absolutely important. Make those words come out clearly, no matter how cloudy the passion they expressed might be. The deep singer in her also began to hear and practice each pitch with many alternate colorings, all of them bent on clarifying the emotional meaning of a passage. Though Maxwell had made her aware of what she had to deal with, the woman had done it herself. She had figured out how to make the idea a fact of aesthetic action. He could lead her to the water but she had to do the bending down and the drinking. She was the one who had to get down on her knees.

In order to open up her ear, Carla sang scales by assigning to each note one of the many sounds a great singer had at her disposal when manipulating feeling and color into a specific pitch—a Billie Holiday C, a Sarah Vaughan C-sharp, a Dinah Washington D, a Bessie Smith D-sharp, an Ella Fitzgerald E, an Aretha Franklin F, a Mahalia Jackson F-sharp, a Helen Humes G, a Shirley Horne G-sharp, an Ivie Anderson A, a Betty Carter A-sharp, an Abbey Lincoln B, and on and on, changing the order, up and down, or using other singers as reference points, until any note, hit perfectly in tune or intentionally just a bit sharp or flat, had many different basic sounds in her mind and places in her body where she could send her voice to get them.

Imitation wasn't the idea at all. Her goal was quite removed from the weird multiple-personality impact had on an audience by a performer with no individual direction, which made the work, even if highly polished, an embarrassing pastiche. The elements of those singers Carla utilized just allowed her entry points; once she got into that color, that vibrato, that way of slurring into or out of a note, the job was making it purely personal.

She also used her sound differently to sing something in the minor as opposed to the major, darker for one, brighter for the other. Curious to bold, she might actually invert matters to hear just what vibration was created by the bright side of her voice singing a minor tune, and vice versa. Such approaches made her realize even more fully that one could modulate in timbre, or tonal color, as opposed to the key and get just about as dramatic an effect.

With those techniques arriving for the artistic purposes of emotional precision, not tricks, Carla's self-assurance kept stepping up until, with her feet on the bandstand and her eyes looking straight into the audience, the scared little girl from the Midwest was gone the way of all lesser evolutions. This woman was there to swing, to invent, to create for herself a place within the sound of the band and tell the audience all that her soul had prepared her to tell.

That old demon of silently bragging was sneaking into her dressing room at Crescent City as she thought about that plateau of her own achievement. It was hard not to feel your ego yeasting up when a Sunday afternoon—or any time—went this exceedingly well. You could begin to believe you were just a bit more than a little special. The mind, always happy to take on the job of self-inflation, could start building you a mirror like the one the evil queen used in Snow White. Evil Gal Blues, she quietly chuckled.

Jed brought the big Texas blonde into the dressing room. Kelsie was her name. He said he just wanted her to meet the lady who swings the band. Kelsie, smoking an unfiltered cigarette and coating the end of it with purplish lipstick, told Carla she was in town for some business, just walking her fat ass down the street when something up and told her this was the best place to be. Right out of the fucking blue. Strange as hellfire in an ice cream parlor. Really was. She didn't know anything about jazz but she sure the hell liked what she heard. Liked it a whole goddam hell of a lot. Carla thanked her. Jed obviously didn't want to take up more of Carla's moments alone, nor did he want to waste any time getting this Texas girl in the ride 'em, cowboy mood. He left by saying to Kelsie that Carla was just marvelous. She always was. Kelsie said that was believable.

It wasn't always like that, by by the by.

As with all professionals, when the last set had been performed and the last note sung, there were those dogging moments the girl from South Dakota might also experience—the unsatisfied late-night feeling, the bottomless annoyance that came of something having gone wrong, song after song. She and Maxwell had often talked about that. It was always something no one could explain. The personnel was just what you wanted. The sound system was good. The audience was behind you. The material was well rehearsed. But nothing happened. It was just a big flop. By the finish, if you had risen to the low end of mediocrity, that was a fabulous victory. Even if the audience loved it, or pretended to love it, you knew precisely what you had sung or played or how the band had sounded. Like pure shit. However consistent he was, sometimes Maxwell was so frustrated he seemed like he wanted to fight. There was nobody to fight, however, which meant that he might pick on some musician and begin insulting him, only to catch himself and apologize for trying to ease the mood of defeat by making somebody else feel bad. Carla wasn't like that. She usually wanted to do something and push her mind off of the failure. She was already thinking about Maxwell too much. The vow should have been maintained. Try again. Remember something about yourself. You have a world apart from him. You *do*. You *do*. Come on.

Down in the blues one night about a year ago because she hadn't been able to satisfactorily bring off *anything* she was trying, Carla went out after her gig to the Russian Samovar, a club on Fifty-second Street, just west of Gallagher's and Roseland.

Now she had it going. The dressing room didn't feel so oppressive. That part was coming back.

If she could only relive that experience for a couple of weeks, every second of twenty-four hours, that would be better than perfect luck. What an appropriate time this was to regain the feeling of that past night of redemption. Oh, she could stand some redemption right now. Plenty. It was a different thing from basically being in such a good interior place because the music was sounding so great in Crescent City this afternoon. A serving of redemption would certainly do. With none walking into her dressing room right now, Carla decided again to summon some up.

The gig that redemptive time was two early sets in the East Forties. There were other people who cared about her. Others who looked out for her. Maxwell wasn't the only one who could feel the presence of her heart. She knew that all along, but New York was a town in which it was always good to be reminded of that little piece of the truth. Manhattan could invite you in, but it could just as easily leave you naked in the snow and notice nothing until you had become a statue of death. Cut the morbid sentimentality. Get to the grits.

The job was done at ten-thirty, Maxwell was out of town, and she didn't want to go home. All she would do there was brood. That was all. Brood, brood, that's my food, don't want anything else when I'm in this mood.

Carla was fortunate enough to be with the inimitable Jed Corsakoff, whom she had become used to and always found funny, a cocky but charming little guy who loved to smoke cigarette after cigarette and say, whenever he could slip it in, that his nickname in Italy was "Il Cavallo." Ah, a centaur.

Jed had the streets of New York stenciled on his spirit and carried himself as though he owned every particle of the town, concrete and glass, flesh and blood, heart and soul. When Carla was around him, she sometimes knew what it must have felt like to see Bonaparte crown himself. There was no doubt in this man's personality. Zero. He had surely conquered that side of himself—if it was ever there. There were those who thought the world was theirs from the moment they learned to walk on it. Jed was like that, moxie from head to toe. Yet he wasn't obnoxious and played with so much drive, heat, and sensitivity nearly everyone loved him. His uncluttered ambition was to always step up on the most swinging part of the beat, especially when he was on a bandstand with some black guys who could really play. "In short, which is not a description of my height, by the way, I don't intend to be up there sounding like 'the white boy.' Never. Not one note. If they are *fair* about this shit, and they *still* don't like me, it will be because I'm *me,* not because I come off sounding like your prototypical non-swinging white motherfucker. To give credit where credit is due—to myself, of course—that is not a problem. Not a chance. Hitler, the dumb fuck, had a better chance conquering Russia."

His heroes were Percy Heath, Paul Chambers, Charles Mingus, Oscar Pettiford, and Ron Carter. Their examples provided Jed with the theory that the best kind of jazz bass line, delivered almost exclusively in swinging quarter notes, was a new horizon in counterpoint because, chorus after chorus, it was a subtle, melodic way of delivering and interpreting the harmony of every chord while responding to the piano, the drums, and the horizontal invention of the featured player or singer.

One time Maxwell—there he was again!—and Jed came back off the road together, took her to a delicious red-meat dinner at the West Sixty-third Street Steakhouse, went downstairs to Iridium, and heard Charles McPherson blow the bell off of the alto saxophone, filling every space in the room with absolute life. Maxwell listened to him with awe and appreciation because he was twenty years older than her man, who would have addressed that sound with interest and competitive disdain had the man been his age or younger. The three of them, overwhelmed by the music, rode downtown to the apartment and had a little jam session, tenor saxophone, singer, and bass. Then, while she had red wine, the two of them sat up late into the night smoking Monte Cruz robustos and drinking grappa—"gasoline in a bottle," as Jed called it.

Maxwell told the one about the musician who goes to heaven and hears Charlie Parker playing his ass off around a corner somewhere. All that swing and blues and melody lets him know how much fun he's going to have in the upper room. Gee whiz, he says to one of the angels, that's Bird playing as good as I ever heard him play on any kind of record or any kind of bootleg recording in a club. I know me some Bird. I'm a collector from down home and way back before way back. Oh, really? *Really.* Well, the angel says, that is something that has to be clarified. Clarify me but don't crucify me. The angel didn't smile. He just said what he had to say. That is not Charlie Parker. It is. It is not. *Is.* Not! They stared javelins at each other. Well, who the hell is it then? Well, it's God *imitating* Charlie Parker.

They all laughed.

Then Jed—whom Maxwell had been egging on in order to get him to deliver one of his monologues, the sort he said made traveling with this little guy so far from humdrum—took a sip of his grappa and came in on cue. He asked, "Carla, have you heard the one about Bach?" She shook her head. "And you, citizen of the saxophone, is this a story you have heard?" Maxwell pulled Carla over to him and put his arm around her, kissing her neck and finding the most comfortable position on the couch as he shook his head. Carla could have purred golden bubbles, she felt so good.

Jed said that what he was going to tell them existed primarily in the world of speculation initially, but proof had come down the line that this had actually happened. No doubt about it. He had to lay down some groundwork. There was no question of credibility in this case. These, however, were still celestial matters.

"It all has to do with Bach's personality. The kind of guy he was. This kind of man would not change. Couldn't do it. You see, if Bach heard Paul Chambers improvising those monster bass lines with Miles Davis at the Blackhawk, his mind would be completely fucked up. Completely. Absolutely. No other choice. But there is no way he would just let all this highly sophisticated counterpoint go by. Couldn't do it. He was Bach, who, in case you two didn't know, was one *very* overbearing motherfucker—by the way. Seriously. *Very.* So he would go to God and beat on His door rather noisily. *God's* door. This guy had *no* tact. Now God, of course, has other things to do and is going full speed ahead with His business, but this noise is even starting to get to Him. He doesn't notice world wars and genocide, but some guy banging on His door irritates Him. What can I tell you? Boom, boom, boom. God can't believe it. He tries patience. In this case, however, patience will not do. It's still happening: boom, boom, boom. So He stops taking care of business and who's at His door but Bach, a guy He has set up pretty fancy in heaven—very, very fancy, in fact. So God wants to know why the fuck Bach is out there beating on His door when He has the whole universe to run and this *isn't* visiting day. Anybody else would take the hint and leave right then. Not Bach. Couldn't do it. So God is staring at him and Bach is staring right back. After all, he *did* write the *St. Matthew Passion*, didn't he? Therefore, this is not a man who takes shit from *anybody*. This means that there is no blinking on either side, not God, not Bach. But, to answer the Big Guy's question, Bach holds up *Miles Davis in Person*—you know: the Blackhawk recordings—which Haydn or Mozart or one of that crew left in his room to *truly* fuck with him. God checks out the cover and says that he heard it. Many times. Yeah, they were swinging. It was Miles Davis and Paul Chambers— what *else* did he expect? Bach turns red and his hair stands up like Don King's. Now God, who was only half paying attention, immediately knows that, as of now, He has a *real* problem. Obvious as a tuxedo on an elephant. Some things are consistent. Like Bach. Whenever this guy went off, when he *really* lost his temper, well, his clavicle would almost pop loose. God could see it coming. After all, His business was being all-knowing. He was good at it, which means He was prepared for what came next. Bach does not ask, he *demands* to be sent back so he could get in on some of *this* shit. That's how it went. He got the transfer, two subway tokens, and some sunglasses. Where is he now? *Where?* You ask, '*Where?*' Oh, he's out there somewhere, still learning how to play. Where *else* would he be? When he gets it together, we'll hear from him. Not until then. This is *still* New York. You can't get credit for a brand name. It's not democratic."

After Jed left, she and Maxwell—uh, uh.

This little guy Jed could also play piano very well, walking extremely inventive bass notes in his left hand when he got loose and inspired enough to keep his right hand going at the same time. This came in handy when he was working with Carla. His keyboard skills made it possible for him to take the place of a late piano player at a rehearsal if it was necessary to hear how some particular chords worked in part of one of her arrangements while she was singing. Those abilities also gave him insights into piano players, his two favorites being Duke Ellington and Thelonious Monk, each for the range of color brought to the individual notes and the startling hues imposed on the chords, something Jed took to heart when he was playing his bass. Carla was sometimes surprised by how much time he had spent learning on his instrument exactly what she had worked on as a singer, which meant that they could have dialogues in timbre as well as melody, harmony, and rhythm. When she had a job and could get Jed, Carla was so delighted she couldn't wait to get to work.

Jed had a sense of her, a *real* sense of her. He could feel her, on and off the bandstand. What a blessing. On that redemptive night Carla wanted to relive so badly as she now sat in the dressing room at Crescent City, Jed knew that the girl from South Dakota was unhappy when they went into the Russian Samovar, which was so Russian the air seemed made of dry vodka. Yeah, he knew. It must have been obvious. She was always moping along after a performance she thought didn't work. Always. It was impossible to stop herself. Yeah, he could tell. No mention was to be made of the job they had just played. Keep that in the background.

After dropping his bass off in his apartment at the Manhattan Plaza on Forty-third Street and Ninth Avenue, the two of them walked up to Fifty-second, strolled east for a couple of blocks, and went in, where Jed told her the food had to be eaten to be believed. You could not take anybody's word for it. You had to taste the stuff. It was very good and it wasn't overpriced. They knew how to prepare something for a plate. These were not slackers in the kitchen.

The smoked salmon he ordered for the both of them was the greatest, but the music got on his nerves, or he pretended it did, saying he was tired of all those minor keys and marching or folk rhythms anybody who could sing and play might perform at the white piano in the middle of the room, booming everybody back to the Ukraine or some such fucking place. Is this a Volga boatman hangout? With a look of indignation so exaggerated that it was laughable, Jed said that he was going to stand up for the Russians who grew up in New York, rose from the table like a general about to leave his tent for battle, then casually took over the piano, playing George Gershwin, Harold Arlen, Irving Berlin, and loudly calling for her until Carla, shy for God knows what reason, had the nerve to go up there and sing with him, turning the whole room into something suddenly American, not in an abrasive way but in a celebration of what the children of all these people would become—if they were lucky enough to get that lyrical grit into their systems. People began clapping and dancing. Russians, what can I tell ya?

Outside, a blizzard was now wailing its way up and down the street, dropping heavier and heavier snow. It had begun following her and Jed in the last block east, the wind getting belligerent, the big flakes covering their overcoats.

To end their little unexpected set, the invading duo improvised something Jed called "Blues for a Moscow Mule," on which he and Carla traded phrases, ad-libbing one insane and bawdy rhyme after another, each phrase eventually getting shorter and shorter as what had been a long blue melody, full of surprise attacks on the harmony, started to withdraw, note by note, until all that remained was one whispered pitch, sexy as hell, to declare what soon became the victory of silence. As if she were his favorite sister, Jed took her hand and they both bowed. The volatile acceptance of the listeners was as thick and welcoming as a brand-new mink coat. Her bad night became a good night. She had been able to redeem herself.

On the way home, in the bone-piercing cold of the snow and the wet New York winter coming off the Hudson that was so unlike the dry chill she grew up experiencing in South Dakota, Carla looked out the window of the cab, thinking only of what a little friendship could do. Oh, God: Jed.

Mickey came in and brought Carla back to Crescent City. He asked her about Maxwell. She answered him. He told her it was time for the last set. Five minutes.

Leeann had arrived with Cecelia and Kelvin Thomson, who were bedding down in her town house for the weekend. What a buddy, what a good, good friend. So supportive.

Carla sang her heart out for her friends. She couldn't stop. The tunes were "Cheek to Cheek," "It's All Right with Me," "If I Should Lose You," "I Should Care," "I Get Along Without You Very Well," "Blue Moon," "There'll Never Be Another You," "Bewitched, Bothered, and Bewildered," "Goody, Goody," "All of Me," "These Foolish Things," "All Or Nothing At All," and "Just Friends." Taking her time, she called every song at exactly the right tempo, and Jed directed the rhythm section from his bass with perfection, shifting gears within the beats in anticipation of Carla or responding perfectly, telling the piano player and the drummer what to do by the way his closeness to her had the sound of friendship so thorough it was telepathic. The cymbals felt like the wind, the piano player's chords were trampolines, and she was so liberated at one point that the embracing emotion Carla drew from her musicians almost made her gasp in the middle of a phrase. Notes and colors she had never heard come out of her body took over and, emotion upon emotion, linked themselves into a story, a drama, the crest of her soul flaring into a line of pitches, of harmonies, of rhythms, of memories and wishes so frisky in their unbounded contempt for self-pity that her swing took on a separation that made Carla into a conduit and a spectator as the music became a thing that had nothing to do with anyone or anything other than the unwillingness of passion to die before it had said exactly what it was. The house went nuts. Some might say apeshit. A guy from a record company was there. He wanted her to call him. It couldn't have been better.

Carla got goose bumps just remembering what had happened up on that bandstand as Mickey, beside himself, handed over the salary, wishing, again, that his father could have heard this voice. "Maestra Carusa," he smiled, and bowed with wit and gallantry. Limp for a little bit in the dressing room, she came around, her heart enlarged by all of that feeling coming out of her and at her. What a life. She took a few moments to thank God for standing by her and protecting her and giving her the strength to keep on keeping on. It all came out. Carla couldn't stop it. Pure gratitude. This kind of affirmation wasn't something that could be taken in casually. That would be a brand of sin that frightened her to think about. Oh, no, there was a God, mighty as all the stories ever told, and that God kept it moving for her, never let her go. She wiped her eyes, trembling, shook out her hair, put on some dark glasses, sat quietly for a while, and was ready for everybody right now.

14

POLKA DOTS AND MYSTERIES

Carla paid off the musicians, gave Jed a special hug, wished him luck with the long, buxom limousine of a Texas girl waiting for him at the bar, and felt as free and as independent as she ever had as she walked west with her friends over to Leeann's place, where they had a few before the subject came around to something Carla didn't really want to talk about but that Leeann pushed everyone into because of the way a table of black people had been staring at one of the musicians and his white girlfriend after the performance ended at Crescent City. There was no redemption here. This was not the Russian Samovar. This was Leeann's place and she was tearing at a point. Maybe Carla could get them back to the good feeling. Smiling to herself, she thought she'd give it the good old Girl Scout try.

"Well, it didn't have to be racial."

"Why didn't it have to be racial?"

"She's a silly woman, Leeann."

"So?"

"So she's always making him feel ashamed of being seen with her in public. That's how she is. End of film. Screen credits. Nothing complex. As for those other people, we don't know what those people were thinking. They could have just been perplexed by a guy that talented being with such an obvious airhead. I've seen musicians look at them the same way. Don't you think that could be true, too?"

"No, I don't."

"So what are we supposed to do," Carla said, "think the worst of people because you feel like thinking that way this afternoon?"

"Look, girl, I know the code. These are my people, or they think they are. Anyway, we look a lot alike, you know what I'm saying?"

"Nobody looks like you," Cecelia said, "and what's the point of talking about something like this?"

"The point could be to educate me," Kelvin Thomson said. "I don't have any idea what you all are zeroing in on at this moment. Cue me in."

"I have to drop some science on my South Dakota buddy first. Now she thinks she can read niggers better than I can."

"Damn, Leeann," Cecelia said.

There was quiet as Carla and Leeann faced each other.

"That's not fair. You know it's not. Leeann, you know I have never said anything like that and you know I don't try to give the impression that I don't know my limitations. I love a black man. No, that's not right. Let me say it right. I love *Maxwell*, who is a black man, and I'm learning as much as I can. I don't think I'm anybody's expert."

Carla was seriously irritated. She had to use all of her will to make her voice come out with no strain because she hoped the subject could shift to something else and because there were those times when she wasn't in the mood to hear Leeann tell her how little she knew about black people. But she had enough experience of that in other places and with other races. People loved to let you know that no matter what you thought you knew about the flesh and blood of their little group or its time in the world, you would never be privy to the nuances. You were not what they were; they were what they were, and that was that. Leeann knew about that manner of closing someone out; in fact, she had said as much.

So how did an afternoon that started off so well turn out like this? She was back in New York only a couple of weeks, Maxwell, thank God, was already out of town, the wonder and the futility of going to Houston were still running through her like a river, there was this easy gig with a transporting groove to it, and Carla was with her friends—but the walls must now go up because of some people no one in this room even knew. So what if they were ostentatiously sneering at a groupie who had too much to drink and was being unpleasantly familiar with her guy when the music was over? The power that petty incidents had over intelligent people. Play the drumroll: it was now evident that Leeann had hammered the nails of a soapbox into place, one with a crystal stair that partially circled the enormous stage which she presently mounted, working her ivory cigarette holder and exhaling mammoth clouds of smoke, speaking with the tone of possession guests must sometimes accept when in the home of a person who has decided to make them an audience to an unexpected line of argument.

"Let me break something down to you, some recent history. Before all this skin-game shit got all-American and everybody turned into racists, you and Bobo, or you and Maxwell, or any other nigger you were in love with, could have lived in the black community. You hear what I'm saying? That's right. I heard about how that was. Things ain't what they used to be. Niggers ain't *always* been crazy. Just around the time you and I were born and mucho-pussy-getting Kennedy took his oath to be the president, then it was different. That was when niggers thought it was nobody's business what you do—unless you were such a pain in the ass you had to be told to step the holy fuck off. But once niggers started wearing costumes and talking that mother Africa bullshit, all these motherfuckers and bitches became proud of their *own* racism. Now is that some shit or is that some very shitty shit? You see the way these black motherfuckers look at you and Maxwell and me and one of my white boys when we're out? I do *not* like that shit. Niggers seem to me like they want to send us to a dating-game camp for some extremely serious reeducation. Up in there, my peepus be wanting to give the appropriate instruction in the composing of the most racially correct two heads on a pillow. Look out now! Macro shit on the Afro side. But the lady don't be interested in no totalitarian conceptions of fucking and sucking, not Leeann."

Her audience laughed.

"Hold up. Are you saying that these people over here are *still* thinking about that kind of chickenshit bullshit? "

"Indeed, Mr. Kelvin Thomson. For real."

"Look: this is the only country left in Western society that has that foot stuck in its own ass."

"Every country in the Western world has its foot stuck up its ass," Cecelia said, "if you ask me."

"That's a different issue."

"It is not. Everything stupid is always stuck together, and when white folks get stupid or niggers get stupid or anybody else who has the capacity to get stupid—which is every goddam body on the fucking face of the earth—when you have concerted stupidity, then you can't see straight because the goo of the stupidity gets in the way. All the lines are gone. It's just one big nigger mess, one big cracker mess, one big some fucking body's mess, and it's pulling you down and you can't do a damn thing about it."

"Hey, sweetest, you're perfectly correct, but let's go one subject at a time."

"You mean this race-mixing?"

Carla did not like that term.

"I mean what Leeann started talking about."

"Yeah. Let's stay on that. I started talking about that and that's what the problem is. Dumb black motherfuckers."

"You people are really very behind over here, if you know what I mean. This is so childish."

"I say 'Amen' to that," Leeann responded.

"My sweetest of the sweet is right, though. Europe has a shitload of problems, as the white boys say. But it doesn't have that one."

"Really?" Cecelia asked with a shitload of deprecation.

"Really. In Europe, if some British man gets himself all tied up in that Spanish culture and loves the bullfights and the Spanish girls, the food and all of that, it's just seen as a taste."

"So anybody who wants to run with the bulls is welcome to some horns in his ass?"

Everyone laughed and Carla's increasing funk was lightened by the way the two sparring lovers hugged before he continued.

"Right again, sweetest, right again. It's just a cosmopolitan taste. No more, no less. It's just a goodbye to all that provincialism. The British guy who comes home with his ass patched up isn't suffering from some kind of self-hatred."

"I'm sure he's not," Leeann snickered, "not with those horn holes in his butt."

"Oh!" Cecelia exclaimed, tears coming to her eyes.

"Oh is right," he said after the laughter eased off. "No one is being rejected. Something is being chosen. Same for a Sicilian in love with

Dutch girls, or a Swedish woman who can't stay away from southern France, or whatever and whoever the hell it is. It's just a taste, just a taste. That's the European way. Who should give an emaciated rat's ass about that?"

"Niggers," Leeann said with uncharacteristic outrage, "that's who the fuck gives a fuck. Niggers. Black, no-thought-having niggers."

"Ouch," Kelvin Thomson said.

"But we're still talking about white folks. That's how *they* look at each other. When one of us comes into the story, the script gets changed."

"Speak for yourself. I never had any trouble across the water," Leeann said. "What about you, Mr. Kelvin Thomson?"

"Not really."

Cecelia stared at him as he finished off the last bottle of Leeann's Irish whiskey with a swig. She seemed to have other things going on in her head as she rubbed her belly. There was now a stoic look on her face that did some arm-wrestling with impatience—the mask of her darkening mood was shot through with holes clearly bored open by her affection for the man. Now and again Kelvin Thomson met her eyes with a bent smile on his face and Cecelia melted for a bit before her battle mask rebuilt itself as she tore off the label of the whiskey bottle with just enough force to express her wish that he rein in his drinking. As had happened before with Cecelia, Carla felt as though she were looking at herself, this time parallel to any of those many occasions when Bobo's focusing of his great power on the hypodermic doom of heroin had her both wanting to scream in terrified fury yet tenderly nurse him into order at the same time. For his part, Kelvin Thomson, somehow, was not drunk, or even tipsy. That was not how he did it at all, which was why his problem, on the surface, seemed so far from what it was. The whiskey had to be taking a toll, but except for a minutely off-balance body position whenever he was six or seven glasses in, the expatriate remained the same, never slurring his speech, only speaking more deliberately when many fathoms deep in his cups, as though this entire stance was a trick of demeanor, manner, and speech that he had taught himself over the many years of waging hard war against his liver.

"Now get this, Mr. Kelvin Thomson."

"Get what?" he asked as his eyes left Cecelia's.

"That polka-dot dating game gets residential, too."

"Residential?"

"Oh, yes."

"Leeann, girl, what the hell are you talking about now?"

"Now you all know I love me some niggers. Right. 'Deed I do. Love me some niggers. Love them deeply. Couldn't consider living without them. My peepus," Leeann said, again drawing a big laugh for her affectionate parody of Southern mispronunciation, which Carla had learned was so basic to Negro exchange—the satire of the talk and the ways below the Mason-Dixon line, which were unlimited even in their hearty provincialism. Each allusion to those ways had the quality of a passage through time to that point where something as far from pure as it was from decadence stood in mean-tempered place or rhythmically walked along balancing a world of trouble on its head with jaunty disregard or remained in such a pea-soup cloud of ignorance that the correct assessment of the world never made an appearance. "But that loving of niggers is something I have to do on a long-distance frame right up in here. Some of these days. Not really: *all* of these days. That's how the cookie gets crushed out here. If I want to be somewhere and not be bothered about how I live, I got to live down here around these boring white motherfuckers and these boring white bitches just to get accepted. Oh, heartless fate, what has you done did to me?"

She put them in an uproar with that one, Carla the first to burst out in a guffaw.

"If you want to know," Leeann went on, "I'm sick and tired of being sick and tired of these tired white people, but they don't seem like they get tired of me or what I am so obviously doing with my earthshaking love life. Niggers, that's another story. Two tears in a bucket: fuck it."

"Oh, come on. Am I to believe that the Negro over here is still such a burr-headed ball of contradiction?" he asked, laughing and embracing Leeann as though she were a baby sister who had just come home crying and a little skinned up after flipping over the handlebars of her bicycle.

"Kelvin, given all the complaining you and Maxwell have made about these Afroid Negroids, you are either playing around or you been across the pond too long," she said, playfully pushing him away. "That's true. Tell him, Carla."

"I don't know if I could say that."

"Yes, you do. You just don't want to say it."

"I don't know what to say."

"That's hard to believe," Cecelia said.

"Very hard," Leeann asserted.

Carla did not like their tone.

"All right. I can talk, too. I can. Fine: Maxwell and I don't have the best time when we're around certain kinds of black people. It's true. All right. It's true. I don't understand why and it makes me very sad. Actually, it used to make me very sad. I could get angry about it. I guess I could have. But I didn't. I just wanted to know why we didn't have the right to have our own lives. There was no answer, of course. There never is. Silent night. I learned that. I also grew up. That's all downriver now, like some Pooh sticks. Now I just look at it as nothing more than another of the unpleasant things about living in the world right now. Leeann, may I use your bathroom?"

"What are you doing? Don't ask. Mi casa es su casa."

"Thanks."

She wasn't telling the truth. Carla, caught off guard, experienced extreme anger when she and Maxwell encountered a snooty quality from some black women, especially those who were indisputably well to do but seemed as though that wasn't enough: they thought it was a genetic right to be condescending to her and to her man, to shower them with their loathing. Even to your face. That must have been what it felt like when anybody at any time in the world found himself or herself suddenly pushed into a social and spiritual spittoon where they had to accept all of the hawking and the phlegm, the insulting slime and the diseased accumulations of philosophical sludge flying into their faces, their hair, on their clothes, their fingers, all over them. You could get all holy as hell and forgive them for they know not what they do—if that was the case. But they do know what they do and they like to do it. One was not forsaken because of that disdain. No, not forsaken. One was tested. Somewhere in that rain of spit and stuck inside the slickened walls of that spittoon, you had to find a way to rise on up, just as Carla had lifted on up after Bobo's death. At that time, reader, if you recall, the method was self-absorption and celebration of herself. The Walt Whitman combination of raincoat and dirigible wasn't enough right now. No. Carla knew that. *Hinden-*

burg immolation was what you risked: a blimp full of narcissistic gas could easily catch fire. Maybe that was what created such a repulsive stench in the air quality of the culture at this moment—the fear of facelessness was met with the poisoning gas of self-obsession, which could be extended out to one's group, stopping at the line of its furthest extremity and refusing admission into the circle by anyone else. No entrance unless that somebody else submitted to an ethos much like the Mafia initiation Mickey told her of, which precluded belief in God, country, family, or law: the closed membership of a vain and pitiless order calling itself honorable and using some variation on the symbol of two bloody palms pushed against each other as the seal of inclusion. That was how she felt any time some of those black couples looked at her and Maxwell. To such people, their being together was a statement about something else as much as it was about them falling for each other. That wasn't for her. Carla didn't want to be inducted into anything, and she definitely didn't want to be all by her lonesome standing there against the entire damn world. Still, two people pressing their wounds against one another didn't fuse a man and woman into some higher or deeper force. There was something more human that community ought to be based on, but there were no words she knew that might name it and none that could describe just what that camaraderie would have to be if it could fit a time in which so many important conceptions of integrity and compassion had been either worn out or so perverted that their initial meanings had been smudged beyond recognition. Perhaps, like any other musician, she had to depend on the quality of notes to say what she meant and express what she needed. Right now yearning had come to mean so much to her and seemed a signal aspect of her moment. Yearning. It was much, much deeper than loneliness because one could feel it and be so far from lonely. There was a purifying definition to it in her mind because the limitless desire for nothing in particular but for everything to be right was probably why the community she could not actually describe needed no description. That degree of imprecise desire unsullied one's soul and was right inside the pocket of the groove you were always after on the bandstand. Carla wanted to sing with every aspect of feeling that was inside her when thoughts of that sort arrived, rolling, she laughed to herself, like Old Man River.

"You can say what you want to say about how hard it is being with a white man or her being with a black man," Cecelia said, pointing at Carla as she returned to the room at the moment that Kelvin Thomson ostentatiously left to go get some more alcohol. Cecelia was pacing again, dominating the room, making each movement part of a ballet or a dance in rumbling code.

"I'm not saying it's hard, girlfriend, I'm saying it's a pain in my ass when it slips up on me and I'm caught unaware that I'll be entertaining some thoughts that are far from angelic."

"Meaning what?"

"Meaning how can they condescend *up* to me?"

Cecelia laughed very loudly, moving her head left and right. Then Leeann put her feet up on her gorgeous living room table as if there was a show coming on and Carla, always taken by this woman, awaited what Cecelia was preparing to say. There was a color to her voice Carla had not heard before, and it seemed as if Cecelia were writing in a diary and reading aloud, each word summoned with the intensity of van Gogh's brushstrokes, thick exclamations of—

"All of that could be true. I know it's true. It's funny the way you say it. People below you will look down on you. But it's not the only thing that's true out here in this world. I'm going to say what I have to say about nothing except one patch on the quilt. One patch, you know? Black women *are* angry."

Leeann rolled her eyes.

"No, we don't like all of this race-mixing. We don't, never did, and might never ever grow to like it. Over and over, I was told never to bring anybody home darker than me. That was the *first* rule. Then there was the *second*. I could bring home somebody light and damn near white, but I had better not ever put one foot on the property of my family with a completely white man on my arm. Somebody without one drop of nigger in the bloodstream? Uh-uh. Never. No sir."

"Well, I couldn't have found somebody darker than me unless I found one of them niggers darker than smoke, and as you might not know, Carla, such niggers are in short supply."

Carla couldn't *avoid* laughing with Leeann. Cecelia let that one go by and looked from one of them to the other, then abstractedly turned her head. For a bit she stared at one of the velvet paintings Leeann had hung around her house to scandalize her wealthy friends, always claiming they were true black art and beyond the measure of common high quality. This one was called *Dancing with the Devil* and had two nude interracial couples, white woman and black man, black woman and white man, all four with horns sprouting from their heads and forked tails giving off electric sparks. They were embracing and dancing on a huge table that was covered with used condoms, crack pipes, dominoes, blood-spattered aces and eights, pistols, knives, and white mountain ranges of cocaine. A band of skeletons was playing for the revelers. In the sky above them were dreadlocked black angels at war with serpent-tongued white angels. The name of the artist, painted in red and green on the black velvet, was—his own quotation marks—"Brother Down." Cecelia gave off a soft grunt of derision.

"If you like that one, you should see the one called *Holiday for a Hankty Heifer,*" Leeann said. "Now that one is truly awful. This Negro is destined for the top. Want to see it?"

"I think I can do without that."

"Suit yourself, cuz. It's your world."

"What I would like to do is get back to the point."

"Well, hurry on. We're here just a-sitting and a-rocking."

Cecelia freshened her drink. She started pacing. Court was in session.

"Look, there are only so many men available as it is. Think about that. Besides, you might not want to take that extra step in the direction of getting your heart wrecked up and down by crossing the color line, *too.* You and Carla can do that. That's not the way I choose to go about doing my romantic business. I don't go that way. It doesn't pull my interest. But, to be honest, I sat here all this time since we started this conversation, *all* this time, trying and trying to think of a white man—*any* white man—who could be attractive enough for me to dream about him even if I didn't want to. I still can't think of none. Still can't. Sorry. Can't. I'm just an old-fashioned brown-skinned girl. I'm a dinosaur who hasn't turned into a bird yet—standing at the edge of the cliff, not knowing what the hell to do. Maybe I dream too much. All I want in the world is one of those kinds of men I saw when I was just a little kid. Those kinds of men, *oh,* they could make me feel safe just by being nice to me. Just a little kindness, you know? A little sugar in the cup of my heart. There I was, dirty as a mud pie, and they looked at me like I was as clean as purity on its very purest day. A man back then didn't seem like the existence of his species was threatened by the internal presence of just too much goddam, trifling-assed, motherfucking bullshit. That kind of man is what I want, and he can't be white, not for me. So I'm stuck where I am. And where that is, my friends, is a very, very funky little place. Little and funky. Just me and a whole lot of stink. In my own little corner of the blues, the hardest thing to get is for a man to meet me with the same amount of feeling that I have."

"Oh, Cece," Leeann said, nearly gasping.

"Yeah. You know what I mean by *meet?* I know you do. I'm talking to you, too, Carla. Don't feel excluded."

Those words pierced Carla's breastbone.

"I think we all want *somebody* to meet us just one time *somewhere* and to let us know that *somehow* on this earth the fullness *can* be equaled. Somebody to look me right in the eye, straight, and see Cecelia for everything I am. Someone to look at me and look to me and hold me so close I become nothing but myself. If somebody ever stood up and met me with that much feeling I might go crazy. I have no idea what I would do, none at all. It has never happened to me and it has never happened to any woman I know. Uh-uh. This drunken Negro I'm in love with right now—what did I fall into *this* time? On wand off for seven years now. Him over there, me over here. Everything just so goddam sophisticated: open enough for me to be dissatisfied with him and me, and with every *other* man I got close to in Washington, D.C., when I didn't have *him* near me. Well. What can I say? The truth, I guess. Sometimes I almost feel it from him, almost—not really *that* close, but close enough for me to *almost* know. Then all this hard-hearted Hannah shit granulates, every last bitter piece of it, and I'm nearly a mess of sobbing and begging for more love and more love. If he ever answered that question before I asked it, if Mr. Kelvin Thomson could meet me right here in the middle of my heart, right where I've dug in and hidden everything soft in my entire being, from my childhood to this very second, *oh,* my sweet God in heaven, I don't know what I would do. I don't. I don't know if I would ever be right again, and I don't know if I would ever want to be. It's a mystery, girls. Yep, that's what it is. And I don't know if I will ever be lucky enough to know the answer to it. Well, to say things the way they seem to me, I doubt it. I doubt it all the way down the line."

15

MY KIND OF TOWN

LIFTING THAT magnificent copper-colored face, with her eyes glistening, Cecelia stood, brushed off the front of her dress, excused herself, and went upstairs to use the bathroom, leaving a train of melancholic radiance in her wake.

"I need me a cognac *right* now," Leeann said, and went to her reduced liquor cabinet, which had been under siege by Kelvin Thomson. It was a five-foot-tall rectangular structure of metal and glass, the bottom third black seamless metal, the rest transparent with three shelves of bottles. The black bottom had a hollow compartment where Leeann kept her private stuff so that she never ran out of liquor, even if her guests did. Once they were gotten rid of, the long black South Carolina girl would make herself something particularly good and contemplate the havoc, the tales, and the feelings that had been left in the atmosphere of her town house.

"I almost feel like something strong myself," Carla said, looking toward the stairs, figuring that Cecelia was probably muffling her crying in a monogrammed towel, having so suddenly caught herself off guard in the middle of the kind of talk that could make more come out than you wanted, even among the closest friends, none of whom would be able to help you actually carry what you spent so much time trying to keep from smacking you down in public, some long condition of emotion and desire treating you as though it were a pimp or a cruel, cruel lover who hadn't the slightest regard for how helpless you were made to look and sound.

"Mark my words: You better stick to the light stuff, little Miss South Dakota. The last thing I need now is a drunken white woman crying the blues about her and her black boyfriends."

"Is that so?"

"More than so."

"Well, shut my mouth."

"Shut it indeed. We need to get this *meeting* shit off of our minds as fast as we can. Start thinking about that and the two of us will be up there with Cecelia, having a tear feast. Sobs and sniffles and snot and shit. And, believe me, there is nothing a man like Kelvin Thomson or any other man can do when this many women fall apart about nothing anybody on the face of the earth can do the least little goddam thing about. Shit, we might scare that nigger into permanent sobriety."

Laughing, Carla settled for a cold, cold beer as Leeann put on some festive music from Brazil before going out of the living room and up the stairs to her bedroom for some darn thing.

There Carla was, all by herself, one of her friends in one place, the other yet someplace else, and Kelvin Thomson out buying what had to be an enormous bottle of Irish whiskey, his thoughts surely nowhere in the vicinity of what the subject had become once he left.

Meeting: that had been what made so much difference for Carla with Bobo and what she had fought for with Maxwell before they were on the way to Houston and she was so afraid that he was going to leave her. Now she was sure that he was. She wasn't so afraid now. She wasn't relieved either. There was pain in her heart but it didn't seem torn or broken. It was a little woozy and it was floating, traveling to a time that was lighter, so much less of a burden, back to when initiation had come about so freely and oh, had she learned so much about the solid grace of people and about another kind of pride in just where she had come from. Feeling, like Rondo Jackson said in his blues club, was an unpredictable thing.

Such affection had been felt for men since Jimmy Joe and sweet home Chicago, where there had been none of these looming Manhattan difficulties since Jimmy Joe's world had no political elements to it, just people living through the blues and all of the Mississippi particulars that had been carried North, in bags, in suitcases, in pockets, minds full of the old business of that segregated world but on the lookout for the first time a tall, tall building filled the train or bus window and all of that concrete let you know that most of how you lived down South was over, at least for now.

Jimmy Joe's mother and sisters—Carrie, Mamie, Bessie, and Dinah—had taken her in, and Carla learned how to cook those sweet potato pies, those cobblers, the fried chicken, the chicken and dumplings, the barbecue, the pig feet, the ham hocks, the chitlins, the collard greens and the turnip greens, the corn bread, and so on and on. She had never felt more proud than on that Saturday night when she took over his mother's kitchen on the South Side and prepared a feast for Jimmy Joe and his family, one of baked capon chicken, greens, mashed potatoes, candied yams, and a blueberry cobbler. They loved it and was Carla glad that she was a regular jogger, otherwise the woman could easily have ended up as fat as a Dutch wife.

The Chicago winters had created a card-game culture and Jimmy Joe, who possessed a highly retentive mind, was part of it. He knew many different games, those he could entertain kids with when he had to watch the children of one of his sisters or of a cousin or a next-door neighbor. Jimmy Joe had the same kind of fun playing cards with kids that her dad had playing math games with Ramona, who was going into the sciences before she was swept off her feet by the debate team as well as its captain and decided on going into law, which was where the man her big sister loved was headed.

There was a communal sizzling in the air when Jimmy Joe was showing the kids how to play fish, war, slapjack, aces, crazy eights, acey-deucey, and knuckles, in which the loser was whacked across the game's namesake with the deck of cards, something Jimmy Joe discouraged the kids from going into with the expected sadism of the young: just a tap; you won; that's all they need to know; they were beaten. "Yet in still," as he would say if her Chicago man had one of those mean little boys around, some little Johnny who thought he was too bad, there could be consequences. After the kid had done his dirt, beating up his little sister or something of that nature, Jimmy Joe would call him out to play a game of knuckles and go quite a bit beyond tapping the boy, just to let him know that, "son, pain is a serious thing; it ain't to be played with for fun." He didn't have to do that often. Blood might be left on the edge of the cards.

For his own adult pleasure he also knew pinochle, hearts, tonk, dirty hearts, cooncan, bridge, gin rummy, spades, which was a variation on bid whist, and—Oh, Lord, Lord, Lord!—dominoes, or "bones," a game that he and Carla teamed up on, playing against others in both the domestic version of four sides and the international version of one long line, known that way among the Spanish as *la culebra,* the snake. The quick-draw math of the players was very surprising, the velocity with which they could see how to make scores that ended in five or zero. More than a little sophisticated. It was exciting, too. Jimmy Joe gave the impression he was going to split one of those bones when he smacked it down on the table and called out the point. She adored those times of playing the game with Jimmy Joe's relatives and their friends because another side of her own mind lit up and he was so easygoing but could explode when he got hot at the domino table.

There was no greater fun, even so, than the all-night whist parties—deep into the greasy South Side world of 7UP and Seagram's, Colt .45, unspeakably sweet wines, beer sipped through straws, bowls of fried chicken, potato salad, popcorn, rice pudding, and corn bread—where she and Jimmy Joe would battle the other members of the blues band with "froggy-bottom whistology." He taught her to play and she had such a knack for it that the two of them worked with the kind of intuition Carla later found on bandstands when you and another musician started hooking up on the accents and the harmony right out of the air, improvising as though it had all been declared somewhere far above this little world we live in. She loved to look through the cigarette and cigar smoke and across the whist table as Jimmy Joe said "Coming into Boston" with the sound of a conductor on a train but meaning that the whist opposition would not get one book to its name, zero points. He usually stood up then and started whipping down his cards as though they were thunderbolts. "Now how you snuff-dippers like that action?" Jimmy Joe would ask as the two they had defeated rose from their chairs, starting with nothing and leaving with nothing.

There was now, a strain not of nostalgia but of reverie, glow upon glow. Carla stood up, hearing nothing in Leeann's home but dancing as she had in her tennis shoes with the ponytail bouncing off her shoulders as she recapitulated the passions that were absorbed and the elevations that went with them. This was not something she yearned for; she had possessed it completely; it was part of her soul now.

That reverie strummed the soft blue guitar of her memory as she thought more of how it had been during those Windy City times, even when the funky dressing rooms of Jimmy Joe's gigs would be invaded by the self-involved white girls who turned up with this black musician or that and gave the impression that the ambition they each shared was to become a peroxide blonde in the middle of the jungle, lording over some babbling Africans as she sat on a crude throne in a leopard bikini and monumental earrings with unexplainably shaven armpits and legs. Carla now laughed to herself that those white back-stage Chicago girls were only looking for a biracial version of the adulation she had enjoyed beyond all bounds during her high school years at the top of the social heap: the casting and the fantasy set built for their script might have been different, but the movie sure as hell made the same point.

Those Sheena of the Jungle white women, the parties, and the world of the music clubs were only part of it. There was also that energy of Chicago with all its ethnic neighborhoods and the hangover of gangster violence still throbbing at the temples of the town, which sometimes seemed a huge person intent on blowing the blues away or sauntering a different rhythm against the inevitable speed of a metropolis that had battled itself into existence by taking on all comers—the weather, the immigrants, the industrial needs of the nation, the appetite for slaughtered meat, appliances, and whatever else could be brought in or shipped out by railroad, truck, or plane. Sometimes when they were walking at twilight on Michigan Avenue, a misty chill in the air, the lake to the left and the skyline to the right, Carla thought that she and her blues-playing saxophonist were at the center of something sensational. The girl from South Dakota was sure that few were they who had come to Chicago at some time or other and not felt the special atmosphere of the town in which the skyscraper had been put on display for the very first time and where—after staring at the big screen in the impersonal air-conditioned chill that prefigured his condition—John Dillinger, coming round the mountain of assumed anonymity, entered the land of the dead through a door of blood outside of the Biograph Theater, which was still showing pictures, by the way. She dreamed of so many things late at night when she and Jimmy Joe were taking the El back to the South Side and to his apartment. Everything was perfect. This was the thing she needed at the time. The girl from South Dakota was doing extremely well in her studies and this straight-ahead guy, just by being himself every second of the way, helped her reestablish a sense of wonder, one so strong that the accident in the high school cafeteria came into proportion and Carla felt a bit of shame at just how important she had thought herself and her suffering were.

Yes, she and Jimmy Joe had their fights. Doozies, believe me. For no reason at all that she could see in retrospect, since not even the subject of one came to mind now. Some, however, were actually stirring because the girl from South Dakota felt the sweet resurrection of her stubbornness, a quality very reminiscent of Mom. It was a personal favorite. In high school, she hid it reasonably well, but in Chicago, assuming herself at the verge of becoming a woman, she flaunted it when alone with Jimmy Joe. What great times! Carla enjoyed whamming her ideas against his as well as the unveiled respect this man had for her, which came out as he said, "Baby girl, you need to change your name to Caldonia, your head is so goddam hard." It felt delicious to modulate the mood after getting her point across, to take control and make up to him, snuggling and kissing and imposing her intimate femininity as he tried to push her away. No, now Caldonia in another frame, she wouldn't have it, breathing on him and putting her hands under his clothes, teasing out all of the affection until they went at it like a couple of minks, over and over until there wasn't one place inside her soul that didn't fairly drip with peppered honey.

Hey, the City of the Big Winds was very, very nice, but it wasn't paradise by anybody's measure. They were occasionally looked upon with something mighty close to hatred by the racists among the Poles, Irish, Italians, and Negroes who made sure that nobody forgot the spiritual dirty drawers worn under the well-cut suit of spirit that represented Chicago to her. But as Carla became more and more alive again, her loss of potential Olympic glory in perspective, those irritations amounted to what Dad said, "Some people are like poison ivy.

They keep growing, but in a nasty way, and if you come in contact with them they always have the same effect. These are the kind of people who don't really have many choices on their menu, so to speak. No taste for variation. Kind of narrow. Usually ignorant types. Wads of gum stuck under the desk of society. So you have to realize that the effect they have is never good and neither are they. Well, at least they're not good in some areas. But if those areas are important enough, they might as well be evil from the peak to the dregs of the valley. Anyway, you just watch out for the poison ivy. Sometimes you're right in the middle of a bush of it and don't really know. That's the kind of ignorance—ha, ha, ha— that doesn't last long though. Pretty soon you're scratching like hellfire is under your skin and you know exactly where you really were standing."

Carla looked out for those kinds of people and moved herself along, fascinated by Jimmy Joe's obliviousness. He never discussed race and could never be drawn into talking about it. People could go on and on and trade this theory against that one, that atrocity tale against this one, but the blues tenor man would just sit there with a face devoid of passion, drinking his drink and smoking his Pall Mall. Under no circumstances would he give that color trouble even the time of day. If Carla's conservatory buddies were the insistent types, determined to be Christian or Jewish or atheist soldiers marching onward against bigotry, Jimmy Joe always said the same thing, "I haven't thought on that too much. I'm going to start, though. Soon as I think of something worth you all listening to, I'll get right in there with you."

In private he told her once and only once, "I don't have that kind of thing going on in my head. You know I know about it just like everybody else knows about it. Got to know that just to cross the goddam street. But, suffice it to say, you and me trying to find out some new fun is what I get interested in. Besides, baby girl, when I get to talking about that with some people, especially some white folks, it seems to me that I'm all of a sudden in the hospital in traction with both my arms and my legs broken. I was a man just a minute ago. Snap: now me and some white people are wondering when the damn plaster casts is going to come off. I used to talk that talk, though, to be honest—especially when it could help get me some bed action from a white girl who was doing penance by opening her legs to a black man. But now I'm in long-dick retirement from that now."

Carla began laughing so hard she started choking. He brought her some water in one of the jelly jars he preferred to glasses and spent the rest of the evening telling hilarious stories about his experiences on the road. His words took her right to each town and specified the ways of the audiences—told of where you went or couldn't go because there was no there to go looking for—and clarified for his baby girl that if you were the kind to pay attention, you saw one thing in every place that you couldn't have imagined before it happened but that nearly always led to another extraordinary laughing matter when you came down to it. Geez, Jimmy Joe was so *fun*.

When her Windy City time was finished and she graduated from the conservatory, a composition major and a voice minor, Mom and Dad came in for the ceremony but Ramona, down with the flu, was unable to make it. As Carla became pushy during the telephone call and urged her to just put a little more effort into trying to come since her little sister would only graduate from music school *once*, Ramona, who did not sound sick at all—*not at all*—became brusque, wished her a happy graduation, and bid her goodbye. So much for Ramona. That one hurt. It lay inside, pulsating like a wide cut. *Anyway*, she and Jimmy Joe took her parents to dinner graduation night and then the four of them went to his job, where Mom and Dad danced to blues and walked with the two of them some fifteen or twenty blocks in the soft and warm Chicago night after the last set, then caught a cab back to the Drake Hotel, a place where Mom had always wanted to stay. The four had a late breakfast together the following morning. It was simple and easy. Jimmy sent in a sub that night so that he and Carla could take Mom and Dad to eat at his parents' house. Wow. Wow. Wow. What an evening that was. As it turned out, Jimmy Joe's mother and his father, Splanky, had been at that party on the South Side all those many years ago when Joezell Taylor had these four white kids in his full house dancing and eating the chicken and waffles after daybreak. *Can you believe it? Unreal. Just what she and Randy Jr. used to dream about after it had become part of "the Saga of Mom and Dad."* Splanky, a supervisor at the post office and a collector, broke out some of those old records from that time so that he and his wife as well as Mom and Dad could cut some old-fashioned rugs. Jimmy and his graduating girl picked up on the steps immediately and were into the ballroom flow. Carla's heart almost cracked with joy that night. If the book of this world had been hers, she'd never turn the page.

In a borrowed friend's car, a big shiny red Pontiac, Jimmy Joe and Carla took Mom and Dad to the airport, where they bid something of a lonesome farewell to their daughter and her guy before heading back to wahoo territory. The baby girl was still more than a little disappointed that Ramona hadn't been able to come out and be with all of them, but there was such a good atmosphere in the car on the way to the airport as the weather drizzled until the sky cleared up to an extra kind of brightness. A sob evaporated in her chest as she was embraced by Mom and Dad kissed her on the cheek before they both shook hands with Jimmy Joe and headed for their seats on the American Airlines flight. She and Jimmy Joe held hands in silence as they waited at the window to watch the plane take off into the Chicago sky.

A few weeks later, traveling light, Carla stood with Jimmy Joe in the train station. She had to move on out East to New York, where her luck might lead her into more of a career there than Jimmy Joe had experienced in the biggest of the big towns. It was all settled in her mind and had been settled for more than a year. She was going to sing; she was going to write music; if she failed, she could come back to Chicago or go someplace else and lie down on the rack of music education, where she would teach until she retired and died, disappointed in herself and feeling that she had been the queen fool of all time. There would be no Jimmy Joe in that future, whether there was success or failure. Both knew it was done. They had had their fun if they never saw each other anymore. That was built into the way he was and the way she was. He was exactly where he wanted to be, but that wouldn't do for her and he had no intention of trying to get her to say it was good enough for what she wanted to do with herself. That was all passed back and forth without words. The two had gotten that close. With him it was the first time that Carla learned the intuitive feeling Mom had for her could exist between a man and a woman. Jimmy Joe, Jimmy Joe. He hugged her so, just before the train got to moving, that the pomade in his hair and his Brut cologne were embedded in her nostrils for half an hour. The sweet sorrow of goodbye was over. They were finished. Carla didn't cry on the train to New York but was aware that she had been next to something so good that the memory of it hurt in that way a woman—who was not too long ago a girl—begins to feel the pain of endings.

That train ride backwards to the starting point of so much immigration into America, all the way to indifferent Manhattan, went by swiftly. She didn't see anybody she knew at the station but she sure felt a change equal to her expectations, as if the energy of the city was an invisible man at a river ready to baptize her into a victor or a victim. Carla, anonymously looking for an apartment along with everybody else, could surely have told the world that she had been born again as a stranger, another person who meant no more than what she looked like. This wasn't salvation but an identity she enjoyed. The puny celebrity of public school, the kind her talent gathered on the campus in Chicago, what she experienced as Jimmy Joe's girl, were both inside her and behind her. What came Carla's way now would arrive not through reputation or through friends but through her own ability to magnetize respect. That is, if she could keep this place from driving her so crazy she didn't even notice the world around her.

It was easy to remember but impossible to forget when that hit home.

Not long after she had arrived in New York, Carla found herself standing, as you often did while waiting for a public phone, listening to someone talking so loudly about intimate business the impression was given that neither you nor anyone else on the planet were within a country mile. This didn't happen in Chicago unless the person was addled or imperially young and acting vulgar in order to either draw attention or make it clear that what you thought or felt didn't even mean do-diddly-squat. What was going on during that unseasonably warm fall day in midtown was special to Manhattan, where the sheer size of the population made each person who went wild in front of other people feel as though it was impossible to ever be embarrassed by revealing information that most others in America held very close to the vest. It was that bizarre similarity to screaming your head off if you wanted to out on the plains back home, the endless horizon creating the same feeling as being just another unacknowledged speck in New York. What Carla heard in a sentence or two made her think about Jimmy Joe with a touch of longing and also wonder how much time in this town it took before strangers knowing your aches and desires was of no concern at all. Was it gradual? Like the proud but bitterly sad violinist in the story who thought that he was a neglected major talent until, while playing one night in a filthy dive at the very bottom of the business, the ragged musician heard what he actually sounded like and committed suicide, essentially apologizing to his soul for having allowed it to undergo so much anguish when the ignoring world was not cruel in his case but absolutely correct.

The head and face of the woman on the phone were distinguished by red hair and freckles, blue eyes, and an aquiline nose. Under her eyes were large, dark bags that must have been hereditary because she couldn't have been more than forty, but the woman had what Carla would eventually recognize as the pouches common to obsessive readers of newspapers, magazines, quarterlies, and books. New Yorkers such as this one were up late at night angrily telling themselves they should be asleep while possessed by an unrelenting anxiety at the thought of not awakening with a crisp, insightful opinion about this fascinating but far too fucking long article some writer, so dazzled by his or her wordsmithing gifts, had written in such a way that the reader was made to suffer one unnecessarily detailed but well-turned description after another. The red-haired woman was smartly dressed in one long piece of flowing gray cotton, a necklace of polished stones the color of pomegranate seeds, with earrings to match, and kept switching her gray purse from beneath one arm to under the other. She hunched over as she made some points, stood straight as she listened, took deep breaths when whatever was being said on the other end of the line threatened to suffocate her in the open air of Times Square. It was loud outside on that afternoon of Carla's first Manhattan fall, but the woman on the phone was louder.

"Don't be such a petty, tiny Jewish snit, I wanted to tell him. In all confession, I must say that I didn't *want* to tell him this, but even so, I told him. I *did* tell. What do you mean you don't believe? I'm lying about this? For what purpose? Tell me for what purpose I'm lying? Can you? No: obviously. I'm glad on *this* we agree. So *now* you believe, *now*? Good. Let me continue. Can I continue? Is that at all possible? Are you prepared? Can you lounge back and listen for a moment? I assume this is good. *What?* No, this is not a loungey story. I'm about to hang up this phone. There are people waiting here, you might imagine. Yes, for the phone. Can't you hear the traffic? *Traffic.*

Can you hear the traffic? Fine. I have been patiently wanting to continue. Sorry: impatiently. Just one second. Do you think you are providing a good or a bad imitation of a best friend? Yes, that's what I said. If you would like, I can tell you more than that, in all honesty. Do you want *my* opinion? *Do* you? *Now* you want my story. Oh, you! How contrary. My God. You *are*. Is this a conversation or a competition? So I—what I was saying—is not so horribly difficult to understand. It is *not* boring. I am now prepared to never speak to you again. Never in life. In this one, the next one, any that are provided. Is it all right to continue now? *Now.* Appreciated. Appreciated. See if this makes sense to you. What I am giving you is a direct expression of something I finally saw in this man and, unfortunately, *very* unfortunately, in myself: After he insulted me—after he insulted *me*—in his typically snide way—a way that I hate from these unattractive little Jewish men who have to cut off your legs to make themselves taller than you—after all of this, after being so very, very nasty, *he* had the look of someone stunned. *He* had. Un-*fucking*-believable. If I were trying to describe it in something written, if I were the writing type, I would say that shock spilled out of his face. I *would* say. That's good, isn't it? It *is* good. Thanks. You're so sweet. Yes, I would say that. That I would write. It would capture this. Then it became sad. Extremely. Very much so. His confidence started falling on the floor right in front of me. Yes, terrible. And, as I'm sure you know, the ongoing guilty person I am pushed—very, very hard, I might add, very—I had to push against *any* kind of will *whatsoever* to do better by myself. Pathetic. For *me,* just once for *me.* Oh, sure: by better I mean to put myself in front of the line for once. I mean to not cringe, to not bow down in fright and continue to ask to be excused for getting in the way of the people who are in the line jumping ahead of me. I am there, standing like everyone else. I should not have to apologize for being there—as if *I* am the one so cavalierly wrong doing. The cavalier is what I cannot stand in the least bit, the least bit. Fortunately, so hurt by this tiny, this nerdy, this cruel little Jewish piece of shit, I asked myself what the fuck I was doing. That was the hurting. No other question could be so true or so cruel to me. This time, of all times, I had the right answer for once. For once I had. Yes. I refused to be just another female weenie and apologize to this person who had insulted *me.* I refused. What does he say in reply? No, you guess.

All right. What *would* he say? He says nothing. *Why* does he say nothing? Because there I am in front of him. I am *there*. My back to stab is what he prefers, the twitty little know-it-all. I hate such people. I hate him so much I have no idea how, in the name of Jehovah, I ever married him. True, true. Horrible. Absolutely. You are right. You are. Yes, I know why. I can say. I can say. Yes, I can say. He was so *sweet* to me at the start. I had never been treated sweeter. Never. Ever. Not by anyone. Never at all. It was then that I knew love. It was then. Now I long for this and it is gone. Via col vento. Via col vento. What? Yes, I am crying, what *else* should I be doing?"

1 6

THE LAST DANCE

After wondering what the hell Leeann and Cecelia were doing as she *still* sat there by herself, the Brazilian music back in her ears, Carla got up and walked around the town house, seeing nothing. Via col vento. Oh, God. Please. Panic ripped up inside her. What was she going to do? That one was easy. She was going to inhabit the existence that had been given to her. Like anybody else a long way from the way she wanted her own home to be, she felt that she was the child of her life but that it was treating her as if she had no mother, no father, nobody to stand up for her and say what she deserved. What, by the way, *did* she deserve? What does *anyone* deserve? Do sorrow and happiness move on in or out on the basis of some signal of inflated self-worth, deciding to arrive or leave on the basis of what you fucking think you *deserve?*

Carla didn't know *what* she deserved, but with the light creeping away outside and the shadows in which she had smiled and laughed moving through in a montage of faces and places, she couldn't stop remembering the good and ascended into a reverie for the dance floor. Her body was doing part of the recollecting. Soaking in rhythm and stroking it and coming to know herself through it was what she had done—each ounce of her body carrying and sending the beat, from her big toes all the way under to the heels of her feet and up her ankles, then her legs, around the horn of her behind, up her spine and shoulders, scaling the vertebrae of her neck, the round back of her head, across her scalp, down her forehead, zooming off her nose, swinging back to her lips, gliding on down to her chin, dropping to her breastbone, then to each of her full but not heavy breasts, moving onto her belly, the beat crossing the pubic thatch that guarded her lower lips until, all its accents in place, that beat disappeared through the invincible space between her vagina and the tops of her thighs: that concave cupping of air, never less than open, regardless of how close she held her legs together. It started like that.

Once you had been bathed in those rhythmic differentiations of the dance, those syncopated distinctions functioned as but one side of a conversation. The other was the dance itself, the retort. Carla could now feel her feet going through the steps upon steps they knew, her calves and thighs riffing back over all of the moves they had flexed and tightened themselves in order to execute, the lower back remembering how a hand felt on it and the way sweat made the part of the dress over her Hottentot into a skin of wet cloth, the belly noting how some of the dance beats seemed to arrive right in its center and syncopate out from there, her palms reliving the texture against them as she rubbed down the front of her dress between her breasts and her waist and alternated sensually holding one or both in place, the breasts reassuming the presence each took on inside her brassiere while moving to the rhythm or resting against the partner when it was slow and close, her neck understanding the sense of distance it had as the long, dewy column between her head and shoulders, the head traveling again through the infinite nods, turns, and snappings with which it responded at varied speeds to the beats and the phrases. Those were rhythms she could have experienced only that way with that man.

The Midwestern woman by herself in that Manhattan room in Leeann's town house now thought for a bit of how she and Maxwell had soared through a phase of swing, Latin, and tango dancing, going from studio to studio and into the ballroom-dancing world, practicing the steps. He had promised they would do it and he wasn't just talking, as some men will, bringing up a thing that would take some effort to enjoy but never really getting around to it because they were too lazy or too stupid to know that keeping the promises you make to yourself and to others might be the two most important things you can do in the world. As much a man as Bobo was, he could never keep the promise to himself and to her that he would get off the drugs and bring the same disciplined freedom to his life that he did to his music. Maxwell edged him that way, which was no small edge. The result was that they, like two time travelers, found themselves dancing to swing bands among groups that included some old heads who went all the way back to the glory days of the Savoy Ballroom up in Harlem and Roseland in midtown. They encountered, among the younger ones, ancient Argentinians who told tales of Carlos Gardel at the milongas, or tango parties, in the Triangulo way west on Fourteenth Street or in Belle Epoque with live musicians upstairs on Broadway, not far from the Strand bookstore. In the red-hot rooms uptown where the Latin situation was such a rich cross section of colors and hair textures, the movements so percussive and feline, the two danced until their clothes stuck against their bodies.

Carla's man was already graceful on his feet, but he had read something Duke Ellington said about how important dancing was to playing well and that was it. He was on a mission. Maxwell had proven, under the challenge of all the instruction, to be such a good dancer, and Carla—in his arms or standing apart and doing the intricate steps that put her toes, the balls of her feet, and her heels on the drumbeats—was, for the very first time, sure that she knew exactly what Mom and Dad felt when they were together and making themselves mirrors of the music.

What a year of great fun. Just one of those things you came to count on. Foolish woman. You were not foolish. Don't shit on the past just because you're living in shit right now. Try being an adult, sultry person, she laughed, almost aloud, rubbing her hands on the insides of her thighs one or two times.

Maxwell, of course, couldn't do anything partially. Oh, no. Sometimes his life was lived as though he were an ongoing Method actor. He loved the theater of everything, which was why he was sometimes late for his gigs, standing there pondering his shirts and ties and shoes as though he was doing something as serious as putting together the strategy for a brain operation. Boy, the time he spent trimming his mustache, oiling and brushing his hair until the wave pattern was to his liking, and, at last, palming on a mixture of three luxurious colognes so that his preferred scent was inimitable. The warmth of his smile in the mirror then was actually a blowtorch of ego.

It was all of that same preparation when they were hoofing the night away. They dressed up for it. The evening would begin at an old-fashioned delicatessen on Twenty-second and Tenth Avenue if they were going swing dancing. The same for the other styles. Start with the clothes and the grub. He figured if you put yourself in the clothes, ate the food as well as did the dances and learned about the music—even some of the language if you had the time—you could get further into what the people were thinking about and how the world seemed to *them,* not you. Maxwell wanted to get as close to the actual spirit of it all as he could. Then he would keep what appealed and discard the rest. In order to find that essential element, the one line of transcendent strength that wove through the whole thing, you had to get a lot of specific information. Carla could never have been that extreme about it on her own, but, hey—even if he didn't appreciate it now on this Sunday night wherever the hell he was in the world—they were *so* much alike.

When he was done with it all and they only went into those worlds every now and then, Maxwell would adopt what he learned of the cultural DNA into his own art. Other angles of expression arrived and Carla noticed how the classical excitement and romance of the city that went with swing dancing and the sounds of the baritone and tenor singers were summoned into the timbres of his tone. The Latin melancholy, tenderness, delight, and pugnacious sexuality left their imprint as well. The dramatic eroticism of the tango, in which love was simultaneously a buzzard picking at your liver for learning its secrets and an angel of spirited, graceful uplift, didn't get left out. All blended with the wide, blue sound he had, which already rippled lightly at the edges with a wisp of vibrato, touching each note like the breath of a whisperer against an ear. More than that whispering, he once said to her, was getting to that *sigh,* which was what Ben Webster, Harry Edison, and Miles Davis did better than anybody else, the sound that expressed the most transparently delicate side of the spirit, the happiest or the saddest, the one lighter than a moan because it was actually just breathing with emotion. The rhythms, from swing to the tango, were studies for him in what Africa had become in the Western Hemisphere, how the epic miscegenations had created something fresh.

Miscegenated spice is where you find it, big boy. There were also quite wonderful, saucy blends of his black beans and her white rice when they got home from those dancing whirls, him sometimes carrying Carla in his arms up the stairs and wondering at how light somebody with an ass that big could be. She would be laughing then and the two of them, their clothes wet and salty, started to undress each other. He took off each of her shoes, massaged her feet, rubbed the backs of her calves ever so lightly before squeezing them as though they were his, not hers. In the process, however, Maxwell's hands, captured by her flesh, became hers, not his own. Then, with her skirt off, he slid his palms against the insides of her thighs until they started trembling. He smooched her belly, his little soft pot of ivory. She couldn't get rid of it once she turned thirty-five and he didn't want her to. Her guy liked it just like it was. A belly didn't diminish her looks one tiny bit. It made her womanhood more full, as far as he was concerned. That little pot gave her body another sensuous and vulnerable swell. Ooo, that Maxwell.

He stood and put his hands in her damp hair, which had—if you asked her—no character but *felt,* even in its flatness, as though each strand of her whole story was growing from her skull into his fingers when the mood was like this. Such was the Midas touch that led to softening a woman, not hardening her. That's what it was. It let Carla possess every drop of the swampy goo inside her own soul. She was all steam and boiling sugar. She knew it then because she couldn't breathe and she couldn't stop breathing. There was also no better feeling in the universe than the way his warm hand would rub her wet back so gracefully as he turned her around to unsnap the moist brassiere. Standing now in her panties only, which Maxwell always made a production of removing once they got to the bed, she loved taking off his shirt, kissing the back of his neck, repeatedly but carefully nipping his shoulders, then unbuckling his belt and experiencing the scintillation that came as her thumb and forefinger pulled the zipper down slowly so that each metal tooth had its say in the night air.

They then met in the place where men and women meet, the place they both have to arrive in, her one way, him another, both bringing the syllables of feeling necessary to create the rhyme of all time. That was what her man jokingly referred to when he called either from somewhere in the city or out on the road. There was no greeting when she answered, just a pause. Then it began. He asked, his voice low and soft, almost like that of an aroused stranger. Sometimes he was inventing a way into something close to mischief, what Carla considered a cute brand of teasing:

"Say, is this here the palace of the crown princess of the posteri-orotti?"

"It could be."

"Hey, baby, how's the fuzzy-wuzzy school of South Dakota Kama Sutra moves?"

"Just what, exactly, are you referring to, sir?"

"Viking Hottentot. Serious business."

"As in?"

"That's what I'm talking about—as *in*. How is that blonde Hottentot institution? I'm talking about that rump roast, which also offers hot velvet courses in marine polyrhythms."

"Excuse me. Excuse me! Have you got the correct phone number?"

"How is that finishing school for high-class boudoir action doing—right about now?"

"Oh, *that*. Well, well. What can I say? Let me see. It's doing all right. There."

"You think you can still be sweet enough to get your heart *all* the way down there?"

"You got to bring a heart to meet a heart, big boy. Mine will be right there waiting. In the Kama Sutra steam room, where the fish smell fresh and clean. Just for you. Sweetheart."

There was then a pause and some contemplative breathing she found exciting.

"Carla, baby, aw, *baby!* Whew. Now *that's* exactly why I love you, baby. *Exactly* why."

"Come on home, honey boy. Come on home to me, daddy. I'm so hot I can't stand it. I want to feel that thrill when I hear your feet on the steps and the key turn in the lock. I want the touch of your lips, Maxwell. I want us to make love to each other until we turn into two balls of fire."

Well, now *that* was over. No more playing around and having silly, cutesy-poo pornographic conversations that would have embarrassed the both of them out of New York if anybody else had ever heard them. How long had it been since he talked with her like that, or she had listened to herself saying things to him nothing out of the past foreshadowed at all? He was different this last year and didn't care to sneak behind her in the shower, his shirt, pants, and shoes on, saying he just couldn't wait to be against her skin, which made him seem so foolish and childish but so much *her* man as the two of them removed his clothes until he stood before the girl from South Dakota in all the rippling bulk of his masculinity, washing and turning her and whispering her name, the two of them so free of everything but each other.

There were no more times when his eloquence startled her as she lay on her round stomach in the sensually itching blackness of the night and he told his baby how beautiful her form was to his hands, that the rise between her waist and the top of her thighs was a full hill of romantic dignity, that the down on the back of her neck was a beard of sunlight, that she was perfect because each nuance of honeysuckle tenderness was equaled by a spear of smokeless fire that made lying against her feel like he was moving across the top of a sugar cake covered with lit candles that didn't burn but gave him fresh, impeccably luscious sensations, that the two of them making love was another kind of talk, a conversation in which the flesh and the words of love and the wordless noises of love summed up what Ellington meant when he said that a man and a woman going steady were the world's greatest duet.

That wasn't all. Not with Maxwell. In the afterglow, there were experiences that touched Carla so wholly she might find herself transported close to a sob by the sentiment in his body. She and her man would lie there together, wet and salty from all the action, and he would embrace his deliciously exhausted baby, hugging her as though his heart had become his arms. The succession of hugs were of different pressures, slight to powerful but never even close to hurting her, only one statement after another of emotion beyond even the realm of whispers, emotion so clear in those embraces that her own insides became more evident to Carla as they tingled, bells of fresh feeling going off at the prompting of those increasingly expressive hugs that misted her up. Maxwell would then delicately move his hands across her back, her thighs, her bottom, her calves, her shoulders, her waist, the half-moon crest of her belly, her forehead, her temples, her cheeks, and her neck, made to seem so much longer by the quality of the way he put his fingers to each inch of it. All of these subtle things for maybe an hour, kissing her here and there so, so softly and somehow coaxing both of their bodies to relax, from the forehead to the feet, until the skin of each one became porous enough for even more feeling to breathe itself back and forth, his to hers, hers to his, the slightest touch both an unscented perfume of spirit and an entire tale of passion in gradation upon gradation. She quivered against him then and her heart stood still and sometimes she couldn't stop crying.

Carla needed no help to understand that whenever that happened, the weeping in his arms, it meant that she was in yet another depth of nakedness, responding to the satisfaction of hungers for the unrelenting strokes of romance, hungers their love revealed to her when the intensity of the joy was that gentle. There were still pleasures, yes, but not those, and those leisurely times were the elite moments of recognition that made the arguments as well as the periodic, self-involved moodiness expected of two artists define themselves as nothing but difficult intermissions. It no longer seemed like old times. Romance was a vacation from the way they were living now, not the essence that they always returned to, sometimes full of apologies but always more aware of what had put them so firmly inside of each other. She didn't like the long death of it but faced the truth that the tone of surrender was gaining power in her heart.

Carla, the cooling taste of beer going down, felt both satisfied with her increasing fatalism and alienated from it. Tired of herself and everything that dominated her thoughts, she took in, once more, the glorious place this wild and very good friend made her home.

On this homecoming Sunday, before everybody else had unassed the area, they were all relaxing on the first floor, where Leeann would have people over for drinks in the room that opened to the right of the staircase and provided the gateway into her garden and lawn, the place for barbecues, teas, light suppers, and hanging out under the moonlight with just a few other people, talking and talking. The next floor had a kitchen, comfortable chairs of cloth or leather or wood, the long dining table which sat in front of the tall glass doors that opened to a balcony one third the size of the room, from which you could look at the other buildings or on over to the Hudson River. One floor up from that were Leeann's quarters, half the space taken by aisled closets in which she had her clothes, jewelry, and shoes organized by color and then broken down into specific fabrics, furs, and distinctions of leather. (Leeann had a fanciful story of wearing her mink one winter and catching a fat white girl who was about to spray-paint the back of another woman's fur coat. According to her, she snatched the animal rights advocate around and offered to let her spray the mink she was wearing so that there would be an excuse for flipping this tub of guts on her head before dragging the culprit to jail or waiting for the cops to make an arrest for destroying private property.) There was an elephantine brass bed covered with pillows that were inside cases made from kimono silk Leeann had picked up in Japan. Above the bed was an Abstract Expressionist portrait of her in the nude with large words in vampire red across the middle, "Abandon Hope All Ye Who Enter Here."

A long table was against one wall and on that table were pictures of Leeann and her family, a file with every report card she had ever gotten in grade school, her framed first-proof sheets from when she had been discovered while majoring in English in college, and a ceramic Picasso dish she used for an ashtray. Her bathroom was marvelous, with a black marble bathtub easily big enough for two people and a red marble shower that had a showerhead the size of a sunflower and made to look like one, with polished brass petals. The sliding window doors separated the bedroom from a patio balcony with a couple of chairs. Leeann, who could float off from her own gatherings, was probably up there on the balcony, sipping something and looking out over the roofs of the other town houses, forgetting anybody other than herself and maybe, provoked by Cecelia, remembering some experience so full of sting she had to massage her insides before coming back downstairs. One floor up from there was Leeann's swimming pool and the two guest rooms. Carla was welcome to come over anytime she wanted to and get in the heated rectangle of water, thirty feet by ten, and swim until she got tired. That was always relaxing after a long rehearsal or a lesson with her singing coach or when she felt lonely and had walked until she wanted the intimate company water could provide a swimmer. No matter how much of a hair shirt Leeann could be sometimes, she was a friend and always looked out for her buddies. *Always.* Who could ask for more than that?

With the sambas maintaining a light position in the atmosphere, Carla, observing that she was forever Dad's contemplative daughter, stared at Leeann's sound system and, actually hiding out in the defensive caves of her intelligence, experienced all those nights when there had been recorded music and learning in her life. The three kids, in or out of their pajamas, had watched Mom and Dad leave puffs of stardust behind them as they danced near the Christmas tree during the holidays. Carla and her girlfriends had listened to their favorite records over and over, she and Randy had practiced all the steps of the new rhythm-and-blues dances, Ramona and her little sister had danced together, one pretending to be the boy, the other the girl, the older sister imitating what Mom might be saying to Dad about having too many drinks, the younger daughter answering as he might, joking about the whole thing. That whole way was done for; the technology had moved on.

Kids today didn't even know how recordings felt in your hands before compact discs, or how weirdly evocative it was when you were a kid in somebody's basement thirty years ago and found a small envelope full of the needles they had screwed into the tone arms of the old units with the turntables that revolved the easily broken shellac records 78 times a minute. Kids today never have the chance to feel hoisted up out of their bodies and into another era as you sit on the floor in tennis shorts with the wind wild outside the window and examine a stack of actual albums from the forties, that ancient world of black-and-white movies, that era when each record was in a brown sleeve and bound together as if part of a collection of photographs but with the picture of the musician on the cover and some innocuous statement on the back bracketed by musical staffs. Poor kids; the only thing they can relate to is each other. They don't know how it was when the album had become one long playing record, an LP, and there was no end to excitement when you got to unwrap the cellophane in which it was sealed, back in the day when a single large record meant more sound than a smaller single record.

Well, she wasn't that old, even with this very little pouch inexorably descending under her chin, but she had seen some things. Now, knowing what she knew about making a recording today, Carla thought of how compact discs had changed her conception of time. It used to be—in her days of reluctantly but proudly wearing miniskirts when the hemline had risen as far as it could and she hated the fact that she *always* had to sit with her legs crossed—that the album had twenty minutes or so on each side. When that side came to an end, or another album dropped from the spindle, you knew just about how much time had passed. She couldn't judge right now, listening to Leeann's sound system.

Of course, she had a watch on, but that wasn't the point. Well, there *was* the watch, which Maxwell had hidden as a parting surprise inside the pocket of the turquoise skirt she was wearing; it had a turquoise face and a silver band. He still did things like that, even now. Yes, even now. How strange a species of heartbreak the gift invoked. Carla rubbed the band of the timepiece with her thumb and thought about how sweet it was to have a guy who always did those little kinds of things to remind you that he had you on his mind and wanted you to feel happy.

As her consciousness rose up out of a sigh, it struck her once more how the compact disc put a new pressure on musicians to create an overall sound, the impression of a suite. There was no longer a side one and a side two. The dividing pause necessary to turn the recording over was no more. The compact disc keeps playing. Part of Maxwell's success came from his ability to put his recordings together so that they didn't seem like episodes in different moods. His albums were each one statement in which the modulations, the meters, the colors, and the harmonies led right into each other, shifting with a natural feel that he sweated red for, worrying over sequencing all through the night, his mood becoming distant and irritable when he was getting the recordings right. They didn't sell like pop material but they did so well that the royalties came in and they weren't discontinued due to low sales.

Why couldn't she just think about *herself*? Why *not*? Well, because she *couldn't*. If so, Carla would be another person and her blues would be somebody else's. She would get it together, eventually. Maybe there was no point in doing anything other than letting a terminal love get out of town on its own, since, quite obviously and obviously again and again, no amount of willed eviction notices was working. The hideous term "Jewish lightning," meant to describe those New York landlords who burned down their own places, had no place in this homecoming Sunday. An honest act of will might. It might not, too.

Anyway, the compact disc, to the learning delight of so many like herself, also made it easier for musicians to study. That was truly a blessing. The details were more accessible. Now you, with your thumb, could program the repeat of a couple of seconds and listen to them over and over and over until you understood what was going on, what the notes were, where they fell in the time, and the harmony.

Carla had done that so many times with Billie Holiday and Ben Webster, her two favorites and the biggest influences on her singing. Except for Louis Armstrong, nobody could equal Billie when it came to making a sung note sigh. Wow, what a thing to be a part of, living inside those phrases that were magic trails. Programming those bits of music to repeat and repeat was near about the same as continually rereading a touching but mysterious passage in a book. Yes, Dad, you were right. You were right. The honor of being his daughter primped up her sensibility. That was *another* of his theories: "Everything imitates writing. It has to because, so far as we know right now, we are the only species obsessed with telling stories. Our whole human story, everywhere on the earth, comes down to a narrative that defines every kind of meaning in the continuum. That narrative, when you think about it, comes down to two words: how and why. That's the point of writing, finally, the book. The words on the page and the freedom you have moving back and forth. That's the tip-top of the matter. Hugh Kenner said that about James Joyce. Kenner's a very smart guy, you know, not your average professor by any means. This guy *thinks*. Now he says that Joyce wrote *Ulysses* based on the fact that the reader could go back to better understand where he was at the time. He could pick up something that explained what was going on. These connections could be made. You can't really do that in music. It keeps going. Not in a movie. It keeps going. A play and so on. They exist in *active* time. Writing exists in *perpetual* time. The previous pages of a book are always there. That's what a recording is. You can reach back and get those notes like you can reach back and get those passages in a book. What did that kid call it? You know, the one you all had when you were kids. It used to drive Mom and me crazy, the one that was always playing *over* and *over*? Gee whiz. His name. The record. Gee. Something or other. Oh, my gosh, did I come to hate that song this guy wrote. You know, Carla, the one about looking for another pure love or something like that. But the title of the album, now that brought home the bacon. *Talking Book!* Stevie Wonder. Blind kid. How Homeric. He was right, you know. Now, living in a modern world with these videocassettes and these compact discs, you have the book of active time. Students can study the way they study writing. But writing is the supreme, you have to understand that. Writing is the symbol of man speaking in meditative silence or in a passage read aloud or a play. Can't be outdone."

Only Dad would have the nerve to say that so casually to a couple of musicians, she and Maxwell sitting there with him drinking coffee and looking out the window at the snow falling into the Manhattan night the time he came to New York for a conference and had to deliver a paper on emotion as improvisation in the writing of Greek drama: "We know what is going to happen, but it is how the playwright makes us *feel* about it that gives us a charge or not. That's the essence of it."

"That's the same thing musicians do with chords in jazz," Maxwell said. "You know what the chord is, how it goes, and like that. Then you wonder what the next guy is going to play on the same chords you did. It's a world of difference depending on which person is going through the harmony. You look like you don't know what I'm saying."

"Not at all. I'm following you clearly. You know Beethoven did that with the *Diabelli Variations* on a silly waltz, one surprise after another."

"Well, Dad, you know that could be the first time something like a jazz conception came into Western music. Jazz musicians have been doing that with popular songs, some of them pretty fluffy, since Louis Armstrong."

He seemed not to have heard her.

"This might be something I can use in my lecture. If not this time, later on when I have the good old chance to work it in. Continue, please. No, Carla, not you: Maxwell."

Let's go bonding in the male room, she thought.

"Okay. Let me see how to say this. The harmony is the story in a Greek play. Each chord follows in the same order. Oedipus, Medea, Electra, whichever one of those people. I had a few lit classes back in the day. Same thing. Oh, yeah. In fact, you know what I always liked about reading was you could sit in one place and travel anywhere the words took you by moving your eyes on the page. In music, you stand right there and tell a story as you follow those chords. What makes one musician more interesting than the other is how he makes the chords *ring*. That's where you get the feeling. Somebody can make some chords you know feel another way. You're saying the same thing about playwrights, right?"

You're also, guys, saying what I was saying.

1 7

BACK-HOME BLUES:
LUCK BE A LADY IN RED

C ARLA WAS beginning to feel unwanted in Leeann's home. No one had come out to see how she was and there was no Kelvin Thomson. She began to worry. He had been gone for nearly forty-five minutes now. In those bars where she learned how to serve people, Carla also found out that it was very easy for a drinker to stop along the way and have a quick one, get in a conversation or an argument or a period of self-questioning, then abruptly realize that someone was waiting, gulp down the liquid trouble that would surely bring more imprecision to his condition when he got where he was already supposed to be, silently or not silently rue the decision to try and quickly wet one's whistle, reach for the money—usually in the wrong pocket the first time—pay the bartender, and hurry out.

But Carla got herself another cold beer and sat back down. She was curious as to how things would turn out and now, in unexplainable contrast, was oddly enjoying enough of the privacy of her contemplation to feel as though she were at home. Yes, even though she wasn't shooting the breeze with two friends she loved, Carla now appreciated how peaceful it was after all of that emoting among buddies. Just a little bit of that good old calm—calm, what calm?— was something that couldn't be overvalued at certain times. A chance to smooth out your mind and get a sense of where you were, free of both the impositions that came with fury and the tragic dissatisfactions that were always lying in wait. You got that right. There was an explosion if you went one way; in the other direction was a dousing bucket of ice water when you needed to be reminded of the cold, cold limitations built into your life and everybody else's. You could glide by both of those with a little relaxation on a day just like this one, your sail in the wind, the spray in your face.

There was still no Kelvin.

He had to get there fairly soon. If not, she would step upstairs, gather Leeann and Cecelia, and leave in a posse, searching for him. She had done that before with Bobo. The drill was familiar. There might be no other choice. These kids in the bodies of men left you with no selection long and worthy enough to handle their taking a powder. They popped the whip. You got up and went tracking, anxious every goddam second. All you wanted, when you did that, was for him to be close by, not swept up in a disappearance that kept you awake late into the night when you returned with nothing, wondering what had happened, so relieved when he got back but full of anger at having been exploited emotionally because you didn't even get a phone call to let you know just what to expect, that he would be next to you soon or that he was out in the wilds of the New York night and presently trying to reassure you that everything was all right, which was some total bullshit but still better than not hearing his living voice and finally edging up into the panic of wondering if you would ever hear that voice again.

She eased back into her recent past. Once more, she stopped resisting. It wasn't all bad. No, it wasn't. There were financial and career blossoms. *Hers.*

Money was coming in for arrangements that other singers had commissioned from Carla. All the training in Chicago and all the listening to the masters of the jazz pen were hitting pay dirt. Lazy about it, impatient but too full of pride not to do a good job, she worked all through the day and all through the night on those commissioned arrangements, using subtle counterpoint, hip little retrogrades, and surprising combinations of the voice and the instruments in harmony—the singer who paid for the music was sometimes on the bottom, sometimes in the middle, sometimes on the top of the chord. It was all an irroyal pain until the rehearsals and the recording dates came around. Then the girl from South Dakota was in charge and loved it beyond description. With her music in hand and her professional face in position, Carla conducted those arrangements, her headphones on, her hands in the air, and made use of her ex-waitress ability to put people at ease. That was a big help, especially when the drummer couldn't immediately get a rhythm right. She could instruct the percussion man and not muss the hair or thump the head of his ego. Bobo would have had no problem.

She started getting those commissions after she had recorded her own arrangement of "The Days of Wine and Roses" with Maxwell three years ago. One Carla was especially proud of was "Cassie Mae in Satin," a recording of ballads done for an equally large-bottomed Negro singer from Mississippi who was so sensual her singing was breathlessly erotic but the romantic soul brought to the delivery made sure that the music never even resembled pornography. When they were in the studio going over one of the arrangements and Carla felt a little nervous, Cassie Mae relaxed everything by creating loud, conspiratorial laughter between them when she said, "Girl, with you and me in here at the same time we got enough boody to bounce this building down!" The girl from South Dakota was nervous because she had discovered something new. Carla had heard the drummer Lewis Nash's band at the Village Vanguard and was struck by a passage in which he used the violin and the soprano saxophone in harmony. For Cassie Mae's recording, which was originally supposed to be for strings and voice, Carla went bold and wrote for four soprano saxophones and four violins, creating textures she and no one else had never heard before. They were light but vocal and substantial, their freshness so appealing in combination with Cassie Mae's singing that the album became a strong jazz hit. So Maxwell's shadow was no longer smothering her and when they were among insiders, musicians or no, she didn't get that look of pity and dismissal reserved for the tagalong and untalented females who took advantage of the respect that their men had earned.

Her money and his money brought in a nice income they kept in a joint account, checking and savings. Yeah, but. Exactly: yeah, *but.* There always was one, wasn't there? The two of them still didn't have enough money, and not only because he spent like water running down a hill anytime she went out on the road with him. It was a tendency. Maxwell got angry with her and would pout if she said anything about how often he decided to pick up the tab when they met another couple for dinner or were hanging out at the bar of a club with a few people, laughing and having a very good time.

And, as life will have it, crashing the party at will, there were also things Carla hadn't even told Leeann about, thinking it was nobody's business. She could have been more honest when they all arrived in this house from Crescent City earlier. She could have been more precise, even with herself. Well, it was something she tried to avoid the specifics of and shuffle under a deck of philosophical overviews that, while hurting, didn't pour a more burning sort of recollection into the cut. It took a while to get there—to what it was all the way down in her bitterness—because of what she had concluded about him. *Raise Up off Me:* That was it. Hampton Hawes had written that when he and his bebop boys were strung out on heroin and couldn't get any dope they pushed lit cigarettes into their arms to vary the pain of the withdrawal. Perhaps her desire for control over how she would experience the disillusionment had been no more than protective selections of choice, emblems of weakness. Her face went hot: a deprecating vision of herself stung inside.

Yes, as it really was, her very being seemed to heckle or embarrass him, notably when they were in public together or he was working a club and the black women interested in Maxwell began to look at this handsome man as though he had become a leper the very second Carla stepped forward and made it obvious that the two of them were a couple. Maxwell himself had said—how many times, huh?— that they didn't spend any time listening to him before he started becoming a lightweight celebrity. So what did he owe them? Nothing is what he owed them. Were the two of them, once so above it all, now reliving a romantic variation on that tired story in which the woman supports the guy throughout college and medical school? Then, when he's ready to make his name, the one who has stood by him come rain or come shine is informed that another woman who understands him so much better than she *ever* could has won his heart and all he now has to offer is an apologetic and philosophic goodbye as well as, at best, a thanks for the memories! Carla was boiling in a pot of fury and being cannibalized by the very idea of it. There he was on any of those nights. Any one of them. Any. Take your pick. He had an apologetic look on his face when these black women would get cold and huffy. Her man should, very calmly, have told them to fuck off or go find their own men. That's what he should have done. That's what Bobo would have done. That's what he would have done if he was who she thought he was.

"You brothers need to come on home," one said to him as though Carla was a stain on his tie he needed to clean off, "and get something real. You know what I'm saying? Put some brown sugar in your coffee. That African sugar. It'll wake you up. That tired European ice milk is putting you brothers to *sleep.*"

Carla wanted to kill that woman. Peanut brown and buxom with splendidly contoured legs and long slim arms, her braided hair black as a hawk's wing and her eyes the color of cider, this round-faced professional Negress with an attractive gap in her teeth was unabashedly proud of such contemptuously bad manners and gave Carla a dismissive glance as she turned and walked off, her high, sensual backside seeming to chant, "Kiss this black ass, you tired white bitch."

Maxwell, quaking Carla's heart with rage and insecurity, said nothing, merely had an empty expression on his face that was soon saturated with a cast of indecision and tiny, tiny bubbles of anger. He closed his saxophone case without automatically putting the neck strap inside of it.

Carla could not have been more humiliated if the woman had thrown a bucket of phlegm in her face and Maxwell had given off the attitude that he was irritated because she was standing there drenched. For the rest of that evening she didn't speak to him and waited for an apology, then began to nearly hate the man for remaining silent and found herself sobbing in a late-night shower because it was so obvious that he had, after all they had lived, become no more than a coward. That was one of the most painful revelations of Carla's entire life, but her pride would not allow her to even mention just what a pathetic vessel of uncertainty he seemed to her that night.

Maxwell alluded to all of that the evening before they left Houston for New York, but she didn't feel like trying to get him to talk about any of that sorry business at that time. Nor was she now interested in thinking about the other ways he had begun to show the changes in his racial attitudes. The week with his parents had been something so far from anything she could have imagined that, well, all Carla wanted to do was ask herself the question of just how much of what she had experienced would become part of her way of being and how much would remain purely as memory. She could think about that rather than what was going to happen to her and Maxwell. That was pretty clear anyway.

Oh, Houston, Houston, Houston. Eunice. Ezekiel. The best. What a time, what people. So much kindness and vinegar. Was she grateful to God that she had met them. Such resonant hospitality. She knew that they had been central to the most entrancing element of Maxwell's tone, which was the sound of welcome. That level of invitation always separated the big souls from the little ones. But some, as it turned out, had bigger tones than they did souls when it was time to count off, face the music, and show them. What a chickenshit.

Anyway, the day prior to Carla and Maxwell flying home to New York, Ezekiel picked up their cleaning and Eunice insisted on doing all of their laundry herself, which was now matchlessly unsoiled, fluffy, sweet-smelling, and neatly placed in the drawers so that there would be no trouble at all packing. Maxwell and Carla had both become expert packers. They found hardly a wrinkle on their belongings when they opened their suitcases or traveling bags upon arriving at a destination.

That was another good thing that would last after he was gone: Maxwell had taught Carla something that made her wish Mom was alive so she could pass it on as another way to handle a problem. He always put scented soaps in his luggage so that there was never an unpleasant smell, even if his clothes were in need of cleaning and he hadn't had time to get them taken care of before moving on the run to the next part of a tour. Mom used the little sachet bags of herbs or sandalwood, but the soaps were was just as good and one got them free from the bathrooms of the better hotels.

Mom would have liked the scented soaps, and there was no doubt that Mom would have adored Maxwell as Carla had when it was good. Dad did and Ramona would have liked him, too, if she had ever been able to pull herself away from her job in Cleveland on the couple of occasions when the two of them had taken Northwest Airlines out to South Dakota for the holidays. Ramona was as bad about keeping in touch with her sister as Maxwell was about calling or visiting Ezekiel and Eunice. She didn't answer letters; she never returned phone calls. Carla had heard about people becoming that distant once they left home, but as close as they once were, she hadn't expected her big sister to ever be that way. The feeling of *always* getting left out really hurt, which was why there weren't too many calls from her side; not hearing back over and over and over would have made it that much more humiliating. Could that silly argument about men have left such deathless anger in her big sister's heart? Apparently fucking so. Sometimes, however, Saint Superior Ramona went out to see Dad and, he said with plenty of galling pride, bragged about how well she was doing. Of course, her big sister didn't have to worry about returning *his* phone calls because Dad *never* called anyone long-distance and didn't write or send out holiday cards either. Mom always did that, and it seemed as if he thought she was still doing it from the other side of the grave. If you wanted to get in touch with him, the whole thing was on you. So Ramona probably got some of that from their dad. If Mom were alive, she would set everyone straight, absolutely no jiving and jacking around. Whatever the circumstance and the logistics, it was still so nice to go back to the big plains. So simple.

Out there, the two of them didn't do much other than look at the eternal snow and sit around discussing national and world events, with Dad showing Maxwell the family albums and introducing him to his theories. Carla would cook dinner for them and experience a deep and private sorrow about there being no Mom, no Randy Jr., and no Ramona.

Dad, always trying to frame the world he was in, had lately become obsessed with what was going on on the cable sex stations. That was what he claimed anyway. She didn't accept that his sex drive was gone. Carla remembered too well those sounds she and Ramona used to eavesdrop on. Then, though both virgins, they would knowingly eye each other as Mom and Dad came to breakfast with a particular brightness in their faces.

On cable, Dad said, everything was depicted as fine and dandy— one man with two women, two men with one woman, three women together, women in leather dresses putting nipple clips on each other and getting their bottoms spanked red, women mailing in home videos of themselves stripping or couples sending cassette footage of themselves in the act, or women using dildos or licking whipped cream off of each other, orgies, voyeurism, and on and on. Pretty raunchy stuff, all of it pretty much the delirious worshiping of the taboo, just the totally puritanical burden of the nation flipped inside out. What Dad found most fascinating, however, was the fact that women *still* got a raw deal. In interviews or monologues they did panting, whining, and instructing phone-sex acts right before your eyes, or they talked about being prostitutes or nude dancers or porn stars or having been centerfolds in sex magazines as though these were just regular jobs and glorious achievements. These were their bodies and their selves. They had a right to choose. Their work was nothing special, no more outrageous than a mechanic explaining how he used his tools to fix cars or, in detail, describing what kinds of problems were specific to certain kinds of vehicles. It was odd to Dad how sexual liberation had led, in this increasingly popular lane of depiction, to a kind of glossy denigration. Women finally had the barbed-wire straitjacket and the chain-mail cowl of the Virgin Mary lifted from them but remained, according to these leering cable stations, pretty much no more than whores, exhibitionists, and braggarts who were supposed to be calmly or giddily proud of it.

It's a crazy country, he said, laughing as he stood before the fireplace and looked at a picture of Mom. While saying what he thought, Dad also did his hayseed act. It's hard to get free of your old position of service. Full freedom for the individual is still our longest dream. You can be one full-time crusading fool but you still get a goose egg for every strike you make at the end of the alley. Get your back up if that's the way you want to react. We can all understand that. It is pretty much discombobulating, more to some than others. You can lose all your marbles over it, go off the deep end like a crazy blind man in the streets with a pistol. Postal worker type. Those are still the rules of the game. Sometimes, there's just more hogwash than there are hogs. So our nation swings as far as it can in one direction, like a wrecking ball, then it swings in the other direction—or sideways or up and down like a yo-yo—still knocking the hell out of something else that was traditionally stationary. After all of this, it just hangs there. It's all sticky, like my wife Susan used to say. Her idea was that it was mixed with the blood of our suffering, sure, and what she called the honey of our human understanding. Well, you can be sure she didn't forget to mention the sour cow juice of pieties.

Cow juice?

Milk, Maxwell.

Now I got it.

You have to learn to speak *Midwestern,* sweetheart.

All three got a big laugh out of that one.

You know, Dad went on, it's not quite still. It can't be; the old wrecking ball is forever rattling on its chain. Somewhere out there in the middle. Until the next gold-rush tornado of social revolution starts doing some whirling and it spins into a vengeful dreaming swing again. That's the way of our country. Well, sad to say, it's got things in it that are too bad and too late to change, like the inevitable destruction of the Indians. You know, Maxwell, the Indian Wars ended right here in South Dakota when they massacred the Sioux in the winter of 1890 at Wounded Knee. They weren't there to fight; they were sleeping and they were slaughtered. That's the cruel way, the fake way. A terrible burden on the soul of the country and one we should never fool around and forget. Fake patriotism is what it is. Fake as you can make it. You take some bad things the other guys did—doesn't matter when they did it—and you use those things as an excuse to dehumanize people so you can feel fulfilled and noble when you abuse them. That's fake patriotism for you. But, when we don't fake it, when we don't drop the ball and forget about our complicated and collective humanity, it's a *good* way. It is. To tell the truth, it's the best way, the last best hope—if, as my wonderful wife always liked to say, we remember things like those frozen bodies in the snow of Wounded Knee so that we don't become so satisfied with ourselves that we forget we could always do a little better. We could be a little fairer.

She was so proud of her dad out there when he talked like that, being himself and filling in for Mom's point of view as well—and as he gazed at her photograph! *Mom,* whom Dad, on the odd and stormy occasion, affectionately called "the velvet War Department." Carla's heart became the twin of a hot fudge brownie fresh from the oven when Maxwell nodded at Dad, smiling in that way that he did whenever something special was said.

As for that whole other thing, on those occasions when she and Maxwell spent a little time looking at one of those sex programs, the two of them got a good laugh because their intimate life was pretty simple, naked skin and naked feeling. What they really found ominously hilarious for a bit were those late-night cable movies in which men and women on secret missions killed off mountains of villains with explosives, hundreds upon hundreds of bullets, brutal, repeated martial-arts kicks, and twistings of their evil heads to break their necks. What a way to parade equality. No wonder there was such a love of disorder in the streets. That had to be part of it. Male or female, in combat gear or with implanted breasts partially or fully exposed at every opportunity, you settled things by becoming as merciless as the totally no-good opposition. If on the right side, well, you were allowed. Spill your gallons of blood where you wanted. That made Carla and Maxwell kind of cynical and angry the more they thought about it. The funniness was gone.

Then Maxwell, just about a year ago, had become unbelievably enraged one dull viewing night when he and Carla, flipping the channels to one silent set of images after another, saw two nearly nude black women in obvious wigs of Shirley Temple curls sitting on a cheap couch with a telephone in front of them on a crappy table while another, her hair in a long, false ponytail, did a clumsy stripping routine. He wondered what was going on and turned up the sound. As soon as the dancing girl sat down, a call came in, "Janky Bo from the Bronx," who wanted to know how much one of the girls whom he knew by name would charge him to lick up in his ass. The girl went bonkers, haughtily explaining that people saw her on that show and approached her in the street like she was a prostitute, which was all the way wrong because, yes, she would lick your ass, suck your dick, and you could fuck her in the ass, but you had to be her boyfriend, not just *anybody.*

"That's what this country is doing to black women," Maxwell almost bellowed, standing up and shocking her. "These bitches are so stupid they humiliate themselves and think they're defending themselves. A whole lot of older brothers told me most black women haven't been having oral sex but for about twenty-five years anyway. Last to fuck and last to suck. Now, under the influence of these goddam motherfucking decadent-assed white people, they're doing *this* kind of dumb shit. That's not the *real* them. They're not like *that.* They shouldn't be in this. That's not *black.* They should be like those black people in *Satyricon,* just looking on and *laughing.* Fellini knew

357

what the fuck he was talking about. He's Italian. In his country, fuck, they elected a stripper to be a mayor or city council or something like that, and she pulled off her top when she won. He was showing the *real* history in *Satyricon*. That's *their* shit."

Maxwell turned off the television, went into a sulk, put on his clothes, and left their place. The cracks were starting right then.

Thinking of that television blues and his disproportionate anger as she sat in Leeann's comfy place, the underlying melancholy of the Brazilian music now totally obvious, Carla massaged the upper bridge of her nose and, mortified by the memory, wished she had something stronger than her white wine. She also wanted to be somebody else in another world but there was no model that appealed enough to let her dream about no longer answering to the troubles or having the emotions of the stumbling and evolving person that she had been for nearly four decades now. If she could simply forget how stunned she was on that evening and how obvious it was that there was nothing to say to him that he wanted to hear from her. Yet Carla had those kinds of ways herself, when she was just snitty or in a mood and didn't want to hear his words or those of anyone else.

Maxwell gave her the kind of wide berth she *needed* at those times and Carla—so, so wrong!—thought herself returning that favor the night that he exploded at some stupid girls on a public access cable show that didn't have one thing to do with race. Zero. They were only imitating some topless white girls who did the same thing on another channel. Well, that was his point, wasn't it? Yes, and it wasn't a very smart one. She'd have to say it was pretty silly. Your people always let you down if you looked at them long enough. Nobody could get away from that. No one on *this* earth.

Carla had never told Maxwell of how Baby Aaron had begun sobbing over the phone when he called from his home on one whistling and storming San Francisco night. It was late on her end, but he felt like talking to that old big-butted white girl he considered his play sister. She wasn't asleep anyway, just lying there in bed thinking about some Monk chords. Maxwell was out jamming with some of the kiddies at Small's on 10th Street. He told her of the evening that he had gone into a club in the West Village on one of his visits from the Bay Area, back in the early days when the shame was gone and homosexuals were finally becoming free to do whatever they wanted. Whatever. Guys were out on the streets everywhere. God, were they out there and were they busy! There was sex everywhere, in doorways, against cars, under trucks, against trees, in parks, slipping and sliding on the greasy floors of the empty meat trucks that delivered sides of beef, even on the corners under street lights. In your face, baby. The world was being told that there were men who loved men or who didn't even love them but wanted to have their flesh immediately. That was the point. It was pure desire and public recognition of that desire. This was unrestricted masculinity. Dogs in ready heat. Woof. As for you, whomever you happened to be in the outside world of the breeders, you were going to find out what this whole new freedom was about if you crossed into the cruising territory of the West Village. The closet doors were gone. Off the hinges. It had gotten to be like that.

Baby Aaron had never felt so liberated. Pure D paradise. He was still a gleaming young thing—a boy's boy—living in San Francisco and missing none of the restrictive stuff one had to go through back home just to get next to a man. On the way out west—once he had grown fed up with sneaking around and becoming the focus of married men who couldn't stay away from him but couldn't acknowledge his existence either—Baby Aaron had a wonderful night with a Texas Ranger. This big pink sonofabitch stopped him for hitch-hiking and, before you could say, "Drop your pants," the two of them were in the bushes to the side of the road. There is nothing in the world like the sweaty arms of the redneck law. Especially one who called him "Three Cock Monty" because the range rider had loved him some Montgomery Clift in *Red River*. There's a copper in the grass with a darkie in his ass, make it good, make it good, like boy's boy should. And, Carla, do you know the baby boy of the Davis family had to stay there with this delicious, big-hatted officer until sunrise because Mr. Ten Gallon had lost his gun in all that turning and twisting? If they had been two tumbleweeds they couldn't have rolled any better. The couple might never bump again. Yet in still, they had the rhyme *that* time.

But the point, Aaron continued, was that he went into one of those West Village clubs full of men over near the Hudson River and the docks. In there it felt absolutely incredible to be surrounded by nothing but your own kind, faggot balls to the wall. The club was called Hot Rod and had black painted windows illustrated with figures of men in leather jackets and tight jeans walking away but looking over their shoulders. The bartenders were naked except for black leather cowboy hats, black leather aprons, and black cowboy boots. Cigarette and reefer smoke were in the air as was the biting scent of amyl nitrite.

Aaron loved the feeling of danger and brash masculinity. He never let anyone hurt him but it was something of a rush to be in the middle of all that fire and theatrical toughness, some of which he knew amounted to nothing more than soft-boiled eggs in leather shells—pure, limp-wristed sissies, sweet to the taste and touch as cotton candy, hiding their delicately wired hearts and nerve endings behind masks of stern faces. *Okay?* Down a sticky corridor beyond the bathroom in the back were other rooms where all kinds of things took place. He didn't really want to go back there and never had been close to the acts themselves. For some reason, he felt his first mind saying it was bad luck on this particular night. Aaron didn't even look in the direction of those other rooms when he went to relieve himself in the urinal, which included dick-high holes in the wall behind which ugly men could wait to suck something they would never get between their lips if anyone saw their faces and how they were built. That hole, he laughed, was a different kind of confession booth. I'm confessin' that I'm ugly. But, for all that, the boy's boy from Texas got so drunk on cold straight vodka his nerve lifted him up and before he knew it he had turned all the way around after admiringly staring at himself in the mirror behind the bar as his face changed under the influence of the alcohol and seemed disembodied in the swirling white lake of cigarette smoke.

Now, as though he wasn't even walking but being carried along, Baby Aaron gave himself a one-man tour of the most forbidden part of an already liberated universe off limits to breeders. Nothing really struck him as much to write home about. He was prepared for the rather light whippings and the shouting and even the golden showers that excited some men. Humiliation was never something attractive to him, but there obviously were those who fully loved every nasty little bit of it. For the pretty black thing that he was, cringing and calling somebody *master,* especially a white man, was absolutely *out* of the question. Hody howdy hoody hum. One room had a door so heavy and a knob so hard to turn you had to think a little bit about *if* you really wanted to go inside. Near that door was a half nude guy with rings through his dark pink nipples and a skull above an X of two crossed spears tattooed on his chest. He was involuntarily moving his mouth and grinding his teeth, obviously coked up and playing with a lemon yellow yo-yo that had a light inside it, rising and falling, rising and falling. How cute.

Well, he was there now and what could he lose? Baby Aaron, feeling challenged by the pretty boy with the yo-yo, went in. How dare that Rosie of the Rings challenge *me?* Faggot bitchiness, as you should know if you don't already, is *our* version of macho. No violence, baby, just a shitload of *attitude.*

Broken glass, like a glittering powder, was all over the floor and the crunch of shoe leather on it was ominously soft in the blue and red light. There were naked men with bleeding feet hoisted up from the floor and held by chains that formed seats from which their asses hung out. On the floor were cans of Crisco. Men were slowly and carefully rubbing it on their forearms and the backs of their hands. Then they would work their balled fists up the rectums of the wailing bitches sitting in the seats of chains. Baby Aaron had no intention of being intimidated or shocked but soon spewed his dinner up against the wall when his true reaction took over. He was running out of the place before he realized what he was doing, continuing across the street until he was on one of the docks. He sat there crying and crying and crying. There was so much livid mourning in his heart. The smell, the corruption, and the weight of that room sat upon his soul as though his spirit were a toilet. He returned to San Francisco immediately and was morose for days. For *days.* You just had to face it. You couldn't get under it; you couldn't get over it. No matter what you were or what you wanted, there was a version of it that couldn't be described as anything other than monstrous. That room was now an island in the soul, a land to which he would never return, only recall when memory became the tinkling dissonance of split bells telling him something about corroded liberty. Now, Aaron said, every one of those liberated sissies who were so free to sit there and have fists rammed all the way up their ass are probably dead. A death train was all their freedom amounted to. All aboard. Bitches.

Perhaps, if Carla had told Maxwell what Aaron said to her, he would have understood. He understood so much. He really did. Geez, he had been so smart and many times she had far too pridefully come to believe that they were preordained to be together. Yes, those many times when what they spoke of had the intimate empathy and shared level of exchange that enlarged her soul.

During one particularly cold visit to the big plains—surely the last one together—they just missed being held up by the blizzard that forced the diverting of the flights only a few hours after theirs arrived. As the storm continued to grow and howl its indifferent power, closing the airport for a couple of days, Carla sometimes fantasized about Little Randy having an athletic and brainy Jewish girl from Northern California. This fantasy girl was red-headed, sandblasted with freckles, full of tough, smarty-smart opinions and wet-eyed, endearing sentimentality, the kind who would stand up to her brother's love of the cold outdoors once she stopped complaining about the weather and began hiking with him or throwing snowballs or going sliding like a couple of kids. That sort of playing in the wonderland of winter was something Carla got Maxwell to enjoy once the blizzard subsided. Oh, but she had to put a hell of a lot of tickle in her ways so that she could charm Maxwell beyond reluctance into a manner of fun he had never associated with people from his background—as if the snow and the clean wind gave a damn about anybody.

The cold itself didn't make a bother. He loved walking in it. That had nothing to do with being a Negro as far as he was concerned. They had even been skating in Central Park, day after day, his athletic grace allowing her man from Texas to get the rhythm down very quickly. But throwing snowballs and sliding? No, no. Well, yes, yes. I don't think so, baby. Come on, just once, just for me. Just for you? Just for me, sweetheart. They could have been eight. Boy, was that a great one. Hugged up with her man, the cap and the hair on her head wet fom the melted snow, she came back to the house laughing and looking at Dad and everything around her with that confident and affectionately regal feeling for life that Carla had possession of a few flat-chested years before puberty—but this time thickened up by all that had made her every inch a woman.

Out there, back home, with that dark and bulky man listening in her father's house for the last time, Carla told him about her brother, sometimes nearly breaking down, Maxwell holding her, petting and coaxing her along, knowing that she wanted to tell someone how that whole relationship with the youngest of the three kids had felt to her, that she wanted to unburden her heart. That last visit was about six months before things started going bad between them.

At the time, with Maxwell so close and so sensitive, she felt something crumple in her and simultaneously rise as they sat up at night looking out the window into the cold, moonless space of South Dakota. That deep freezing night couldn't touch them. They were ready. These two knew how to be prepared. Maxwell had stacked the firewood perfectly. He told her, between Santa Claus ho, ho, hos, that the crackle of the flames was the sound of dreams returning to heaven and, he said in his normal way, that her voice was always the sound of an angel flying into his ear. She just looked at him, almost dazzled, and he smiled, knowing that he had rubbed up inside her and poked the firewood with the subtle delight of that recognition. She knew she was his baby.

Carla, padding around in some heavy ski socks, made them some hot toddies and they got comfortable. Dad was asleep. It was the right time. She could do it. Maxwell was with her. He was ready for it. So was she. She didn't have to travel back there alone.

What an odd thing, so queer and peculiar that a story could be so much like music, that just saying how things were, just using the unseen presence of sound, could pull a ghost right into a room and show him off to someone else. That was how it seemed when she began talking to Maxwell, hearing almost her little-girl voice come back, the higher pitch that she had fought to lower as she grew up and became a professional in show business. It was very near to embarrassing, noticing her voice break upward like that, leaving behind the almost husky register that had become so second nature to her speech. Maybe some stories remake you into what you were when you lived them. Gosh, she didn't know. She didn't know if she was regaining something or displaying something or exorcising something. Whatever it was, it wasn't easy. What a spirit her dead brother had. What a spirit.

Little Randy, never fully in the adult mode, always gave the impression that he wanted to chase life down. That was his aura. You would have thought he was a hunting dog waiting to be let loose. His energy seemed to be panting against the air. He moved like he couldn't wait. He was a physical guy, one side of him was. Nothing meant more to that part of Little Randy than going out there and doing something either meaninglessly thrilling or demanding of skill, patience, speed, and strength. By himself or on a team, he didn't care. Let's do it. Swimming. Baseball. Football. Basketball. Yeah, he definitely had the mindless, irritating fervor of a jock.

His early career plans were, well, weird—in comparison. He wanted to be a forest ranger when he didn't dream of earning his living in horticulture. There were boxes of leaves he had collected. Randy had learned far more than the names Mom had taught her and Ramona when she walked them outdoors. The name of every kind of tree and flower and bush was waiting on the edge of his tongue when the family went on camping trips, sometimes into Wyoming, sometimes up into Canada. How boring and stuck-up and insulting that all was to the competitive Carla whom he always seemed to smirk at with that I-know-but-you-don't look on his face as they came upon some more foliage and Little Randy decided to display, another obnoxious time, what green or brightly colored piece of God's creation he had connected to a name given by men. Well, he might know all that, but he still covered Q-tips with brown mess whenever he got around to cleaning his ears. So there.

History was always the best story as far as Little Randy was concerned. It wasn't foliage. So there back! The old ways were so far away from his own time, but he took to reading and became a time traveler who comprehended more and more of what those worlds were as he grew from childhood to early manhood. First it had been fairy tales, then the dinosaurs were the best fairy tales, with him asking what happened to the titanic reptiles and Mom saying that they, like every living thing that can leave something behind, were out there represented now by no more than two things—their bones and those paleontologist people who put the bones together and tried to understand which ones ate plants and which ones ate each other. You could only get so close, Dad explained, because they didn't know how to write down who they were and what they had been, not like human beings—and even that, if you want to think about it, only goes back a short bit.

That did it. Little Randy loved the idea that people could let you know how it was and you could have that fairy tale and it could be true. So the growing kid lived in the Egyptian desert of the pharaohs, in ancient Rome, in Greece, on horseback with the Mongolian conquerors, in the ships of explorers, walked side by side with Marco Polo into the oldest civilization known to humankind, argued the subjects that heated the royal courts from London to Moscow, found out as much as he could about the Norsemen from whom he was descended, became fascinated by the many Indian tribes of America, could draw a map of exactly where Hernán Cortés landed and describe in imposing specifics just how the Aztecs fell, knew the men who had made the Constitutional Convention an intellectual hotbed of revolutionary democracy, had a solid grasp of how technology had defined and extended the parameters of one society after another, yet, for all that, her little brother maintained a certain level of insecurity that mixed an inevitable tenderness into the mood he brought to a room. This gave an attractive ballast to his brashness and convinced the girls who were smitten that he already knew something delicate that they wouldn't have to teach him. He wasn't too shy to take advantage of that, by the way. The calls from the girls drove everybody in the house crazy. Mom gave him a time limit per night on the phone. He was not living in the house by himself. That was that.

She paused. The flames in the fire were getting a nice even burn going, the smell of the logs was buoying, and the comforter covering their legs became perfectly toasty. Maxwell told her that during his own time as a youngster he had cut out the pictures of saxophone players and kept them in a special book. He would look at them and wonder what it felt like to have those people sitting there in clubs and concert halls listening to you. He loved their suits and the ways they wore their hair. Each one of them held the instrument differently, his fingers sitting on the keys in a certain way. The saxophone itself was a mysterious thing to put your eyes on. There was a mystical quality to it. The saxophone looked as if it might decide to talk to you when nobody else was around. It was hooked into spookism. But when he was sounding like somebody dying a terrible death as he learned how to play, starting with the clarinet, moving to alto, and settling in on tenor, Maxwell didn't know anything except that he wanted to be in on that number with all of those famous guys who had the kind of sound that he liked—Coleman Hawkins, Ben Webster, Don Byas, Lester Young, Lockjaw Davis, Lucky Thompson, Paul Gonsalves, Johnny Griffin, Charlie Rouse, Sonny Rollins, John Coltrane, Wayne Shorter, Joe Henderson, Clifford Jordan. As he got into his instrument, the thought arrived that on the illuminative days of serious playing he somehow roamed to all of those places where all of those saxophone players had been and was reclaiming for himself and for his moment all the glory that was so romantic and so powerful, as if every whisper a master had pushed up out of the bell of the horn and every fat-backed shout and every kind of passage in between was waiting in the ether to take an encore in a new body with a new story. When he became sufficiently proficient, Maxwell knew he had to compete with all the old guys who had become invincible through high style and immeasurable soul. It was a magic circle. You competed by trying to get in it. Once you were there, it was over. You couldn't be removed.

Carla understood exactly what he meant. Her brother would have known, too. Little Randy was forever in competition with Dad, but not the brutal, hysterical kind. He wanted to be as good; that was all. He just wanted to be . . .

Maxwell agreed.

Competing with the old heads was figuring out how to become as good as they were—if you had the right spiritual level of talent and the will to release it through hard work. Sonny Rollins was so overwhelming to him at one point that Maxwell thought there was no other way to play the saxophone. He held the saxophone like Rollins, had the same posture when playing, became equally taken by all of the different kinds of tones and colors the tenor could be cajoled or bullied into making audible. Getting past that awe and inventing himself was a big job because Rollins had the whole history of the saxophone in his horn and you could travel to the beginning with him, to the moments when Negroes started manhandling the instruments these white folks had invented with very different intentions on their European minds. Coltrane went back further, traveling through time to the field-hollering era of slavery and across the water into what he imagined the primitive majesty of Africa must have been. That wasn't for Maxwell. The blues went back far enough. It was the summation. It was the identity. A Negro was not an African nor a West Indian nor a South American. The Negro, as Kelvin Thomson said to Maxwell in Paris one night, walked out of the lion's mouth of slavery and turned the king of the jungle into a house pet. Well, Maxwell laughed, that *was* stretching it quite a bit. You must consider the context. They *were* drinking and anything was subject to be said once the cups were big enough and the two of them had their diving equipment on.

She didn't care about any of that, not really. All the autobiography was getting in the way. So there was a light whiff of steam and sulfur coming out of her ears. Carla wanted to tell him some more about Randy, about the boys he used to beat to a pulp after Dad taught him to box and then struggled to keep his son from becoming nothing but an educated bully. Maxwell asked her to excuse him for going off and talking about himself. This was her time. He was supposed to be listening. He apologized. He rubbed her back and kissed her on the cheek. This man could feel her so clearly. Sometimes she didn't have to say one word, not even one. Carla put her head on his chest and continued.

Randy was the same way about his father that Maxwell was about Sonny Rollins. She didn't tell him about the satisfied arrogance her brother had on his face after abusing the pugilistic skill he gathered from Dad and how he didn't get control of it until Mom, tired of the constant fighting and the calls from school and the astonished parents of the battered kids, said to her boy she was becoming so ashamed of him that hatred of her own flesh and blood was just one more brutal scrape away. *You want to fight about that,* Mom said, moving right up on Little Randy, her voice as hard as a saber, *try me. I'm the hard case you have to face out here, young man, not these boys you treat with such conceited savagery. Oh, mark my words, you can be this sort of bullying person if you think that blue suit fits you. But if you choose to be childish trash like that, I promise I will never speak to you again as long as either one of us is breathing. **Try** me.*

No, Carla kept that to herself. What she said was true but it didn't include the vicious period. The predatory look in Little Randy's eye was otherworldly to her one afternoon when just the two of them were in the house, she drinking some milk and eating a few oatmeal cookies in silence while this brother of hers wrapped some ice in a towel around one hand. It was swollen from the fight he had with the Jensen brothers, beating one down and knocking the other out, all of it beginning with an argument that was less important than the chance he had to let the bloodlust free, his own cut lip, split eyebrow, and scraped ear meaning nothing other than false proof that the Jensen boys had a fair chance but weren't up to the game that was afoot. As she thought about that over the years, Carla grew to believe that all of civilization, all resistance against teenage anarchy, is based on creating the rituals and the exhausting games that handle the destructive urges arriving in newly strong young men at the same period when they are almost suddenly capable of getting girls pregnant. So weird, the ability to share in the beginning of life through the act of love and the appetite to destroy coming into existence together. With a red face and wide violet eyes, Ramona confided to her baby sister that she thought Randy was on the outskirts of becoming a murderer, that she was having nightmares about it but had told no one else. The mark of Cain was all over him. He would kill someone and be banished to the land of Nod, just like in the Bible. They were both so afraid and started crying. Maxwell didn't need to know all *that*. Her brother had gotten over it. He gave up being a werewolf. Maxwell would never know him anyway. So, incapable of revealing everything, she told him other stuff. All of it true, all of it true.

Once, when he was very small, Randy walked around saying "Dad" over and over. And over. Carla, the pugnacious little girl, wanted to bop him one. He was so loud and irritating and had such pleasure on his face as he got his one syllable out of his mouth, his mantra of paternal recognition, pointing at pictures, at clothes, knocking over an ashtray as he reached for his father's pipe. The direction was clear: later, whenever he would observe, "But *Dad* said . . ." you would have thought a point of order in the universe was being acknowledged. As he grew toward adolescence and the father and son played catch with either baseballs or footballs and the two sisters were made to join in until they enjoyed it as much, Randy began to imitate Dad's physical style so thoroughly that Mom, braying, would point out how they seemed like a comedy team in a silent movie over by the garage as her husband's every personalized movement was responded to with the same gesture from her son.

Randy had no interest in being a kid once he found out that there was such a thing as manhood and that it meant knowing about a lot of things other than all of the aspects of the physical world he was so partial to and born to know. He never got over Dad telling him about the Greek ideal of a sound mind and a sound body. That stuck. He was afraid of Ramona but never stopped teasing Carla. His troubles with math and Latin were handled by Mom, who sat up with him in the kitchen and drilled her son as though he were preparing for battle. Dad, who knew Latin backwards and forwards, let it go that way because he didn't want Randy to feel that he owed his father too much and didn't want to intimidate his son in the slightest bit. Dad was good at such things. He knew how to handle you.

Carla floated off. She wanted to pause for a bit. She sipped some of her toddy, nearly finishing it, then nodded to Maxwell and asked him if he knew what she meant.

Well, Maxwell said, as far as he was concerned childhood was overrated. Randy was right. Hype. The two of them could have lined up on that. They could have lined up on those maps, too. They were his favorite things for a while. Maxwell used to love to study them and turn the bas-relief globe in the school library, imagining what it would be like to know beforehand what was coming up and then react to it, or plan for it before you took off. He saw now a close relationship between chord symbols and the maps that had mountain ranges, deserts, rivers, woods, and what have you drawn in symbolically. So when you were playing, certain chords could make you feel like you were mountain climbing or taking a canoe across a big river or sloughing through sand or being in the cold or burning up in the sun or just being in the middle of a feeling that wore no label of explanation, which was the main thing that took over in the music. Like in music, a map couldn't tell you what to do or think or *feel* when you got someplace. That was your freedom. The big difference was that a musical symbol was like the word for the wind; it was a symbol of the invisible, not like the words and symbols on maps.

Carla really, *really* liked the idea of that, the idea of making the invisible audible.

He said, well, that was the business they were in, sweet stuff. He was playing from that; she was singing from that.

Carla said that she had always wanted to be grown-up, too. I was always a fake sophisticate, she laughed, always. I might not have known what it actually was like, but I enjoyed working my way into the role. You can believe that.

Of course, Maxwell replied, why wouldn't she? Being a kid had always seemed a waste of time to him.

It wasn't a waste of time to Carla, but her age and the town itself, its dry, dry summers and its equally dry winters, the long stretches of nothing, her booming popularity, even the secret trails she used to love to learn from the Indian kids because you could go on them and hide out until you decided to come back because nobody outside of a special little group would have any idea where you were—all of it became something like a tightening choker by the time high school was finishing up. Moody and ready to go out there somewhere, *Is this all there is?* she found herself asking.

Me, too. What Maxwell wanted to do was get in on the grown-up stuff. Adults had so much more going on than what he and his buddies were doing, which was a whole lot of goddam fun, though—skating noisily on the sidewalk, fighting, riding bikes, throwing papers, going swimming, playing baseball, football, basketball, running track, popping firecrackers, collecting spiders, and eventually, with all that very tender butter an objective, chasing adolescent girls. He was in training for Carla, that far back, but just didn't know it. Meeting her straightened that out. He was walking that way all along.

That put it on her. Maxwell seemed part of her skin and all that was under it. He was deep in the heart of her and that heart felt as vast as the Lone Star State from which he hailed, or the plains of her own background. It was encompassing, an everywhere thing that made her feel sort of foolish, asleep to reality, too, too sentimental, suddenly—and suddenly—pushed all the way back to her teenage years when she was so adolescent in her intensity. It was as uncomfortable as it was abundant and delectable. She whispered his name, said, "Oh, sweetheart, sweetheart," then hugged him and experienced her chest filling. He had given her a fever with just a few words. There it was. All she could do was hold him.

After a bit, Carla got up to make some more toddies and felt as if she was right in front of herself. It couldn't be as good as it appeared. Nothing could. Maybe so. It could be. There was a simpatico rhythm in the house which reminded her of how it was when

Mom was there and you didn't need to try to hide because the trick always fell on its face—if she was focused on you. If she wasn't, you might get by for a little while. But not for long. Maxwell was focused on her.

Yeah, he said as she returned with fresh hot toddies, he knew about all the awe and the discovery and that line of blah-blah about childhood or youth. But anybody in the arts, like you and me, Carla, anybody knows that creating *and* recognizing other people's serious creation is your own cartography. You get a real chance. You get a real chance to understand. I think that's why we get so excited about what we do. The understanding. It's a personal way of getting with all of the explorers and the scientists, those ones that kept getting it together until they knew exactly how something everybody is aware of *actually* works, no made-up explanation necessary. The thing that always stuck in his mind wasn't the detailing of the natural wonders themselves but the wonder of people being able to map out what the fuck was going on for *real*.

As much as he liked to exaggerate and even make things up in order to tease or make fun of somebody, how could he not be captured by the idea of making up an explanation? Or had she just missed the meaning of what he was doing?

Of course not. He was just playing. That was true, but something else was going on then, in his kid years. The first time he really saw some aerial footage—the first time he really thought about it—his heart started coming down in heavy beats, faster and faster. What excited Maxwell enough to make him start shouting, which he didn't, was the fact that while the Wright brothers had broken the heavier-than-air barrier, somebody else had invented a machine that could capture a view nobody in history ever had before—and *pass it on!* Compared to those kinds of things, his lightweight boyhood discoveries about the world were spiritual chump change. Beyond that, his father and the men that his father knew were men. His mother and the women she knew were women. He wanted a fast horse to where they were. The groove was too wide and too deep to ignore. They were so strong about what they knew that his mother and father didn't seem to him that they had ever been kids at all. But, of course, they had, which was what Ezekiel reminded him of every time Maxwell tried to argue a point from the perspective of his generation, the *young* generation. "Boy," Ezekiel would say, as if dropping pebbles on his head from a high window, "seem like you don't know something. Don't know why you *would* know. But you talking that mess make me know you *need* to know. Listen here, boy. I already been your age but you still ain't been *mine.*" Maxwell never had an answer for that one. Ezekiel knew how to handle him, just like Carla's dad knew how to handle Randy.

Nobody, however, can necessarily handle you when your will is strong and your luck is bad. The time Randy had decided that there was somewhere out there that he had to climb by himself, not with Dad, not with anyone, was the end of everything to do with him other than the memories of the way he was and the dreams of how he might have been. Broadway songs his most recent love, he was whistling—flat as usual—"The Lady In Red" the day he left.

A big storm, hungry and predatory, impersonal in its appetite, had come howling and stalking a few hours after her brother had passed two New York Irish guys who had been sent out West a few years earlier because their parents thought they were doomed to become criminals. They grew up in town, Eddie Gallagher and Jimmy Walsh, one cute with big ears, dimples, and hair as dark as a night lit neither from above nor below, its shining blackness a key to his good looks; the other not so handsome and muscular but surely benefitting from wavy brown hair, that starlight in his eyes, and a way of turning his head when he spoke that Ramona found magnetic but could never do anything about, other than moon over him on the debate team, imitate his career decision to go into law, and hope that she would somehow get him away from his small-breasted and wide-hipped girlfriend Elaine Sage, who always wore her curled hair short and could be counted on for witty, street-smart remarks many boys considered very, very sexy. Well, not the *utmost.* Jimmy, kind of joking, made a pass at Carla one time, which she handled just right because he was a bit too old for her and not her type anyway—but Ramona heard it and became very cold to her little sister. Gee whiz, it wasn't *her* fault.

Anyway, Eddie and Jimmy were camping on a plateau, having breakfast and easefully preparing to move on up the side of the mountain. These were those kind of guys. You know the kind, not rich but might as well have been. That's how they were. Loafing along and taking it all in was their speed. Life had to be served to them on a platter at the club bar, where they each stood with one foot up on the rail, everything smooth but something inside that was ready to put a sweet bite on you. Some athletes, those two! It was just fun to them. Something else to do. They were in no rush; the mountain was going nowhere. It had never gone anywhere.

Carla chose not to remember how many feet up there they were, but she didn't ever forget the feeling of a hole opening in the air of the house when the fatal word got back that Little Randy was missing. The storm was so rough that the Irish guys he passed on his way up into eternity were just about done in themselves. The flying ice felt like it could cut off your ears.

Carla never paid attention to the sounds of car motors starting and wheels turning on snow or gravel, but in the kitchen on that morning when her father slowly stuck each arm into his overcoat and stood tying the flaps to the top of his winter cap, everything seemed very loud, from the soft way he spoke to her mother to the little squeak when the back door opened, to his boots going down the steps, to the way the van door sounded when he closed it after getting in. There was a shriek to the ignition when he first turned the key. Then he paused and started the motor up perfectly.

That was one lonesome morning as she, Mom, and Ramona stared out the window in silence.

When Dad brought the body back at twilight the next day, it seemed as though the funeral had already started as he parked and sat there with his head down against the wheel for a long, long time. Mom actually squealed as Dad, seeming a foot shorter, opened the door and said, in a jagged whisper, that the boy gone home was out there in the van.

Ramona remained in her room for the three days until the morning of the funeral. She didn't eat until everyone else had gone to bed. Carla, incapable of sleeping until she got accustomed to the sorrow harshly pinching her insides, heard Ramona going into the kitchen. No one knew what Ramona was thinking or feeling and everybody left her alone. This was not the time to tell anyone what to do or to ask what something meant. Moving through the day was enough. It was even more than that.

But in that house on that morning Ramona was up first and

responsible for the bear claws, muffins, and coffee that were ready to eat and drink when the rest of the family made it to the kitchen, thanking her for being so considerate and going out to the bakery.

The always peculiar scent from the cleaners that was on her black dress reminded Carla of formaldehyde, which allowed her memory to speed into biology class and the dissecting of frogs, no one wanting to get a female because of the trouble one had to go to in order to remove all of the eggs in the belly.

Mom's eyes had been ladles since the body came home with Dad. She was always crying or on the verge of it, but still going about taking care of friends from the neighborhood and family that came in, driving or flying, the house filling with them, gloom periodically turning tail as the stories began, too many of them hilarious to hold back natural laughter, Mom's sometimes the loudest. Carla thought at that time of how Little Randy had spent years trying to get Dad's baritone guffaw until he gave up and responded to the comedy of life with a percussive sound that came from the top of his voice. She missed him so.

Dad told her the night before the funeral that he had no idea this sort of thing would ever happen. There was nothing he could measure it by in his own world other than all of the terrible stories of infant mortality and short life spans that went with their Norwegian forebears coming to this country. He said, until this, he was just kind of philosophical about all of that history, never really feeling it, only knowing it and emotionally responding to the person talking or writing about it. Now he felt the pain. No man should ever have to experience the death of a child. He should not have to own that sorrow.

Ramona fainted during the eulogy. As her sister was carried into another room of the church before the family got into two of the dark cars, her with Dad, Ramona with Mom, Carla was encircled within herself by the welting sensation that she had no sibling with whom her loss could be mutually exchanged, acknowledged, soothed. Each bleary second of the funeral and the trip to the cemetery made it more true than ever that there were only two children now.

Carla, now still alone in Leeann's, felt her eyes stinging and her cheeks getting wet as she recalled how Maxwell had held her that night back home, how attentive he had been, and how he somehow, perhaps because of how he then felt about Aaron, knew exactly what it was like to lose a brother.

On that last visit home with him, Carla also told Maxwell of how she and Ramona had always waited for the winter, after excitedly becoming brown as they could get during the summer—covering themselves with baby oil and lying atop blankets drinking ice tea on the grass in the backyard, swimming, hiking, bike riding, and wearing as little as Mom would allow—pooh-poohing with adolescent insolence all warnings about what too much sun would do to their skin by the time they were in the territory of middle age. *I don't care if I look like a turkey when I'm forty,* Ramona said to Carla after Mom walked back in the house, *I'm a spring chicken now!* Autumn, if it weren't for school starting and her academic social life kicking back into place, would be a nothing time for the little sister. When the smell of winter came into the air, the young Carla thought of the moisture freezing in her nose and lightly rattling as she breathed. Then she and Ramona could skate and skate. That was a slice of heaven.

She took Maxwell to her high school, which was under big drifts of snow, like something rising or sinking into a chill past. There was no wind, there was no sound. They stood at the metal fence in exactly the place where she had watched the football players practice, proud that Paul Munger, the handsome quarterback—easily as good-looking as Eddie Gallagher—was her senior-year boyfriend. She didn't say anything else, just inhaled and exhaled all of those memories and knew that whatever her sense of herself had been those twenty years ago, there was no way on God's green earth that one second of what had happened after leaving home could have been imagined as it actually came to be. The wind was in their faces now and the blowing snow was turning upward in circles and circles, erasing everything from view as the invisible whistled and got louder in its unmanageable power.

After the two had put their heads down and walked from the old high school fence back to Dad's Range Rover, Carla caught her breath, feeling—out of nowhere— so separated from her sister since she hadn't seen her in such a long, long time. That emotion queered the moment with a slash. She told Maxwell that it was impossible to imagine what kind of a man would be with Ramona now that she was such a successful lawyer, her time clerking in Washington, D.C. having paid off once she went into private practice and worked her way up into that powerful firm in Cleveland, where she had become a partner at forty.

Well, come to think about it, that was not all that Ramona had become. Forty was only a few years away for Carla and there was still so much unresolved. At least, she was now on the—

Kelvin Thomson came in the door.

18

JOHNNY TOO BAD

H E DIDN'T HAVE any liquor and Kelvin Thomson seemed sobered. "That boy, my God."

The pain in his face was of a different nature from the dread, melancholy, and bitterness that could rise up in the lay of his eyes and the turn of his mouth when he had the last few drinks before floating to the deep end of the drunken pool, where he inhabited a veritable poise and, with no more than the very slightest lisp, became hysterically funny, or so lucid that whichever of the many subjects he knew a great deal about now took on an easily absorbed presence in the discussion through one eloquent sentence after another. He was a good addition to the crew.

Kelvin Thomson had come into the circle through Leeann, who met him in Europe when she was running around with the German filmmaker named Ekkehard, whose passion of the moment was to make a film out of a play that had become very famous on the Continent. It was called *Boredom* and Kelvin Thomson had written it with a German woman who escaped from East Germany before the Berlin Wall came tumbling down. The play was set in two places, in America and behind the Iron Curtain. The stage was split. The story told of a Negro who had been picked up by the police in Los Angeles and a woman who had been arrested in East Berlin. The Negro, alone in the streets when he was stopped by two cops, had made the mistake of being just a little flippant on a late night and the police took him in. The woman was whistling a song one evening and laughed when a man in dark clothes told her that she was humming out of tune. She was arrested.

At the police station, with the background music of "Old Devil Moon," the handcuffs were removed from the Negro, who heard the two dicks talk with their buddies of how dull their shift had been until they picked this guy up near a fish market that stunk up to high heaven. The car got smaller and smaller the longer they drove in the wet night looking for *something*. There was nothing going on. Dead night. What a bad piece of fucking luck. One joked that he couldn't stand to hear the voice of his partner say another single thing in that car as the empty sidewalks made fun of their job. One street after another saying screw youse guys. The other, as the music changed to "Angel Eyes," said that his head would burst open if he had to listen to his partner in law and order reiterate how much weight his wife had put on and the big mistake he made by buying aluminum siding for his house. The music stopped. Suppositions about sports took over the conversation. As he was fingerprinted, the Negro became quite angry but said nothing, merely used the cleaning solution to remove the ink and dried his hands with such deadpan rage that the paper shredded into the trash can. Their uniformed malaise started to dissolve, their guns didn't seem to weigh so heavily, their badges ceased to seem pinned through their shirts to their chests as the two cops joked around and flirted with the girl on the switchboard. They smoked cigarettes and talked of moving to Australia after retiring so as to be outside the reach of the Nubians. At once, all of the police officers looked at the Negro and moved toward him. That side of the stage went black.

The woman of East Berlin smacked her forehead in the police station for being such a dunce and not finding out who was criticizing her before she started laughing. Too low for the words to be heard, the Rolling Stones' "Sympathy for the Devil" began. Outside the room where she was sitting, the undercover officer who brought her in gave a long monologue about how dull a night it was, so, so dull, and the things one had to put up with in the building where he lived, no matter that his status as a man who had done his part to protect the regime should have guaranteed better. There was a pair of plastic shoes that came into his rambling. He found them disgusting. What was one to do in this strange time of our now, he asked, when people who believe in the structure of new things find themselves feared rather than respected by people such as this woman? Ho, ho, ho, his friends at the station said. Respect is not a necessary thing. This is the stuff of the fairy tale. Perhaps; however, there is also another side. There is never another side. There is only a mistake. No, no: what if all ideas of goodness and order are fairy tales, but fairy tales that cause many of us to make decisions? The others looked at him and began to parody interrogation. Is there meaning to this? Why are you pausing? Jaunty, he answered them. I am saying that we do this to prove that our minds rise so high, in these sacrifices, above the crustations of despair and anarchy. What words, what words: a bit too intellectual, you sound this evening. Are you going back to reading books? In my entire life I have never read a book, only those pages required to give the right answers. What answers do you think this woman will have? Oh, she has none. Nothing. She should be let go. The stage went black as a door opened and a light, extremely harsh, came across the room like a knife and fell upon the woman.

So you didn't commit that robbery? Of course not: it was miles away from where you picked me up. You guys said that yourself. Yeah, but we're not criminals. You might be the criminal, my friend, which means you could have zipped over there in a car. I don't have a car. That was how it began with the Negro. The number one inter-rogator, who had been pacing from the left to the right of the stage on a platform above the two stations, fully lit at times, in half or blue light at others, moving with a grumble in his rhythm, listlessly toying with a paper or with truncheons, came down the stairs rather deliberately and stopped the woman at the door just as she was about to leave the station. I must ask you some things. They said I was free to go. It does not matter what they said. You are not going. You will be asked and you will answer and then you will go. Look, I know you guys used me as a ticket to come back here so you could bullshit with your buddies. Now you read minds? Huh? Isn't that what you're saying? I know you had no reason to pick me up. We'll see about that. You have a record. We know who you are. Young lady, is it customary that you walk alone in a part of the city at night where it is known that criminals spend a lot of time? I was just walking. The interrogator slapped her face. Answers are preferred to statements. All right, Mr. Innocent Man, why do you have these arrests? I live where you get arrested. A cop slammed his billy club on the table and asked him if he lived where someone could get his head cracked open in a station house if he didn't learn how to speak the fucking language clearly and answer what the fuck he was asked. You've been seen with dubious men. You seem afraid to respond. I am. I am quite afraid. You shouldn't be. You were just walking. People who are just walking are never afraid. They hum out of tune and laugh when they are told so. I meant nothing. I'm very sorry. Fine, but as it is now, that is not enough. Meaning nothing doesn't complete this inquiry. We are all, young lady, quite sorry. Apology is in our mouths the moment we rise from the black lake of sleep. I don't know why you guys want to do this to me. I was minding my own business. So now you're in business? How about that. You have a store? A parking lot? You sell clothes? What the fuck do you do in your fucking business? I didn't mean—

If I were you, buddy boy, I would shut up right now. The number one interrogator began to probe into her life, her job, the way she felt about it, what she dreamed, teasing her forward until the talk became angular and intimate, shards of her childhood stumbling into language, her feelings about her family, her fear that her supervisor didn't like her, the few drinks she had some nights because the light intoxication was perfect company, then she was pushed to speak of the very first time she had been touched in a sexual way by a young man. If it were up to me, if I was running this screwed-up city, if they didn't have so many goddam restrictions on my carrying out the demands of my job, you might be dead right fucking now. Why? There he goes asking questions again. *You* don't ask questions. *We* ask questions. This is leading up to a question and you had better have the right answer or you are going away for a very long time, buddy boy. You have been identified. Yes: someone recognizes *you*. That's right. Ha-ha. *You* were identified by a woman as a rapist. Take that shocked look off your goddam face. Don't say one word yet. You still have a chance. We're trying to decide if she's crazy. Could be. She acted a little odd. That's the God's truth. A little. That's not enough for you to get out of here. Yeah, she seemed like a fruitcake. But guess who she saw today? She looked at you through that mirror and she saw *you*. She described *you*. She said what it felt like to be snatched by *you* when *you* put that chickenshit wooden matchstick in her lock so she couldn't get her key in the front door. Then, when she got frustrated and went around to the back of her house, *you* were right there waiting. *You* had your plan in place. Yes, you were like a slick black panther in a white Stetson and you *pounced*. The interrogator said that they had letters of hers in which she had lusted for abnormal pleasures. The woman, trying her best to sustain her dignity, lost out to the way she felt and began weeping. All I asked for was some tenderness. What, young lady, makes you think that you or anyone else in the world deserves to be treated with tenderness? You *bit* her on the neck. You *bit* her arm. Now you know what we're going to do? No, he answered, with his head down. We're going to get an imprint of your teeth. Those jungle chompers. If they match, you're finished, kiddo. Molasses in the cold, cold ground. You can speak now. There was a long silence. The Negro began to murmur in nursery rhymes, babbling into statistics, stuttering the names of his victims. We must search you now. He pointed to the floor. The woman went to her knees and removed her blouse. More. She stood and took off her skirt. The stage went black. Then the lights came back up. Everyone on both sides of the stage was in the same place as before the dark. This is the first time this boy has begun to make sense. I wouldn't have believed this fucker if I wasn't standing here myself. You started off as an animal, Mr. Innocence, now you've made yourself into a *man*. Bravo. A mind is a terrible thing to waste—especially on a nigger. This is enough. Yes, that is what I said. Yes. We are done now. You can dress yourself again as you were. This time, fella, you were very, very lucky. Lucky is right. We're letting you go. This time. You can straighten up and act like a man. No one was raped. There's no fucking rape victims. But you had the *balls* to take the weight. We like that. Volunteerism. This will go on your tombstone. "He could be counted on." Young woman, you must now stop this crying. These measures are necessary. You may continue your night. We now know enough. Fully enough. Our file is complete.

The Negro, mad as a hatter, comes to center stage. So does the woman. They each begin sobbing. Then they turn and are facing. In three-quarter time and a minor key, the song "Lover" begins very softly. The Negro takes her into his arms. Spastic at first, they begin to waltz. The music rises in volume and they become more and more gentle and cultivated in their steps and turns. The black backdrop begins to quiver with color in cloud formations, moving very slowly, going into darkness and reappearing. Those colors become a silhouette against a blue sky. The silhouette is a bridge, with golden cables and beautifully designed, like the one across the Mississippi in Alton, Illinois. Water is heard lapping. Then the musical sound begins to reduce in volume until "Lover" is a whisper and the light onstage has become quite dim. It goes black. A pin spot comes up on the chalk-powdered face of the number one interrogator, who is back on the platform above the two station houses. He laughs quietly but with a bitter and violent tinge. The spot on his face becomes red, then blue, then all goes black. The play is concluded.

The Europeans loved it.

"When I saw that play, it scared the *shit* out of me," Leeann told Carla. "But I knew I wanted to meet the nigger who wrote it. Ekkehard was down with the nigger, and when I met him and the three of us talked for a couple of hours, I knew I wanted to figure out how to get in a situation where I could drop these drawers on him."

"Oh, Leeann."

" 'Oh, Leeann,' my ass. Don't look like you don't know what I'm talking about."

"It wouldn't occur to me to say it that way."

"It would occur to you to think about doing it, though."

"Oh, I don't have any idea."

"Is that right?"

"Well. All right. Let me be honest. It might, if the guy was *really* interesting."

"Oh, I see. It's like *that*. Very good. I think we can get this straight right quick. You know the George Bernard Shaw story about the guy in the big party in a Bavarian castle?"

"No, I don't."

"You should."

"Is that right?"

"Stop trying to be so sarcastic. Let me tell my story."

"Let's hear it."

"Exterior: Bavarian castle. Interior: party too fancy for words. This guy goes up to this countess he's had the eye on for the whole evening and asks her—after some preliminary charming and all that—he asks the woman if she would sell him some pussy for ten dollars. Her face turns red. She almost throws her drink in his face. But she *is* a countess—you know how *they* are. The lady has too much class for that. The answer is in the negative. Her voice, *how-somever,* is so cold an icicle is hanging off his nose and his eyebrows are covered with snow. The countess did not like that shit at all. He smiles. Then this guy asks the royal lady if she would sell him some pussy for a million dollars. It gets quiet. The red leaves her face. She giggles a little bit. Then the countess bats her eyelashes and tells the man, 'Of course.' Her voice is so warm it melts the icicle off his nose and makes his eyebrows slick and shiny. He replies, 'Now that we have established *what* you are, all we have to do is haggle about the price.' "

They began laughing so loudly that everyone else in the Oyster Bar at Grand Central Terminal looked in their direction.

"So you know what I'm saying?"

"Yes, I know exactly what you're saying," Carla answered, a sparkle rising in her as she took a drink of her white wine.

"So, as you can imagine, there was no way I was going to miss the chance to find out how cool this ice-cold nigger would be once I got these legs around him. I had to put him to the test. There was a reason for this. When me and Ekkehard rolled up on him, Kelvin Thomson was profiling so hard on them Europeans—hanging back Dog Town fonky—with an old-time gangster lean and talking more shit than the radio. Every fastball they threw at this man he was hitting over the fence. This brother was *serious.* He kind of had that thing that gave me a fantasy. I felt like there might be a roar in his rhythm, you know what I'm saying?"

Carla understood Leeann exactly because any time she had been embraced by a man from whom she felt the weight and heat of love it seemed as though there was more than a vibration in his arms and his hands; life itself seemed to be roaring from inside him and through her flesh, pouring like the cascades of notes that would enter her body and create a chill whenever she was on the bandstand and the music was really going on.

"Primitive is what I'm talking about."

"You're darn tooting. Primal."

Leeann smiled bright at her buddy.

"But I could imagine him saying something I would remember when I was walking down the street and nobody was there but me. Or me laying up butt naked in my brass bed and not wanting to do anything but cuddle up with a memory, the thrill of it all dissolved into something spiritual. Just a man's voice saying the right thing that you wanted to hear and you *needed* to hear, but you didn't know how much you needed to hear it until those words came out, and you knew the moment you heard them that nothing short of some goddam brain damage would ever, ever let you forget them. It could be gentle, too, you know, the kind that can make you cry you feel so tender. I felt all kinds of fantasy and I had me big fun just feeling that way. Not only that, the nigger knew how to *dress*—oh, that nigger was *sharp*, baby: rust brown shoes, chocolate brown pants, an oatmeal-colored shirt, a tan suede jacket, and a bright silk rust brown tie, with a goddam tan-faced watch with a chocolate brown strap—and he even smoked some small brown cigars in a way that made me lathery in the pink palace. He had it going *on*. I didn't even let myself smell that alcoholic smell I know came from his insides being soaked in whiskey every day. All I wanted to do was get my message over to this Negro. Well, Ekkehard finally got his ass up to go to the bathroom or something, so I got to the brother that same night in Berlin, where we were at this party celebrating the first year of the play's opening. Those Germans loved them some *Boredom,* baby. Oh. The German woman who wrote the play with him was there, too, getting ready to marry a nigger from Atlanta, Georgia. She was another story. I won't go into all that. Leave it at the fact I found out that the man I had a crush on was going to be in Paris at the same time that Ekkehard had to go to Japan and I had to do a show of some dumb-looking shit for them fucking frogs. Now, meanwhile, Cecelia had just become the principal of her own school in Washington, D.C., and was trying to bring niggers back to civilization. She had a semester break coming and I decided that I would treat her, since she was my favorite cousin. So, I bring her pretty ass over and put her up in the Georges Cinq, too. I go do the fashion show and am supposed to meet Mr. Kelvin Thomson that evening in the bar, where all of those stupid movie types and those kinds of assholes hang out when they hop the pond. I dressed for that nigger. Oh, I was looking *good*. I had on a blue leather skullcap with rhinestones around the edges, some polished blue stone earrings, an ice blue feather boa, a blue silk dress tastefully slit up to the knee on the right side, some cobalt blue nail polish, some open-toed blue shoes an angel would trade her wings for. I'm ready to get *rocked,* baby."

Carla always lingered before the mirror for a good while as she decided what would best complement her when Maxwell was playing somewhere and there was the intention to capture his eye back in the time of their starting to get nice and cozy. Her behind had been quite an ally then. Among Negroes, it had always been. She sipped her wine.

"So what do I see when I get down there in the bar? Cecelia is all up under the nigger and he got his hand, lightly, mind you, on her thigh and they're laughing like it's too late for me to get in on some of *that* dick. It *was.* Now what the fuck was I supposed to do? I couldn't fight her for him because I still liked Ekkehard."

"You couldn't prove that by me."

"The hell with you. You too old-timey. Let's face the fucking and stop all the bullshitting. See, I have never been the kind of woman who didn't *know,* okay, that you can give away all the pussy you want and you still have enough left for yourself."

Carla laughed in awe but there must have been some kind of camaraderie in the cast of her eyes because Leeann nodded with a wink that was parallel to the way two men slapped palms in acknowledgment of something they were both fully aware of.

That was how it had begun seven years before. Now, Kelvin Thomson, so long Cecelia's boyfriend but never her husband, was standing there in the house and the power of his presence called Leeann down from her place above the first floor. Leeann was followed by Cecelia, who must have gone back to the room where she and her man were bedding down. The women, certain something was wrong, wanted to know what had happened and he stunned them all by asking for some water before beginning the tale. This man drained three glasses before the words started coming down from his brain.

He was on the way back from Imperial Liquor on Hudson Street with a big one of Irish whiskey, some vodka for Cecelia's martinis, a bottle of vermouth, and a brace of Pouilly-Fuissé perfectly chilled and intended for Leeann and Carla. The sellers of spirits and the serious drinker had been joking and laughing, making the exchange a bit more human than the dull ritual of asking for something at a counter and paying for it, the cash register supplying a metallic interlude of mercantile percussion, and neither customer nor merchant coming into warm verbal contact. Yes, with the taste of sugarless grape bubble gum in his mouth, he was feeling absolutely flawless, inhaling the light as the Manhattan sun prepared to make its exit until dawn, and the thought of another drink made him even more intent on wetting his whistle than he already was.

This scowling kid was coming toward him, wearing an oversized coat, a baseball cap turned with its bill pointed in a diagonal just the other side of his right eye, drop-down pants ready to give up the fight and fall around his ankles, a pair of spotless untied workman's shoes sporting their tongues as if exhausted from carrying the boy's weight. Refusing to budge an inch on the narrow nineteenth-century sidewalk, the kid strongly bumped into Kelvin Thomson and knocked his bag from his arms. The bottles broke and the liquor began spreading through the bag and onto the sidewalk. Oh, me, oh, my. Wow. This was a catastrophe of immeasurable proportions. All he could do was stare at the place where his bag had fallen. There was no one else on the street.

"Say, man?"

"Huh?"

"You bumped into me."

"Yeah."

"Did you hear what I said?"

"Yeah."

"I said that you *bumped* into me."

"Sorry."

"*Motherfucker,* are you deaf or something?"

"Not at all. I'm sorry. Guess I have to go back to the store. Oh, well. More where this came from."

"Hold it."

"What?"

"I said, '*Hold it,*' nigger."

"Something wrong?"

"*Yeah:* you *bumped* into me."

"I said that I'm sorry, young man."

"Sorry don't stop the rain, mother*fucker.*"

He saw the look in the boy's eyes. That was a *look* he knew.

"I don't know what else I'm supposed to do."

"Oh, now you don't know, huh?"

"Actually, no. I apologized to you a couple of times."

"Look," the kid said, moving up on him, his scowl now a flesh-and-blood battle cry as he stood there, pulling open his coat to reveal an ugly nine-millimeter pistol stuck in his belt, "I just want you to know what I'm representing. I want you to *see* this shit. I *let* you go. *Let* you go, motherfucker. I could *smoke* you right here. Yeah. *Yeah.* Blood on the concrete. *Finish* your old ancient ass. Prehistoric moth-er*fucker.*"

Kelvin Thomson, who had been wheezing as the kid became more aggressive, began coughing violently.

"Can I get my handkerchief?"

The kid, street-smart and ready for a trick, patted the breast pocket.

"Fuck you and fuck your handkerchief. *Bitch.* Get the motherfucker. *Ho.*"

He reached into his breast pocket for the soft piece of silk. The kid, ready to move on, was full of himself as he stepped forward and looked, with the thorniest contempt, at this old nigger about to cover his mouth with the handkerchief. Then a cough turned into a huge gust of breath and the kid's eyes were full of red pepper, his pistol was gone, his right arm in a hammerlock. He heard the old man tell him to shut up complaining about his eyes as he was marched into the police station, coughing and sneezing. There the older and the younger sat next to each other, one cuffed to the bench, the other free. Illegal firearms guaranteed a year in jail. Did he know that? The kid told the cops that he was bored as a motherfucker anyway and didn't give a good motherfucking goddam *what* the fuck they did to him or where the *fuck* they sent him.

"Oh, Kelvin, Jesus Christ, you could have been killed."

"By whom?"

"That stupid kid."

"I'm an old dog. He wasn't nothing but a puppy with rubber teeth."

"Brother Kelvin," Leeann said, "uh, I don't want to break ranks with your fantasy but I do believe that gun was real. It was not rubber, brother."

"So?"

"What if you had missed, baby?"

"Not a chance. He felt no danger. That's why he wasn't paying attention."

"Where'd you learn that trick from anyhow?"

"An old bebop singer. The land of ooo blah de. He, he, he."

The three women stared at him.

"But that wasn't all I learned this evening."

"Come on with it," Leeann demanded, as though he was toying with her and her alone.

"Sure. Sorry, ladies. Anyway, whew. It was so tedious. Believe you me, this is some bullshit. So much goddam money and time spent on this kind of simpleminded shit. The whole thing started getting to me. I felt alone all of a sudden. Don't know why. So I wanted to talk to somebody and the cops weren't interested in talking to somebody who wasn't a cop. So there I was. All by myself. Waiting."

"You could have called here and let us know where you were."

"Look, baby, if I had called, you all would have come running around there and it would have been a bigger mess."

"So it was better to let us worry?"

"Were you worried?"

"No."

"There it is. You know you're used to me taking forever to get back from some place. I get distracted."

"Sure the hell do."

"Thank you, Leeann. Anyway, as I was saying, I wanted to talk to somebody. *Anybody.* What the hell? I sat there next to that boy and talked to him."

"You talked to *him?* Well, I guess bull dooky is just reaching up through the clouds now. Kelvin . . . *what?* This fool who was about to *kill* you?"

"Sweetest, he was in the cage then. He was going nowhere. This battle was over for him. All had been done and all had been said. But I wanted to know what was on his mind."

"His mind? His *mind?* God doesn't waste *minds* on niggers like that," Cecelia said, her fury tantamount to a three-dimensional force in itself.

"Calm down, cousin, calm down."

Her man rose and rubbed his hand across her forehead and around her face, calming Cecelia and opening into plain view her affection for him. Carla couldn't explain what she was seeing, but she could sing it. She knew that. He continued.

"Naive or not, I wanted to know why he would want to kill somebody he bumped into, why he couldn't apologize, what it all meant to him, you know, that he could kill a man right there over nothing, just a couple of inches on the street. Maybe I wasn't paying attention; maybe he wasn't."

"Look, Kelvin, you know good and well that little savage nigger bumped himself into you on purpose."

"What difference did it make? It meant nothing. It meant nothing. There was no meaning. There was none. It was a moment that hung on a zero. I said all of that to him. I wanted to know what was going on. This kid looked at me with amazement. Then the amazement turned to an extremely bitter scorn. I felt like he had a giant brush that he was dipping into a spittoon full of all kinds of shit and that he was sitting there painting me with all the fucking slime in the world. I don't know if I had ever seen a pointy-nosed redneck cracker look at me like *that*. That boy put the fear of God in me. I felt like praying for something to save him or save me or save the whole world. He sent me all the way back to the Baptist church, every last blessed and unblessed step. I'm not kidding. He took me into another dimension of fear. It was an odd, odd feeling. Oh, it was a moment in *my* life. At that point, his eyes stopped being so dark and angry, they had a flitting glint of tenderness. That softness, maybe even some compassion, a spark of reflection, was gone fast. *Zip.* He was cool as a cucumber now, almost like an Asian statue. His eyes cleared to sort of a hypnotized blank quality. Then he started laughing at me, laughing his ass off, laughing like I was the biggest fool there is."

Cecelia put her arms around her man, saying, "Baby, I'm so glad you didn't get hurt. I couldn't stand it. It would have broken my heart in two." Then she led him up the stairs. Leeann and Carla looked at each other. This party was over. Without a word, they embraced each other and the lonely woman from South Dakota left the town house.

THE ME AND YOU
THAT USED TO BE

Patriotism. Progress. Culture. A MONUMENT CONCEIVED AS A
TRIBUTE TO THE IDEALS OF CLEVELAND BUILDED* BY HER CITIZENS
AND DEDICATED TO SOCIAL PROGRESS, INDUSTRIAL ACHIEVE-
MENT, AND CIVIC INTEREST.

Inscription on the wall of the Cleveland Convention Hall

As SHE WALKED from Leeann's on that heavy Sunday that had
begun so well, Carla thought about all that had been said, that had
then happened, and knew she had experienced a real New York day,
when so much singing, talking, thought, feeling, and action took place
in a brief time that the whole of it seemed impossible instead of the
common Manhattan thing it really was. Then, upon arriving at
Bleecker Street, she turned east and began wandering back in the direction of where she had lived so many years. She turned on Tenth Street,
crossed Seventh Avenue, and stood at the window of Three Lives
bookstore, one of the places where she most loved to buy books and
browse. It was closed; she couldn't distract herself there. There was
nothing to do other than keep walking. Carla paused at the west side
of Sixth Avenue and Eighth Street, allowing the street to take her in.

* You read right.

It was still early evening and there were plenty of people out having themselves a time, visiting tourists, bridge-and-tunnel types from New Jersey, camera-laden Japanese, local Italians, Jews from the Upper West Side, middle-class black people, from their late teens to middle age, and some of the kinds, male and female, who had given Kelvin Thomson so much trouble just a short while ago. The gang was all there. There was a change in the air toward the direction of impending autumn and she felt herself waking up another way inside, feeling as if some kind of a song was coming on.

But there was no song. Her day was ending, the bandstand was behind her, Leeann, Cecelia, and Kelvin Thomson were doing whatever they were doing, and there was an empty apartment that she didn't want to go into just yet because it would remind her of what was on the way out the window. There it still was: no hiding place down here. Then, as if there were no choice, while Carla felt the air playing with her hair as if it were wind chimes, she experienced the redemptive power of the town in the lights, the shops, the restaurants, the other walkers, and the noise.

She almost stumbled while crossing Sixth Avenue and found her mind returning to the Oyster Bar that time she had lunch with Ramona. The preference would have been to think of something much less complicated, but that mind had a destination of its own and was pressing in that direction. She had held it back long enough. She was by herself. She could think about it. She had thought about damn near everything else.

Her big sister called a few days after Maxwell left for the quick tour that preceded the two of them going to visit Ezekiel and Eunice. It was a month before they went to Texas. What a surprise piece of luck. There she was, forever whining to herself about how badly things were going with Maxwell and hoping she would learn something in Houston that would help her hold on to the life she had made with this man.

The phone rang.

Carla was so excited to hear Ramona's voice, even though she spoke to her younger sister with kind of a distracted business tone that didn't have all of the warmth that Carla instantly felt, the phone itself seeming to take on literal heat counterpointed by the chill coming through her body as this voice she had wanted to hear agreeing to see her was now, finally, saying that the two of them could meet the next day. She could barely sleep that night. So many memories. So many.

It all started so well. That was normal. The place couldn't have been better. Any visit to Grand Central Terminal put Carla in an avid mood—spring, summer, fall, winter—because it was such a symbol of the way things had gone when technology changed and engineering went to another level. She loved to get out of the East Side train on Thirty-third Street and walk toward Grand Central Station on Park Avenue, looking at the big Forty-second Street structure that was dwarfed by the far more contemporary Met Life building, which stood behind it like the flat, glass-faced symbol of either a far less poetic age or a straightforward connection to the slabs raised at Stonehenge by those primordials who worshiped the sun, not commercial rental space. Still, Grand Central itself cast such a feeling over that part of the city, hovering in its own visual frame with the quality of something ancient but made possible in the fullness of its function only through the same kinds of leaps forward or developments of precision that had allowed the pyramids to rise in such imperial mystery from the faceless landscape of North African sand.

Beginning around the turn of the century, it had taken years and years to build the blessed thing because the whole system of travel by train was shifting from thickly smoking engines to electricity, and the air-fouling section of real estate that became Grand Central Terminal was a gathering place that changed its form from above to below ground in order to best make use of the limited space of New York, which meant that this station had to accommodate a universe of rails that essentially had no model. Smokeless trains would come and leave, come and leave. The activity, in its dense force, amounted to the Sistine Chapel ceiling fallen into three dimensions on the floor. It was a gargantuan American enterprise that came into existence through dreams, the icy facts of math, the hotly improvised, imaginative expansions of what was known, the politics of a city ever willing to swallow corruption, hook, line, and sinker, the rivalry engendered by individual egos perhaps larger than the Western Hemisphere, and the idea that functional monuments within a United States context should somehow rival the mythological powers of the classical world, which was why the statues of Minerva, Mercury, and Hercules around the clock at the top of the edifice were appropriate, not pretentious. American technology, Yankee know-how, an endless labor force, the steel mills, the makers of concrete, those able to cut window glass in overwhelming measures, and everybody responsible for the electric cables, the rails, the walls, the paneling, the tunnels, the floors, the plumbing, and all of it were part of something that barked so loudly at the moon of Mount Olympus that a fortissimo echo bounced back. The big ticket-buying area inside the station and the light that entered through the high windows were on a scale that seemed to chant out the identity of Manhattan, where so much energy was compressed into small spaces, just as it had been on the three-minute jazz recordings of the old days, a stack of which was like a cylindrical aesthetic skyscraper of dormant sound, each recording a floor of artistry or mediocrity or fluff or tomfoolery that individually submitted to and personalized the available area in the way various businesses and dwellers did the floors of commercial spaces and high-rising apartment houses, or just as a stack of compact discs was the same as the old three-minute records except that the vinyl circles were smaller but the space for sound was more than twenty times larger. Carla often contemplated those things as she looked at the Manhattan skyline, and sometimes concluded to herself that the human body was all of that, too. It contained, she thought, entering Grand Central Terminal, such capacity for information and feeling, mythology and comprehension. How sweet it was to be in one of her favorite places, tarted up to look her best and anxious to see her big sister. In that vast, shining space, the girl from South Dakota had the same feeling that walking through a great museum or a great cathedral gave her, that she was inside a compartment of inspired human recognition made physical by stone upon stone and image upon image.

Carla arrived an hour early so that she could wander around the station and look at the people while wondering what Ramona would be like after all these years of only hearing her voice over the phone and always being so disappointed that she could never seem to appear when she and Dad and Maxwell or any of her guys were together. The last time she had seen Ramona was when Carla thought she was such hot stuff and they had gotten into that tiff about men when both had returned home to get Dad off the bottle after Mom died. Ten years, my Lord.

While she had tried to pretend that it didn't mean much, that she could get along without her very well, Carla actually missed Ramona so terribly and wanted to discover a way to restore the closeness that they once had, those moments in their teens and their twenties when all of the crap that they put on each other washed off and they were just one sister younger and one sister older and the two of them feeling that love only a couple of siblings can ever have. Her longing for the love of her sister made her eyes well up and Carla felt that strange feeling of being marched nude through a public place as she took a handkerchief from her purse and applied it to where the tears were on their way. Before anyone decided to express valor or concern, Carla scooted off, quickly making her way to the Oyster Bar, where she got to the reserved table and sat there, settling herself with a glass of white wine as she awaited Ramona's arrival.

When Ramona came into the Oyster Bar she looked much like a soldier of some sort. Her hair was cut in a very butch style and her olive drab summer business suit made her seem more like a man than a woman. Her face had a restrained seriousness to it and a smug sense of personal accomplishment. She had surely done what she wanted to do in the world, and one would have to be deaf, dumb, and blind not to recognize that this was a woman who had made something of herself. The little play that had been in her step, which made her move as though she were either nearly skipping or dancing, was gone. Each foot moved forward with a severe ease, as if part of a drill Ramona had done so many times that it was now intrinsic to her and not something she had learned. It probably went with being a lawyer. One couldn't be too physically jaunty in court.

Carla noticed that Ramona didn't take in the room as she had so long ago, always looking for friends or enemies, interesting or silly things to talk about; she walked into the Oyster Bar and through it as though she owned every bit of the space. What was on the right or the left, what was beyond her younger sister was of no interest. This was a characteristic of the wealthy. Wow, Ramona had that, too. Her demeanor was that of one on a frosty mission. Her medium-sized rectangular purse of beige leather matched her shoes and she wore a big—but not vulgar—diamond wedding ring. There was clear polish on her manicured nails.

Ramona's aura destroyed Carla's intention to get up and embrace her. It made the younger sister feel as though she should raise her hand to even get permission to speak, as if she were in a class with a stern grade school teacher. Carla fought to give a sunny greeting.

"Hello, Ramona."

"Hi there. How you doing, baby sister?"

"Fine, I guess. How about you?"

"I don't like these damn business trips to New York. I prefer Cleveland."

"You come here often?"

"Four or five times a year."

"Really?"

"Oh, sure. What a bother."

"Why don't you ever let me know? You know I would love to see you."

"We'll talk about that later. Let's order."

Carla did not like this. She still worked at maintaining a pleasant demeanor. It had been so long. Ramona, as if she felt expected to give an account of herself, brought her younger sister up to date with no prompting, warmth increasing with each thing she said.

Carla was told that she had been married for seven years and had two children, one named after Dad, the other after Mom. Her breathing shallow, an anger in Carla nearly matched the unexpected hurt of just being told that she had a nephew and a niece, two children she hadn't seen as babies, didn't hold and smell and kiss, hadn't watched toddle, didn't hear speak her name, hadn't known the voices of, and didn't see look first like one of the parents, then the other, then some combination of the two. This was so wacky it left her stunned. When Ramona, her face lustrous with pride, pulled out the pictures of the two towheaded kids, both looking so lively and pugnacious, there was nothing she could say at all.

Carla excused herself, got up, and went to the rest room. She sat in a stall and sobbed, wondering what she had done to her sister that was so bad all of this had been kept secret. Did she hate her little sister? Was that why, for all these years, she was never there when Carla came home and never returned the phone calls that were left on her Cleveland answering machine? Why she never answered one goddam letter? What had Dad done that deprived him of the simple right of knowing that he was a grandfather? Ramona went out to see him sometimes, after all. Dad had told Carla. But she never even told him? What kind of a person was this sister of hers right now? Carla cried until she felt as though she had been swallowing ground glass. She willed herself past the boo-hooing. Well, well. Let it all come down. So this was what she had to face up to this afternoon. Very good. Let's get it on. She would find out what was what. Carla got herself together, washed her face with cold water, put in some eye-drops and watched the red clear out, applied a little rouge and pow-der, a bit of lipstick, then returned, determined to be gallant but feeling rejected in a way she had never felt in her entire life.

The food was on the table.

Ramona was eating and had risen into a shining mood. Good for her. She wanted to tell Carla more. Why shouldn't she? Feel free. Somebody should.

Her husband, Bob, was very successful in real estate—*very* success-ful—and they lived outside of the city in an expensive and very exclu-sive suburb. The house was wonderful. The lot was great. They had two classy cars and a fantastic sports van. A young live-in nanny from England. Perfection. Nothing but luck. Well, maybe something more. She had met him by chance in a bookstore in Seattle, when both were there on business. It was *so* strange. Ramona hadn't wanted to go and could have gotten out of it by letting this *other* eager beaver go to a conference she knew would be boring and would supply her with nothing that could move her career forward in the law firm even one inch. Being that reasonable was a full-fledged waste. Fate kept push-ing and kicking her until she went, not aware of why it seemed she just had to take that plane, go to that hotel, put on her name tag, and get in there with everybody else. So, thank God, she met Bob.

Ramona was between guys and the form of her life had set in with them anyway: either she was too strong for them or they were too weak for her. Some top-notch sex every now and then seemed about as good as it was going to get. This was not like that. She and Bob were immediately like ham and eggs, butter and toast. It was magic. They talked and talked and talked about everything, from society to surfboards. The constant hum of romantic failure that droned way inside her finally shut its goddam trap. For the first time, Ramona knew she had been seen and felt, heart and soul, by a man. No one had ever made her feel that she was so attractive, that her touch was so precious, that the sound of her voice had music to it, that her opinions had so much merit, that her passion could triumphantly cross the big territory that stretched from the whispers to the wild, very private things. With Bob, who was an Oregon boy originally, she had finally become unclogged. Freedom had a fresh dimension of meaning now.

But it wasn't all so nicey-nice and serious! Their life together was so fun. Her love for good, clean air and exercise was reborn outside of the obligatory context of the goddam gym, where everybody was trying to keep control of their bellies, avoid those cottage-cheese thighs, and fight off love handles. This was much better. She and Bob had their own pool, a basketball court, and their own gym, but they also took long, long walks after dinner, never missing quality time and always maintaining intimacy. Or they rode their bikes together, singing soft-rock classics to each other. They even had a custom-made bicycle built for two that was great and made you feel like you were in an older America, when things were sweeter and better. The two of them went out on camping trips, hiking and sometimes hunting, often practicing with their pistols and their rifles.

"I'm a lady who knows how to lock and load," Ramona said with a giddy but scornful pride.

"You really like guns?" Carla asked, glad she had a place to get a word in edgewise and trying to camouflage her abrasive envy on every level, especially motherhood.

"I *love* them. Never thought I would. But we all change."

"I guess we do."

"Yes, we do. That's for sure."

"The next thing you're going to tell me is that you're a member of the National Rifle Association."

"Almost fifteen years. Around the time that you graduated from music school."

"The NRA. Incredible. For what purpose?"

"I don't think you would understand that, Carla."

"Try me. I might not be so bad. I know whatever you have to say couldn't be any worse than not knowing I had a niece and a nephew before today. Try me."

"All right."

"Go ahead. Tell me."

"At first, well . . ."

"Yes?"

"Stop acting like a prosecutor."

"Oh, sorry. I just want to know."

"All right. I thought there was going to be a race war and I didn't want to be a casualty."

"Be serious, Ramona."

"I am serious, little sister, serious as an autopsy."

"Did Mom and Dad know anything about this?"

Ramona looked at Carla as though she was searching for something in her younger sister's face.

"If they did know, they didn't tell me, and I can't imagine that."

"No, I never told them."

"Can I ask you why?"

"Sure. Sure you can. Nothing to it. That's not true. Well, here we go. They wouldn't understand. You know how they are. They live in a very small world. I live in the great big world out here."

"You don't mean *Cleveland,* do you? That's not my idea of very sophisticated."

"Have you ever been there?"

"I passed through with Maxwell."

Ramona now had the look of someone who wanted to start a fight.

"Oh. Maxwell. Right. He's the nigger you're with now, isn't he?"

"What did you say?"

"I said what *they* say all of the time. What they scream. In the streets, on television, on the radio. Lingua franca. Niggers. Or haven't you heard?"

"I find that word offensive."

"You mean your black friends don't use it?"

There was a silence. Ramona continued.

"Just as I thought. Exactly. But if we call them what they call themselves, since they *do* know what they are, then we are supposed to be in the wrong. Isn't that how the thinking goes?"

"Ramona, I feel like slapping your face."

"That would be a grave error, little sister. I am quite well trained in hand-to-hand combat and I wouldn't want to embarrass both of us in this restaurant."

There was a very nippy pause in the talk.

"I can't believe how I feel. This is very, very painful. Jesus Christ. I don't know this person."

"What do you mean, 'this person'?"

"You, Ramona. You. What have you become?"

"What have *I* become? You should be the one talking. I pity you. You are just like Mom and Dad. Lost."

"Your mother, *our* mother, was almost a saint. Now you're making fun of her?"

"Now don't try to pretend right now that you loved Mom more than I did."

"And you think Dad is *lost?* Of course you do. He's not good enough to know he has grandchildren. Must be a loser."

Ramona tightened her lips.

"Why haven't you told him you got married and became pregnant and had two adorable-looking children? Why?"

"I have my reasons."

"Sure you do. Because he doesn't have your racist views?"

"Racist? Here we go. Hardly. You don't know what these people are and you think I'm sick and all of the people who think like me are sick. Well, let me tell you, we are *not* sick. By the way, I love Dad as much as you do."

"That's easy to see."

"There you go. Judging. You're so much better than me, aren't you, Carla? Just so much better. You have no idea what this has done to me inside. You couldn't or you wouldn't look at me like that."

"So now I'm supposed to feel sorry for you after you locked me and Dad out of your life, kept your kids from us, and have lived this fucking secret life? What do you want, *everything?*"

"No. I just would like some peace of mind. I have a deep hurt inside my heart. Yes, I have. Very deep. I *do.* That surprises you?"

Her emotions twisting and cutting like metal shavings, Carla remained silent.

"This has been nothing but turmoil for me. Nothing but. I didn't know what to do and I didn't know what not to do. Bob is just as strong in his beliefs as Dad is. I didn't want the trouble. You think I didn't want to tell Dad or send him pictures or bring my children to visit? I did. I still do. I still do. Every day God gives us. But I don't want to fight and I don't want Randy and Susie in the middle of a fight over what's right and what's wrong. Besides, I love Bob absolutely and I will hear no other man's opinions over his, even those of Dad."

"So the wonderful Bob—when he wasn't going about being just the greatest guy in the history of the world—I guess he took a little time off and put a racist whammy on you."

"You are so snide. So snide. Ha. Whammy, huh? You would like to believe that."

"Well, you didn't get it from Mom and Dad."

"Let me tell you something, Carla. *I* learned about your wonderful niggers when I went away to college."

"Oh, really? That was part of your college education?"

"Oh, yes. Sure was."

"College. Wait. Now it's coming in. You started changing then. You *did*. Yes, Ramona, I remember. The music you listened to and the crowd you ran around with. Those terrible people from Trelstad Heights. They probably loved the smell of their own shit. What a self-important bunch. Mom and Dad—who were absolutely correct, *obviously*—thought those people were socially backward."

"Of course they would. We liked each other. Each other. Big fucking deal, right? We didn't need anyone outside of our group to make us feel good. We could get along just fine without the approval of a bunch of snotty minorities."

"I don't know what you're talking about. Nobody in our family ever tried to prove something by associating with *anybody*. That *never* happened. It never happened and you *know* it never happened. We were just reared to have natural relationships with other people. Mom and Dad believed in individuals."

"Well, the niggers at college didn't. Hold it, Carla. Time-out. Don't say it. Sorry: the *African*-Americans. That's what they call themselves *now*, isn't it?"

"They do change their names a lot, don't they?" Carla joked, which surprised Ramona, who laughed. This odd moment startled the younger sister into wondering if she, too, harbored, some kind of racist resentment. All she would need was to find a Ku Klux Klan hood hidden in the attic of her heart.

"Anyway, distinctions aren't something they are very good at. They just aren't. They are not a subtle bunch. That was why, no matter how sweet and liberal we tried to be—coochie, coochie, coo—we were all just one horrible, horrible person. Horrible. Hopeless. One white person was all of us, *all* of us. They were *so* confident. The great Caucasian code had been broken. They could read us like a book. They knew how willing we were when it came to taking all of their crap. That was why they stopped fooling those of us who *could* see. They went on and on until, eventually, they showed their *real* character. They revealed just how they *really* think. They segregated themselves. Separate student union. Separate dorm floors. Separate eating tables. They beat up white kids who just made little social errors but weren't trying to be nasty. We didn't know anything about their hair . . . or how were we supposed to know they didn't eat rare meat? I mean, well, who could know they wanted all the flavor cooked out of their steaks?"

Carla wanted to laugh but held her face straight as a razor blade. Revolted at first, now she wanted to see how long this would go on, how much pus would come from this boil of memory.

Plenty.

"Everything was racist, racist, racist. Poor little things. The slightest little trouble and we had to hear another tirade. They stole until your stuff wasn't safe in your dorm room. They gave rallies where they screamed about hating white people. All you heard about, over and over, was how much they hated the United States. At *our* expense, they brought these niggers on campus in African costumes and overalls."

"You were there on scholarship, Ramona."

"Whatever. These speakers they brought and paid loads of money wanted to murder people. They even wanted Jews exterminated. Talk about turning on your friends. Real weird stuff. This was the cause of black freedom. And, it didn't matter a smidgen how nice we tried to be, made not a do-diddly bit of difference. All the bending over backwards right there, well, excuse the hell out of the truth but they *never* gave us a chance. They just *wouldn't.* They treated all of us white students like we were nothing but one big stack of shit. All of us. That included the white girls who were going to bed with the leaders of the black revolution. You know, the ones strutting around in army gear and African robes. Jesus William Christ, it was *so* insane. It took some time—because I had been so goddam *brainwashed* by Mom and Dad—but I slowly grew to face reality and that is when I fully began to *hate* them."

"Ramona, grow up. You can't mean that."

"I do mean it. I mean it with all my heart."

"This is sick. It really is. Sick. Why didn't you talk about this when you came home?"

"To you, to Mom and Dad, to Randy Jr.? You don't mean that. You can't be serious. What good would that have done? You just said it. I would be the one who was sick, the sore thumb."

"We could have given you a better perspective than the one you have now, I can tell you that."

"I'm sure you could, but it wouldn't have been related to the facts. Yes, the facts. I'm accustomed to that look on your face. I'm not impressed. Not right now. All of you are so far from the way things are. I made the right decision. Oh, I'm sure of that."

"Didn't you know we loved you? You didn't know that?"

Ramona's eyes suddenly misted and her face went flush as if she had been slapped.

"God, Carla, just because we see things from different perspectives doesn't mean I'm *crazy*. How could I *not* know you all loved me? Why would you even ask me that? That's really not fair. It really isn't. That's why I was in such a goddam turmoil. It all started right there. There was no lack of love. That wasn't the problem. I was lost in there. Alienated. It was something totally different. At times, I *hated* being in that house. I didn't want to be there. I was *so* alone. I had no one to talk to. I was all by myself. Don't interrupt. That's how it was. To me. But I wasn't going to be crushed. I wasn't going to be blinded again. I knew I had to save myself from being humiliated right in the middle of my family. So I kept my big mouth shut. I had to. There was no other choice. Every single one of you would have tried to make me feel guilty for not turning my eyes away from the truth. I had to make my own way."

"I hate to say it, but it sounds pretty much like you got lost to me."

"It would. Of course. But I had to find my own people. I didn't quite trust what I was hearing from you all anymore. I found a new circle of friends and they understood what I was experiencing. Some heavy stuff was coming down. I had to create my own answers."

"Create your own answers? Everybody creates their own answers. You make this sound like it was some sort of a religious revelation when all you have done is—"

"I'm almost finished. Let me finish, Carla. Try to listen to me. Just see if you can understand my experience. It's not yours, but it did happen. I'm not making it up. I suffered through this. It was my life."

Carla was trying to understand what she should do. There was an emotional sprain, a vast ache, in Ramona's voice, and this thing was so deep that if it had been water in a well, the bucket would have been lowered a long time before it touched anything wet. The insistence of this feeling was new to Carla and it was out of line with the confident posture Ramona had when she entered the Oyster Bar. So much of all this wacko stuff was out of line with that grand entrance. She surely loved her husband, her children, her father, and, maybe, even Carla. Yet what communicated itself as an unmendable loneliness was all she could hear in her big sister's voice, and it seared Carla's heart to such a degree she almost began to shudder with a recognition that was very close to guilt.

Ramona, after wiping her eyes, was staring at Carla like a prosecutor.

"You remember that time you called me in the dorm, just to see how I was doing, and I had to get off of the phone very quickly and called you back?"

"Why would I remember something like that?"

"Sorry, Carla, *why* should I expect *you* to pay any attention to someone *else?*"

Ramona knew how to get her. She couldn't sense the nature of Carla's emotion. It would have been unimaginable that her little sister, even while arguing against those repugnant ideas, was feeling such convoluted compassion and so much regret. Bob's wife was giving back all the hurt she had gotten and Carla knew it was her duty to sit there and take it. Ramona was her sister. That's how it was. Nothing would be accomplished by merely looking down on her and leaving in a huff the way Carla would have when she was so full of herself in high school.

"I'm sorry, Ramona, I just don't remember."

"Well, I will never forget it. Never. A week doesn't pass when I don't think about it. It's part of me. Kind of disturbing. Anyway, you had called and I was talking to you and thinking about how we used to skate together and talk about Sonja Henie. It was so clear in my mind right then. I could feel the whole thing sitting right there—the wind, the temperature, the feeling of the ice and the snow. Gee, the things that go through your mind sometimes. Shoot the duck. The needle. Those kinds of things on the ice. Boy, oh, boy, oh. Hot cider. Sitting on the bed, singing together. I was always the flat one, but that was okay. There were some sweet times we had back then."

"Yes, we did, Ramona. I haven't forgotten."

"Then these two black *fucking* bitches started telling me to get off the dorm phone or they were going to kick my white bitch ass."

"They said that to you?"

"That's exactly what they said."

"Really? What nerve."

"Exactly. Big mistake. Big. Oh, they didn't know. They stood over me like two angry shadows. I wanted to respond in kind but I said nothing. I just wanted to talk to my baby sister. The taunting kept on. I tried to be nice about it. How dumb of me. No way. No way. They weren't going to let it be nice. That was a mistake. They didn't know right there. All of those times that Dad had taught us to box right along with Randy—"

"I thought that was so silly. Boxing. Very unladylike."

"Me, too. I hated it, punching and all of that stuff with those big fat padded gloves. But right there it came in pretty handy."

"You know, now I do remember. I was going to use some of my savings to pay for the bill for the call when Dad, the eternal cheapskate, went through the roof. I knew he would. He did, too."

"He's *so* cheap, isn't he?"

"He *is*. It's funny. Anyway, I was enjoying that call. I was imagining being a college girl someday. You were so grown-up, Ramona. And so funny. We were laughing about how silly those girls looked wearing those helmet hairdos. It was night back home. Late. I wanted the best long-distance rate. I did call you, Ramona. You're right. But you didn't call back."

"Yes I did."

"No, you did not. I'm serious. I remember it now. You put down the phone. I could still hear. There was a commotion and some screaming. It didn't go on for very long. Then you came back and you sounded winded but said it was nothing. You said you had to run and get something. Didn't you say that?"

"You *do* remember. That's exactly what I said. Oh, Carla, sometimes . . ." Ramona looked down at her food. She drank half her glass of water. Then she continued talking as she ate. "Anyway, that wasn't the truth that I told you. The truth is that I knocked the hell out of *both* of them."

"Really?" Carla asked, immediately hoping her unforeseen pride in her sister wasn't obvious in the sound of her voice.

"Yes, really. And I *loved* it."

"You loved beating up a couple of other girls?"

"Yes, the same way you used to love to defeat other girls in skating competitions."

"I was pretty vicious, wasn't I?" Carla asked, smiling but not understanding why she was trying to identity with what Ramona was saying. Was she losing her mind?

"Yes, you were vicious."

"Oh, I wasn't that bad."

"You were worse than that."

"Well, oh, I guess so."

"Don't be coy. I hate that."

"I'm not being coy."

"Yes you are. Stop it. Be what you are, Carla. You were a competitor. You were a winner. Heaven for you was defeating people. Face it. Now, if it doesn't bother you, let me *finish*. That night in the dorm when I smacked those black girls in their guts and in their mouths and made them submit to *me* was the first time I knew how you *actually* felt. I never felt better in my life. To be perfectly truthful, I came alive right there. I used to have so much anger inside, so much. I was choking every single day out there. But they were such pissy little cowards. Contempt isn't strong enough to say how I felt right there."

Ramona stopped. Carla could see the weight of a time that still cut into her big sister. They both just went on eating their soft-shelled crab and sharing a Caesar salad. Suspense was a mood pacing around the table because Carla didn't know what to say and didn't know what Ramona was going to tell her. As if taking a breather, they compared appreciative notes on the food and the atmosphere, gave some attention to the other people there, and were just a bit catty about how these or those overly or badly dressed women looked. That took a load off. Then, with the other subject returned to front position, Ramona went back to what she had been talking about. Carla wished she hadn't gone back so soon; they were like old times for that bit of conversation and her heart was filling up for Ramona. She tried to keep things where they were. Nothing doing.

"Like I said, I can't get those black girls off my mind. I have been thinking about them for *years*. Years and years. Sure have. They were strange ones, you know? A few were real ghetto girls. Some. No more than some. You know the kind—crude, insecure, obnoxious, and with the worst taste in hair you could ever imagine. I mean, black women and their hair, is that some kind of a joke or do they just not know how really terrible they look? What about those monster-movie nail jobs? Claws. Yuck. Now the pickaninny effect is in, which, I guess, is another way of stating their ethnic identity. Anything not to seem like us. Give the world a fucking break. But I'm off the subject. Way off. Most of those girls, those black girls in college, their backgrounds weren't slummy. Hardly. They were just middle-class girls like you and me trying to put on an act. Guy. Oh, brother. These girls would dress the part and they would talk the part. And, believe me, it was a part. I know they had to practice saying 'ax,' instead of 'ask.' I guess I studied them. Urban anthropology. I got it. It was a haunted-house show. They wanted every day to be Halloween so they could scare us in an unlimited way. Terrify the white people. Make us fear for our safety, our lives, and our country."

Ramona, her humanity reaching out, seemed to be discovering something right in front of Carla, but her face, once again, changed and became so stubbornly cold.

"I messed up their little fake ghetto game. They couldn't have that going on right there. So it turned out that once wasn't enough with this one. Not Ramona from South Dakota. They still wanted a piece of this white girl. So I got tested a few more times. I stood up to them. I whipped the girls from the streets and the other ones, too. Such a bunch of chickenshits. They were black and they were loud and they were supposed to be so proud, but they didn't know *anything* about fighting. Not so much that I could see. They were pathetic. Pussies. I punched them out. What an irony. It makes me laugh. If Dad could see what his liberal training had done for me. Ha. What a hoot. From that point on, I was known as 'the crazy white bitch' and they left me alone. Crazy, they called me."

"I don't know what to say to you, Ramona. I don't know. It seems that you took a few incidents of some silly kids in college and created a whole worldview."

"Yeah, right."

"Oh, come on. Grow the hell up. Everybody in college acts strange. Oh, I saw the same things. I'm not somebody who was on another planet. I was down here on the ground, too. I saw what people said and I saw what they did. But it's like you said, those kids were just acting out. Let's face it. You already said it. They love everything you and I love. Be honest. You know they do. They were just confused. So many of us want to get revenge because life doesn't turn out to be what we think it ought to be. We do stupid things and we hurt other people because we don't think we should have to pay attention to them. We're Americans. We hate to respect anything. Our dead are more important than anybody else's. Our hurt is number one. That's the way it was. It was the times. White kids and black kids had so many doubts about this country and they acted them out. Both sides did. *Both* sides. That goes back as far as the McCarthy era. It's all connected to the pain of the Civil Rights Movement. Everybody lost faith in the FBI when they found out what a lunatic J. Edgar Hoover was."

"What a pervert. Do I know stories."

"Right, right. But as I was saying, things fell apart. Hard times. Really hard. So much *death.*"

"Sure was."

"It touched us all. It did. Don't forget that you were just as sad as everyone else in the house when Martin Luther King was murdered."

"It's true. I was hurt. Yes, I was. I won't deny that. I felt like I had been hit in the chest with a sledgehammer. But Dad said something when all of those niggers—"

"I don't want to hear any more of that. Cut the bravado. You don't have to talk like that to me."

"I'll respect that. I will."

4 0 7

"Thank you, Ramona," Carla said, embarrassed but satisfied by the humility that was in the sound of her voice.

"Oh, sure. But let's try to be a little logical here."

"Let's."

They both laughed, a bit more ease coming into the air around them. Ramona continued.

"Here's what I want to say. All of those riots across this country, these are black people tearing up their *own* neighborhoods in protest of King's assassination. Is there something just a teeny bit crazy about that—even to you? Doesn't it say *something* about the oddball mentality of these people? Wait. I'm afraid it does. They're very destructive. That's what they're proud of, like punk rockers, heavy-metal types. If they're not destroying themselves with alcohol and drugs, they're destroying this country by polluting it with their stupidity and the love they have for anything ignorant."

"That's ridiculous."

"Dad *knew* that the week that King was killed. It was so unmistakable. He couldn't face it, but he knew it. You remember he said that this country was going in a direction that no one could explain? We were lost and were going home by a road we didn't know."

"I kind of remember it. I remember it a little. What I remember most, Ramona, is that you and I were holding each other and crying. There was so much sorrow in the house. The radio was blasting; the television was on; everything was crazy. It felt like the world had come to an end. Randy had the flu or something and he was asleep. But this crazy feeling was everywhere. You and I had nothing to hold on to except each other. Mom and Dad were so dazed. We had never seen them like that. I know we hadn't. I remember that and I remember everything like that about us. Those are the feelings that come back to me. This, what you're saying right now, is very frightening to me and I feel very bitter right now. Here we are two worlds apart, so goddam far apart, and all I wanted was to reunite with the love of my sister. It's not fair. It's so fucking unfair."

Ramona looked away and began talking to the air.

"We've gone in directions that aren't compatible, little sister. Bob feels like I do, and so do our children, and you are with this black guy, which makes me want to *barf*. Not only that, he's what—the third one in a row? Oh, I know what you're doing. I have my ways of knowing."

She felt too far above that garbage to talk about Barton and the other guys. Carla wasn't going to defend herself. Ramona wasn't as informed about her little sister's past as she thought.

"Well, I wish I had my ways of knowing about you so I wouldn't be so surprised by all of this. Shocked, actually. It makes me feel so alone. Mom's gone. Little Randy's gone. Dad's growing older and older. I just wanted to be back with my sister. I only have one sister. One. It doesn't matter if I sound naive and sentimental. That's the way I am about these things. We used to be so close our periods came at almost the same time. Do you remember that?"

"Yes," Ramona said, her voice sounding as it did all those years ago.

"Then we got messed up. We went apart. I didn't know why, but we did. So you have no idea how happy I was when you called and we agreed to come here and meet. All I wanted was for the bad part of the past to disappear and for the two of us to get together and just be nice to each other. Just be nice. I just wanted it to be sweet."

Ramona was pretending to look her sister in the eye but was actually focusing on her forehead. It was obvious. It was evasive. It offended Carla. She wanted Ramona to look her in the eye and see the person she had become.

"Carla, you know, for all the pain you caused me over the years— you hurt your big sister so badly sometimes, you know? I was shattered inside sometimes. I was the oldest. Never was good enough, though. I couldn't be. It was all about you. Mom thought so; Dad thought so; and you, most of all, *you* thought so. Let me stop. Let me stop right now. Matthew, Mark, Luke, and John."

Mom used to say that when she was exasperated.

"I have to catch a little bit of my breath. Whew. I can't get my emotions straight right now. My heart feels like a bag of worms."

With a brave shyness, her violet eyes met Carla's.

"You reveled in my jealousy of you, Carla. You did. I could see it. Even so, there is something so sweet about you right now. It is. Just so sweet. So loving. I can't help it. I know you love me. Oh, God, what the hell am I doing with my life? Carla, Carla, Carla, you're *so* loyal. You're my little sister. I . . . oh . . . I . . . love you," Ramona said, her face softening and tears suddenly gushing out. She rose to her feet as swiftly as a switchblade opening and went to the ladies' room.

Carla didn't know what to do and she didn't know what to think.

There they were, somehow close but even more estranged. She felt a headache coming on. When she wanted to cry but couldn't—or wouldn't—that sometimes happened. Her mind was free of all expectations by the time Ramona, looking exactly as she did when she arrived, seated herself again. It was then as if her older sister hadn't ever said what she said just before leaving the table. Probably in the same bathroom stall where Carla sat and let all of the hurt sob free, Ramona had made her own decision. She was not going to give in. Her mission had not been accomplished. Both ordered coffee. There was more to say and there was a conclusion that Ramona was seeking, even if it didn't contain all of her actual emotion. That family characteristic, that tenacious side, was back in action and Carla, no matter how separated they had been, knew her sister and could feel what was coming.

Ramona went on to explain. She became an iron maiden of bitterness, each of her words a spike. Somebody had to be honest. It was all about race. Nobody ever heard the *honest* other side. Never once. It wasn't allowed. Oh, how she resented that, because there were things that she knew. She had covered the waterfront. This wasn't some stupid and trashy Aryan Nation bullshit. Not drunken bigots with no front teeth and tattoos, the kind Mom hated. This was real. But the trick that had been established in the media and in the political arena was to make the truth seem like some racist insanity. Shut up or we'll put a hooded white sheet on you and burn you at the stake. She wasn't backing down from what she knew. The flames in hell would turn to strawberry ice cream first.

You see, no one could tell her *anything* about black people because she had been around them for *nine* months out of *every* year in college all the way through her passing the bar exam. Everyone with their theories and their statistics forgot *that*. It was never part of the media equation. Hard facts were in place. Uninformed people like Mom and Dad didn't really *know* any black people. Not really. They didn't take into consideration that these black college kids Ramona had studied and endured were *truly* representative. They *were*. They didn't come from a crappy background in one tier of black society in one state. Oh, no. These people came from across the country, the Eastern Seaboard, the South, the Midwest, the Southwest, and the West Coast. They were the sons and daughters of welfare mothers, of blue-collar workers, and of doctors, lawyers, pharmacists, entertainers, realtors, career military men, educators, mathematicians, scientists. But almost every last one of them despised anybody and anything white. If they didn't, they were ostracized. What about performance standards? Basically, out of laziness—*not* inferiority!—they couldn't measure up, so they wanted to destroy every standard of evaluation.

Yes, it was clear if you weren't afraid to look. Once you got close to them and heard them when they felt free to be themselves, you thought about them in a *completely* different way. If those black college students, so full of hate and so disdainful of America and such self-righteous, inferior students were the cream of the crop, what must the *others* be like? Who would want to know *that*? Catfish Row Goes to Harvard. If those bullies actually thought white guilt was endless and that they could crap all over people as if *they* were the majority and *not* the minority, then they were much dumber than anybody ever thought they were. For all they talked about the past, their so-called legacy of the lost, stolen, and strayed, their fall from the makers of civilization to the tasteless wad of gum stuck under the desk of society, it didn't seem that their sense of the future was very rational. Sort of insane, actually. Someday, some of the people—a lot of the people—whom they had fooled and screamed at would be in charge. All of the time. Then there would be hell to pay for their goddam vanity. It didn't stop at their black eating tables, dorm floors, and student unions.

Why should it?

When she had done her legal clerking in Washington, D.C., Ramona, burdened by her anger but hoping to experience something that would justify the perspective in her family's house, had never seen so much black corruption, so much stealing, so much arrogant ignorance, and such disdain for the truth. They were always talking about how the white man couldn't stand to hear the truth about himself, but this chocolate town could have a dope addict and hustler running their city and not care a damn about *that*. He could get caught and put on some African stripes and say he was a new man, and they whom he had shat on would elect him *again*. That wasn't all.

How surprising.

It could hurt you personally. Ramona would never ever forgive them for the guy who was placed so high in the local government. He was so perfectly tailored and well spoken, so egotistical, such a past master at assessing everyone in a room. This man was an insider who could walk the walk and talk the talk across the spectrum. Having gone to the best schools with the liberals *and* the conservatives, he later found himself helping those whites in power get their wives and their husbands and their children free of addiction to food, liquor, and drugs.

This was the fellow with the best list of deprogrammers of kids caught up in cults, the source of all the best tutors and the finest therapists for children who had been abused in those degenerate situations where even countless money meant nothing. At the podium, he became both an embodiment and the fount of eloquence and church rhetoric interwoven with the lyric and knowing textures of the worlds of politics, law, and the sophisticated traveler.

This man loved to call her big sister in the middle of the night saying that he had a woody, eight inches of big hard black dick, and wanted her to help him do something about it.

The humiliations were endless. Yes, her penance had been rugged. Yet, as with so much of her hardship, she had been left stronger at its end. Everything resolved with clarity. Now that Ramona was in her Cleveland law firm and had some stationary power, there would be *no* black people rising to the positions of partners. Not if she could help it. And she *could* help it.

"I know how to do it and everybody around me has the know-how. We don't end up in court. Never. You know you have to have them around. You must. You can't avoid that. It's the law. They saw to that. But they didn't see to everything. It's all right now. Things are mending. Ways have been developed. We know just how to make them feel as though they aren't wanted, and eventually, they accept where they are or they quit. They get out of there. You see, people like me and Bob run the country now and we all remember those years in college. We know the facts. These aren't just feelings. This is the reality."

"It doesn't sound very real to me. It doesn't even sound human."

"It doesn't have to, little sister. It's like a Lutheran eating applesauce out of a Mason jar. No one cares. You do what you do and we do what we have to do. We know what we are confronted with and we know the exact best way to get things done out there. If these black people want so badly to be independent right now, they should *be* independent. Instead of building one social latrine after another, they should really work for each other. That'll be the day. Anyway, they should build their own society inside ours like the Chinese did in Chinatown. Bob and I would definitely support *that*. America is a silk handkerchief, not a piece of toilet paper. Fuckers. We have spent almost a trillion dollars in this country trying to raise them up from the mud over the last thirty years but they keep slipping back. In reality, they keep *running* back. That's because they're lazy pigs and they love it."

Carla looked at Ramona and knew then that there was no need to sit there any longer. She didn't have a sister. This woman right there with the mannish haircut and dressed in military colors meant nothing to her. Ramona became quiet and sipped some water, her face flushed. For an instant, she looked as though she wished she could take a deep breath and pull all of those words back out of the air. Such things are not possible. You cannot unbomb Hiroshima.

The sadness at the table firmly squeezed them both. Carla gestured for the check. They sat there not saying a word as the bill came. They split it and left a twenty percent tip. Each of them, looking as though she was at a funeral for someone who had died prematurely, moved to the door. There was nothing they could say and nothing they could do. They would never speak to each other again. Sure thing. Never tomorrow, never next week, never next month, never next year, never any time at all. If that was Ramona's mission, it was accomplished.

But who could say?

Carla had no idea what this woman she knew and didn't know at all had intended to get out of that lunch. Still, her older sister's secret lunacy was safe with her; she would not burden Dad with it; that would only be a way of trying to ease one's own hurt by hurting someone else and pretending that a bond against something terrible and mutually threatening was being created out of absolute necessity. Some of it you had to carry all by yourself.

Maybe not. Maybe Dad should know.

Hold your horses, girl. That might be a trick.

A trick?

It could be. Oh, it could be a trick.

If the big sister's intention was to get to Dad through the little sister because, when you got down to it, after all the howl and bluff, she didn't have the sheer nerve to break his heart by revealing what she had become—not a chance. Let Ramona stew in her own stuff. She was deserving. Ah so. How Pyrrhic. Even if Ramona was spiritually boiling to death, up to her neck in the slowly heating bile, longing, and guilt that sat on a low flame, the loss experienced by her younger sister wasn't accompanied by even the lightest scent of any kind of satisfaction. So this was what she had to face today.

Sure, Carla understood that life didn't really love *anybody* but were she to step up to her own truth, life had done its best to trick her pretty good some of the time. Right then, however, on that balmy day outside Grand Central Terminal, the girl from South Dakota felt as if she were a human piece of soap standing in the rain and melting. She knew she was a volunteer sucker and she hated it.

2 0

YOU TURNED THE TABLES

Carla was decidedly exhausted when she got home that Sunday night. The stroll down that high-noon street to meet her memories of Ramona and all they made rumble around inside her right now were, to say it plainly, taxing. Thinking about the details and the finality of that lunch at the Oyster Bar had taken her on a long, long walk when she left Leeann's, all the way over to her former neighborhood on the other side of Tompkins Square Park, where the old East Village, rising from its stoic squalor, was no longer the old East Village.

This was just as true of Eighth Street. Once so wonderful and filled with many businesses distinguished by the quality of their merchandise, it was now a strip of third-rate places and fast-food joints because the loud black teenagers, Puerto Ricans, and white rowdies from New Jersey had repulsed the old clientele. On weekends, the police had come out on Sixth Avenue to close off the side streets between West Fourth and Fourteenth streets so that residents wouldn't be driven loony by cars and Jeeps blasting obscene rap recordings. That all infuriated Maxwell no end, and it was good that they lived west of Seventh Avenue and didn't have to be bothered by other than the occasional group of Negro kids riding in a Jeep with smoked windows rolled up only so far, allowing you to see the tops of their heads as they nodded to the angry chants of the rappers played at volumes which would certainly have long-term effects on the hearing of the partially hidden passengers.

Given what that part of Eighth Street had decayed to, everybody who remembered the way it had been must have felt the loss. Had to. Couldn't be any other reaction. Hardly. Why, when Carla had first gotten to New York, those in the East Village dreamed of someday being able to shop on Eighth Street between Sixth Avenue and Broadway. She and other waitresses talked about it. They walked those few blocks and looked into the windows imagining themselves up on another plateau of comfort and acquisition. Another American dream gone by the wayside. What a dumb dream.

What a pointless walk through two ghost towns. This woman made into a New Yorker by time spent in this urban geography knew nothing had been resolved by footing it around until she was tired. Her soul was encircled by a zero. She couldn't lose herself and she couldn't forget and there was no one waiting for her at home or for her to wait for. Going back out didn't appeal to her. Appearing in clubs by herself was always a problem anyway because there were those musicians and other guys who acted as though Maxwell being on the road meant that she was available. It was tricky since she might call to hire one of those musicians for an engagement of her own and didn't want to have sexual rejection get in the way of his taking the job or prompt him to accept the work but perform below his talent in order to get revenge for her not laying back and letting him try to fill this body with his fantasies about himself and about her. Home was it for tonight. Hungry as a lioness who had missed one kill after another, Carla made herself a hearty portion of pasta with butter sauce and salad, ate, and sat around for a while. All the wonderful places where they had eaten together arrived in smells and lights and interior design—Cent'Anni on Carmine Street, Pesce Pasta on Bleecker Street, Anton's on West Fourth Street, where Maxwell sometimes went during the day and jammed with the Viennese owner and master chef who also played alto saxophone, La Ripaille on Hudson Street, Toon's, the Miracle Bar and Grill, and the Paris Commune on Bleecker. . . . There were more but there was no point in thinking about them. She took a long shower, at least until the water unexplainably started getting cold and her anger functioned as a distraction from the loneliness that had come over her.

Ramona's image in the Oyster Bar, as if rotating behind and in front of other subjects, went through her mind with the heat of a knife wound. Oh, Ramona, Ramona. Tsk. She was a subject Carla had hidden from herself all through the visit to Texas and most of the short time since she and Maxwell had come home from Houston. And there was no way she was going to tell him. It wasn't her style. Some things happened that you couldn't talk with anyone about. You lived through them, maybe even nearly to the point of death, then you went on, pushing the horror down as far as possible so that there was only a sharp edge of it left, a blade you made sure not to finger with your memory, which could then take you back on a jet of blood. Enough. There were plenty of things she could have said at the Oyster Bar, but they wouldn't have mattered. What would her big sister have thought if she heard Cecelia complain about the trashy influences from pop culture on the children in her school? The trouble was just some more promotion of the bottom as the best, the nastiest as the purest. Somebody always did it like that, somebody always had a way of making the condition of slime a prime aspect of existence. Refinement meant a loss of soul. Such unadulterated bullshit.

What an unrelenting bitch Ramona was. It was still the other side of belief. Who was this pillar of Cleveland to look down on her? The contempt Ramona had expressed and the way she had talked about Maxwell as though he were interchangeable with Bobo and Jimmy Joe. What a cold hoot in high hell. This was one big sister who would never know. If she even vaguely recognized. If she could feel how complicated it was and how frail things were now with the man she was in the process of losing. Houston hadn't made any serious differ-ence. It was just a gorgeous blip of light. He was still sliding away. Nobody had to tell her that. It was as obvious to her as the golden gleam of the city that had taken her breath away once again as she looked out the window while their Delta flight from Texas slowly descended into La Guardia Airport four hours after sundown the night they returned. They were at the end of something Carla could never have imagined devolving as it did.

Love, like Mr. Handy said, careless love. Some had other ideas about that. They always did, didn't they? Guidebooks through the safari of your life. Pick it up today. Dial right now. Have your credit card ready.

One of her friends, Doreen Gopstein, a feminist writer who was small, Jewish, and as charming as she was intellectually combative, had once accused Carla of living for love, of putting too much stake in men, of not realizing that the whole romantic shebang was just another of the many mirages a woman had to recognize if she were ever to find satisfaction in the oasis that was herself and her work, the two things she could count on being there every morning, every afternoon, and every night. Your own consciousness and what you had done or needed to do never left you; they were there on your deathbed. *When you are dying, Carla,* Doreen said, *you will probably be thinking of some recording you could have made a little better or some song you intended to sing but didn't. You might even begin to think of an original melody. That's exactly what could happen. You could be humming it to yourself when you are dying. Then you will be free. You will be beyond the mirage of romantic love.*

The girl from South Dakota didn't look at it that way. She found the whole idea offensive and defeatist. She wasn't living for love; she was trying to live for life. There was no way she was going to accept deprivation as a normal condition. If there was anything to fight against, it was that. Sure, we are all lonely and caught in a screwed-up world run too often by the stupid. Yes, we are always arriving alone and dying alone and so, so, so. But if you love someone and that someone loves you, that is just as true as being yourself and having an art you have dedicated yourself to, or an ideology, or a corporate job, or the secret power to influence the nation and the world, or whatever it is you have. Isn't the dual loyalty to yourself and to someone else just as much an accomplishment as discovering who you really are and exactly what you can really do?

Maybe so, dearie-dear, and so what? Life still didn't give you a break, not a fucking break. Here she was, alone in their apartment, Houston, Leeann, Cecelia, Kelvin Thomson, Ramona, and all of them rampaging through her mind while her heart was slowly splitting because the man she loved didn't want her the way he used to and would soon not want her at all. She couldn't sing her way out of that, just as a woman without talent couldn't love her way into being an artist by standing soul to soul with her man. Carla wished she had the bravado to say, Two tears in a bucket: fuck it, and believe she felt like that. She did not, not at all. She could not. That, in her case, would have been cowardly. What the hell had happened? For all that bitter blather with Ramona and all of big sister's proud details about the perfect life with good old romantic and racist Bob, they hadn't spent one second talking about what Carla had made of herself and her own situation. What an emotional cheapskate. It was too costly to try and learn anything real about her little sister. What a cheat. What a goddam cheat. It was so easy for Ramona to judge. She had her ways of knowing, did she?

As far as this NRA warrior queen of Cleveland was concerned, her little sister lived in some faceless spiritual squalor, overwhelmed by the erotic tales and powers of equally faceless, shiftless, and cruel black men. Hmmph. And, to be sure, there was probably a cure for that, which, fuck you very much, was unknown to any of us other than the anointed. Had to be. Big solutions coming from Ramona.

But there was none for careless love. It, like music, went the way it was going to go. Love and music were eternal; you weren't; you were just a tenant, who might have toiled enough to earn the luck that underlay getting a suite. You might have been so full of self-satisfaction that you actually believed that you deserved that suite. Fool. You had no way of being sure that the suite, the hotel, and the whole block wouldn't disappear. You could lose someone through who knows what the things are that actually do something deadly to a portion of your fate, and if you had the very worst fucking luck, your talent could go, leaving you with no more than recollections of the short or long period when there was something special to the way you said how it should be in the aesthetic part of your own sky. To get and hold on to both, who exactly in the hell did you think you were to expect a portion that large?

It had even been hard at the very start. That's right. Sweet but hard. They were so much alike and she was surprised to find that his New York story had parallels to hers, which she didn't think about at all when looking at how he was regarded by other musicians and listeners. You never know too much of what is going on. Never. But part of what they get you with is the way they are and the story they have to tell. The sensibility and the biographical report. He had pulled her in like that, if pulling was what it actually had been.

As it began, Bobo was still all over her soul like thick, thick foliage, but Maxwell was charmingly cutting his way through, with each word, with aromatic silences, with his own touch, the way he made love, the comfort he gave her, the encouragement to continue working on her music, which was support that she didn't ask for but considered mandatory at this point in her life. There was also his sense of humor. He could make her laugh and she so loved to laugh.

What brought her closest at the start were the tales he told of his own first years in New York. She went to meet him out in Brooklyn at the Botanic Garden the spring just a year after Bobo was dead. He looked so masculine among the plants and she reveled in the fabulous collective smell of all of those different kinds of flowers and greenery. It was a perfect place for her to fall in love. She didn't know that much about him then but felt both her force and his weaving together as Maxwell went autobiographical on her. Her future man spoke of when he had arrived off the bus in some tennis shoes with a box of chicken and a fairly good sound but not enough information, only the ability to squeak and honk with the avant-garde players, which he rejected fairly soon out of boredom and a contempt for a circle of musicians who couldn't really stand next to their predecessors; they could only talk some kind of relativism garbage designed to make up for the fact that the craft they supposedly worshiped so devoutly was not at their command. Maxwell did not want to be one of them. He was too proud. Slowly, humbly, those chords and their resolutions were learned over a decade as he went through every kind of harmonic system, from Jelly Roll Morton to Wayne Shorter. His sense of melodic line was most affected by Louis Armstrong, Lester Young, Charlie Parker, Sonny Rollins, and Ornette Coleman.

With Bobo, who could net rhythms out of the wind, he had learned so many road maps in and out of beats that he could come into and move out of rhythms like a phrasing wisp, toying with the time but always swinging, now lagging behind at the end of the line, now right in the middle, now up in front, looking over the cliff, now floating, like a big brass bird, over the whole business. Maxwell was one who sometimes shaped his improvisations so that each eight bars in a standard song was approached from a specific point of rhythmic entry, chorus after chorus, something Maxwell had picked up from Bobo, who would play like that, orchestrating and evolving his rhythms.

Yeah, man, he had walked all of those long steps, up that treacherous staircase to the top of the bandstand, where the respected ones laid their wares on the air. So he knew precisely how Carla felt when she had been so insecure. He had been that immigrant novice, too, hoping he wouldn't mess up onstage, looking for the approval of the other musicians, even developing the kind of paranoia that made him learn every new scrap of music in every key so that if he found himself faced with a strange piano player who wanted to play games by suddenly switching the trumps, Maxwell could get there before he finished his first trick. At those moments, he took joy in cutting a motherfucker who was trying to cut him. So part of his imposing skill was spurred into place by fear and suspicion.

That he had made so much of those feelings instead of letting them make him into a lesser person caused her to see Jimmy Joe in a different light. Her Chicago bluesman didn't have the conqueror's spirit, which Maxwell had and which she knew was her kind of spirit as well. Inside, under it all, they spiritually rhymed, her and this man from Houston. She knew it that afternoon in Brooklyn. That was the connect. Then they were caught in a whirl of steam and she was sweating inside for him and before she knew it—or that was how it seemed—she had agreed to move in with him. Actually, it was a year, but surely the fastest year she had ever lived.

It began, as it should have, right inside the art that was becoming a room of her own, the place where she was getting to the freedom of being exactly like herself every second. Up on that bandstand. That was the signal point of her arriving in the emotional big time. Clarity was the issue, sweetheart, nothing else.

When Carla first declared herself as completely available to him, body and soul, was about six weeks after that spring day in Brooklyn. It was the Sunday afternoon that Maxwell came to hear her sing at the Blue Note brunch job she had on weekends. A full decision had been made, no aspect of wimpishness holding a strong spot in her heart. All of the music was prepared and rehearsed. Did she have a surprise for that man!

She had been waiting for him to get off of the road and come to the Blue Note like he said he would. There had been calls and Carla found herself sniffling when she hung up, his voice sweetly coiled around her and the wonder of the telephone such a blessing for lovers separated by great distances. How had men and women ever been able to stand it before this technology? Some said it made them into eloquent writers of letters. Still, God, that must have hurt. It hurts enough when you hear from the one you want right here. It sure does. Good God, it does.

Her insides began skipping along as she left home on that Sunday an hour and a half before she went on, which allowed her to stroll out of the East Village leisurely, cool out when she got to the job, and pick every song in exactly the right order.

Walking west on Third Street past New York University and into the block where the club was had been a whole lot of fun, her thinking about him and what he had said to her that day in Brooklyn before they left the Botanic Garden and went to Keyr N' Deye, an African restaurant near the Brooklyn Academy of Music, eating in silence and staring at each other as though words were fruitless. It was simple, Maxwell said, his eyes nearly snatching her to him and squeezing the breath out of her just an hour or so prior to their finishing up the delicious Senegalese food. Very simple. Neither one of them would ever be able to forget Bobo because he was inside of them for good, but that didn't mean that they couldn't get inside of each other on their own. *I mean I'm right here for you, Carla, right here, and I hope you're right here for me, he had said. I am, was all she could answer.*

While she was upstairs in her dressing room, one of the few real dressing rooms you could get in a New York club, Maxwell, back in town only a couple of hours, came up to wish her well and brought the gift of an orchid. It looked so delicate Carla was almost reluctant to pin it on. What a guy. If how he really felt for her was anything close to how that flower was shaped, well, there was nothing more to say. She thanked Maxwell, kissed him, and said she needed some privacy to get herself together before going onstage.

Carla was up on the high bandstand and Maxwell was down in the audience but the serenade came from above, not below. There was a nice crowd there to eat and listen, New Yorkers and Japanese tourists. It didn't matter to her whether the other listeners knew what was going on or not. A story had to be made clear this afternoon. She was not there just to sound good or look good. A man had to be told something and there was no better way or place for her to say what had to come out than singing from this stage on this Sunday afternoon. That man was right there, sitting against the mirrored wall across from the bandstand, sharp as two tacks in his light, caramel-colored suit of silk and wool, beige shirt, yellow tie, and brown Allen Edmonds shoes, with his head back and his eyes on her, the atmosphere of confident musical prestige rising from him in combination with a big taste of romance.

Carla felt solid as a teakwood cup and light as the air inside it. This was going to be something special. She opened with "I Didn't Know What Time It Was." She started it as she did all of her songs, always singing the verse, which, depending on her arrangement, was delivered a cappella and out of tempo or accompanied in time only by piano or bass, sometimes that verse with just the drummer's brushes on his open or closed sock cymbal or his ride cymbal alone or, if she had a catchy little syncopation that worked, on his bass drum. All by herself was the way this one began. That first tune was followed by "Anything Goes," "Every Time We Say Goodbye," "All Through the Night, "Night and Day," "In the Still of the Night," "I Get a Kick Out of You," "All of You," "Easy to Love," "It's All Right with Me," "I've Got a Crush on You," "I've Got You Under My Skin," "I Concentrate on You," "Change Partners and Dance," "Let's Do It," and "From This Moment On." As she sang, putting a story into every word and note, swinging through different tempos and stretching her heart out on ballads, Carla felt herself maturing right inside the music and saw Maxwell captured by her ardor, which brought a fierce response from the audience.

She had been right. Each of those good old good ones, those American songbook tunes, was perfect as a vehicle for singing, for improvising, and for making herself well spoken and explicit. The girl from South Dakota had pulled the covers off of herself, she had gone naked in public, all of her right there in plain sight, perfectly and proudly audible, no jacking around, no blushing doing the flutters inside. The lyrics and the notes had let Carla allude to her adolescent time with Paul Munger as well as the Chicago time with Jimmy Joe, the time with the various guys on the way to Bobo, and there was the freedom to satirically sing of the history behind American outlandishness, only to discover that accepting the right proposal transcended all of it, which led her to get as soft as she could contemplating the look Maxwell had in the Botanic Garden, then go on about the little bit of hurting expiration that went with saying farewell to that big guy over there, push a phrase of notes and lyrics toward how it was when she was against him and they were rutting with such rawness she believed the gorgeous delirium would split her wide open, a belief that, from another position, allowed her to soar toward the way the very thoughts of him tempestuously subjugated her spirit in the light and in the dark, how the tom-toms of vivid adoration forming a per-cussive choir in her heart pounded his name out in rhythms that hum-bled her in the moisture of a teasing joy, pretty much because the fact that this pure female flesh against his pure male force was so much better than any of the drugs or the black leather or the crazy and eva-sive things that people used to kick and whip themselves into inten-sity, not to mention this lady's searing wish that everything about him was hers to own and to keep and to tame and to spoil and to make laugh and to set aflame, plus the fact that it had become so easy to fall for this big old boy once she let her heart have its head, that now it was all right to move away from the ghost of Bobo into the diverse and textured world of a living man who had the right face and rhyme and rhythm for this particular lady, why it all came down to some-thing as old-fashioned and sweet as a crush multiplied up from child-ishness into the vast desire of a woman made ready for life by the fire and terror of life itself, the gift of it all having traveled far beneath her skin while that very skin panted for tenderness and the barely liquid whispers against her ears and her neck and her breasts as this she and he lay on the black and flying carpet of night made dense and humid by the polyrhythms of romance, a state of living so important that if she had been in the kind of pinch that meant she had to resort to moving him out of another's fortunate arms, this girl from the big plains would have shown loyalty to nothing other than her own long-ing for him to change partners, a decision, given that special guy's comic sense of living, she could be sure included all of the wit and the sensual humor that joined this him and this her to every kind of species—even jellyfish—all that had to come close to one another in the sticky exchanges that made them more alive and put them in the hugging position to perpetuate life, all of it, at this moment, a song presently ready to take sail out into the world, possessed of the sound like this her and this him, looking groomed to luminosity by the old-est story ever told, the one in which high cold loneliness, hard smacks, and the funk of grief taught you what you most viscerally wanted and caused you to ask God that someone be sent to love you and to watch over you and to see you as just what you were, a mottled and private grown-up walking inside the yearnings that were realized only by please and by yes and by always.

She bowed and introduced the musicians.

The way the audience now stared at her made Carla a bit uneasy as she turned to leave the stage. Maybe she had gone too far. Maybe she hadn't. Maybe it wasn't any of their business. Maybe she had made it their business by putting her business in the street. Whatever, it was too late now. They were staring at her like she was an exotic zoo animal. Then the audience stood and clapped for her as no audience ever had. So did her musicians. She almost burst into tears. Her professionalism stopped that from happening. This wasn't a time for minorleague sentimentality over being liked. Let's get down to the get-down. The singer's encore was a slow, slow "You're My Thrill," which segued into a medium-fast "My Romance," her head, chest, and diaphragm working for the kinds of colors and swing she really wanted to come out this afternoon, swing that enunciated nothing but affirmation. The audience responded even more powerfully this time. Carla bowed again, thanked them again, and walked off the stage.

Wow: this was not something she had ever done before, and hopefully, would never have to do again for the same reason she had on this Sunday, since this was one affair Carla hoped would hold up, make its way through the travails that had to be coming but could never be predicted. She was thirty-three years old and she wanted something she could count on as long as she lived.

After the set, he came up to see her, handsomely dawdling around at the gift shop until she had finished accepting compliments and signing autographs for the Japanese tourists.

"You sound like you're talking about us."

"I am."

"Nobody ever put that much feeling on me in public before. I have to say I got a little embarrassed."

"I didn't. I loved it."

"I don't know what to say, baby. You are some kind of woman."

"I know what to say. I only have one thing to say. I love you."

"I love you, too, baby."

She locked the dressing room door, unpinned the orchid to keep from destroying it, pulled Maxwell next to her on the couch, and held him a bit, kissing and sighing but not going too far because, after all, she had another set to do and didn't want to look like the satiated cat who had swallowed the blind goldfinch because it sang too beautifully.

Still, when it came time to move, to actually take all of her things to the *his* place that was to become *their* place, she didn't feel all that good about it. Not at all. She was, by the way, pretty goddam ambivalent about it. There was just no playing past the truth that this East Village, this holiday space for a graveyard of memories, had been unalterably important to her early experience in the town, both as a newcomer learning the city and as a singer mastering her craft.

This was also where Bobo had lived. His old place was only seven blocks away and she couldn't ever forget how it felt walking over to see him, where she, too, was taught so much about rhythms and spent as much time in the middle of her apprenticeship as she did in the middle of her romance with that magnificent but doomed man.

New experiences never erased the old ones anyway. Maxwell was right about that; people stayed inside of you. They couldn't take away from her those nights when, thinking she was asleep, Bobo would practice with his brushes at three in the morning, playing so softly the cymbals sounded like wind chimes, alternately delicate as the single petal of a rose or as powerful in force as a drum choir while remaining in the arena of percussive whispers. Bobo hated anything loud and always told drummers that you pushed a band with swing and feeling, not a whole lot of goddam noise. The louder you played, the less sound you got. There were no gradations of timbre and nuance, only rhythmic volume. Carla never got another feeling like the one he gave her when they were making music together in his loft, just the two of them, especially after she began to truly hear the beat.

So it had not been easy to leave, not at all. No matter how much Maxwell had gotten to her, she didn't believe that she could ever love a man more than she loved Bobo. Yet her childish side was outgrown by then and she knew that a woman loved a man or a man loved a woman on the basis of how he or she was. Otherwise, there was nothing individual to it and maybe nothing individual to you. If that certainty was the case, you obviously wanted something you already knew or that you planned on, not another flesh-and-blood human being who made you feel fresh things about yourself. Yes, she had been sent someone to make her feel fresh things. Maxwell was like that. Oh, was he.

That, even so, was not enough for her to experience comfort about giving up her own place. How the hell could it be? Considerations had to be taken into account. That's right. There was simple stuff. Basic as a blue sky. If things went bad, there she would be, another New York woman struggling to find an apartment, since there would probably be no way she could kick *him* out. The stories she had witnessed when that happened to somebody she knew made her even more reluctant. It wasn't insurmountable. It was just a tight spot. No, she did not want to find herself in a situation tight like that. Still, he had convinced her. Maybe, after all, Carla wanted to be convinced. Maybe a big risk and a leap of faith were what she wanted right about then. Something else to live for, an addition that would only complement her iron reverence for her art.

In a moment of unsentimental assessment, when she halted the Evangeline echoes springing around inside, she had no doubt that there would be plenty of privacy and a number of days when she had the apartment to herself, given the professional fact that Maxwell was so frequently scheduled to leave town and blow his horn. Not a bad deal. Hey, even as much as she was loving him then, Carla didn't really want to be around a man every goddam day. Mom had sometimes seemed as though she was imprisoned by the constant presence of Dad and the kids, which was why she might bathe, hum, and sing in the bathroom for what seemed hours to the children, or close the bedroom door and read, hanging a "Do Not Disturb" sign from the doorknob, or take eternal walks, or visit out-of-town relatives by herself, leaving Dad to manage things, which he didn't do very badly, by the way. Mom knew. You couldn't beat it. A little solitude in your own house was always a good thing. Definitely.

That Carla was assured of having some time to do nothing but be herself, intruded upon by the flesh-and-blood energy of no one that she didn't invite—what can you say?—it helped her make up her mind as much as the idea of being with a guy who was reminiscent of no one and brought her up to the penthouse of her emotion, where the view stretched for a great distance.

Then there was the day that Maxwell, one soft May afternoon in an unbuttoned red and white shirt, blue jeans, and Air Jordans, arrived with a small U-Haul truck and some buddies who were helping him take her piano down the stairs, all five flights, the same piano she had seen in the street ten years before, waiting for somebody to get it home or tear it to pieces. As soon as she fingered all the keys from top to bottom and knew it was good, Carla went mad, immediately running to the bank for some money and gathering some young guys whom she paid twenty dollars apiece to grunt that set of ivories up to her apartment. She thanked God at every flight that no one else had gotten to it first.

That was why the exit day from the East Village was both traumatic and magical. That piano represented her commitment to her music and her own space. It was not great and didn't hold a tuning very well, but that was where the girl from South Dakota methodically went through songbook after songbook, learning all of the Broadway tunes, the Ellington tunes, figuring out the Strayhorn songs, those wonderful harmonies in Tadd Dameron, the jagged Manhattan skyline of Thelonious Monk's chords, and so much other music, period upon period, steeping herself until she sometimes felt as if every molecule of her body had at least one note in it, one drumbeat, one chord. After all that work in her embarrassing little place, Carla's lungs felt weighted inside her body as Maxwell and those other guys began moving her piano down the stairs, each landing—four, three, two, then the first floor—taking her a good distance from what she had kept and protected for so many years in New York, always holding on, always returning, always making sure that she had that room of her own, that keyboard, that life in private.

This was truly an occasion of the blues two different ways: she then wanted to go and she definitely wanted to stay; joy and loss were the moving pedals on a bike inside her, one up, one down. The sky that was hers through the single window, the noise she had become accustomed to, Tompkins Square Park, where Charlie Parker once sat and played his saxophone to the neighbors at night, long before the street on which he lived became Charlie Parker Lane. Mmm: there were also the Chinese-Cuban, Jewish, Italian, and Indian restaurants; the little art galleries, the bookstores, the marvelous Russian steam bath she went to once a month or so, the Italian bakeries, the record shops, the used-clothing stores, the many different bars, the army of police officers who were in the area once the city brass decided to stomp the neighborhood's drug trade into a pulp—and all that she had forgotten but that was undoubtedly integrated into her sensibility, gliding below recognition in the misty aspects of the brain.

Yes, she was hung up on that spring day in May as the parts of her neighborhood and the six or seven or eight blocks beyond it in every direction gathered in her heart as a medley of experience and were as hard to leave as they were uncomfortable when she dreamed of moving somewhere, having a spacious apartment west of Broadway, a good piano, perfect light, and all of the quality neighborhood things that went with leaving the East Village, which was, actually, in the middle of becoming a much better place to live just at the time that she was getting ready to go.

Quite simply, New York always re-created itself by turning dumpy blocks into attractive ones since there was only so much real estate and the well-to-do would live anywhere if that anywhere was safe and had enough going on to qualify on a posh tip. There it was. Exactly: once the builders and realtors got their intentions in order, a slum like hers was in its last square miles of time, but so, in an icy way, were the people who didn't have the money to keep up with the well-to-do immigrants into their environs. Like the Indians, they were surely destined to be pushed out and forced to find another low-income district with disorder at its borders.

So there had been a kind of reverse talk for years about the neighborhood being ruined by improvements and the reduction of its criminal presence. "I think it's good to have some junkies on your block or even a crack house because that keeps pretentious people out of your social space, man," Carla heard one middle-aged guy in a torn Marilyn Manson T-shirt say to another almost as sloppily dressed as he, both balding yet sporting greasy rat's tails held in place by rubber bands and drinking cup upon cup of coffee. Maxwell overheard the guy, too, made an outlandishly funny face as commentary, and she laughed more loudly than she would have liked to, throwing her head back and feeling as though a big laugh was the best response to such absurd ideas.

She was still living over there then, about a year before accepting the proposal to move west with her guy. She and Maxwell were enjoying some hot chocolate and moist sponge cake at a restaurant across the street from Tompkins Square Park after having walked all the way down to Battery Park City at the south end of the island, talking away, mostly about music and each other, about songs they loved, about chords, about rhythms, a bit about what it was like growing up in South Dakota as opposed to Texas. As they sat there, almost consuming each other through their orifices and their skin, Carla knew it didn't matter what anyone said. The rules were in place. New York, as impersonal as nature itself, was just changing again. Reconstructive neighborhood surgery was at work. As this specific process went on while she was getting enjoyably used to this new man, the rich and the poor could be right next door to each other, closer than they would be at a sporting event, since those on the low side of the bucks line never had seats as good as those on the upper side.

She said goodbye to all that she had lived in the East Village. She helped Maxwell and the guys organize her stuff and get it down the stairs. She took the chance.

Their clean and well-lighted place was very neat. His shoes were in a rack, his clothes other than his suits were folded and organized on some shelves he had built himself. His music was in order, as were his vinyl recordings and compact discs, his many books and his dozens of videos. He was not averse to mopping and cleaning. Dirty dishes never piled up and he had a monthly credit arrangement with the Italians at the cleaners and the Chinese who did his laundry; both delivered. Maxwell was that kind. So was she.

This meant there was no picking up behind each other. They were both so orderly and willing to do chores that Carla never ever felt as though she was Maxwell's girl servant. They were partners and he was just as good a cook as she was. He loved to challenge her in the kitchen and alternate nights of making dinner for a week, adding up the score on Sunday as they walked up to Central Park, traveling north on Fifth Avenue and stopping at Rockefeller Center, a good place to get a snack, a drink, a cup of coffee. When they had what Maxwell called "the battles of the cook pot," Carla usually edged him with a dessert, something she had learned from Mom or from Jimmy Joe's family in Chicago. It always adds up.

That sense of order she so enjoyed, when arriving at their place or looking at it before leaving for a trip, came from their childhood homes. Neither of their households was at all sympathetic to messiness as they were growing up so far away in miles but so near in sensibility. Mom and Dad, Eunice and Ezekiel had that in common: dirty houses, dirty kids, and dirty rooms were against the law of the domicile. Mom hated white trash and Eunice didn't have any time for black or white trash. Both were so religious. Each stood tall and strong in the household.

When Carla looked at the pictures of Maxwell's parents at their wedding and posing in a photographer's studio not so long ago, she got a feeling of earth and sky from Eunice, a distinction much like the interior width of character Mahalia Jackson has on the cover of the *Black, Brown, and Beige* album as she stands next to a seated Duke Ellington. Eunice, also like Mom, seemed to know things that had preceded the beginning and would continue after the end. Ezekiel gave the impression that he was made of chuckles in the wedding picture, but in the later one, with his face scarred, there was the seasoned compassion that appeared to have done much battle in order to maintain itself.

Having only so much confidence in what a camera could capture in an instant, Carla wondered at the time what both of those Houston people were actually like and sometimes tried to imagine what a conversation between Eunice and Mom would have been about. Now she wondered how it would have hit the ear, whether or not they could have really gotten to know and appreciate each other, if two women that strong could individually find the way to give up enough air so that the other could comfortably breathe. Death had made sure she would never know that.

The apartment was L-shaped; the long and wide central room contained a Steinway upright Maxwell had gotten from an old Italian woman on the Upper East Side who was dying but had heard his playing on the radio some fortuitous afternoon and got in touch to let him know that the album with strings reminded her of the good old days and that he deserved a medal for that, which she didn't have. Hence, the wonderful piano that he kept tuned.

Bobo's drums were there, set up for rehearsals. They spooked her when she first started coming over, and sometimes, when she spent the night, Carla would sit there and look at them as the streetlights and the moon created odd, geometric shadows behind those drums.

The day Carla moved in, Maxwell said that the drum set was incomplete with the cymbals he had bought. He asked her, quietly, if she would let him use those cymbals of Bobo's that were in the cymbal bag she had kept in the closet of the place that was no longer hers. This guy was confident. She nodded and he put the cymbal bag next to the drums since there was still work to do.

The kitchen area near the window at the front of the building had a view of the street if you wanted one. The refrigerator was full of beer, which Maxwell passed out to the buddies who had helped him load her stuff in the U-Haul truck. Her piano was put in their sizable bedroom so that she could practice at the same time that he did. He also bought a compact disc player and Sennheiser headphones for the bedroom so that either of them could lie in bed listening and studying a particular recording if the other one was in the main room working at the Steinway.

Day by day, Carla had watched him work all of that out as he talked her into living with him, but it still seemed like a surprise when she arrived there and he was so ready for her. For that first night, Maxwell had even gotten his lady a cotton nightgown with pink angels on it like the one she wore as a little girl. She found it hanging on the back of the door to the bathroom, which was right next to where they slept. He was doing it for her in layer upon layer at that time.

Their abode was right next to a parking garage, and the space in which they lived was over a bar frequented by cops, which Maxwell got because the bar was so well soundproofed he could practice or have rehearsals at any time and knew that you also wouldn't have to worry about burglars or riffraff wandering up and down your block with all those plainclothes and uniformed officers of the law wetting their whistles in Big Little Joe's. The place got its name because the Irish guy who owned it had the same name as his scarlet-faced and strapping father, Big Joe; but as junior got older, the son became a rather sizable man himself, which led to the name he put on his bar. Maxwell hung out in Big Little Joe's drinking Killian's beer, watching the sports channel, loving to listen to the blue and grimy tales told by the cops, and always happy to tell them about his travels through Europe, South America, the Caribbean, and Japan.

Carla didn't like the bar down below too much and rarely went in there because the guys were just too much into being guys. Even the women who were cops seemed like they were guys with vaginas as far as she was concerned. At least they did at first. But when things of the heart hit them, family or romantic joys or troubles, she could see that they, too, were the same as she, just that the job they had imprinted them with an emotional steeliness and sort of a rowdiness that was much like the way those boys used to be on the football team when she was a cheerleader back home. It touched her that the job of facing danger, learning that no one was above suspicion, and having so much pressure on you made the racial lines dissolve to such an extent that everybody was just a cop, whether Italian or Jewish, Irish or Negro, Asian or Spanish.

The space between life and death was thinner than the edge of a Gillette razor blade, one of the cops said one night, and there were other times when they told tales of how the enormously respected priest had deflowered young girls or buggered little boys, how the woman constantly weeping and spending the Christmas season nights in the station house while her missing children were looked for turned out to have brutally murdered them with her boyfriend because the little bastards made too much goddam noise, how the great Brooklyn judge, after he retired, was discovered to be a child molester himself, which explained the odd speech he gave before going light on a fellow molester while still on the bench, how this terrible and that terrible and all of it came together to make you not so much truly cynical as fairly sure that life *had* to be protected and that protecting it was a job much more complicated than you imagined while fooling yourself into believing how tough you were becoming when the training in the Police Academy was going on.

There were prejudices and tensions in the department, like everywhere else, the old demon of internal bias prowling through the precinct house and out in the squad cars and in the rooms where promotions were decided upon. But, one older black cop told her, the old gray demon wasn't as spry as it used to be, which was how the hell it went if you kept your foot in the white man's ass until he learned how to do right, which was a very slow process for a whole goddam lot of white folks, a whole lot. None of it made a difference when a cop was disabled for life or killed, which turned the air somber in the bar as they drank there in their funeral finest and white gloves. Then, even the ones she suspected of being racist and brutal rose, in the shadow of death, to something approaching the noble.

His hanging out in the cops' bar was an example of an aspect of Maxwell's personality that Carla really felt in sympathy with, that commitment to New York. He loved it, its rugged elements, its difficulties, its suave qualities, and its explosive tendencies. This was even shown in his affection for every season. That gave them plenty to do, no matter what the weather was. Nothing kept them inside if they wanted to go somewhere. They could get out there and feel the way things were, cooling off when it was hot, warming up when it was cold, walking in the rain as the city was being rinsed clean of its dirt, strolling somewhere together when it was just right, enjoying the city in its full stretch. Off to the movies, to the museums, to the park, to sales, to flea markets, to street festivals, to concerts, to the Big Apple Circus. He was always ready for Manhattan, come what may. She discovered this about Maxwell her first winter with him when he was hoping for a blizzard, which she considered strange since black people often found extremes of cold oppressive.

"I don't give a fuck what other niggers think. That's them. This is me: Maxwell Davis, born in Houston, Texas. But I didn't come to New York to live in goddam Texas. I want me some snow, plenty of it. I want it piled up *high*. I want to put on my action from the army surplus store. Get me my quilted long underwear, my insulated socks, my waterproof boots, flannel shirt, my heavy sweater, and my overcoat with my beaver hat and the flaps down. I want to get into it. I love this shit. Blotto absoluto: you heard what I said. Snow? Are you kidding? Hell, yeah. It comes down and it makes the city beautiful. Pure white for one night. Or it keeps that white going if the snow doesn't stop falling. Then, like everything else, it gets to be a pain. It turns into filthy slush. Then we are in official grayland. With all kinds and colors of shit here and there because the dog owners, the selfish motherfuckers, use snow as an excuse not to clean up behind their goddam-assed pets. Are they a bitch, or what? Then, after mashing all that cold on you, Mr. Winter gets knocked flat on his icy ass. KO. He melts down and spring, who caught him with a left hook, starts lifting up. Ah, wilderness of slush, get thine ass the fuck away from here. Scat! Soon, you look around with the trees blooming and you can't even believe there ever was a winter with all them goddam wonderful blizzards full of fat snowflakes. That's a deep change in itself. Gone, gone, gone. All that cold seems like a legend somebody told you and you just experienced the whole program in your mind by listening to it. Never were there. Strange feeling. Weird after that icy time gets on up the way. Next! Smooth entry, yeah, spring. Stepping itself up over knocked-out old Mr. Winter. Perfect for you and me, baby. The season is standing under a balcony singing right on up to you, a coloratura of feeling. Delicious up under your skin, you know? You get that fever and feel romantic another way, not cuddled up when it's cold outside or sitting at the end of a bar with the fog on the windows, you and me, or walking in that winter air with you looking so fabulous and both of us sloshing through all of that until we get where we're going and stomp the snow off, take off all that heavy stuff, and get all the way down to some hugged-up *fun*. I mean some yum-yum. Spring is another kind of thing. It blooms outside and you bloom inside. But that doesn't go on too long. Why would it? Soon the New York summer, unbearable, oh, my God, steps up on you. All this hot-assed concrete. Can you believe that? Lord have mercy. You sweat through that and the fucking pollution of all those cars making you feel like you know something, a little bit anyway, about the gas chambers some of these Jews always use as an I've-been-fucked-over-more-than-you credit card. I'm waiting for some of them Pol Pot Cambodians to come over here talking that yang. Later for all that shit, race cards, gassed cards, flabby pussy cards, short cards, tall cards, fat cards, red cards, yellow cards, disease cards, short dick cards, whatever kind of game card you're running. It does not matter because, in the summer, there is a reality beyond every bit of that. Every bit. That's right. It passes up the Rhineland *and* the Whineland. Beyond it, I say. Beyond it. Every public swimming pool in this town is full of young cuties and guys trying to learn how to swim. They are handling some very hot hormones. They are gone from puppy love to dogs in heat. They are growing up the way you do every summer when you're a kid. That'll charm the beak off a buzzard. But from the angle of hot, it's still hell on a daily basis. Then that foul summer gets its ass on up the road and you are right here in autumn in New York. Now is the time to be starting to dress a little heavier and feel the friendly kiss of that New York wind. What a beautiful season. Fall all over the place. Not too much. Then Old Man Winter gets like

Lazarus. He starts stalking the city, dogging it. And when he's got his groove right, he lays the white on just right, heavy and cold. So I want me a blizzard and I want one *now!*" he laughed.

After what were a very good four years of coming to know and have faith in each other, it had begun to go so, so sour shortly after they returned from the marvelous party down in Washington, D.C. This last year made her life lopsided. Pure on one side, polluted on the other. Not pure in terms of perfection but in the human terms of being right where the best of the real things always were. She had learned a lot from Maxwell about purifying her voice, which was about developing the skill to liberate the emotion, let the feeling breathe itself right out, free of the excess that led to the melodramatic, the sentimental loss of confidence that made you overdo it—or lose faith in the power you had to reach for way down in the soul bucket and fully pull out when it was time to raise the heat and meet the moment with a spiritual risk. You had to know how to be subtle and you had to know how to get hot.

One time, in the middle of the night, she heard Maxwell playing the *Leibestod* in unison with Leontyne Price. He got his tenor saxophone into her range and, instead of squealing, made this voluptuous blue tone of melancholy and transcendent grief take its place in the air, as if the burial earth itself were speaking to the waters of the world and to all the fire the heart ever held dearly and felt diminish when a loved one crossed over into the perpetual night of extinction. His diligent and constant practicing with great singers of all sorts gave Maxwell exceptional flexibility and was part of the reason he moved audiences to such an extent. This man had discovered the voice inside his tenor just as she was discovering the instrument inside of her voice while never forgetting she was a singer. She, too, wanted to deepen her identity, not dislodge it.

Yeah, right: they were so close in what they were doing, but her way of going through a song and his were very, very different. She had been able to find her own methods. Had she not, Carla couldn't have looked Maxwell in the eyes when they were talking about music. She would have been ashamed of herself. That was not how it was. She was proud of herself but fought against her tendency to gloat and preen inside.

That was no small battle, especially when Maxwell was in the brunch audience at Good Henry's listening to her, or when other musicians she respected were there and everything was working so well up on the bandstand that she felt herself inside a kaleidoscopic miracle of pulsation.

On afternoons and nights like that, she was ready for a crown. But Maxwell, noticing that her ego was going fully astronautical, would always tease her into place or play some choice, choice Billie Holiday and Dinah Washington records just to calm her down about herself. After she returned from the full moon of ego and landed on earth, he would hug her and whisper, "Let me tell you something. This is something I know. I know this very well. You sound damn good and you keep on sounding better. You remind me of none other than myself," he would then joke and they'd laugh and laugh.

Maxwell was above the pack as a musician in his age bracket and had always been so above the silly aspects of race, but in that last year before they traveled to visit Eunice and Ezekiel, he began hanging out with a different crowd. Instead of being philosophical about on-duty cabs passing him up or calmly telling off white people who tried to step in front of him in lines, Maxwell became extremely angry, returning home with one tale after another of how tired he was of eating shit because his skin was dark.

One of the recurring modes of behavior that most outraged him was the way white women clutched their purses when they saw him coming down the street, even if he was walking toward them as dapper as Beau Brummel and had maybe a thousand cold cash dollars in his pocket. Fucking self-important bitches trying to pretend that somebody black who was obviously doing all right still gave enough of a damn about their pocketbooks to ponder making victims of their asses. From his first days in New York he picked up that white women on the street averted their gaze as if he was an attack dog who would become aggressive or vicious if their eyes met his, the black man as mad pit bull. Woof. Eyes: More about them. He really didn't like the attitude in the spiritually emaciated stares of the white people when they debated within themselves whether or not to buzz him into their shops. That pissed him off while he was searching out something to get for himself or for her; it almost riled him as as much as one lightweight salesman did at the old Barney's on Seventh Avenue, which deserved to go out of business because of people like him on its staff. Here he was, Maxwell Davis—*known* the world over for being sharp as a mosquito's peter—dealing with a chump who knew much less about clothes but gave the impression that a favor was being done by letting a black man shop there and spend so much of his money. It wouldn't have done much to suggest that those kinds of puffed up people often lose their jobs for overstepping their bounds with customers as good as Maxwell. He would not want to hear that in the middle of his disposition.

Carla was told that once he and Bobo, at the drummer's high and fiery urging, had beaten the dog shit out of a big proper-looking nigger they saw suddenly push a white lady to the ground in the West Village because she seemed so proud of herself in a new fur hat and coat. "You ain't so much!" the nigger bellowed as he knocked her over and walked off. Maxwell and Bobo, the only other people on the street, helped the lady up. She seemed revulsed by them and relieved that they weren't going to add an ass-whipping to having been pushed over for absolutely no reason at all. Catching her breath, she started an embarrassed apology yet couldn't look them in their faces. After making sure the lady was okay, ready to tell some kind of a racist tale about the dangers of darkies when she got wherever the hell she was going, they ran and caught that motherfucker in the snow. Vapor rose in clouds from his head when his knit cap was knocked off. Ice was left freezing red because they wanted this nigger to know, punch by punch and stomping foot by stomping foot, that he was fucking it up for the rest of us. Now, however, this new person—growing inside Maxwell like a spiritual cactus—said that *he* understood just how much anger that brother felt toward her totally and typically arrogant whiteness, even though *he* sure the hell wouldn't do some shit that dumb himself. Carla didn't know which of those two things were more appalling to her—the vigilante violence or his empathizing with a crazy person. It made no difference anyway and the girl from South Dakota said nothing, just let him keep opening his steam valve. This subject was his bully pulpit. Her assignment was that of an ear.

He reminded this tympanic membrane with two feet of the springtime they had been in a cab stopped at a light near Houston and the Bowery when a young brother with a backpack who looked like a college student gave the car an odd once-over. Then the kid walked up to the driver's side and snatched the cabbie's folded money from his left shirt pocket. Throughout the rest of the ride, the driver kept looking back over the seat at Maxwell as though he was somehow responsible for the theft and the cheetah-speed with which the brother ran off, as if every nigger was in ace-boon-coon cahoots with every other nigger. Maxwell now failed to remember that Carla had been so angry about that accusative turning around that she almost cursed her guy out for still overtipping that asshole, whom he laughed off as just an example of some more nonsense you couldn't let get you down.

At this point, he wasn't laughing about anything having to do with race. He started using some of those clichés that he used to make fun of, that "us versus them" philosophy that usually demanded certain kinds of ethnic costumes and body oils and hairstyles in order to make the clear point that these Americans were neither white people nor black people who had been overcome by white society. They were not anybody's black Anglo-Saxons. Or so they thought. To her dismay, especially since she was still dreaming of having a child, Maxwell sneered about the "almost niggers," "the not quite niggers," the "I-wish-I-was niggers" who had been so bleached out inside that their skin was just a husk, an ethnic mirage. They were black on the outside but corny as Kansas in the summertime. The contempt he showed for such people in his conversation when they appeared on television or in restaurants or came up to him asking for an autograph after a performance was incrementally frightening. It was as if, out of nowhere, he began to accept some old-fashioned idea about the complete separateness of black and white.

He stopped hanging out at the bar downstairs, asserted that all of the white cops down there were racist, and disappeared either into the East Village or somewhere in Harlem or over the bridge into the African and Caribbean settlements in Brooklyn, usually returning home as though he were in possession of a secret that had nothing to do with her whatsoever, which was furthered by the fact that he would only say that he needed a break from the West Village and wanted to be around some "real people." There were other kinds of Negroes hanging around him on his jobs, and Carla got the impression that they didn't like her at all, no matter what she tried to do. Instead of Maxwell calling them on their rudeness, he ignored it.

Then there was the aura of entitlement to the way some of the black women spoke to her man and stood in his presence. One took a gold handkerchief from the breast pocket of his tan suit and wiped her face and his own with it, far too intimately. That made Carla wonder if Maxwell was playing around on her, if he wanted a big behind that wasn't white, if he wanted skin so dark no blue veins showed, if he wanted nappy hair next to him and in his hands. Maybe those disappearances into undetermined parts of New York, where he could be with "real people," included him moving inside any one of the many colors those women could be, black as a stallion, almost as white as Carla herself, nutmeg and vanilla, light brown, yellow, dark brown, brown going to mustard with freckles, thin, voluptuous, big thighs and small calves, calves that revealed ballet training, short necks, long necks so perfectly smooth or given to catching sweat in the lines that seemed aesthetic decisions, braids, close-cropped hair, short dreads, thick, flowing hair similar to horse's tails, hair of any texture and any color from blonde to brown to red to black, fleshy arms made sensuous by the color, long arms any dancer would want, lips as thin as Carla's, medium lips, heavy flappers. In the middle of all that, low voices, voices manipulated for accents that came from Manhattan or Brooklyn or the Caribbean or Africa or were some modulating mixture that also took in the South. Did they say something to him she couldn't say? Did they touch him some way she hadn't? Was it really, when the lights were out and there were only two people, not even talking, was it so important what the other person looked like when the lights were on?

In the middle of that, Carla realized that she had never seriously been jealous of another woman or taken seriously the idea that some guy fortunate enough to be with her would take his shoes off next to another bed. God, she had been so egotistically naive! So vain. True, true. Some kinds of naïveté, given the hard way that jealousy felt, were good fortune. They weren't so bad. But Maxwell letting that black woman talk to her the way he did the night that she decided he was becoming a coward was no kind of luck at all. "You brothers need to come home."

She actually said that. What nerve beyond nerve. What a perversion of the idea of home. Home in America was something you made for yourself, not a goddam assignment some haughty crew of bitches decided was good for you. Maxwell used to understand that better than she did. Right: used to. He was such a heartbreaking chickenshit. All he did when that woman insulted her was forget to put his neck strap in his saxophone case and say not a mumbling word. Still, her jealousy was kept miles down under whatever she said. Laughing at the idea inside and silently, Carla was not going to give him or any of those women the satisfaction of watching her become Othell*a*. She couldn't give in to that. There was nothing less dignified than a musician's wife or girlfriend arguing with him about some woman he was talking to or some woman screeching on the street about being disrespected because her man held another woman too closely at a party or the incredible fights she used to hear in her East Village building, the women going crazy and throwing stuff or braying on and on while the men ignored them or shouted even louder. Fine for them but not for her.

And on it went. For a while.

When Carla finally said something to him about all of that other stuff because her pride evolved in the other direction from refusing to acknowledge ignorance and the slights of consistently bad manners— when that proud sense of herself wouldn't allow the girl from South Dakota to ignore the abuses one millisecond longer—Maxwell only shrugged that these new friends of his weren't trying to do anything to her and that she shouldn't be so paranoid. That was not what she had wanted him to say. She didn't want to be blamed. But she had been. It was a muggy evening and he was playing beautifully at the Village Vanguard, perhaps even more beautifully than she had ever heard him play, but she knew her face, refusing to cooperate, was flushed after that conversation, and she also knew this was not just a passing phase, she knew that they were beginning to lose whatever it was that they had had.

Only three or four months ago, when Carla told him as soon as they got home after a job he did at Birdland that she became particularly exasperated by some of his new friends always treating her as though she weren't there, Maxwell said he couldn't understand why white people were always so paranoid if black people weren't kissing their ass. That one hurt so much she would have preferred that he hit her as hard as he could with his fist and she told him so.

He had his wide back to Carla and was silently drinking a glass of water. Did he hear what she said? No answer. She repeated herself. Silence, as if he was in the house all by himself. Did you hear what

I said? No reply. This disregard was new. They could always talk, even if arguing at the tops of their lungs. Carla now hated Maxwell and everything in this apartment. She pushed him with all her might. The glass came down on the kitchen counter. It cracked. He turned quickly, so quickly that she knew he was going to slap her down. She braced herself, refusing to lift a hand to stop the blow, already prepared to be a martyr, pack, and get the hell out. No, he stood before her, hands at his sides, staring down into that white face with unlimited frustration and something unfamiliar to her. This man did not even look like Maxwell. The emotion brutalized his face. He was a stranger to her. The air, under the power of this stranger's nameless feeling, turned into long bristles, drawing blood as she inhaled, drawing blood as she exhaled. Then the facial features Carla once knew in every single mood fought their way out of the emotional disfigurement. This, goddamit, was *her* guy. It was. He had come back. Maxwell was all around her—kissing her forehead, her lips, her cheeks, the back of her neck, her shoulders—and he was apologetic, soothing, promising everything she wanted to hear, everything, nothing she wouldn't have told him to say if she were controlling his words. She wept; she went along; she hugged him; she whispered; she kissed; she made drenching love, but, alone next to him in the foul cavern of that night, Carla was confused, spiritually trembling, and more than sure that their life together was going down slow, doomed by the cannibalism of an ethnic identity that removed everything personal and remade you into a pile of meatless bones rattled by the most imbecilic dictates of the tribe. What a tired fucking stereotype, what a *cliché*, she thought, and remained awake, sullen, throughout the night.

Yes, it had been like that when Carla and Maxwell left for Houston but it had not been that way a year before. Then the world was still, for all its troubles, theirs. She wished Ramona could have seen that. The self-centered bitch.

CAPITAL CITY BREAKDOWN

UNDRESSED NOW, in bed, incapable of reading or watching television or studying or practicing or sleeping, this whole day back in New York so screwed up, Carla, calming herself, wondered on this gloomy Sunday evening what her big sister would have thought if she had gone to Washington for the surprise birthday party that Leeann had for Cecelia in the spring of last year. It would have been more than a little interesting, she knew that. Ramona's solid gold suburban knees might have buckled. She would have seen something. It would have been hard not to, even the Queen of Cleveland might have had to step down from her throne and kick off her Aryan shoes.

That May, as she just couldn't stop herself from thinking, it was still so sparkling with Maxwell and the younger sister had nearly succeeded in weaning herself from the fantasy of giving birth to a golden-faced child with hazel eyes and dark blonde woolly hair. Actually, she dreamed of having twins like the British couple she saw in *Jet,* one child white like the mother, the other Negro like the father, paddling the hell out of everything anybody in the world knew about dominant and recessive genes. Whew. It was good that no such thing had happened because, at this point, on this Sunday night, the idea of being a mother at her age with a small boy or girl or a confounding set of twins when your man decided that you weren't the right color gave Carla the clammy shudders. There you go. Her fortune had been good again. After all, there were stoic or embittered white women around the East Village, some of them with children, who had been through the whole thing, the *whole* thing, all of it beginning when the guys they were with discovered their "blackness" and slowly but undoubtedly moved away from them into another world altogether. Those brothers went home. Ugh.

She got out of bed, rattled and caught in the fatiguing net of insomnia. Carla poured herself a big glass of white wine from the refrigerator and looked around the place that Maxwell had brought her to, where they had made a life that was theirs, hers and his. It had been something all right. If they could only have remained as they were then. Ha. Only a year ago. So many surprises. So goddam many.

When they were taking the Metroliner down to Washington as part of the conspiracy to surprise Cecelia, she was so happy that her recording of "The Days of Wine and Roses" with him had gotten her a lot of arranging work over the last two years. She wanted to talk about it but didn't, since there was no way, given his mood, that Maxwell wasn't going to look out the train window and make some kind of a joke, which she didn't feel like right then. Made slightly melancholy by that, she had focused on where they were going. They speculated together. Knowing Leeann's imagination, neither she nor Maxwell had any idea how the whole deal would work out. As it was, the party had taken them into another loop of history and the present, the place Carla always liked to be, a feeling she had become accustomed to back home. Right now in her beloved Manhattan, the memory of that ride on the train to the nation's capital and the talk with her man made her feel so much less alone. So did the white wine.

She had never heard words like nigger, spick, kike, wop, or any of that before she got to New York, which made it sound kind of idyllic to Maxwell, who laughed that he had heard every last one of those words in Texas, either from Negroes or the white folks who talked about those crazy people in New York, where children smoked cigars and drank the blood of the parents they murdered.

Carla knew that he was exaggerating from the shimmer of mirth in his eyes, but she let him know that South Dakota had its full sky of blues, too. There was Mr. Finnestad, who had lost the top joint of the first finger on his right hand because he had stood in the bathtub and tried to kill himself by putting it, wet, in the light socket. A beautiful red-haired and ruddy woman who swelled up into a drunken barrel after she came back to her husband, Mrs. Heinz ran away with Leon Manheim but the car had unexplainably stopped in the middle of the empty winter night, and when he got out to see what was wrong her lover man was eaten alive by wild animals. Some young guys, such stupid young guys, just so stupid, usually jocks, were always breaking themselves up into permanent disability while driving drunk, or kids were killing themselves speeding, or handsome girls flew through the windshields of those cars, got plastic surgery, looked like somebody unrelated to anyone in the family, and remained glum for the rest of their lives.

She changed the mood as he was surprised by her portrait of home as so dour. As if he were able now to lay his listening burden down, Maxwell said he deeply appreciated that shift from South Dakota Heavy to South Dakota Lite, and she gave him a fake push and he gave her a real kiss. Nothing exceptional ever took place back home, but there was so much a feeling of community, with the kids having a lot of good times playing with each other, no matter what their race was. As hard as things had been when it came to putting that part of the country together as a unit of the United States, South Dakota seemed as free of a lot of the troubles of the nation as the horizon was of intrusive building and overcrowding.

Maxwell gazed at her as though she were a bit too willfully inno-cent about the ways and wherefores of what he called "THE white man. That's the one you have to watch, the one with the T-H-E in front. All caps. That article declares his goddam constitution. Three letters. Watch him now. He's the one who makes it bad for all the other white people. He marches mud on their reputations. THE white man. He lives in South Dakota, too. Believe me."

If he was out there, and he might have been, she hadn't met him and her parents hadn't brought him home. Maxwell silently clapped and made the sound of a stadium cheering.

That wasn't funny.

Besides, where she grew up was just a different piece of America. Out there, one could get in on the start of things, come in contact with the origins of the land. You could not have greater fun when you were a kid than riding those Indian ponies with the Lakota young-sters, pretending it was a hundred years ago and the buffalo were still traveling in herds that stretched all the way to where the sky lay against the earth. Nothing had a sadder quality than the alcoholism that did these first Americans in slowly the way the wicked interstate highways finished off so many drunken white kids swiftly. Sometimes the funerals came as though a plague was upon that South Dakota earth. But, in general, they just lived American lives out there.

Maxwell laughed and teased her when she said that, but he wasn't then the kind of guy who would try to make you feel smaller by pulling out a scroll of atrocities that he had seen or heard about. He said one thing, "Indian reservations," then switched the subject, declaring that he didn't want to argue, even lightly, about some place he hadn't been to, didn't grow up in, and cared about only because someone he loved with all his heart had come from there. He knew that when he was a kid, for all the good, good times he had, playing athletic games, enlarging his mind through learning, diving deeper and deeper into the bell of the saxophone, chasing girls and discover-ing how to get them out of their panties, there had always been a feeling of being all by himself, a feeling as wide as those plains Carla told him of every so often. He knew it wasn't loneliness because he wasn't neglected; he wasn't unpopular among the kids; he got as much pussy—uh, had sex—as anybody else; they loved him in the church. It was all going on just fine. But loneliness is what it was and it was wide. The answer he had to the loneliness he felt as a kid, and could still feel as a man, arrived in the saxophone more than any-thing else.

As Maxwell got up and went to the bathroom, Carla sat back in the first-class Amtrak seat of the club car wondering if they should have spent this much money going down to Washington just because it was a private car, comfortable, the food was far, far better, and you got service. Well, that was her man. Mom would never have put up with the kind of spending Maxwell did if Dad—who was a full-blooded Norwegian Scrooge—had tried that. Mom loved quality but was rather austere. The best whenever you can get it, but never excess. She always had disdain for the rich who were too showy, but even more contempt for those who couldn't afford it but strained to give the appearance of doing much better than they actually were *when everybody knew exactly where they were on the financial scale anyway, since whispers about loans and second mortgages and drunken outbursts about spendthrift ways moved in concentric circles of gossip around those who lived too far beyond their means. Well, that might have been well and good for Mom but —*

Maxwell sat down beside her, took her hand, and kissed it. There were a bunch of college kids on the train headed back down to Washington, he said, some of them Africans, some Asian. His thoughts about race didn't exclude her then. Or anybody else. Not really.

Her man had heard somebody say that America grew up with the Industrial Revolution and that niggers grew up with America and with machinery, which was what made them different from other black people. They were central to the making of their part of the Western world. They weren't strangers in the modern village; they helped design it, create its personality, influence its laws and all of that, how people laughed and danced and everything. Niggers were not just some colonials way the fuck away from the mother country that was exporting one or two raw materials and already had an identity. The Negro was all up in it. That's why all this "one black people" is truly some bullshit; it's just a way for black people who aren't up to date niggers to neutralize the way American niggers stuck their thumb in the ground and turned the world around. They want to reduce us to them, outsiders, Johnny-come-lately nappy-headed motherfuckers. What were these other black motherfuckers doing when niggers over here were inventing couplers for trains and traffic lights and developing blood plasma and inventing ragtime and all of that? They might have been doing something but they wasn't doing **that** *fucking much. It wasn't that they were inferior or anything like that,* **nobody** *was inferior. That's some* **very** *stupid ego shit to think like that.* **Very** *stupid. It was just that the world they were in didn't have those kinds of possibilities.*

This was a point Kelvin Thomson told him and he had only read it somewhere, not thought of it himself, but it still made sense to Maxwell. We're all mixed up with each other over here. Black, white, Indian, Mexican, and whatever else you got. Europe is just now getting like that, with all those unwelcome guest workers. They got a long way to go. They'll get there. That's inevitable. But the first modern black person is from here, not from over there. We don't need to look up to **nobody**—not in Europe, not in Africa, not in the Caribbean, not in South America, not in Asia or Australia or any fucking place on the face of the goddam earth. Oh, no. But niggers, whoa, niggers over here now, these goddam niggers, these all-day suckers, these chumps on the run, oh, my Lord, my Lord, these niggers are **always** looking for bullshit backup. Bullshit. Backup. Naive and wrong as the day is long, niggers in the NAACP even got the white folks to break down the preferential American immigration laws. Oh, yeah. Broke them down. Now all these other Third Worlders that used to be shut out of this country come over here looking down on **us!** Everything we get, they're **supposed** to get because of being some kind of nigger or some kind of near-nigger or maybe even, by not being white, a **cousin** of a nigger on the racism scale. Is that the meanest hustle of all time or what? See, that's what happens when you get tired of kissing **white** ass and **decide** to kiss black ass. You end up tied up in a trick by your own rhetorical bullshit.

Don't blow a gasket, sweetheart. This country is crazy and always has been crazy. But it's so crazy you have to be in love with it. It just so happens that we're Americans, and an American is a human being way out on a limb, looking for something. Who knows, babe? This decade, the next one, maybe a hundred years from now, this is going to be a better place to live. It just might take a whole lot of our bones in the ground before that can happen. The observation tower that lets you see the greatest distance is always made of rib cages, femurs, skulls, vertebrae, and the rest of those skeletons.

Damn, Carla.

My mom used to say that, and she was right. Oh, I don't know. It's all going to get mixed up and get better. You know that. So, as far as these immigrants go, I mean who the hell can expect somebody coming into America to be sane when they get so many maps to the nuthouse as soon as they get here?

He laughed softly, actually snickering with a conspiratorial charm.

It's wack, sweetheart, but it's still wonderful. I couldn't have met you anywhere else. My God, my God, what I would have missed if I had been born in Norway and grown up there. I might be married. I might have children. But I wouldn't have my man.

She couldn't keep from kissing him and he didn't deny her an abundant hug. She liked it like that. Really liked it.

*They let the seats back and gazed out the train window for a while, Maxwell sipping on some beer, Carla enjoying her white wine and the rhythm of the train, which she never failed to recognize as such a central influence on the blues and on jazz. She could hear it in any station and in any seat: that unplanned rattle, those shakes, the metal wheels rolling on the metal tracks, that iron horse, which told those Indians—as if these primal giants of the range were soaking wet and spoken to by a cold wind—that the jig was up; the mean fireman and the cruel engine, cruel engine, engineer, the mean old fireman and the cruel engineer represented the Empire State Express. Carla knew the turth of all that. She had read the history of her part of the country and had listened to Dad talk about it both during family camping trips and when he sat in the living room or the kitchen making the land come alive with the brand of intensity men like Son House brought to the blues. So she knew what a doggone train would do. It was a vehicle of destruction, of escape, of delivery, of farewell. Those galling railroad boys traveled and worked on the metal bones of John Henry, the rails themselves and the old wood-burning and coal-burning locomotives symbolizing the noisy and cloudy disruption of the Indian Nations that got their revenge and rebuilt themselves not on dysentery from water and food south of the Mexican border but through millions felled by lung cancer from the gift of tobacco to the white man and the yearly untaxed billions gleaned from the contemporary casinos in which white folks lost their shirts, their underwear, their cars, their homes, and their families to the red-faced demon of chance. Those galling railroad boys they could get you out of Mississippi and up to Chicago real quick. Sure the hell could. But the Empire State Express—**any** Empire State Express—chugging and lugging and hootie-hoot-owl howling all kinds of smokestack lightning, any old precision-engineered train, any one that was traveling where it was traveling, each of them had that thing about it that an evil piece of machinry would get so lowdown dirty and **do**, which was take your sweet, sweet baby and huff that smoke right black at you. Yes, right **black** at you. Those big skies out where Carla had grown into late adolescence, those wide heavens that had watched even her as she left for Chicago, those expansions of firmament had seen plenty. All she said to him, pointing out the window, was that the skies of America had seen plenty.*

Maxwell agreed.

We lived another thing. Tricked up, mixed up, and fucked up. It was like your people, Carla; they come from cowboy country. Now what is that?

Farming country, actually.

Anyway, they fought Indians out there. They had those badlands, too. Sam Bass and them motherfuckers. I'm a buff on this shit. You seen all of those books I got on the West. They didn't call me the Kid once upon a time for nothing. I know some of that story.

Funny, I never think of the badlands as part of back home.

Mighty white of you, he joked, and she smiled, her entire personality caught up in that curve of lips and teeth.

Maxwell could be so much fun and carry all of the stuff with such a light touch. He really had it together then and made Carla experience the bitter goodness of his memory and feeling, even when he didn't care to have all of the facts right, which was odd, given how precisely he wanted to command each aspect of his music. What could you say? People weren't coherent. They had their sensibilties and their inclinations and you either got with them or didn't care to or turned your back on the whole mess and went looking for something that made life feel better in the way that you wanted it to feel better. As could happen, she had missed some of what he was saying and he hadn't noticed. That was consistent.

So that's cowboy enough for me. I mean a little bitty nigger from Watts riding broncos and bulls and winning him some rodeos? You figure out how he wanted to do that. But what I want to say is, what is a goddam cowboy? Just some white motherfuckers? Not hardly. Obviously. There ain't no fucking cowboys in Europe; there ain't no fucking Indians; no Mexicans coming up with the vaqueros, who was the first cowboys. And, no niggers inventing fancy roping and bulldogging and all that shit. All of those people made the Wild West and the cowboy story. They made it exactly, when it got down to the emotion, exactly like that movie—good, bad, and ugly. The blues. That's what I'm talking about. It's a goulash groove. Hey, Levi Strauss invented the pants. Who can mess with that? Jed Corsakoff said that if a cowboy hates a Jew he needs to remember a Jew is why his ass is so well covered.

They laughed. Jed, as he would surely say, had put it in again.

So what's the deal? Mixed up. The biggest intersection in the world. We still trying to get the story straight. The who's who is missing a lot of pages. It's that T-H-E publishing house. Not to be trusted. In fact, Ezekiel, my daddy, he told me some niggers chased Geronimo's or Vitorio's or some famous Apache all the hot-assed way down into old Mexico and brought the red butcher **back**—**then** *the white people pushed the chocolate drops out of the picture and posed with him like* **they** *had caught him. That was how it was. The music comes from all of that. What I'm playing, what you're singing. All of that. The big intersection. John Lee Hooker called it "the big feeling."*

Maxwell, his eyes radiant with emotion, said that if he had been born two hundred years ago and rich and white and a musical genius, he would never have the satisfaction of blowing a saxophone because there was no saxophone. All of the giants of music from anywhere in the world had their say about the pulse of the human soul, and said some profound things, but if they didn't get here after 1840 they didn't know what it felt like to have a balanced-action Mark VI tenor saxophone under your fingers and a rubber mouthpiece with a personally sanded reed in your mouth making the sound that was your sound.

She looked at him intently as he said that, mostly talking to her in profile.

The sound he made come out of the tenor was a companion and that companion grew along with him. That was the sweet flypaper of the matter, the tar baby, the velvet mousetrap. It caught him good. That tone. As he came to understand things about life better, his tone became more expressive of knowledge, even if it was only a kid's knowledge. Actually, the sound was precocious; it took him places that had no names and no dimensions other than the feeling of the ancient, which meant something that happened more than ten years ago, Maxwell laughed. Whatever it was, that sound gave him a sense of place in the world and it brought with that place dreams of becoming a professional, of getting on out to New York, where all the heavyweights were playing and singing and writing music. As soon as he got out of high school, Maxwell was gone.

God, they were so much alike.

The surprise birthday bash so well calibrated by Leeann was held in a mansion that had been the childhood domicile of a very wealthy woman who was part of D.C. high society and had come from a long line of those people intent at one time on making sure that houses weren't sold to Negroes within certain parameters. The only darkies they wanted to see were the statues of the jockeys holding the addresses of their homes way out in horse country. Well, actually, it wasn't quite that bad. There was also work for the living ones who spent time either in the servant quarters out there or did their duty within the capital city, preparing come the morning to meet the demands of the rituals and the whims that went with keeping a big house going and everybody who wasn't black feeling as good as it was possible to make them feel.

The ghosts of old power and the huge portraits of men and women who had done the Republic well and hadn't done themselves badly either were still on the walls of this huge place that Carla now walked through in a dream, holding Ramona by the hand, both of them looking at the walls and the high ceilings, the hardwood floors, the rooms that opened so perfectly one into the other, the back porch that was large enough for a number of tables, and the bountiful lawn on which croquet mallets had struck balls that rolled through wickets during the summer parties. At such events, there were all the white ladies in big hats and the spiritual lace of unbanked privilege, the pink or chalky girls with ribbons in their hair and the men in bright ties, July blazers, tan britches, and straw boaters, punch of some sort in their hands, the females wondering how powerful the men they were to marry would become, the young guys inhabited by dreams of how they should live up to what was expected of them or, seriously caught on the barbed wire of ineptitude, these guys just now out of college by virtue of a fix, an academic inside job, were full of the fear that they would be discovered as men worthy of nothing more than the special inheritances measured nearly to the penny and intended to keep them far enough above the middle class to solidly disguise their fundamental mediocrity. No one—definitely not these two Norwegian girls from South Dakoka—would ever know just how many jokes had been told in these environs or how many lies or to what degree the truth had been stretched for the purposes of entertainment or the exact details and emotional contours of the affairs initiated so that the force of life would have some purpose other than to carry a body from here to there and there to here.

So there was the incense of sadness inside this estate, a twisted-up set of human energies that didn't haunt but spoke of how much generation after generation had overestimated the stationary meanings of entitlement. Those meanings weren't necessarily so clear until the dust kicked up by programmatic happiness settled and refused, like the blues, to move on down the way. So much of it was like the saddle soap that was applied to the riding boots, not to mention the laundering, the careful ironing of the pants, the tailored jackets, the caps, the saddles, the riding crops, the dogs and all the galloping noise that went into pursuing the fox until that panting streak of burnt orange or auburn and white fur was cornered and reduced, after all, to a sticky scruff of blood and pelt. This nasty leftover was nobody's trophy, which meant that it was all hopped-up pomp, nothing less and surely nothing more.

Women standing nude before their full-length mirrors and watching their powdered bodies sag into time knew that as well as they knew what each minute of labor had felt like as they suffered to deliver their children. Men, recalling what had been the thrill of all that was now tedious, were equally aware of just how many things had to be put in place so that full moons wouldn't encourage madness or reveal the nightly meltdowns of spirit that had begun with the early deaths of siblings or of children or of favorite friends and relatives.

Every last unexpected demise was proof, no matter how beautifully restrained the funeral services were, that neither you nor anyone else could say exactly why the pressure of life would never relent in its war against these cultivated souls that so fiercely shuddered and were never ever able to successfully hide behind the witty conversations with the servants, the latest bits of gossip, the new sailboats, the trips to Europe, the gatherings of diplomats, the clubs, the private planes, the impositions of will and strategy on the politicians who ran the town and the world. Alone before the light or the darkness, each one of them knew that something charged with the glory of all answers was neither his nor hers to have.

Well, there was something else lined up now.

Carla and Ramona, caught up in a Manhattan singer's fantasy, were inside with Maxwell and everybody else when Cecelia came in the door behind Leeann, expecting to drop by a stuffy gathering with her cousin for a drink before they went on to dinner. At the collective shout of "Surprise," there was a presence of feeling that came from her which was so precise Carla could see just the way Cecelia had been so many years ago at the point when she was the little copper-colored girl who discovered affection as something unexpected but knew it was, always, out there somewhere.

On the staircase, dressed as if ready for class in their white tops and black pants or black skirts, were all the kids from her school who could sing. The musical director was lean, dark, with a shaved head rising on a long neck above a tuxedo outfitted with kente cloth tie and matching cummerbund. A diamond earring sparkled from his left lobe as he raised his hands and led this choir into a loud and richly harmonized version of "Happy Birthday" that was joined by all of the assembled.

As Cecelia stood there twitching and crying, other students brought her bouquet upon bouquet of flowers. A stuffed purple velvet chair fit for a queen was carried in and she was seated with a crown of orchids placed on her head. The choir then was led into "Lift Every Voice and Sing," which was followed by "Go Down, Moses."

"Okay, cuz, I know we don't need all of these people here to let you know how we feel about you, but we have them anyway. I put the word out and somebody gave me a special list and I said they couldn't come if they didn't love my cousin as much as I do. Some of these people started acting like they loved you **more** than I do. Ain't that a blip? Now that's something I can't hardly believe, but you have obviously touched a whole heap of folks down here in this town of plentiful potholes and capital disasters. Oops, I didn't say that, did I? Can't take me anywhere. Got to be like that. Anyway, Cecelia, this is a gathering of love. Now we know nobody knows what the heck love really means but we do know it makes you want to be nice to somebody and everybody here wants to be nice to you."

Leeann hugged her cousin and began crying herself. Then, standing straight with her eyes looking smeared, she gestured to the servers of the party.

"Bring forth the champagne! Take one glass apiece now. I said **one** glass! Good. Lift that crystal in celebration of this woman whom I have known since I was a girl and have admired all of these long years. They might come a whole lot worse but they cannot, under any circumstances, even approach coming any better than my cousin. Not in this world. Happy birthday, baby."

The party was filled with all kinds of people from Washington, D.C. Cecelia seemed to know everybody. There were bellmen, firemen, cops, lawyers, teachers, architects, cooks, restaurant owners, plumbers, beauticians, writers, politicians, actors, dancers, painters, computer whizzes, clothing designers, mailmen, cabdrivers, choreographers, barbers, and just about any kind of somebody you could name, with the exception of the kinds of hustlers that Ramona **said** were the only kinds of people she had encountered while serving her hard time in this town. Had Leeann mistakenly invited any people like that, Cecelia would surely have pitched a bitch and had them thrown out, or would have, as she once said, "put my titty on her titty and motherfucked that baby shit-colored heifer all the way out the goddam door," referring to a teacher at her school who had spoken far too disparagingly of some of the kids because they were either dark-skinned or from backgrounds "just too poor for her."

This wasn't that kind of party. The feeling of light-skin privilege was definitely not in the air. Further, few of those in the house were white. At least, they wouldn't have called themselves white, though it would have been impossible to pull them out of a crowd for the high crimes and misdemeanors of blurring racial lines. In that dream of seeing them all so clearly in the company of her sister, Carla and Ramona wouldn't have been able to tell that such people weren't what was considered white. This fact made the girl from South Dakota wonder to her man just how many influential people in the history of the country's racial story might have been "passing" for white, using their skin tones as passports into social stations of imposing influence.

"Now that," Maxwell laughed, "is really funny. That's actually a bitch of an idea. What the fuck? All these white folks reaching down to help out the niggers and getting patted on the back and all kinds of invisible niggers hiding out in their blood and falling out of their faces on the floor and running around in the room making fun of **all** this shit. I think you called that one, Carla. Me, I used to think about that another way because, you know, I'll tell you a serious secret. Sometimes that hair between the legs of those kinds of women is a little **too** nappy to be from a pure line of white folks. Mm-hm. That would *mean that the kinds of white men who* **know** *about all of that, they could be having some big fun on the illicit side. Oh, yeah. They probably get a kinky little thrill from the fact that they're lying down in the Alps and the jungle at the same time. Hey. Yeah. Check this out. You're an imaginative person. I know you can see this one. Just think of one of those rich crackers from old Virginia. It's the nighttime, it's the right time to investigate the tight and slippery element. It's time to get* **all** *the way down. He's made his midnight creep and there he is in the saddle, sweating and sweating, with his face turning cherry red. Old massa about to come on home, his ass sucking wind and him howling, 'Hannibella! Hannibella! ' "*

With the memory of that night taking on ever-greater clarity in the Manhattan apartment above Big Little Joe's, the colors in her eyes, the air on her skin, and the feeling of the grass under her feet, Carla wished so much more deeply that Ramona could have been there laughing with her, Leeann, and Maxwell as they assessed the gathering. All right. No matter. She was not about to be straddled, once more, by her disappointment.

So in this wide-awake dream about that great Washington party, her big sister **was** *standing right there as Maxwell sang, imitating Jimmy Rushing while Leeann had her smoke out in the soft, late May night air, thirty yards or so from the tables on the veranda of the mansion, where the kids from the Excellence Academy had their ice cream and cake after wearing out the catered Ethiopian food, a favorite of Cecelia's, which was served by those North African people who look like no other human beings on the face of the earth.*

Enjoying their dessert, the kids were taunting and charming each other, some bragging about how that Ethiopian hot sauce didn't scare them off like it did you all, others talking of the wonders they had seen in this house where somebody used to really live and stuff, you know, with this big old backyard and all of those rooms upstairs and the huge kitchen and all of that space with these grown people walking around. Some of the kids were saying they would have even **bigger** *houses when they got through with school, and others said you mean you going to be* **cleaning** *houses this big, and on it went.*

"All right now, here we go. This is the right one. This is the perfect rag on the nighttime and the right time. Let's call this 'The Plantation Tom Cat Blues,' " Maxwell said, patting his foot in a very sensual tempo:

Oh, Hannibella Lee, oh, Hannibella Lee,
Come down here and do the nasty with me!
Hannibella Lee, oh, Hannibella Lee,
Get on down here and do the nasty with me!
Oh, I might be light, oh, I might be white,
But when you feel this johnson, you will know that I'm right.
Mmmm.
Hannibella Lee, mmm, Hannibella Lee, mmm.
Please come on down and do the nasty with me.

Leeann, of course, was dancing as close as she could to the moves of a hoochie-coochie girl while not being too far out to draw the kind of attention to the lewd that Cecelia would have found abominable in front of the kids from the academy, who were, still, looking over at her with curiosity, too polite to laugh but also puzzled as Maxwell continued to invent more and more verses that must have sounded like muttering from that distance.

After a couple of choruses, Carla found herself beginning to sing backup harmony to Maxwell and trying to keep from laughing as she thought of a note to hit with the one she could feel he was about to sing. Something happened between them at that moment, the comedy blues and accompaniment to Leeann then turning a corner so suddenly and with such subtlety that the both of them were now talking to each other and planning the caresses that would arrive when they were in their suite at the Willard Hotel, her harmonic choices and his melody line foreshadowing in their invisibility that three-dimensional moment of actual love, the point at which a woman could experience the touch of power in an uncharacteristic way.

While the female orgasm was supposed to be a number of times more intense than the male's, Cecelia had said once to Carla that there was much more to what women knew about the orgasm that arrived **right** with all kinds of squishy rocking and rolling. They knew that when a man **loved** you he used all of his power **for** you, so you came in contact with male force absolutely untainted by negative bullshit and abuse and all of the fear that went with getting touched *the wrong way by the wrong person for the wrong reason. Once a man put the motion of that fire into you with the finesse that symbolized just how much he felt **for** you—all the empathy that put sweet blisters on your soul—you could never **ever** stop wanting to experience the right masculine rhythm of **that**.*

Every waking day, Carla thought about that at least one time since Cecelia had said it to her. Power *for* instead of *against,* what an idea and, best of the best, what a feeling when it was going on and you were receiving the same intensity of force, sweetened, that those who took the blows of domestic violence suffered in all their bludgeoning bitterness. She often flipped that in her mind like a coin when she was listening to Doreen Gopstein or any other ardent and brilliant feminist. They were right about a whole heap of things, but *that* part they never, *ever,* got. There were, however, things they would have something to say about. Carla, chuckling, recalled that she dreamed once of the political consequences following a conversation she had with Leeann about fellatio in which her friend took the seasoned position that uncircumcised johnsons were more enjoyable because their heads had a silky texture that the other ones didn't. In the dream, word had gotten out to Doreen Gopstein, who instantly organized a movement called KIO, or Keep It On, which resulted in a manifesto declaring that male circumcision, now revealed, functioned, with the far more terrible female circumcision, as part of an overall affront to the sexual pleasure of women, and that men, always trying to give women the short end of everything, were so well aware of this that the whole supposedly hygienic reason for the clipping off of foreskins had sinister, even sadistic, intentions. Outside of New York Hospital, Doreen and her friends, carrying signs which read "Don't Take It Off," "Off Is Oppression," and "Don't Dare Cut It," were arrested, chanting, with dignity, "Give Me Some Skin, Give Me Some Skin," as they were hauled off. Carla, now belly-laughing and enjoying her wine as much as she was hating her insomnia, went back to Washington, D.C., on the Memory Express.

Kelvin Thomson, flown over from Paris as a special treat, was giving a toast to Cecelia and everyone was gathering back inside. His shoes were red, his silk pants with three thin shining stripes cobalt blue, his dress shirt eggshell, his dinner jacket white, his bow tie red. He stood on the step that separated the front of the house from the large, sunken gathering room that evolved the other side of the windows into the red brick veranda. The big arch of a front door now a backdrop, Cecelia a few feet from him, and everybody looking his way, with some of the smaller kids frustratedly trying to see through all of those people, Kelvin Thomson spoke, his champagne glass something Carla thought he could hold in place, somehow dive into, with his entire body other than the hand and the wrist disappearing down into the stem, then return, bone dry, his feet coming down on the floor in a one-two accent, the glass empty and a priceless calm over his face as he wiped his mouth with his sleeve and said, "Ah!" Were Ramona actually there, Carla couldn't have explained that to her big sister in any way, shape, or fashion. Just one of those weird things that went through your mind. She wasn't telling Maxwell either. Too many cartoons during childhood. What a back flip in time.

"We are always looking for something good to say about something out here in the world. We don't always get much of a chance. But this here is a goody. This chance is fat. We all know how great this woman is and we are all happy to be able to use a word like 'great' and not be even close to exaggeration. She knows how to hold on. You can't make her back up. What she wants to do will be done. This woman is a maker of manners. People who come into her realm will learn how to believe in the wonder of being human. She is willing to bleed the blood, to sweat the sweat, to cry the tears. It is always hard for us to believe that a woman this beautiful, so fine all the time, could be so sweet and work so hard and have so much heart, but— what can you say?—some people are able to live up to their looks. As the Italians say, 'May you live a hundred years.' "

Both Carla and Maxwell heard his words the way two lovers on a dance floor absorb the tango emotion that makes them a magnificent beast of four legs and two backs and two heads and four eyes and four ears and four arms, tied together by the golden notes that gleam inside them and outside them, the invisible bow of emotion that is music seemingly tailor-made for a broiling pair of souls gone home to the house that is close, close dance.

Cecelia, all heated formality, briefly embraced her man and, still laboring under the shyness uncovered by all of the affection she was being shown, could say nothing, only kiss each of her hands with meditative intensity, then wave with an encompassing gesture to all the assembled, much like one of those women lifting an arm in church during a passage of the sermon that took her far the other side of words.

What she saw looking at Cecelia was turned in another direction by a sound that welled up inside her at the same time that it came into her ears. The kids who could sing were now being led through "Deep River," Carla feeling each note and living each interval as another pure reiteration of her unstated belief that the impersonal beauty in nature could only be equaled by the aesthetic forms given to the human heart.

The way those cadets sang that song for Cecelia gave Carla the same spiritual smooch and instant condition of gooseflesh she got when the recording of "Just One Of Those Things" with Billie Holiday and Ben Webster clarified for her what she would do in music— the time on the bus coming back from West Texas when she was dead tired and full of sadness because the sound of any version of country music had nothing to do with her and everything decided upon over the last couple of years had been absolutely wrong for a certain girl from South Dakota. Her feet hurt terribly, she yearned for a long, long bath, the food throughout the bus trip had been bad, but the grandeur of the landscape held its own and spoke to her in the silent way that images do when one is so far down anything suggesting the lovely feels like a gang of giant steps upward.

The sound she had started trying to make come out of her body in Nashville and gave up on in El Paso was behind her, along with all the Southern and Southwestern feeling that had been baked in the tropical part of the nation or out in the dry cattle and oil country that so often gave over to huge stretches of nothing other than land. Why she had tried to get into that made no sense to her as she sat with her face absorbing the outdoors while holding a cheap little portable radio to her ear and listening to whatever came on, mostly static and garbage.

Then she heard those two musicians, that little female voice and that big tenor sound, as the bus crossed into that zone where the transmitting was clear as you could ever want it. Her eyes smarted because, after so much defeat, Carla knew there was a place in sound for her. Just for her. There was no doubt at all. Snap. She was then awakened on that bus ride and less tired but no less sad, aware that a change was waiting for her and one that she, like any singer, would have to make happen by becoming strong enough to deserve whatever you got.

Watching the kids assembled once more on that staircase in Washington and looking at the movements of the choir director made her wonder what position Holiday's body was in and how Webster held his horn while those notes came out. As always with music truly expressed, the physicality of the singing kids varied itself so that, upon looking at how these children heard the beat, this one or that one or another seemed to be in front of, behind, standing on, alongside, and under every note—pushed by the pitch, trying to catch up with it, lifted by it, leaning a head on its shoulder, looking at it just above his or her head and following purely celestial instructions.

Carla, Maxwell, Leeann, Cecelia, and Kelvin Thomson, all in need of some further celebratory libations, went over to the bar at the Willard after everything was done, each man, woman, and child personally told goodbye by the guest of honor, the serving staff thanked, and the mountain of presents packed up. The Willard was only a few blocks from the White House, and when Ulysses Grant was president, those wishing political favors would descend on him in the hotel's lobby, hence the term lobbyists. Maxwell always wanted them to stay in the Grant Suite but Carla never let him go that far out of economic line. But she would have liked to be in there, too. How did it look, since the smaller suites she held her man down to were so marvelous? It must have been something. There had been a time or two in Washington when they were there together and she had lain awake at night wondering what that suite was like as she went through her satin and patent leather fantasies about the two of them going all the way to the top, where money was no object and where they had maintained, somehow, the integrity that both believed so essential to making the same kind of music that had touched them when they had come to understand exactly what kind of human business it was that defined each of them. She knew she was being silly, but what American girl of her generation hadn't been imprinted by the 1930s world through which Fred and Ginger danced, the comedy, the romance, and the fire all resolved in that universe of fantasy privi-

lege made real by those breathtaking duets, every one televised on the Million Dollar Movie when she was a child and never missed by the King and Queen in Carla's household. That was why one of the songs she sang with the most feeling was "Cheek to Cheek," meeting the challenge of its two bridges as she improvised and finding a way to pull the yearning of mythology together with the real grit of the swing that her musicians would lay down when everybody was up off their asses and getting to where the blue heart of the down-home-in-the-soul matter truly was. All right now.

Ramona would have liked the Willard and had her own dreams there, thought her own thoughts about what she had accomplished if she were there and couldn't sleep, but it would have been hard for her to get into partying with Carla's friends on that night. The little sister couldn't imagine her enjoying the company and opening her heart to them. No, she couldn't. That was pretty final. But had Ramona been able to do that, maybe it would have changed her way of thinking about all of this. Getting up and walking to the toilet, Carla sat there in the dark as she relieved herself, angry and confused again. Had Ramona a peculiar capacity for this kind of xenophobic and cult thinking? Maybe. Well. Don't stop there. You can't get by with that. Carla then asked herself if she was somehow the guilty party. Could she have been so self-absorbed all these years that such elements of the emotional mix that was Ramona padded by unnoticed because the little sister had headphones on blasting her narcissism so loudly that she *never* heard the spiritual limp of her big sister? She flushed the toilet, her face now hot, her cheeks fluttering. No. No. Not quite. There was something snaky in there. Very snaky. There was the question of whether Ramona *actually* thought the way she so adamantly claimed she did. Let's look at that a little bit, dearie. She might just be another one of those weak women ruled by the openings between their legs and the desire to have somebody love them so badly that all home training, all morality, all reason is given a stiff kick in the pants. So step the fuck off. All of that stuff about guns and that bravado could have just been a front, couldn't it? Yes, a front for an insecure woman who had finally been wooed the right way when she was in the mood to be wooed. Hadn't she actually made it sound that way? Sure the hell had. She could be that way. That was possible. But maybe she actually was the brazen racist bitch she presented herself as. Oh, God, Ramona.

*At the Willard Hotel, Leeann, refusing to let anybody else spend **any** money, announced, Hattie McDaniel style, that everything was on her and that if anybody didn't like it, she would never speak to them again in life. Everyone laughed at the way she made fun, as she loved to, of the bossy servant image, which was one of the things she told Carla had been on her mind when she was becoming as sophisticated as she could: "I decided when I was a little girl and my mother would bring me magazines home from the white folks she worked for. I knew which way I was going. She couldn't give me anything but love and dreams, what with my daddy killed out there gathering that goddam tobacco before I could even remember him. He must have been something. It didn't matter what anybody else said. I could tell by the way my mother called his name, girl. He was some kind of man. Then when m'dear subscribed to **Jet** and **Ebony** and I saw Negroes with some money and traveling all over the world—besides getting lynched and shit—I was clear on what Leeann was going to do. I was going to study my way up out of the South, take flight on the wings of English literature, but the flashbulbs got me and I'll never be the same again."*

Leeann ordered the bar's best champagne and, at his prompting, an Irish whiskey chaser for Kelvin Thomson, which Cecelia clearly did not like but which Maxwell diverted tension from by asking for one himself. Carla did not want Maxwell to get drunk and would have to figure out a way to make sure that he didn't try to keep up with Cecelia's man, which would leave the girl from South Dakota with a breathing corpse up in their suite once he used all of his strength to get to the elevator, remain standing as it rose, put one foot in front of the other, hand her the card key so that the door could be opened in less than ten minutes, then, while making some grand statement, pass out and hit the bed like a falling sequoia.

After toasting the birthday girl, Maxwell had some questions about the school itself and so did Carla, which Cecelia rather proudly spoke of in detail, beginning with why she had those kids learning the music that they sang. It was all part of her philosophy. Maxwell—who had *grown up just as the comet of great rhythm and blues passed across the sky in the best of Motown and in the Philadelphia Sound—was extremely disgusted with popular music at large and had been so for over a decade. He felt that joy was the real rebellion since life was nobody's mink-covered stairs. The anger and disruption in popular music got on his nerves, not to mention the exceedingly low level of the musicianship. He had even come to conclude that Negroes were themselves becoming such Xeroxes of third-rate definitions that their soul power, on a mass musical level, had been drained off. This made him angry and irritable when he thought of it, but seeing all of those kids coming in the right musical door at her birthday party made Maxwell wonder if Cecelia was thinking the same kind of thing.*

She was.

Songs like "Deep River" were sung because part of Cecelia's idea about the Excellence Academy—EA to you—was that all of these children had to be reminded not only of who they were but of what living meant at its best. Those Negro spirituals arrived from a time when black people were more in touch with the spirituality of their culture and of life itself. Now niggers didn't even have a spiritual position in the culture. From a cultural perspective, they now took their position next to, or below, the crudest Jews and Italians. They represented the most crass kind of materialism with their gold chains and their gold teeth and their obsession with brand names, like one fool who called himself Travesty Ex-Lax because, as he said, "I pumps out all the shit and all my shit turns to gold, yo."

Carla, intending to let everyone know that she, too, was well aware of what was happening, recalled to the assembled how she and Maxwell had been looking at a televised pop music awards show. One of the winners was something else. Jimmy Wham and the Ho Flow. This rapping Wham did a number called "Bust That Boody" before accepting his award. The loud and static energy of the performance immediately alienated Carla because the mood was so masturbatory it had none of the communal emotion of art. Focused purely on himself, a human flame concerned with nothing other than his own burning, Wham did some kind of aggressively spastic dancing comprised of twisting and turning and going into splits. His six light-skinned backup girls—the Ho Flow—all had their hair dyed in three shiny colors—crimson, emerald, and black. They wore see-through outfits with neon pasties over their nipples and panties. Rolling their eyes and lewdly sucking their thumbs, the yellow girls of the Ho Flow were constantly turning their abundant cabooses to the camera and grinding them against the air. The leader concluded his act as they formed a semicircle around him and chanted, over and over, "I got to bust, got to bust, got to bust that boody." He humped the floor with mounting force while the Ho Flow moved as though each of the girls was in bed and having sex. At the peak of humping fury, the award winner let out a howl so loud it seemed as if he had achieved the climax of the century. Absolutely still, our boy lay flat on the stage as the Ho Flow bowed. Rising in one snaky motion, his body polished with sweat, Jimmy Wham came to the microphone, his gold rope chain dangling long from his neck and the diamonds in his nose ring, in his earrings, and on his fingers glittering. He grinned gold and diamonds, took a bow, then his voice suddenly soft and nearly humble, Wham said to the audience that he wanted to thank his moms, his pops, and, most of all—

—his merciful Lord: Jesus Christ! Maxwell interjected with a tone of repulsion, disbelief, and embittered satire.

The laughter and head-shaking were immediate.

I guess these up-to-date decadent darkies put a hole in the gut-bucket of your theory about the blues people and the sacred and the profane, **don't** they, Mr. Kelvin Thomson? Leeann asked with an emotion that pushed a very thin blade of defeat up through the comic timbre of her question.

I think you're right, he answered as if he were a priest who had lived every second by the Word of God for decades, but had come to be so overwhelmed by the density and the speed of evil that the idea of an invincibly moral supreme being was now enough to make him retch.

Quiet took over the table. It was dark with the blood of silver-bearded illusions bashed against the wall until their heads cracked wide open and what were once the sources of thought became no more than a putrid yield ready to be scooped out by the curved beaks of scavengers.

Yeah, like she already said, it was pretty bad out there, but Cecelia, trying to change the mood, declared that it wasn't about losing your memory just because somebody else did. Being quiet isn't enough.

Somebody got to tell. She recalled how those songs, those spirituals, used to open up the sky when she was a girl. They might not have been somebody but they told. There was something ancient in those notes, she said, almost gulping down her champagne. From way back before way back, beyond Africa or anyplace else. Those notes put you in touch with the touching place. Kids attending the Excellence Academy would, therefore, sing them.

Still on point, Carla wondered if the day would arrive when all of these Negroes who had become wealthy in the most abominable ways would have to, as had so many others who rose from the mud in filthy ways, face a hellfire of wrath from an unexpected direction.

Maxwell asked her what she meant.

Well, perhaps the same fate awaited the gangster rappers and their record producers that had awaited so many of the rapacious pluto-crats and the ethnic gangsters—the Irish, the Italians, the Jews. The very worst of the industrialists were neither shy about destroying the environment nor brutally breaking strikes, while the organized or dis-organized thugs hustled every illicit commodity in order to achieve prosperity and murdered whenever it was coldly considered neces-sary. Perhaps these gangster-rapping Negroes would become one with they of the upper crust and the underworld who, on some merci-less day, found that their children, spiritually nauseated by the deeds of their parents, were absolutely ashamed of them and wanted noth-ing to do with what they represented or how they had made their bloody fortunes.

Maybe so, said Leeann, since niggers were **always** running a fast last to everybody else when it came to getting over. But, after all, cor-ruption is old as the devil rapping Adam and Eve out of paradise. Maybe, she went on, the whole story of niggers was just the story of how it went in America if you robbed your way to riches. You started off trying to be good, built a considerable reputation for being good in face of all kinds of obstacles and prejudice, then got corrupted, **enjoyed** being corrupted, rose to power on corruption, became guilty, took up philanthropy, and, Lord, dear Lord, hoped down on your knees every single night that your kids didn't know what a dog-assed motherfucker you had been on the way up. It could be some kind of American cycle, yeah.

Carla, getting back to the subject of the academy, was surprised to *see the children so neat, since schoolkids today usually had such bad taste it was comical when you saw them. One bakery she and Maxwell loved to go to on Bleecker Street because of its cranberry bread had a girl working there whose hair was shaved off except for a circular thatch on the top. She had one arm tattooed almost entirely blue, piercings everywhere, and filthy teeth, but she shaved under her arms!*

Cecelia said that kids might do that kind of stuff on their own time but not on hers and not at her school. There would be no weird clothes at the academy. Her school separated itself from empty-headed popular trends and Cecelia wanted to make sure that the kids knew that, however they might carry themselves after they got home. Boys would be gentlemen, not street-corner jerks. Girls would wear no lipstick and no makeup. They were girls, not hoochies. Everything great that had ever been taught and could be communicated in a reasonable fashion would be part of the curriculum, kindergarten to twelfth grade. You had to get them at the start and hold on until they left for the world.

How did you get your kids in?

Well, the academy didn't take just anybody. It was run like a private school but was actually a public school that parents got their kids into through a lottery.

It was right in the middle of run-down D.C., but the gangbangers and the others had come to learn that they would have to give the kids who went there a wide berth or that crazy-assed woman who ran the school would be out there in their faces, leading posses of mothers and grandmothers demanding that those corners be given up. The fucking bitch. Somebody should bust a cap in her ass. But if somebody did send her to the graveyard world of St. Dusty and got seen, well, the ho was liked too much and a snitch would send your ass all the way down. Fuck her and fuck her school and fuck everybody going to it. There's plenty of D.C. They can have them blocks. Bitch-assed motherfuckers.

Toying with her ivory cigarette holder that was carved like a crocodile, Leeann drew in what reappeared as a wide cloud of smoke and got stone-faced all of a sudden. She told Cecelia that all the good manners and the nice clothes were just fine but she had met plenty of well-groomed white boys and girls who were not worth as much as a piece of flea shit. Leeann knew all about the "gentleman's C" that the best colleges used to give to those dull-brained white boys with money. So what she wanted to know was if those young knotheads had anything throbbing between their temples. What the fuck were they learning, by the goddam way? Were wide country feet kept appropriately deep in their asses?

Reading scores were rising like the Mississippi and the kids were on debate teams, had music classes, and were doing everything that had fallen into disregard when schools became tawdry day care centers staffed by the dull and the lazy. They learned Latin, literature, history, math, science, art, and how to read music. Every kid had to keep a journal and read it to his or her English class on Monday and Thursday. They read a book a week.

How is this whole school set up? Carla wanted to know. She was infatuated with the idea of staking your own claim to education right in the midst of all this madness, poverty, and terror. She couldn't completely repress a certain envy as Cecelia explained how she went about doing her job and laying out a strategy to meet the demands of her task.

Right at the center of Cecelia's design were both the kids and their parents. She had found out that the school had to support the parents because of all that had happened in the world since drugs and teenage pregnancy had worked hand in hand to strangle the civilized nature of the communities. Dope is what destroyed this country, she said. Dope. Getting high. Deranging yourself until you didn't have any sense left.

If the kids had problems, they were usually traceable back to the troubles had by their mothers, such as drunken, drug-using, abusive men. Cecelia stared for a second at Kelvin Thomson, who, upon finishing his Irish whiskey, said, Don't look at me. I don't live in D.C. That drew a laugh from everyone, even a resisting Cecelia, who went on after catching her breath and taking a sip of the champagne.

So there it was. Fine. SOFUS, baby: Same Old Fucked-Up Shit. Well. Then the social services had to be connected to the school so those women could be helped and not get in the way of their children being superbly educated.

This had become most apparent to Cecelia when she couldn't sleep one night and was out walking, her head full of schemes for EA.

You never know, she almost muttered, leaning toward Maxwell, *the time when life is going to put some fresh hickeys on your ass.*

That's right, Maxwell said, *you never do know.*

Why, Carla wondered, was this woman talking to him so intimately all of a sudden? She listened now with a spray of huffiness wafting around inside.

As if waiting for it all to come back into her head, Cecelia was silent for a moment. Then she went on about that sleepless night.

Just wearing some old jeans too comfortable and faded to look good, some dirty white tennis shoes, a crimson scarf over her hair, and a navy sweatshirt, Cecelia felt that freedom only her most private times at night brought, when she was not under the pressure of the promises she had made to herself.

Whistling and humming the verse of "Sleepy Time Down South," her favorite part of the song and the part nobody ever sang, Cecelia turned a corner and saw one of her kids out in the street, which she did not goddam like at all. It was late. The boy was supposed to be at home studying.

Hearing his complete name called out, Roland Ray Beasley turned and faced her upon command, his attempt at getting away nipped. He looked at the ground until she told him to lift his head when she spoke to him and tell her what in the ham sandwich he was doing out in the streets at this hour.

He said nothing.

She asked him if he had lost his hearing.

There was no response. He looked down.

The boy was told that looking at the ground was not an answer in **this** world.

His face was almost blank when he raised his head.

The impassive weight of anger and resentment in Roland Ray's eyes was now visible and something in Cecelia felt smothered and threatened. She knew how to keep her mask up but she felt it all the same. He was a boy but he was still a healthy male and had to be much stronger than she was, what with that solid athletic build. Oh, he was angry. Mad as he could be. So?

He even added some more pissed-off to the bucket of pissed-off she started carrying the moment she saw his not-supposed-to-be-in-the-

streets ass walking into the middle of her late-night sliver of relax-
ation. Moreover, this mediocre-looking teenager actually had the
audacity to act as though he was going to walk away. That was easier
to deal with than the emotion in that boy's eyes. Hell if it wasn't.

She then told the child that she would not let him go wherever it
was that he was going. He had better stand right where he was. This
is serious business right here. He had better not even **think** *about*
leaving. I'm not playing, young man. Further, his mother would have
to know that he was out here and the two of them were going over to
see her right now. This very minute.

He started crying but he was so proud he couldn't look at her but
had to look at her. He almost imperceptibly trembled as if the truth
was so cold it made him shiver. The tears came out alone, not a mum-
bling sound, a whine, a moan. He sucked in his cheeks and stood
there. Then he began to speak.

Roland Ray couldn't talk with any ease, but, horrifying bit by bit,
staring at his twisting foot on the sidewalk as though he was crushing
out a cigarette, with his hands in his pockets and his voice getting
lower and lower, softer and softer, he said to Cecelia what was wrong.

If she was lying, she wished a moon-mad dog would tear out her
throat right now.

Young Beasley was unable to go home and do his studying, the boy
had to stay out in the streets, he couldn't set foot in his house, the
premises were off-limits to him, there was no way he could be there,
his presence was not allowed in that house, because his mother lined
men up, any men interested, and sucked their dicks between six and
midnight every evening to get the money for her drugs.

Oh, my God, Leeann and Carla said almost together as Kelvin
Thomson and Maxwell simultaneously snapped their heads up and
cringed as if a gunshot had been fired in the bar.

Her soul a blast furnace, Cecelia, walking so fast she was almost
running, took the boy home immediately, had him sit on the porch,
went inside, and told the men gathered in that funky house, all of
them laughing and farting and bullshitting, that she ran the Excel-
lence Academy and was boon coon buddies with just enough rough
police to make it very hard for every last one of them to get from
Monday to Tuesday if they didn't stay the hell away from there.

Say what?

I said what I said. I do not have to repeat myself.

*Already low as a snake in wagon tracks because of what he was waiting for, one of those greasy niggers in a dirty old blue cowboy hat had the nerve to look at Cecelia like he was thinking about letting her have one right in the mouth. A big fist busting her right in the teeth. This bitch right in here was so good at sucking dicks he had had to wait awhile and now he got to hear all of this motherfucking bullshit from some goddam fucking schoolteaching bitch with her ass all the way up on her shoulders and her mouth full of fuck you motherfuckers. Fuck yeah, she needs her ass whipped **good**. She needs the **shit** kicked out of her. She needs some bones **broken**. Begging for this stomping to **please** stop is what she needs to be doing. That's what he was thinking. He wasn't trying to hide it either. His eyes were red and his grease-spotted white clothes smelled like they were woven on a loom of corruption.*

*Looking straight at him and lifting her head to an even more contemptuous angle, Cecelia said if that was not enough, she would come down there every night—nine-millimeter-**strapped** if necessary—to take pictures of one and all in order to make sure that whoever they were and wherever on God's earth they came from, their wives and families and employers and whoever else would find out how they entertained themselves.*

They scattered, like the roaches we have been told will survive a nuclear holocaust.

Aw, Leeann laughed, Cecelia, you lying, girl. Ain't nothing like that near to happened. You just want us to think you're some kind of St. Louis woman turned into Joan of Arc. She then burst into song about that St. Louis woman pulling those men around by her apron strings, which the table joined in, until Leeann changed it to for she's a jolly good fellow. There were a few people at the bar and they all looked on in nettled amusement. Leeann poured another round and said, Girl, I'm scared of you. You really don't give a damn.

No, Carla said, beginning to feel tipsy herself, she does give a damn.

No, Maxwell chided, she gives a goddam.

The damn-givers have it, Kelvin Thomson concluded, and their party laughed again with unfettered rowdiness.

The bartender came over and asked them to hold it down just a little. No one wanted to cramp their fun but they were getting a little loud.

All right, Leeann said, we can stop showing our ass. Pull up your pants, everybody.

This drama cannot have ended on that note, Kelvin Thomson said.

No, no. It hadn't. Not at all. It kept going.

The boy's mother, coming out of the bathroom in a cloud of crack smoke, started cursing and wanted to fight but, looking at the brick outhouse with the warrior's eyes that was Cecelia, thought the better of it and, after a whole lot of screaming and hollering, broke down into a shambles of incomprehensible degradation, every sound that came from her full of the spiritual pus she floated in day by day.

Cecelia, while wanting with all her heart to ease these revelations by bursting into a sob, hung tough and bullied the woman into a drug program, loudly and coldly threatening to have her jailed and her child taken away from her. That was not all. She was one who walked the whole distance. Whenever necessary, no matter the hour, she stepped down into that valley of dry bones with this mother whom, at certain times, she envied to the point of tears for not having been born barren, which was the aching life sentence of her own condition.

Carla felt that one like a long needle pushed through her chest. It was too late for her to have a child and she knew that Maxwell didn't want one. Actually, it wasn't biologically too late. That clock was still booming like Big Ben and she had been through two abortions, one with Bobo and one with Maxwell, never forgetting the wet sound of the fetus sloshing in the bag but thanking God she didn't have to go through what one of Jimmy Joe's older sisters had told her about this friend she and another woman had to walk around through the night so many years ago after a black nurse with a medical bag—name of Johnetta Eagle—had appeared in the Robert Taylor Homes, her overcoat hanging from her shoulders like something dark and awful, her manner cold, her exit a relief. It had taken Carla a while to get over those two operations. Bobo never knew. She took care of that as soon as her period was late enough to know a child was in her body. What would that be, having a child with a man who could push death into his arm anytime? Stupid, that's what it would be. With Maxwell, it was different. That was secret, too, but she left a receipt from the clinic where he could find it. The receipt disappeared and he never said anything. She had already assumed he didn't want a child. Anytime she brought one up or talked about how beautiful some boy or girl of mixed blood was, Maxwell never said anything. Or another subject was raised, as if she had said nothing. Her heart fell on a sword every time that happened. So she stopped it from happening. The case was closed with silence, but another unmentioned element of her inner life took its place in the catacomb of her soul. Nobody knew all of her troubles except her. Her and God were good enough. Most of the time. Envy, yearning, bitterness, gratitude, and the desire for Maxwell buffeted her around. To get her mind free of herself, Carla asked Cecelia what had happened to that woman.

Good question, Leeann said. Is she still sucking dicks by the dozen?

Cecelia did not like that but she smiled.

Sweetest, she's just kidding.

Negro, do you think you know my cousin better than I do?

I might.

Be serious.

I am.

Nigger, please.

*He might, cuz. He could have a crystal ball in his soul. But even if he doesn't, just answer the question. I'm dying of suspense over here. I retract that insult to the poor woman's character. Let me restate myself: Is she still sucking dicks by the **half** dozen?*

Cecelia, ignoring the laughter at the table, answered.

On this birthday night celebrating a half century of soul in the world, buck-toothed Katie Mae Beasley, now a teacher's assistant at the Excellence Academy, had stood next to her plain-faced son at the surprise party. Cecelia vengefully smiled that Katie Mae had had the look of one who needn't ever avoid anybody's eye because, when it called for the strength to rise up from that basin where all of the skeletons of her dreams had been picked clean by the buzzards of her own appetites, she had done it. She had learned, second by second, bitter goddam drop by bitter goddam drop, that she could take the pain.

*Saying her intention was to feel **no** pain, Leeann ordered another bottle of champagne and Kelvin Thomson his third Irish whiskey.*

Maxwell, having picked up on Carla's irritation, had stopped at one and stuck with the bubbly.

What I wanted to do at EA, the birthday babe continued, was to kind of get something just like what we have right here in this bar. You know, this kind of feeling.

Of a bunch of drunks? Leeann asked.

No, Cecelia said, incapable of not laughing in a country-girl pitch Carla heard as yet another side of this woman unknown to her. Where did she stop? Where did any of us stop?

I had to go back to the village. That was what we needed. I got it when I was a girl. I knew it could come around. I knew you could **bring** it around.

Sparked by the hard blues of stories like Katie Mae's, Cecelia slowly created an extended family that included all the parents and the grandparents. If a mother had a problem with a man or with herself and didn't want to fall back by the wayside, she could call the school and get immediate counseling or get some from the social services or get some attention from another parent or from a grandparent. The same was true for the kids with troubles and the fathers battling screwed-up wives or their own demons. Sometimes all you needed in the world was some talk with a little sympathy in it.

Cecelia, on the verge of bragging—or already across the goddam line, as far as Carla was concerned—said she was going to have a civilized community if she had to build it herself. Being down below sea level didn't mean anything to her. The world started underwater. But it got going. It did that. Nothing stops the story anyway. The story can get its ass whipped something terrible. It can end up in traction. But it's still breathing; its heart is still moving. The story can be disabled but it can beget. Her grandmother had said to her one day when Cecelia was so confused she didn't know what to do, "Cece, we're all stories waiting to be told with the grace of God."

There it is, said Leeann, there it is.

Carla had no idea what the hell they were talking about.

I think I read somewhere, Kelvin Thomson mused, I think I read those same words. Maybe the same idea.

Gran Ruth didn't. And even if she did, her saying that at the right time got me on my way. I was straight then. The stars fell in my *apron, which Gran Ruth used to say, too. I saw the light. That's when I decided my arms weren't too short to box with darkness.*

Damn, said Maxwell.

Carla wondered if Maxwell was getting a light crush on Cecelia. She didn't really care. He was in love with her. Nothing could step in on that. One thing in which she had unrelenting confidence was their love and their intuitive closeness. It was touching in no way that she had been touched, even by Bobo. In her mind, no two people could be more different and so much the same. If that was so, why was she so irritated by Cecelia? Not a bad question. Well, there was that jealousy that sometimes came up because the only woman she wanted Maxwell to appreciate on an emotional basis was herself. It wasn't out of insecurity, just greed, her dog-in-the-manger side, or a variation on how she felt when listening to another singer who sounded extremely good and moved the girl from South Dakota but then got on her nerves. This was because Carla so loved being the cat's meow on the bandstand that the audience was related to in a possessive way, no matter that she wasn't on the bill and had no stake in actual competition. Uh-oh: she had lost her place in the conversation and now had to catch up, having turned the dial to station ME while everybody was so busy amening the birthday girl.

*As far back as Cecelia could see, falling was basic to the story of everybody who had ever walked this funky earth. This was a stinkbloody and numbing fact from the first almost monkey motherfucker who built up a little bit of something, just a **little** bit, and saw every last speck of it destroyed—every last one!—all the way up to people like herself, who witnessed the barbarians sacking their own communities and getting patted on the back for the hell they raised and the money they made in the streets or in the recording studios where they celebrated nihilism and were now defended in the academy by chicken-hearted niggers who couldn't stand one second on a street corner at night and step up to the kind of trashy assholes they used as references to whip the white folks into submission. "Academic slave traders, I call them," Cecelia said.*

They are some truly sad motherfuckers, Maxwell stated with a razor blade of anger in his voice. All the ones I met are punks. These black studies motherfuckers never did anything for jazz. Not on a

consistent basis. That takes too much heart. But they have confer-
ences on Africa and hip-hop and shit like that. They supposed to be
so involved in culture, right? Black culture. Ain't necessarily so. They
don't even recognize what Bobo used to say. Which was they always
running around talking about how the white man took away the
drums when we came here as slaves and now these black studies
motherfuckers are helping to talk up some rap shit that took away
the drums and put in electronic beats. Slaves to a mechanical rhythm.
*Ain't that a **bitch**? What about **that**? This **truly** pisses me off. These*
college faggots started having these departments in the late sixties
and they still aren't dedicated to jazz. If they had of been, our audi-
ences wouldn't be ninety-nine point nine percent white most of the
fucking time. These Jews and Italians and every other kind of white
folks who run the music business and write about us wouldn't be able
to look at us with that arrogant little smile because, deep down, they
know that we have been abandoned by niggers and left out here to
*depend on **them**.*

Boy, you sound like Caliban with a saxophone, Leeann said.

Not quite, said Kelvin Thomson, he's not speaking a language
those people taught him.

Whatever. You all can argue that whenever you want to, but I want
to finish what I was saying.

Well, excuse the literary hell out of me, Leeann laughed in a way
that made Maxwell and everybody else follow suit. Maxwell saluted
her and gave Carla a little peck on the lips before speaking.

What I'm saying is serious. If these black studies faggots had some
heart, we could get another mix. They too busy kissing the asses of
the kids. Faggots. I don't know what else these niggers are doing, but
they sure the fuck are bullshitting on the music. They just a bunch of
*almost-niggers anyway. They can't get down with **us**. Sissy punk-*
assed faggot motherfuckers.

I didn't know, said Leeann, that all the directors of black studies
departments were homosexuals. I thought that was only true of jazz
musicians.

Maxwell laughed the loudest. Then he blew a kiss at Leeann before
saying, You right. Ain't no use to getting pissed off. Why should we
expect anything other than what we're getting? These niggers are just
disgusting.

Carla knew that Maxwell was caught up in the theater of his own anger because he had a few friends who taught in those programs, whom he had invited to their home and to whose homes the two of them had gone, where, in the postdinner private of contemplation among intimates, those professors and their wives or husbands, putting on the blues garb of collegiate sack cloth and ashes, said that white people at the colleges didn't care whether the teaching and the courses were good or bad as long as the student natives were kept from becoming restless, which was equally true of the women's studies, the homosexual studies, and the other ethnic studies. One version or another of slave dances and career molasses on the academic plantation. Sheer racism toward some; icy, conceited disdain toward others. Back up a bit, let them eat cake. Back up a bit further, bread and circuses.Carla felt an accomplice to an exaggeration as everyone looked at Maxwell.

Some nuts were brought to the table by the waiter to refill the bowls emptied by this drinking party, which went into silence as everyone reached for something to nibble. That silence didn't last long. Just before it broke, Carla recalled what Bobo had said about the drums becoming lifelessly mechanized and wondered if, with the new morphing techniques in film, more and more actors would eventually stop acting and sell or lease their voices and their images from different times in their lives to the studios so that they could be any age in any movie, allowing the control of directors to become as total as that of writers and painters. The art of makeup would largely die off. Then everything would be the same as cartoons. Not really, since film, like recording, was the animate presence of the living dead once the performers were gone. This morphing had to become something different because the performance would **begin** with death, with no feeling from the source, only the manipulation of persona. Acting without actors. How hideous. At least until some genius came along and showed, again, just how technological dross could be turned into aesthetic gold. Carla almost burst out laughing as she chewed some nuts and silently muttered to herself that you can't keep a good species down. Leeann eyed her as though she could read the mind of the girl from South Dakota and they both smiled. What a buddy.

Maybe, Leeann said, those college darkies in charge don't understand what Mr. Expatriate Writer calls this burr-headed, hammer-headed, bullet-headed, Hula-Hoop-headed Negro is about. You got to *fool* these niggers. You **better**. They love them some conspiracies, just like everybody else. But they want theirs custom-made. Just like everybody else. That's the high mark of ethnic identity, isn't it? All over the world. I don't eat **your** conspiracies raw now. Bring me a gutbucket of conspiracies and let me put in my **own** seasoning, goddamit!

They all laughed.

Leeann—looking at Carla with her eyebrows raised and a pattern of irony squirreling through the light from her eyes—said, Then, my children, I feel free as a rich Southern white woman on her knees with a nigger chauffeur's dick in her mouth and a nigger cook's dick up her ass. That's right. Did some chickenshit somebody say conspiracies in this room? Oh, yeah. That's the key.

I don't know exactly what the fuck you mean, Maxwell said, taking Carla's hand.

Yes you do.

If I did, I wouldn't say what I'm saying.

Don't be dense.

Carla felt like slapping Leeann's face.

All right. Here's the niggergram delivered right to your door, Mr. Bandstand Caliban. About all this black studies, or coon studies or whatever the fuck they are, you must lift every voice, Maxwell, my brother. You got to get the dickhead niggers in charge to tell the kids the white man don't **want** you to know about this. Affecting a podium rabble-rousing Negro accent that was, by turns, pulpit, street, West Indian, and ersatz African, Leeann went on: Low-down crackers. I'm talking about rednecks. I'm talking about flat asses this evening. Faye Dunaway with that boody. You saw **Network**. Help me somebody. Seem just like yesterday. I'm talking about how the slave trade snapped off the great black umbilical connection to Mammy Africa. Cut us off at the ass. Don't let me get started.

Pouting inside, Carla knew no one could stop her. Such a good time and then this race and sex stuff had to be pushed into her face. What a weird friend. Maxwell took her hand and kissed it. Oh. Nice. Nice. Together, rain or shine, they could handle whatever they had to handle. She didn't care if the sky itself acted on the impossible notion of dropping all the way down to the bottom of the deep blue sea. Nothing mattered. The two of them were ready. Maybe nobody else could overcome race but they could. Leeann winked at her as she continued her oration. So strange.

Oh, don't let me get to going home to where my soul is. I feel a grass hut over my head this evening. I hear me some drums. I'm getting ancestral. I feel the slave ship swaying across the mighty Atlantic Ocean. Seem just like yesterday. I feel the cries of the crammed and the damned. I smell the toe jam. I'm all the way back to the bushwack. I feel a cotton sack on my tired black back. I'm feeling a feeling this evening. I'm talking about Daddy. Papa De-Dada. Dada. Dahomey. Home, down home with my homeys is what I'm talking about. I'm talking about something **actually** black right now. I don't mean **almost** black. I don't mean **half** black. I don't mean **nearly** black. I don't mean **passing** for black. I'm talking about jazz.

Did you hear what I said? Did those four letters—bless my bones—did they cut through the rain forest of your ignorance, my brothers and my sisters? Spirit, come on down here and pop the whip on these people. Lift the wail from under that veil. Let them know. Let's get real snappy and all the way nappy. Jazz. That right there is the point. Black claimed by white. Help me somebody. The white man. Oh, you got to watch him. You got to watch that carrot-nosed cracker now. You got to watch that blonde beast with a devil's tail poking out of the back of his pants. Oh, he's a evil thing. He'll get you to move and then you'll lose. Like at the Grammy Awards. Huh? Grammy my mammy done told me is a whammy. I mean can you believe that these crackers got **two** categories now? Gospel and **Soul** Gospel. That lets the white folks win in a category our people **invented** and we supposed to be a black version of something that was black from the very beginning of the beguine. That's the white man. Oh, that's him. If it's good, the white man **wants** it. If it's better than good, he goes **crazy**. If it's great, he must take it away and claim it as his own and **disown** your black ass in a cloud of laughing gas.

Tarzanism. Tarzanism. That's what he's about. Watch that cracker. He'll swing on those vines and yodel you out of business. Keep your eye on the prize of your rhythm. Don't let them walk off with your shit. They **will** do that. They walked off with Egypt, didn't they? Made it white as a KKK sheet. Hannibal, too. First they made him white, then they made him a cannibal. Tarzanism.

Do they believe in the truth? Do they believe in being fair? Do *they believe in the greatness of African people? You know they don't. What they believe, and what we got to teach, teach, teach, is that they believe in bleach, bleach, bleach. Peroxide is genocide. Help me somebody. So here it is. Now they doing that with **jazz**, my brothers and sisters. They trying to keep you **away** from Louis Armstrong and Duke Ellington and whatnot. This is too **great** for them to want **you** to know about it. That's why they don't **let** you hear it on the radio. They don't **want** you to hear it. These are not the things that happen by **accident**, if you feel like really knowing right now. Not hardly, me brothers and sisters—or should I say dicksters and disters? Listen with a close ear to me now: the mighty white man up here, he know just what the thing they doing is. That's why they're **glad** when **none** of you dead monkeys are in the audience. They got it going on then. They know that the deculturalizing cultural conspiracy has worked. Laughing behind your back is what they're doing. What did the great man Mr. W. C. Handy say about this, **huh**? **What** did he say? What did **he** say? I'll tell your dumb donkey arse what he said. First they get you accustomed to the feel of silkless silk, then the taste of milkless milk, then, by God, the sound of soulless soul. They love the illiteracy of you rapping, my handsome brother, my beautiful sister, they love it. You went for the wack and called it black.*

Leeann looked around the table. She put on a somber mask that wouldn't stay in place.

*The niggers will get into it then. Guaranteed. You know my peepus. Tell them they **better** leave something alone and they won't think about anything but fucking with it around the clock. They're disgusted. They're disgusting. They make you feel regusted.*

After they had laughed again at Leeann's concluding minstrel update, Cecelia began speaking, wiping her eyes but also showing the effects of having been upstaged by her cousin on what was supposed to be her night of narrative glory in the spotlight. Carla was hoping her goddam white face hadn't turned red and was embarrassed by her anger at Leeann, who clearly showed no quarter to anyone. The whole world was her target, and if you were around her long enough, you, too, would get a giant hatpin run horizontally through both cheeks of your backside. She enjoyed seeing Cecelia moving to com-

pete with Leeann, however, wondering what she was going to say now. Could anyone top that?

Cecelia took her turn at the ears of the table. She started to say something but excused herself and went to the ladies' room, shortly followed by Leeann, who said, a bit in her cups, Don't you get sick of these bitches who leave to go to the bathroom, saying, I have to go **pee?** Well, hee, hee, hee, heifer. Me and Cecelia were talking about that one time. Think they being cute, assholes across the color line. I always want to say, Look, **bitch,** until you say you're getting ready to take a **shit,** I don't want to hear it.

Leeann is hot tonight, Kelvin Thomson observed, quickly finishing off his Irish whiskey and ordering another. He and Maxwell then began talking about what a true soul sister she really was. None of the money and all that travel had been wasted on her, but she was still full of that special sass and vinegar too many lost when they climbed up into the penthouse. No deracinated Negress was she, Kelvin Thomson laughed, joined by Maxwell. Her soul was still black gold.

Carla wanted to say something but kept her mouth closed. If these black studies people ever woke up and created a jazz supercircuit on college campuses, would they hire people like her? Highly doubtful, Little Miss Blue Eyes. The melanin deficiency would do in your employment chances. But Leeann . . . Good grief. It wasn't clear enough in her mind, and, remaining quiet, she didn't want to give an impression unlike what was at the essence of the whole relationship with this wild South Carolina woman. Feeling an advantage, she mused that Leeann might have been going through all of this because, when we got down to it, round about midnight right now, she was here in Washington all by herself, no one to touch, no one to kiss, no one with whom she could share the whispers and buoyance that followed—

Carla can tell you. She knows.

She nodded, hoping she didn't have to prove she hadn't been listening.

Does Maxwell really—

I have to admit—

Leeann and Cecelia returned.

Look, brother, I already said it. These rap guys get everything. All the attention. All the women. All the money. I don't need the women. I got one of the most beautiful women in the world. But I could go for the attention and the money. Then these no-music-knowing guys, well, I still can't believe that somebody is studying rap in college and listening to somebody talk about how much it tells us about black culture. I really hate this shit. It really makes me feel alienated and outside. It's kind of painful. I feel like an orphan.

A motherless child, eh? Leeann smiled.

No, a brotherless and sisterless and supportless child, Cecelia chuckled.

They are ganging up on him, Carla thought. She also realized, glumly, that Maxwell still wasn't being fair to those professors he respected. He knew there were plenty of them, too, and, like most people, they just went along, hoping it would all blow over. He knew that. What a drag.

That's how it has gone, said Kelvin Thomson. Look, about seven or eight years ago, I went out to a college I used to teach at back when all these black studies were starting up thirty years ago. Thirty years. A long time. Anyway, I was visiting there and living with an old buddy of mine out in the Midwest. Saber Tooth Poody Wah.

Saber Tooth who? Leeann laughed.

It's just a nickname.

I hope so.

His real name is Jasper Lee Jackson.

I don't know if that's an improvement, baby, Cecelia smiled.

*Maybe not. So there I was at his place. I thought I could write a book. I wanted to sum up what had happened to us and to this country. But I had been gone for a long time. I had been in Europe for almost twenty years. So I went out there to this college and they had this Negro who was the supernigger to the black students, history teacher. Hey, man. They loved his dirty drawers. He was telling the students that there was a huge abolition movement in Africa all through the slave trade, which is a **goddam** lie. When I talked to him in his office, he laughed at me like I was the biggest fool there is. What I didn't understand, he said, was that the point was there **should** have been one. Some Africans **should** have cared; they **should** have fought in the interest of their black brothers and sisters. But,* since they didn't give a goddam and didn't fight to abolish the slave trade, he decided to make up an abolition movement. He stood up in his office, looking at a map of Africa, and continued straightening me out. *Cultures need heroes and myths, brother. The white people have shown us that. Besides, this nigger smiled, we now have a power we **never** had before. We got it **all** now. If we got enough **balls,** we can get power and respect and some **serious** money right about now. Alex Haley was the innovator. Great man. A true builder of black kingdoms. Zero to hero. A brother with **true** courage. No dog in him. Not Alex Haley. This brother **deeply** ripped off a white man for **Roots,** which was **fine.** Somebody **finally** had the nerve to turn the tables on these European cave dwellers who've **been** stealing our stuff since we were kidnapped and brought to this **strange** land. I say, Amen. Keep on stepping.*

Carla, intellectually nauseated by the described corruption, wondered what this guy looked like as Kelvin Thomson paused, took a sip of his drink and leaned back. Was the guy lean, handsome, and despotic or a porker who carried himself like an odious version of royalty or might he be something else altogether?

All the muddy water that Negro was talking out his ass, and with the hollow log he was using for a microphone, I guess you have to call this scholar for dollars "The Creature from the Black Studies Department," Leeann said, then asked, while the others were still loudly wheezing and chuckling, Is that all?

Not by a long shot, Leeann, not by a long one, he continued, still mimicking the hortatory tone of the history teacher's voice: *Some **nerve** got put on the table, brother. Some **black** nerve. It was time for some pay**back** and some big pay **checks.** And when brother Haley got sued for stealing, it wasn't no big thing at all. A man stepped in and popped the popcorn so Alex Haley didn't have to break his crown on that hard seed of getting called a liar so loud **everybody** could hear it. He kept the brother out of the dump and got him over the hump! The best friend of a ruthless brother with a **cause** is a liberal white man. One of them was the judge in the plagiarism case and this Moses on the **very** real side said that since Alex Haley had become so famous and important to black people, hey, there was no **need** to expose the brother, to keep him from the promised land and break the believing hearts of his people. Play the blues and go. Give the white boy his*

$750,000 and keep on stepping, Mr. Haley. You got plenty more com-
ing from where that came from. Mum's the word he said to the white
boy—if you want that money. All quiet on the plagiarism front. Now
*that's an alliance made in heaven. There's **always** a liberal white man*
*who has lost all his faith in the system and knows that we **deserve** our*
*chance to get all the way over by **any** means necessary. This John*
*Brown kind of white man will always say, That's **my** nigger, right or*
wrong. You following what I'm saying, brother? So here comes a
judge who thinks he's paternalizing but he's actually perpetrating.
Brother Haley kept his reputation, his honorary doctorates, kept mak-
*ing **big** money, and all of that good stuff. Black victory. So now the*
form is set. The game is up on another plane. Hey, I know a brother
who stole a play from Camus and got over. Nothing happened. I know
*another brother who stole all **kinds** of shit from a white boy in*
Canada when he wrote a biography of a famous musician. Got away
*with it **clean**. Walks around with his head up high, some dreadlocks,*
and some new teeth. Same thing up in here, brother. Right here. We,
*the descendents of they who were once **denied** education, we have*
*come marching on home to the **briar** patch and we have **conquered***
*the academy just like the **Moors** conquered Southern Europe once*
*upon a time. We **rule** this thing. Peep this out: We were hired to pro-*
*vide the students with the myths and the heroes they **want**. The black*
*kids believe **us**, no matter **what** the white people say. White scholars*
*don't count anymore. No more, no more, no more, no more, no **more**.*
*They had to hit the **road**, Jack. Those boxcars of degrees behind their*
*names are empty now, brother. Sidetracked. White authority is **fin-***
*ished**. We have never had **that** power over them before and we can*
*now make the students into what they **need** to be. We can make them*
*believe what they **need** to believe. They are under **our** control. Any-*
*body try to get cuckoo out here, he'll get **clocked**. Mr. Kurtz, this*
teacher laughed, is like the man said—he dead. Damn. This college
teaching nigger put a spell on me. I was so disgusted and disillusioned
I returned to Paris and sat there doing nothing. Everything I had
fought for lacked meaning. I knew then that Negroes were doomed. I
had never felt that disgusted by anything.

That is disgusting, Carla said. It sounds like—

Being disgusted wasn't enough, Cecelia asserted, because some-
body would always sell somebody out in the name of helping them or

*respecting them or submitting to their wishes. Drug dealers did it all the time. They were **helping** you have a good time. Motherfuckers. Con men wanted you to know, just as a favor, how it **felt** to make some money **real** fast. Bastards. A boy with a hard dick, no bubble gum and no rubber knew, dumb little girl, you **needed** to get that brave feeling of showing your unconditional love at any risk. Assholes. That's how things go and that's how they have always gone. So you could sit there whining and crying or you could get up and do what you could do and whine and cry in private.*

Kelvin Thomson looked as though hot water had been thrown in his face. He slowly sipped his Irish whiskey and his champagne.

It was simple, Cecelia went on. People always lied and they have always died. That never made life meaningless. It was just some more hurt you had to handle. If you learned how to handle it right, you had a civilization.

Well, I guess the comedy shop is closed for repairs, Leeann said.

But, Cecelia, look at how messed up we are, Maxwell said. We don't know shit and don't care to know shit and the white man has his foot deep up in a nigger's ass.

Sweetest, Negroes seem to have become happy in a barbarian state. I may not live here anymore and I might be out of touch, but anybody can see that it's all over but the shouting.

Carla was confused: after all that they had seen at the party, those black people so far from barbaric or doomed, those kids, those incredible kids, how could these men say what they were saying? What Kelvin Thomson said about that teacher was terrible but, sure, it was kind of like it was when she was a little girl in school and they used to have a fairy tale read to them before they took their afternoon nap. A fantasy before a pleasant loss of consciousness. Bizarre that the fairy tale putting you to sleep right now was political and demanded in college. So? None of that changed the way those kids they all saw down here were. None of it. Maybe these guys were just playing with Cecelia. If that was the point, it wasn't working.

Cecelia looked at Maxwell and Kelvin Thomson as though they had just shat on the table. None of that was acceptable in her book. She didn't want to hear it. Unacceptable.

See, Cecelia remembered when even being abjectly poor didn't give you the excuse to be a barbarian. Not hardly. Niggers just like these, she said, her head at an angle expressive of pride and agony, just as poor as these, who came from the long suffering of slavery, ignorant, superstitious, facing the wrath of the white folks, and, always outnumbered, niggers just like these made a way where there was no way provided for one man or woman who wanted to be a human being and not somebody's favorite animal on two legs.

She was heated up now. Her sudden power made Carla feel smaller and she didn't like it and she didn't like not liking it.

I say Amen to that, Leeann chimed in, lifting her right arm and snapping her finger. Run it, cuz, run it. Take these two manchilds to the promised land.

Carla knew not to laugh. Leeann did anyway. Cecelia looked the two of them in the face.

Like she said before, somebody had to remember and somebody had to tell. A predator with a jive hustle **always** thought the world started with him or that he could destroy worlds forever and remake everything into his stink-assed image so that one day all you would be were some nomadic Arabs passing the pyramids and listening to some bull as low-minded as rap and not having any goddam idea that once upon a time there were those in this very desert who had stood up against the limitations of flesh and blood to make a civilization. That's right. Stood up. **Stepped** up. Now what those ancient Egyptians had wasn't anywhere near as good as what we used to have in our own good old colored neighborhoods, but the point is that they did something monumental in the desert and somebody forgot it for a very long time. **Very long.**

How long, Lord, how long? Maxwell and Kelvin Thomson said at the same time, which brought a pause to the table.

How long? She wasn't waiting that long. Under no circumstances. How long? They would have to kill her first. Cecelia was about making those children read the Rosetta Stone. How long? Not long. It could all start right in the notes and words of those Spirituals. Yes, their eyes may shine and their teeth may grit, but the moon would turn to green cheese before she would allow those children to think they were nothing but worthless piles of shit. It was working quite well, by the way, and the rest of the city was starting to look at what she was doing. Looking was always a beginning.

All of their eyes were watching Cecelia as if she were a wrathful goddess.

Now let me tell you, Cecelia said, then stopped. You all . . . Her eyes were now overcast with nostalgia and she looked as though she were at the edge of weeping. Kelvin Thomson kissed her on the cheek and she dissolved for a bit, her eyes going from Leeann to Carla to Maxwell and to Kelvin Thomson. What a turnaround. The air was humid with affection. Her love for them couldn't be articulated perfectly enough to be clearly spoken, but it came out in her face, all the gratitude for being appreciated and surprised on this night and having now a little drink or two or three with some people in front of whom she could kick off her shoes and set aside the mantle of authority so necessary to doing the work that she did.

You don't have to say anything, Leeann seemed to nearly whisper, but that was only the effect of the tenderness in her voice.

Cecelia paused, a bit tipsy, then continued, taking all of them into her story from another perspective, something with the kind of intimacy that Carla felt was so accessible to Cecelia. It was something she admired to the point of envy so real it was almost physical. She was not able to do that kind of thing herself, just open her heart like that, allow all of the feeling to get free in some bar with friends. Carla could only go so far and that was the way she was and she wasn't ashamed of it. She was a private person except when she was on the bandstand or with Maxwell. By the way, right now the girl from South Dakota was anxious to get up to the room with Maxwell and have some of their personal fun, but he seemed as interested in what Cecelia had to say as she was herself, even begrudgingly. This made the wait a bit more like the kind of delicious frustration that romance had when you were young and couldn't get enough of everything about the other person. She ran her hands through her hair, feeling like a steam engine about to blow, knowing that when she did, her man was not going to forget this night in Washington, D.C. Let it wait. The time to come will come.

Leaning her head on Kelvin Thomson's shoulder, then sitting straight up and finishing her glass of champagne, Cecelia said that she had experienced the long dream of craving to run something like the Excellence Academy from that first day when she spent so much time putting on and taking off lipstick, dabbing one tissue after another against her mouth to reduce the shine, then deciding not to put it on at all, then concluding that she looked too plain and putting it on, then, afraid that she looked like she was trying to pick up a man, tak-ing it off, until, finally, she put on the right amount to handle those full lips and, trampolining in the thrill of becoming something new, left home for her first greenhorn day in the professional cattle car of public education.

Rising with a light of what her kinfolk said was a special bright-ness, legions of classroom hours behind her, meaning also mountains of chalk dust, the requisite bags under the eyes from reading papers late into the night, the sadness that came with having to face the truth of those who could be educated only just so far, regardless of the effort they put in, the chills that came whenever the spark of fresh knowing transformed a face and the tone of a voice, Cecelia was able, given the courses she took and the administrative experience she gained, to approach the Board of Education and convincingly ask for the chance to experiment with something like her pet project simply because she couldn't ever stop remembering Billetta Straganaw, her favorite teacher when she was a kid and didn't have one fully grown curse word in her mouth.

*Where do these Negroes get these **names**? First we got Saber Tooth Poody Bah and now we got this, Leeann playfully taunted.*

You got to watch that Negro, Maxwell said.

The Negro, Kelvin Thomson said in a mock professorial tone, has labored to free himself and herself. This is a serious matter. These names express the personhood of the Negro. Ah, the wilderness of personhood. To be exact, the liberation from the impositions of Cau-casian naming. Why, pray tell, should someone give a person a rea-sonable name when something like Billetta will do the job? After all, that tar-brushed, barbwire-haired twist upon twist of contradic-tions—the Negro—can regain the primitive in only so many ways.

In other words, Leeann said, they some dumb motherfuckers.

Precisely.

After the very loudest laugh of the night, Leeann looked around to notice that there was no one else in the bar. They and the bartender were closing it down. She ordered a round of the bar's best cognac and coffee for everyone. Kelvin Thomson asked for a quick Irish whiskey while the bartender was getting everything else together. There was no visible sign of the liquor having affected him. Carla was glad that Dad wasn't like that. He might already be dead by now.

Mom would have stopped it, though. He didn't have a chance. Self-destruction wasn't on his menu. Not with Mom around. The cognac was wonderful and the coffee was the very good kind you get in quality places. The smell of that coffee and that cognac. What a night. She was glad it was almost over.

Now what about that Negress with that crazy name?

It was just her name.

Look, cuz, don't get stink on me. I want something to breathe for, some story about this woman that will make my life an indelible dream. I just feel it. I can't explain it. I know that there is something spectacular here. With a name **that** dumb, you have to have something going.

Oh, she had something going.

Well, break it down, cuz. Give us one more tale of black triumph, baby, one for the road.

Leeann, you are a mess.

I know. I work on it.

All right. O.K. You win. This is how she was.

Carla studied Maxwell to see if he seemed sleepy. She didn't mind using her methods to bring him to full consciousness. That was fun, too, making a man arrive at attention. She had her tools of flesh. There were muscles she had patiently developed. She could hold things and she could massage things and she didn't need her hands or her mouth. In her erotic soul, she was a courtesan, and very goddam proud of it. But he seemed all right. He was alert. Was she glad he didn't go **mano a mano** with Kelvin Thomson in the Irish whiskey sweepstakes. He couldn't keep up. She would be furious then. It would be such a disappointing end to a very sweet, demanding, and vital night. But the two of them were safe. The suite was going to be hot tonight. Awful hot.

Cecelia inhaled deeply, sipped some coffee, yawned with an undertone of nostalgic pleasure, and took her tale flying home.

Miss Billetta Straganaw, the daughter of molasses-black Aida Jane and reddish-brown Paw Straganaw, she who was quarter Indian and an educator, and the granddaughter of Saphronia Lillie and Paw Paw Straganaw, the half-Choctaw educator and African Methodist Episcopalian minister, this Mississippi woman, this Billetta Straganaw, had a soul of fire, steel, velvet, and peach cobbler. The example of her *iron eyes and her code had inspired Cecelia to become what she became.*

*That was back when they would get up Saturday morning at seven-thirty, take a bath, dress, leave with everything necessary including a little jar of Dixie Peach, traipse around the corner to pick up Carlotta Johnson and get some freshly baked biscuits with red jelly from her mother, go on and meet at the park on their bikes, all girls with their hair sticking straight up, pedal around as fast as they could until the time came to go to the swimming pool, lay their bikes on the ground, bury a quarter somewhere, go in and take their swimming lessons at nine, wait until noon for the pool to open, splash and go crazy with the boys trying to feel them up, come out and dig up their quarters, buy some wax lips and some wax teeth or some white paper beaded with candy or a Mars bar, a Milky Way, and a pair of Hostess Twinkies, gobble them up, get home in time for their mother or their aunt or their big sister to tell them they had better not have one ashy spot left on them after they had cleaned up and gotten dressed for dinner, sit there thinking about boys and about your books, especially the ones that were late from the library that you couldn't enter in numbers of more than five at a time because the librarian couldn't handle a bunch of giggling, screeching girls, every one of whom looked like the model for an angel come Sunday morning and was nervous as all heck but ready to meet the demands of Billetta Straganaw on Monday, when there would be no kind of jive whatsoever because this woman would call your house or visit and sit there the color of milk chocolate with a rose undertone—staring her power through the hardest eyes God had ever made—and tell your parents that they had a responsibility to the world, which was to make sure that their children did not at any time and at any place fail to understand that something you learned was something that **no one** could take from you, and that if you failed to learn you had betrayed the blessing of ever having been born with the ability to become a fully rounded and well-educated human being who could pass on every form of knowledge that he or she possessed just by the manner in which this person carried himself or herself, which meant, consequently, that this child of yours had to be disciplined with the fierce love necessary to communicate that though there might be plenty to laugh at in this life, life itself was nobody's laughing matter.*

2 2

———

THEY CALL IT STORMY MONDAY

CARLA, NOW oppressed by her recollections and her stomach unexpectedly sour from the cold white wine, knew that the clock had crossed midnight. Gloomy Sunday had passed the troublesome atmosphere to early Monday and she was caught, still, in a squall of memory. If she could get to the port of sleep, things would at least subside for a time. But now there was a headache. She hated aspirin, which would, as always, make her stomach even more sour. There was nothing to do but drink water and cut off a piece of Zito's bread, put some butter on it, and sit down, eating and thinking in order to distract herself from the pain between her temples. Her small bladder guaranteed that once she went to sleep she would be getting up every half an hour or so until all this water and wine took a flush to the sewer.

In a fit of self-deprecation, she stood before the floor-length bathroom mirror and hated the body Maxwell had once loved, the little fat stomach he patted so softly, the navel he kissed, tickling with his tongue, then sucking and letting loose with a wet pop; the breasts that were not yet sneaking downward and had a few blue veins he fingered as if they were alive and sometimes called sweet streaks of romantic lightning; the freckled shoulders Maxwell said were actually lightly covered with tiny droplets of the African mist that rose from her Hottentot; the neck destined to fold and wattle its way into a visual disaster over the next ten to fifteen years, a process she had recognized starting on Mom just before she died; the barely emerging pouch below her chin that sometimes made her sad to touch; and the single line on her upper lip that now had a twin rising on the other side. She wasn't even forty for two years, and now these hardly noticeable little things made her feel foolish for ever having thought herself beautiful. When she was a kid, so in love with herself, the world was falling apart, and now all of those fissures had caught up with her. *What?* The self-pity, so out of proportion to all that had come to her, made Carla as riled as Mom was when her deliberate, tragic pioneer faith in everything had no influence on the talk that was dominating the house in which Ramona and her little sister were too close in their souls to separate.

Dad talked about them all the time. They were barbarians to him. Carla had never seen him more puzzled and so close to being fright-ened about where the society was going. So many of the white kids in college had tried to escape their middle-class backgrounds and embrace some cornpone version of themselves just about the time she was becoming the flower of her junior high school campus. Dad just couldn't handle it and Mom would neither believe it nor make much of it when all the evidence was laid out. They argued because Mom had turned her back on all of it and made no effort to share his trou-bles. As far as Mom was concerned, God had blessed America and it would get through whatever it had to get through. There had been a Civil War, too, for heaven's sake. Refresh yourself on that little situa-tion in our history, dear. The nation was held together by the sticky blood and moldering flesh of all those corpses. Today's insipid blisters on the body politic meant nothing. Mom. She could be like that when she felt above something. If you wanted to make a big deal about it, then go right ahead. She wouldn't even watch. Call her when you were done.

That meant everybody else in the house had to listen. This could be like sitting in a tub of drying concrete. Dad had his observations. Did he ever. She and Ramona just wanted to go out horseback riding or ice skating or walk around whispering about the girls who were using birth control pills and doing whatever they wanted to do. Some of them were rich, some of them weren't. It was all so intriguing. You could tell they were on the demon pill if their breasts filled out, or that was what they said you could do. The almighty *they*. The gossip and the speculations were so wonderful. The two of them were like Harriet the Spy tracking down the mystery of sex and snickering to each other as they talked about two old copies of **Peyton Place** and **Lady Chatterley's Lover** that Ramona had found in the basement at Teresa Sorensohn's house and brought home under her blouse, walking so casually with one stuck in the back of her skirt, one in the front, both filled with anonymous underlinings of the hot parts. What a piece of espionage work. This would help them break the code. They had all of that on their minds. But they were sentenced to listen to Dad's lamentations. That was an unstated order. Be brave. Sit still. Pay attention. These were serious matters.

Let us start with Old Glory.

Sure, Dad, the girls said with such insincere interest only someone as absorbed in his ideas as he was wouldn't have noticed.

In Dad's time as a young man, when he regretted missing World War II but had served in Korea, the flag was something that stood for freedom. How could that be gone and done with? There was something very troubling about how the emblem of the flag was seen a few years back as the mark of Cain or something to patch over holes in your pants. Not to mention something to put on cigarette papers and roll marijuana cigarettes in. It was as spiritually morbid, as horribly ironic, as the way those Southern yahoo terrorists had fused states' rights with the willingness to forever bomb churches or shoot people down in their driveways so as to defend segregation. Neither the new specimens on campus nor the Dixie murderers had the meaning of the nation right. Both of those kinds got in a lifeboat with a drill. He had other thoughts, too. I'm sure you do, Mom said, excusing herself to take a walk. Dad liked the music that wasn't loud but he just didn't get the rest of it.

These youngsters were listening to blues records and folk music and dressing in some version of American Gothic updated to include long hair and psychedelic colors, and as one phase passed, they stopped trying so hard to look like freaks and took to wearing the clothes of blue-collar workers. Carla saw them in the house or sitting on the front porch talking with her father, most all the time trying to speak to her as if she and they were in some sort of conspiracy against *the adult world, which was something this teenage girl wasn't at war with but wanted to get into as soon as she could, regardless of all the fun that was coming into her life as the luck of the genes made that figure and that face so appealing.*

Five feet eight and a half inches, 126 pounds by the end of high school and never more than 131 since—uh, 133, which she was now. She had gained *five* pounds in Houston. Jesus William Christ. Look at yourself. You look like a fat goddam pig. Maybe this is bloat because I'm close to my period. You are, by the way, two and a half weeks from getting your period. You stuffed your face and now it shows. Next case.

*Pieces of their eight or so ideas blew past her. Carla only listened to them halfway because she was learning how her period affected her mood and was reading those two books over and over, looking forward to lying down in the sweet sin of tongue-kissing and **doing** it, plus—thank you God!—she was no longer wearing a t-shirt because her chest had gotten large enough for a brassiere, which made her feel just so much closer to being a grown woman. No, she didn't listen too closely to what those students were saying but she made sure to catch the essences because her father might ask her what she thought of the things they were saying. If she didn't know, well, without a doubt, a bawling out for being so rude as to not pay attention to guests would put the baby daughter in her place. Yuck. The kids visiting Dad believed that the trouble was what had happened once cities got bigger than six hundred people. Meaning? If you couldn't know everybody, then you got too involved in yourself. That wasn't a dull observation. But you should also do your own thing, other opinions be damned. Didn't sound too bad to her; she'd like to do that with them and their opinions right now. There should be no money, no war. What would no money solve? She'd like to know that but didn't ask. Every now and then there was talk of forming new kinds of small cooperative communities and becoming organic farmers. Whew. Or they were all turned around in free love orgies or promiscuity as answers to frigidity and loneliness. Phooey. Or they felt that they could escape the gravity of being who they were and where they had come from by getting high* *as a mountain goat or submitting to an Eastern religion or protesting everything that got in the way of them rolling on back to the soil. Roll on, roll on, tumbleweed, she and Ramona used to chant when even younger, what you got I do not need.*

There she went again, elevating herself above somebody else. Carla, chewing her Zito's bread and drinking some water in the kitchen after stepping off the bathroom scale, abruptly couldn't stand the way she was then or now. Would she ever get out of grade school? Would she? Was it possible? Almost middle-aged and snooping around for a way to be better than other people. How about just being yourself? See if that would do. Stand on your own, not on somebody's head. Stop being a fucking immature bitch.

To be fair, those kids were right about some things, like the war in Southeast Asia and prejudice. Continuing the worst American traditions was something they didn't want to do and kids all over the Western world didn't want to do. But they were, finally, kids given to all the misapprehensions of youth. They deserved some credit, though. They even understood how yucky a lot of the American diet was, which meant that, eventually, when you asked for a salad in a restaurant just about anywhere in the country you didn't get a cold half of a peach that had been soaked in syrup and was now resting on one or two browning leaves of iceberg lettuce with a vile scoop of watery cottage cheese in its hollow. Yikes. Yet back to the earth could mean, if you made a wrong turn, back to the mud or the caves or running across the roofs of the homes in the trailer park. She could prove that easy. There were still enough genial but empty-headed hippies ten years her senior and older, all of them left out there, the last buffalo of their special order, who were actually duh ... duh ... duh, duh ... duh ... duh, duh ... duh ... duh marijuana smoke rings around the Saturn side of the culture. What a goofy mess.

Eek. There was plenty of nothing to think about. Did it have any limits? Apparently not. All of this trouble was so knotted up together. As if acting the sadist of recollection, her memory put her on another rack.

*Not long after the birthday party in Washington, Carla and Cecelia
had been riding together on the train in New York one day when some
loud, loud black girls in early adolescence came into the car talking
about whose pussy smelled and whose didn't and that if one of the
flat-chested members of their crew wanted her breasts to get larger
she would have to let somebody suck on them. Cecelia got so furious
Carla was afraid she would snatch one of the girls and assault her. The
only time Carla had seen a civilized person that angry in the flesh was
when Dad, whistling and singing, came home from a faculty party so
totally plowed he fell and hit his head on the corner of the living room
table, opening a geyser of a cut. Mom, suddenly hurling one of her
favorite teacups into the fireplace, seemed as if she had become a full
two feet taller and could kill him at the same time that she wanted to
stop his bleeding.*

*Shit, bitch, smell like you got a fish market between your crusty-
assed legs.*

*Oh, no. **Ho**. You smell like you got **three** rotten fish stuck up in
your pussy.*

What you looking at, you moonhead heifer?

Heifer is your mama.

You ain't got no breastis.

I got enough.

Let somebody suck on them shits until they grow up.

Yeah, somebody suck on them shits.

Thimble titties.

I don't care. They awright.

Well, fuck you then.

*Yeah, bitch, **fuck** you.*

Yes, they were horrible people or they had terrible manners, but
what did that mean when one got down to it?

It might mean nothing but a socially cumbersome bother. That first
time five years ago when she had gone to meet Maxwell at the Brooklyn Botanic Garden one Friday afternoon, the train had filled up with
schoolkids. Carla always remembered that she was wearing a white
shirt rolled up to the elbows with a hand-painted flower on the left
side of the buttons, some black silk pants, a jaunty, lavender-colored

jacket she had bought on West Broadway, dark panty hose, and some flat shoes. Her hair was pulled back in a ponytail and tied with a purple ribbon. If she were to say so herself, she was looking damn good.

When she wasn't closely reading an article that fascinated her, Carla was having fun, as usual, looking at the lights of the stations and the shapes of the people across the track in the train going the other way. Those over there, a few peering in her direction, seemed passengers in some ghostly conveyance, or appeared to be moving in a strange film between the steel girders that held up the ceiling but flitted, if the pace was right, like the borders that separate the images on a strip of celluloid.

With the sound of the schoolkids faintly in her ears, Carla thought on that good afternoon about her future man and how warm she felt when he had called, inviting her to come out and meet him among the plants in spring after he had finished a sound check for a concert he was doing across the bridge later that evening. Then, with Maxwell's voice in her head and romance prancing through her heart, she took notice of the kids.

Yes, they were terribly dressed with bad, oversized jewelry and abrasive hairdos—their versions of the equally absurd white punk attire and satanic cult chic; yes, they were loud; yes, they blasted flat, vulgar limericks on their radios until the transit cops made them turn them off; yes, they were foulmouthed. But that arsenal of fuck you, like the barbed end of white youth culture, was only one part of the rudeness of an era when the ordeal of civility had been defined as just too goddam much.

How long, oh, Lord, how long, she had smugly smiled to herself, would it be before Americans and Europeans and everybody else who became civilized understood that continually vitalizing the middle class was the issue, not hiding in costumes and bad behavior? There was *always* decadence far above and far below. The sociologists used to be so clear about that. So much for rebellion, not bathing, and bad manners, or ethnic costumes and primitive posturing as tonics for the spirit. Then anger bumped around inside of Carla's heart. These asinine children are not alone. Not by a very long shot. Pissed-off adults wanted to be cynical about everything, leaving *no* point of affirmation standing, then they had the galling, unmitigated nerve to wonder why their kids, why *their* kids, why *their* kids were lost in fantasy

worlds of drugs, science fiction, death, destruction, and obnoxious-
ness.

For all that, the *Oh, no!* of recognition sprang forward on that Friday as some other stuff: these terrible black children on the Brooklyn
train were actually *faking*. Pure counterfeit. Undiluted fraudulence.
How did *she* know this? Was she now the white psychic queen of
America? No quite. Take it easy, *friend*.

At one stop, some real thugs got on, real as the acid rain of dagger
wounds that took Julius Caesar down or the lead globe of a derringer
bullet that, while Abraham Lincoln was laughing, exploded into the
back of his head. Yes, they like that. They were the real deal.

They had blood in their eyes and they moved as though all they
wanted was any excuse to hurt or make someone grovel. Each one of
them seemed ready to slap the air if it touched him in a way he didn't
fucking like. The subway car became quiet, absolutely quiet, as the
true bad boys stood together and vibrated menace or perused the
other adolescents. One of the crew was casually spitting between his
teeth on the window of the subway door. Another—his eyes as empty
as those of a cadaver on the cooling board—was blowing large grape
bubbles of gum. Each of the others, his hair twisted up in odd knots
and rubber bands, merely stared at the intimidated schoolkids,
imposing the mood of a killer on the loose who might someday find
himself running with a smoking pistol in his hand and a cop's voice
shouting for him to halt.

All along, Carla had suspected that the bulk of those kids were
harmless, but had been too afraid sometimes to believe that she was
right. They were such obnoxiously good actors. Academy Award
material. Besides, a woman out here in the world was always on the
verge of danger. It came from so many directions. She remembered
one night eons ago when she and Ramona were sitting up in the
kitchen late at night after a snack of apples and that good sharp Wisconsin cheddar Mom brought back from a weekend trip to see some
cousins. The two Norwegian girls were drinking hot chocolate
topped with whipped cream and looking at the snow. Her big sister
said that once she had visited a college in Southern California and
was walking with a friend across the campus late one evening. So
weird. *Too* weird. They came upon a man who had his belt in his
hand and was hysterically striking the face of a monumental Gaston

Lachaise statue, muttering, in tears, "You bitch" over and over. If the statue could have bled and cried out, it would. Such things terrified Carla. All the baby sister could recall, and not push from her mind in bed that night, was the horrified look in Ramona's violet eyes as she described the sound of the leather whipping against that image of a woman.

So did those black kids, especially since more and more of them were now growing so oddly large because, a painter friend of Maxwell's speculated, all they had been fed by their teenage mothers from earliest childhood were the fast food hamburgers and fried chicken filled with steroids and growth hormones. This made them seem a hoodlum race of Little Johns out to rob the rich *and* the poor, the children of the underclass outgrowing those above them because the garbage they ate came from companies that wanted to get as much meat on hoof and the chicken foot as possible. *A master race from hamburgers and chicken!* the painter laughed in his loft after he, Maxwell, and Carla had marveled at the size and speed of some black athletes on the sports channel. She had been afraid of them back before any of that analysis, from the point she arrived in New York until the awesome day that she learned all she needed to know about the difference between behavior and inner identity. Then, to her good forture, embracing among the horticulture, the girl from South Dakota realized on that afternoon in Brooklyn that she and Maxwell were definitely going to get into something. It had that feeling. Two revelations in one day.

At that subway moment on the way to the Botanic Garden, watching those previously unruly youngsters cower before the authentic teenage makers of death, Carla began to understand what Cecelia made explicit four years later. They were walking on Lexington Avenue toward Bloomingdale's and the creator of the Excellence Academy was still so furious about those vulgar black girls screeching about their purportedly unwashed anatomies: *That's how stupid these niggers are. They don't know that those little things like flushing the toilet behind you, running a paper towel over the public washbasin, saying excuse me, and that kind of thing works racially, too. Please and thank you. When we were coming up we were told that it was our duty **not** to make it harder for the Negro coming behind us. Don't leave a bad impression by acting stupid. Now nobody said take any* *shit because I'm from a long line of Negroes who did not even know how to take some shit. They were deficient, culturally deprived of ass-kissing training. By acting civilized, however, you spread goodwill. You put a little sweetness in the air. A pinch of sweetness, you know?*

Now, these kids today curse at the top of their lungs anywhere and act like savages. They think showing your ass is saying something. That's as backward as the reverse gear in your car. You're right to laugh. Don't apologize. It is funny. Sort of. Maybe. But you probably don't know that Brer Rabbit slapped the tar baby because he thought it was a nigger too stuck-up to speak to him. These black people think the tar baby is the real them and they get stuck to that. It's all crazy and funny. We see what we can see and we do what we decide to do. You're on a different path from this.

I don't know about that.

I do.

I'm not that different from you, Cecelia, just because I come from another kind of background.

Oh, yes you are.

Why do I always have to be treated like an outsider? Can't we just be friends and think about these things together?

Listen to what I'm saying. Relax. This won't hurt a bit. This is a friend. I'm not trying to belittle you.

Bravo.

Carla, come on.

I'm trying to get on board. But I keep being told I don't have a ticket.

Listen. You know if I didn't like you, or if any of us didn't like you, we wouldn't be around you. That's not our style.

Well, I can't argue that. It still makes it uncomfortable, Cecelia. It hurts sometimes. It does. That's all. I wish I could say something else, but that's the way I feel when you say things like that to me.

That makes sense. I can see what you're saying. But I just want you to understand something.

Oh, all right. I'm listening.

Don't say it like that, Carla. Don't do that to yourself.

I'm not doing anything to myself. I'm just trying to be honest with you.

I'm trying to be honest with you, too.

Well, let the honesty keep going.

They both laughed. Then Cecelia's face got rather serious.

As a white woman, you walk through life as though the whole society is on your side.

No matter how she wanted to take it, Carla felt assaulted. Boy, does she not know what she's talking about.

You feel like everybody is out there to look out for you or give up some help or make things nice just for little old you. Don't blush, Carla, it's true. It's clear in everything you do. It is. Second nature. A blind man could see it.

Well, I never think about it.

You don't have to think about it. That's the point.

Carla felt her blush intensify and was also being made to feel silly. That really hurt.

Now I don't think there's a black woman in this country who feels like that, or a black man, or a black child after the child finds out people think he's a nigger—white people and black people and anybody else who heard about niggers. See, Carla, everybody throughout history is trying to figure a way to get out from under being niggerized, which means that you don't count; what always precludes who. When your ass gets kicked long enough for what you can forget all about who. If somebody asks Who the fuck are you? you won't be able to step up. You just roll around in that tar-baby tar and stick out your tongue and start puking in their face. I tell my kids that's not an identity, that's a reaction by someone who doesn't have an answer, and, well, well, maybe, what's wrong with our world is that no goddam body, no goddam body at all, has an answer anybody is willing to sacrifice a single drop of sweat for.

She saw what Cecelia meant and she actually did assume a certain kind of privilege, or, at least, a certain kind of civilized treatment that her black friends sure as hell didn't. What a bring-down. Though enjoying the trip to Bloomingdale's, Carla thought about it through the rest of that shopping time together, noticing, as she had become accustomed to, that Cecelia spoke in an implacable tone to the white employees in Bloomingdale's, which was the way Maxwell always talked to cabdrivers after the two of them were finally picked up, half the time passed by white, black, and Asian drivers until somebody pulled over, an Asian as often as not, usually from Pakistan. Neither Cecelia nor Maxwell seemed to know, and she wasn't about to tell them, that being white in this town didn't automatically save you from those maniacs who were out there somewhere, hanging back and ready to tear you apart because there was no one to help you. Oh, you could get niggerized all right and be just as white and blonde and blue-eyed as you wanted to be. That didn't allow for any kind of mercy at all. You didn't even have to do any puking. You, no matter who you were or how you looked, always had to beware of getting niggerized, which, Carla knew, was what Cecelia was saying. It happened anyway and you didn't need to help it along.

Perhaps that was one of the reasons people like Bob and Ramona of Cleveland felt as they did. Although these black kids wearing the false faces in a carnival of street niggerism were just another part of irritating teenage American style, they played into the hands of racists or, with all their adolescent energy, created so much disgust and fear, they helped breed racism. These bogus ruffians—as unsettling as the bongo-thumping natives who beat out their rhythms all through the night and drove the peroxide blondes mad in the old jungle movies—made it impossible for thin-skinned white people to believe that the society was still on your side.

How *dare* they? Treacherous little sambos. We had a nice little thing going on right here. Shame on them. Shame on them. Now the only ones on your side, as the so insightful Mrs. Bob made clear, were those banded together with you, not certain kinds of strangers. Don't go to strangers. You had to stop pretending. You had to address the reality of the situation. Blow away the illusory clouds and look at the true sky. They hated you and you repressed them and that was that. There was a tradition to this, a way of life, like any other. Awake and get on the right white side. Look up and live.

Carla gazed out the window. Her body was so tired it hurt. She didn't want to know what time it was. If she did, that would make her even more irritated. Across the street there was a handsome Puerto Rican guy slipping along and spraying black graffiti on every other door or so. What a good-looking guy. Scrumptious. Didn't he have anything better to do with his handsome time than that? Apparently not. He wanted to be known. To autograph the world. Latin Kilroy here.

A couple of the cops from the bar downstairs came out and stopped him. A gun was drawn. They must have been drinking; they sounded like it. She became frightened. The Latin guy was patted down and told to empty his pockets. His money and identification were torn to pieces and thrown in his face. You don't need any fucking money and you don't need any ID. We know. We know who the fuck you are. Your kind is common, buddy. *Too* common. Pain-in-the-ass fucking asshole sonofabitch. This is a crime you won't do again, buddy. Tonight, you are going to learn something you need to know. Comprende? Doesn't matter. Fuck you. *Amigo*. One, weaving a bit, took the spray can the Latin guy had been using, shook it like a Molotov cocktail, and told the Puerto Rican to close his eyes. Even at that distance, his terror stepped right through Carla's window and lay on her skin. The cop sprayed his face, neck, and clothes, front and back, emptying the can until the black goo on the perp shone in the moonlight. Now get the fuck out of here and be happy you didn't get the shit stomped out of you. We're letting you go, you dumb fuck. Don't cross anybody's path. Bad luck. Scat! *Amigo*. They laughed.

Ramona's outrage wouldn't let Carla go. Maybe just the sustained memory of it, kicking the kid's terror to the curb, had contaminated her. She hated what she had seen the cops do, but she was glad they humiliated the guy while not hurting him. They had held court in the street. Terribly swift justice. If they had done anything more, she would have gone down the stairs, gotten their badge numbers, and testified against them. But, as it was, she enjoyed thinking of this stupid guy walking home, hopefully to the Bronx or some such distant land, sprayed from head to foot and looking like the irresponsible fool that he was. The problems he would have were perfectly deserved. It was a better sentence than some bullshit in court. He wouldn't even be taken to court for defacing property. Probably not. He deserved it. My God, she couldn't believe how much of a fascist she was becoming there in her own house! Ramona, Carla thought—with more bitterness than she could stand, than she could stand, than she could *stand*—would believe I'm beginning to see the light.

Now Mr. Memory put on the garb of a history professor and gave her a test. She was surely her father's child. History. The nagging past.

That was how it seemed, her mind laying one subject up against another, giving her no quarter, making every millisecond of this insomnia ever more unpleasant.

The European aristocracy must have felt something like Ramona after the French Revolution. Something like that but far different, actually. Ramona, no matter what the Bob of all Bobs told her, was not royalty. Bob: what a splat of vomit. What a priggish idiot for her big sister to end up marrying and having children with in that fucking antiseptic Cleveland suburb. *Them* royalty? Sure. Oh, sure. Definitely. Duke Bob and Duchess Ramona. She found herself, finally, laughing again. Was that a relief.

A yearning arrived, one that came into her heart every once in a while. Randy was wrapped inside that yearning and she was thinking of him as he might be if her little brother had gone on to teach history like Dad wanted. This itch to have him be there for her took over whenever she was shit-out-of-luck lonely. It was always silly. Always. Always because death doesn't give any refunds. But her longing fantasy didn't care about the facts of souls gone from flesh forever. Her desire was there, as pure as the hard truth of that corpse Dad found frozen and had to bring home. No matter that he was dead: what if Randy had married the fantasy Jewish girl from Northern California that Carla had dreamed up for him? Would they have strawberry blonde kids, part Midwestern, part smarty-smart opinions and charming hearts? Where would they be living with *their* kids? Not in fucking Cleveland. Not with *their* kids. She could not believe that that was one she would miss, and that Ramona, of all people, had *not* missed. Two kids. Two kids, a boy and a girl. Shining little critters, too. Adorable.

What a merry mix of bullshit. Why Ramona and not me? Her belly and breasts wouldn't swell and get heavy as a child grew inside this body. The screaming and pushing rite of passage that was giving birth had no future in this woman's life. She wouldn't be able to talk about the skin creams and the struggle to get rid of the stretch marks or how hard it was to get back down to your normal weight. She'd never hear herself say that breast feeding had sagged her bustline for good but that it was worth it just to experience the knowledge that the gift to your womb could live on the sweet liquid sucked from your nipples. Not for you, babe. None of that.

For a second, she felt a satisfied fury. Little Randy couldn't side with Ramona. Never. That was impossible. History was already becoming too serious to him when he went up that last mountain. Carla, now whimpering inside, knew she didn't feel about him then like it would have been nice to feel. He got on her nerves back in his final days, always singing those Broadway songs *so* out of tune and talking about the goddam French Revolution with such a full-of-himself tone. Maybe that was when she first began to think about it. Could be. Well, if Randy was thirty-six this very year—and the kind you would *expect* to come out of the totally sane household they grew up in—all that would be behind them right now. Every resentment gone. True or not, it was pretty comforting to think so. They could be on the phone talking for hours about this terrible change and he could share her horror at what Ramona had become. She needed someone to share this nightmare. Someone from home who hadn't turned on her like a lunatic. Only someone from home should know about this. Her brother would know that what Ramona thought was wrong as trying to carry water in a sieve. She laughed but knew that the suburban regal family of Aryan Cleveland was not real and definitely not funny.

Yet it must have been that snowy day in hell when the *European* aristocracy realized that the peasants not only had ceased to look up to them due to the purported superiority of their breeding but had come to hate them for having run such a successful ruse for so long, for working it so well that they were held in shimmering awe by those on the lower rungs, their surpassing glamour the quality that made it logical and convincing that the underlings *should* submit to them. But. There always is one, isn't there? But. Once the lice-ridden person licking the custommade shoe realizes that there is just another human foot inside it, and perhaps a stinking one at that, things can get a little dangerous. Uh oh: this was something like Maxwell's wack theory about misogyny. File that under "forget."

Even so, what was going on right now was a Reign of Terror in the streets and for all of the same reasons of reverse intimidation; but race, no matter what Duchess Ramona said, was only part of it. The loony versions of black studies that Maxwell talked about in such an exaggerated fashion would fall away as had the Committee for Public Safety that made the Parisian thoroughfares safe for paranoid authority and gutter blood. Randy tried to make her cringe back when he told her about those dog days of Paris not even a week before his final climb. He obviously relished talking about the most repulsive stuff while eating a double-decker peanut butter and jelly sandwich with lettuce and tomato. This was the side of him that used to put worms under the bedsheets to wake her with their clammy crawling. Her feet and calves remembered exactly what the hell that felt like. Such a pill. The winter sun was shining through the back door and her brother's shadow pointed at Carla as she sat demurely eating a turkey sandwich made from leftovers and giving no facial response to what he said. Basking in the gore and drinking one of those Royal Crown sodas just so inferior in taste to Coke, Randy made his voice as scary as he could, first belching like a leopard growling, whatever manners he had shrinking away like a snowman as winter took its leave. He also broke wind around her when they were by themselves, which she also refused to acknowledge. This time the air was clear. His sis was told that so many heads were dropping in the basket a guy could stoop to playfully redden his handkerchief in the gutter while taking his girl out for a night on the town during Robespierre's moment of liquid rubies. This added up to nothing in her book. Zero, pal. Like Mom, Carla believed that there was something in the mighty air of this country that could blow away the blues of the accumulated spiritual flatulence and the dingy clouds rising from the refuse pits of folly, corruption, and vengeful incompetence.

"Each generation is like a baby, Carla," Mom said to her once when she was so exasperated by Dad's fear that the country was losing itself. "No matter how sweet and pretty the baby is—coochie, coochie, cooo—you have to change the diapers and the diapers are always full of the same thing. Wet or solid or both. You just have to stick your hands in and do the cleaning. If you're childish about it, like so many people seem to be, you can resent or even hate the baby because it fouls its diapers day after day and you have to reach into that mucky mess. That's the life we all live in America and maybe everywhere else, and if we don't want to change those diapers, if we get too tired or too darn selfish or too holier than thou to do what we're supposed to do, the filth can become acidic and burn the flesh of that baby. Then you can be pretty doggone sure what kind of a person that neglected child will grow up to be."

23

CALL ME

Carla felt as though she were lying under an icy slab. At least, her headache was gone and her stomach had cooled itself out. She lay in bed again, naked and enjoying the smell and feel of the clean sheets. Jesus: a lifetime ago, she had finished her set at Crescent City over on Broadway near Union Square and had joked around with Jed, whose bass lines on "Cheek to Cheek" she could almost remember note for note they were so pretty and so melodic. After bidding farewell and thanking him for hiring her to work in his place, the girl from South Dakota was walking with Leeann, Cecelia, and Kelvin over to the town house. Since then, my goodness, so much wild stuff. Her fidgeting mind had been on such a long journey and had traveled to so many places. She felt neither satisfied nor dissatisfied. She still couldn't sleep. Thoughts were still pressing down on her. So much emotional cactus in the world.

What it all added up to, she wearily guessed, was too simple to have much chance of working. It meant everybody had to face the truth that no one was innocent or special. Then they had to figure out a way to forgive everybody else and get on with the business of being alive in this uphill time. Of course, forgiving didn't make the world a better place by itself, but it certainly made you a better person if you could actually do it. If your heart could open up to the strength of that kind of humility. But how could anybody become humble in our world? Carla knew she wasn't that good at it. She never had been. Her heart didn't open up all that much. Not as much as she would want it to. Why did she want to try and judge somebody else, even if she didn't agree with them and considered what they thought and felt uglier than the homemade sin of molesting your own children? Who in the goddam hell was she? The white goddess almighty? Face it and know it could have been you. Get down on your knees. You just lucked out. You were blessed. You were nobody special. It could have been you. None of that changes the pain. Private pain always made its own marks. Ramona couldn't forgive those black kids from college, and she couldn't forgive her little sister either. She wanted to rig the game, though. That's right. Rig it. Don't play fair. *Cheat.* Her big sister was just hugging the thorn bush of the past so that the pain stayed alive. If it ever subsided, Ramona might have to suffer through seeking out another perspective on human beings that didn't deny at all their capacity for abject cruelty and one's own inevitable periods of horrifying disappointment. One thing was sure as shooting. There was a throttling waiting for everybody. A big hand around the throat.

The phone rang.

"Hello."

"Hello, baby, I had to call you on the phone," Maxwell's voice sang, imitating Billy Eckstine doing "Jelly, Jelly, Jelly."

"Oh, sweetheart, I'm so glad you called. I was feeling so lonely."

"Me, too. I wish you were out here with me."

"You do?"

"Oh, yeah."

"Well, we can't afford that."

"Right."

"We can't. But that doesn't mean that I don't miss you, babe."

"You need to go to the airport tomorrow and come out here with me."

"No I don't. I need to stay here so that we can start saving some money."

"I don't think so."

"That's too bad, Maxwell, I'm not coming out there so we can spend more than we should and start fighting when we get ready to come back home. I'm not doing that anymore. It's time we started acting like adults. Other people do."

"How many?"

"Not enough."

"Then we would be in the minority."

"Maybe."

"I always liked the elite. I'm with you on this. But you still should—"

"No, I should not. Babe, please don't make me think about something that bad for us. Let me just enjoy talking to you. I'm grateful for this. It's not enough, sweetheart, but I'm grateful for it. I have had a very bad day."

"What happened?"

"Just memories. Sometimes they pull me down. Way low. But your calling right now lifted me up."

"I called you because of something else."

"What's that?"

"I haven't been doing you right."

"Yes you have."

"We both know better than that."

"I guess."

"You were there. You know."

"All right."

"I was letting this race stuff get to me."

"I really don't want to talk about that."

"I have to. Just listen."

She said nothing. She didn't want to hear it. Not more.

"Look, I was backing away from you. I was losing my nerve."

What did two people being together have to do with nerve?

"I got confused. I had to talk to my daddy about this."

If he was like Ezekiel, they wouldn't have any problems.

"That's why I really wanted us to go to Texas. I didn't want to talk with him on the phone, I wanted some hours and some walking and talking, you know? I needed it like that. Well, I went to the right man. My father. Me and Ezekiel talked about it when we were out walking. I told him how, sometimes, I didn't feel comfortable being with you because of the way black folks would act."

"What did he say?"

"He said that was some ignorance he didn't believe in."

"Oh, Ezekiel."

"That's my pop. Ezekiel said he remembered hearing people tell him all the time, back in the day, different stories about the North. They told him—now check this out—they said that if a colored woman loved a white man or a black man loved a white woman, they could live in the black community if they didn't feel like being bothered. Up in the North anyway."

So he was saying the same thing that Leeann was saying—but what was he actually saying?

"Well, that sure has changed."

"You right. It has. That's why we live downtown. I don't want you to be bothered with that shit."

You couldn't prove it by the strange ways he had been acting, a whole fucking year of it.

"And?"

"Ezekiel didn't want none of that either. He said that he liked it where he was and he wouldn't move to the North just to marry a white woman. But now if Eunice was white and that was the best they could do, he would move up there for *her*. Now we know he ain't never met a white woman like Eunice, but if he had of met one, Pops said he would have had to go up to Chicago or somewhere to stay next to *that*. No way he was losing out on being close to the woman he wanted. So he didn't know what the heck was wrong with me. I had a good woman and I was walking around caring about some people who didn't even know her."

"You guys talked about all of that?"

"All of it. I was trying to explain myself. It's just in the air. Some weird kind of way, things can always pull you back. You can want it to be simple. This over here, that over there. Simple. I guess you can pay a lot for that. I just wanted to go to a job and walk down the street with my lady and not have black people looking at me like I had sold out."

"Sold out?"

"Yeah. That's what they call it now when you bow down to something white. You know, you start acting a different way because you're ashamed of yourself. You start liking things because somebody said you were supposed to like them. White people said this was good. So it had to be good. But then you start wondering if what you like is based in your own heart or if your heart is counterfeit, hypnotized by some white bullshit. I didn't know if I was in love with you."

"You didn't know?" she said, some anger peppering her voice.

"Look. It starts on the outside and it goes to the inside. That's how you know a person. In your case, baby, you have that seriously Negroid boody but, Carla, you're as white as a white person can be. There's nothing black about you at all."

There was no help now. She knew he was trying to apologize to her for something but she could feel him leaving her right then. He was floating off. She knew it. Her throat went raw. She could hear herself breathing very deeply.

"Are you all right, baby?"

"No."

"I can't hear you. Speak up, baby."

"I said, 'No.' "

"What's the matter?"

"I don't know."

"Come on, you can tell me."

"Actually, I don't know how to say anything right now."

"Whatever it is, you can say it."

"Sweetheart, I can't be anything else. I never tried to be anything else. I wish I could open my heart up more. I wish I could do that. But, oh, gee whiz, I might be too old now."

"You're still young and fine."

"I'm almost forty."

"Really?"

Giggling, she hated how Maxwell would always find a hole for a joke and make her laugh. The subject didn't matter. The moment didn't matter. Laughing at life was basic to his philosophy; he wouldn't change that, and she wouldn't want him to.

"Well, actually, I'm a few years away, short years, but I'm still not there. I'm not forty yet. But, sweetheart . . ."

"Yes, baby."

"All I can say, you know, is that, well, I finally learned how to sing and I love you and that's all there is to me."

"But, baby, I love you, too."

"Then why is this stuff bothering you?" She sounded too insistent. She was ashamed of herself. There was no dignity in her voice.

"I wish I knew. Damn. But I do know. I wanted to be something somebody was telling me to be. But I couldn't be that and be with you."

"So what does that mean?"

There was a silence. They listened to each other's breathing. The light from the sky was on her face. Then a cloud put her in darkness. She felt as if each nerve in her skin weighed fifty pounds. It was over and she knew it. She had a feeling for that and she had never, ever, been wrong. This was it. He was bringing the pain. He was trying not to, but he was bringing it, little by little, until she would find herself shit out of luck. Her heart would start to crumble when the conversation was over. Then it would turn to powder. The powder, once wet with a new illusion, would become clay. On a splintery worktable, a form would be made from the red globs. It would take shape as a new heart hoisted up and dried out with another adventure's name chiseled in. That was how she was. She was coming to know herself. But it didn't ease her unhappiness.

"Ezekiel made me see myself. I was turning into a coward."

She agreed but said nothing.

"Ezekiel did not like that. He did not raise me to turn and run from a woman I loved. 'Not for no niggers, not for no crackers, not for no dadgum body.' He had a new look on his face. He was disgusted. He never put his eyes on me like that before and I seen him mad enough to tear down the house because I did something stupid. I could tell he was disgusted. He was ashamed of me. It was pure shame. That had never been in his face before. It was so pure, that shame. I couldn't stand my father looking at me like that. I couldn't handle it and he wouldn't stop looking at me like that. He made me feel like a stupid little boy. He didn't say anything either, he just kept on looking and that shame got purer and purer until I could feel it touching me and pushing me away from him. I was losing my father. He was finished with me. Then I broke down, honey. It was too much emotion. I started crying like a baby when he said that to me with his face. I was hot, I was cold, I couldn't run, I couldn't stand there. It hurt so bad, baby. I was in a barrel of shame. So I feel very humble now. You're my baby. You're my girl. You're my woman. I have to be a man. I have to. And I have to ask you to forgive me for trying to pull away from you, Carla. I have to ask you that."

"Do you really love me, Maxwell?"

"Yes, and I want you to forgive me. That's what I want."

Carla didn't speak.

"Please forgive me."

She couldn't say she forgave him. It had nothing to do with her emotions. All she could say was what she felt.

"Oh, God, I love you. I love you *so* much."

"Okay, baby. This has got to be how the truth feels, sweet stuff, and I'm feeling it just like you're feeling it. I mean full love, all the way up to the top. I'm with you. That's how I'm feeling it. You got me in my heart, Carla. I have to be with you. I have to. But I better go now. I got to go. They're calling me. The bus is here to go to the concert. I'm going to keep you in my horn."

She didn't know what he meant, but her response, from way down inside, was very tender: "Are you?"

"Yeah. I'm going to play strong and sweet for the people. That'll be my way of telling them I love you. I love *you*. I'm with *you*."

She said the same thing to him and she was crying and she was on fire and she had come alive again and her loneliness had been put on hold. Ooo, ooo, ooo: what a little mush on a moonstruck night will do. Tonight she would go to sleep with a smile on her face. Unless, Carla's mind being what it was, she began obsessively thinking about never speaking to Ramona again. This, no matter how much Maxwell loved her, was not something she would get over. It was a condition that amounted to a splat of shit in her face she would never be able to wash off.

Interlude

SHOUT CHORUS ON THE WAY OUT

Homesick, tired, all alone in a big city
Why should everybody pity me?
Nighttime's falling
And I'm yearning
For Virginny.
Hospitality, with any,
Calls me.

THE SIZE of the city from a window more than twenty floors above the street at night made it clear just how big the buildings were for business and for living. The lights on those monuments or coming from the windows of apartments gave an organic feel to the evening as one could look down on the Amsterdam Avenue traffic and over to the Hudson and farther into New Jersey or, from a vantage point in the other direction, on up toward the George Washington Bridge or, even somewhere else, see east to the FDR Drive and on down to the exits that let you off into Chinatown, where the soul of a people lay in the space between highly nuanced manners and gruffness. Below that section of herbs, restaurants, acupuncture, and movie theaters with oddly colored marquee pictures, one was eventually in the stations of city government, the courts, and City Hall, then the financial district and among those buildings from decades and decades ago that stood so close to each other there were places where it was always cool in a shadow, even on the day when the highest temperature set a record and numberless air conditioners went on blowing enough hot air out into the streets to sweat birds and butterflies.

Some she or some he could use that city at night or that city in the morning or that metropolis in the afternoon or that helluva town in early evening as a mirror of her energy or his. No one particularly cared what you thought about anything, but everyone actually did because the sentiment of the city was made of those large progressions of harmony and dissonance, those major and minor modes of success and survival that stitched fire into the molecules of the air or had the childish ease of a boy or a girl with his or her head on the shoulder of the equally smitten member of the opposite sex, muttering something barely heard for all the noise of the subway train vainly attempting to beat a beam of light to the next stop.

It would seem, given all of the force that made Manhattan what it was, only those with mental problems would ever conclude that their aesthetic feelings were of the slightest importance, that they could somehow equal a design for living that reiterated, apparently, the laws of perishable goods. The question of maintaining the artistic sensibilities that spoke across the centuries to times that had remained stable for very long periods when you lived in worlds that rose and fell at the tempo of crops—planted, in bloom, picked, and gone—was a question that pushed the timid deep into themselves since their problems and their dreams and their frustrations were the only forms of consistency they could count on. But it was the combative way in which New Yorkers used indifference to express their own sense of the dignity of their individual importance that gave the city so much soul. If you didn't get that, you missed the whole thing and went home with more stories of the rude people who live in New York. It was easy to misapprehend what the city meant, but it was also easy to become so intimidated by its many meanings that one could easily spurn the challenge of paying attention because Manhattan asked so much of the individual and haggled over every scrap of recognition. It seemed interested only in itself. Which was why it was one of the freest places in the world.

When that girl was still new to New York, no boyfriend yet in sight, and had come home late one evening, whistling and humming to herself all the way back in the days after she had quit the waitress job in that Irish bastard's place, refusing to serve some moldy cheesecake, a huge Negro guy was right behind her and put his hand over her mouth.

If you say anything, I will kill you.

She felt urine soaking its way down her leotards. His other huge hand turned her around. He asked her where she lived. What apartment she was in. She didn't know what to do. Her head was bumped swiftly into the wall. Though her apartment was on the fifth floor, she told him she lived on the third, then pretended to faint. He dragged her up into his arms and she could tell that he was high. There was something far off-balance and he smelled of a gross combination of alcohol and marijuana. His breathing took in all of the air from the hall. Bitch, she heard him say. Faint on my ass. You're still going to get fucked. Oh, yeah. I'm not letting you go.

On the third floor, she felt his hands pressing her throat. Her eyes popped open. He smiled. She tried to fight but he was so much stronger than she was. No air was coming into her body. She actually lost consciousness this time. She awoke to little slappings. His face wasn't as clear as it had been and she couldn't hear as well. He smiled. Then his hands pressed her throat. She knew she was dying. Consciousness disappeared. He was rubbing spit across her face. He hawked into his hand and did it again. His face was less clear and she heard even less well. The power of his hands burst the blood vessels in her eyes and did damage to her eardrums.

He asked her where she lived. It was so hard to breathe that she couldn't talk, only gesture, but in the wrong direction. Her box cutter was in the pocket of her skirt. He must have been high. Her dress wasn't on and her leotards were partially down. He was pinching her lower lips. She cried out and he told her that if she made any noise he would snap her neck like a chicken. This is some pain you have to take. He lightly punched her in the stomach. She felt queasy and wanted to vomit but was afraid he would kill her if her insides flew into him. God, please let me hold it down. Where do you live? She pointed, gasping, incapable of getting one word out. Please finally came out of her mouth. Let me. Put. My dress. On. Fuck no. Just pick it up. Her hand was on the box cutter and she was more frightened than she had ever thought was humanly possible. If she tried to cut his throat and missed, he would take it from her and kill her right there. She went limp, making herself into pure deadweight. As he was reaching around her, she cut him across the back of the neck. He grunted and continued in the direction she had pointed. What could she do now? Which one is yours? Don't make me ask you again, he said in a stage whisper as heavy as an ax. She was so close to unconsciousness and so afraid to cut him again that she couldn't speak. He let her down to the floor and squatted over her. Before she could think, she rapidly cut him and cut him and cut him and cut him above his heel. He screamed so loudly she knew that she was dead and blood was gushing from him. He had forgotten her and the pain in his voice swelled until the filthy hallway was full of door latches being pulled back and people asking what was going on. *Oh, God, please God, please God, save me. Please save me. Please, God. Please. I **know** You can save me. I know You can save me. Oh, God. What have I **done?** What am I **doing?** What? This poor little girl? What have I **done?*** he shouted, maniacally turning and turning in a circle as his eyes, even in their bleariness, stared at the ceiling. He stopped, now noticing each of the doors cracking light into the hallway. Hobbling with all the agony in the entire world, he began going down the stairs, speed picking up as he realized that his freedom depended on getting out of that building. She was whimpering and trembling so hard her head was bumping against the wall again.

You got to watch that Negro. He'll upset you.

Later, the body of a male Negro was found just outside of a basement behind an abandoned building near Tompkins Square Park. He had bled to death. His name was Robert Charles, a.k.a. Chili Cheese. Once upon a time he had been a heavyweight boxer. Charles kept in shape and went to the gym five or six days a week. He became feared after pulverizing six of Satan's Angels who attacked him with chains near the fountain in Washington Square Park when they saw him kissing and walking arm in arm with two white women. Chili Cheese managed to hurt them all very badly but come out untouched. One by one, with cracked ribs, snapped collarbones, broken noses, splintered jaws, shattered knees, and knocked-out teeth, they ended up bloodying the water in the fountain. All that those who saw the fight could agree upon remembering was the silver cap on one of his front teeth shining as Chili Cheese smiled while landing blow upon blow. Rough customer. There had been arrests for drug dealing, but he had beaten all of the cases because mistakes were made by the narcotics division. This man had been accused of rape a number of times, always white girls but none of them had ever gone through the whole thing and testified. Once, however, the man was accused of raping a black woman and got into a fight with her fiancé, Algernon Menefield, another male Negro, a.k.a. Moneyfield, a.k.a. Money, a.k.a. Mini-Money. Menefield, wearing a big cream-colored cowboy hat, came looking for Charles at Troy Brown's, a Bowery hangout for Negro artist types and dope fiends that used to be called the Beach Front, itself something of a legend because there were supposed to be tunnels in the bowels of the bar that bootleggers, under the leadership of Meyer Lansky, used during Prohibition to transfer booze arriving on boats from Canada. Both Charles and Menefield were hauled in and there was a big mess down at the station house. Patrick Logan, a known Caucasian pederast with a taste for Negro and Puerto Rican boys, bailed Charles out. As usual for the accused, the case fizzled away. Now he was gone. Dead in some bushes as if he was hiding from somebody.

Some white girl who had tussled with a nigger trying to fuck her one night was almost comatose with shock and had spent some time recovering from the damage to her eyes and her ears. The bastard kept strangling her. Sadistic sonofabitch. We had to go over there to that goddam East Village with pictures of the motherfucker laid out dead in the morgue. Probably ten thousand people were cheering if they heard about his demise. She was spooked for sure. Felt sorry for the girl. Nice little blonde. But we had a job to do. There was plenty of blood in the hall from this nigger who tried to rape her. Somehow he got off and the blood trail ended. He went a couple of doors up the block into another building and through to the back. He got over the fence and that was that. We didn't have dogs or anything. The nigger wasn't a runaway slave. He was just another goddam guy with a woody he wouldn't whack off on his own. Reduce the salami at all cost to somebody else is what these animals think. Now the girl, she was your regular. Still scared. Didn't want to open the door. Big bruises on her throat. Eyedrops in bottles. Eardrops. You could see the shit everywhere. Anyway, it's all simple and private at this point: we're just three white people in a fucked-up apartment house now. Two big lugs with an envelope of some pictures of a nigger corpse and a girl with a story about how the city put a tattoo on her ass that she will never be able to remove, believe me. She's the bride of the monster now. Forever. These punks can do that. When she started crying we were ready for it. The reaction was familiar. These raped girls, these almost-raped girls, they're all the same in their manner; it's just that each of them is her own story and she can't trade her story for the story somebody else has. So she has to bear it. Grinning has nothing to do with it. When she saw this big sonofabitch laid out dead, she was very frightened. She was so frightened that I knew this was the nigger who tried to fuck her and might have killed her if he had gotten her alone. Then this cutie pie, oh, she was a real looker. I wouldn't mind a serving or two of that myself. Actually, I would take a few dozen. But I wouldn't take it. Besides, I'm just in this scummy job world we're in here and nobody really likes us too much. They think they do until they learn we have our own fucking problems and then the glow resides and we're just some more screwed-up New Yorkers who got a job to do. It's just that we go to work carrying guns. That's a **serious** point of difference. But the main point is that I have no doubt in the goddam world. No doubt at all. The sun can burn out and I will still be sure that the nigger on that slab was the nigger who she put a very good cut into with that razor's edge. The fear fell out of her face. She got kind of clinical in those sweet blue eyes. She was cool all of a sudden. Basically, I don't believe she wanted to be bothered. She wanted it to end right there in her tight little apartment. A lot of them are like that. They've had it. But this girl, Carla Hamsun was her name, she looked me in the eye and she looked my partner in the eye, and these are two guys who have seen quite a bit of shit alone and quite a bit in combination, both of us got a big chill from the way she said to us, with her face still as if she was dead herself, **No, that is not the man.** It was all a lie. I know it was. This is my business. There is no doubt in my mind that she was a nice lying little waitress serving us to a pile of shit. But. If she was telling the truth, then the real nigger is invisible out there somewhere, still on the run, waiting to get recognized by pushing his dick somewhere that it's not wanted.

2 4

THE PAINTER OF MODERN LIFE

Some were the times when Maxwell was gone that she would pick up the phone and hope to hear it answered by Bobby Lee Robinson, an artist. She and he evolved into good friends because Bobby had so many things on his mind and always got Carla to see something differently. He had theories about everything, some she agreed with, some she didn't. But none of that mattered because Bobby provided Carla with so much stimulation of the sort that she often found lacking in the world of jazz musicians and avant-garde types once one got past the thrilling to hilarious anecdotes of the traveling music-makers and the contrived eccentricities of the downtown types who wanted so much to be in a place like Paris during the high times of Picasso, Stravinsky, Joyce, Pound, Hemingway, Proust, Diaghilev, and all the others who were giving a new shape to their century by pulling a fresh butterfly from the cocoon of convention. Jazz musicians, no matter how intelligent, usually didn't read books or know much about things outside of their personal experience or the tidbits of opinion about culture and history that they had picked up in conversation. The downtown avant-garde read books but understood them badly and loved costumes as well as the quirks that were supposed to be "pushing the envelope" but were most often founded in the rock-and-roll appropriation of high-art expression, which Carla assumed had come from the electronic rise of fervid amateurishness being mistaken for the vital power of primitivism: someone with green hair screeching and jumping up and down in front of speakers that substituted volume for intensity was not the same as someone from the bush of the Third World or the Indian mysteries of America, a three-dimensional being who was speaking to the living and the dead through a complex system that transcended time and was about far more than using some flat version of shockingly bad manners to grapple with the middle class of the moment. In one phone conversation, Bobby told her that she was right and that all of that had begun when Baudelaire wrote a letter to an upper-class woman who admired his work.

"All of it?"

"All of it."

"Bob, you certainly have all the answers."

"I don't know about that, but I do know that I'm right about this one."

Bob was so nonchalantly egotistical Carla had an amused affection for him.

The letter in question described a dream of his in which the dandy who prided himself on his uselessness climbed up the wall and went into the admiring lady's bedroom one night, where he took a knife and cut a hole in her stomach, then pushed his penis into the wound. "That was the beginning of rock and roll and Andy Warhol and all of that kind of dumb shit. But because Baudelaire was a genius and a great thinker, these sad motherfuckers out here can use the lowest level of his brain fluid to shine the floors of their ignorance. Now, if you have ability, *actual* ability, maybe even *virtuosity,* you are seen as the enemy. They might wish you dead. If they could make you be actually dead, they would probably try that, because that's how they see you. But you have to be seen as *something,"* he laughed.

Maxwell had introduced Carla to Bobby at one of the artists' parties in his enormous loft near Chinatown. Bobby's parties were the best and they always followed his having had a profitable sale that gave him the money to prepare things exactly the way he wanted them. Bobby was big on cooking and preparing and began working on things the afternoon before. He did it all by himself, just as he lived by himself and sought an understanding of the world that was, all by its lonesome, his very own. At that first party, everything was swinging and the painter, who was actually also a clay sculptor and a wood-carver, made everyone feel like paradise was getting ready to knock on the door and walk right in.

"First of all," Bobby stage-whispered to Maxwell and Carla in passing, "if paradise doesn't know how to party, then what does? Give them a taste of paradise, then they'll know what to be hungry for."

On a long table covered with butcher paper were a full poached salmon; a turkey abetted by dressing run through with fried, chopped-up chicken livers; a ham sporting circles of pineapple; astonishing deviled eggs; small squares of corn bread filled with pinches of pork and bits of jalapeño peppers; meatballs in dark brown giblet gravy just waiting to be speared by toothpicks and whisked away to gullets; a crock of yellow rice, a crock of black beans; perfectly sweet watermelon slices; four or five different cheeses clustered near various kinds of crackers; a dressing that was a delectable mix of oil, vinegar, mustard, toasted garlic, and bacon bits lightly covered the tossed salad which was in a chef's metal bowl; and there was loaf upon loaf of French bread that had been toasted and splashed with homemade garlic paste and butter. The host, Carla would later learn, never invited people to party unless there were plenty of eggs, bacon, and sausage in case he awoke to find himself surrounded by those who had not gone home and were quite hungry upon coming to consciousness. Bobby would then serve them breakfast, some orange juice and champagne, waiting patiently for the appropriate moment to let everyone know it was now time to stroll the fuck out of his loft so he could get his black ass some rest.

For that first summer occasion when Carla met him, Bobby had made a special gin punch with Tanqueray, concord grape juice, Mountain Dew, lime juice, orange slices, and enough seltzer water to keep the taste of sugar within delicious bounds. The punch had a covert effect. One wanted more and more until, suddenly, tipsiness made itself evident by some misjudgment of space and proportion or by some piece of conversation starting out well then shattering into near babble as the syllables refused to stand up and do their articulate duty. Once the punch had its way and the classic Nat Cole records were going, everyone decided to become romantic or felt full up with mirth, dancing closely or swinging at easy tempos.

This was when Carla discovered that Maxwell was a fine dancer, very light on his feet and fully acquainted with all kinds of different steps. There had been those late-night dancing times at Good Henry's, the two of them pulled close by a slow blues or ballad, but this was different, since Bobby played many contrasting kinds of music for the party—big-band swing, romantic balladeers, rhythm and blues, tenor and organ groups pedaling through the blues, Caribbean stuff—creating moods and breaking them off, or letting them evolve into other states of partying as tempos got slower and slower or quicker and quicker until something completely different was put on, even a syrupy recording of waltzes that allowed everyone to laugh and laugh as they collectively mimicked what they had seen in movies, perhaps none realizing, as Carla did, that the waltz was once the controversial forerunner of the belly-rubbing slow drags of one sort or another that preceded so many twentieth-century instances of hot or inept or frustrated coupling. For her, the waltz, no matter how terribly played, always, like the tango, had a quality of elevated release and heartbreak, a summoning recognition of all that was meant by the nearly dead mare and stallion of romance, mutually whacked into life this time in measurements of three beats to a bar, each bar an invisible step on a staircase traveling all the way to the moon. Sometimes she couldn't believe how *sentimental* she was!

Maxwell was especially good on the Latin and Caribbean numbers, though he didn't actually follow any of the rules, preferring to invent his own steps from chorus to chorus, intricate patterns of footwork and surprising spins, sometimes triples going in one direction, stopping for another pattern, then a single spin, more steps, two spins, more steps, three spins, all spins in the opposite direction or in alternating directions, from right to left. Then he would take her in his arms and stalk the beat like a predator, lifting Carla into parts of the rhythm and the accents that were almost off, gestures of dance that just barely made it into the meter or were assertive pronouncements of countersyncopation that allowed her to live each second of a song with him and reach, new direction upon new direction, the duality of mobile partnership where the tipsy duet gave this South Dakota girl the impression of living inside the vibrant lungs of civilization, feeling the winds of the world enter and leave with each step. On the slow numbers Maxwell seemed to breathe and seep himself through her clothes until she felt that the two of them, like a couple of kids tentatively playing doctor under a sheet, were inside of her blouse and her skirt, their bare flesh touching. This condition of toying, erotic bliss was achieved not because he pushed against her in a vulgar manner but because he insinuatingly leaned his body against hers with such superbly restrained passion, which would be canceled by four or five ostentatious turns that made them both laugh.

"How did you learn to dance so well?"

"From playing all kinds of dance gigs."

"You could have pretended that you didn't know you were a good dancer. You could make what I said seem like a compliment."

"Okay. Thanks. I'm just doing the best I can. I appreciate that you enjoyed dancing with me. I hope I didn't step on your toes. I can be clumsy sometimes, you know what I mean?"

"I like the other version better."

"Fine. I'm here to please."

"I just bet you are."

"You wouldn't lose any money either. Where were we?"

"Dancing."

"Those pretty eyes threw me off. There's nothing wrong with my mind. But beauty will make you forget where you are."

She had to look him straight in the eyes to say what she felt.

"My, my. So, to answer your question, I've seen all kinds of steps. I've been on some bandstands, you can believe that. Then I read something—where was it? That's all right. Anyway, Duke Ellington said in something somewhere about jazz musicians needing to be good dancers. You could play better if you could get up inside that rhythm. That turned my ass around. The two of us should look into that sometime. Take some lessons."

"I wouldn't mind. I love dancing. I always have."

"You move like you do. But, you know, dancing wasn't always important to me, though. When I was a kid, I didn't care too much about dancing. I was an athlete. I ran the two-twenty and the anchor on the mile relay."

"You seem pretty big for a track star."

"The dancing bodyguard."

"You said it."

"You got to watch that Maxwell Davis. He might upset you. Anyway," he chuckled, "I played football, too. Middle linebacker. I could smell those plays coming. I knew where the ball was going and what the quarterback was going to do. Being fast, I could create some defensive hell. For my time and for where I was at, hey, I had it going on. I was a little appetizer version of what Lawrence Taylor became when he turned his position around. You know Lawrence Taylor cut football history in half—what it was before him and what it was after him. But I was better at track. I liked track better, too. It didn't have contact. I liked winning at football but I didn't like snatching guys and getting blocked and all of that shit. Track was clean. Just you, your track shoes, the gravel in your lane, the chalk dividing up the track, and then that finish line up there. The end always seemed a million miles away when you were stretching a little, down there making sure you were loose, and you know you were hoping that you wouldn't pull a goddam muscle. Paranoia central. But I could get up to the finish line with some speed. I beat plenty of guys. If I had been just a little better, I mean just a little, I would have been Olympic material. But over in that fast lane, over in that Olympic lane, well, a little is a whole hell of a lot. You know, Bobby—"

"Bobby?"

"The painter, the guy who's giving this party."

"Oh, him."

"Him. Him pointed out one time that black athletes changed our conception of mass and velocity."

"That's interesting. You mean big guys moving faster than you expect?"

"I mean that exactly."

"Good for you and Bobby. Him. But you aren't the only two in the universe who thought about that."

"You don't say."

"I do say. I thought about that myself because my dad was such a big fan of Muhammad Ali, even though he liked it better when he was Cassius Clay. Dad's old-fashioned like that, which is all right, too."

"Well, it's all right with me."

"Thanks."

"You're very welcome."

They laughed.

"Any*who,* Dad told me that when Ali and Joe Frazier fought in Manila—"

"The greatest heavyweight fight of all time."

"My dad thought so. Anyway, the size of those two men and the speed they had was something new."

"Yeah, white guys made you think big and slow were always supposed to be together. Siamese twins."

She put the stare on him of one who had been lightly violated. He picked it up.

"But, hey, that's not completely true. Let me stop lying. A cousin of mine said to me that he also saw that coming with a white . . . track . . . high school guy named . . . Forrest Beatty. This was a long time ago in California. This guy was from Northern California and ran sprints, the hundred and the two hundred. He was big like a football player but ran dirt in many a nigger's face."

"Please, Maxwell."

"Fine: many an athletic Afro-American's kisser."

"I like that much better," she said, and pecked him on the lips.

"You see, a perfect lesson in American history: drop a nigger and you never know what you'll get."

"Oh you!"

"I see what you're saying, sweet stuff, and I'm going to work on it. I will. Trust me. The last thing I want to do is make you uncomfortable."

"Most of the time you don't even come close to making me feel uncomfortable."

"That's good. I'm getting my job done then."

With the music going and the people dancing, she and Maxwell took a breather and began looking at Bobby's work. The host came over and walked around the loft with them, now and again excusing himself to take care of something. Carla was impressed by his manners and the thick power of his presence, which reminded her of what Dogpatch Daisy McCord had called "a nice comfortable pillow of a man. Muscular. Soft. Bulky. Yum yum." The furniture and the doors as well as the cabinets, his desk, and the iconic rectangles of wood around the windows were all done by Bobby. He had begun his fascination with form when he was taking wood shop as a kid, and never lost his love of the smell of sawdust and the transforming of what had been a tree into something that, in his opinion, needed to try and catch up with where the wood had begun as it stood within its visual position of natural power in nature. To that end, Bobby's wood pieces and furniture were as often starkly poetic as exquisitely gnarled or geometric challenges, which remained as comfortable when functionally used as they were intriguing when perused. He wanted to put the boot to the Bauhaus. All of this evolved from when he had seen the Chinese banyan tree: there was no doubt in his mind that nature was the greatest abstractionist, always making statements and then making fun of its own seriousness.

"If you looked at a banyan tree and were told a story that this was really what had happened, you know, to a family of snakes that had been cursed to live forever in an almost petrified fashion, you would believe it, dependent on where in the world you were and who you happened to be when you heard the story. If you lived in a culture that was always trying to get in on God's cosmic jokes, you might laugh every time you saw one. You might fall on the ground. But, actually, that's the reason why screwed up people are sometimes the best at things."

Carla was lost as Bobby was called to greet some guests who had just come in. Then he came back.

"I know: I left you hanging."

"I'm doing pretty good myself," Maxwell responded.

"Good."

"You know me. I only halfway listen to what people are saying at parties anyway. People always leave you dangling. That's how you know it's a party. No continuity whatsoever. If you can't handle that, you should stay home. Besides, I come to a party to *party*. If I wanted to listen all goddam night, I would go to a concert. Or a lecture. Now, however, I'm ready for the explanation."

Carla couldn't tell whether there was hostility in what Maxwell said or not. Then he and Bobby looked at each other in silence. Maxwell raised his eyebrows in a comical way and they both burst into laughter.

"Well, guys, I would appreciate some clarification."

"I knew she was the intellectual."

"She ain't no more intellectual than me. Goddamit. In fact, I want to hear what you have to say *much* more than she does. Please,

Bobby, please tell us." Then, turning his cap sideways, Maxwell began to imitate the hard-jive gestures of a rapper chanting into an invisible microphone, "I need some illumination yo to wash the razorback of my salvation yo and get me off the plantation yo and prepare the way for my immigration yo to the fat land of elevation. Yo. Ah so. Imminently."

All three laughed this time.

"Boy, you crazy. What I meant about screwed-up people, right, having a reason for doing something better than almost anybody else you can find—or anybody else you can think of—is, actually, about comedy. Everything they do is ugly except this one thing they do with such beauty. I mean serious, serious beauty. Beauty that will buckle your knees. See what goes on when you find yourself trapped and forced to experience that. Then, what really happens, is *you* have the covers pulled off yourself. The joke is on you. You are absolutely reduced to the state of awe and childish envy in the presence of their creative abilities—these weird, nasty, cruel people—which is quite something, actually. So what happens is that's God telling you that *He* leads the band and picks the musicians, not *you*. That's a cosmic joke."

He, Carla thought, *He.*

Beyond that, as they went from one section of the loft to another, moving around people and putting their attention on various works, Carla saw that Bobby had taken on, in his own way, the entire history of painting and sculpture. Maxwell excused himself and wandered off into the rest of the party when it became apparent that Bobby was going to say a number of things he had already heard. Bobby then told Carla that he worked in clay because he wanted to deal with the primal materials of plastic form. Dealers had advised him to have his pieces bronzed, which made them durable and raised their selling value. Bobby told them that when he fired his clay work inside the kiln that occupied one end of his loft, he was all the way back to earth, water, flame, and air. That was it for him. Market be damned. His paintings displayed an enormous scope, some, to the sloppy looker, like children's drawings and finger paintings, others extraordinary studies in juxtaposition, portraits that transmogrified in style but remained the same in feeling. There were very basic works in clay, others that appeared to have arrived from ancient kingdoms or rituals, then tragic or comical ones that leaned against so many layers of time and style that they could only have been done now. All efforts were attempts to realize Bobby's heat theory, which was that a very good painting or piece of sculpture emitted about six feet of palpable heat, the magic of emotion and spirit arrived at in pigments and control of light, or through command of three-dimensional structures. A great painting or sculpture shot out a stream of fire that extended at least twenty feet.

Carla became excited at that statement because that was exactly her experience when she and Mom had gone to Europe that summer after the high school cafeteria accident. Mom, always ahead, had some money set aside "for dreams and emergencies." Perfect for this situation. Randy Jr. was glad to spend those three weeks with Dad, but Ramona, who said nothing, nothing at all, was jealous as Cain must have been when he bashed Abel's brains out. Mom had to know it but she had chosen a way to handle things and that was that. With Mom, that was always that. Her charm and good cheer were as inflexible as the streak of mule-like stubbornness anybody discovered who wanted to go will to will against her. Yep, as Carla often thought, pioneer women must have been like that. Cactus roses. Perfumed instruments of puncture.

Carla was elated by the idea of going abroad. She needed that private feeling she always got with Mom and it made her psychologically recover much faster. They drove to Chicago, where the car was left with a cousin, then they rode the train to New York, taking off and crossing the Atlantic so smoothly that Carla lost all fear of crashing in the water. What a wonderful way to lift up from the depression that Mom must have known she had all along, even after her daughter had been so stoic about it, such a real aristocrat, so superior in her apparent rejection of that superiority.

The tour worked perfectly, in terms of emotion, in terms of intellect. Stepping into all of those museums and looking at art from the world over, going to restaurants, walking the streets and the parks of Europe, seeing where so much history had actually taken place, from the marvelous to the horrific, gave Carla a reprise from the coming-and-going inclinations toward self-pity. She felt rejuvenated and also saw herself, actually for the very first time, as part of some process both furious and run through with finesse, the motion of life and civilization, the battle in which the tale of beauty and the beast didn't necessarily have the same outcome every time around, not the pretty version at least. More often than not, beauty was mangled by the beast, converted into his extension, something ugly, malicious, and brutal. But some person somewhere always felt an indelible passion and went the many steps necessary to make that passion take form, and through that form civilization found its way into light of indeterminate length, somewhere between a match and a permanent flame. Listening to Mom, reading the guidebooks, and arriving at her own conclusions, Carla saw Europe much more clearly on that trip—even wound up as she was in her adolescent image of herself as a princess who had been victimized by the rigorous unfairness of fate. Europe, the best of it anyway, was a huge storehouse of light, illumination from all over the world, from any place where human beings built a net capable of snaring sunshine or moonlight, from the outside world or from the inside world of the self, or even from the animated strength of existence that arrived out of those cultures where there was no self of the sort Westerners believed in.

In either London or Paris or both—as they strolled (at the slowness determined by a special curiosity) through one of the Third World collections of masks, spears, fetishes, and bizarre geometric shapes decorated with feathers, straw, and animal hair—Mom said, "Most people on the earth, they don't exactly cater to the idea of the individual life. They just believe in life. I guess we might think of them as primitives but that makes them kind of like scientists. So queer, isn't it? You know: the people who just follow the big patterns and see the little parts as ingredients. We believe in the importance of the carrot or the pinch of salt. The individual soul. Everybody else, just about, believes in the stew. Mmmm. That makes me hungry. Let's go get some lunch."

The quest for a meal meant that Mom looked at the list of eating places, country by country, that she had gathered in a little notebook from her old college friends who traveled a lot and were all happy to let her know the best places they had found in the European cities. Mom never lost contact with anyone she liked and was obsessive about sending out birthday cards and Christmas cards and whatever went with letting her buddies know that the bond was never about to loosen—not if she could help it. That made eating in Europe a transforming experience. Mom preferred her gourmet stops off-the-beaten-track and was particularly happy when one of the lists had the name of a little restaurant where the chef, if you saw him outside smoking or just taking a breather, stood in his apron as proud of himself as some virtuoso magician who knew that his tricks began and ended with him because, no matter how well the cook had been taught, even starting the apprenticeship as a little boy making sauces, his own imagination and sense of taste had demanded variations that became edible triumphs of personal expression.

The masters, regardless of profession, were everywhere, and Mom told Carla that these people usually disappeared into history without leaving a track but were part of what made each period sacred and each time its own time, guaranteeing that not even the tip-top scholar could experience or imagine a previous era with complete fullness. "The present, Carla, is a pure gift from God. Happens once, happens only once. If it was any other way, birth would be a big fat waste of time. The point I'm making is we will never know the present of anyone who lived before us. Never. That boat was filled and left before we got to the dock. If we actually could get on that boat, my God, static is all the world would be and the individual life would have no consequence at all. How hideous. Each of us would just be living proof of no more than maybe a law in physics." That was why the idea of time travel was ridiculous: once anybody who had not been there entered the previous time, it would no longer be itself and the entire period would probably turn into a force that immediately vaporized the threatening intruder. The great artist or storyteller or actor—or whatever—provided the glorious approximation, which allowed everybody in the audience to fill things in with their own particulars. But the very thing that Sophocles felt when he sat in an audience and listened to his own words, or that Shakespeare heard in his mind or saw when he looked at Elizabethans, or Titian felt when he put his kaleidoscope of European skin tones on canvas, or Caruso sensed when he was warming up his doomed golden tenor, or Bill Robinson experienced tapping up some stairs, or Shirley Temple experienced tapping up them with him, those were absolutely personal and private and mysterious—only because there was just so much of a moment that could be translated into the grand approximation, no matter how inclusive a genius might make it seem. When Mom explained things like that to Carla, the world seemed far less harsh and more of a blessing, even with all its bloodstains. Carla was curious about her mentioning Bill Robinson because she never seemed to care much for Negro expression.

"It's usually overstated, as far as I'm concerned. Louis Armstrong and all that business. I was never touched, even in a small kind of way. I felt a little bad for them, to be honest. It was sad that they had to live their lives in such a world of exaggeration. Bing Crosby and that smooth baritone was more to my way of appreciating music. I also loved Tommy Dorsey. What a tone *he* had. Even the very, very smooth ones, the colored people like Duke Ellington, they seemed to be invested in crude distortions, like those bathroom plungers on trumpets and trombones. Such beautiful, beautiful brass instruments and listen to what they *did* to them. Can you imagine? How ridiculous. Anyway, there's a place for everything. Live and let live. Well, so much for that subject. Smelly."

Then, as they walked out into a lifting fog from the British Museum, Mom took off her trench coat, folded it over one arm, and began saying things that gave Carla the thrill of returning with her to a past age that maintained an open invitation through the lilt in the sound of a voice that became more communicative, year by year, as the daughter listening evolved in her own comprehension.

"So odd. The things you remember. Back when I was a girl during the Depression and Shirley Temple was everywhere you turned, she made me Heidi one moment and Bill Robinson's dancing partner in the next movie. When you saw her there on the screen, wearing the curls you *had* to have, it all felt like a miracle. Fred and Ginger were too much for me then. I could never imagine being what they were. Ginger was up on a different cloud from the rest of us. But Shirley Temple was all of us, every little girl in America. I thought her and Bill Robinson, the two of them dancing, was one of the best things I ever experienced. I still do. It was so fun! Now when your dad and I met and he turned out to be one of the best dancers who ever walked on a ballroom floor, I felt like Ginger Rogers then. It was one of those college dances partway through the evening when everything had lost its charm because the boys couldn't make you feel the way you wanted to feel. I was pretending to enjoy myself but I was in a blue funk. Then I saw him and he saw me. Your father seemed like sunshine in the middle of the night. He was so Norwegian and so much out of this whole Midwestern history. If he couldn't have spoken a word of English and had gotten off of a covered wagon with dust all over his clothes and that Lutheran look in his eyes, I wouldn't have been surprised. He made me feel like our Norwegian time in America had come to court me. Rough. Simple. Direct. Religious. Dreamy. Graceful when lucky. And I mean when lucky!"

Carla imagined the dance was held in a gymnasium, like a lot of the dances when there were plenty of people and the shine of the polished floor seemed like a flat moon of wood you were walking and dancing on.

"What a young man your father was. He wasn't a clod and he wasn't, by the by, always making snide remarks about this abundant backside like the other guys. Sometimes they made me think I was misshapen. I felt just terrible. But, as a woman, you never know what will pull your heart to a man. Your father, I still can't believe it. Wrong as trying to eat rice with a pitchfork. Your father. He showed me something so stupid once that I fell absolutely in love with him. I did. That was it. Verdict in. We were juniors in college then and he was going in the direction of trying to be sophisticated and kind of slummy—you know how guys try to be. We were on the way to a fancy dance and he looked so handsome in a white dinner jacket. He seemed like he was made out of life. So he reached in his pocket with this knowing wink and showed me this paper napkin he had gotten from some place. It had a little cartoon of an exhausted donkey sitting on a Luther Burbank tomato. Enormous tomato. The caption, which was just so stupid it was charming, it said, 'Look at the ass on that tomato!' "

Carla blushed and suddenly found herself hysterically laughing with Mom, who wiped her eyes and twisted her mouth with an affection that was at least one part amazement.

"Signed, sealed, and delivered. Can you believe it? Something so silly as that and I was unconditionally in love with your father from that moment on."

After that first party, Carla and Bobby immediately became good friends. He knew so many things about so many things. The two would go to the Museum of Modern Art, the Metropolitan Museum, the Guggenheim, and the collections from one end of Manhattan to the other that might specialize in art from one particular place in the world. East Side, West Side, all around the town. Bob loved to sit outside in the café section of the Hotel Stanhope and either joke as the two of them watched the doings on the steps of the Metropolitan or change to a funereal tone when he speculated about the day or the night or the morning or the afternoon that Charlie Parker was supposed to have died inside the Stanhope. Carla loved Bob's jokes because they were always wicked and full of mimicry as he created conversations between some people they were looking at, or who passed and gave the two of them a quick once-over. One time, when Charlie Parker came to mind, Bob went through the stories he had heard, weighing the truth of them, any of them. Maybe so, maybe not. There were so many tales circulating around his demise, some saying he was felled by an overdose of dope or a heart attack, others that he was shot dead in a scuffle and one of the hotel's staff members saw the bullet wounds as his body lay in a bathtub. There was even one in which Parker had taken a punch to his ulcerous stomach in Brooklyn, then died on the way into New York, where the corpse was abandoned until a story was patched together in order to protect the drummer who had killed him accidentally but could forever count on the mythologizing word of a wealthy Jewish baroness who had once driven ambulances in North Africa during World War II and loved her some jazz Negroes. Bob audibly wondered how much suffering Parker had gone through and how he felt, from one sunrise to the next, about the balance of that pain on the scale of beauty that came out of his saxophone.

"Charlie Parker's music is always about warfare."

"Don't you think that's pretty one-dimensional?"

"No."

"I do. I don't see why everything has to be put in such narrow terms. Didn't he have more things on his mind than warfare?"

"I seriously doubt that."

"I don't. It would have made the emotions of his music pretty limited in their scope. Sure, warfare is, unfortunately, basic to what has happened in civilization and in barbarism as well, but I don't see how you could conclude that about someone as great as Charlie Parker. It's kind of melodramatic."

"I played the alto saxophone. You didn't. I wasn't good, but I know something about it, and if you will listen to what I'm saying you will see that I'm making a different point from the one you assume I'm making."

"That's good to know."

"The alto saxophone, it will give you nothing, not do-diddly-squat. It's a mean, stingy motherfucker. You might even say that, as an instrument, it *likes* to sound fucked up, sour, tinny, and all that kind of stuff. You have to *take* whatever you get from it. Now Charlie Parker, he understood that reality perfectly. Charlie Parker kicked the alto saxophone right in the crack of its ass and kept his foot up its ass until he died. He beat the shit out of that motherfucker. You could even say he brutalized it. That's why it sounds so beautiful when he plays it. You get the sound of pure submission, imposed submission. In order to free himself he had to enslave it. There was no other choice."

Carla didn't like what Bob was saying at first, but her friendship with him didn't have a lot to do with arguing different points, especially when she heard a particular sort of passion in his voice. She had already gone far enough. One turn more and he might storm off, leaving her with the bill. You had to be careful. Bob was known to start shouting and screaming if someone disagreed with him at certain moments. Don't trample on his theories. Don't call them names. No, no, no. At other times, discussion was easy. You never knew, unless you paid close attention to the sound of the emotion. Still, what he said meant something other than machismo, as Carla put actual thought on it later when she was alone.

She concluded that Bob was right because what he said reminded her so much of what she had seen when Bobo revealed to her so, so, many things about the drums, a good portion of them determined by the sounds he pulled from the instrument through his touch. Bobo played the drums differently if the song was in a major key as opposed to a minor, using a brighter sound on the former and a darker on the latter. His will and his skill did enslave the instrument to his quality of feeling, all in the interest of expression. Bobo always said he wanted the drums to get out of his way so that the invisible quality of his mind, his heart, and spirit could take wing. He wanted to inhabit sound, which is already invisible, with something that is far more substantially outside the world of sight: "It's the invisible *inside* the invisible that means the most. That's always a warm room. You can cool out in there. I never want to go any other place when I'm playing. I'm lost if I miss that room. Besides, that room travels on its own. It doesn't bullshit."

Carla would never forget the moment she and Bob were at Asian Antiquities on East Eleventh Street looking at a bronze piece from Thailand and he observed it was Gothic, from bottom to top: the edges of every smaller square inside another square rising to where the figure itself stood, every ascending bas-relief version of a Chinese box had at its edge a series of very small, flat pyramids, each right next to the other, much like teeth. The toes of the shoes worn by the statue were turned upward, the open palms that faced the viewer as they pushed forward, the patterns of the attire, and the hat itself. "Up is all you get here. Something, huh? Up. The sky is always a destination. I like that. Yeah. All right. Very good. I should do something about death . . . in which, right, everything points *down*. Maybe just a carved wooden skull on the end of the shaft of a spear stuck into a platform. The symbol of death supported by the instrument of death. Better, hey, the platform should be raised up on four legs that are spears themselves and the spear that the skull is on should be coming through the platform. Five Gothic points going in the opposite direction. Wait. I got the skull in mind: no lower jaw and all the teeth in place on the top. Maybe just the canines. Who knows, jaws might be Gothic, too. Could be. Except that when you're eating something you find yourself crushing the food with the top and the bottom. Maybe that's why the smile is international. It's that moment when the top and the bottom teeth point at the tongue—ah, ha, ha. And the lips curve upward. Bone, flesh, language, the Gothic kiss. Wow, Carla, you're good luck. I can work for a week on this stuff. Maybe longer. I'm pleased as punch," he said with a sarcasm intended to undercut his own enthusiasm.

She could always get stimulation from him, and now that Maxwell was back out there playing his tenor saxophone, leaning his body and his notes into his listeners, and Leeann was out of town doing some modeling in Europe, Carla wanted someone to talk with and called Bobby. But she would have called him anyway, since this was an afternoon when hers was the appetite for a conversation with a man who was a friend and who, because he had been introduced to her by

Maxwell, sort of reminded her of the man she was missing in a gentle way, secure but still with that little sting of wish you were here.

"Artist's studio."

"Hello, this is Carla."

"Oh, hi, Carla. Back in town, huh."

"Yes. I've been back almost two weeks but Maxwell has been gone for the last ten days. He called a few nights ago."

"How was your trip?"

"Full. Incredible. There is no way I have digested all of it yet. It was really a revelation to me. What a family Maxwell has. His parents are wonderful. I learned so much, and the two of us, Maxwell and I, we got so much closer that . . . that the whole experience was like a gift."

"Hey, that's wonderful."

"So what are you doing?"

"Just some work."

"Oh, you know I know that. Painting, sculpting, wood carving? You know I always want to see what you're doing."

"I think this might demand all of that. Everything I know how to do. I'm after something that is kind of hard, and it just might turn into a series, sort of what Picasso called a suite. You know, some work around a few themes or images."

"I always loved that Vollard Suite."

"So did I. Something, huh?"

"Certainly, certainly. You going in that direction?"

"Not really. At least, I don't think so. Probably not. What I wanted to do at first, you know, was paint Achilles' shield because I had just read that poem of Auden's again and it inspired me because of this thing I have with masks. The whole world, actually. You know, the river is a mask for a riverbed; ice caps are masks for the ocean; the night is a mask for the day—and vice versa; the field of corn, grass, cotton, trees, sugarcane, rocks, boulders, all of them are masks for the earth; the surface of the earth is a mask for all of the different kinds of underground activities you get from insects, rodents, and all the various kinds of, uh, uh, the, well, you know, the churning forces that, uhhhh, sooner or later turn out to be earthquakes and volcanoes. Pavement is a mask. A family, of course, well, a family lives inside the mask of a house. Each room inside a house, if it has a door, is a mask. The glove is a mask for the hand; in fact, all clothing is a mask for the flesh of the body; hair is a mask for flesh; flesh is a mask for the skeleton."

"Okay, Mr. Mask Man. So what is the skeleton a mask for?"

"The skeleton is a mask for nothing."

"Nothing?"

"Right. Which is what you get when you go far enough. Moving away from nothing and toward nothing is all that ever happens, actually. That's the whole story right there. It doesn't matter who you are. But that is why I moved along to Menelaus and Paris's helmet. That is the beginning of the argument with the gods for being some unfair, dirty motherfuckers."

"Oh, I remember. Homer. Gee whiz, it seems like I was living another life when I read him, another life. But I know what you mean."

"You do? That's very good."

"I should think so. My father is a classics scholar. *And* a history teacher. Have to pick up something along the way. You are talking about that moment in the *Iliad* when what you men now call *mano a mano* would have ended the Trojan War."

"I guess. Whoever calls it whatever they call it, that's what it was. Two men. The Trojan War could have been ended. Very, very simply. All the killing could have been averted. Troy could have remained as it was."

"But Paris would have had to die."

"You're very correct. Paris would have had to die."

"But Paris was the man *Helen* chose. She didn't *love* Menelaus."

"Helen, actually, was put under a spell and given to him as a trophy."

"I don't believe that."

"Well, if your father's a classics scholar and you have read the *Iliad* I don't see what you mean. It's right there. No one is making this up."

"The people who wrote it made it up."

"Of course, it's literature."

"Bob, listen to me for a second. I believe that this is something made up by men to explain why a woman married to a king would run off with somebody else. They always explain things that way. He put her under a spell. Under a spell. Always under a spell. It couldn't have anything to do with the guy she's leaving. Even if she's unhappy, she wouldn't leave on her own. If something was challenging their system, the way those Greek guys wanted to pretend things were, they would reduce it to that hoodoo that you do."

"Oh, I see: that old black magic."

"What else? Helen wanted to be loved and the man who loved her wasn't somebody she wanted to die."

"Paris *should* have died since he, coward though he was, agreed to meet Menelaus and settle everything in single combat. But then the gods stepped in, and while Paris was being dragged and strangled by his chin strap, he just disappeared. In a mist."

"You're darn tooting. Right over the wall and back into Helen's arms. She didn't care about the way some stupid warrior societies conducted themselves. Paris was hers and she wanted him and that was that. I mean that's what I think the *real* Helen felt. The woman behind the myth wasn't embarrassed. Besides, women always learn that men aren't all that they say they are. They love them or they don't. We have a great capacity for diminished discovery. That's why his being spirited over the wall is a fabrication for a guy running when the going got too rough."

"Well . . ."

"Right over the wall. What a hoot! I always thought that was kind of funny."

"Funny?"

"Funny. I'm serious. I saw it differently. Like something in Buster Keaton. *Sherlock Jr.* or one of those incredible things of his. You know, where the steps he's standing on in *Sherlock Jr.* disappear and Keaton falls flat on his bumpty-bumpty as the scenes change."

"Is a bumpty-bumpty what I think it is?"

"Sure it is. And Keaton falls on his because he's *not* in the story; he's just dreaming. Keaton is a pathetic projectionist trying to put himself in the story on the screen. A party crasher. Surreal slapstick is a pretty good name for it. The same with the *Iliad*. Bob, don't you think it could be that, too?"

"I guess so. But what really happened was absolute anguish. That's what it turned out to be. Menelaus stands there with the empty helmet and then begins to search for Paris like a wild beast with his nose full of scent and nothing in sight. That searching, to me anyway, is a cry out against the fact that you can do what you agreed to and *not* cheat but the gods will look at you and *still* cheat you, like the dirty motherfuckers they are. When that came to me, I lost it. I went a little off. The inside of my head could pretty easily have been mistaken for a beehive. So many subtle things. I knew I had discovered something but I couldn't figure out how to depict it. This was a curious problem. That's because we have all of these images of decapitated heads being held, blood dripping down and all that kind of stuff, but I wanted to have something empty being held and the look of horror on the face of Menelaus when he realizes that this whole thing could go *any way whatsoever* because the gods don't *give* a fuck about being fair. They actually don't, and . . . never have. So that's what I'm working on right now. I want that moment of horror, you know, which is also a moment of glory because what really happens right then is that man, through the reality of his anguish, declares himself a moral creature of the sort that separates himself from the gods as they really are, the dirty motherfuckers."

"Well, I don't know about how *they* really are and I don't believe in a *they* in the first place. Mess around with that stuff and you can find yourself in just another conspiracy theory."

"Conspiracy theory? How's that?"

"Pretty obvious right now."

Oddly, her mind went blank and she couldn't grasp what she was saying.

"Is this," Bob asked, "what they mean by a pregnant pause?"

Carla laughed.

"This happens to me, too," Bob said. "You have to—"

"I just lost my bearings for a minute. Excuse me. I know where I'm going. All of the nutball conspiracy theories, well, I don't know. I mean they just probably go back to something like what my mom called 'the shenanigans on Mount Olympus.' People being pissed off about that. Yes, of course: that's what I mean. It doesn't matter what culture you're talking about either. I don't think so: when you find yourself holding the crappy end of a stick right there and you thought it was going to be perfectly clean, well, you could kind of begin to believe there was a cosmic plot."

"In that case, Carla, all human plots, when you come down to it all the way, they would have to be mirrors of cosmic plots, wouldn't they?"

"I could agree with that. But I was thinking of how, if I totally accept what you're saying about masks right here, I could see the mirror itself as a mutating mask. Mutated by the image inside it. That could be possible."

"You're right. But there's something else, actually. Well, see, the mirror is actually a clean piece of glass treated so that it will hold an image. If you scrape off the treatment, it becomes a window, which is, in the final analysis, a solid piece of nothing."

"But that's not all."

"Oh?"

"When a window becomes dirty, it wears a mask, too, doesn't it?"

"Dirt is definitely a mask."

Bob began laughing and told "the diva from South Dakota," as he jokingly called her, that it was now time to get off the phone and go back to work. The empty helmet awaited him.

For the rest of the afternoon, Carla lounged around in that set of ideas, thinking of the infinity of masks and the inevitability of nothing, but the continuity didn't seem depressing to her, the very form made life have an order, not a chaotic set of thrusts that could wound or kill you at every step. Nothing is not the story. Death was hardly the issue either. So what? is what they amount to. The fact that we live and we *want* to live gives life all the meaning it will ever need, even if God, in all His so inarguably tender and torrential mercy, didn't exist. That, from her perspective, put a gag on all the whining about meaninglessness. It was also tiresome to her that so many things had to be handled in that Greek way of fighting and fighting. Helen didn't care if Paris was a chump; he was *her* chump, her coward, the man who made her feel alive when there was no Greece and no Troy, only a room with two people, swords and armor and all that crap either outside or someplace else, every bit of it so irrelevant in comparison to the freedom she felt with Paris and had never known in the company or in the arms of Menelaus. That whole male business of looking at things only one way was why nobody realized that the real hero of the *Odyssey* was Penelope. While Odysseus was running around acting this way and that, part wily and part childish, Penelope has to deal with all of those suitors, a bunch of drunken fools, and keep them from destroying everything, year in, year out, exhibiting just as much wiliness as any Odysseus and facing much more loneliness. Penelope had none of the sex toys her long-gone man got so much fun from and screwed—*every* chance he got—which increased the thousands of days and nights it took him to get all the way home.

At one time Carla thought Winnie Mandela, with her twenty-seven very real years, was an even better Penelope, so noble and unswaying. What a thumbed nose at all of that Greek patriarchy. So beautiful as well; no Greek woman could have looked any better. This was a real Penelope with far more terrible suitors dominating her house, her land, the home that was her country taken over by colonizers. What these suitors wanted wasn't just land and wealth; it was utter submission. The Xhosa prince who was her man wandered through time behind bars for shouting the word freedom into the tribal face of xenophobia, which was color-blinded to humanity at large. Her Nelson wasn't an egotistical fool who had called his name out to the Cyclops whom he had blinded, bragging on himself and incurring the wrath of Poseidon, the god of the sea and the Africa-visiting mack daddy of the used-to-be-one-eyed boy, his son Polyphemus, who liked to have his guests for dinner. Perhaps the Cyclops was an ancient and inflated Jeffrey Dahmer, the cannibal murderer who inspired the spiky joke in which his mother told him that she didn't like his friends and he said, "Then eat the vegetables."

This contemporary tale of trouble, however, was purely human in size and everybody on earth was lucky enough to be alive when someone lived out a set of principles that demanded even more than mythology had defined as an ultimate test of will and endurance. So Winnie Mandela was an angel of integrity to Carla, who read everything there was to read about her, who hated buttons but sometimes carried one with her picture on it, who had more than a few dreams of one day standing in the great lady's shimmering presence. She and Bobo had such heated arguments about Winnie the wonderful, of whom he said, "Bitch look evil to me. Look in her eyes. I seen *that* look before. Oh, I seen *that* one. It ain't got *nothing* to do with liberation and all that shit she talking and *you* talking. Bitch look *evil*. I'm sorry." Carla's fury at his saying such mean things was boundless and circular, as if an unending plain scorched black by anger and stinking with the smoke of destruction were turning and turning around her and inside of her. Who was Bobo to judge a woman by her eyes, or a man or anyone? Intelligent people on juries couldn't do it: what made him think that *he* was so far above everybody else put in positions of judgment? Bobo was dead by the time the angelic Winnie fell from heaven—her wings so heavily soaked with blood—and turned out to be a xenophobic, hate-filled monster who couldn't do any better than say, when the murders, kidnappings, and tortures were displayed, "Mistakes were made." They sure were! You've got to watch those masks. So many kinds. Oh, brother.

Carla had been extremely depressed by all of that for quite some time. But the reversal of positions between Nelson and Winnie gradually awed her as she thought about the two over the years. He had remained faithful to her while, so the rumors went, she lived in a bacchanal and butcher shop of sexual boy-toys and revolutionary hit jobs. During his nearly thirty years in penitential bondage, Nelson had grown more wise while she, after almost five hundred terrible, terrible days in prison, had sunk down into the very xenophobia that her man stood so tall against, even creating for his century a new kind of Odysseus, one who could endure so much, suffer for so long, miss the many small things that go with watching the growth of one's children, then emerge from incarcerated exile and address a stadium full of South Africans—the spectrum of color, the spectrum of kind— with a lyrical sense of grandeur and forgiveness that did not compromise any ideals at all, only turn its back on the mechanics of homicide that were such conventional aspects of revolution.

The prince who returned as king—but would prefer to be *elected* president—left Carla bawling in front of the television as his address to the assembled progressed: she felt herself witnessing a miracle of the sort only those who had lived in a time as cynical as hers would ever understand. Before 120,000 people in Soweto, Nelson Mandela descended in a helicopter then stood on a taller mountain and saw much farther and much further than all the mythological gods who had ever inhabited Mount Olympus. He strung an impossibly difficult and brand-new bow for Africa, eloquently proving that he, no one else, should begin the movement of his nation toward the expanded sense of democracy and universal humanity that was immeasurably beyond the world of Odysseus. But that was not all. Each word, every pause, the overwhelming nostalgia in his eyes, and the quality of the gestures that magnified his stance were subservient to the force of all his now old man's years pulling that freshly strung bow back and back and back and back and back. The arrow made wide by age and sent into the world from his throat flew through and beyond the ax handles, spears, machetes, rifles, guillotines, lynching bees, purges, gas chambers, cultural revolutions, killing fields, and ethnic cleansings that expressed the variously interpreted tribal will of an international family of kissing and killing cousins, so, so many millions gone. Lord, Lord, Lord. Darkness all day long. Seemed like ten thousand at the burying ground. Nobody loving somebody knew how much had been lost until they laid all the corpses down. But this elder returned to the troubles of the world understood exactly where his feet were set. As his image shot round the world and the Xhosa timbre of his sound was heard in all the tragic optimism of its power, Mandela stood up there on the mountaintop with Gandhi and Martin Luther King, Jr., socially favored men whose disdain for imposed human boundaries had taken them so far beyond all those ancient or ideological gods, the quirky, heartless, dirty motherfuckers.

"All you need is a dream that's packing some shit, grit, and mother wit. That's all you need," Bobo once said, "and you can be goddam sure that's all you're going to *get*. The deck is stacked out here, baby low. The cards are razor blades. You got to get cut in order to pick up your cards. You got to get cut in order to play your cards. And you damn sure got to get cut in order to *deal.*"

The South Dakota diva was also depressed for another reason during the period when the covers had been pulled off Winnie the drop-dead gorgeous promoter of burning rubber necklaces. There was an unshapely melancholy doused in guilt because, although Bobo had not been gone for all that long, she was, against her will, beginning to imagine herself loving another man and being loved by someone she didn't know, someone who could liberate her in the way only one who feels profound affection can free anybody. Carla knew by then that love and independence were two different things. For love, you could sacrifice yourself and accept it, feel larger rather than smaller as you learned that difficulty, fear, and pain were part of the role something in your soul told you that you had to play if you were up to the game you had also told yourself you were spiritually training for all of your life. Contrary to know-it-all theory, masochism had nothing to do with it. That was where her feminism and her heart always collided. Carla set aside all ideas about women submitting to the will of men and their needs and their definitions the moment her insides swelled up and her heart had full possession of everything the splendor and stink of romance meant to her. Women redefining themselves beyond the narrowest traditions of submission while achieving the freedom to completely love a man might have been the biggest task on her side of the sexual line. It surely was the trickiest one. Who knew how much it took to muster the strength to say *I won't stand for this shit* as well as *Baby, won't you please come home?*

Then, as her mind turned, she felt rather jubilant thinking about the earth and people putting on and shedding masks. The idea of farmers planting and harvesting masks tickled her. She toyed and toyed with the conception because it was applicable to so much. As Carla's playful contemplation moved over into the human world, she gamely concluded that men were the greatest lovers of masks and that they went into the forest seeking the sturdiest wood. Poor materials, after all, give poor impressions. Once they chopped and chopped and grunted and grunted until it had fallen, the guys had their basic material. Men carved out their masks and decorated them with the plumes of the most handsome birds and the most substantial and communicative dyes. They then spent the rest of their lives asking you what you thought of their facial shields, not of *them*. Men figured that the effort put into the making and the upkeep of the masks stood in for personality or intimacy. Actual recognition was irrelevant. Submission, applause, awe, and love would do. Women, almost always, wanted to be seen as what they were and known as who they were, and sought, when given the chance, to strip everything away until all they had left was their nudity in its very fullest meaning, which might have been a mask for nothing but a nothing that was more than a little something. Perhaps that was the essence of the so-called battle of the sexes, the struggle between the nudists and the mask-makers.

Carla was satisfied with thinking. She felt inhabited by a delicious yawn. The workings of the world had been deduced. Sure they had, she laughed at herself. All was as easy and in place as the feeling you had driving through the Great Plains, when pure expanse was a companion that asked no questions and gave no answers, when there was nothing but sky in front of you and nothing but sky behind. As Mom used to bray when Dad got all wound up in one of his theories about math, language, athletics, and cuisine, "Jabberwocky. Jabberwocky. Talky, talky, talky." This day's binge of intellectual inquiry was over. The woman was ready to get on up the way. Her spirit was now a sparkling medley of emotion. While putting on that big guy's gift of the ritzy star sapphire earrings with the silver bells, she heard herself humming "No Regrets" until it filled her body, then felt her Viking Hottentot, that alabaster black ass, jauntily bouncing to "The Best Thing For You (Would Be Me)." Dancing full heart into one of her favorite songs, "My Ship," she began appreciatively wailing and wailing their home full of music, just her and those notes and the soul of those words. The emotion that those tunes allowed her to free nearly lifted Carla up off the floor and sent the girl from South Dakota safely sailing out of the window, like the very first dinosaur who ever learned how to use her wings. Now was the time to go out and have a glass of wine near the end of the bar, any bar where she could look into the street and think of just how good she would feel when Maxwell got back off the road and they were, once again, alone together.